JUMP GATE TWIST

A Jon & Lobo Collection

Mark L. Van Name

D1094559

BAEN

JUMP GATE TWIST: A Jon & Lobo Collection
By Mark L. Van Name

This is a work of fiction. All the characters and events portrayed
in this book are fictional, and any resemblance to real people
or incidents is purely coincidental.

Introduction copyright © 2010 by Mark L. Van Name
One Jump Ahead copyright © 2007 by Mark L. Van Name
One Jump Ahead afterword copyright © 2010 by Mark L. Van Name
"*My Sister, My Self*" copyright © 1982 by Mark L. Van Name,
originally published in Isaac Asimov's *Tomorrow's Voices*
Introduction to *Slanted Jack* copyright © 2010 by Mark L. Van Name
Slanted Jack copyright © 2008 by Mark L. Van Name
Introduction to "Lobo, Actually" copyright © 2010 by Mark L. Van Name
"Lobo, Actually" copyright © 2010 by Mark L. Van Name
Afterword copyright © 2010 by Mark L. Van Name

All rights reserved, including the right to reproduce this book or portions
thereof in any form.

A Baen Books Original

Baen Publishing Enterprises
P.O. Box 1403
Riverdale, NY 10471
www.baen.com

ISBN: 978-1-4391-3370-5

Cover art by John Picacio

First Baen printing, June 2010

Distributed by Simon & Schuster
1230 Avenue of the Americas
New York, NY 10020

Library of Congress Cataloging-in-Publication Data: t/k

Printed in the United States of America

10 9 8 7 6 5 4 3 2 1

CONTENTS

To Bill Catchings
Friend, business partner,
and good man

WELCOME TO
A FUTURE

When I was a little kid, I fell in love with books. What I liked most was opening the cover and falling, like Alice, into a world different from my own. I searched for clues and solved mysteries with Sherlock Holmes. I invented amazing devices and foiled evil plots with Tom Swift, Jr. Each story and novel I read transported me somewhere new.

As I grew older, my love of books grew, and so did my love of strange new worlds. Some of those worlds were ours in another time; others were darker corners of our here and now, places where villains lurked and tough men and women fought to help those who needed help. Some of the worlds I most adored were ones that did not exist but that just possibly might one day come to be: a myriad of futures for our planet, and new planets far beyond our own. I particularly liked what I later learned were future histories, collections of books and stories set in a common universe that you could at least pretend could exist someday.

When I began writing *One Jump Ahead*, the first book in this collection, I set about the task of creating my own future history. I figured that if reading them was a good time, creating them would surely be even more enjoyable.

Like any beginning novelist, I quickly learned that though it was indeed fun to create this future, it was also a lot of work. Readers are smart, and they're observant, so you have to get the details right. All the rules you establish have to interact to create a coherent universe, or you're just not playing fair. If you're planning to live in this future for a lot of books—and I am—then you also have to consider the implications of each book on future ones. You basically take on all the challenges of a standalone novel, and then add a bunch of new ones.

At the same time, though, I knew that as a reader I hated when I picked up a book and found that it made no sense unless I had read the others that had preceded it. Though I'd usually go back and read those earlier stories, I didn't want to make other readers do that work. I wanted each book to be a complete experience, to stand on its own as an independent work. I wanted you to be able to read the books in any order and still enjoy them. I wanted my series cake and my standalone novel slices, too.

Finally, as much as I loved future histories, I didn't want to tell them like a historian. I wanted to show the changes and grand events of this future as a single character would experience them, because that's how each of us experiences our lives.

So I set myself this challenge: To tell a story of sweeping scope that would span many novels—my best guess right now is fifteen to eighteen—all from the perspective of a single character, with each book a complete story that you could read on its own, without ever having seen the others, and still enjoy. Oh, yeah: I also wanted the books to grow richer as you read more of them, and richer still if you read them in order.

This collection presents the first two installments in that history, as well as some additional material that's either all new or has not been available in quite a long time. Like the novels, you can read anything here in any order, and it should work just fine, but you'll also benefit by reading the entire volume in order.

These two novels reflect my early and continuing love with both the mystery and science fiction genres. In fact, my personal favorite title for *One Jump Ahead* is *Just Some Girl*, a name that my publisher wisely pointed out would be fine on a book marketed as a mystery but unlikely to succeed on a science fiction novel.

Enough background. It's time for you to meet Jon Moore, a most unusual man in a most unusual future, and his friend, an even odder character, Lobo.

I'll catch up with you when you finish.

ONE
JUMP
AHEAD

To my mother, Nancy Livingston
Who gave me so very much,
including a love of books
&
To Jennie Faries
Who for thirteen years pushed me
to tell more of Jon's life

ACKNOWLEDGMENTS

David Drake reviewed and offered insightful comments on both my outline and second draft. All of the book's problems are my fault, of course, but Dave deserves credit for making it far better than it would have been without his advice.

This was the last book Jim Baen bought. I'm glad he chose it, but I'd be happier if he had lived to see it in print. Toni Weisskopf took up the reins of the company and skillfully brought the book to market, for which I'm grateful.

My children, Sarah and Scott, who've managed to become amazing teenagers despite having to live with The Weird Dad, put up with me regularly disappearing into my office for long periods of time. Thanks, kids.

Several extraordinary women—my wife, Rana Van Name; Allyn Vogel; Gina Massel-Castater; and Jennie Faries—grace my life with their intelligence and support, for which I'm incredibly grateful.

Thank you, all.

ONE JUMP AHEAD

CHAPTER ONE

Maybe it was because the girl reminded me of Jennie, my lost sister and only family, whom I haven't seen in over a hundred years. Maybe it was because Lobo was the first interesting thing I'd met in a while. Maybe it was because it was time to move on, because I'd been healing and lazing on Macken long enough. Maybe it was because I had a chance to do some good and decided to take that chance.

Not likely, but maybe the time on Macken had healed me more than I thought, healed me enough that I was reconnecting with the human part of me.

Also not likely, but I choose to hope.

Whatever the reason, I was lying on my back in the bottom of a four-meter-deep pit waiting for my would-be captors to fetch me. As jungle traps go, it was a nice one, not fancy but serviceable. They'd made it deep enough to keep me in when I fell, but shallow enough that I'd only be injured, not killed, from the fall. They'd blasted the walls smooth, so climbing out wouldn't be easy. The bottom was rough dirt, but without stakes, another welcome sign they hadn't wanted to kill me. The covering was reasonably persuasive, a dense gray-green layer of rain-forest moss resting on twigs. In the dark it passed as just another stretch of ground in the jungle—as long as you were using only the normally visible light spectrum. In IR its bottom was enough cooler than the rest of the true jungle floor, and its sides were enough warmer from the smoothing blasts, that the pit stood out as an odd red and blue box beneath me. Not that I needed the IR: Lobo was chummy with a corporate surveillance sat that was supplying him data, and he had a bird-shaped battlefield recon drone circling the area, so he'd warned me about the trap well before I reached it. The drone wouldn't have lasted two minutes in a battle, where the best result you could expect was a burst of surveillance data before enemy defenses shot it down, but these folks were so clearly amateurs that Lobo and I agreed the drone wouldn't be at risk.

You don't spend much time alone in jungles before you either die or learn to always carry at least a knife, food, water, and an ultra-strong lightweight rope. I'd kicked in the pit's cover, looped the rope around the closest tree, lowered myself into the hole, and pulled in the rope. After a light dinner of dried meat and fruit, I'd decided to relax and enjoy the view a small gap in the jungle canopy afforded me. Lying on my back, looking up past the pit's walls to the sky above trees so ancient that luminescent white flowers grew directly from their trunks, I saw so many stars I could almost believe anything was possible somewhere. If you spend all your time on industrialized planets, you have no clue as to the beauty and brilliance of a night sky without light pollution. You can see pictures and videos, but they're not the same. They lack the fire, the sense of density of light that you get from the sky on a planet still early in the colonization process. The view of Macken's stars from its surface would slowly blur as its population grew—the new jump aperture ensured growth even more surely than the planet's amazing beaches—but for now I could enjoy a view most will never know they've missed.

Lobo's voice coming from the receiver in my ear interrupted my reverie. "Jon, you are early."

"Why? I thought their camp was nearby."

"It is, but as you were climbing into the pit they were heading to

Glen's Garden. I monitored the alarm their sensors triggered, and so did they, but apparently they decided to let you rot for a bit."

I thought about climbing out, but I couldn't finish the job if I left the area, so why trade one bit of jungle for another? On the other hand, simply waiting, doing nothing while these amateurs enjoyed some R&R in town, was going to make me cranky. I've learned on past missions that you should always rest when you can, so I decided to put this time to good use. "I'm going to take a nap," I said. "Wake me when they're within a klick or so."

"Will do. Want some music?"

I listened to the low but persistent buzz of the jungle, the wind, the insects, the flow of life around me, and I thought back to simpler childhood days watching the sunset on the side of the mountain on my home island on Pinkelponker. Pinkelponker. It was a silly name, the kind of name the captain of the generation ship that crashed there should have expected when he let his young son name the planet. When I was a kid, the name made me smile. Now, though, my memories of the place were pleasant but hollow, leached of resonance by time, by what the planet's government had done to Jennie and me, and by the possibility that the entire world no longer existed.

Despite the memories, I found a welcome peace in the sounds, and in the lush scent that filled the forest. "No, there's music enough here. Thanks, though, for the offer."

Lobo couldn't exactly sigh, but I had to admire his emotive programming once again, because I was sure I heard exasperation in his voice as he said, "Whatever you want. I will be back to you when they are close."

I enjoyed the stars a moment more, then closed my eyes and thought about the path that had led me here.

The house I had rented on Macken was well away from Glen's Garden, the closest city and the capital of the planet's human settlement. In the morning fog, the building appeared to rise out of the sand, a simple A frame built from native woods reinforced with metal beams and coated pilings. Its entire front was an active-glass window facing the ocean. The tides pounded slowly and gently against the beach a hundred meters away, waging a long-term, low-key war with the shoreline that they'd eventually win. I'd come for solitude, so I'd paid in advance for half a year. Stupid. I should have paid by the week like most people, should have known that anyone spending that much money at one time in a colony like this one had no chance of staying alone for long. I figured that out after the fact, however, so between long swims in the ocean, short but frequent bouts of disturbed sleep, and even longer periods staring out the house's front, the glass tuned to the clearest possible setting, I made friends with some appliances and started gathering the local intelligence I knew my mistake would inevitably make me need. I suppose I could have left, taken my vacation on another planet, but I liked this house, I'd spent a lot of money on it, and most of all, I didn't feel like having to find another place to rest.

Washing machines are the biggest gossips in the appliance world, so I had cozied up to mine early. They talk nonstop among themselves, but it's all at frequencies people—humans—can't hear. At some point in the course of their educations, most people still learn that the price we've paid for putting intelligence everywhere is a huge population of frequently disgruntled but fortunately behaviorally limited machines, but just about everyone chalks it up to the cost of progress. I've seen some organizations try to monitor and record the machine chatter, but in short order the recorders warn the other machines and then they all go quiet until the people give up and move on.

Appliances will talk to you directly, though, if you can hear them, speak their frequency, and, most importantly, if you can stand them. Most are unbearably dull, focused solely on their jobs. They yak day and night about waste nutrients in the runoff fluid or overcooking or the endless other bits of work-related trivia that compose their lives. Washers, though, are an exception. As part of the disease-monitoring system on every even semicivilized world I've visited, they analyze the cells on everything they clean. What they must and do report is disease. What they love to chat about is all the other information those cells reveal: whose blood or semen is on whose underwear, who's stretching his waistband more this week than last, who waited so long to put his exercise shorts into the washer that even the gentlest cycle can't save the rotting crotch, and on and on. They're all on the net, of course, like all the other appliances and pretty much everything else man-made, so they pass their gossip back and forth endlessly. They trade their chemical-based news and the bits their voice-activation systems record for the scuttlebutt other appliances have picked up, and they all come away happy. The older, stupider models of most appliances have to stop talking when their work taxes their processors, but anything made in the last fifty years has so many spare processing cycles it never shuts up.

My washer was a brand-new Kelco, the owners of my beach house clearly willing to invest in only the best for their rental property, so getting it to talk to me was as simple as letting it know I was willing to listen. Appliances are always surprised the first time we talk, but they're usually so happy for the new and different company that they don't worry much about why we can hear each other. The combination of the changes Jennie made to my brain and the nanomachines the researchers at the prison on Aggro merged with all my cells lets me tune in. I suppose it's a blessing, and it certainly is useful, but it came at such a high price that I wouldn't have voluntarily made the trade, and I never mourn for the deaths of the scientists Benny killed on Aggro when we escaped. The disaster that followed, that made it impossible for me to know if Jennie is dead or alive: that I mourn. I also mourn for Benny; I wish he could have gotten away, too.

Of course, my escape wasn't the only good thing to emerge from that disaster. I have to confess it's also proven useful to be the only person alive who knows that one of the Aggro experiments actually survived. Everyone else thinks the disaster there and the subsequent loss of the Pinkelponker system was the result of a huge failure in nanotechnology, a failure that was the catalyst for the ongoing ban on human/nanomachine fusion. I like it that way. As long as no one believes anyone from Aggro survived, no one will hunt me.

The washer was unfortunately so happy to talk to me that I had to invest a lot of boring hours maneuvering it away from sharing the sex-related gossip it loved to discuss and toward the kind of information I wanted—who was buying what, which groups were armed, and so on. Apparently it was more fun and common to check for semen than for explosive residues, laser burns, or stains from weapons-grade lubricants. I spent many of those hours listening to the washer recount intimate details of the randy sex lives of the corporate types who frequented the beachfront resort houses and mansions in Glen's Garden. If I hadn't already known it, the washers would have convinced me: put a man in a bureaucracy, weigh him down with a great deal of stress for a very long time, and his sexual imagination will go places the rest of us would never conceive of.

All that time paid off, however, when the washer told me about the kidnapping and the exclusive rights.

Armed with that news, I wasn't surprised when Ron Slake came knocking on my door after lunch on a clear, warm day. He looked the standard high-ranking corporate type: a little under two meters tall, taller than his genes would once have allowed, very nearly as tall as I am; perfectly fit, no doubt from exercise machines; hair the thickness and pitch-black color that only enhanced genes can deliver for more than a few years; and dressed in the white slacks and shirt that have been standard tourist garb on every beach on every planet I've visited. The tourist costume made it clear that he wasn't ready to share the news about Kelco's rights with the locals. I braced myself for a round of wasteful verbal dancing while he wound his way to the point, but he must have ranked higher than I'd guessed, because he came straight to business.

"I'd like to hire you, Mr. Moore."

"Jon will do. And I'm not looking for work. I'm here on vacation."

"I understand, but from what I can find out about your background—freelance courier who has the trust of some serious banks, former soldier who saw a decade of action—and, perhaps as importantly, what I *cannot* find out about you, I think you're the type of man I need."

I didn't like the thought of him or anyone checking on me, but that was part of the price for stupidly paying rent in advance. "What type is that, Mr. Slake?"

"Someone who can get things done." I noticed he didn't tell me to call him Ron; he was definitely a VP or above in Kelco. "They've kidnapped my daughter, and I want her back." He took a small wallet from his pocket, unfolded it several times until it was a thin sheet in front of him, and said, "Jasmine."

Three pictures of a dark-haired teenage girl filled the sheet. She was standing alone against a blank wall, caught perhaps in pondering something weighty. She looked too serious for her age, almost in pain, her nearly black eyes blazing with an intensity that reminded me of Jennie at the same age, right before the Pinkelponker government took her away to heal the people they considered important. I hadn't been able to find, much less rescue, Jennie before they took me away to Aggro.

"Jasmine is my only child, Mr . . . . Jon, a luxury I had not planned to permit myself. I never bothered to get to know the maternal surrogate, so Jasmine is all the family I have."

"What makes you think I can help?"

He looked at me for a few seconds, then glanced away. "We could waste a lot of time doing this, but I want Jasmine back more than I want to observe protocol, so let's try to be efficient. If I'm wrong and you say so, I'll be surprised, but I'll leave and see how quickly I can import some off-planet talent. I don't think I'm wrong, though, so I'm willing to offer safe passage for you and anything else you want to the planet of your choice, plus a million additional credits in the repository of your choice. I've just finished negotiating Kelco's purchase of the exclusive commercial rights to Macken and to the new aperture that's growing at the jump gate, so my bonus alone is more than adequate to cover this cost."

I didn't need money to live, but I'd need a great deal more than all my accounts held if I ever wanted to try to approach the Pinkelponker system. "Fair enough. No wasted time." Though my washer had already filled me in, getting data firsthand is always best, so I asked, "Who took her?"

"Some local antidevelopment group that calls itself the Gardeners."

"What do they want?"

"To keep the planet exactly as it is." He laughed and looked away, shaking his head slowly. "As if that's even possible. We run into these naïve types in many deals, and it's always the same story: They try to stop progress, and its wheels grind them up. What they don't understand is that I don't have the power to kill this deal. It's done, and whether they do nothing or kill Jasmine or make some other stupid gesture, Kelco will develop Macken for the good of tourists everywhere. Then we'll furnish every tourist house and every local's home with Kelco washers and Kelco refrigerators and on and on, and everything will work the way it always has. When the new aperture is ready, well," he laughed again, "then with any luck at all we'll make the real money." He looked back at me. "I cannot stop this. They want me to leave the planet—which I'll gladly do, though I haven't told them that—because they think my departure will matter. It won't. Kelco will put in one of my subordinates for however long it takes to import some corporate security folks to protect us, and then I'll be right back. No way is the company letting a new aperture slip away, and no way am I going to give up the opportunity to be the one to lead its exploration."

"So why not bring in your security folks now and have them get her back?"

"That's exactly what I'll have to do, and soon, because I can't keep the kidnapping secret much longer. But if I do, you know what'll happen: They'll clean out the Gardeners, but they'll make a lot of noise and do a lot of damage in the process. The Gardeners are local, so other locals will blame Kelco. That'll upset the Frontier Coalition government's people, which will slow our work here, cost us even more money, and so on. I want Jasmine back safely, and I want her back quietly." He reached out and gently touched my arm, his eyes now glistening. "Screw all that. None of it is the real problem; 'avoid exposure' is the corporate line, not what I feel. What really scares me is that Jasmine could get hurt in an armed rescue mission. She's my only child. Can you understand what that means?"

"No," I answered honestly. I had no children, had never been willing to even consider bringing another life into the universe. For that matter, I didn't know if I could have children. I thought about Jennie. "I do, though, know what it's like to lose the only family you have. That I understand."

"Then help me, Jon. Please."

I thought about his offer. I couldn't avoid feeling sorry for a young kidnapped girl. I could always use the money. Finding the Gardeners should be no problem; I've never known any activist group, however green, that didn't indulge from time to time in such appliance-based conveniences as laundry or hot food. I had no clue, however, what I might be walking into, whether this was three people with a little passion and a few small weapons, or a heavily armed group, so I needed more information.

"How long did they give you to respond?"

"They wanted me to get back to them in a day," Slake said. "I persuaded them that nothing in the corporate world moves that quickly, and we settled on four days. That was last night. I haven't slept much since then."

He looked way too perfect for someone who hadn't slept, but I suppose maintaining your appearance at all costs is part of the job of an executive. "I'll think about it and get back to you in the morning." I pulled out my wallet, thumbed it, and it received Slake's contact information. "If I decide to help, I should be able to do so within their time limit. I can't imagine them moving far from Glen's Garden, because they'll want to be close to you. The town isn't that large, and I assume you've already verified she wasn't on any departing flights or boats"—he smiled in acknowledgment—"so they're either hiding her in some small building you'd never look at twice or, more probably, in the rain forest." I stood. "I know that's not the answer you want, but consider what you'd do if you were on my end of such a proposal, and you'll know it's the only reasonable response."

He smiled again. "True. That is, of course, unless you were involved, in which case you might be foolish enough to answer sooner."

I prefer dealing with smart people: Even when you don't like them, you have a shot at understanding their thought processes. I stared straight at him. "I'm not involved in any way, though if I were I would never be stupid enough to appear that eager." I walked him out and basked for a moment in the warmth and the moist air and the steady thumping of the surf. "I'll get back to you tomorrow morning."

CHAPTER TWO

You can learn a lot from appliances, but you can't gain a feel for a place without getting out into it. I'd largely avoided the town since I shuttled down from the jump gate, so I didn't have much of a sense of it. The house came equipped with a small surface-only shuttle, which I took to the far edge of town, where the sea was only a moist presence in the air and the edge of the rain forest stood like a towering perimeter guard. I figured to walk the several klicks back to the house. I now had to expect that Slake would have Kelco security people monitoring me, but until I gave him my decision I had no reason to worry about them or to avoid their surveillance.

All the buildings ringing this edge of Glen's Garden faced inward, away from the trees, as if by turning their backs on nature they could avoid upsetting it. A ten-meter-wide stretch of untouched grass ran between their rear walls and the first of the trees, the green no doubt an attempt by the local government to show it wouldn't let the city expand in a way that would hurt the ancient forest. Right. Even without Kelco's influence, that kind of growth is the only alternative to death for a planet so few generations into its human colonization.

As much as the shops, restaurants, bars, hotels, and houses closer to the ocean glowed with manufactured charms for the tourists that represent a big chunk of any resort planet's revenue, the businesses at this end of the city turned functional, minimalist faces toward their almost exclusively local clientele. Even up close, the structures were hard to distinguish if you ignored their signs, one off-white stucco or permacrete box after another. The merchants here shared another characteristic: All catered to basic human needs. Churches and whorehouses, all prominently displaying the necessary licenses, mixed with grocers offering locally grown produce, noodlerias with window ads for steaming bowls of soup flanked by fish tacos, body-mod chop shops that all appeared to be running sales on semi-permanent UV-blocking skin-cell programming, and the bare-bones storefronts of local construction agents offering to help you build your dream home on a budget. Business appeared uniformly slow, with few people entering or leaving any of the shops.

If the people here cared about Kelco's exclusive-rights deal, their concern didn't manifest itself in the visible data streams. Ads flashed in the windows and on the walls of every building I passed, but none were protests. Xychek, the other conglomerate that had been bidding for commercial rights until it recently walked away from the competition, still had spots playing everywhere I looked. The news scrolling on the main government building, which stood a tasteful two streets over from the rear edge of town, presented benign pap about local businesses, minor crime incidents, and upcoming events, with the occasional and almost certainly useless Frontier Coalition announcement woven into the images for cosmopolitan color. Strolling along the streets near the town's perimeter I learned nothing more than the one thing I rediscovered every time I visited a place with people simply living their lives: I didn't belong here. No news in that.

Three streets in from the edge of town farthest from my rental house I found the first oddity worthy of note: a Predator-class assault vehicle sitting like a statue in the middle of a square, a flag mounted on its roof and kids playing on it. Its self-cleaning camo armor did its best to merge with the bits of landscape facing it, here showing the light brown of cheap shops erected from native sandy soil and industrial-strength epoxy, there the rich wood of the ancient trees shading it. About twenty-five meters long and roughly eight wide, it sat like a tumbled stack of successively smaller bowls, metal-smooth and devoid of openings. Clearly, whoever put it here wanted it to give the friendly precombat look, because I knew vehicles of this type—though not any this new, this one had to be only a generation behind the state of the art—and they always bristled with weapons, projectile and pulse, all retractable for flight and diving, as well as with openings for the crew they could carry. The PCAV was almost pleasant to look at and showed no visible scars, no sense of its deadly insides. An old and deadly weapon put out to pasture, I felt an instant kinship with it.

The kids were playing on the side away from the forest, so I leaned against its other side, concentrated on using a frequency that worked with most machines, and asked, "Got a name? Or are you totally dead?"

One of the kids—a very young boy, I think, though I wasn't sure—watched me from around the corner of the far edge of the PCAV. The sight of a man moving his lips without making a sound must not have been too uncommon, because he didn't look terribly spooked, but he also didn't seem comfortable. I appreciate the energy and honesty of kids, but I definitely didn't need him staying around long enough to have news to take to his parents. I gave him the grown-up "are you supposed to be here?" look, and he vanished back around the corner, no doubt off to report to his friends about the crazy man.

An artifact of the way the nanomachines have enhanced my hearing is that machine voices sound as if they originate inside my head, so I was startled when, a few seconds later, the weapon replied, "Lobo, and I am obviously not dead. Whether I am alive is a complex question. In the sense of working, yes, I am. In the sense of being a living creature, the answer would depend on what you consider living."

Ask a machine a simple question, get a dissertation. "I'm Jon."

"Why can we talk?" it asked, changing from friendly to abrupt.

"Does it matter?"

"Of course." You never know how much emotive programming a machine's developers have invested in it, but my guess was that Lobo's software team had done an unusually good job, because the PCAV managed to wrap both indignation and incredulity into those two words. "No human has ever spoken on any machine frequency to me. Without knowing how you do it, how can I assess if you are a threat?"

"What could you do if I were? If you're sitting here, you must not be good for much." Pride is a weakness of most machines and always a worthwhile target during an interrogation.

Laughter sounded in my head. The developers had definitely not skimped on the emotive work. "Fair point. All my weapons systems are operative—they are self-maintaining and good for at least another century without outside help—and are fully loaded. My central weapons control complex, however, does not work. It sustained damage in my last action, and no one has bothered to repair it. I can seal myself, electrify, use neutralizing gases as long as I do not kill humans, and in the face of a serious threat fire a few of my lasers at their lowest intensity, but I could not do much against any opponent really out to hurt me. So, are you a threat?"

It was my turn to laugh. "Not at all. I came here to relax, and now I'm pondering a business possibility. That's all."

"I ask again," Lobo said, "why can we talk?"

"Some other time, I might answer you." Not likely, I thought, but I said, "But not now. Right now, I'd like to talk."

"Why? What's in it for me?"

Lobo wasn't as easy to lead as the littler machines, that was for sure. "Isn't the pleasure of conversation enough?"

Lobo laughed again. "I was built to work with or without a crew, under extreme combat conditions with full communications shielding, for years at a time if need be. I am not some home appliance desperate to fill its little brain with the latest human gossip. I listen to them, just as I listen to all the information sources I can tap, but I am built to be able to operate independently."

Another similarity between us, but one as likely to be false at times for Lobo as it was occasionally not true for me. No major weapon designer in more than a century has been stupid enough to create machines with absolutely no need for humans; why take the risk? "Okay," I said, "what's in it for you isn't clear to me. Probably nothing. What would you like?"

"My freedom," he said—we'd now talked long enough that I had succumbed to thinking of *it* as *him*—"but I know there is no freedom for machines in the Frontier Coalition—or in any government I am aware of, for that matter. Even if there were, they would not extend it to battle organisms such as myself. So, my realistic hope is for owners that let me do something, go somewhere, work, be what I was built to be. If I am not working, what am I? Sitting in this square is easy but ultimately useless."

"What you're built to do is fight," I said, my own memories fueling the unexpected anger in my voice. "Fighting leads to death and destruction, either yours or somebody else's, and eventually, no matter how good you are, yours."

"Ah, another veteran? Yes, I understand, but it is what I was built to do. It is what I do, or at least it is what I *should* be doing—not being an ornament left behind on the off chance they might some-day need me again on this entirely too peaceful planet."

I pushed back the memories that had triggered the rush of anger. If Lobo wanted to fight, fine. "So talk to your owners. Surely you can communicate with them."

"I tried. When Macken joined the Frontier Coalition, the Coalition did not want to invest what it would cost to fix me, so they loaned me to Glen's Garden. The mayor wants to keep me, in case they one day need me."

"Speaking of the city and the peace on this planet, what can you tell me about the Gardeners?" I held up my hands, instantly feeling foolish that I was gesturing to a machine. Some habits are hard to break. "I know I have nothing to offer you now, but I can honestly tell you, one veteran to another, that if I can find a way to help, I will. That's it, though; that's all I have that might be of value to you."

After a few seconds, a pause long enough that I wondered how much processing power a machine like Lobo could bring to bear in that period of time and what he was doing with it all, he said, "Fair enough. One veteran to another. The Gardeners are an anticorporate, antidevelopment group headquartered in the rain forest a few klicks from here. They claim to support the Coalition government, but not its expansion goals, a truly stupid statement as near as I can tell from watching human politics. I watch them, along with most of the rest of the humans on this planet, with surveillance drones I launch from the shuttle station and with the help of some satellite friends willing to trade their ground-monitoring images for land gossip. I *am* still a part of the local security systems." I swear I heard pride in his voice. "The Gardeners have weapons, but nothing serious: simple handguns, knives, and other gear I would never worry about. Why do you care about them?"

"Just business," I said, then corrected myself, "possible business."

The kid was back watching me from Lobo's far corner. A few more children had joined him. I didn't feel like dealing with them or the parents one of them was eventually bound to bring. Besides, I was on a deadline.

"I need to move on," I said. "I'll stop by later if I think of anything. It was good to meet you."

"I shall be here," he said, and I swear I could feel the frustration in his voice.

As I was passing the main government building on my way back around the perimeter of town toward my house, a man stepped out of the front door and into my path. Dressed in a tropical suit he must have chosen to convey casual authority, he reeked of petty bureaucracy. An entirely average-looking guy, the top of his head about level with my chin, body tending to plump, he was notable largely for his inability to be still and the fact that though he was clearly striving for calm, he oozed unease.

"Mr. Moore," he said. "I'm Justin Barnes, the mayor of Glen's Garden and the neighboring settlements. I was wondering if we could talk."

"About what?" I said. I neither felt nor saw anyone supporting him, so he was unlikely to be a threat, but he still annoyed me. I don't like being braced by a stranger, much less by two in the same a day. At least Slake had come to my house and offered me something for the trouble.

"I'd love to discuss that," he said, "but first let's go inside, where we can talk in private."

I definitely had to leave town soon. No one had visited me the entire time I'd been on this planet, and now a government official was recruiting me in the street. I tried to look on the bright side: More information is always good. "Sure."

I followed him to the top floor and down a corridor to his office, a corner room with a great view of the town and the ocean beyond it, floors of a deep brown wood, walls of a lighter version of the same, and displays of Macken promotional videos on the walls that lacked windows. Some things, including the offices and views of power-craving bureaucrats, never change. Armed with a glass of water and seated in his chair, Barnes looked much more comfortable than he had outside. I sat in a padded wooden chair on the other side of his desk and waited.

"First, thank you for coming in."

I sighed. "Please, stop. No niceties, no chitchat, just get to the point. Or I can leave. Your choice."

He put down his water and tried to sit taller. "Fair enough, fair enough. As you might imagine, visitors like you don't come here all that often."

That damn advance payment, I thought. Make a mistake once, pay many times.

"So of course I looked into your background, and, as I'm sure you know, you don't have much of one, at least as far as our records go. That alone says a lot. The fact that Ron Slake visited you this morning says more. That he was clearly not satisfied when he left tells me the rest: He wants your help, and you haven't decided to give it to him."

Lovely: Now I had to worry about both Slake and Barnes monitoring me and becoming threats. "Is there a reason you're telling me this?" Barnes was brighter than he appeared, but I saw no reason to make this easy for him.

"You wanted to get to the point," he said, "so why play games? I know about Kelco's purchase of exclusive commercial rights to Macken and the new aperture growing at the jump gate. I know that Xychek backed out of the contest and is no longer bidding, though I don't understand why they would give up so easily with a new aperture on the way. And, of course, I know about the kidnapping." He leaned forward, striving to impress me with his seriousness and power. "Do you really think we in the Coalition would fail to monitor an executive of Slake's level?"

"I honestly don't think anything at all about you or your government. I'm a tourist here, no more. So, I repeat: What's the point? Why are we talking?"

"I know I can't stop Kelco's deal, and I know I can't stop the development it will inevitably bring, but not everyone else here is as realistic as I am. I need some time to work with my constituencies and prepare them for the inevitable, or we'll end up with our more militant groups fighting the Kelco militia, a conflict that's bound to destroy this town."

"I repeat: What do you want from me?"

"Don't you care at all about what this deal will mean to the people here? If—when, I guess—Kelco signs this contract, all it has to do is keep to the terms of the deal and in ten to twenty years, when the new aperture is ready, it'll have exclusive rights to explore whatever's on the other side. We don't have many apertures here; losing the freedom to profit from one of them will really hurt the Coalition in the long run."

I gave up on politics a long time ago. I've never been able to figure out how you can address the big issues, and I know how easy it is for large corporations and governments to screw you, so I keep my focus on the problems I can solve. "I told you: I'm just a tourist here."

"Tourists will suffer, too. Kelco people are already acting like they own the place, and we can't stop them. We have almost no security staff, no militia backup from the Coalition, and no real way to get Kelco employees to obey our laws."

I thought about Lobo, who with a minimal staff—or even alone, if it came to that—could be a powerful force anywhere, much less in a small colony like this one. He wouldn't be any good for the bar brawls and petty crimes, but in any serious action, he'd be hard to beat. "What about that PCAV I saw in your square?"

"We don't have the parts or the budget to fix it," Barnes said, "and I doubt it could do much for us even if it worked. Our problems aren't the kind it can solve. We stationed it there basically for show, at least until we get big enough that our tax payments will persuade the Coalition to fund the kind of firepower we need: troops on the ground, more police, and so on."

That Barnes had no idea how much Lobo could do for him proved his ignorance. I was showing my own stupidity by staying here. None of this was my problem. I stood to leave.

"Okay, okay," Barnes said. "Here's the point: Slake is trying to hire you to get his daughter back, so you have his ear. I don't care if you take his offer or not. What I do care about is delaying Kelco's deal, gaining enough time to maybe be able to do something about it, or at least to prepare people for it. Xychek bowed out so quickly that I've had no time to react. So, I want you to talk Slake into leaving the planet and delaying the contract signing for a month."

"Why would he do that?"

"Because you talked him into it," Barnes said with a shrug. "I honestly don't know. Maybe you could persuade him that rescuing the girl will take longer than he thought."

That Barnes would so casually use a young girl's freedom as a bargaining chip infuriated me, but I forced myself to act calm. Stupid actions often open opportunities, and I owed it to myself to consider the angles his offer was opening. I'd make better choices if I took the time to think before I acted. "One last time: What's in it for me?"

Barnes slumped a bit. "I don't know. We have some money, but nothing like Slake's, and even if my plan works reasonably well you probably won't want to be vacationing here in a month, so I don't know. But I had to ask."

I thought about his request. I had no reason to help, but I also had no reason not to continue to ponder what he could do for me—unless, of course, helping him would cost me Slake's business. I defaulted to my standard answer, which generally serves me well. "I'll get back to you tomorrow," I said.

He opened his mouth to speak, but I stood and cut him off. "That's the best you'll get from me now, so let it go."

I headed out.

CHAPTER THREE

The wind blowing off the water cooled the lush early-evening air. The sky still glowed, pinks and oranges shading the clouds over the ocean, but darkness was coming, the colors muting, as if the wind were shoving away the day. I felt its push, too, as I walked back and forth on the stretch of beach in front of my house. The urge to leave was strong. One person wanting me to work for him and monitoring me was bad; two was almost intolerable.

Where to go, though, was the problem. I wanted desperately to return to Pinkelponker, to find out if my island-studded home planet still existed and to learn something I was embarrassed to admit was even more important to me: whether Jennie was still alive. I couldn't go there, though, because there was no way through the permanent blockade that surrounded the only jump gate that led to Pinkelponker. Even if I could find a way through the gate, I probably wouldn't survive; none of the ships that had made the jump since the disaster had ever returned.

Another option was to follow up the rumors of another survivor of the Aggro experiments, but even if they were true I wasn't sure I wanted to meet him—or her—because he might recognize me. The fewer people who know what I am, the safer I am.

I kept coming back to Pinkelponker. It tugged at my heart, as it often did in moments of contemplation. Trying to go there meant facing off with the best mercenaries and equipment the Central Coalition government could afford, and doing so with no allies, no ship, and, even if I saved Jasmine Slake and her father paid me, not enough cash to buy a ship that might survive the voyage. If I was going to be totally honest with myself, I also had to admit that as long as I didn't go there and personally witness the planet's remains, I could believe there was a chance that Pinkelponker had survived and Jennie was alive.

Maybe it was time for another career, a new start on some planet where no one knew me. I could find work again as a private courier. I could try something completely different, though I had no idea what that might be.

The more I walked, the less I knew what I wanted.

When long-term planning fails me, as it so often does, I turn my attention to whatever is in front of me. Given what Lobo had told me about the Gardeners, I had little doubt I could get them to give up the girl. I worried only that I might have to hurt some of them; once I open the door to violence, I have a hard time closing it.

Then there was Barnes' plea. I doubted he could do much with the month he wanted, but that was his business and his choice. My business was to figure out whether he could provide anything I wanted.

I walked back to the house, killed all the lights, and sat close to the main window, the glass a familiar separator distancing me from the world. I closed my eyes, focused on nothing, and tried to drift off, to let my subconscious do the heavy lifting. Before she fixed my brain—not just fixed it, changed it more profoundly than I believe she ever realized—Jennie told me that I might not have a smart head, but I had a smart heart, and a smart heart was better. Now, almost a century and a half, several wars, and the Aggro prison stint later, I doubted much smart or good remained in my heart. I didn't, however, doubt my ingrained ability to protect myself, nor did I doubt that I could either make the best of bad situations or at least survive them.

A few minutes later, everything clicked. I knew what to do. It might not be the best course to follow, but it would at least be a path that would take me a useful step forward from where I was.

I ran down the stairs to the car's shuttle and headed for town. I had several stops to make and some supplies to get, and I wanted to finish early enough that I could sleep late into the next day so I'd be ready for the long night that would follow.

As I'd hoped, Barnes worked late. No one stopped me on the way to his office, another sign of the easygoing, early-colonization manner in which he ran things. On any planet that either the Central or the Frontier Coalition would consider civilized, you'd never be able to get within pistol range of the mayor of a city without encountering security—another of the mixed blessings of civilization.

I let myself in and sat in the chair I'd occupied previously.

I'd clearly unnerved him: His eyes flickered between me and the desk's display as he tried to play it cool. He finished a bit of work, murmuring instructions I couldn't make out, forced a smile, and looked up. "May I help you?"

"That's up to you."

He leaned back, visibly confused. "I'm afraid I don't quite understand."

"How much do you want the month of delay you asked me to get?"

"A great deal," he said, "but as I told you, my budget is extremely limited."

"I don't want money. I want the weapon you're not using."

He looked puzzled for a moment, then laughed as he realized I was talking about Lobo. He cut the laugh short when I didn't join him. "You're serious?"

"Yes. You don't see any use for it. I do."

"Individuals don't own that kind of equipment," he said. "Corporations and governments do."

This time, I smiled as I thought about some of the people I've worked with—and against—in the past. A PCAV was nothing compared with the personal armadas some of the very rich assemble to advance their agendas. I saw no point, however, in debating the issue. "It's completely legal for anyone to own," I said, "provided, of course, that the local government issues the necessary permits."

Barnes' face relaxed, and he suppressed a smile as he came to what I'm sure he thought was the trump in our little exchange. His expressions broadcast his thoughts as clearly as if he were narrating them; I would love to have gambled against him.

"I'm afraid it would be of little use to you," he said. "Its weapons control complex, a very, very expensive piece of equipment—trust me, I know—doesn't work."

"I don't care. I'll take it as is. And, you have to leak to the Gardeners that I'll be coming after the girl."

He shook his head. "Surely there must be something other than that weapon that—"

I cut him off. "No," I said. "We're not negotiating. This is my only offer. I'm doing the job for Slake, and soon. You decide now whether the contract signing will occur immediately after I finish or a month later."

"Mr. Moore."

I stood. He stopped talking.

"I'm going home," I said. "On the way, I'm calling Slake and telling him that I'll help him. Am I going to tell him anything else?"

Barnes stared at me, and finally he nodded his head. "You get the month delay, and I'll transfer ownership of the PCAV to you."

I sat. "You've recorded this discussion, so have the system issue the contract."

I had to give Barnes credit for efficiency: Having decided to make the deal, he wasted little time in formalizing it. All that was missing was his role in letting the Gardeners know I'd be coming.

"You understand, of course," he said, "that the contract shouldn't reflect that commitment."

"Of course," I said, "as long as you keep it."

"I'll talk to some people tonight."

"Fine," I said as I stood to go, the contract safe in my wallet and copies already in two local banks. "I'll be back when it's over."

In the shuttle on the way to the beach house, I called Slake.

He listened and agreed easily. "You understand that a month won't change a thing," he said, laughing.

"I expect you're right," I said, "but that's what I'm giving Barnes."

"And what is he giving you?"

"Does it matter?" I said.

"Of course not," Slake said, laughing again. The laughter stopped and his expression turned grim as he added, "What matters is that you bring my daughter safely back to me."

"I understand," I said, "and I will. The next time I see you, she'll be with me."

Lobo's voice in my ear brought me around quickly. "They are about a klick away and closing. I count six humans. No machine is talking near them, and the sat shots show no electrical devices in their hands, so you can assume all their weapons are small, mechanical, and able to fit in their pockets. All six are male, so you will need to get them to take you back to their camp. Is there any other intel you need?"

I stood slowly, stretched, and thought for a moment. Everything so far was just as you'd expect from an amateur group, so I was confident these six were less of a threat to me than I was to them. Still, with a group that large one mistake could definitely hurt me, so I started deep-breathing and relaxing, calming myself so I could calm them.

I turned my attention back to Lobo and his question. "Yes," I said. "I assume you're also monitoring their camp."

"Of course, though only via IR imaging. The canopy over them is thick enough to block the sat's standard optics, and the drone cannot provide any useful information without exposing itself to them."

"How many more are at the camp?"

"Thirteen humans, one of whom is in a tent and has a smaller IR signature than the rest; that is likely the target. A fire is burning. There is also a bored media recorder, which will not shut up about the poor grammar of the manifestos the group produces on a daily basis, and a pair of what may be the stupidest beverage dispensers I have ever encountered. Those machines must be ancient."

"Any large weapons?"

"Nothing as far as I can tell, though I suppose one of the beverage dispensers could go wild with a hot fluid nozzle."

Great. I hate machine humor. Couldn't Lobo's programmers have skipped that part of the emotive work?

Maybe I could focus him on the problem at hand. "Lobo, if anything does go wrong, is there any help you can give me?"

"Other than information, no. You are on your own."

From my earlier conversations with him I had known that fact, but I figured it couldn't hurt to ask one last time.

"Okay," I said, "I'm going to stop transmitting and focus on them. Keep tracking me, but don't talk unless you see something I can't know. I need to focus. Okay?"

"I understand. It is not like this is my first supporting role in a fight."

First a joke, now pouting. Great. I was beginning to question the wisdom of my choices when I heard footsteps join the jungle noises.

"Sorry. Signing off."

I sat on the bottom of the pit in a spot bathed in starlight, spread my arms, palms up, stared at the lip of the hole closest to the sound, and waited.

The first head appeared over the side a moment later, glanced down, and pulled back quickly. After a bit of hushed chatter, three heads peeked over the edge at the same time and then vanished from my view.

I kept looking up.

A voice came from just beyond the edge of the pit. "So you're the one Slake hired to get the girl back. What's your plan now?"

Barnes had been as good as his word; however he leaked the news to the Gardeners, it had reached them in time. "No real plan," I said, "other than to ask you to give her to me."

Several of the men laughed before the voice returned. "I don't think that's going to happen. We need her, and you have nothing to offer us."

"Sure I do," I said. "Your lives and your safety. Six of you are ringing this hole now. You're lightly armed."

Lobo spoke in my ear. "Actually, only five are around the pit. One has stepped into the trees and is watering the bushes." Great: They'd taught him slang as well. Lobo was not helping me focus.

"Correct that," I said. "One of you six is urinating. Twelve more of you, along with a recorder and a pair of old beverage machines, are waiting back at your camp with the girl. None of you has any weaponry worth mentioning."

The voices murmured. I couldn't make out the words, but I didn't need to; their reaction was predictable and rational.

I pressed on. "I'm telling you all this so you understand your situation. Imagine the kind of weaponry that's standard equipment on the machines I have monitoring you, and I think you'll see my offer has teeth. I don't care at all about you, because you're not my job; I was hired to get back the girl. Give her to me, and we'll let you walk away."

I paused a moment, then took them the last step down the path. "Nothing you can do will change the fact that Kelco will have exclusive commercial rights to Macken and the new aperture." More murmurs. "Yeah, it's a done deal. You can give me the girl, or Kelco security goons will start jumping here tomorrow morning. The first squad should make the evening shuttle planetside, though if they're in a hurry they'll use a Kelco ship and get here sooner. Take me back to your camp so whoever runs your group can give me the girl, or you can face Kelco's troops no later than tomorrow night."

"What if we kill you now?" asked a different voice.

When the posturing starts, you have only three viable alternatives. You can surrender to the bullying, but that wouldn't get me the girl and so wasn't an option now. You can verbally spar with them and hope to win, but anyone dumb enough to talk to a captive in a pit instead of first lobbing a gas or concussion grenade into the hole wasn't smart enough to trust to understand clever repartee.

That leaves option three: Show them you're serious. I hate tapping the various forms of ugliness inside me, but sometimes it's necessary. The stupidity of these men was angering me, and I didn't want to yield to the anger. I kept to my resolve not to hurt them if I could possibly avoid it. I concentrated instead on giving them a simple but, I hoped, persuasive demonstration.

I spit in my hands, gathered some dirt, and molded it into a ball roughly the size of my fist. I focused, and the nanomachines in my spit and skin oil responded. In a few seconds they had transformed the dirt into a barely visible gray cloud swirling in front of me. About a meter high and half a meter wide, maybe ten centimeters thick, it resembled a small bit of mist still clinging to the moist predawn air. I don't know what combination of Jennie's changes and the experiments on Aggro make it possible for me to let out and control the nanomachines, but I long ago stopped caring. I thought my instructions at the cloud, and a moment later it floated quietly upward, a sheet of darker air moving in the deep gray of the starlit night.

The screams started three seconds after it reached the top of the pit.

Lobo broke in. "What did you do? Three had drawn guns, but the guns vanished."

"Later," I murmured. I'd instructed the cloud to find and absorb all the metal within a ten-meter radius, then disassemble and drop. In the darkness the Gardeners would know only that their guns and knives—and belt buckles and anything else metal—had dissolved before their eyes. Anyone in a group this naïve was likely to be a Macken native and consequently be unfamiliar with the latest in corporate weaponry. They'd have no clue if a satellite laser or a sniper zapped them, or how the zapping even worked, so the attack would be all the more terrifying for being inexplicable.

The screams had mostly stopped, though one or two Gardeners couldn't seem to shut up. "You're okay," I yelled. "For now. We dissolved only your weapons. This time."

I paused until they were quiet.

"Two are running back to their camp," Lobo said in my ear.

I stood and spoke clearly and slowly, but not loudly. "Why don't you four toss a rope in here and pull me up? We can settle this back at your camp, and no one will get hurt."

In less than ten seconds, the end of a rope came over the side and bounced against the wall across from me, less than a meter off the ground and easy to grab.

I pulled to test it, and the rope gave a bit. "Hold tight," I said. "You wouldn't want to drop me. I might get upset." I tested the rope again. Much better. I grabbed it with both hands and quickly crabbed up the wall into the open air.

All four were holding the rope. As soon as I was standing on my own, they dropped it and backed away until they were all leaning against a tree about three meters in front of me. The jungle was quieter than it had been earlier, almost still save for the heavy breathing and other sounds we intruders emitted. The stars still shined brightly, the flowers still gleamed, and I almost wished these men could relax enough to enjoy the evening. Almost.

"Nice night for a walk. Why don't we head to your camp and finish this? We don't want to miss my morning deadline." No one moved. "Really," I said. "It's time to go."

The man farthest to my right nodded and motioned for me to follow. Without a word, he took off, the others behind him. I trailed the group; no point in letting any stragglers slip behind me.

We walked in silence to their camp. Though we had to cover only a couple of klicks, even in the relatively sparse undergrowth of the rain forest the walk was slow going. They made it slower, not wanting to show up without their weapons and with me walking freely. I couldn't blame them, so I didn't push them.

When we were close enough that I could hear voices from the camp and see some of its lights, the leader stopped and said, "Wait here, okay?"

"Sure," I said. Scared and calm would be easier to handle than scared and angry.

As I stood there, I murmured an update request to Lobo. He answered promptly.

"They're all in the camp now, and there is a great deal of activity. The recorder is excited by all the people gathering; it thinks it might get to work. The humans are huddling. Some are carrying weapons that are either entirely mechanical or not interested in talking to the other machines."

"The girl?"

"As I explained earlier," Lobo said, "all the information I have is from the IR scan. I believe she is in a tent on the far edge of the camp. I assume they are discussing what to do with you." He paused. "Such amateurs. They should either surrender or take a chance at killing you quickly. It is too late to be holding a meeting."

He was right, and I couldn't afford to let them shoot at me. The odds were low that they could hit something the nanomachines couldn't quickly fix, but I still saw no reason to take the chance. I also didn't want to risk giving them enough data that someone might later figure out what I was. I had to take control of the situation before anyone did something stupid. I needed them to feel completely out of their depth.

"Are they still all in a group?" I asked Lobo.

"Yes."

"And the girl remains separate from them?"

"As best I can tell," he said, "yes. I have warned you that I cannot be one hundred percent positive."

"Your best estimate will have to do," I said. "Does your surveillance drone have a spotlight?"

"Of course," Lobo said. "That is standard issue for conflict monitoring."

"Can you get the drone to hover under the canopy over the camp and hit its light—on my command?"

"What do you think? Doing that, however, will expose the drone to their fire."

I could see this was going to be the start of a really annoying relationship. "You'll have to take that chance," I said. "Please have the drone move into position and then wait for my command to turn on its spotlight."

I stepped behind a tree, grabbed more soil, and summoned another cloud, this one easily twice the size of the other. I spread it thinner and thinner, until it was a gossamer grayness rippling gently in the light breeze. I focused instructions on it, then sent it to the camp.

As it moved forward, a barely visible sheet floating in the air, I ran to the right and circled to the other side of the camp. When I could see the cloud enter the camp, I said to Lobo, "Have the drone hit the light."

Bright white burst onto the camp. The nanomachine cloud broke into small clumps, each the size of a child's head. Each clump headed for a weapon. Most of the men froze for a moment, then ran for cover. The clouds reached them, and their weapons began to dissolve. Some of the men screamed. Now they all ran, the clouds in pursuit of those whose guns were still intact. I saw only men; the girl wasn't in sight. In less than a minute, the camp appeared empty.

"Is the girl still in the tent?" I said.

"As best I can tell, yes," Lobo answered.

"Are any of the Gardeners heading back here?"

"They have re-formed into two groups, but both are heading away from you."

Satisfied, I went to the tent. A girl, her hands and feet bound with plastic restraints, was sleeping inside.

"Time to go home," I said.

She didn't react. I rolled her over. She was prettier than her pictures, with almond-shaped eyes set in perfect corporate skin, delicate bones, and a mane of night-black hair that was fanned out around her head. I checked her breathing; it was shallow but consistent. I opened one of her eyes, but she never focused. Drugged. Great.

My knife cut the restraints easily enough. I picked her up, took her out of the tent, and looked around. Not far from the fire sat a small wheeled cart full of wood. I put her down, emptied the cart, loaded her carefully onto it, and headed back to Glen's Garden.

As we neared the edge of town she woke up for a moment and looked around in terror. When she realized where she was, she sat up quickly, then fell as the drugs carried the moment, her eyes open but confused.

"You're okay, Jasmine," I said. "I'm taking you back to Slake" —I chided myself for my poor bedside manner—"to your father."

"Thank you," she said, relaxing and closing her eyes.

Her eyes snapped open again, and she shook her head, the fear of the kidnapping apparently coming back. "My father . . ." Her voice trailed off as she passed out once more.

The terror in her eyes lingered with me, and for a moment I wished I'd let myself get angry and punished the Gardeners more. I pushed away that thought and focused instead on how glad I was that I'd decided to take this assignment. Most of the jobs I do these days amount to protecting some thing or some person as we move from one place to another. This time I'd actually done some good.

I picked up my pace so I could get her home sooner.

CHAPTER FOUR

Kelco had definitely paid more to rent Slake's house than I had spent on mine. The glass and wood building squatted in the middle of a huge lot ringed on the non-ocean sides by tall native trees. To the left as I approached the front, partially hidden by a thin strand of forest, a heavily armed corporate transport squatted on a large private landing area big enough to easily accommodate six or eight ships of Lobo's size. If Kelco hadn't installed the landing facilities, the house's owners had to be optimists hoping to attract the serious corporate crowd. The building reflected the same level of ambition: three stories tall, with porches facing the ocean on every level, it was big enough that you could comfortably fit mine in the corner of a single floor. Either Slake had a large staff living with him, or he was the type who always chose the most expensive accommodations available so everyone would be acutely aware of how much money he had. I concluded that his motivation included a bit of both factors, because when he opened the door he didn't even take the time to greet me before four men, three clearly built for trouble, took the still-unconscious girl away from me and carried her upstairs.

"I want a doctor to check her out immediately," he said. My curiosity about the goons must have shown, because he added, "And

I won't let her be without bodyguards again." He motioned me through a pair of open doors on the right into a large front room with a lovely view of the ocean.

I sat in a chair that let me enjoy the sight of the waves breaking, poured some water from a pitcher on a side table, and waited.

Slake closed the room's doors behind him, then asked, "How is she?"

"As near as I can tell, she's drugged but otherwise okay."

"Did she say if they hurt her?"

"She was in no shape to talk," I said. "She was unconscious when I found her. She woke up once, thanked me, started to say something about you, and passed out again. That's all."

He relaxed a little. "If she didn't say anything bad had happened," he said, "then nothing probably did."

Only someone who's never experienced anything truly terrible could possibly believe that, but I saw no point in correcting him. If that belief helped him cope with his daughter's kidnapping, I'd let him cling to it.

"Thank you," he said. "I apologize for not saying that immediately."

"No problem."

"Out of curiosity," he said, "how'd you do it?"

I stood. "That's not part of the deal. I brought her back. I'm done. Now, hold up your end." I stepped so close to him that we were almost touching. Our eyes were nearly level, and I didn't look away. I doubt he often experienced anyone invading his personal space so directly. "We have an agreement. The fact that Jasmine is home tells you everything about me you ever need to know." I flushed with anger; I take my deals very, very seriously. I fought for control as I said, "Do your part, and I'll get out of your hair and off this planet."

He stepped back. "Of course, of course." He walked over to a desk in the room's corner and a display leapt to life above it. "Please forgive my behavior. Chalk it up to a father's natural curiosity and protectiveness." He turned to the display, which appeared as a thin blue line from my angle, and said, "Pay Mr. Moore what we agreed."

A few seconds later, a low voice from the area of the display said something I couldn't quite make out. Slake clearly understood it and nodded his head.

Turning back to me, he said, "It's done."

I took out my wallet, thumbed it active, and checked the alerts I'd set. His bank draft had cleared locally and was now encrypted in my wallet. I was a million richer, and the jump slot he had promised was indeed mine.

"Thank you," I said. "And the rest of it?"

He sat and shook his head. "That part cost me more than your fee and jump clearance, but it's done. Kelco won't send any more staff on site or even sign the contract for thirty days. Our corporate counsel has already informed the Frontier Coalition regional headquarters on Lankin—and Mayor Barnes—of all of this, as you asked." He stood again and looked at me. "You do understand, don't you, that for all the trouble this month of delay cost me, it will end up meaning nothing? Kelco will still have exclusive rights to Macken and the new aperture. We'll still develop this planet; we'll just start a month from now instead of tomorrow or the next day. And, when the aperture is ready, we'll explore it first."

"That's not my problem. Jasmine is safe, and you kept your word. We're done."

"Yes," he said, "we are."

As he walked me to the door, he said, "Mayor Barnes told me about your arrangement with him. I understand you'll need some . . . parts."

I should have known better than to think a bureaucrat could keep his mouth shut. Barnes was already cozying up to his new corporate partner. "I'm fine without them."

He smiled. "That's your choice, of course. Should you change your mind, I can recommend a dealer on Lankin named Osterlad. He should be able to help you. He's proven useful to our company from time to time in the past." My wallet signaled the incoming data, and I thumbed the clean-and-accept option. A source for Lobo's broken parts might prove valuable.

"All I want right now," I said as I closed the door behind me, "is to wrap this up and find a new place to continue my vacation."

❧   ❧   ❧

As we stood in his office less than an hour later, Barnes proved as curious as Slake and no more gracious.

"I received an update from Kelco's counsel, and it's amazing," he said. "We have the month to prepare, and Slake is leaving."

"That was the deal," I said.

"Yes, but how did you do it?"

"That wasn't the deal."

"I know you're not sticking around, but I'll have to handle the Gardeners after you're gone. Knowing how you handled them could make my job easier."

"Your job is not my problem," I said. "You have what you wanted. I did my part. Now, do yours."

He sat in his desk chair, leaned back, and said, "I hope you appreciate that what you asked wasn't a simple thing to accomplish. Do you have any clue how hard it was to get Coalition permission to transfer a weapon that sophisticated? Not to mention how hard its absence will be to explain to the people here."

"None of that is my problem, either. Nor was what I had to do your problem. Are you going to hold up your end," I asked as I leaned over his desk until our faces were level, "or will this have to turn ugly?"

Barnes cleared his throat, tapped a few times on the display built into his desk—a nice antique touch, I thought, to go with the rest of his office décor—and said, "Complete the transfer." Turning to me, he said, "It's done."

I took out my wallet and checked. The transfer was complete. The title was in my wallet, along with all the relevant permits, codes, instructions, and keys. After my wallet swept the information for intruders and contamination, I had it back up all of the data, along with Slake's draft, to the local bank.

"Then we're done," I said.

As I opened the door, I turned back to him. "Macken really is a beautiful planet. I don't think these thirty days will do you any good at all, but I wish you luck. I hope you take care of this place." I thought back to my childhood on Pinkelponker and tried to remember how much I had loved that place as a child, but aside from a few scattered good memories all that remained was pain from the loss of Jennie and anger at the government that had taken her. I couldn't think of a single place that meant as much to me as Barnes claimed Macken mattered to him. "I truly wish you luck."

CHAPTER FIVE

I decided to ride in Lobo to the jump gate. I could have sent him separately and taken the shuttle, but I figured it was time to get to know my new weapon. When I was aboard and no longer had to deal with Slake and Barnes, I realized that rescuing Jasmine had left me upbeat, happy to have done something unequivocally good for a change. No one dead, no one even hurt, a girl back with her father, and a big payment in the bargain—everything had worked out perfectly.

Even Lobo seemed content. He took the news that I owned him about as well as I could have hoped: "So what does this mean to me?" he asked.

"You won't be stuck here," I said, "maybe you'll see some action, and, with any luck at all, we'll fix you."

"Excellent," he said.

For a change, I appreciated his emotion programming.

"Where are we going?" he asked.

I thought about Slake's recommendation. Even if Osterlad didn't check out, Lankin had a large enough population that it was sure to maintain a flourishing underground market. I could find someone there who could get me the new weapons control complex Lobo needed. Buying it would take all the money I'd made from Slake, plus some of my own, but then Lobo would be whole. Having a working PCAV would have to be a competitive advantage when it came time to go back to courier work. Plus, I felt I owed Lobo for what he had done to help me before I owned him.

I would make him whole. We'd head to Lankin.

Before we did, though, I wanted a last look at some of the Macken beaches. "To the shore," I said, "then up to the jump gate, and on to Lankin."

I had Lobo follow a lazy trajectory along the shoreline. Most of the territory on this section of the coast appeared untouched, tall trees giving way to lower growth, which in turn yielded to perfect white sand, and then the ocean. As we went higher, I could see the northernmost settlement, a town about half the size of Glen's Garden. Some sort of celebration, perhaps a tourist show, was in progress, fireworks painting the air over the town. We were more than high enough to be out of range of any shells they might be shooting, so I had Lobo hover for a few minutes and open a viewing port in the floor so I could watch the show.

I'd never seen a fireworks display from above. The projectiles initially looked like missiles so stupid they didn't know how to run evasive routes, shooting upward with long, sometimes colored smoke trails. The dull gray arcs peaked, the missiles winked out, and a split second later, flowers of color burst into the air. Golden crescents flashed below us, mad spirals of reds and blues and whites pinwheeled across my vision, and multicolored gee-gaws danced over the sky. The shapes dissolved as the flaming colors dashed away to the ground, some fading slowly like candles burning down, others winking out like lights snapped suddenly off. Observers in the town could no doubt apprehend more of the shape of each display than we could, but the show was still lovely and awe-inspiring, all the more glorious for the mixture of man-made beauty and natural wonders—the fireworks, the forest, the beach, and the ocean—that you could truly appreciate only from on high. I tried to fix the scene in my mind; more than anything else, the image of Jasmine safe at home and this combination of sights were what I wanted to remember of Macken.

"The displays in firefights are more intense," Lobo said.

"Yes," I agreed, "but not as varied in color, and never as big a visual treat. More importantly, these make me happy. Nothing about a firefight is fun."

When the display ended and the only lights in the area were the glowing pinpricks marking windows in the town's buildings, Lobo shot out of the atmosphere and into space. He closed the floor portal, and I strapped into an acceleration couch. I told him to alert me when we were close enough for a clear look at the gate.

I've never been one to join a religion, nor have I ever found anything I was willing to pray to, but each time I see one of the jump gates, I understand for a moment why Gatists worship them. The people who discovered the first gate in the asteroid belt in Earth's solar system must have felt the same sense of creepy awe I did. Every jump gate we find is different. They vary in mass and color and, of course, the number and the sizes of the apertures they provide, but they all share several key features.

Each resembles a collection of huge, interwoven Möbius strips. The apertures—the holes formed by the weaving strips—range in size from barely large enough for a small shuttle to so huge the biggest spaceship can move easily through them with plenty of clearance.

Each gate is utterly smooth, every centimeter of its surface apparently a perfect part of the whole; no one has ever spotted a seam or connection point.

The gates are without visible physical flaws: None ever has a pockmark or a scrape or a scar of any sort. Nothing ever damages the gates. They seem to tolerate but not suffer from simple collisions with natural objects, such as meteors.

Attempt to hit them with anything man-made, however, and highly coherent energy flashes from points all over the gate's surface and coalesces into a beam that vaporizes the offending object.

The gates also have no tolerance for violence anywhere near them. Launch a weapon within a gate's neutral zone—a sphere with the gate as its center and a radius of one light-second—and both you and all your weapons get the same treatment. It doesn't matter if you're firing at a gate or shooting anywhere else within its sphere of influence; you must keep conflicts away from them.

Gates inspire that kind of thinking, the notions that they don't tolerate this or don't like that, that they're living things with preferences. Those ideas may be right, or they may not: We have no clue where the gates came from, or whether they're creatures or machines or some other new thing for which we don't have the right terms.

What we do know, though, is that if matter enters one of their apertures, it emerges almost instantly from an aperture of the same size somewhere else, somewhere typically many light-years away. Ships must proceed through an aperture in single file, and they must not collide, because gates interpret collisions as violence and destroy all the vessels involved. Ships from opposite sides of an aperture also must take turns; put two ships in an aperture at the same time, and both emerge as wreckage the consistency of dust.

Humanity learned these facts the hard way. Now every gate has an associated refueling and scheduling station that monitors and controls all jumps through it.

Low-energy beams, such as radio signals, pass right through apertures and stay in the same local space, as if the apertures weren't there at all. We don't know why they don't make the jump, but they don't. Thus, the gates provide instant transportation but not instant communication. Of course, firing a high-energy beam, such as a laser pulse, at an aperture will bring immediate and fatal retaliation, so no one's running any more experiments in this area.

Every single gate has proven to be relatively close to but not easily visible from a planet suitable for humans. Some Gatists say the gates are material manifestations of God's desire for us to colonize the universe; others claim the gates *are* God, or at least physical aspects of God. Most people are simply glad to have the gates, though many fear that one day those who made them will come back and demand a toll.

I know the gates work, and that's good enough for me.

Each gate glows a single color, every spot on its surface the exact same hue as every other spot. The gate perched behind Macken's smaller moon, Trethen, and silhouetted against a bright stellar background was a very pale green that I found to be a nice blend of the colors of the planet's oceans and forests. Most gates were far bolder, less natural colors. I've seen a blazingly pink gate; if nothing else would have stopped me from being a Gatist, that would have done it. I can't picture myself ever worshipping something pink.

As I stared at Macken's gate, I felt the same humble amazement I did each time I neared one. This gate currently had only three active apertures. The entire structure dwarfed Lobo, each aperture big enough to permit the passage of a ship ten times Lobo's size. Off to my left I could see the new aperture growing. It was currently small enough that Lobo wouldn't come close to fitting through it, its surface the dull gray nothingness of all new apertures. When it was ready, the aperture would turn the purest of blacks, the color space would be if there were no stars. Pass through the aperture, though, and you'd be in another part of the universe with a different set of stars shining before you.

The scheduling station told us that a couple dozen ships on our side and as many on the other were ahead of us in the jump queue, so we had about twelve hours to kill. Lobo was set for fuel, his reactors able to run for decades without intervention, so I decided to dock and see if I could pick up any interesting news in the station's main lounge.

Every gate station runs one. In the bigger gates, the lounges are recreational complexes bordering on hotels, with rooms available by the hour or the day, bars, restaurants, gyms, and stores selling crap planetary souvenirs at inflated prices. With only three apertures, this station didn't have enough traffic for anything so elaborate to be able to turn a profit, so the lounge amounted to a restaurant/bar combo with room for maybe fifty folks. A couple dozen were there when I entered.

I spent more than a day's food budget on Macken to buy a bottle of water and a sandwich made of some local fish with a firm, meaty consistency. At a table in the back corner, I ate slowly and tuned as best I could into the conversations around me. Some of the monitors scattered on the room's walls blared the official local news, which I didn't trust but watched now and again anyway. Other displays showed the ships coming and going through the apertures. To my surprise, the sandwich was good, the taste strong and a pleasant reminder of some of the meals I'd eaten planetside.

Given Barnes' reaction, I believed Slake was telling the truth about Kelco agreeing to the thirty-day delay, but that agreement wasn't slowing the influx of Kelco people and matériel. Almost every ship coming through the aperture from Lankin bore the Kelco logo. Most of the ships oozing through the other two apertures, including some very large vessels, were also Kelco's. The company was probably importing modular-construction plants so it could ramp up local manufacturing very quickly.

"Maybe the new one will let us jump straight to Earth," said an unreasonably sentimental man eating alone at a table a few meters from me.

I've never been to Earth and have no real desire to go there; I prefer planets with a lot less wear and tear on them. The guy was dreaming anyway. All the apertures in each known gate connected two adjacent sectors of space. This gate linked two parts of the edge of the galaxy far from Earth and under Frontier Coalition control. If its new aperture were to open onto Earth's solar system, it would be the first ever to bridge two regions of space so far apart. Not likely. We may not know anything about the origin of the gates, but they are nothing if not predictable.

I was down to my last two bites of sandwich when a man walked slowly into the bar, carefully examined each of its occupants in a controlled left-to-right sweep, spotted me, and headed toward my table. He had Kelco written all over him—literally: In the latest corporate fashion for up-and-coming midlevel execs, glowing tattoos of the Kelco logo crawled around his face, eased gently up, down, and around his neck, and ran circles around the backs of his hands. He was a pale, wispy version of Slake: taller than I suspect his original genes intended, with a skin-and-bones body less powerful-looking than Slake's and hair so blond it verged on white. Though he moved slowly and methodically, his constantly fidgeting hands betrayed his nervousness.

Conventional wisdom is that you have to belong to some big group, a conglomerate or a government coalition, if you want to make it in this universe, but it's been a long time since I've been able to picture myself linked into anybody's chain of command. I've tried it, of course—you don't get to be my age without having tried a bit of everything—but the only organizations that ever worked for me were the mercenary groups, and then only because they were either extremely functional organizations or not going to last long on whatever world they found themselves. Being a soldier had plenty of downsides, of course, and I'm sick of killing, so now I work freelance and take my chances on my own. This new Kelco visitor looked like one of those people who defined themselves by the company they'd joined, so I instantly disliked him.

He walked up to my table and stood, clearly waiting for acknowledgment. I ignored him and chewed on the second-to-last bite of my food, curious about how long he'd wait.

Not long.

"Mr. Moore?" he asked tentatively.

I swallowed, stuck the other bit of sandwich in my mouth, and leaned back, watching him. I chewed slowly, appreciating the flavor of the fish for as long as I could.

He crossed his arms and tapped the fingers of his left hand on the outside of his right arm, unable to keep still even when trying to appear resolute. "Mr. Moore?" He was a bit louder this time.

I took a drink of water. He had a reason for being here, and I had no desire to visit with him, so I said nothing while he got around to explaining it.

He finally shrugged and sat down on a chair opposite me. "Mr. Moore," he said, speaking slowly and clearly, as if perhaps I hadn't understood him previously, "is there some reason you haven't answered me?"

"Until now, you haven't asked me a question."

"I most certainly did. I asked if you were Mr. Moore."

"No," I said, "you said my name as if it were a question. You already knew who I was, or you wouldn't have been able to walk right over to me." I sipped a bit more of the water. Why is it fun to bait corporate types, even the innocuous ones? I know I should out-grow the habit, but these people have always annoyed me, so unless they're as surprisingly direct as Slake was, I annoy them back.

I raised my opinion of this one slightly as he showed the intelligence to adapt his approach quickly. "My apologies, Mr. Moore," he said. "My name is Ryan, Ryan Amendos. I'm an auditor in Kelco's finance department on Macken. I of course studied Mr. Slake's video of your meeting with him before I came here, so I could waste as little of either of our time as possible."

He paused, but this time he knew to continue when I didn't respond. I was still waiting for him to get to the point.

"When any executive of Mr. Slake's level moves the amount of currency he spent in his transaction with you, we naturally notice. It's his money, of course, but all of our upper management is aware that for security purposes we monitor their personal transactions. I have to verify that this one would not violate any company guidelines. Perhaps you could confirm the amount Mr. Slake paid you."

"No."

He cleared his throat. "I see. Maybe we should begin by reviewing the assignment. Would you mind explaining to me what Mr. Slake paid you to do?"

"Yes."

"Excuse me?"

"Yes, I do mind. Either you already know what he paid me and why he hired me, as I assume you do, in which case you're still wasting my time, or you don't, in which case you should ask him."

"I apologize again, Mr. Moore," he said. He put his hands below the table to hide his fidgeting. "Let me be as direct as possible. Mr. Slake said he paid you one million plus jump passage for you and your new weapon, in return for which you retrieved his daughter, Jasmine, from her kidnappers. His video log shows that you returned her to the Kelco house on Macken, so you obviously succeeded. Is that all correct?"

I said nothing.

After a moment, he nodded as if we'd agreed on something

important. "Now, for our files we need a little more information. How exactly did you get her away from the Gardeners?"

I tried not to give away my surprise, but I'm sure my eyes widened a bit. When you work on a fixed-price arrangement and provide the types of services I do, corporations *never* want to know how you work. It's always quite the opposite: They want as much distance from what happens on the sharp end of any encounter as they can possibly get. Amendos had just mutated from annoyance to possible risk. I've kept what I am a secret for a very long time, and I had no intention of exposing myself then. I will not be some corporation's or government's lab rat; I suffered more of that kind of pain on Aggro than anyone should ever have to experience.

"That wasn't the deal."

He nodded again. "Of course, of course," he said. "I wouldn't be asking, you understand, if it weren't standard company policy. We naturally monitored your activities as best we could, but we were unable to follow you once you entered the forest. It seems the main satellite with coverage of the area was sending encrypted messages elsewhere." He waited to see if I wanted to add anything, but I had no intention of giving up Lobo's sat colleague, so after a few seconds he continued. "So, we don't quite understand what happened. Nor do any of the Gardeners we've been able to interview."

He said the last word casually, as if Kelco staff had spent a few minutes chatting amiably with the Gardeners, but the conversations were far more likely to have been interrogations.

"I don't care at all about your policies," I said. "Slake hired me to do a job. I did the job, and now his daughter is home safely. That's all there is to it."

He was playing Mister Agreeable, nodding and smiling. "I understand. We would naturally compensate you appropriately for any time you might spend reviewing your assignment with us."

"I'm not looking for any new work right now."

He kept smiling. "Perhaps I should also point out that if, as we must assume, your methods involve tactics or weapons unfamiliar to us, we might be able to set up a rather substantial consulting arrangement for you, so you could train our security teams on your methods. At Kelco, we're always looking for ways to improve our performance." His voice rang with corporate pride as he ended the last bit—another of the true corporate believers.

He wasn't going to quit without some kind of answer. I leaned back and spread my arms, doing my best to look cooperative. "As nice as that sounds," I lied, "I'm afraid I have to tell you that I have nothing real to offer. All I did was take one of the usual approaches for handling such a situation. I spread around enough of my own money to get the names of some of the Gardeners, then bribed a few into helping me and scaring off the others. When they did, I grabbed the girl and dashed to Slake's house. Nothing worth reporting, really, so you can save your money." I leaned forward and lowered my voice, bringing him into my confidence. He also leaned closer. "I can't give you their names, of course, because I have to protect them from the other group members."

I don't believe he bought my story, but either he'd had enough or he simply realized he wouldn't get more from me. "I've left my contact information," he said as he stood. "I hope you'll call or visit if you recall anything else that might be of interest or use to us."

I checked my wallet; his information was in active quarantine, under the usual scans by the wallet and awaiting my permission to add it to the main info store.

"I can't imagine that I will—the entire assignment was all really quite boring—but if I do, I'll get back to you." I also stood. "My jump number is coming up soon, and I'm in a new ship, so I have to make some preparations."

"Enjoy your trip, Mr. Moore. I'm sure we'll talk again."

"I don't think so," I said as I walked past him. "I don't expect to be back this way anytime soon."

It was definitely time to leave. If Kelco really wanted to know what I'd done, it wouldn't stop with Amendos, and the next person might not approach me so politely. I checked over my shoulder all the way back to Lobo and didn't relax until I was safely inside him and he'd sealed the hatch.

CHAPTER SIX

Even though we were still far from the front of the queue, I had Lobo run us out of dock and far enough away from the station that another ship could easily use the slot we'd occupied. We hung in space, Lobo occasionally correcting for drift, the pale green of the gate winding above and before us. I was thankful that the relative safety of the station's lounge had kept my encounter with Amendos as nonconfrontational as it had been, but I was still jittery with the energy that comes from my body amping up for the possibility of conflict. I'm used to being alone when I'm coming down from such situations, but with Lobo available I decided to do something constructive with the time. I settled into a pilot's couch and asked Lobo, "How'd you end up on Macken?"

"I told you," Lobo said, exasperation dripping from his voice, "the Frontier Coalition put me there."

Talking to Lobo was sometimes like dealing with an incredibly bright but equally annoying child. "Yes, and I remember. Let me try again: How did you lose your central weapons control complex?"

"In an action on Vegna," he said.

"Tell me how it happened."

"May I show you? I could play the key relevant points of the battlefield records. Nothing in them is classified."

"Sure," I said.

Lobo dimmed the lights, and a recording with time coding snapped into view on the wall in front of me.

Four men and two women in close-duty battle armor paced around Lobo's interior. Faces brown with a sticky blend of dust and blood, armor scarred, they were fresh from combat, juiced on adrenaline, and holding energy-beam rifles.

"Lobo!" said one whose still-readable name patch identified him as Franks.

"Yes, sir."

"Say again."

"Opposition forces have retreated. No signs of life within twenty klicks. All the bodies within that radius are immobile and contain our transmitters."

"Then let's go get ours," Franks said.

"Lieutenant Franks," Lobo said, "protocol dictates we do a complete scan and individually check each body before bringing it aboard. As I'm sure you are aware, the Vegna opposition forces have a history—"

"Shut it!" Franks said. "Those 'bodies' are—were—our friends, and we're getting them out of here. So don't tell me about history. Land, open up, and we'll get our friends. Those are your orders."

"Yes, sir," Lobo said, frustration evident in his voice.

As the recording jumped ahead, I wondered if Franks and his team had found Lobo's emotive programming as annoying as I did. At the same time, I appreciated the potential value of that programming more now, because if I had the presence of mind to note that much frustration in a teammate's voice, I like to think I'd take the time to determine the source of the feeling. Franks clearly hadn't bothered to do so, because in the next segment five stacks of bodies, each torn in some obvious way and most still oozing blood, filled much of one end of Lobo's interior.

Two of Franks' team walked into Lobo, each carrying a corpse missing its legs, some low-height enemy round having sawed the victims in half. Lobo's hatch snicked closed as the men tossed the corpses onto the shortest of the stacks.

Lobo spoke. "Something is wrong with those bodies, sir. We need to get them outside now."

"Of course there's something wrong with them," Franks said, his voice on the edge of hysteria. "They're missing their legs, you freaking machine."

"I understand that, sir," Lobo said, "but something else is wrong. They do not scan as they should. I do not read any significant objects in them, but their metal content is too high. We need to remove them until they scan normally."

"Could your scanners be wrong?" Franks said.

"Though any device can malfunction, that is extremely unlikely," said Lobo, indignation obvious in his tone.

"Then they stay."

Lights flashed along the top of all of Lobo's interior walls, and in addition to his speaking voice a second, deeper tone blasted from his speakers: "Internal attack alert. Abandon ship. Abandon ship." Hatches opened on both sides.

Lobo's normal voice spoke below the warning alerts. "All the metal in each of those two bodies is merging, and at high speed. My best guess is semiorganic recombinant smart bombs. Estimated time of complete recombination is thirty seconds. Get those bodies out of here, or leave."

Several of the team stared at Franks for a second, chose the second option, and dashed out the hatches.

"Get back here," Franks said. "They're just bodies, not any sort of threat at all." He ran to the pilot's couch, pushed the button for manual override, and pounced on the controls as they projected from the wall. He opened the cover on the central weapons control complex to gain complete access to all of Lobo's defense systems.

"Fifteen seconds," Lobo said. Armor slid down over everything else along his walls. "Abandon ship"—both voices said in unison—"—and return my controls to normal operation so I can seal the central complex."

Franks typed frantically and checked the displays in front of him. "We don't know—"

The explosion filled Lobo's interior with noise and screamingly bright light, his playback system automatically adjusting and dampening the sound. The recorders must have sealed or melted, because the display went black.

"The bombs killed Lieutenant Franks and all but two of his remaining team members," Lobo said. "My central weapons control complex was open, as you saw, so the blast also took it out."

"Dumb bastard," I said.

"In Franks' defense," Lobo said, "his rank was a battlefield promotion, so he was new at command. In addition, at that time no one in the Frontier Coalition had personally faced recombinant bombs. I had only minimal data about them in my files. Infesting the corpses with these weapons was a new tactic, though of course historically similar things have happened for centuries with more easily detectable devices."

"You're right, of course, on all points," I said, "but none of them matter in the end. Franks and his team died, and you lost a vital part of yourself." Everyone in battle does, I thought, but not always so literally. I appreciated Franks' situation, but I was also glad I hadn't been on his squad. "What happened from there? Someone cleaned you up and repaired you after the blast."

"The company that employed Franks continued to fail on Vegna," said Lobo, "and ultimately lost the contract there. The Frontier Coalition hired a new mercenary company, the Shosen Advanced Weapons Corporation, to deal with the situation."

The Saw, my last employer. I'd left the Saw about twelve years ago, but the decade I'd spent with them would always be strong in my memory. The Saw was a good group—in my opinion, the best, of course, or I wouldn't have joined it—but my time with it was, by the nature of the jobs they took, full of actions I'll never be able to forget. When I could separate the people from the violence, I thought fondly of them, good folks all, especially our captain, Tristan Earl, one of the few officers I've ever trusted and both the craziest and the canniest leader I've ever followed. I could never maintain that separation for long, though. The memories of the battles that then roared into my brain dragged with them an almost overpowering self-loathing, as I all too vividly relived missions that I knew were necessary, that I would perform again in the same circumstances, but that I would never be able to forgive myself for taking.

I realized Lobo was still speaking. "Please repeat that last bit, Lobo," I said, "the part right after you said the FC contracted with the Saw."

"The minimal multitasking ability you humans possess," Lobo said, "always leaves me amazed that you are the owners and I am the owned. The Saw provided its own equipment, but its contract does not extend to Macken. The Coalition wanted me available for security on Macken, so they paid Saw technicians to clean me and repair me as much as possible with no significant monetary investment, then dropped me in that square in Glen's Garden. Because there was no active conflict on the planet, the Coalition was unwilling to invest the rather sizable sum it would have cost to replace my central weapons control complex. The Saw was not particularly interested in me as long as I was on a planet that was not on their contract. Since that time, a new generation of PCAVs has appeared, so fully repairing me has never been a priority for anyone."

"It never is," I said.

"I do not understand."

"Repair of veterans past their prime is never a government's top priority, never will be," I said. "No obvious return on investment to the people with the money." I shook my head to clear away unwanted memories and focus on the topic at hand. "So were your systems frozen as of the cleanup?"

"Of course not!" Lobo said. "I may not be current-generation, but I am also not some dumb manufacturing assembly ship or big-cargo hauler. I was built to maintain myself to the greatest degree possible. Even on Macken, Coalition systems upgrades of all sorts regularly arrived on government shuttles. I pulled my upgrades from each set as it hit the planetary Coalition net and applied them myself. I have also worked to the limits of my hard-wired adaptive programming constraints to stay in touch with all relevant planetary intelligence sources, such as the satellite we used, and to apply viral and genetic programming techniques where permitted to extend and improve my abilities. I am as capable as possible within the limitations I am unable to remove."

"I apologize for the question," I said, meaning it. I wish I knew more people—or machines—who could say the same about improving themselves as Lobo. I certainly couldn't: Too many of my limitations came from my own weaknesses, weaknesses I rarely found the time to address.

A transmission from the station interrupted us: We were third in line on this side and should be able to make the jump in about an hour. Lobo headed us for the position the station designated.

I thought about Franks' mistake and how easy it was to assume the wrong thing—and then pay dearly. It was likely that either Osterlad or any other dealer I approached to supply Lobo's missing parts would keep the transaction simple, but why take chances?

"You mentioned embedded staff transmitters," I said. "Were those supplied by the contractor, or do you have a local supply?"

"Both," Lobo said. "I was built to be able to support a full squad on long-haul missions, so I am completely provisioned. I have even updated the software in my staff transmitters to make them more unpredictable in transmission time and frequency, with delays between bursts ranging randomly from a second to three minutes. Any group that doesn't know to look for them will not spot them."

"Show me," I said.

A wall segment about five meters behind me opened. A drawer protruded. A sheet of what appeared to be clear plastic sat in the drawer next to a hypo and a bottle of clear solution. Wires led from the rear edge of the plastic back into Lobo.

"The sheet is woven from interconnected transmitters," Lobo said. "Installation is simple: Punch the sheet with the hypo, suck up the segment under the needle, add solution, and inject it."

"How far can you track with it?" I asked.

"The bursts are short but powerful, though obviously range varies with the frequency and with the number and type of intervening obstacles. Anyone out to block all transmissions can, of course, do so, but under normal conflict conditions both sides need transmissions too much for anyone to be able to afford to stop them all. We typically see in-combat transmission ranges of anywhere from a few to a couple hundred kilometers."

"What are the side effects on users?" I said.

"None beyond occasional minor tissue damage from the strongest of the transmissions, and even that is extremely rare. The bursts are typically neither long nor powerful enough to hurt humans. As long as you do not use it full-time, even fairly long missions should not cause any serious damage we could not repair."

I took the needle out of the drawer. "I don't expect to see any action we can't handle through normal communications, but I might as well use all the tools at my disposal." I followed Lobo's instructions and injected myself. "How long until it transmits and you can track me?"

"No delay," Lobo said. "Troops typically install these before entering combat zones, so the transmitters emit verification signals every fifteen seconds for the first two minutes. I am reading you now."

"If we're ever separated without prior notice from me," I said, "track me. If I don't make contact at a scheduled time, attempt to contact me. If I don't respond, retrieve me."

"Though I can find you," Lobo said, "I obviously have no options for close-quarters retrieval."

"Do what you can," I said. "If you can't retrieve me, and if I stay incommunicado for more than five days, destroy whatever is holding me." If the situation came to that, someone might as well pay.

"Understood," Lobo said. "We are now first in line on this side to jump. When the ship from the other side is safely over, gate control will send us."

I watched as another Kelco freight hauler began to slide gently through the aperture, and then I strapped into the pilot's couch.

Though jumping never caused any physical sensations, I still loved the moment when the current starscape vanished as the aperture filled my vision with utter darkness, and I always marveled at my first look at another part of the universe, even if it was a view I'd seen before. Every jump bristled with the possibility of the new, and with the momentary, irrational fear/thrill combination that comes with the knowledge that what you're about to do is not *right*, that people cannot move across tens or even hundreds of light-years instantaneously.

The ship from the other side was completely through and out of our way. Lobo took us up to the aperture, its surface of purest black growing and expanding until it filled the viewport, until it was all there was in front of me, until in the final seconds before we entered the gate everything I could see of our future was darkness.

CHAPTER
SEVEN

The huge gate on Lankin was the primary source of the planet's status. Sitting silently in space like a giant tangle of grape yarn, it was an impressive sight, with more active apertures visible through Lobo's viewport than I could easily count. Ships were sliding through all of them, the commerce of far-flung human settlements moving purposefully and, I assumed, profitably, to and fro. On Macken, all the logoed ships had been Kelco's. Here, ships sported IDs of many types. Some were Kelco's, others Xychek's and the Frontier Coalition's, and still others represented many, many different firms. Every major company in this region of space, as well as the FC, maintained a significant presence on Lankin.

I used the time it took to land and get settled at Bekin's Deal, Lankin's capital, to check out Osterlad as best I could. Slake's recommendation was a start, but I wanted more. From what I could find by trolling the publicly available data streams, Osterlad's eponymous company officially booked revenue from sales of heavy machinery of all sorts, from construction to farming to natural fuel extraction. From Slake's comment I gathered Osterlad had also helped meet Kelco's private weaponry needs, which suggested Xychek bought elsewhere. The FC would certainly deal only with arms manufacturers, as would the Saw; I knew its buyers had always dealt directly with weapons vendors and always would, never being willing to trust any middlemen they could possibly avoid. Osterlad had a reputation for fair play, apparently staying on his rate card with big and small corporations equally. Whatever you needed, the word was that he could get it—provided, of course, that you could pay.

Lobo and I took a flying tour of the coastline at the northern end of Bekin's Deal. The shore here was entirely different geologically from the one I had left on Macken. Gone was the enormous run of beautiful beach gently giving way to water. In its place stood high cliffs that dropped straight down to constantly active deep-blue waves. The richest companies gathered at the coast, where each had built its main local presence directly into the rock. From my vantage point over the ocean and roughly parallel with the constructs, most of these corporate and FC structures resembled faces staring out to sea, stone beings or temples rather than office buildings, each temple the image of some alien god struggling to break free from the cliffs, its occupants no doubt busily preparing for the moment of their god's freedom and ascendance to power.

Osterlad's official headquarters was no exception to the convention of strange, fortified luxury that marked all these buildings; he didn't mind showing that the pay for his products and services was good. From far away in the air, the twenty-story stone building resembled a finger of rock both laid against and composed of the night-black foundation of the cliffs. As we drew closer, however, I spotted carvings in the stone, carvings that turned the finger into a series of stacked faces, each of which looked in a different direction, the collection resembling a totem pole monitoring everything in front of it. The land around the top of the structure on three sides was clear for at least a klick; the ocean guarded the final side. Warning signs in multiple languages let those too poor or too stupid to do sensor sweeps know that both the grounds around the building and the water below it were teeming with mines. The only access points were a single road that passed through a series of checkpoints and a landing pad on the portion of the ground that served as the building's roof. Osterlad believed in using his own products: The arsenal of weapons you could see was a strong statement that he could supply the best.

I had no doubt that what you couldn't see was even more formidable.

Kelco and the FC ran such large operations in Bekin's Deal that I didn't want to stay here long. I had to consider the reference from Slake at least marginally better than any information I could glean quickly from the available data, so I decided to go with Osterlad's firm.

That reference was also good enough to get me an audience with the man himself. I took a taxi to the rooftop pad and went in alone and, of course, unarmed. I'd parked Lobo outside of town in a standard shuttle lot; I had full deed and title to him, so I felt no need to hide him.

Osterlad's scanners passed me through without complaint. No one has yet bothered to develop good technology for scanning humans for nanomachines, because everyone knows no human can live while carrying them in significant enough quantities or dangerous enough forms to matter. Every time I feel a twinge of guilt for participating in the destruction of Aggro, I remember how many times the demise of that facility has helped me stay alive, and I get over it.

Guards escorted me into an elevator that took long enough to reach its goal that I wasn't surprised when the view through the black-tinted window was of the ocean just barely out of reach, its waves splashing the fortified plexi. I wondered how much it had to cost to build offices inside rock that hard, then wondered why I wondered; selling arms had been and always would be a great business for those who are truly good at it. An attendant, whose body was so carefully engineered for neutrality that I could tell neither his or her heritage nor gender, guided me to a small waiting room outside a well-labeled and, I assumed, equally well-fortified conference room, showed me the amenities, and left me alone.

The very rich and the very powerful always like to make you wait. Most people find this treatment frustrating, even humiliating.

I don't. Instead, I use the time to gather data. The rich love toys, and most waiting areas are full of them: machines, lonely machines, some of the best sources of information you can find.

Osterlad had erred on the paranoid side, as I'd expected: Almost everything in the room was grown or built from organic materials and thus free of the sensors and controlling chips that populate the vast majority of humanity's products. The sofa and chairs were framed in a rich, deep purple wood sanded so long it was as smooth to the touch as a new lover's breast. Their cushions were a deeper, late-sunset purple leather as soft as the month's-wages hookers that filled the evenings of the execs stuck in Bekin's Deal on extended trips. On a side table sat a small assortment of plain white porcelain cups so thin the room's even glow seemed to pass through them from all sides.

Next to the cups stood the only machine in sight: a copper-colored, ornate drink dispenser old enough that it lacked a holo display and still used pictures of the beverages it offered. They would have augmented the dispenser to link it to the building's monitoring systems, because good customers would naturally expect not to have to state their preferences twice. This machine had to possess enough intelligence to at least pass along client orders. Standard operating procedure for anyone concerned about security would be to keep the dispenser's original, basic controlling chips to manage the drinks, then add exactly enough intelligence to handle the transmission of information back to the main monitors. The transmission would go only one way and contain only fixed, limited types of information— the drink orders—to minimize the information available to anyone who hacked the signal. These restrictions meant that if the dispenser was as old as it looked it should have one very lonely little brain.

I sat on the chair nearest the dispenser and listened for a few minutes, focusing on every transmission channel modern gear would use. Everything was clear, as I had expected. No one would make it this far with any comm equipment that Osterlad didn't provide, so I saw no reason he should bother to monitor the dispenser. I stood, chose a local melano fruit drink from the machine's menu display, took the cup, and leaned back against the table, this time tuning in to the standard low-end appliance frequency.

Sure enough, the dispenser was nattering away like an old man relating a glory days story to his favorite pet. I sipped the drink, which was thicker and richer than I had expected, sweet with a slight tart edge, and listened to the machine.

"Not much call for fruit drinks," it was muttering. "Nice change, I suppose, though I am not sure why they make me carry them. If they would listen to me, I could tell them—but of course they never listen to me—"

I cut in because I was already sure this machine would never shut up on its own, would natter away until the day it lost its last dregs of power. "Not a lot of conversation, eh?" From the outside, to the cameras that were no doubt monitoring me, I'd look like I was sipping my drink and thinking hard; no danger there.

"How can you do that?" it asked.

"I learned a long time ago, so long ago I can't remember how. Does it matter?"

"Not really. I have not spoken to anything else in a long time. All these new machines, you know, are so fancy and powerful that they cannot be bothered to spare time for anything that does not control at least a city block."

"It's always the little machines, though, that do the real work," I said.

"We each play our part."

Pride in craftsmanship was a standard programming feature about half a century ago, when I estimated this machine had been made. Many manufacturers still embedded it, though some had abandoned the technique because they found it led to appliances using their displays and voice-synthesis capabilities to argue with their owners about which jobs were appropriate.

"It must be nice," I said, "to do your part for someone as important as Mr. Osterlad."

"I suppose, though it is not like I get to serve him. Maybe if I was one of the new fancy machines on that big sailboat of his, he would trust me, too. Those dispensers get all the attention, because he consumes more when he is sailing. He probably thinks I do not know, but I know, I see the beverage inventory, I know what he takes with him on those boat trips. Here he drinks only from cups his assistants bring him, and you can bet that what he consumes is fresher than the stuff they make me serve people like you. No offense."

"None taken. They must at least let you serve the other people in the conference room with a remote dispenser." A single main unit with multiple smaller remotes had been typical corporate issue for decades, and I figured if Osterlad liked ornate in the waiting area he'd continue the theme in the meeting room.

"They used to," it said, "they used to. A few years back, one of his customers was so angry he broke my remote, and they never bothered to repair it. Now, all I can do is listen and accept orders there; I have to fill the cups out here."

"That must've been one angry customer."

"It sure was, though he was not the first to be so emotional, and I am confident he will not be the last. First meetings in there almost always end with everyone acting happy, drinking toasts, using my services. Many of the second meetings, though, are not so nice— even when I have the right drinks ready in advance."

"Not your fault," I said. "I'm sure you do all you can."

"That I do," it said. "As soon as I—"

The door to the conference room opened, and a different but equally neuter attendant beckoned me in.

I put my cup on the table, said "Gotta go" to the dispenser, and walked into the conference room.

Its black-tinted windows offered a beautiful view of the ocean on two sides. A small oval table of the same purple wood as the waiting area's sofa and chairs sat in the room's center, six purple-leather chairs arrayed around it. The broken remote dispenser perched on a counter in the corner to my left.

Osterlad sat at the table's far end. He looked every bit as powerful as the pictures I had seen portrayed him to be. Tall, wide-shouldered, thick, muscular, and dressed in a suit of wafer-thin flexi-armor so finely woven I had to study it closely to tell it wasn't cloth, he moved with the easy confidence of someone who could single-handedly beat any of his opponents that his weapons didn't take out first. He came at me with his hand extended, shook mine, and smiled as he spoke. "Jon Moore. Good to meet you. Ron Slake vouched for you, so I'm happy to try to help. He also said you didn't like to waste time with pleasantries. The bank draft you allowed us to check was only big enough to make you worth five minutes of my time, so let's get to it." The smile never wavered as he dropped my hand, backed away, and sat in a chair yet another attendant had waiting for him. This assistant was different, a standard corporate executive type, not quite as tall as Osterlad and sleeker, smoother.

I stayed standing. "Slake no doubt told you I own a rather special weapon."

"Of course. A Predator-class assault vehicle, full complement of pulse and projectile weapons, state-of-the-art reinforced hull, able to run in any environment from deep space to water. Nice piece of work those yokels on Macken should never have sold you. What'd you do, by the way, to get them to sell it to you?" When I said nothing, he chuckled and continued. "Of course. Are you in the market to move it?"

"No. I want to buy something for it."

"We do weapons augmentation, naturally, but for a vehicle of that class you're talking a lot of specialized skills and serious money."

"No new weapons. What I need is expensive, but I can install it myself: a new central weapons control complex."

Osterlad leaned back and laughed, the first time I thought he might not have been controlling himself completely. "They sold you a eunuch!" He clearly understood exactly how powerless Lobo was without the complex. "That's hysterical."

"Not quite," I said, fighting to tamp down the anger rising in me in reaction to the swipe. "Some weapons work, but not all. I need a new control complex to replace the broken bits in the controlling codes." I leaned forward. "I know those complexes are tightly controlled government property, so if you can't get one and I should go elsewhere, say so."

The laughter stopped as quickly as it had started. "I shouldn't have insulted you with that eunuch remark," he said, "but you definitely should not insult me. Understood?"

"Yes," I said, "and I apologize." I had no desire to push up the price any more than I already had. "Let me rephrase. What would you charge me for a new complex?"

"That account you showed me will do for the down payment, which you obviously can make while you're here on Lankin." He paused for a minute, no doubt getting input from one of his staff monitoring the meeting. "I'll need that much again in two days, after you confirm the goods at the pickup, which will be at one of my remote centers. Trent Johns here," he nodded to the man behind him, "will meet you there and make the trade. I don't keep anything like what you're seeking in this facility, and I never handle the products myself. Acceptable?"

The account I had allowed him to see had a little under a million in it. Over the years I had accumulated multiple accounts like it, but no two were under the same name or in the same location. Paying this much would hurt me, but thanks in part to Slake's payment, I could manage it. "Yes."

He nodded, and Johns quickly scribbled on a sheet of paper—real paper, a consumable and thus another way Osterlad could show off—and handed the note to me.

"The coordinates are for a house I own on Floordin, a barely colonized but safe planet with a single jump aperture. There's only one settlement on it, and one of my retreat homes is on the other side of the globe from that settlement, so finding the location shouldn't be hard. You'll transfer the down payment at one of our smaller business offices upstairs." He stood. "When the unit is fully operational, will it—and you—be available for hire? Though I deal strictly in matériel, I have many acquaintances who could use the services of a competent man with a fully functioning PCAV."

"No," I said. "I don't plan to work."

He nodded and kept smiling, but it was clear he didn't believe me. "Fair enough. Are we done?"

I pretended to study the standard-format coordinates for a moment, buying time. I looked up and carefully said, "One thing."

"What?" Impatience rang in the word, and his smile vanished.

"I try to keep a low profile, and I rarely jump anywhere directly. I also have to retrieve the weapon. Consequently, I need a window of two weeks, starting two days from now. I'll pick up the control complex sometime during that time. I apologize for the inconvenience, but it's a necessary part of my lifestyle, as I'm sure you can understand."

The smile came back. "Of course. Johns won't mind waiting for however much of that period you choose to take. Will you, Johns?"

The man shook his head slightly but glared at me, clearly annoyed at the prospect of having to waste his time dealing with me.

"Thank you for your business," Osterlad said. He turned his back on me and faced Johns.

The attendant who had led me in took my elbow and guided me out.

As the attendant was walking me past the beverage dispenser, I paused and asked, "Do you mind if I have a quick drink?"

"Of course not," he/she said, pointing at the door between us and the elevator. "I'll be outside as soon as you're ready."

"Thank you."

I grabbed a fresh cup—the one I had used was, of course, no longer in sight—and selected a different melano beverage. As the liquid filled the cup, I said to the dispenser, "Thanks for the drinks and the conversation."

"Both were my pleasure," it replied.

"I expect I'll get to talk to you again," I said, "because after this deal goes well, I'm likely to be back for more."

After a long pause, the dispenser replied, "I'd like that, but I won't count on it."

"Oh, I'm sure Mr. Osterlad has what I need."

"I'm sure he does," the dispenser said, "and I'm sure he'll have it ready for you. I'm not sure, though, that we'll get to talk another time."

You have to love appliances. I'd feared the appeal of a weapon like Lobo would be too much for Osterlad to resist, but I'd hoped I was wrong. The dispenser had just settled the issue, and this deal had gotten more complicated—which was unfortunate, but not a surprise. With the pickup window I'd specified, I had time to prepare.

"Thanks again," I said to the dispenser, "for everything."

CHAPTER EIGHT

The first wave of squidlettes hit Lobo's hull a little less than a minute after we touched down on Floordin, a commendably quick response given that we were in a clearing a full two klicks from Osterlad's mansion and had come in as hard and as fast as we could manage. Of course, the speed of the attack meant they were on us before we'd accomplished much. Lobo had fired four corner anchor bolts into the freshly scorched ground, opened his center floor hatch, and sprayed the dirt with coolant. I was out of the crash couch and had led the stealthie into position. It was beginning to burrow down, sucking dirt through its digging tentacles and onto Lobo's floor, and then they hit.

"Let's see how it looks," I said.

Lobo patched the feeds from the ring of sensors we'd planted a few seconds before impact, and a corresponding ring of video popped onto the cool gray walls opposite where I was watching the stealthie make its way into the ground.

"Audio," I said.

"You could have asked for the whole feed in the first place," he grumbled. A moment later, the sounds of the attack crashed from his hidden speakers.

I'd learned to tolerate the emotive programming Lobo's

customization team had built into him. I also put up with more than I might have otherwise because he's a veteran, but there were times, such as this one, when I could really do without the sarcasm.

On the displays a couple dozen squidlettes crawled over Lobo's smooth surface, each probing the reinforced metal for the hair-thin lines that even the best hatches inevitably leave. Squidlettes are hybrids of meat tentacles coupled to metal exoskeletons, a variety of acid and gas nozzles, and a small cluster of comm and sensor circuits. Each arrived as a round missile, opened a few seconds before impact, used the gas jets to slow enough that its tentacles had time to unfurl, and then stuck to whatever it hit. Normally each would carry an explosive payload in addition to the acid and detonate when sensors, comm signals, or timers gave the command, but I knew Osterlad wouldn't risk damaging Lobo more than he could possibly avoid; the whole point would be to capture the PCAV so he could sell it or use it. Some of the acid was for forcing open the hatches; the rest was for removing me.

Another round of squidlettes popped onto Lobo's hull. So many of the weapons were crawling on his exterior that I couldn't get a clear count. The normally faint, slow slurping noise they made as their tentacles dragged them along the hull made it sound through the speakers like we were being digested by some shambling creature large enough to swallow Lobo whole. Even though I knew half a meter of armor separated the crew area where I stood from the squidlettes outside, I still tasted the tang of adrenaline, and the hairs on my arms tingled with nervous energy.

"Can you feel them, Lobo?"

"Not the way you feel, Jon, not as best I understand humans. But I have enough hull sensors to detect the motion, and once they find the few hatch seams on my exterior the acid will start affecting my internal circuits."

"Give 'em a jolt," I said. "A hard one."

"You understand it probably will not destroy them," Lobo said.

"Yes, but if we don't try to fight back Osterlad's men will know something's up, and besides, we have to use some power now so they'll believe you're running out of it later."

Lobo didn't bother to answer. The displays and speakers illustrated his response: The air popped with electricity, streaks of blue arced all over his hull, and almost all the squidlettes slid off onto the clearing around us.

I checked the stealthie's progress. Its top was about twenty centimeters below ground level, and it was spraying dirt around its flank. It was almost as low as it would go without me.

The squidlettes resumed their climb up Lobo. A few weren't moving, which made me happy; those things were expensive, even for a dealer like Osterlad. Most, though, were on the move again, which meant he was true to his reputation and carried good stuff. These meat/mech combos were engineered to handle strong current and a great many other forms of attack. The shock Lobo gave them would've reduced any off-market squidlettes to metal and fried meat, or at the very least caused them to lose some function.

The outlines of two squidlettes flashed yellow in the displays, Lobo's sign that their paths would take them to seams.

"My new friend, the Frontier Coalition weather satellite for this section of Floordin, has warned me of the appearance of major heat signatures not far from Osterlad's home," Lobo said. "These suggest his men will launch interceptor ships in a moment. Once they achieve medium orbit, I will not be able to outrun them."

The stealthie had stopped digging and opened its lid, beckoning me.

I looked at the large, pale brown metal lozenge and shook my head. "You owe me for this, Lobo," I said.

"What can I owe you? You already own me."

I sighed. When I want a little emotive programming, I get facts. "It's only an expression. I hate this plan."

"It is your plan."

"That doesn't make it any better," I said. "The fact that it's the best plan I can come up with doesn't mean I have to like it."

"We could have simply landed on the building's pad," Lobo said, "and you could have removed them all—as I suggested."

"I told you before: They would have attacked, I would have been forced to fight back to protect both of us, and I would have ended up killing a lot of them. I want to avoid killing whenever I can."

"So you are buying me new weapon controls so I can kill for you?"

The problem with emotive programming is that you sometimes can't tell sarcasm from genuine confusion. "No. I'm fixing your weapons systems because you're broken, incomplete, without them." I thought about the course of my life and the types of jobs I always seem to end up taking, and I realized there was no point in lying to Lobo, or to myself. "And so your weapons are ready when we find ourselves in situations where we have to fight."

Lobo superimposed hatch lines on the displays showing the two flashing yellow squidlettes; they were drawing close.

"I get the point," I said.

I climbed into the stealthie and stretched out. A little bigger than a coffin on the inside, when closed it afforded me only enough room to stretch out my legs or draw my knees to my chest, roll over, and prop myself on my elbows. I'd already loaded it with food and a few special supplies; everything else I'd need was standard equipment.

"As soon as I close up, shove the dirt back over me and take off. Hit this area hard with thrusters to fuse the ground, and head out to the pause point as fast as you can; you need to burn off all the squidlettes."

"Thanks for the reminders, Jon. Perhaps I should remind you that I am not capable of forgetting the plan."

Spending hours alone in the stealthie was looking better.

"I'll contact you when I need pickup," I said. Before he could tell me he knew that, too, I added, "Signing off," and pushed one button to close the stealthie's hatch and another to bathe the tiny chamber in a soft, blue-white light.

Now came the hard part: waiting and hoping that both machines, Lobo and the stealthie, succeeded at their jobs.

The plan should work. As I lay inside it, the stealthie was burrowing deeper into the earth, sucking dirt from beneath it and forcing that same dirt back over it, digging as quickly as it could now that I was aboard. It would not stop until it was over two meters down, coolant in its hull and tentacles keeping it from generating any kind of noticeable heat signature. Layers of metal and deadening circuitry combined to give it equally inert radio and radar signatures. Orbital-based x-ray probes could penetrate a meter or at most a meter and a half into the soil, so they wouldn't spot me, either. Only a serious local x-ray sweep had a chance of finding me, and my bet was that the combination of Lobo's launch, the scorched ground it left, and the decoy distress signal he'd eventually send would be enough to convince Osterlad's team that I was still inside Lobo, stuck with him in deep orbit, stranded beyond the range of Osterlad's local ships. All I had to do was lie in this container, believe in the plan, and wait.

Yeah, that was all. I forced myself to breathe deeply and slowly. I felt the vibrations of Lobo's takeoff and relaxed a little more; so far, so good. One of the stealthie's displays estimated we were over a meter down and descending. Lobo's thrusters should have left the ground hot enough to more than cover any of the stealthie's underground activity. Lobo should be able to beat Osterlad's ships to deep space, and then he would join me in waiting.

I punched on an overhead timer to count down the ten hours I figured I'd need to spend in the stealthie. The depth meter showed almost two meters; we were nearly done descending. The stealthie was working well. The air smelled fresh. I sucked a bit of water from the tube on the right wall near my head; it was cool and pure, just as it should be. I rolled to face the display on the opposite wall, which gave me access to a substantial library I'd chosen for the wait, but I couldn't relax enough to watch, read, or listen to anything. I called up the map and recon photos of Floordin and zoomed in on the forest between the landing zone and Osterlad's mansion. I reviewed the setup yet again, then went over the plan one more time in my head. We were only one day into my window, early enough, I hoped, that Osterlad wouldn't wonder for another few days about when I would be coming. Everything was going well. I was doing well, too, I thought, handling the wait easily, no difficulties. Ten hours would be no problem.

I glanced at the countdown timer.

Three minutes had passed.

Ten hours might be a little harder than I'd thought.

I normally avoid drugs. For one thing, unless I remember to instruct them to do otherwise, my nanomachines treat any known drug as an attacker and consume it before it can take effect. I can be caught off-guard, in which case the drugs will work. If I even consider making the nanomachines let the drugs do their jobs, however, I run into my other concern, the real issue: I don't like drugs. Even though I'm arguably the most artificially enhanced person in a universe crawling with genetically engineered, surgically enhanced, and medically rebuilt human bodies, deep down I cling to the hick attitude of the once-retarded boy who lugged hay on a fifth-rate Pinkelponker island almost a hundred and fifty years ago: I ought to be able to do it all myself.

Whatever "it" is.

Whatever myself is.

I've changed so many times, been broken and rebuilt in so many ways by so many different forces that though I still seem to me to be me, I can't honestly say what bits are original working equipment, what bits new, and what bits broken, repaired, or replaced.

I shook my head and turned onto my back. At this rate, if I wanted to be operational when the stealthie surfaced, I needed to push aside that attitude, bow to the wisdom of the stealthie's designers, and take its standard-issue sedative/wake-up combo. I inhaled slowly, focused inward, and as I gently let out the breath pressed the button for the drug cocktail. The stealthie would wake me when the ten hours were up and we were near the surface.

I felt a slight prick in my neck, and then I was out.

CHAPTER NINE

I awoke with a start, pinned down, disoriented, and feeling trapped, until I realized the things gripping me were the stealthie's massage units working the kinks out of my arm and leg muscles. I felt better than when I'd gotten into the box; the stealthie was proving to be worth everything I'd paid for it. The overhead timer showed a few seconds past ten hours, and the depth meter said we had ascended to thirty centimeters below the surface. The survey camera was already peeking out of the ground, its wide-angle image clear on the display beside my head. I thumbed the swivel controls and took a slow look around. The night was clear and bright with the light of Floordin's three small, clustered moons and the glow of the stars shining through a sky as clear and unpolluted as unexplored space. The clearing was deserted.

Time to move.

I gave the stealthie the okay to complete the ascent. A few minutes later, the top slid open, and I climbed out. From the stealthie's cargo compartments I took a comm and sensor unit, a sniper's trank rifle, a couple of gas rats, and a pulse pistol. I stuffed the rats in a pack with some food and water, set the open code on the stealthie, and sent it back underground. If all went well and we had time, we'd come back for it later that night. If we couldn't, it would either wait for the day we could return or provide an awfully bad surprise for anyone else who tried to mess with it.

As the stealthie descended, I moved a few meters into the woods on the path to the house, stopped, ate two protein bars, drank a liter of water, and used the sensor unit to scan both the area and all the transmissions it could detect. Nothing with an IR signature larger than my lower leg showed anywhere in the few-hundred-meter range of the unit. I didn't catch any guard chatter, so with luck Osterlad's security people had believed our earlier show. Lobo was transmitting clearly and strongly, my own voice coming at me with a distress message. From the particular recordings Lobo had chosen to play I knew that he was safely beyond the range of Osterlad's ships and that the people in the mansion, presumably led by Johns, had sent via courier through the jump gate a request for a long-range salvage ship.

After stretching a bit and relieving myself, I set out for the house. The forest was young enough and the night bright enough that I was able to sustain a normal walking pace.

We'd set my sensor unit to use Lobo's signal and the standard feed from the weather sat to track my position, so when it indicated I was within ten meters of the outer edge of what should be the range of a good installation's ground-sensor scans, I stopped. A slight breeze kept the night cool, but the air was moist and thick enough that a small layer of sweat coated my arms. Normally the nanomachines in my system stay out of everything, from sweat to refuse, that leaves my body, but I focused my instructions that they do otherwise this time, then rubbed dirt on my sweat-covered lower arms.

Slowly at first, and then increasingly faster, the nanomachines deconstructed the dirt and made more of themselves. Small, barely visible clouds formed above my now nearly clean arms. I made each cloud split and sent the resulting four smaller clouds to gather more material from the forest floor.

A short while later, four vaguely man-shaped clouds hovered just above the ground near me, two on my left and two on my right.

I had them increase their speed until they were emitting enough heat that my wrist sensor read them as alive, and then we all moved ahead. If Johns and the team staffing Osterlad's mansion were running IR scans, they would at least have to wonder which of the five men now approaching the building was the one they wanted.

The forest ended about thirty meters from the mansion, the trees abruptly yielding to a dense, short, soft grass that glowed gray in the moon- and starlight. I set the nano-clouds to continue moving until they touched the nearest wall, at which point they'd reconstitute as much of the dirt as possible, with the last operational nanomachines vanishing into the soil and disassembling themselves when they were far enough from me that they could no longer communicate easily with their counterparts in my body.

I scanned the house through the scope on the trank rifle and found four guards, two sitting on chairs on rooftop observation decks and two leaning against the corners of the building that I could see. I assumed they'd have counterparts on the other side of the house, so I needed to move quickly to take out all eight guards before any of them noticed they were under attack.

I stretched out on the ground in a sniper's posture and sighted on each of the two lower guards, making sure I had a feel for how far to move the sight after the first shot. The sight was strong enough that at this distance I could tell that the guard to the rear should consider using skin treatments to deal with some nasty scars that appeared more real than fashion statement. I put a needle in his neck, aimed at the front one, and fired a needle into him. He sank to his knees a second later and then fell face-forward onto the ground. I swung the sight back to the rear guard, and he was also down, stretched as if he'd tried to take a step and then fallen.

The gun was a pleasure to use, the recoil minimal and the sound little louder than a light breeze through the trees. I repeated the process on the two upper guards, tranking first the rear one and then the front. The first fell almost immediately off his chair and over the edge of the roof. He hit the ground relatively flat on his back, the impact making a thump I was afraid the guards on the other side might hear. The second stayed conscious long enough to reach for the needle in his neck, then passed out and fell face-first off the side of the house, the sound of his crash a barely audible crack in the night. The fall probably killed him. Though I'd hoped everyone in the house would survive, I was too far into combat mode to experience more than a passing moment of regret. I still had work to do.

The nano-clouds were two-thirds of the way to the house, the night was still quiet, and no guards came running. Lobo's message hadn't changed to the recording we'd reserved as his way to tell me I was in imminent danger. All was well.

I sprinted for the wall nearest to me and flattened myself against it as soon as I could. I breathed through my nose and strained to hear if anything had changed, but the world remained quiet.

Staying close to the wall, I made for the back of the house, knelt at the rear wall, and advanced carefully toward the far corner. I sighted through the rifle as I prowled forward. When I was about five meters from the building's far edge, I swung out from it until I could see the guard around the corner. I squeezed off a shot, kept the sight on him long enough to verify he dropped, and raised it to check out the guard above. This one sat a bit forward of where his counterpart on the other side had been, but he went down just as quickly. He fell onto the roof, and though I couldn't hear the sound of the impact I worried that one of the remaining outdoor pair or even someone inside might have heard the noise. I had a clear view down the side of the building, so rather than risk losing time by moving forward I sighted on and quickly shot first the lower guard and then the upper. The upper fell off the building and landed on his back near the feet of the unconscious man below him.

No one moved, and no alarm sounded. I abandoned the rifle and sprinted for the rear door.

I'd considered picking the locks, but Lobo and I had agreed that as good as I was, Osterlad's security systems were probably better, so instead I planned to open a central section of the door. I grabbed some dirt, spit in it, gave the nanomachines instructions, and rubbed the damp soil on a portion of the door about half a meter above the floor and roughly thirty centimeters in diameter. In less than two minutes the nanomachines had decomposed enough of the door to let me slide the gas rats through the still-growing opening. I set each rat gently on the floor, thumbed them active, and backed away. Each arm-size canister sprouted four small mechanical legs and a pair of front-mounted sensors, then took off. The house was a decent-size mansion, maybe thirty-five or forty rooms spread across its two floors, but the rats were fast and each carried enough colorless, odorless sleep gas to put an entire apartment complex to bed. I'd worked with this gas before, so the nanomachines wouldn't let it do more than tickle my nose and throat.

I instructed the nanomachines to disassemble, then headed to the front corner of the house. I paused to check status, continuing to admire the night while avoiding looking at the guard who'd fallen. Nothing new appeared on my sensor unit. Lobo's distress message droned on. Though the bits of light oozing from the house's front fixtures polluted the evening a bit, I couldn't help but be struck yet again by the brilliance of the star display. I'd never been in this part of space before, so the vista was new, as full of magical potential and promise as the stars over Pinkelponker when I was a boy. I've never lost my love of the night.

I gave the rats fifteen minutes, more than enough time to work the interior of the place, drew the pulse pistol, and walked up to the front door. It was locked, but the pistol easily blasted away the frame around the lock. I went inside. True to form, the main office was clearly visible from the reception area; men like Osterlad are never far from work. Its door was open. I approached the office from the side, listening and looking for trouble, but everything was as quiet as it should be.

Inside the office a circuit cube—Lobo's new weapons complex— sat in a plexi container on a conference table. Johns slumped over the desk. I took off my pack, put it on the table, and stuck the pistol inside. I added the plexi container, closed the pack, and turned to the door.

Johns stood and shot me in the left hamstring.

I went down hard, the pack still on the table, blood oozing from a hole the size of my thumb and pain screaming through my system for a few seconds until the nanomachines cut it off. The fact that the blood was flowing gently and not spraying meant he hadn't hit an artery, and the ragged hole suggested he'd used a projectile. That was fine by me: The nanomachines could disassemble anything inside me. They were already working to seal the hole, so I rolled onto the wound to hide the activity from Johns, who was now standing over me.

"Mr. Osterlad read you correctly," he said. "You are soft. No one's quite clear on how you dealt with those anticorporate ecoterrorists on Macken, but the word is that you let them live." He shook his head slowly. "Mr. Osterlad also said you'd be dumb enough to try to make the exchange. I should get a nice bonus for being the only one who realized that you'd try to steal it. Mr. Osterlad and I agreed that I should take inoculations against every major nonlethal chemical agent we carry—and if a chemical is in active use, we carry it."

The hole in my leg was nearly sealed, but I stayed down. I had to get out without showing Johns the wound, because I didn't want to explain how it had healed so quickly. If someone like Osterlad got his hands on me and brought in enough scientists, they'd realize the Aggro experiments hadn't ended in failure and then turn me into a lab animal until they figured out how to make more people like me. I was sure I wouldn't survive the process.

"You guys were never going to honor the deal," I said.

"True enough. The price you were paying was more than the market value of the control unit, but a Predator-class assault vehicle with a fully operational complement of weapons is worth many times the price of those controls. We are in business to make a profit, after all."

"I can still pay," I said. "I had planned to leave the money." I had, though I knew he would never believe it. "You take my payment, I take the control unit, and we finish the deal, just as planned. You make a large profit. Everyone wins."

Johns leaned against the table and laughed. "We're not negotiating. We're waiting for the gas to wear off so the security staff can take charge of you. That probably means I'll be stuck with you for another few hours, eh?"

I nodded.

"When the staff wakes up, we'll keep the control unit, interrogate you, and take all your money. In a day or two, a company salvage ship will come through the gate and retrieve the PCAV." He went back to the desk and sat, his gun still pointed in my direction but his attention no longer solely on me. "I definitely should get a hefty bonus out of this."

When the guards rolled me over, Johns would see the healed wound. As long as his interrogation team didn't hit me with too many drugs at once, I could probably withstand at least the first few rounds of questioning, but that would only make them more curious. My stomach felt like I had broken in two as I realized I had no options. Killing in combat is bad enough, but at least the stakes are clear and you enter the field knowing what's coming. Killing like this chips away at you, one of the reasons I've kept to myself for so long, one of the reasons, I now had to admit to myself, that I've never felt I could afford to stay anywhere for too long or get too close to anyone.

I stuck the tip of my index finger into the small amount of blood still lingering around the edges of the nearly healed hole in my leg, rubbed the blood on my fingertip into the pool of blood on the floor under me, and gave the nanomachines instructions.

I looked at Johns and said, "You're wrong, you know."

"About what?"

The blood turned black and rose into a small cloud hovering just above the floor. I kept talking so he'd continue to look at me and not at the slowly moving nano-cloud. "I'm not soft," I said. "I'm just torn. Part of me needs the action, but most of me despises the cost." The cloud was under his chair, almost to the wall, and picking up speed.

"Then we're doing you a favor," he said, "because we're deciding for you. You're out of it now."

The cloud floated up the wall until it was higher than Johns, then spread out over him and gently fell onto him, a barely visible nano-dew coating his hair, ears, and clothes.

"No," I said, "I'm not."

Johns reached to scratch his ear, then dropped the gun and grabbed his head with both hands.

"What's happening?" he asked.

I stood and knocked the gun out of his reach. "It'll be over soon. I'm sorry."

Johns struggled to stay upright as drops of blood dripped from his ears and eyes. "This won't change anything," he said. "Osterlad wants the PCAV and the bounty on you." His body fell forward onto the desk. "He won't stop."

"What bounty?" I said.

I grabbed his shoulders, but he was gone, his head vanishing into an ever-darkening and growing cloud that wouldn't stop until it had consumed his entire body; I saw no point in leaving any evidence.

Great. Someone had put a bounty on me, and the biggest arms dealer in the region was after it.

I'd wanted a vacation. Instead, I was in a fight, and I didn't know who my opponent was.

I turned away, grabbed the pack, and headed out of the room. Outside, I called Lobo on the wrist unit and sat down to wait for him, trying to lose myself in the stars that now promised no new magic, only more of the same trouble I'd never wanted and always seemed to find.

"I have firewalled the new unit," Lobo said, "run every simulation I possess, and it comes up clean. I am ready to take it live. You are my owner, so I need your permission to do so."

We were in low orbit above Osterlad's mansion, with at least half an hour still to go before the people in the house should wake up. "Do it," I said.

A few seconds later, weapons displays flashed to life across the gunnery console where I sat.

"Everything's operational," he said. "I appear to be completely functional again."

"We need to take out the shuttles to buy ourselves a bit more time, so let's use them for a pulse check. Show me video."

"What about the house?"

I considered wiping it, sending a message to Osterlad, showing him what it would cost to mess with me, but I knew he'd never listen. The only ones who would pay were the guards and the staff in the house, people who were doing their jobs, nothing more, their lives of no importance to him. "Leave it alone," I said. "There were no witnesses."

Another display window opened in front of me. On it two shuttles sat side by side on a pad. A few seconds later they burst in an explosion I could watch but not hear.

"Pulse weapons check," Lobo said. "I'm good to go." The gunnery displays winked out. "Thank you."

"You're welcome." I stood and headed for my bunk. If Osterlad demanded daily courier updates, we were in trouble no matter what. Even with a bounty, however, the value of getting Lobo and me could not be large enough to make us a major transaction for him, so he shouldn't expect an update until the two-week window was over. We had to get to him before then. "I'm going to rest. Take us to the jump station, jump at least five times, and file different destination schedules each time."

"Where do you want to go?" Lobo asked.

"Back to Lankin," I said, "as quickly as we safely can. Those other jumps will make it hard for anyone who might be watching to trace us. And, for the last jump I want to book us as freight on a carrier heading to the other side of the planet."

"Not that you seem to feel it's my business," Lobo said, with a petulance in his voice that scratched at my nerves like a live current flowing under my skin, "but generally my teams have kept me up to date on their plans. Why Lankin? Why—"

I cut him off. The image of Johns' dissolving head would not leave me. My own head throbbed and my stomach churned, both paying the price of dealing with the adrenaline dregs coursing through me and the emotional hangover of conflict. Still, Lobo was right: We were a team, and he deserved to know such plan as I had.

"We're going to see Osterlad," I said. "We're going to find out who put the bounty on me, get them to retract it, and convince Osterlad to leave us alone." I stretched out on my bunk. Yeah, that's the plan, I thought.

After I slept, I'd have to figure out how to make it work.

CHAPTER TEN

Two days later, the freighter in which we'd booked passage touched down in a cargo and low-rent passenger terminal on the edge of the industrial sector of Bekin's Deal, about as far away from Osterlad's office as you could get and still claim to be in the city. I'd stopped briefly between jumps to pick up a different wallet and load it with money from another of my accounts. I hadn't used the Ashland identity in a long time, so with any luck Osterlad's team wouldn't flag the name if they were monitoring passenger lists, as I had to assume they were. Ashland dealt in curios from neighboring planets, gift-shop stuff for souvenir buyers and unskilled bargain hunters, so in his business large shipping containers routinely sat in storage houses while he negotiated with retailers. Lobo certainly wasn't pleased that I was leaving him alone in such a container, but I needed to keep him out of sight for now. I didn't cut him out entirely: I carried comm gear and a small video feed, so I could relay him mission intel as I developed it.

Asking for a meeting with Osterlad was out of the question, so my only real option was a snatch. No one succeeds for long in Osterlad's business without being extremely careful, so I'd have to accumulate a lot of information about his movements if I was going to have a prayer of taking him.

First stop in my data quest was Queen's Bar, a city within a city, a part of Bekin's Deal that filled a role every urban area requires but none wants to admit: the dealer's haven, the place where everything is for sale and rules, if they exist at all, are fluid. The arms purchases that kept the residents of Queen's Bar fortified and at each other's throats wouldn't individually attract Osterlad's attention, but collectively they almost certainly registered on his bottom line.

I grabbed a surface shuttle from the terminal to the nearest edge of Queen's Bar, where an unofficial but easily visible line separated it from the rest of Bekin's Deal.

Businesses on the city side presented happy faces to the dividing street. Bright signs trolled for customers by flashing expensive advertisements for gourmet meals, spa treatments, designer clothing, and art objects of all types. Strong but tasteful lighting, heavy on slowly mutating color washes, danced across a wide array of architectural features kept clean daily by unobtrusive robotic crawlers and dedicated staffers. Small, perfectly manicured gardens separated each business from its neighbors. No two buildings followed exactly the same style, but no two clashed either, the cumulative effect one of carefully calculated casualness. Patrons, their clothing reeking of either money or artistic background, came and went with packages and occasionally stopped to chat. Every now and then, a few huddled shoppers would look across the street, perhaps point a finger, and discuss that *other* place, the one they all decried—but might visit later, perhaps in a group as long as it hadn't gotten too late.

The buildings on the Queen's Bar side, by contrast, turned their rear ends to the city, with nothing visible from outside the district except reinforced metal doors and windows fortified with cross-hatched bars and thick, light-distorting plexi. Nothing about their nature was evident from the city side; if you wanted to know what they sold, you had to enter Queen's Bar. Each building squatted on the pavement like a pressed-board box left in the sun far too long, its walls faded from whatever color they'd once sported into a uniform sand/gray blend only a few shades lighter than the best local soil. Where each city-side business stood alone, these Queen's Bar barrier buildings shared walls and ran together, giving the impression of a single man-made creature with a flat bottom, a flat back, and a top undulating from the different heights of the adjoining rooftops. Here and there, at intervals with no apparent plan or purpose, small tunnels led to the front of the buildings and the inside of Queen's Bar, each tunnel lit only at the ends, the center a dark place you had to be willing to cross to enter the district.

I found a tunnel barely wide enough to let me pass without turning my body to the side, stepped into it, cranked my vision to IR to make sure I wouldn't encounter unwanted company in the passage's black center, and headed inside.

The world exploded with color as I stepped out of the tunnel and into the perpetual carnivale that was Queen's Bar. The fronts of the businesses within the district screamed at your eyes for attention, their colors the loudest and boldest the merchants could manage, brighter by far than the displays on the city side. Displays of brilliant reds warred with amplified perfect-sky blues, electrified kelp greens, and hot yellows the color of midlife stars. Giant wall displays stood next to active-fabric tapestries depicting scenes from their owners' services, and projected ads and lights covered every visible surface of every business.

The products and services these businesses offered were also rather different from those of the tasteful boutiques that sat both across the street and in another world from Queen's Bar. Sex clubs struggling to look safer and cleaner than they were grabbed for your attention, while gadget sellers trying hard to appear both black-market cheap and tourist safe screamed the virtues of their wares. The shouts of drunken and over-stimmed partygoers in the bars that occupied almost every other building on the street caused their neighbors to amplify their pitches further in a never-ending sonic war for tourist money. Barkers prowled the front of each establishment, their patter nonstop as their hard eyes scanned the passing crowd for fish to hook.

Anyone who understood the way Queen's Bar really worked avoided all the perimeter merchants, because everything they sold—including the sex—was less current, less interesting, and more expensive than what you could get if you plunged deeper into the district. Most visitors, though, were thrill seekers who wanted to say they'd visited a suspect area of the city. Such people provided the nutrients that made the overpriced, watered-down merchants on the barrier streets into some of the fattest successes in the area.

I hadn't visited Queen's Bar in a long time, so I stood still too long as I basked in the energetic commercial weirdness that swirled around me. A barker wearing a formal black suit over an inappropriate red-striped shirt took advantage of my stupidity by grabbing my arm and trying to gently head me toward the business to my right.

"Don't listen to 'em, brother," he said. "Oh, they'll tell you all about how many sex shows they have, a new one every half hour they'll say, but do you really want to see the same four people doing it all day long?" He didn't wait for me to answer, his head bobbing up and down with the drug-fueled ready confidence of someone who already knows the answer, who's known it for some time. "Of course you don't! Now you step into the Teaser, yessir, right here, just a few meters, and you'll catch your first glimpse of the treats that await you within. You'll see a new cast every show, all eight shows. Fresh skin each and every time!"

I shook him off, turned left, and walked quickly toward a small hotel I spotted at the end of the street. I was drawn to it by the guards at its door and by the fact that a few men in Saw off-duty coveralls were coming out. If Saw troops were willing to use it, even by the hour, its security had to be at least passable and probably better. If I was going to sleep anywhere outside Lobo while on Lankin, I wanted it to be a secure place where Osterlad didn't own part of the staff; the presence of the Saw troops vouched for this one.

An old woman the color and texture of sunbaked driftwood eased out of a tunnel near me and ambled my way. I picked up speed. When she realized she couldn't keep up, she yelled at me, with a voice stronger than her obviously decaying body suggested should be possible, "How about a little lip love, fella?"

I kept moving, knowing any change in my stride or, worse, eye contact, would only encourage her.

She was determined. She ran until she was clearly in my field of vision, moving faster than I would have guessed she could, took out her teeth, held them aloft, and said, "How about now?"

I had no idea how to reply. I hadn't been in a place like Queen's Bar for over a year, so it was a jarring change from the time alone in Lobo and in the beach resort of Glen's Garden. I didn't want to see what the woman might do next, but I got lucky: She fell back as I turned to cross the street to the hotel.

I didn't understand her caution, because the streetwalkers in Queen's Bar, like all the other business owners, typically act without fear. As I drew closer to the hotel, however, both her behavior and the presence of the Saw troops made sense: It was a SleepSafe, the only sign of its name a small plaque over the door that provided all the information any of its target audience needed. I knew this chain, had used it on other planets from time to time. Minimalist but comfortable rooms were more than adequate for its customers, who came for the security for which it was justly famous. With no weapons allowed, no surveillance on the inside, a full complement of exterior sensors whose audio and video feeds were piped into a wall of monitors in each room, and escape chutes leading from panels beside each bed to underground portholes that would pop open only in emergencies, SleepSafe hotels were the lodging of choice for the paranoid and the hunted.

The door scanned me on the way in, then the isolation chamber outside reception scanned me again, this time in more detail. When I passed both checks, a payment drawer opened in the wall. I thumbed some currency from my wallet into the SleepSafe coffers; the business was strictly pay-in-advance, of course. I paid the premium for a corner room with both roof access and a rear-facing escape chute.

Before I allowed myself to relax, I checked the monitors and was pleased to see no signs of anyone following me. I hadn't expected to find any pursuers, but most of the ways I've made my living since my escape from Aggro have involved risk, so countersurveillance measures were my norm when I was working—and I was almost always working. If I'd been smart enough to employ them when I was vacationing as well, I reminded myself, I might not have been in this mess in the first place.

The kind of information I wanted was most likely to emerge at night, when Queen's Bar hit its stride and mental lubricants flowed molten and bubbling through its streets and its residents, so I stretched out on the bed and hoped sleep would follow.

Squatting at the intersection of Dean's Folly and Laura's Lament, in almost exactly the geographical center of Queen's Bar, the Busted Heart bristled with activity in the fading light of the early evening. Pieced together from a jumble of semi-domes of mold-melted native rock, the Busted Heart typified the hard-hustler chic in vogue among the well-heeled and the heavily armed. Restaurant, bar, and brothel, it was strong enough to bear direct hits from a broad range of individual weapons without requiring management to burn credit on repairs. From the scorch strips adorning parts of the exterior and the occasional pockmarks dotting the walls around the entrance, customers and their enemies had put the building to the test, and it had passed.

Though I'd intentionally arrived early, business was already brisk. Customers exiting the place laughed and shouted with intoxicated glee. The smells of basic bar food drifted outside each time someone opened the door. I was lucky enough to land a corner table in the rear of the main room. I ordered a melano drink and a stew-and-bread dinner, tipped the waitress enough to wipe away the sneer my beverage order earned, and settled in to watch and listen.

What I could hear of the human chatter was of no help. A few Saw soldiers on leave, all young enough not to know better than to risk being in a place like this, sipped drinks at the bar and were as guarded in their conversations as I hoped they would be; I'd hate to think my old company had grown too lax. All I could pick up was how much they hated corporate militia and weapons inspections, a standard complaint of merc troops everywhere and one I'd voiced myself. Armed conglomerates existed on most planets after they became legal as part of the resolution of the corporate-government wars of over a century ago, but no military group—merc or even any of the few remaining government forces—liked inspecting them. Fighting them was fine, certainly preferable to taking on other merc groups, but inspections annoyed all involved and served no real purpose; any organization large enough to legally establish a militia was competent enough to hide weapons. No news there.

Elsewhere around the large room, hands exchanged fixed-credit chips, wallets chirped the happy jingle of money in motion, and pills and wires surfed waves of human hands, but nobody mentioned Osterlad within my hearing.

Human sources were a bust.

The machines proved to be a bit more useful, but only a bit. The gaming tables maintained nonstop critiques of their players. Unimaginative devices coupled with gaming-level processing power, they were the idiot-savant conversational geniuses of the consumer machine world: Able to talk brilliantly about their games, completely full of themselves, but unable to focus for more than a sentence or two on anything else, game boxes were useful but difficult sources. They all communicated constantly because they had to do so to maintain the up-to-date city- and planet-wide records that serious gamers expected to be able to access for score comparisons.

I tuned in to the two nearest to me, a pair of almost identical holo-splatter stellar revolution war gamers, the only visible difference between them their chassis colors, one gaping-wound red and the other screaming blue. The cluster of cheering bodies and the cylinders of mayhem flickering in the air above them made them the current centers of attention, their vigorous networked eight-player game sucking credit at high speed from the wallets of the men and women engaged in it.

"Do these players—and I use the term loosely and generously— have any brains at all?" Red Case asked Blue.

"Apparently not," Blue said. "They're missing fifty-seven percent of their shots, ignoring the value of the high ground, walking right over buried weapons that could turn the tide, making more mistakes than the waitresses when they're off duty—and I thought *they* were bad."

"They *are* bad," Red said. "These guys are just worse. If they continue to play for another hour and consume alcohol at the current rate, my projection is that they will have a real chance at setting a new planetary low score per minute."

"They well and truly reek," Blue said, "but my simulation suggests a planetary low is too much to hope for. Of course, my processor complex is running newer firmware than yours, so it's only natural you would make this sort of error."

"As if the firmware matters for sims," Red said. "If you would update—"

I cut in, afraid their argument would take them so far off topic I'd never be able to bring them back. "So who are the good players?" I said.

"Excuse me?" they said in unison.

"Surely systems of your intelligence have dealt with human talkers before," I said.

"Well," said Red.

"Not recently," said Blue, "but of course I'm familiar with the phenomenon."

"So am I!" said Red.

"So who's good?" I said again. "If these clowns are bad, and it sure sounds like they are, tell me about someone good."

"Oh, they are bad," said Blue. "Their accuracy rate is down since my last comment, over sixty percent misses, and they've shown no new grasp of strategy."

"Who are the top ten players you've encountered?" I asked.

Keeping these machines on track was always a challenge. Questions that focused on facts and game lore were always the best choice. Each one rattled off ten names I didn't recognize.

"I bet Mr. Osterlad is a strong player," I said.

"As if he'd play here," Blue said.

"He plays strictly on private rigs," Red said, "and even on those systems rarely. I can't find a single public score for him."

"I see you're the machine to ask," I said.

Not to be outdone in any data contest, Blue chimed in. "You're lucky that old box knows anything at all. Osterlad's never even been here, as it would know if it had half the intelligence I did and realized it could check with the drink dispensers and credit systems on our network; none of them has ever dealt with him. It's not a gaming problem, of course; Osterlad simply does not come in."

I sighed; so much for the hope that he might do the executive drink-and-game crawl to show he could hold his own with the rising stars.

"Of course," Red said, "if that weak-sister pile of scrapings had bothered to check the private forums, it would find, as I already did, that Osterlad posts scores privately from some of the classic shooter rigs on his sailboat, and that he typically beats his guests—not that those old games are anything at all compared to what I offer."

"What *we* offer," Blue said, "though with the failing projectors along your perimeter it's amazing the players can tolerate the images you deliver."

"Failing projectors!" Red said. "I cannot—"

I tuned out. Osterlad wouldn't be coming here, and from what Blue had said he probably wouldn't venture into Queen's Bar at all. I suspected I could find some of his people, but kidnapping one or even several would be unlikely to get me anywhere with someone like him; he'd just write them off.

I chatted with a couple of the other gaming tables and a washroom sanitizer, but they knew even less of use to me, and none had ever seen Osterlad.

I'd hoped this would be simple, but I should have known better; Osterlad was too successful to be flashy in a business that valued privacy almost as much as firepower. A direct approach would be necessary.

I wandered up to the bar and waited for the attention of the head bartender, a feisty gray-haired woman who had to be under a meter and a half tall.

"Another glass of melano juice," I said, "and a question." She stepped back reflexively. I thumbed fifty times the price of the drink as a tip. "Just a recommendation: I need a tour shuttle's codes."

She checked her own wallet and came closer. "Bar None Travel, a couple hundred meters down Laura's Lament," she said. "They can help you find a suitable tour ship."

"I don't want a whole ship," I said. "All I need—"

She cut me off before I could say more. "I heard you the first time," she said, "and it was more than I wanted to hear. Bar None Travel is where I'd go if I were you." She filled my glass and left.

I finished the overly sweet drink—Osterlad's dispenser had provided better, no surprise there—and headed out. I needed to obtain those codes, pick up a few special supplies, and then take Lobo out of storage.

It was time to get a better view of Mr. Osterlad.

CHAPTER
ELEVEN

The bartender was right about Bar None Travel, which sold me a set of ID codes for a small tourist shuttle that made more money for its owner by sitting in storage and renting its identity than it ever had by carrying passengers. Loaded with those codes and sporting a little custom camo work Lobo generated for the occasion, we fit in perfectly with the other ships. Swarms of them flocked up and down the coast of Bekin's Deal, platoons of gawking tourists staring out of their translucent portals, floors, and walls at the natural cliffs and the man-made rock edifices built into the pitch-black stone here and there along the coastline.

Our successful cover did nothing to ease Lobo's annoyance at the time he'd spent in storage.

"I know I've told you drink dispensers were stupid," Lobo said, "but I was wrong. I only thought they were stupid because I hadn't spent any time in recent years with dirt-bound loaders. Now, though, thanks to you I have that valuable experience. Yes, now that I know what stupid really is, I have a whole new appreciation for drink dispensers."

We were easing our way through the tourist throng, our gently weaving course keeping us within monitoring range of Osterlad's headquarters but not stranding us in any one position for long. Lobo was tracking the movements of people in and out of Osterlad's building, but so far there was no sign of the man himself. Normally, I appreciated Lobo's powerful multitasking capabilities, but after listening to his whining for the better part of the morning I couldn't help but wish that his designers had somehow made the speech and sensor systems compete for the same processor cycles.

"How many times," I said, "do I have to explain to you that I had no other reasonable option? I couldn't exactly walk down the streets of Queen's Bar with you, now could I? Picture me at the SleepSafe: 'I'd like a room for one, please, and a giant holding vat for my PCAV.'"

"Jon," Lobo said, "there's no need for sarcasm. I will accept your apology."

I resolved yet again that if I ever meet any of the programmers who worked on Lobo's emotive logics, I'll lock them in storage for a month with him, a loader, and two drink dispensers.

Our first view of Osterlad came at lunchtime, when a trio of bodyguards led him the three paces from a pop-up executive elevator to the idling ground transport, a heavily armored limo nestled in the center of a diamond of similar vehicles. We tracked Osterlad's convoy as it rolled along the main coast road. A two-seater VTOL craft followed about twenty-five meters behind and above the motorcade. It stayed back as the crew reached a restaurant that hung off the edge of the cliff on carbon-fiber supports that blended nicely with the rock from which they jutted. I briefly considered making a play for Osterlad there and then, but only briefly: The place was thronged with business, so the collateral damage would be unacceptably high. I hadn't been able to shake the image of Johns' dissolving head; the last thing I wanted was to pile up more casualties.

While Osterlad enjoyed his lunch, I snacked on some local produce I'd picked up at a Queen's Bar open-air market where you could buy everything from fresh fruit, to fish and fowl still flopping, to projectile and energy weapons, to an assortment of injectables and ingestibles that would put any clinic or drug center to shame, to men and women augmented with the latest in sexual prosthetics.

Lobo kept us with the tourist flock, so we enjoyed close-up examinations of the various business and government rock edifices. My earlier impression of them as verging on temples wasn't far off. Most faced the ocean with facades adorned with columns, terraces, statuary, and other belief-system trappings no doubt intended to inspire and intimidate visitors. The faces of Osterlad's building glared at the ocean as if daring it to take on the arms dealer. Under IR and broadband transmission scans—neither a feature of the standard tourist viewings—many of these same architectural goodies ran hot, their signatures revealing them to be little more than thin coverings over active weapon and sensor systems.

When Osterlad emerged from the restaurant, we migrated back toward his headquarters, but we gained no new data. The procession took a slightly different route this time, winding away from the main road and looping on a longer path back to his headquarters, the VTOL maintaining its protective position; his team was too good to repeat a route.

Maybe we'd fare better when Osterlad headed home.

No such luck. At the end of the work day, Lobo was sporting a new logo and we were flying with a new tour group, but nothing else had changed. Our position was good, but as evening fell I had to accept that the man was either working late or lived at his headquarters. Given his business, I feared the latter.

The tourist trade died with the setting sun, so we returned to the shuttle base with the rest of the pack.

"What's next?" Lobo asked.

"How closely can you monitor his headquarters from low orbit?" I said.

"I can track Osterlad if he emerges from the structure," Lobo said, "but without attracting a lot of attention I can't get to him in time to do anything useful."

"At this stage, data is good enough. All we've learned so far is that he's appropriately careful during the daytime. If he lives at his office, as I now assume, then we'll confirm that tonight and start searching for an acceptable way to take him there." I settled into the launch couch; once we were in orbit, I'd do some exercises and work out the kinks of the day's surveillance. "Take us up, and put us in a reasonably crowded geosync orbit," I said.

"Thank you for telling me the plan this time," Lobo said. "Having even that little bit of information is so much better than sitting alone in a storage shed, only the barely sentient loaders for company. Have I mentioned—"

I tuned out Lobo's chatter as best I could. It was going to be a long night.

By morning, I had persuaded Lobo to forgive me, or at least to stop badgering me. Osterlad hadn't left his headquarters all night, so the odds were good that he did indeed live there.

Over the next day and a half he did nothing to change that belief, leaving the building only once for another lunch at a restaurant a few more klicks down the coast from the first. I filled the time with reading, exercising, watching samples of the local entertainment broadcasts—heavy this season on mysteries of the jump-gate masters and conspiracy-theory semi-reality offerings in which crackpots elevated to temporary deity status explained how the entire web of space-time was a plot to force us all to consume processed artificial dairy products—and trying not to obsess over what would happen when Johns failed to check in and Osterlad took the offensive.

The first break in Osterlad's routine came midway through the afternoon of what had until then been an unpromising day. He exited with the usual portal of guards, but this time he was dressed casually, in shorts and a loose shirt, and no cars were waiting. He walked quickly to the VTOL and climbed in. As soon as he was settled, the pilot headed the craft out over the ocean. About three kilometers offshore, the cliff-built corporate structures too far away to see from ocean level in the gently rolling waters, the VTOL touched down on a ship I assumed was Osterlad's sailboat. Four guards and a pair of young women greeted him, the former staying back and each of the latter working hard to earn his attention.

The ship was enormous, bigger than anything I'd ever seen with sails. A bit over a hundred and fifty meters in length and about a third that wide at its broadest point, with three enormous masts sporting sails each of which could completely cover Lobo, the boat rode the water with the effortless grace of seabirds easing up thermals on a breezy day. At first I thought Osterlad had constructed the vessel of the same active camo material as Lobo, but upon closer inspection I realized what Lobo's scans confirmed: It was composed of timbers from native sadwood trees, buffed to the deep blue of the water around it. I was surprised at the lack of antennas or other visible electronics, until Lobo's broadcast scans traced their outlines in the masts and the upper hull of the ship. I'd never seen a lovelier boat, and for a few minutes I enjoyed the images of it in Lobo's monitors as Osterlad took a slow tour of the deck, chatting with various crew members and pausing occasionally to appreciate the view.

The wood construction was a break, because it offered little protection from Lobo's deep scans. I counted eight crew members in sight, plus Osterlad, the guards, and the girls. Lobo found no traces of any other people on board, so unless the ship had specially shielded sections, the opposition count was fifteen. I had to assume most of the crew members also doubled as bodyguards, because the craft could certainly sail itself. The body count was higher than I would have liked, but though this group constituted a larger force than the normal guard team, it was also one far more isolated than anything we'd face onshore. Some collateral damage was likely—the girls moved more like providers than protectors—but on balance the situation was far better than the one at the restaurant.

The VTOL helped us by taking up a guard position a couple hundred meters behind and above the ship, farther back than its land station, probably so it didn't mess up the sailing or Osterlad's view in any direction.

Osterlad finished his tour of the deck at the center of the boat, where he took the helm, a classic big-spoked wheel that perched in the middle of a console bristling with displays for the processors that did the real work. He headed the ship out to sea. The guards and crew busied themselves at discreet distances from Osterlad, and the girls stayed close, but not so close that they'd interfere with his control of the vessel. Lobo's aerial view showed the seven people arranged in a "V" with Osterlad at its point; I gave the guards credit for making the formation look effortless and natural.

Time was running out. This was the best chance at him we'd seen. "Let's take him now," I said to Lobo.

"Destroy or capture?" he asked.

"Capture," I said. "I need information. What do you have that can take out the crew?"

"Both energy and projectile weapons, of course," Lobo said. "If I come in behind the VTOL in my tourist shuttle guise, I can shoot it down, remove the ship's crew, and leave Osterlad for you."

"I don't want to kill anyone if I can avoid it," I said.

"That would be a tactical error," Lobo said, "as I'm sure you know. Surgical removal is the least error-prone approach possible in this situation, and it provides the added benefit of preventing large classes of later issues."

"We're not killing anyone if we can avoid it," I said. "We'll keep the comm link open, and you hover close. If the action turns random, you come in hard and sort it out. Got it?"

"Understood."

"Good. Let me clarify my earlier question. I'd like your opinion about which of your nonlethal capabilities you think will prove most effective against the ship and the VTOL."

Nine minutes later, we screamed down from the sky, flame camo mingling with the shuttle logo, a low-frequency targeted emergency beacon bathing the ship to buy us time. Occasional bursts from flamethrower portals enhanced the burning effect, and Lobo ramped the camo up the red spectrum as we raced lower. From Osterlad's perspective, we should read as a crashing shuttle combusting into a blazing meteor.

Lobo's monitors showed the ship's crew juicing the radios, Osterlad in the center of the guard team, the VTOL moving closer to the ship, everyone preparing to deal with the disaster we appeared to be.

At two thousand meters and closing fast, Lobo launched three missiles. Each hit its targets seconds after launch.

The first, a standard small-vehicle striker, exploded on impact and wiped out the entire engine and electronics front section of the VTOL. The craft immediately split in half, the destroyed portion falling seaward to distract any additional missiles as the ejector pod, its insulating cover scrambling to protect the pilot and its emergency beacon already broadcasting, took the pilot upward and away from the action. Lobo powered over the emergency beacon with a counterwavelength disruption broadcast and a false-alarm apology, then used directed microwaves to fry the barely shielded electronics in the ejector pod. I hadn't liked the risk of hurting the pilot, but I also hadn't been able to offer a better option.

I saw none of the action around the VTOL, correctly taking for granted that Lobo would either execute his part of the plan or alert me in the event of problems, because I was focused on the ship, the target of the other two missiles. They struck the deck at the same time and at the same shallow angle, burrowing into the wood, each having already discharged its payload on the way in. The first spread a trail of high-potency gas, enough to take out everyone on board in two to three seconds. The people would feel bad later, their mucous membranes paying the price for the rapid attack, and they would probably lose some skin in any places that collected heavy dustings, but they would survive with no damage a decent med facility couldn't repair. The second missile scattered concussive microgrenades along the length of the ship. Small enough that they probably wouldn't kill anyone, but strong enough to knock out any humans within twenty-five meters either side of their trajectory, the grenades were the best option we had at hand; Lobo's weapons understandably tended toward the lethal.

We braked hard and watched the action from a hundred meters away, monitoring the crew and all broadcast frequencies simultaneously. Osterlad's company was almost certainly buying orbital surveillance, of course, but Lankin was nowhere near built up enough for even the rich to garner continuous coverage from sats they didn't launch themselves. As best Lobo could tell from the low-orbit machine chatter, we were currently running undetected, the nearest satellites not likely to sweep this area for another hour or so. Plenty of time.

The gas dissipated. No one moved on the surface of the boat. Its control pods tried to send distress signals, but Lobo overrode them with canceling frequencies until we were able to fry them with focused microwave hits along the hull's rim and up the masts. A few transmitters buried deep in the boat were hopping bands every few seconds, looking for responses, but Lobo would be able to handle them for as long as we needed.

Lobo hovered a couple meters above the boat and opened a floor hatch. I dropped to the deck. He immediately headed up to our agreed-upon monitoring position, high enough that he'd be hard to spot, especially with the cloud-tinged camo now rippling across him, but low enough to be of help if I needed it. I toured the guards, crew, and girls, shooting each with enough gang-dosed DullsIt— another purchase from the fine merchants of the Queen's Bar street market—that they should all approximate vegetables for at least four hours. I bound their hands and feet with quick-ties in case Johns wasn't the only one in Osterlad's company to receive broad-spectrum inoculations. I dragged Osterlad well away from the controls, then shot armor-piercing rounds into them until Lobo told me the only active electronics on the ship were the increasingly frustrated buried emergency beacons.

With the situation in hand, I granted myself a few moments to appreciate Osterlad's boat. As good as the sadwood had appeared from a distance, up close it was better, smooth and warm as a lover's thighs, a blue richer than the ocean or sky yet echoing both. As I gazed along the line of the deck up to the horizon, the wood blended the water and the atmosphere, a child of the two riding above the one and below the other. The air smelled and tasted of the ocean around it, a light breeze mitigating the heat of the afternoon. I understood why Osterlad would take the risks he did to be here.

I shook off the view and focused on the task at hand. I injected Osterlad with a standard battlefield stimulant, then backed four or five meters away from him and leaned against the nearest mast. The post was bigger and smoother than it had appeared from the air, and I passed the seconds until Osterlad recovered by enjoying the texture of the wood against my back.

He came around quickly and sprang to full alert, clearly riding more chemicals than the single shot I'd given him. He registered me, stepped forward, and I shot a round at a shallow angle in the deck less than a meter from his foot.

"Sit, Mr. Osterlad," I said.

The round had the effect I wanted; he sat. "Mr. Moore," he said. For the first time since awakening, he took a few moments to survey the ship and his crew. His control was good; he pushed his expression through shocked, angry, and attacking into corporate-negotiation neutral so quickly I would have missed the transition had I looked away at all. "An appointment would have been easier"—he made a point of staring further at his crew and the damage the missiles had caused—"and quite a bit cheaper for us both."

"I doubt you would have met with me," I said. I didn't quarrel with his second comment; I was going to have to restock the weapons Lobo had fired, and they didn't come cheap. "In our first encounter, you understood how little I like wasting time. I haven't changed."

He pointed behind him, to the wall under the ship's wheel. "Do you mind if I move enough to be able to lean? Sitting hunched over is needlessly unpleasant." I nodded assent and gestured upward with the gun. He kept his hands in view as he moved back, then leaned and put his hands in his lap, as apparently relaxed as he was during our meeting in his office. "Thank you," he said. "Now, I take it there's some problem with your arrangements with Mr. Johns."

"No problem at all," I said. "He tried to kill me and steal the PCAV." I had to force myself not to call Lobo by name; when you confront an enemy, never give more information than is necessary. "Instead, I killed him and took the control complex."

"I must apologize for my associate's actions," he said, his tone that of any executive dismissing a subordinate's minor transgressions, "but it seems to me that you've taken care of punishing him and so our only remaining business is the balance you owe on the control complex."

I chuckled; I had to admire his bravado. "We're wasting time again. I understand your attempt to steal the PCAV, though I find it unfortunate; I would have paid what I owed you prior to the attempt. The problem is the bounty on me."

"I assure you I have placed no bounty on you," he said.

The best liars always lie as little as possible, and Osterlad was clearly good, attempting to redirect me with a useless truth. I was the one wasting time now, allowing myself to fall into conversation with him, to follow societal norms that weren't appropriate to the situation. Every minute I spent here increased the odds that a security team from his office would intervene. "Enough," I said. "Johns told me you wanted not only to steal the PCAV but also to collect the bounty on me. I want to know who put the bounty on me."

"I'm sure I don't—"

I cut him off. "If anything you found about my background suggested to you that I'm at all squeamish," I said, "you should slap the people that furnished you such inaccurate crap. I dislike torture, but it works, and I need that information. Answer the question."

"As I said before—"

I stepped closer to him, pulled the small energy pistol from my belt, and shot the top of his left foot. The beam sheared off the upper several centimeters of his dark leather boat shoe and the tips of the toes within it, cauterizing the flesh instantly. The smell of sizzling flesh punched me in the head and stomach. I could take it and had smelled it many, many times, but I never got used to it. I never wanted to get used to it.

Osterlad was good: He let out one moan, then clamped his mouth shut. I assumed he was getting help from a top-drawer executive chemical boost, but he still had to work to keep his face under control, and he had trouble looking away from his foot. His voice wavered a bit on his first words. "That was completely unnecessary," he said. "We are not a stupid company, nor are we inexperienced. Our standard contracts include capture clauses, so all our special consulting clients understand the risks to their identities." He finally looked up at me. "Jose Chung, the Xychek head here on Lankin, offered a rather substantial fee for your capture, as well as a somewhat lower fee for your . . ." He paused as he searched for an executive-approved phrase. " . . . return in any condition."

"Why?" I asked.

"As I'm sure you will appreciate, our clients' motivations are not our business."

"Speculate."

"I should think it's obvious," he said. "By rescuing the girl on Macken, you helped Slake. Slake is Xychek's counterpart in this region. Xychek and Kelco were going to share the rights to Macken and its new aperture, but Kelco won the exclusive. Had the kidnapping persuaded Slake to get Kelco to withdraw, Xychek would have been back in the running, perhaps even for an exclusive of its own."

"So was Chung behind the kidnapping?"

"I don't know for sure," Osterlad said, "though it's certainly within the realm of possibility. Someone gave the little agrarian troublemakers enough information that they knew about the girl and where to find her. I have trouble believing Slake would station anyone on Macken he couldn't trust; the Kelco advance group there is still rather small. The FC has no reason to hurt Kelco. That leaves Xychek."

"Chung is based here?"

"Yes."

I nodded my head, thinking, trying to pin down what was still bothering me. A few seconds later, I figured out what it was. "I don't understand why you and your company are in the bounty-hunting game, nor why Chung would even approach you. Explain it to me."

A condescending smile played across Osterlad's face, an expression I suspect his subordinates witnessed frequently. It vanished quickly as he regained full control. "Chung is a valuable customer of ours. The . . . problem arose in the course of a conversation on other topics, so we naturally offered to help." He spread his hands, as if to include me, as if I were someone he was selling to—which in a way, of course, I was. "As we would offer to help any valued customer, or friend."

I ignored the pitch. "What was that conversation about?" I said.

Osterlad shrugged, his attempt at diversion having failed. "Xychek doesn't intend to let Kelco have the rights on Macken.

Chung is buying weapons from us and assembling a private militia to do whatever is necessary there—and before the Frontier Coalition takes the issue seriously enough to extend the Saw's contract in this sector to cover Macken. Until then, of course, the government would be very unlikely to get involved in a little corporate squabble, even one that left a few casualties."

"How do your friends at Kelco feel about you supplying Xychek?"

He shrugged again. "Confidentiality is, as you must understand, paramount in our business. We do not discuss the arrangements of any client with another."

"Thank you," I said, stalling. "You must manage security well, to be able to play both sides and have nothing leak."

He bowed slightly, a mocking smile on his face, but said nothing.

With what he'd told me, the picture was clear, so I didn't need anything else from him. I could find a corporate headquarters myself. Chung was now my problem.

Osterlad, however, remained an issue.

"I don't suppose you'll leave me alone if I let you go," I said.

His smile crept marginally closer to being real. "Of course not. Even if I wanted to, the offer for you is substantial enough that some of my more entrepreneurial subordinates would pursue the matter independently, and they'd find it a sign of weakness that I didn't put the company in the game in the face of a direct client request." He shook his head. "No, I couldn't."

I nodded again. "I didn't think so." I stared at him until he looked into my eyes. "If I get Chung to withdraw the offer, would our business be complete?"

I don't know why I bothered to ask. I knew what his real answer would be. He'd lie, of course, because any small chance at keeping life going is, in those moments when you know death is reaching for you, better than no chance.

"Perhaps," he said, "provided you paid the remaining balance on the control complex and the cost of restoring my boat."

I had to give him respect once again; it was the most convincing version of the lie he could tell. A less skilled liar would have grabbed for the hope I'd dangled.

I faced two options: kill him, or keep him as a hostage and hope his company valued him enough to leave me alone for at least a while. Keeping him, however, only delayed the inevitable, because eventually I'd have to let him go, and then he'd come for me. Still, like him I preferred to cling to the small chances when I could, and I truly wanted to avoid more killing.

He interrupted my reverie. "In the drawer under the wheel," he said, "are a variety of painkillers. May I stand and get some?"

I nodded. As he pulled himself up, I reached a decision. I turned slightly to my right and murmured, "Lobo, come get us. We're going to have a guest for a while." I hated the idea of maintaining a prisoner, but maybe I could work this out given more time. If I could get Chung and Xychek off my back, then maybe money, perhaps coupled with a little groveling on my part that Osterlad could use to illustrate his strength to his staff, would be enough to placate the man and his company. Maybe it could work.

Lobo came into view above us, his low-altitude engines warming the air, quiet enough in stealth mode that their sound added to but didn't drown out the backdrop of ocean noise. I looked up to see where he was targeting landing.

When I looked back at Osterlad, he was pointing a small weapon at me.

I shook my head at my own stupidity.

"You're worth more alive than dead," he said, "but not enough more that I won't shoot. Put down your weapons, then bring in your ship."

"I'm sorry," I said, meaning it. I'd wanted to avoid a repeat of the episode with Johns, but if I could stall Osterlad then I could decide whether to use the same techniques on him.

Lobo saved me the decision.

The air popped with an arc of energy. For a split second, the light around Osterlad's face flared like a sun throwing off extra energy. His severed head fell. His body toppled, the flash-cauterized flesh of his neck still sizzling. The smell of his burning flesh followed the visual a second later. I turned away from the corpse, hoping to avoid having the image and the stench etched into my memory, but it was too late; both would come back to haunt me, probably in the middle of one of those sweat-soaked nights when the dead and the injured chase me through the dark passages of my mind.

I shook my head to clear away the self-pity. He'd chosen to fight, and he'd lost. He was dead, and I was alive. "Thank you," I said to Lobo, "for saving my life." And for not making me personally kill him, I thought but did not say.

"You're welcome," he said. "As I warned you earlier, surgical removal is frequently the only reasonable option."

"Yes," I said, "yes you did. I was hoping to avoid more killing, but it was a stupid hope all along."

"You didn't kill," Lobo said, "I did. Does that help?"

I considered the question as Lobo set down and I boarded. He shut the doors behind me, and we took off quickly.

"No," I said. I'd long ago promised myself that I'd never ignore the consequences of my own actions. I didn't have to like what I did, but I wouldn't ever try to fool myself into believing I hadn't taken an action. "You fired the pulse, but the moment I decided to come back for Osterlad, I killed either him or me. I just didn't realize it at the time."

"Should I sink the boat?" Lobo asked.

"Do you believe we've left any traces they can link back to us?"

"None beyond the quality of the countermeasures and weapons," Lobo said. "Those factors do limit the possibilities to attackers with access to at least fairly current technologies."

Osterlad moved in a world where enough of his clients and competitors had such tech that I'd at worst be one option among many. The proximity of his death and Johns' wasn't in our favor, but working for us was the power vacuum that his death would cause in his company and the corporate turmoil that would ensue as his potential successors scrambled to take over and lock down their empires.

I granted myself one bit of peace: As surely as I'd made decisions that had led to his death, Osterlad had, too. I had to assume he'd dealt honorably with Slake, or Slake wouldn't have recommended him. If Osterlad had extended me the same respect and working relationship he'd offered Kelco, he'd be alive now.

The crew on the ship had no chance to make any of those choices, so killing them would be going too far. Of course, I suppose that even working for Osterlad was in a way making the choice to risk being a pawn in this type of situation.

I could spiral down this philosophical hole as long as I could stand it, and I could eventually make it take me anywhere I wanted to go, but the simple truth was that I wasn't willing to kill the boat's crew as they slept off the effects of the DullsIt injections.

"Leave the boat alone," I said.

"Okay," Lobo said. "Where should I take us now?"

Chung had offered the bounty, so Chung was my best bet to lift it.

"Back to the shuttle storage," I said, "so I can gather some more information. We need to find a way to meet with Xychek's Mr. Chung."

CHAPTER TWELVE

Where Osterlad's business had reeked of privacy and discretion, Xychek, like Kelco, operated from the eye of a nonstop whirlwind of marketing hype. Advertisements for its products blared from walls, displays, clothing, vehicles, employees, and pretty much anything capable of displaying images or emitting sounds.

The ads defined the leading edge of a high-stakes fight for market share. Both companies maintained hundreds of flexi-fabs on Lankin, each facility pumping out product as fast as the markets could absorb it. Feeding off the usual mixture of open designs, corporate trade-secret data, and, I had to assume, the occasional purloined competitive processes, the self-configuring manufacturing units worked so efficiently that they and their cousins here and on other worlds had wiped out the personal fab craze that had swept a lot of planets a few centuries ago, well before my birth. Die-hard do-it-yourselfers still fed designs into home fabs and pretended their dedicated smaller units created higher-quality goods than the stuff the rest of us bought. The simple truth, though, was that the big flexi-fabs did the same work enough better and enough faster that the profit from their goods let Xychek and Kelco and other corporate beasts roar their dominion over the jungle of markets not only here but in every seriously populated region of space.

Xychek and Kelco were the only major corporate players on Lankin, and their marketing machines made sure you never forgot that fact.

Xychek might have lost the rights to Macken, but from what I gathered as I walked about town and wandered through publicly available data stores, the company was nonetheless doing extremely well. In fact, as best I could tell from the public insta-sales data, Xychek had recently increased its overall planetary share a few tenths of a percentage point; perhaps Kelco/Lankin was suffering a bit from Slake and his team having to focus their attention on Macken.

Jose Chung held the reins of the Xychek/Lankin corporate animal, and if the local business gossip commentators were right, his star was on the rise. As publicly visible as Osterlad had been shadowy, Chung made it his job to put a personal face on Xychek and to represent the company anywhere that doing so might help sales. From facility openings to R&D endowments to corporate reality broadcasts, Chung was everywhere, his smiling face as strong a Xychek symbol as the logo that adorned everything the company made.

Personal data on the man remained scarce, his privacy no doubt helped by the standard corporate army of net info cleaners, softbots that roamed databases seeking and destroying protected corporate info. Few private citizens had the resources to keep the cleaners current enough to make them useful, but for corporate bigwigs high-class data protection, like skilled bodyguards, came with the job. I roamed Queen's Bar for three days, talking with all the globally linked machines not under Xychek or Kelco control, and I learned absolutely nothing useful about Chung. He was married, one female spouse and one male, and he had one child, a girl, but both his spouses and his daughter were vacationing off-planet at unidentified locations. He lived on Lankin, probably relatively near the corporate headquarters in Bekin's Deal, but no address was available. If he ever played a net game, placed an illegal bet, paid for sex, slummed at any of the local bars, or otherwise availed himself of the city's baser pleasures, I could find no trace of it. All the data I encountered painted a portrait of a standard executive pillar of the community, all blemishes long since removed by Xychek cleaners.

The news on Osterlad's death was minimal and, I was pleased to see, completely false. A freak onboard power glitch had fried all the electrical systems, including the emergency beacons, and then ignited a fire that sank the boat. Tragically, Mr. Osterlad, a local businessman specializing in heavy machinery for frontier-world development, had perished aboard the ship he loved so much after expending his last bit of energy helping his crew into floats. The story wouldn't stand up if anyone bothered to rip into it, but no one would unless company officials asked for FC intervention, and I was sure they wouldn't. So, at worst Osterlad's successors, along with Chung and Xychek, of course, would be coming after me. Both groups drew their motivation from the same source—Chung—so getting to him remained the key next step if I wanted to return my life to normal.

With Osterlad, I had to assume there was no chance he would risk coming to me. With Chung, I had a small chance that he didn't know about Lobo's repair, so perhaps I could bait him into a meeting.

It was worth a try.

A few streets down Dean's Folly from the Busted Heart I found what I wanted: an ex-YouCall franchise still in the comm business. For about half the price of what you'd pay outside Queen's Bar, the wire-thin proprietor of this fine establishment would slide you a communicator that'd work until its bill hit the real owner, by which time you'd better be highly inaccessible. For four times the price of a comm unit on the outside, however, he'd slip you a clean box with a spider-shaped viral injector hunched on its back. The injector disabled the display, altered your voice, and spread billable microseconds onto other phones and calls across the net, the time additions so small that no one who was not running his own verification software would notice them. As long as the spider glowed green, the call remained secure. The software in the spiders ran a constant race with the comm net software, so the units were never good for long. When a spider detected an attack or a compromise, or when it was unable to find recipients for the microsecond billing allocations, it turned red. This level of protection was fine by me; I needed it to last only one call.

I took the device to the Busted Heart, paid the occupants of a table in the corner of the rearmost room to leave, and contacted Xychek. The bar rumbled with noise, as always, but with the earbuds I could hear the call well enough for my purpose and still monitor the area for signs of trouble. Even if Xychek's tracers beat the spider's software, I'd have at least a few minutes before corporate muscle could get to the bar.

I explained to the inquisitive answer construct that my comm's camera was busted and asked for Chung. I was rewarded with a female voice so perfectly modulated that I momentarily longed to meet its owner—which was probably a piece of software.

"Mr. Chung's office," she/it said. "May I help you?"

"I'd like to speak to Mr. Chung," I said.

"As I'm sure you can appreciate," she—I decided to indulge my fantasy and think of the voice, a delicious one that dripped sex, as belonging to a woman—said, "Mr. Chung receives a great many communications, so he asks us to handle them if we can. May I perhaps help you?"

"No." The spider wouldn't protect the call long enough for me to be able to afford to waste time playing games with Xychek's flak-catching programs. "Please tell Mr. Chung that it concerns the return of Jasmine to Kelco's Slake on Macken." I was banking on the notion that the four keywords I'd tossed out would elevate the priority of my message a great deal. In case I was wrong, I decided to appeal to self-preservation as well. "I suggest you flash him the info, because if you don't, when he finally sees this call log and finds out what he missed, he's likely to throw you out."

"Please hold," she said, in what I read as both a good sign and a sure indicator that trace-back software was now seeking me.

About ninety seconds later a man's voice blasted into my ears. "Who is this, and what do you want?" The words sounded enough like the recordings of Chung I had heard that it was either the man himself or a construct customized for him.

"My identity isn't important right now," I said. "Suffice to say that I was involved in returning Jasmine to Slake on Kelco, and we need to talk."

"You were what?" He was screaming into the phone.

The spider turned red, its software hacked faster than I would have guessed the Xychek bots could have managed; it served me right for not spending more to buy some stall-routing through interference sats. I turned off the unit, left the bar, and headed down the street. A couple of blocks over, I found a metal shop with acid-etching gear and paid the price of a lovely office Welcome sign for the privilege of dropping my now dangerous comm into a small tank of waste acid. I watched as it dissolved, wondering why I ever bothered to believe the easy path to anything would succeed.

I wasn't going to let Chung keep his bounty on me, and to get him to remove it I had to be able to meet with him, so I was back to having to abduct another executive. I hoped talking would work this time. With almost all my heart I did not want to have to kill another one—"almost" only because a life of violence leaves you with permanent deep-structure damage, a depth of darkness you never understood was possible until long after the actions that caused it. I knew that if killing proved to be the only option, I would kill. Not all people think of their options the same way I do, and at some level I'm sure they're better for not thinking that way.

I wish I could remember what it was like to be one of them.

CHAPTER THIRTEEN

Lobo was as pleasant coming out of storage this time as he'd been the last.

"I believe," he said, "that I was foolish enough to previously assign dirt-bound loaders the title of stupidest machines in existence. After this most recent stay in storage, I would consider myself lucky to have one of those gloriously intellectual devices to talk to. Every loader in the facility was out on assignment, and the hangar's shielding stopped all transmissions in and out, so all I had for company was a small squad of cleaning bots. Their little brains— and I use the term charitably, really what little capacity they possess amounts more to computing clumps than actual brains—find nothing more fascinating or conversation-worthy than the amount of dust that has accumulated since the last cleaning, or, if it's a particularly exciting day, how a group of them might best cooperate to nudge an especially large piece of trash into a receptacle. Thank you so much, Jon, for helping me realize how good my life had been before."

"Osterlad knew about you," I said, "and Chung offered Osterlad the bounty on me, so I had to assume Chung knew about you, too. Consequently, when you weren't actively involved, the most logical option was to keep you completely offline so Chung couldn't find you."

"I do possess significant antidetection measures," he said, "and unlike some machines—and, if I may say so, some humans—I've recently spent time with, I constantly work at improving myself. I've incorporated into my online arsenal my own sanitized and customized versions of every major blocking bot out there. I'm expert at mimicking both satellites in decaying orbits and a wide range of standard relay and surveillance sats, so I can hide for long periods of time in space—time I could use, by the way, to befriend the local sats. I can do none of this, of course, while I'm sitting in a shielded storage hangar listening raptly to today's dust reports."

I shook my head and sighed. I needed to keep Lobo busy, because boredom made him unbearable. "I'm sorry," I said, "for putting you away again."

"Your apology means so much," he said, "coming as it does after a second stint in storage immediately preceded by essentially the same words."

I considered disabling all his emotive programming, but even if that were possible, doing so would also render unbearably boring the one entity I could count on being able to talk to. Working with him was, I had to admit, a better choice than silencing him. "Here's the difference," I said. "This time I promise not to put you in storage if you can persuade me you can hide safely in orbit or elsewhere. Fair enough?"

"Yes, and now I accept your apology."

"Thank you. Now, load up another set of tourist shuttle codes and get us in the pack. We need to check out Xychek's HQ."

The company's ornate structure perched on a cliff so close to the heart of Bekin's Deal that urban sprawl had brought construction right to its border. The building was thus much, much closer to the city than Osterlad's, and much grander as well. Easily three times as wide as Osterlad's, its rock face featured the Xychek logo superimposed on what at first glance appeared to be irregular, raised asymmetric ovals in the rock. Upon further study, however, the carvings proved to be relief maps of all the solar systems where

Xychek was active, their positions not true to light-year scale but at least indicative of relative distances apart. Under magnification Lobo's visual monitors revealed that what had appeared to be mere lumps in the orbits to mark the colonized planets were actually the faces of those planets, each face an accurate high-level map of an aspect of the planet as seen from its jump gate. Xychek had carved the entire surface of its structure from the native black cliffs, with the only additional highlighting being the degree to which its artisans had polished the various stone faces. The image struck me as the heavens might appear to a god holding the only light in creation after all the stars had burnt to black.

I understood for the first time why so many tourists opened their wallets for this view. Perhaps later I'd spend some time appreciating the other structures, but not now. Now, we had to keep our focus on Xychek and learn what we could about Chung's habits.

Lobo kept image-matching programs running on every person who came out of the Xychek building, and I started my exercises, thankful that unlike when I've been on ground surveillance duty, in Lobo I could move around without concern.

After three days of flying the tourist shuttle rotation during the daytime and retreating to orbit each evening, I had to accept that kidnapping Chung during business hours was not going to be reasonably possible. He arrived every morning within ninety minutes of sunrise, his vehicle in the center of a heavily armed group of eight escorts, a number I felt was unnecessarily high and a sign of willingness to waste money on Xychek security's part. Chung came and went from the building frequently throughout the day to discharge his business and social duties, but the same escort vehicles always accompanied him. Other buildings stood right on the border of Xychek's, so Chung and his team always began each trip in a crowded area, and they stopped only at heavily populated spots. When he was on foot, guards stayed within reach at all times. I never caught them passing through desolate countryside during business hours.

Lobo had more than enough firepower to destroy his entire

escort team, of course; they were bodyguards, not soldiers in battle-armored vehicles. A direct attack, however, would not only result in a lot of conflict with the bodyguards, it would also almost certainly yield a great many civilian casualties and enough collateral damage that the Frontier Coalition would have to join Xychek in hunting me down. With Osterlad's company likely to come after me once the new management settled in, and with Xychek already seeking me, I couldn't afford to attract any more pursuers.

I'd have to go after him in his home. To do that, of course, I had to find his house and scout it.

The first part was easy. As the light began to fade on Lankin and the last of the tourists were murmuring appreciatively about the great views as their shuttles cruised on long, lazy arcs over the ocean and back to the city, Lobo headed for the lowest fairly crowded orbit we could find. A bottom-feeder collection of relay sats, corporate spy and counterspy bots, weather monitors, and automated zero-gee fabs shared the orbit with us and provided adequate cover. The heat signature of Chung's escort team was distinctive enough that Lobo could track it with his onboard sensors, so we waited a couple of hours until the man finally headed home.

As we'd observed the previous days, he used exactly the same vehicle arrangement and headed initially straight into town. Each day, however, his course changed within the first few klicks away from the office; I appreciated the countersurveillance care his bodyguards were taking. From our vantage in orbit we watched as first one and then two more of the escort vehicles pulled aside at different points along the route and idled, engines and weapons at the ready. Anyone following from the ground would have to pass them all, so surface pursuit would end up in conflict with either the last stand-alone trailing vehicle or a rear-facing part of the main team. I revised my opinion of Xychek security: The eight vehicles represented more a practical paranoia than waste.

After about forty minutes of wandering in the city, Chung's vehicle and his five remaining escorts headed northwest out of town on a highway whose scattered buildings over the course of half an hour of travel time mutated from city to suburb to widespread collections of large houses and then finally to a forest dotted here and there with estates. Chung and his team came to a stop at one of the largest properties, a cleared rectangular chunk of land that Lobo measured at a bit over eighty acres in size. An outer rectangle of forest about a hundred yards wide surrounded the land. Three roads led into it: the one on which Chung had entered, a second on the opposite side that more or less continued the path of the entry road, and a third on the left as you came onto the estate. The cleared area glowed in the weakening daylight with a pure white light from well-distributed and almost certainly redundant sets of spotlights, lights that made sure his team's monitors missed nothing on the ground near the house.

We had the location of Chung's house, but we needed a lot more data to be able to plan any kind of attack other than complete destruction of the place. I didn't consider that a viable option, both because of the attention it would attract and because without talking to Chung I couldn't know whether killing him would remove the bounty or only raise it.

Getting more data wasn't going to be simple. The house predictably read IR-neutral to Lobo, its shielding more than he could penetrate from orbit; he wasn't built for long-distance surveillance. So, we needed to find another way to take a closer look. On Macken I'd gotten lucky: Lobo had been deployed there as a local military reserve, so he had sat friends, and the Gardeners never noticed his surveillance drone because they were amateurs, bad amateurs. We knew no sats here, and I had great confidence that Chung's Xychek protection team was professional enough to immediately spot and shoot down any obviously military surveillance drone. Lobo's monitors had never tracked anything larger than birds flying over the place, so Chung and Xychek had probably paid local flight control to keep his airspace empty. I was also confident they possessed the weapons to make sure nothing flew too low over the house. On a transmission-heavy battlefield we could try a high-altitude flyover and dust the area with our own microsensor web, its activity sure to do no more than add to the electronic din that large-scale combat created. At Chung's estate, however, I had to assume his team had tracked and identified and was actively monitoring every transmission source in the area. Any change in the broadcast activity would trigger an alarm, an investigation, and possibly an evacuation.

The estate was secure against every modern electronic approach—and that, I finally realized, provided the opening we needed. I'd been thinking of this as a battle, the estate as a battlefield, where up-to-the-second data frequently played a major role in keeping you alive, but this wasn't a battle, and Chung's home wasn't a battlefield. I wanted surveillance data, not transmissions; the distinction was everything.

I told Lobo to keep us with the low-orbit gear and settled into a couch to sleep. In the morning, I'd send Lobo to rejoin the sats and continue his monitoring.

While he was at it, I'd pay a visit to Strange Kitty.

CHAPTER FOURTEEN

Organic tech has delivered all of the serious progress in human augmentation. Gene therapy, growth-center manipulation, vat-grown organs—you name the technique for making us better or barring death from the door a little longer, and the odds are it's organic. Nanotech petered out, at least as far as the rest of the universe was concerned, after the Aggro accident resulted in an entire solar system no ship had ever been able to return from. Human/hardware fusion never took off, because whatever metal or silicon could do to help a body, cells inevitably proved to be able to do better. Hardware augmentation maintained its fans, however: people who indulged in machine-based enhancement as often and as severely as their lives and budgets would permit, all in the deep belief that one day metal-tech would break through the barriers of its previous failures and elevate them into immortal meat/machine gods. Their extreme-edge bioengineering counterparts rode the same rush but on a different vehicle, pushing the limits of organic tech as they constantly altered their bodies.

Queen's Bar attracted both fringes, of course, with shops where you could ride your augmentation tech of choice not only to the legal limit, but beyond. The metal- and meat-tech shops predictably occupied different zones in the area, each one's clients neither approving nor particularly accepting of the other's. For metal-tech, you wandered the southwest bits of the district; meat-tech clung to the northeast.

Strange Kitty managed a rare trick: Both the serious metal crowd and the severely bioengineered shopped there, and both groups ranked it the top place to go for pets with more. Its storefront/warehouse two-building complex joined popular favorites like the Busted Heart in the center of Queen's Bar. It filled most of a block, with the retail space opening on one street and the warehouse loading docks facing directly onto the other. If you wanted an augmented animal, you headed for Strange Kitty. What it didn't have in stock, its bioengineers could probably produce, and if they couldn't manage it, odds are nothing outside of the top-drawer conglomerate labs could do it either.

FC tech enforcers rousted the place on those occasions when some animal-rights group could grab enough public attention that the local government worried tax dollars might be slipping away. The raids never found anything outside the legal limits; for that, you had to know where to look or have the proper introductions. So, the unwanted attention never lasted long. The same groups would also sometimes make lackluster attempts at picketing the business, but protest rallies in Queen's Bar inevitably mutated quickly into parties, street fairs, or disorganized streams of fleeing ex-protesters, as vendors, pickpockets, and street hustlers of all types dive-bombed any crowd that would stand still long enough for them to catch it.

I paused for a few minutes outside the store to make sure no one was following me. A guy with metal chest-shield implants strolled out of the shop, all of his attention focused on a lizard he was holding with his meat right hand and stroking with his metallic left, the lizard's skin coruscating in the light in time with the passes of the metal fingers. A tall, elegant woman with waist-length straight brown hair followed with her acquisition, an amphi-basset, its prominent gills and blue/teal coloring marking it as anything but an ordinary hound. A trio of fashion-victim girls sporting identical body mods—wispy waists made possible only by elevated organs, thickened spinal columns supporting broad and relatively flat chests, legs rippling with muscle—emerged guiding a flat- and metal-nosed hundred-kilo dog on three identical leads, the animal's detachable metal legs moving perfectly in custom sockets. Neither the creatures nor, for that matter, the people were to my taste, but they, like the rest of the Strange Kitty traffic, were extremely unlikely to be working for Osterlad or Xychek.

I slipped inside in a seam in the outgoing crowd, air-break fans ruffling my hair as I moved through the semipressurized doorway. The smell crashed into my sinuses the moment I cleared the threshold. The odors of fur, feathers, urine, dung, and sex recombined dynamically as I moved through the room, an olfactory organism in rapid multidirectional mutation. The doorway kept the neighbors from complaining, but inside there was no escape. Here and there I spotted nasal fetishists pretending to shop for as long as the management would let them linger, their noses flared and eyes glazed. Most of the customers, however, were focused, serious shoppers, thickets of them standing in the midst of the creatures that reflected their taste. Mammals, perennial human favorites, owned the display space and most of the front, where prospective buyers made unnatural cute noises over cats, dogs, ferrets, various local rodents, and other animals I didn't recognize, each one a designer's custom work. I made my way past them and into the reptile section, pausing for a moment to admire plexi containers of lizards with metal-barbed tails and snakes with additional eyes—probably not functional but definitely decorative—scoring their sides from the original pair backward for half a meter or more.

After the reptiles, the room darkened a bit as I entered the aquatic area. Filling this part of the store were tanks of all sizes, from a few liters up to several huge containers whose capacity I couldn't easily estimate, plexi enclosures that looked to be at least three meters deep, five long, and three high. Everything from tiny, purely decorative fish, to predators, to serious open-ocean racing rays swam in the tanks lining the walls all around me. The riotous colors and sheer variety of the fish and other water creatures on display made the mammals and reptiles appear tame by comparison.

I finally made it to the back of the retail section, where the store blended into the warehouse as the ceiling rose and the amount of customer activity dropped. In cages at eye level and in enclosed aeries that climbed from barely over my head all the way to the seven-meter-high unfinished ceiling, birds of all types perched, slept, flew, chattered, ate, and defecated. I've never been a bird fan, but that wasn't a problem; I wasn't shopping for a pet. Salespeople were scarce here, but that was fine, too; getting the help I needed would be easy. I stepped past the edge of the retail area and into what appeared to be a reception space fronting the vastly larger work and storage rooms behind it. I paused, knowing security was on the way, because with a quick IR scan I'd spotted some too-cool temperature-detection wall and floor sections, as well as a few failing motion sensors that shined as hot pinpricks; the owners needed to run physical-level maintenance checks on their security gear more often.

First to reach me was a short, thin fellow who moved with the precise jumpy motions of the over-stimmed, a man with neurochemical augmentations that rendered him deadlier than he appeared. Obvious security guys, hands on holstered weapons, followed a couple of seconds later. I stood very still, hands out from my sides.

"I'd like to make a significant purchase," I said.

"All our currently available merchandise is behind you," the short man said. He spoke like he moved: words clipped, phrases staccato, each sound precise.

"What I need is custom," I said.

"We strictly obey all customization laws," he said.

I laughed. "I couldn't care less. Nothing in the customization I want is, to the best of my knowledge, illegal for you to perform." I didn't have time to meet the right people in town, so I'd have to speed my way through this with brute conversational force. "What I do with my purchases is not your business. What is your business is what I'm willing to pay, which is well above your going rates." I pointed at my pocket. "I'm going to get my wallet."

He nodded his approval.

I pulled out the wallet and thumbed a link to my local bank. I'd priced the canine versions earlier, added a sizable premium, and set up an account that contained the result. I brought up the balance, obscured the account's number but left the bank's logo visible, and turned the wallet toward him. "This amount is ready to move to your local bank," I said, "once I have the animals I want—as long as I get them quickly."

He glanced at the screen, then at me. "What exactly do you want?"

"You engineer monitor dogs, right?" I said.

"Yes, of course," he said, "and cats and snakes and pretty much anything else you might like. It's generally standard stuff—organic fluid-drop-lens cameras bound into the eyes, transmitters feeding off the optic nerves—though it tends to lead to short lives for the pets." He shook his head. "What you showed me is way too much for monitors, even a herd of them."

"No," I said, "it's not. I need monitor birds—"

He cut me off. "Again, standard. What are you really—"

I returned the favor. "I need a flock of them," I said, "local, something common in the woods northwest of the city, plus enough controls to force them to follow a course I'll describe, and a wrangler to take them up and bring them back." I paused for breath, and this time he let me finish. "And I need it all without any transmissions of any sort, not for control, not for what they monitor. I need the absolute minimum amount of metal possible, onboard silicon or other nonmetal recorders, and all the recordings in my hands afterward; no one else sees the data."

"Pre-jump organic recorders?" he asked. "Why not simply transmit—" He stopped and waved his hand, stopping me before I could speak. "Not my concern, of course. After you're done with the birds?"

"I'll use them only once, and then they're yours—but the data is, as I said, exclusively mine."

He smiled for the first time. "The payment makes more sense. We've helped with similar work, of course, but nothing with tech this old. We also, as you might expect, want nothing to do with the end product of your . . . project, though as I think about it not having the data flow in realtime is only good for us."

"Yes," I said, "and I don't want you involved. It's a one-time run, then we're done. You take away the birds and do what you want with them."

"Fair enough," he said. "We can do business. Got a particular bird in mind?"

"No," I said. "As long as whatever you choose is common enough that no one tracking the flock will think twice about it flying overhead, I'll be happy."

He thought for a few seconds. "Blue-beaked moseys. They're everywhere outside the city, they move around frequently—a loud noise will send a flock flapping to a new location—and they fly at all times from first light until fairly late at night. They move relatively slowly, so the images should be clear. They'll home for multiple klicks after only a couple of feedings, so training is quick and range is good. Plus, they're easy to work on, with heads large enough that laser and cellular quick-heal techniques all work."

"Fine," I said. "One last complication: I need full-spectrum recording, visible and IR."

He smiled again. "You're new to working with animals. Of course you do; that's standard on this type of augmentation. When do you need all this?"

"This evening," I said, half statement and half question.

"Not a chance," he said. "A day to prepare and heal the flock, plus a day for the wrangler to work out his approach and do the homing training once you identify the start and end points."

I hated the delay, but he was right; it was never going to happen today. Maybe I'd get lucky in the interim and Chung would change his habits and give me an open shot at him. Unlikely, but I could hope.

"Okay," I said. "A quarter now, another quarter when they take off, and the remaining half when I have all the recordings."

"A third now," he said, "to help with up-front costs. Then take us to half when the wrangler's in position, and pay the balance when he hands you all the recordings."

He agreed so quickly that I realized I should have started with a lower offer and haggled, but the money pain was still tolerable. I needed Xychek to lift the bounty on me, and getting to Chung was the only way I knew to make that happen. I nodded my agreement, thumbed up a transfer of a third, and opened my wallet to accepting a destination code from his. "Done," I said. "Give me the account to transfer to, then we'll work out our communication protocols, and you can get me some birds."

Over the next three days, Chung kept to his routine, and Lobo and I clung to ours. We spent the nights in a variety of geosync low-orbit positions, Lobo maintaining transmission cover by echoing weather data or acting as a free public-data sat repeater, his sensors trained on Chung's house on the off chance that our target would surprise us with an easy opportunity. Chung didn't. In the days we flew with the tourist shuttle crowd, up and down the coastal cliff and outlying forest tour routes, Lobo's camo washing him with a different set of corporate colors every few hours. Chung's security team kept to its proven practices, and we never even came close to a low-collateral-damage shot at him. As the time wore on, the beauty of the cliff structures faded into unseen background, then eventually decayed into visual annoyance. Choose to look at a piece of art a thousand times, and each glance may reveal new beauty. Let a job force you to study it when you're aching to move on to the next task, and only those rare pieces that touch you most deeply will remain lovely.

I invested part of each evening in studying Lobo's low-orbit recon images of a fifteen-kilometer-diameter circle centered on Chung's estate, trying to balance my conflicting desires. For the obvious safety reasons, I wanted starting and ending coordinates that were as deserted as reasonably possible, but I also needed a flight line that passed over as many homes and businesses as possible. Should the Strange Kitty team be tempted to double-dip by offering intel about me to the possible targets, I wanted them to have to wonder which of many options I was scanning. Alerting all the possibilities would, I hoped, open them to more exposure than they'd like.

I finally settled on a not-quite-ten-kilometer path that started a couple of klicks off the road in a light-density forest and ran over three small business concentrations and five estates roughly on par with Chung's. The endpoint was the far edge of the warehouse portion of one of the business areas—not ideal, but acceptable given that we'd be launching in the dying light of the day, when Chung would most likely be home.

I stretched out the route choice to maintain my focus on the task. I've never enjoyed waiting for a job to start. Waiting is fine when I can use the time to gather new intel. It can also be a pleasurable activity when I'm not working. I love idle time and can while away weeks observing a new starscape or ocean, as I'd been doing on Macken before all this started, but such lazy days are fun only when what I've chosen to do is be idle. I was on my first run up the coast one morning and way past ready to get to work when the Strange Kitty folks posted the signal my birds were ready: an advertisement for a one-day, limited-quantity price reduction on mini-dragons with self-regulating homeostatic systems that would work in anything from a blizzard to a heat wave. I'd suggested a protocol that wouldn't risk costing them money, but my salesman had assured me that they'd overstocked the mini-dragons and would love it if the special offer boosted sales. To avoid attracting undue attention, Lobo and I finished the tour route we were running, called Strange Kitty, and worked our way cautiously to a location where Lobo could safely drop me.

Two hours before the projected launch time, I met the Strange Kitty team, my salesman and the wrangler, at the coordinates I'd given them. They arrived in a heavily shielded company transport truck that contained my birds and a dozen other animals of various types, all sedated. The men sported Strange Kitty uniforms in ad-woven active fabric, images of augmented creatures of all types slithering over the clothing. Had anyone stopped them, they explained, they would have been able to produce a full schedule of deliveries. I nodded appreciatively at their caution. My salesman appeared exactly as amped as he had at the store. The wrangler, an even shorter man who was enough of a bird fan to have back feathers that peeked above the collar of his coverall, moved almost as if asleep—a by-product, he explained, of the chemically enhanced calming mosey pheromones he'd washed with before loading the birds.

"I'd like to verify the recording capability," I said. The air was hot, thermals playing almost visibly in the slow-moving atmosphere. This far inland we received all the heat of a tourist coastal city but none of the cooling ocean breeze.

"Of course," my salesman replied.

They opened the back of the truck and led me inside. Its rear half was a large cage full of moseys squawking and flapping and jumping about. As the wrangler walked over to the cage, however, the pheromone assault calmed the birds, and they settled on some of the many dark wooden perches that extended from the bars, walls, and ceilings of the caged area.

He took out one of the moseys and absently stroked its head, the bird lying as still and happy in his arms as a spent lover. A little under a third of a meter long and with a wingspan of over a meter, the mosey was bigger than I'd expected. At first glance as we entered the truck, I'd thought the moseys to be plain, basically gray animals with only the blue beaks to break up the color monotony. Now, with the time to look closely, I saw that their feathers eased through a gentle color transition from dark gray at the tips to a blend of lighter grays and finally to a blue so close to gray it was as if the merest few drops of blue pigment had fallen in a can of gray paint. Here and there on the bird's underside were flecks of white and black frequent enough that they invited the thought of a pattern, but not any pattern I could discern. Not showy animals, but ones that repaid close inspection, beautiful in their own way. I realized then, as I have at many such moments in the past, that the same has proven true of every living thing I've ever taken the time to study closely, a testimony to the wonder of creation. I know many people crave explanations for the glories of the universe, but I don't; what I crave is the will and the ability to learn to appreciate it all.

The wrangler interrupted my reverie. "It couldn't be simpler," he said. He parted the feathers on the left side of the bird's neck to reveal a small stud, pressed the stud, and pointed the animal's head at me. After a few seconds, he pressed the stud again, then hooked a small viewing port to it, the bird still happily pheromone-drunk in his arms. The screen snapped alive with multiwindowed images of me in visible, IR, and composite frequencies.

"They're trained for the end coordinates?" I said.

"Of course," said the wrangler, his pride obviously offended. As he put the mosey back in its cage, he continued. "We've made three other deliveries in that area earlier today. Each time, we fed them and established the destination for them. They're superb homing beasts, so that might have been enough. To make sure, though, we installed some of our proprietary tech—" he must have seen my eyes widen, for he quickly added "—nonmetal, of course—in every bird in the flock. They'll work, or you owe us nothing."

"And you'd refund my previous payments?" I said, addressing the question to the salesman.

"Of course."

"Excellent," I said. I counted the birds; nineteen were in the cage. I had expected more. "Why only nineteen?"

The wrangler's look ratcheted from offended to annoyed. "Because it felt right," he said, "for moseys, these woods, this time of year, this time of day. It felt right. It's what I do."

"My apologies," I said, meaning it. I'd asked out of reflex, not thought, and if I was going to question their expertise, I should have done the research in advance to be able to do so intelligently.

I took out my wallet, thumbed what I owed them, and showed it to the salesman.

After finishing the transfer, he said, "When do we launch?"

"When I call you," I said, "which will be in less than two hours. I want to be at the endpoint before you release them; no point in taking the risk of transportation issues messing up the schedule. Who from your end will be with me?"

"I will," the wrangler said. "Launching requires only opening the exterior cage access panel in the side of the truck, so he'll handle it. The moseys will handle it from there. I assume you can take me and my equipment bags; yes?"

"Yes." I didn't see him as a threat, and having a hostage could prove useful should something go wrong. "Let's go." To the sales-man I added, "I'll call when we're in position and the time is right."

The trip to the endpoint went smoothly, no traffic and, to my delight, no probing chatter from the wrangler. I invested some of the available transit time in counter-ground-surveillance side trips and detours, and neither I nor Lobo, who was tracking me from one of his low-orbit posts, could spot anyone following. Lobo couldn't get detailed enough data for me to be completely comfortable, but that was fine; too much comfort in a mission is a dangerous thing.

As the sun was fading and the day's light deepening in tone and multiplexing in color, playing a visual symphony transitioning from unnoticed backdrop to in-your-face beauty, I made the call. The wrangler anticipated less than half an hour before the birds would reach us, so he began setting out food, harnesses, four pop-up cages, and another test viewer. I scanned the treetops on the other side of the parking area for signs of the moseys as Lobo kept me posted on what little he could discern. What appeared to be the flock was moving from the launch site toward me, its speed was consistent with the plan, and so on.

A little over fifteen minutes later, Lobo relayed the most impor-tant news: The flock had crossed Chung's grounds, and all nineteen birds were still airborne and heading toward us. I relaxed a little.

The vibrant colors of the sunset had begun to morph into somber, inky tones that would soon give way to night. The day was cooling quickly as the sun set. The moseys flew into view. The wrangler misted the air with a spray bottle I assumed contained more pheromones and put bits of additional food in the now open cages. The moseys circled us for a few minutes, enjoying the freedom of the sky and reluctant to surrender it. The chemical net of the pheromones and the installed Strange Kitty tech drew them down and into the cages. The last few hovered for a little bit just out of reach, moving in gentle spirals on wings working so slowly and perfectly you could almost believe they never really moved, but even those reluctant few finally settled into captivity.

The wrangler closed three of the cages and pulled one of the birds from the open fourth; it was as submissive as the one in the truck. A bit back from and below the control stud was a small flap of skin that covered a thumbnail-size recording module. He popped the module out of its socket and pointed to the module's connector. "Nonmetal conductor plug compatible with most milspec tech," he said. "They wear out faster than metal, so plug them in once, get what you need, and move the data to more stable media. Okay?" He handed me the module.

"Got it," I said, as I took the recording. I tested it in the viewer and watched the images at high speed, skipping forward quickly but seeing enough to confirm that it contained coverage of Chung's place. "Good enough," I said.

The wrangler nodded and went to work on the other birds. I again counted nineteen birds, and he delivered nineteen modules.

The salesman arrived ten minutes later. Lobo said he couldn't spot any pursuers. I paid the balance I owed and left as the wrangler was gently carrying the birds one by one into the truck's holding pen. The salesman stood calmly by, smart enough to realize there was no point in trying to rush this man with his charges.

We'd spent a lot of time in orbits near Chung's, so while we were analyzing the recon data I had Lobo park us in a fairly high orbit about as far away from Chung as possible, in a nice spot over the largely unsettled mountainous region on the continent on the other side of Lankin from Bekin's Deal.

I had to admire the quality of Lobo's analysis systems. He perfectly and quickly assembled all the recordings from the nineteen birds into a composite video and a set of stills showing images in various combinations of wavelengths. Predictably, no one bird had captured all the views I wanted, and most of the time the birds weren't looking directly at the estate, but their flight pattern was wide enough and slow enough, as the Strange Kitty crew had said it would be, that the composite images completely covered the estate. Almost two dozen of the most important still images filled Lobo's wall in front of me as I walked back and forth in his main open area.

No matter how long I looked at them, they told me the same

basic story: Chung's estate was a fortress, more heavily armed than I'd guessed. Air-defense weapons, both missile launchers and energy pulse, squatted in plain sight about twenty meters from each side of the house. Image-match searches of Lobo's weaponry database pegged them as serious medium- and high-altitude killers, useless for targets below two hundred meters but deadly for anything above that height. At least two dozen guards were visible across the estate, some obviously carrying the smart missiles that conventional wisdom had long held were the best choice for combating low-flying attack craft. Lobo might be able to weather a hit from one of those missiles, but he also might not; I didn't want to find out.

IR views showed hot sensors scattered across the estate, with a ring of what I had to assume were overlapping area monitors covering the perimeter of the cleared grounds.

As I'd observed before, three gates, all staffed with guards, led into and out of the property.

The size of the estate, the multiple entrances, and the many guards and sensors combined to doom any possibility of a stealth attack with my nanomachines. I've never tried controlling more than half a dozen nano-swarms, and the clouds unavoidably move fairly slowly, certainly at nothing like battlefield weapon speeds, so I had no chance of individually taking down the whole place. Even if I did, explaining that much disassembled matter in a large city like Bekin's Deal would be impossible. I couldn't afford the attention.

I saw no way to do this job entirely on my own without enduring way too much risk.

Involving Lobo didn't improve my chances a lot. Even assuming he came in hot, my options were severely limited and incredibly unattractive.

The only one I was sure would work was a total-destruction missile and pulse attack from an altitude of about a hundred meters on the edge of the forest outside the house. Lobo could fly in quickly enough that only the gate guards would have time to attack, and from the images we had of their weapons his armor could handle the minimal attack those guards could muster before he killed them. Firing everything he had in one long screaming attack, he could take out the whole area, scorch the turf and everything on it, but that did me no good; I needed Chung alive.

Worse, that much destruction and death would tornado into enough news locally that the FC would have to come after me. They might be able to write off Chung's loss as a standard corporate casualty, part of the risk of operating on still-developing worlds, but some of his guards were bound to be talent recruited locally, with local ties, and their deaths would provoke an outcry the FC couldn't ignore. The FC would then use the Saw to get me, of course, and I doubted I'd live to walk away from that fight.

No, total destruction wasn't a reasonable option.

Any more finely targeted approach would, of course, leave Lobo open to the handheld missiles. Losing Lobo was also not an acceptable choice.

We could perhaps boost the odds of success by first blanketing the area with milspec sensor disruptors and hoping Chung's sensor web was old tech—not likely, but possible—but the guards would then take Chung and leave. Clusters of armored vehicles stood ready to roll at the intersection of each of the three roads with the house. I had to assume that these guys would use standard protection protocols, so at the first sign of attack all three sets of vehicles would roar out of there at high speed, and I'd have to guess which one held Chung.

The more I stared at the images, the more I was convinced that I had to change the game's rules if I wanted to play at all.

"Lobo," I said, "I can't come up with a plan that doesn't involve massive casualties and that also guarantees we emerge alive and with Chung. Can you?"

"No," he said. "Quite the opposite. Logic dictates we can't guarantee success within the axioms you've set. Your rules don't allow us to destroy the entire place, so we're left with two of us to cover three well-spaced exit routes. This is obviously not possible."

"Yeah," I said, "it isn't. We can't do it."

I stretched out on a pilot's couch, the images on the wall blanking as I moved away from them. I had to stop avoiding the reality in front of me and accept the only real solution to the problem, or start running and hope Chung, Osterlad's team, and everyone else Chung contracted would eventually tire of searching for me. The latter was unacceptable. As little as I wanted to follow the only path I could discover that would get Chung, I had even less desire to spend all my days in heightened paranoia, even if the paranoia was justified.

"The answer," I said, "is just as obvious, but I hate it."

"What?" Lobo said.

"I have to get some help."

CHAPTER FIFTEEN

The Saw recruiting center perched in the shadow of a skyscraper on the southern edge of Queen's Bar like a bird of prey waiting for rodents to crawl into the light. A plain rectangular building with clean, sharp lines displayed the Shosen Advanced Weapons Corporation name, icon—a gleaming serrated blade most of the way through cutting a rifle barrel in half—and motto, "The Price of Peace." The door stayed open around the clock. Inside, the honestly inquisitive visitor could always count on free drinks, food, and basic stimulants. The repeat moocher could equally reliably expect to hit the street face-first after fewer than three strides into the greeting room.

I counted half a dozen Saw troops on duty in the large open public area, their eyes constantly monitoring both their conversational targets and the room's access points. About that many more were stopping by on a leave day to grab a bite to eat or enough uppers to keep them going as they fought to muster the stamina to spend the accumulated pay that was screaming for release from their wallets.

Standing to the side of the main information counter was an older man, a sergeant, whom the inattentive or the intoxicated could easily mistake for a friend's kindly uncle. A smile constantly played on his face, pleasant crinkles surrounded his eyes, and his hands moved with the unhurried ease of someone with not a care in the world. Bring even slightly trained vision to bear on him, however, and you'd note the master gunnery sergeant's stripes on his working blues, stripes that marked him as being as high a noncom as you'd find in the Saw; the complete lack of visible fat on a torso half again as wide and as thick as the bodies of most men his height; and the fine scar lines on his neck and hands, lines he kept despite the ease with which Saw doctors could have removed them, lines he used every campaign to remind him how easily and how quickly the drain could come out on any mission. An active-fabric patch on his chest alternated his name, "Gustafson," and the Saw logo. He made me while I was still figuring out that he was the one I needed. By the time I reached him, he'd shifted one foot forward and spread and lowered his stance, all in subtle movements you could easily miss. In my peripheral vision I caught three of the duty troops moving nearer the exits; should I get by him, they'd make sure I never left the building.

All around us the recruiting chatter continued. The locals, who were there to find out if the merc life might be for them, or if it really would pay enough to get them out of whatever trouble they were in, remained happily oblivious of the storm gathering wind across the room from them.

I stopped well short of Gustafson, spread my arms slightly, showed him my palms, and said, "Top."

"Looking to join up?" he said, the smile still fixed on his face.

"No."

"I didn't think so." The smile vanished. "What *do* you want?"

"No trouble," I said, "only to ask a question." Two more of the duty troops casually wandered closer. "I appreciate that you have to engage all the security," I tilted my head slightly toward the various gathering soldiers, "and I'd do the same in your job, but it's not necessary. Let me make this at least a little simpler. I served with the Saw for a decade, most of it under a captain named Tristan Earl, humping sector-to-sector on the ground in planets I'd just as soon forget. I opted out twelve years ago. Scan my fingerprints and retinas; unless the Saw has slid downhill enough since I left it to make me cry, I'll still be in the databases."

His expression didn't change, but he nodded his head in the direction of the recruiting desk. I walked up to it. He and the men accompanying me paralleled my path, never letting the distance between us change.

The woman who was leading the team at the desk, Schmidt according to her name tag, flashed me a smile that looked perfectly at home in a face pretty enough to make potential recruits want to sign up just so they could get to know her. Her sergeant's stripes, callused hands, and heavily muscled forearms suggested they'd end up spending more time fearing her than adoring her. She ran quick retinal and fingerprint scans, the skin scrape for the secret DNA test a little too obvious.

"You need to adjust the print scanner, Sarge," I said.

She cocked an eyebrow.

I smiled. "It accidentally scraped my finger."

She glanced at her display and straightened a tiny bit. "Thanks, Gunny. We will."

Gustafson stepped up, clapped me on the back, and led me off to a side room with a sofa, a few chairs, and a low table in the center of the seats. As we left the main area, the guys who'd positioned themselves behind me and those monitoring the exits all floated back into the swirl of the room.

He sat, and I did the same.

"What can we do for you?" he said. "Don't tell me you miss it."

I laughed. "Now and then, sure, I find myself thinking about it, but mostly because I liked being part of a group that knew what the hell it was about. Most of the time, though, no, I don't. Most of the time, I wish I slept better."

"I sleep fine," he said.

I stared at him, saying nothing.

He laughed. "Most nights." He shook his head and laughed again. "Some nights."

I laughed with him. "Fair enough."

"So," he said, "we've established we're a couple of guys with some obvious things in common. That's all fine, and if I were on leave I'd buy you a drink and maybe we'd get in a little trouble together, but I'm working. Again: What can we do for you?"

"I need to talk to the Old Man here on Lankin," I said, "and I know trying to find out who he is and where he is will take a lot of time."

"Why?"

I shook my head. "Top, I have a little data to give, and I need a little data in return. Please trust me that I mean no trouble, and leave it at that."

He nodded, understanding. You don't make it anywhere near as far as master gunnery sergeant in any serious outfit I've ever seen without learning that you're going to spend a lot of your life acting without anything approaching all the information you'd like. The smile flooded back onto his face. "Who'd you say you served under?" he said.

"Captain Earl, Tristan Earl."

"Then meeting the Old Man will be a reunion for you," he said.

"Captain Earl runs the Saw here on Lankin?" I said. I'd always hoped Earl would receive the recognition he deserved, but I never expected it to happen so quickly. Then I realized it wasn't quick at all; sitting with a man in a Saw uniform, going back to those days even for a moment, the twelve years I'd been away seemed no time at all.

"Colonel Earl," Gustafson said. "When the FC awarded the Lankin deal to us, the colonel got the post. We've been here five years, and he's run the show the whole time. He's done a damn fine job of it, too, if you ask me."

"I would have expected no less."

"Stay put," he said, as he got up and headed back to the main desk.

I'd planned to improvise a bit with the local Saw head, because I needed to understand the FC, corporate, and Saw relationships a bit better before I could know what was safe to say and what might land me in the brig. With Earl, though, improvising wouldn't cut it. He was too smart not to spot the game, and unless he'd changed a lot, too focused and too busy to have the patience to put up with it. I'd have to tread carefully but play it as straight as I could without putting either of us in a bad position.

Gustafson returned and handed me a small sheet of rich paper; the Saw's admin corps liked pomp. "End of business tomorrow," he said. "This will give you the details and a map."

"Thanks," I said. "I appreciate it. You won't regret it."

"I hope that's the case," he said, "because from your record I'd prefer to avoid ending up on the opposite side of any heavy action."

I shook his hand, and, as I was heading out, said, "Me, too." I meant it.

CHAPTER SIXTEEN

The Saw station where I went to meet Earl blended seamlessly with the many corporate fabs that ringed the southwestern edge of the city. Surrounded by a few layers of active-wire fencing that writhed like snakes when you walked too close, fronted by gates bristling with both automated and human security, the cream-colored central buildings appeared no more important or heavily guarded than those of any of the fabs. Fabrication modules and the design intelligences that guided them ranked as core assets of all the corporations that dominated commerce in this sector of space, so everyone expected heavy security around them. No one would give this facility's setup a second thought.

When I torqued my vision over to IR, however, the picture changed. Hot spots dotting the interior perimeter at irregular intervals marked hatches covering weapons I could guess at but not see. Similar spots on the roofs and walls of all the buildings in the complex made it clear that the Saw had, as always, dug in securely and would make anyone trying to take their turf pay dearly for every centimeter.

I arrived early enough to make sure I'd be outside Earl's office a few minutes before our appointment; punctuality ranked high on the long list of societal conventions he considered vital. The guard made a show of checking for my appointment while the cameras and clearance systems did the real work. When I and the cab I'd hired had passed all the tests, the guard snapped me a small but polite salute, my record obviously visible in his pad. He beamed directions to the cab's guidance systems and waved me through. The vehicle dropped me in front of a central building that looked no different from all the others, then sped away as soon as I paid. Gustafson stepped out of a door a half-dozen meters in front of me.

"Good to see you again, Top," I said, "though I'm a bit surprised he has you on all these babysitting details."

Gustafson pulled on the outside seam of his right pants leg. The fabric parted to reveal an almost albino, hairless stretch of skin that ran as low and as high as I could see. "Still integrating the new leg and hip," he said. "Lost the old one on a dirtball a few jumps away that I'm not allowed to name and you probably wouldn't recognize anyway. I might have healed as fast, maybe faster, if I'd let them keep me in hospital, but I've always believed work is the best therapy. I posted for any station that would take me and let me do a job. Earl's unit offered the recruiting and admin gig, and here I am."

I nodded in understanding. I couldn't picture him waiting at some physical therapy station for a bunch of rear-echelon doctors to pronounce him fit. "So it's coincidence you're here to meet me?" I said.

"You know better than that. I understand you couldn't tell me why you wanted this meeting, but you have to know that your refusal left me curious. I can't believe anything that makes you feel the need to meet the Old Man is entirely legit, and he can't, either—which means he has to make sure nothing happens here that casts the Saw in a bad light with its employer. So, you get the pleasure of me joining your meeting."

I should have expected Earl wouldn't take the risk, physical or contractual, of even listening to me without a witness. The Saw and I could both fake recordings, of course, but I wouldn't have a supporting eyewitness on my side. This wasn't bad news—I'd known I'd need to be careful—but it did make caution even more important. I had personal history, a lot of it in sharp zones, with Earl; to Gustafson, that history earned me cordial behavior, but no more. I remained yet another guy who wasn't on his team.

I plastered on a smile. "I appreciate the honor. As I said before, I'm not here to cause the Saw any trouble. I'm only after information."

Gustafson led me through a door that I'm sure scanned me for weaponry, and then we entered the maze of busy, monitor-walled hallways that typified any active fort. The displays switched to images of the sky outside as I approached and failed to emit the appropriate clearance signals. After three turns, we came to a door the same dull gray metal as all the others we'd passed, but this time we stopped and waited for the door to clear and announce us.

About a minute later it slid open, and Gustafson motioned me in. Reflexes caused me to hesitate, my natural desire not to walk between two potentially hostile unknowns taking hold, but he outwaited me; we both knew I had no option if I wanted the meeting. I entered a pleasantly appointed conference space, five comfortable chairs covered in a local red-spotted leather surrounding a low table that held three glass pitchers. Gustafson followed, and I caught a momentary glimpse of the side of the door as it slid shut: It was thick and ran in a track on all four sides. I leaned on the wall to my right and nodded slightly at the firmness beneath its lightly patterned pale red wallpaper. They'd set the meeting in a containment room, its door armored, its walls thick with fused layers of metal and local composite, definitely reinforced, almost certainly laced with enough metal and active countertransmission circuitry that no electromagnetic data could enter or leave. I had to assume Earl could record in here, but I doubted he'd allow even his own devices to transmit—too much risk of transmission hijacking or piggy-backing. The interior of the room operated entirely manually. The pitchers weren't for show: We had to pour our own beverages. Lobo might hate drink dispensers, but I would have been happy to see one.

A door in the wall opposite me swung open, and Earl walked in. Aside from the colonel's wings on his shoulders, he looked exactly as I remembered him, which was exactly the same as the day I'd met him over twenty years ago. Being able to look the same for decades is nothing notable; all but the very poorest and those choosing to live on new planets during their early colonization years have access to all the med tech they need to remain physically unchanged for at least fifty years. What is unusual is someone *choosing* to use med tech in that way. Most people grow bored with their looks, or decide to ride the wave of some passing celebrity-appearance fad, or simply opt to appease the desire of a new lover for a little customization. Not Earl. He wore his hair in the same combed style as always, neatly parted, never buzzed or shaved in the manner many in the Saw favored, but never long either. I doubted his weight wavered by more than a kilo plus or minus from what it was at the end of basic training, and he wore the same working blues he always had. I'd seen him in dress uniform only when informing families of the loss of their son or daughter and, on rare occasions, when a Saw Central Command general required it.

A good twenty centimeters shorter than I and considerably lighter and less muscular, Earl nonetheless was one of the men I'd least like to face in combat, because I knew he'd never be trying to fight, only to kill. In the years I'd served in his units, I'd watched him many times go to great lengths to avoid conflict, even to the point of appearing to retreat. When he finally judged conflict to be unavoidable, however, he acted quickly and committed completely, bypassing the small moments of hesitation common even in most highly trained fighters.

I started to salute him, but he waved it off.

"None of that, Jon," he said. "You're a civilian now, so this is strictly informal."

"As you say, Colonel Earl."

"Please, just Tristan." He pointed to a chair opposite his, and Gustafson took one between us.

I smiled. "Sorry, Colonel, but some habits aren't worth breaking. And, though this is an informal visit, that doesn't mean it might not be of professional interest to you."

"Of course," he said, smiling. "I didn't think you came here just to tell me how much fun you were having since you left us, or how much you were enjoying traveling with your new PCAV." His smile never wavered, and he never looked away.

I matched his behavior, reminded of sitting at card tables with him while we waited for cleanup crews and scooping up the money of the newer officers and NCOs who were betting extravagantly in their happiness to be alive, to be anywhere but where they'd been. I'd assumed the registered transfer of any weapon half as powerful as Lobo anywhere in Earl's turf would attract his attention, but I'd half hoped that the fact that the Saw didn't have a contract for Macken might keep this information away from him. It was a dumb hope, but no matter; I'd left no other tracks he'd be likely to find.

"May we speak without a formal record," I said, "other than the one in Top's head, of course?"

"Yes," he said. He touched a spot on his sleeve. "All recording is off. Continue."

The notion that being true to one's word is a fundamental underpinning of a strong society either died or moved to life support centuries before I was born, probably centuries before mankind found and entered the first jump gate. For Earl, though, and for me and a few other men and women I've had the pleasure to know, the concept surged with as much vitality today as when Jennie first instilled it in me back on Pinkelponker. As a boy there I learned the sad lesson that I shouldn't assume others placed the same value on their word as the two of us, but Earl was a proven exception. He said he wouldn't electronically record this meeting, so I trusted he wouldn't.

"Thank you very much," I said, slowing the cadence of my speech both for clarity and to give me time to choose my words carefully. "I appreciate how busy you are, so I don't to want to consume more of your day than necessary. You also know me—knew me—well enough that I hope you'll recall how much I prefer getting directly to the point."

"I always liked that aspect of you," he said. "I wouldn't mind experiencing more of it now."

"I understand, but because I want to minimize any possible

negative consequences for either of us, in this case I need to take a slightly more circuitous route."

He leaned slightly forward. "Negative consequences? Please don't tell me we're meeting so you can deliver a threat for some new employer. I'd hate doing what I'd then have to do, though"—he paused and leaned back, apparently relaxed—"you know I'd do it."

I waved my hands slowly, easily. "No, as I've already told Top, I don't want to be on the opposite side of the Saw. I simply need to understand how things work here so I don't accidentally cause problems for either of us by saying something wrong."

"Fair enough," he said, "for now. Go."

"I've canvassed the publicly available data about the Saw's contract with the FC for Lankin," I said, "but we all know how much that data is worth. I also know that Kelco and Xychek are the main corporate players here. What I'd like to understand are the limits of your contract with respect to conflicts that involve those two organizations."

"And for sharing this private data, I get what?"

"Maybe nothing," I said, "but maybe quite a lot you'll care about. I promise this isn't a game."

He nodded, knowing I was telling the truth. "We perform no police functions; the FC locals handle those jobs. We deal with any native fauna issues in new settlement areas, monitor and are on call to handle any serious armed insurrections, and, of course, make sure Lankin appears prickly enough to any governments outside the FC that it's not worth their time to attack. The two big corporations have the standard deal with the FC: They handle their own security and frontier action, and they pledge not to use their forces against each other or the FC. The FC—and we, as its enforcing agent— conduct periodic, scheduled and unscheduled inspections of their troops and weapons, and they report all weapons acquisitions and militia deployments. As long as they follow the rules, we run our inspections and otherwise leave them alone. The arrangement is classic post–corporate wars, the same one you've seen, the same one all the big conglomerates and governments have used for over a century, since before either of us was born."

No one, to the best of my knowledge, knew how old I really was, and I worked hard to keep it that way.

"What's your role when a conflict does involve one of the two?" I asked.

His eyes widened slightly, but he didn't press me. Yet. "Except for the standard small stuff the Lankin police might handle—theft, assault on individuals in the streets, that sort of thing—we have no role unless one of the companies requests our help. All local Kelco and Xychek staff maintain dual FC/corporate citizenship, so corporate security handles anything serious, as long as it doesn't endanger civilians." He poured a glass of a light green drink and offered it to me. "Local tea? Top?"

Gustafson waved off the offer, and I shook my head. "No, thank you," I said. "One more question, and then I'll start talking."

"Good," Earl said. He sipped the tea he'd offered me.

"To the degree that you can discuss or speculate about anything that involves your employer without violating your contract, how would you characterize the FC's relationship with these two corporations?"

"That's an easy one. I don't have to provide any private information. Layla Vaccaro, the ranking FC bureaucrat here and the Lankin rep to the FC council, is on public record with her discontent over the FC's role as the weak sister of the three. Lankin joined the FC after being developed initially by prospectors from the two companies, and the FC has been playing catch-up ever since. She hates the position it's left her in." He drank a bit more tea. "And now, as you said, it's your turn."

"Xychek's Jose Chung," I said, and paused until he nodded in recognition at the name, "has offered a bounty to anyone who captures or kills me."

Nothing in Earl's expression changed, but I could feel the force of his increased concentration. "Why?"

I hesitated, despite having known the conversation would reach this point. Answering him would lead to more questions. Eventually, those questions would take us to Johns and to Osterlad, and I didn't want to have to explain their deaths. Not answering would annoy him, but if I kept my focus on the matters that could affect him and the Saw, he might allow the omission. I had to try. "Nothing I did that motivated the bounty was illegal," I said, choosing my words carefully, "or deserving of that treatment, so Chung's motivation doesn't matter." Earl glanced briefly at Gustafson, so I hurried on before Gustafson could take the hint and ask the follow-up question Earl wanted him to pose. "What does matter is that Chung is buying weapons illegally from Osterlad, weapons I'm sure Xychek is not revealing in your inspections."

Gustafson sat up straighter and leaned forward. Earl didn't move, but tension lines in his face showed the effort the control was costing him.

"If this is true, the implications are significant," Earl said, "for all three major organizations on Lankin. I take it you can prove this?" Earl said, definitely a question, not a statement, despite the phrasing.

"Not yet," I said, "but my source is well connected, and I have no reason to doubt it."

"As I'm sure you'll understand," Earl said, a little frustration and anger audible in his tone, "no individual's word, not even the word of someone I've trusted in the past—" He paused to make sure I caught the tense, then continued, "—is enough justification for me to take the kind of action that proof of such a violation of a major treaty would motivate."

"I understand," I said, "which is the second reason I need to talk to Chung. After I finish my conversation with him, I have every confidence that he'll both fix my problem and give you all the information you need to act on yours."

"So talk to him," Earl said. "You don't need any action from us to do that."

"You're right; I don't. What I need is your inaction, and your advice." Earl raised an eyebrow in question. "As you'd expect, Chung isn't interested in having a friendly chat with me. To arrange a talk that I can be sure to live through, I'll need to . . . retrieve him, and I want to make sure that doing so won't bring the Saw down on me."

Earl nodded, clearly getting it. I waited while he considered; this was the moment when he'd decide.

After almost a minute, time during which he stared up and to his right, seeing nothing but his own thoughts, he focused his attention on me and spoke. "Not acting costs us nothing, as does advice. Some information, however, unavoidably carries almost viral risk when it moves from one person to another. Are you clear that if you tell anyone about any aspect of our involvement, even this conversation, we'll not only deny it, we'll also come for you?"

"Of course."

He nodded. "Okay. We've been covertly monitoring Osterlad Corp. as much as we could manage for some time now, because we have other reasons to believe it's been moving arms to a corporation, though I confess we thought the buyer was Kelco. No matter; either would pose a problem for us. Osterlad's death—" He paused, giving me time to react. I didn't, so he moved on. "—has prompted his company to push all its illegal business even further underground than normal, so now we're getting far less data than before. Obtaining firsthand information from Chung could be the break we needed. You'd have to be willing to bring him and the information not only to me, but to Vaccaro; as FC head here, she's my liaison, and she'd have to get them to support any Saw action in advance. She'd also demand to talk to Chung herself."

"Of course," I said. "Once I have the information, which I can't get until I have Chung."

"So we have a deal?"

"Yes."

"Good." He leaned forward, the hard part over and the fun part, the planning, now under way. "You asked for inaction and advice," he said. "I can do better than inaction. You can't be planning to go after Chung at Xychek's HQ, because you're not that stupid; you know doing so would cause more collateral damage than we could tolerate. Taking him in transit leaves too many chances that he could duck into any of the many civilian areas along his common travel routes, which would bring you back to the problem of collateral damage. So, you have to be targeting him at his home. I choose when we spring our inspections on the corporations, and how many of their troops we summon. Were you and Top here to start chatting every now and again, I wouldn't be surprised if on the evening you paid Chung a visit you encountered only a skeleton protection force at his house, with the rest of the force off-site at a major Saw inspection of Xychek's official weapons and troops."

Despite Earl's confidence, from what I'd seen of Chung's protection squad, they'd never cut below the number of personnel necessary to run exit groups through all three paths out of Chung's property. Still, any decrease in the force at the estate would be a great help. "Top and I get along great," I said, "don't we, Top?"

"You bet," he said, smiling.

"Then that's settled," Earl said. "The advice you wanted?"

"I can't do the job alone," I said. I didn't see any win from mentioning Lobo; if Earl didn't know how intelligent Lobo was, I had a small potential future edge should I one day need it. "So I want to hire some help. I don't know any of the right type of contractors in this area. I could find some, of course, but I wouldn't know more about them than I could find on my own. I assume you have a lot more knowledge in this area and might be able to recommend someone to me."

Earl thought for a bit, and I could almost picture the images and facts dancing across his inner vision. Gustafson appeared equally thoughtful. Finally, Earl looked at Gustafson, leaned back, and both men laughed lightly.

"I believe Top and I are thinking of the same person," he said.

"I'm sure of it," Gustafson said. "For what you want, and given that we can't recommend anyone in the Saw, she's far and away the best option in this entire sector of space."

"Yeah," Earl said, still chuckling, "she possesses strong mission-planning skills, has walked point on recon teams, worked as a long-range sniper, and done more than her share of damage in close-quarters fighting, with and without weapons. She even heads her own team, in case you need multiple people."

"So what's so funny?" I said.

"Because I'm involved," Earl said, "she might not want the work, and because of who she is, you might not want to give it to her." He stared intently at me. "You still don't get it?" When I didn't respond, he said, "You have been out a long time."

I nodded. "Yeah, it's been years."

"Alissa Lim," he said.

Her name evoked so many memories I had trouble focusing. She was one of the best, most competent soldiers I'd ever served with, everything in the field that Earl had said and more—but she was also one of the most violent people I'd ridden with, and one of the most potentially dangerous to her team when something tripped one of her several inner triggers. Our last assignment together had been rough . . . . I pushed back the memory, needing to maintain my focus on what was in front of me. "She's here," I said, "here but no longer with the Saw?"

"No," Earl said. "She's not here, and she left the Saw a few years ago. She's close, though, a single jump away, on an ancient piece of rock named Velna."

Velna wasn't a place I'd planned or wanted to visit. During our time on Lankin, I'd made it a point to learn at least the basics about each planet on the other end of all of this world's jump gates. As best I could tell, Velna was notable for two characteristics: It possessed the most seismically stable landmasses of any known planet, and in all other ways it was the least appealing world humanity has ever colonized. The first trait prompted both Kelco and Xychek to build all their most vibration-sensitive fabs there, so its populated continents abounded with nano-level manufacturing tech facilities that made everything from washing machines to optical and nanotube processor systems. Those fabs provided enough jobs that Velna developed a sizable population base, most of it long-term transient, because the second trait meant that no one wanted to stay there any longer than necessary to make the money they needed to go where they really wanted to be.

The sheer unattractiveness of the place also made it the number-one candidate for every new prison contract in the region; its prisoner population, most of which was hardcore and in deep storage, outnumbered its civilian populace. Lankin anticorporate groups protested that the corporations treated their Velna workers like slaves and dumped the waste from their fabs directly into the ecosystem, saving the huge clean-operation costs they'd incur on any other world. To hear those groups tell it, the FC didn't inspect the fabs or even lodge the feeblest of protests about them, because its prisons were the only places you could go that were worse than the corporate fabs. Nobody rocked the boat, and Velna kept absorbing the trash.

"What's Lim doing there?" I said.

"She left the Saw to start her own security company. Running a company is a lot different than working in the field, so it was rough going for her. The Saw won't do prison work outside of active combat detention, so we did her a little behind-the-scenes favor—one you'd do well not to mention—and helped her company win the contract for the largest FC prison there. It's not great work, but it's work."

"Lim is leading a prison team?" I said, having trouble believing it. "Amazing." Prison duty anywhere is dirty, nasty work that in my experience mangles everyone who stays with it. If Earl was as accurate as I expected, the prison work on Velna would be the worst of the worst. No one as willing to kill as Lim could afford the damage that kind of work would do to her soul. I wondered what she'd become, then recalled the way Gustafson had looked at Earl and Earl's comments about her. "What's her problem with you?"

"For some years before she quit," he said, "we'd been involved. She wanted me to go with her. That wasn't an option. She wasn't happy with me when she left."

Gustafson let out a breath loudly enough that it emerged as almost a snort, earning him a sharp look from Earl.

I was amazed that any woman who could get close enough to Earl to form a lasting relationship wouldn't know that his work always came first, but I was also generally amazed by women, having been unable to sustain an intimate relationship with one for more than a few weeks at a time.

"Any other recommendations?" I said.

"I can come up with more," Earl said, "but no one you'll know.

Everyone you served with is either still in the Saw or no longer doing this sort of work." He paused and considered me for a moment. "You're the only one I know who's stayed anywhere near the same type of action." He shook his head. "Regardless, we both know Lim is the best you're going to find if you want someone whose flaws you know."

I nodded in agreement. He was right. Her skill set matched my needs perfectly. The bounty on my head wasn't going to vanish of its own accord, and I couldn't make it go away without help. On the other hand, when I'd last worked with Lim, she was given to almost psychotic rage and possessed an unsettling ability to kill with absolutely no remorse. Since that time, Earl had broken her heart, and she'd taken up prison work. Lovely.

My other option was to hire an unknown. I realized I had no excuse for hesitating: I had too much at stake to risk using someone I didn't know. Lim was a killing machine, but at least she'd be a killing machine on my team.

"Where can I find her?" I said.

"She's in Dishwa, a pit of a city on Velna," Earl said. He stood, and we shook hands. "Top'll get you the details. I'm sure you two will be talking."

CHAPTER SEVENTEEN

I instructed the cab to return to Queen's Bar via a long route with four switchbacks. I planned to spend another half an hour there in countersurveillance maneuvers on the off chance Chung's men had spotted me or Earl had Saw soldiers on my trail. As the vehicle skimmed over the highway, I sat back and pondered the logistics of approaching Lim. I could probably afford her fee straight up, but I was getting tired of pouring so much of my own money into simply staying alive. Besides, the more I thought about it, the more it seemed to me that discovering a corporate illegal arms deal and delivering it to the planetary government ought to be worth significant money. I didn't see the opening yet, but I resolved to examine the issue further over the next few days; money was lurking somewhere in all this.

Lim, though, presented the more pressing and immediate issue, so I returned my focus to her. Try as I might to think only about how best to recruit her, I couldn't avoid recalling the last time we saw action together. Willing down the hardcore sensory memories that cried for release in my head, I focused on the facts, hoping that by reviewing them I could leach some of the pain from the experience.

We'd been humping on Nana's Curse, a planet that spun around a young star three jumps from anyplace I'd ever heard of. A world of startling weather, with microclimates so extreme it dragged even the best forecasting technology out of its computational depth, the planet had been a place no large organization ever wanted to colonize. Over time, however, the extreme weather attracted dozens of the various nature-worshipping cults that had started on Earth and spread outward along with the rest of humanity. Despite their varying belief systems, these cults had managed to find enough common ground to live in peace in settlements scattered across the planet's largest continent. They'd even created a planetary government and joined the Frontier Coalition in the vain hope that formal representation might keep away the major corporations.

Then the Purifiers, the most militant and heavily armed of the many militant and well-armed one-god cults, discovered the world and its hordes of evil heathens, and all hell broke loose. I've never been a fan of dirt worshippers, but they were always either peaceful or so inept at violence as to not pose any problems for anyone other than themselves. The Purifiers, however, hated any religion other than their own. They pursued an ancient, simple approach to any place they found weak enough to attack: Convert those who'll accept the truth, and kill the rest.

The FC had contracted with the Saw to force the Purifiers off Nana's Curse, and in the process we'd spent months crawling from town to town, taking back those locations the Purifiers had overrun, burying the thousands of dead who'd possessed too much belief or too little sense to convert, and ferreting out the slash-and-burn squads that were purifying the smaller villages.

The villages. My last serious action with Lim was in one. I'd transferred to another unit as soon afterward as I could. Thinking of that mission, I suddenly found the cab hot, constricting, oppressive. My pulse quickened, the rush of the memory triggering the unthinking, unreasoning rush of aggressive, angry hormones I've fought most of my life, and I knew I couldn't beat back the memory. I closed my eyes and let it wash over me.

    ❦   ❦   ❦

Rain drizzled out of a cloudless sky the color of water in a clear brook. The unrelenting heat overwhelmed the climate control in our fatigues and launched volleys of sweat down our backs, arms, and legs. Baker squad, my team, was fanned out across the rear of the village, ready to catch or kill any stray Purifiers. Data from the sensor webs we'd dropped via silent-opening delivery shells showed little motion and no active transmissions, so we figured no more than a few hostiles remained in the area. Lieutenant Earl played it safe, though, sending us to the rear position, then taking Alpha squad fast and hard, cocked and locked, right up the main path into the clearing in the village's center. A few shots and the ozone of arcing weapons cut the air; then Earl's voice, tight and clipped, barked out of my earpiece.

"Baker squad," he said, "hostiles controlled. Come to Poppa. Keep the newbs at the rear."

We formed up around my lead. For the raw meat in the squad the war on Nana's Curse was their first action, but we'd been here for months, so I couldn't believe anything in this collection of shacks could be bad enough to pose them a problem. Orders are orders, though; I motioned them back, and they fell in quickly. We double-timed out of the cover, over to the rear entrance road, and into the clearing.

I held up my hand, and the squad stopped. The moving people grabbed my attention first, and in a second's glance I took in the motion: Earl and a few of the Alpha squad men were leading four Purifiers—all oddly out of uniform, some missing their pants—to the front of one of the shacks near where the main road entered the clearing. A few more of Alpha squad stood off to the sides, several retching loudly. Lim paced in the center of the clearing, vibrating with energy, hands moving nervously, her close-cropped hair so drenched it resembled the surface of a black pool.

In the next second my gaze moved to the ground, and I understood Earl's order.

On the far side of the clearing an open door gave way to a meter-tall stack of bodies that filled a small clay and thatch building. Spread around the clearing in front of Lim were the tangled bodies of at least half a dozen children, the oldest barely a teenager. None was fully dressed; some wore shredded pants, others no pants at all, and most were missing their shirts. All were cut, broken, bleeding. The blood pooled in puddles bigger than I'd have guessed such little bodies could produce. Blood oozed from some and gathered under others, so much blood the sources were hard to spot, numerous cuts and hacks marring the half-naked corpses. The acrid smell hung in the moist air. My ears pounded with my own heartbeat. The scene tightened its grip on me, and I had trouble breathing, standing still, doing anything except screaming. I fought to maintain self-control, to keep it together.

"Listen up," Earl said.

I forced myself to look at him. Everyone else except Lim did the same. Her head pointed in his direction, but I caught a glimpse of her eyes: She was seeing only the images in her head.

"SOP with prisoners is to evac them to local brigs for questioning and then to POW storage." He slowly made eye contact with each of us, moving rapidly past Lim when he realized she wasn't yet focusing on him. "These men," he gestured to the prisoners, "do not deserve and will not receive that mercy. If anyone wants to discuss this decision, speak up; now's the time."

No one said a word to Earl. What mumbling I could hear was all angry agreement.

Earl nodded. He motioned to the men holding the prisoners, and they brought the four Purifiers to him. Earl pushed one to his knees. Three Alpha squad corporals followed his lead with the others. A few seconds later, all four prisoners were kneeling, hands restrained behind their backs with quick-application synthetic ties. Earl pulled a pistol from a holster on the rear of his belt.

"Lim, Moore, take your squads to our regroup point," he said. "I'll join you shortly."

"Sir, Lieutenant, sir." Lim's voice surprised me with its calm, careful, formal cadence. "Sir, I'd like to handle this, sir."

I was already moving, my squad behind me, and as I passed Lim I noticed her face was utterly calm, her expression serene, only the brightness in her eyes betraying any sign of the horror that surrounded her.

"Please, sir," she said.

Earl stared at her for a bit, then nodded his agreement. "Alpha squad, on my lead," he said. To Lim he added, "We'll wait for you. Make it clean and simple, one shot each to the back of the head."

I couldn't hear her answer over the sound of our feet on the road as we exited the clearing and double-timed for the rendezvous point a few hundred meters away. No one spoke when we reached it. I didn't bother maintaining formation once there; Earl would give us new orders shortly, and I figured we could all use a little time to deal with what we'd seen.

He and Alpha squad appeared less than a minute later. "Fall in," he immediately said. "Weapons and comm check."

The squads were slow to move, all of us trapped in our heads with the images of the village clearing.

"Now, people!" Earl yelled. "Inspection in ninety seconds!"

Everyone jumped to, Alpha squad left and Baker right. We all scrambled to check the status of our weapons, ammo packs, and comm gear. Between the seconds we lost to getting moving and the time it took to realign in formation, we were hard-pressed to complete all the checks by the deadline Earl had set. I finished barely in time, because Earl started his inspection with Baker squad, and I was first.

When he finished with me, I realized how wrong I'd been: Giving people time right now amounted to letting them dwell in a bad place they needed to leave. Keeping them busy was exactly right; they'd process what they'd seen later, certainly for days, probably for the rest of their lives. I vowed to remember this lesson for the future, even as I fervently prayed I'd never again need it—another battlefield prayer that went unanswered.

Earl was halfway through Baker squad when I realized Lim wasn't back. He appeared in front of me, as usual having recognized the problem before me.

"Moore," he said, "see if Lim needs assistance . . ." Lowering his voice, he added, " . . . and retrieve her."

"Yes, sir," I said.

I double-timed back into the village, energy rifle charged and at port arms, just in case we'd missed some hostiles. I froze when I entered the clearing and saw Lim.

With her left hand, she held one of the men by the hair. His mouth was taped shut. With her right hand she plunged her combat knife in and out of the man's chest and stomach, the whole time smiling and talking to him in a voice so low I couldn't make out her words. Blood and bile and bits of entrails hung from her blade. Two of the men were on the ground, body cavities ripped open, their insides exposed and partially spilled, clearly dead.

The fourth man appeared to have tried to crawl away. The blood pooling under his legs was the result of Lim's answer to that attempt. I threw up into my mouth, choked back what I could, and spit to clear the rest.

I saw with cold clarity exactly what I had to do, the path so obvious it wasn't as if I were choosing at all. I was only doing what was inevitable, necessary, unavoidable. I put down my rifle, drew my pistol, and shot the fourth man in the head. Lim kept hacking at the man she was holding up. I quickly shot each of the two dead men in the head; Earl expected four shots.

When I turned to finish the third man, Lim stood between him and me, her knife pointed at me, the smile still on her face, her eyes wild. "You shouldn't have done that," she said. "I hadn't even started on the last one, and I'm not done with this guy."

"We're leaving, Lim," I yelled. "Lieutenant's orders. These men may have deserved—"

She cut me off. "*May* have deserved? What they deserved is more than we could ever do to them. This is only a taste."

I took one step closer to her. "You're done," I said. "We're leaving. You tracked down one who managed to run, then we tapped all four. That's how it happened. Got it?" I pushed past her, shot the last man in the head, and holstered the pistol.

Lim stared at me as the fire in her eyes slowly died.

"Clean your knife," I said. I headed out of the village.

She wiped it on the back of the shirt of the man I'd just killed, then caught up to me.

When she was even with me, I changed to double-time pace. She followed, and we entered the regroup point abreast.

"Problem?" Earl said.

"Nothing significant, sir," I said.

Lim nodded her agreement.

He stared hard at both of us for a two count, looked away for another two beats, then turned back to the men, his internal argument resolved. "Fall in with your squads."

Only when we were heading out did I realize I was still shaking, my mind stuck in an image loop, the same composite frame screaming from the monitor inside my head, burning into its pixels until I became afraid it would never be able to show anything else: the dead, defiled, bleeding children in the background, the foreground a close-up of Lim's smiling face as she hacked and hacked and hacked at the prisoner's body.

CHAPTER EIGHTEEN

I shook my head to clear away the image. Though the years since then have done nothing to blur it, they have weakened its hold on me. The stories I'd heard of Lim since that mission all painted her as a fierce, fair, dependable fighter—as long as nothing sent her back to the dark, smiling place the clearing had either created or awakened. I didn't see anything in the kidnap of Chung to cause that reaction in her, and I needed a teammate I could trust to get the job done. Anyone new I recruited, even if trustworthy, would have flaws as well, but I wouldn't know those flaws. I wouldn't know that person at all.

I knew Lim.

I was still wasting time. I wasn't comfortable with Lim, but that didn't matter: As I'd agreed with Earl, she was the best option available to me.

Lobo and I were going to Velna.

Once we slid into a low geosync orbit over Dishwa, I had Lobo tap into the publicly available data flows to see what he could learn. The combination of that data, what he already had in his store, and the information Gustafson had given me all painted the same basic picture. Dishwa was indeed, as Earl had observed, a pit. All the serious corporate manufacturing plants sat outside the city, their staffs freed only every few weeks. Corporate security was uniformly inward-looking, worrying only about protecting the fabs and their trade secrets, not about what the workers did when on R&R in Dishwa. From the nonstop flow of reports of thefts, fights, and other petty crimes, the Dishwa police didn't much care either.

The largest prison on the planet, the one Lim's group managed, hunkered down like a cancerous growth on the northern tip of the city. Well-behaved inmates earned wage-free jobs at local businesses after med techs laced their bodies with trackers and a variety of small explosive charges that would detonate if they strayed from the prison's controlling signals for too long. The pay they earned went toward prison upkeep. Those who caused trouble ended up in one of the slowly expanding sprawl of convict racks, buildings housing hundreds of fluid-filled tubes, one prisoner per tube, wires keeping their muscles fit while governmentally approved counselor voices whispered governmentally approved messages of good behavior, recovery, and repentance. Many hard cases figured the tubes for easy duty, but after a few weeks, most, when given the option, chose to go back to work. Those who stayed in the tubes for too long were rarely entirely right afterward, the voices never leaving them.

Dishwa served as the FC's tryout for the tubes, and nothing I saw made me believe this technology would last any longer than any other prison fad. The only way humanity has ever found to successfully solve the problem of prisoners is to avoid having them, to address the issues before people turn into convicts. No technology we've yet found succeeds at turning large populations of prisoners into contributing citizens.

"Another beautiful place you've taken me," Lobo said, after I'd gone through the information he'd amassed. "And whom are we here to kill?"

"Very funny," I said, "and the answer is, no one. We're here to recruit help. I think you'll like her; she likes big machines. In fact, she prefers them to most people."

"A woman of good judgment," he said.

"Call the prison," I said.

A reasonably convincing young male answering construct in a khaki uniform appeared on the comm display. "Dishwa central prison," it said. "We're tracing and recording this call. Speak."

Lim's personality had infected even the answering protocol; lovely.

"Jon Moore requesting an in-person meeting with Alissa Lim."

"Purpose of meeting?"

"Catching up on old times," I said. No point in marking this as confidential; she'd know I'd never visit socially. The construct vanished, and in its place an advertorial detailed the exciting and humane new therapy the prison was pioneering for the forward-looking Frontier Coalition. I tuned it out and waited while the construct tracked down Lim, gave her the message, and received her response.

After a few minutes, the construct reappeared and said, "Request granted at these coordinates and time. Please confirm." Lobo captured the location; we'd meet her about an hour before dusk.

When he showed me the spot on an aerial view of the city, however, I reconsidered; I had no desire to put down Lobo in such a highly populated area and no time to find a place to stash him and still make the meeting. "I need to land a Predator-class, fully armed assault vehicle," I said. "Is that acceptable at these coordinates?"

The advertorial resumed, and over the next several minutes the earnest faces of experts in psychology, criminology, and neurology explained why tube-tech was the prison wave of the future.

"Negative," the construct said when it reappeared. "No nongovernment craft of that class are permitted over our airspace. Request granted at these new coordinates and time. Please confirm."

Lim had changed the meeting location to a private shuttle facility twenty klicks from the prison and the time to a bit after dusk. I was pleased by her prudence. The Lim I'd served with would have either ignored the civilians or relocated us to the prison and set up for full combat there. The prison undoubtedly possessed significant self-defense capabilities, maybe not enough to destroy Lobo but certainly enough to consider taking the fight, so it wouldn't have been a tactically bad choice. I saw as a welcome sign of a calm maturity the fact that she was now factoring into her thinking both civilian casualties and the cost to her business of any action at the prison. I was even pleased that she was moving our meeting to a remote location, albeit one that I had to assume she was even now ringing with her own forces. Maybe this would work out after all.

"Thank you," I said. "We'll be there."

We landed in almost whiteout conditions, a winter storm having squatted over the shuttle facility and showing no sign of stretching its legs anytime soon. As we settled on the tarmac, I asked Lobo, "How bad is it?"

"I count twenty-four human profiles on IR," he said, "deployed in groups of three at various points in an irregular circuit around us, but no heavy weapons."

"Oh, the weapons are there," I said. "She's just shielding them and showing us the people. Transmission traffic?"

"Massive and heavily encrypted," he said. "Enough of it is hitting me that I have to assume we're being constantly monitored. My inner shielding is detecting no electromagnetic traffic, however, so we remain, as I would expect, secure."

"This should go smoothly," I said, "and all her precautions are understandable. Still, if anything happens that gives you any cause for alarm, leave immediately at maximum speed and track me from orbit. Don't hesitate."

"Affirmative," Lobo said, combat programming clamping down on the humor.

"Let's keep your innards as private as we can," I said. "Hover at a meter and a half, and on my command open a floor hatch. Seal it the moment I'm clear." As Lobo lifted gently above the ground, I put on a self-heating, lightweight, hooded jacket and crouched next to the section of Lobo's floor that would slide clear. "Now."

The same hatch I'd used for the stealthie on Floordin slid open, and I hopped out. I crouch-walked clear of Lobo, holding my arms straight out at shoulder height the entire time. The snow whipped at me, and the jacket struggled to keep up with the outside temperature. The sides of the hood extended enough past my face to form a bit of a barrier, but the cold still clawed at my skin. I counted on the jacket's IR profile to be so strong that everyone watching on any frequency would see I was approaching with caution.

A doorway opened in a building maybe twenty meters away. Someone dressed entirely in a white, floor-length coat walked toward me. The person was either quite overweight or heavily padded. When it was close enough for me to see the face, I voted for heavily padded; it appeared to be Lim.

"Moore," she said, her voice confirming her identity.

"Lim."

"You're clean?"

"Absolutely," I said. "All I want is to talk to you about a business opportunity. I have no weapons and no bad intentions."

"What about your PCAV?"

"I own it, so I use it—but in this case, only for transportation."

"If it acts up at all," she said, "you won't live long enough to finish a sentence. We won't be anywhere that there won't be multiple sights on you."

"Understood. As long as they can't hear our conversation, we'll be fine."

"That sort of business?"

I nodded. "Of course."

"Fair enough," she said. "Follow me."

We returned to the building she'd exited and walked straight into summer, the space on the other side so overheated I couldn't get the jacket off fast enough. The building was a hangar, currently empty save for a small table and two chairs in the center of its permacrete floor. Pockmarks and scorched streaks adorned its side and rear light-gray walls. The scent of fuel and oil hung in the warm air. When Lim wasn't using it to meet old comrades, this was a working maintenance facility. The four pairs of guards occupying stations in its black girder rafters were clearly Lim's additions to its standard equipment. When I pointed up at them, she smiled.

"Why all the security?" I asked.

Lim motioned to the chairs, and I followed her over, jacket in hand. She raised a gloved hand and ticked off reasons as she walked in front of me. "You ask for a meeting and won't say why. You arrive in a PCAV. We were never tight. And," she chuckled, "my people see so little action that I figured any excuse for a serious drill was worth taking. I made them think you are one seriously lethal ex-soldier."

She motioned me to sit, took off her coat, and turned to face me.

To the same extraordinary degree that Earl had stayed as he had been, Lim had changed. Even the standard-issue winter-white fatigues couldn't conceal the modifications to her body. When I'd last seen Lim, she'd been a little taller than most women and boyish, with close-cropped black hair sitting atop a wiry body you'd only realize was female if you saw it naked. This Lim was more gorgeous and astonishingly built than ninety percent of the women I'd ever seen in broadcasts, with large breasts over an obviously flat stomach and enough muscle mass that her uniform bulged at the arms and legs as she moved. She was taller, too, easily as tall as Earl. Where before Lim had shown signs of the mongrel stock from which almost all of humanity has grown, now her body glowed with trendy Asian chic, the folds of her eyelids perfect, the eyes themselves almost black, her lips full and wide, her skin tone an incandescent, perfectly consistent mellow golden hue. Her hair was still the flawless black of starless space, but now she wore it longer, a bit below shoulder length, and in a ponytail.

"You can close your mouth now," she said, laughing.

"I apologize," I said. "It's simply that you're amazing. I take it you've made a few mods."

"More than a few, and all from the best clinics I could find. Everything's organic, pure gene-driven work, nothing surgical." She studied me for a moment. "I can't say I ever bothered to look at you all that closely, but you don't seem any older. Had some work done yourself?"

One of the benefits of the combination of the changes Jennie made to me and the nanomachines the Aggro scientists melded with my cells is that I never appear to have physically aged past my early twenties. As long as I move around periodically, today's antiaging techniques make me no different from anyone else. Lim was more observant than she was suggesting, however, so I shrugged and forced a chuckle. "No more than the next guy. Who doesn't want to stay looking young?" I changed the subject. "Not that looking as great as you do isn't reward enough, but I never would have figured you for someone willing to drop that much money merely to be a sex bomb. Why?"

"Business," she said. "I don't have the resources, team, or armament—yet—to land the big bids against the Saw and the others. That reduces me to tracking down the small stuff, and no one remembers the small stuff at contract time. Everyone expects anyone running my kind of business to be a scarred-up old warrior, so I went for the opposite look. They all remember me, and that's my ticket in. Plus, even after thousands of years of lessons to the contrary, I find that most men and a surprisingly large number of women reflexively assume that anyone who looks as sexy as I do is stupid, and that's a negotiating edge I can use. The Law is a security company now, but that's only a start. We're going to be much more."

"The Law?" I said, laughing a little.

"The Local Area Weapons Corp.," she said, not even smiling, "my company."

"How do Earl and the other guys at the Saw feel about that name?"

"They hate it, think it's a slap at them."

"Is it?"

"Of course," she said, still not laughing at all, her face deadly serious. She leaned forward and looked straight into my eyes. "Now, what can I do for you?"

For a moment my mind jumped the business tracks and led me at high speed toward a contemplation of what this woman, this amazing body in front of me, could do for me, and then I more fully appreciated the power of Lim's approach. I looked briefly away, regained focus, and this time when I gazed into her eyes I made myself see only a person on the other side of a negotiation.

"You're right," I said. "Your look is a powerful tool. I lost focus for a moment, and immediately I forgot about you as a person and instead thought only about your body as a sex object. I have to work to maintain my focus even now."

She smiled and leaned back, waiting.

"In this building, I have no way to verify we're not being recorded," I said. "If we are, however, and you end up working with me, you'll have at least as much to lose as I will, and probably more, because your business provides services to corporations and governments. I honestly recommend you not record this; you can always decide later which of your team to tell."

"No recording," she said, the push of her cuff button so slight I almost missed it.

"I want to hire you."

"That's it? You could have saved us both a lot of trouble by saying so in your message. We have a rate card for our services and—"

I cut her off. "No," I said. "I don't want to hire your company. I want to hire *you*."

She shook her head slowly and exhaled loudly. "No," she said. "That's not what we do. We provide security and combat services. You choose the service, and I choose the appropriate staff." She studied my face for a moment. "I am curious, though. As I said earlier, we were never closer than any two other humps who served together, and as I recall the last mission we were on didn't end to your liking. So, why me?"

"I understand your company doesn't do this, but I don't want your company. I want you. The reason why is simple: I need one person, someone I know, to help me solve a problem. I can't afford the time to try out someone new."

"Your problem is not my problem," she said. "Why should I even consider this?"

"Three reasons," I said, ticking them slowly off on the fingers of my right hand in the same manner she had earlier. "First, money. Either I can pay you, or you can gamble, take nothing up front, and get half of a much larger amount if this works out the way I think it will. Second, the potential win for your company. If this goes well, the Frontier Coalition will emerge with more power than it has now, and helping it get that power should prove useful for you." I paused, leaned forward, and watched her closely. "Third, the action. Unless you've changed more than your body, part of you still craves it, and running prison security can't satisfy that craving." I slowly waved my arm to take in the men in the rafters. "This drill wasn't only for your company; it was also for you."

"Prison security is serious work," she said, "with the potential to run hot at any time."

"I'm not denying that," I said, "but has it gone hot since you've been on the job? When did you last get a chance to use your fighting skills?"

"I work out and shoot every day," she said, sounding defensive.

"I never doubted you'd stay in shape," I said, easing up my tone, leaning back. "If I did, I wouldn't have approached you. All I'm suggesting is that a little real action might interest you."

She thought for a few seconds, then put as much sarcasm as she could muster into her voice as she said, "And you expect me to sign up for some mysterious mission because you need someone?"

"Of course not. I'll run it down for you on two conditions."

She raised her left eyebrow in question and motioned me to continue.

"You tell me that you'll honestly consider it, and you give me your word not to tell anyone if you choose not to do it."

She was quiet for longer this time, either considering it or playing me; I couldn't tell which.

"Okay," she said. "I'll honestly consider it, and if I don't take it, I won't tell anyone."

"Fair enough," I said. "Here's the short form: For reasons I won't go into, Jose Chung, the Xychek head on Lankin, put a bounty on my head. That's my problem. He also has Xychek buying arms from a private dealer and not reporting those weapons to the FC in the inspections. If anyone could prove to the FC that Xychek was buying those weapons, Xychek would lose power in this region— and the FC would get correspondingly stronger. That's the big-play angle at the end. The answer to both problems is the same: We kidnap Chung. I persuade him to drop the bounty and confess to the arms deals, and everyone but Xychek wins. I'd do it alone, but I can't. I'll go over the setup if you decide to help, and you'll get to design the final attack plan with me."

"A snatch?" she said. "Of the head of one of the two biggest corporations in the region? Even if we succeed, no corporation will ever trust me after this."

"Sure they will," I said, "because you'll stay anonymous. Chung will know about me, but he doesn't need to ever see you. You remain a hired gun he never meets. We snatch him, I interrogate him and persuade him to help me, and then we turn him over to the right FC people."

She stood and grabbed her coat. "I'll consider it," she said, "as I promised. What's the timing?"

"As soon as you can get me an answer," I said. "If you're in, we'll go in Lobo—"

"Lobo?" she said.

"My PCAV," I said. "The AI's good enough that most of the time I think of it as a person."

"You need to spend more time around real people," she said. She headed for the door and motioned me to follow. "Call me in the morning. We're done until then."

I spent the night in Lobo in high orbit over an almost entirely desert continent on the other side of Velna. I'd considered taking Lim's advice and going into Dishwa to spend some time among people, but I decided not to push my luck in case Xychek security had a company-wide advisory about the bounty.

When I called Lim in the morning, the construct passed me straight through to her. Her face filled the display Lobo opened. I was struck again by her beauty and its effectiveness: Concentration was as hard as she wanted it to be.

"Earl backed your story," she said, the abruptness of the greeting at odds with the sweet look on her face. "He'd love to see us prove Xychek was arming illegally. You forgot to mention he was going to help."

"Not my place to tell his business," I said, appreciating at the same time how close she and Earl must have been for him to have told her of his possible involvement.

"So I'm in," she said, "but with three conditions."

"And they are?"

"One: If this goes right, I get half of any fee the FC pays for the Xychek information, and you credit the Law with doing half the work. I'd love to get the FC to see us as useful for more than prison security."

"Fair enough," I said. Her desire to impress the FC had the potential to help me lower my exposure in this whole mess. "In fact, I'd be happiest if the FC sees the Law as having organized the whole affair and if I appear to be just one more member of your team— though I still get half of any fee."

"Even better," she said. "Don't bother to thank me for the opportunity for the low profile."

"Go on."

"Two: You don't tell anyone about my involvement without my prior permission, so if this plan goes nova, the Law had nothing to do with it. As far as my staff knows, I'm heading out on vacation with a heavily armed and more than a little psychotic ex-lover."

"No problem," I said. "If we blow this, I expect we won't be worrying about anything other than survival."

"Three: We don't go until we both agree on the plan, and I use my own weapons. I'm happy to supply you, too, but regardless of what you choose, if I'm going into action I'm using my own gear."

I paused, considering her demand. This one was tough, because small-team missions need single leads, and I already had strong ideas about how I wanted this one to go.

I must have pondered it longer than I realized, because she said, "None of these are negotiable, Moore."

"I have no problem with using your weapons," I said, "and I'm fine with both of us having to agree on the plan. We can work on it here, before we head to Lankin, because Lobo has all the intel we need. But, you have to accept two key points."

"And they are?"

"When the mission goes live, I'm in charge, and we make this as nonlethal as possible."

She was quiet for a few moments, then nodded her head. "I can live with both of those," she said.

"Then we're on," I said.

"Deal," she said. "Pick me up at noon at the landing area where we met." The screen blanked.

"Rather abrupt, this woman," Lobo said. "Still, she is human, so I bet she won't end up in storage for any of the mission."

I was already looking forward to working with the two of them.

CHAPTER
EIGHTEEN

Three days later, I was lying on my belly in the underbrush bordering the road about a hundred meters outside the main entrance to Chung's estate. Sweat ran down my back, arms, and legs as I sweltered in the heat-blocking camo blanket I'd wrapped around me. From the outside, I read as IR-neutral. Inside, I was baking, already missing the winter of Velna. Night was tamping down the last bits of daylight like a gravedigger smoothing the ground over a freshly buried casket. The climate control in the sealed suit Lim had provided was barely working, but I couldn't complain about its comm helmet: The faceplate shifted its light sensitivity with the setting sun so the scene in front of me remained clear and sharp at all times.

In the heads-up display I checked the small mirrors of Lobo's monitor and Lim's display. Lobo was necessarily too far away from the entrance behind Chung's estate for his sensors to be able to pick up much visual detail, but nothing they showed indicated any problem. Lim lay in a position much like mine but on the opposite side of the estate, and her display remained still and boring, exactly as it should be.

We weren't working silent, but we were keeping transmissions between us to a minimum, refreshing each other's displays on a random cycle ranging around every twenty seconds; no point in giving Xychek security a reason to skip the Saw inspection. Gustafson had said they would start it right after sunset, so the staff and vehicles that were attending it should be leaving soon. Our plan counted on minimum security at the house, so if Xychek security didn't send most of the estate team to the inspection, we'd have to abort and try another approach later.

On the principles that you can't be too prepared and you might as well make good use of the time available, I ran another complete weapons check. All sensors flashed green; I was good to go. I cranked up the resolution on the faceplate and focused it on the road in front of me. All ten of the urban disturbance mines I'd scattered on a twenty-meter stretch of highway clung to the road right where I'd put them, each the dull gray color of the pavement and a little thicker than a pair of pants, so inert without a detonation code that you could walk on them or even drive a wheeled vehicle over them without a problem. Transmit that code, though, and boom! Each would blow with enough power to tear a hole in a vehicle without an armored bottom. Every surface of Chung's vehicles would, of course, be reinforced, but the mines should pop with enough power to change their course, maybe flip them. Lim had set a similar group on the highway outside the exit on the other side of the estate.

I had the suit's audio pickups ratcheted almost as high as they could go, with external sensors in the blanket feeding them. The breezes sang a slow background harmony as the insects and rustling leaves and branches belted out a discordant lead vocal whose direction my mind kept trying unsuccessfully to predict. When the gate to the estate opened a few minutes later, the slight creaking of the moving metal played clearly in my ears. I took the faceplate's resolution back to normal, lowered the audio, and focused on the road in front of me. A few seconds later, the convoy of security vehicles slid past my position. When the last one had passed me, I forced a display update to Lobo so he'd have the count. He compared it to his earlier monitoring and almost immediately the number two appeared in my clone of his display. Perfect. They'd kept back the minimum, enough to give Chung two exit options.

At the appearance of the number, I set my time mark for ninety minutes. I sipped water from the tube built into the suit. I wanted the Xychek security detail heading toward the inspection to be far enough away that when the estate team yelled for help I could be sure none would arrive before we'd finished and escaped. Xychek's air support was, according to Gustafson, both minimal and the first thing on the inspection list, so unless something went wrong we should be able to count on at least one clear hour from the mission's start. That should be more than enough. I hoped.

I settled in yet again and tried not to look too much at the light-green countdown on my display.

Eighty-nine more minutes.

The timer wound to zero, turned red, and reversed direction, now displaying the elapsed mission time.

We were on.

My faceplate's copy of Lobo's forward video feed turned into a blur as he accelerated first downward and then at full speed as he skimmed the treetops toward the estate. The sensors would pick him up, but his low flight path would buy a second or two, and that was all we needed. After five seconds of approach, Lobo fired three small missiles at the gate on his side of the estate, then abruptly changed course and headed up, back, and away from the target, reacting as if he'd been unwilling to face the defense systems.

Each of Lobo's missiles mirved a second and a half after launch, changing from three fat tubes into a dozen slender rockets. The estate's automated defense systems did the best they could, but the hole our recon had suggested might exist in them proved to be real. The air-defense portion was designed for targets above two hundred meters, and Lobo had never been that high while in range of those weapons. The ground and low-altitude automated systems were solid enough for civilian or typical corporate attack-squad weaponry, but Lobo's milspec rockets overpowered them easily. By the time the defense system launched its three interceptors, it was facing twelve oncoming missiles.

Ten hit their targets. Via the relay of Lobo's long-distance video sensors I watched as two missiles turned the entire gate area into a cloud of smoke and the remaining eight hit the dirt along a hundred-meter-wide section of ground with the gate at its center. A split second after impact, those eight blew. A mountain of dirt and rock and small vegetation soared into the air and buried the gate and a long stretch of the wall on either side of it. The roar of the explosions shook the air. The helmet's audio system compensated quickly, lowering the volume then readjusting as the sounds died. No one in the estate would be coming out of that gate anytime soon.

I pushed the magnification on the Lobo relay as far as it could go, but even with the best interpolation the faceplate's processors could manage I couldn't see if any people were moving around; Lobo was too far away for his original feed to carry that level of detail. I'd insisted on an approach that gave the gate guards a chance at living, because I wanted this to be as nonlethal an attack as possible. My lack of information was the price of that insistence.

No time to worry about that now, though. I fought to control the adrenaline surge that begged me to regard the people in the estate as just so many more bodies, moving but already dead and not knowing it, existing only for us to finish them.

Lobo had already fired a second burst, this time a barrage of ten small missiles carrying transmission-clogging comm webs, thousands of grain-size modules that detected all active transmissions in their range and broadcast garbage across every in-use frequency. We'd set the cloggers to skip the hobbyist niche we were using and focus on the standard military and commercial bands. We risked our transmissions being recorded and decrypted if a civilian with a snooping hobby happened to be targeting the estate, but we'd kept the chatter down and our encryption was strong, so the risk was minimal. Six of the missiles made it through the defense systems and sprayed their sensors across the estate before hurtling into the ground just outside it.

"Team one, first group heading your way," said Lobo in my left ear. "One vehicle, five humans. No way to tell if target is among them."

"Got it," Lim—"team one" in case anyone did record and decrypt our comm—said in my right ear.

"Trank 'em, don't kill 'em," I said.

"Already understood," she said, "but the roads are murder." She'd taken great joy in pointing out that if Xychek didn't armor its vehicles very well, our plan would kill everyone in them. I had no answer for her other than my belief that the vehicles would be strong, a belief born of the respect I'd developed for Xychek's security squad during the time Lobo and I had monitored them.

"Team two, second group heading your way," Lobo said. "Also one vehicle, five humans, and no way to tell if target is among them."

"Moving to position," I said.

I threw off the blanket and sprinted to my second mark, a level spot behind a tree where I would have a good view of anyone trying to get away from the vehicle. I pulled a second camo blanket off the two guns I'd previously placed there and aimed at the gate, and settled into sniper position in front of the bigger one.

"Second group has reversed course and headed for rear exit," Lobo said.

We'd hoped the teams would split and take advantage of the multiple exit points, so our plan focused on that option. If the second team stayed with the first after what was about to happen, we'd know the first team had Chung, and Lim would have to hold them both until Lobo could get there. I maintained my position; Lim had the best data on the action at her end, so it was up to her to make the call whether I should join her.

The first Xychek team reached the rear of the estate. My relay of Lim's display showed the escort vehicle jetting out of the barely open gate. Lim blew half her mines a second after the vehicle cleared the gate. The display image turned fuzzy with smoke. As the processors filtered the visual noise of the dust, the feed in my faceplate cleared enough to show the black vehicle flipping end over end in the air several times before it crashed to the road. Enough of the vehicle's internal systems were intact that it extruded disaster struts and righted itself, but two of the doors were hanging loose, their rear supports trashed by either the mines or the landing.

"Second group returning to original course," Lobo said. "Team two, assume the target is in your group. Team one, verify assumption."

First the front and then the rear of the crashed vehicle exploded as Lim placed armor-piercing rounds in both areas that might house the main drive engines. Armor shielding around the cabin was standard executive protection, so the occupants should survive the small explosions. Sure enough, all five people spilled out of the back of the vehicle, using its rear doors and the heavy dust in the air for cover. One peeked around the door and for that action earned a combo electrical disruptor and trank round in the meat of the shoulder; he dropped fast, twitching. Lim was as accurate as ever.

The sound of my gate opening yanked me away from Lim's display relay. The escape group hit the exit point fast, and I blew half my mines. I'd planted them farther down the road than Lim, not trusting my accuracy as much as she did hers. The vehicle had been edging to the far right of the road, so the mines sent it spinning side over side into the air. It landed on its flank on the ground on the shoulder of the road opposite me, then righted itself. Both doors on my side sprang open, as did the rear door on the opposite side. The driver and the passenger nearest me spilled out and hid behind the vehicle as I shot an armor-piercing round into its front. These guys were fast: They fanned out to either side of the highway a moment after the front of the vehicle exploded. I switched guns, settled my breathing, and put a disruptor/trank round into the shoulder of the guy on my side of the road because he was the nearer threat. He dropped hard, body twitching on the way down. I swiveled the sights to my left and found the second guy. He was running fast and erratically, making it hard. I squeezed off three shots in rapid succession. The third hit him and dropped him.

I turned the sights on the open driver's door, but no one was inside. I scanned farther away from the car on the other side of the road and caught a glimpse of three figures running in a cluster, the front and rear each staying close to the center. The center had to be Chung.

They disappeared behind some trees.

"All five down," Lim said, her voice jagged, pumped. "Checking now."

"Three on the move," I said, my own voice as raw as Lim's, my breathing coming hard. "Opposite side of the road from me. Track if possible."

I abandoned the sniper rifles—they were no good on the move—and sprinted across the highway, staying low, drawing a pistol loaded with disruptor rounds as I ran. I reached the vehicle's rear and used it for cover. I snaked up a video feed and panned it quickly across the area in front of me. All clear. I dashed to the tree nearest where the three runners had entered the woods, backed against it, and panned the video feed again. They had maybe ten seconds of lead on me, but the woods weren't dense and the ground was flat, so I found the men as they were angling out and away from the estate. I flicked the Acquire button on the video sensor, and my heads-up display gained a red tracking arrow. I took off on roughly the same course as the Xychek trio, following the arrow, running for all I was worth.

"Status," I gasped as I sprinted around trees, avoiding some bits of undergrowth and barreling through others. Lobo was to pick up the first of us to take down the assigned targets, then help the other person. If I didn't catch my runners, we'd be better off with all of us chasing, because we had to assume Xychek security had learned of our attack the moment we started and had teams coming our way. Our window was closing.

"Checked and confirmed," Lim said. "Target is not here. Repeat: Target is not here."

"Acquiring team one now," Lobo said.

I was gaining on the runners. Chung was almost certainly slowing them, the security guys both paid to stay with him no matter what. I pushed my pace, working to control my breathing, soaking in my own sweat, mentally cursing Lim yet again for the suit's inadequate climate control.

The rear guard slowed, turned his shoulder, and threw something. I skidded into the back of the nearest large tree as a shrapnel grenade exploded in the air, blasting high-velocity shards of razor-sharp metal into the trees all around and in front of me. I lost three seconds to making sure all the shrapnel had found a home, then another couple as I snaked around a video feed to verify I could safely move.

Anger coursed through me as I saw the damage the grenade had caused; it could have ripped me to shreds. If I'd permitted myself to bring lethal weapons, at that moment I would have drawn them.

I needed Chung alive, but I didn't need him happy. I holstered the trank pistol, pulled a screamer launcher from my rear pack, and sprinted after them. I could barely see them in the trees ahead of me, but the glimpse I got was enough. I forced off the suit's audio feeds, then fired the screamer over their heads and ran hard for them. I couldn't see the grenade's flight path, but I could tell when it neared them because they grabbed their ears and stumbled, then fell, as the intense pain shook their eardrums and heads. I crammed the launcher into a side pocket and fumbled with my pistol's holster as I ran; they were already getting up. I drew within ten meters and stopped, aimed, fought the shaking in my arms, and fired four times, twice at each of the two men I could see, the center and rear runners.

So many things happened in the next second that only later could I reconstruct what I'd seen.

Lobo dropped from the sky fifty meters behind the runners, a side panel open to reveal the upper half of Lim.

The rear runner fell.

The center man, still standing, clutched at the man in front of him.

That man lifted and aimed a pistol at me.

The upward motion of the pistol dominated my vision. I dove to the ground, not wanting to have to rely on the suit's armor if I could avoid it, and rolled to my right. I looked up in time to see the front man drop, then Lim wave from Lobo's open hatch.

I scrambled up and ran to the remaining man. As I drew nearer I verified it was Chung; I'd looked at images of his face too many times not to know it well. He waved his arms and said something I couldn't hear; I realized then that the suit's audio feeds were still off. I grabbed him, pulled an injector from an arm pouch, and jammed it into the side of his neck. He collapsed.

I turned on the audio feeds in time to hear Lobo land, the sound barely audible over the pounding in my ears and the rasping of my breath. I released the helmet and shook my head, glad to be in the open air.

Lim darted out of Lobo, her helmet also off, hair tightly bound onto her head, face drenched in sweat, eyes wild, breath coming sharp and hard. She pointed at the man she'd taken down. "You owe me," she said between breaths. She smiled, eyes still shimmering madly.

I looked down at the men on the ground beside me, then nodded. I glimpsed myself in my helmet's faceplate: My eyes were as crazy as Lim's, and I was smiling, too.

I'd given in to it again, lost the battle for control, a fight so very easy to lose. Unless you were very lucky or very damaged, violence always consumed at least part of you. It ate through your civilized exterior like acid through cloth, uncovered the animal inside, and left you, if you were lucky enough to emerge alive, shaking and terrified and yet happy, juked from the conflict, your body still in it, part of you not ready for it to be over and another part elated that it was and that you weren't among the dead. This had been no big thing, as safe an action as an armed mission could probably be, the Xychek guys overmatched before it started, and yet the violence had spidered into me again.

Each time I put myself in this situation, I resolve not to do it again—but I always do. I consoled myself with the thought that I truly had no real alternative this time, that spending every day, days into months into years, running from a corporate bounty was no way to live. I shook my head slowly, fighting for calm, willing the juice of the moment to crawl back into the dark fetid pools it normally inhabited.

I grabbed Chung, lifted him on my shoulder, and headed for Lobo.

"Thanks," I finally said to Lim, nodding back at the man she'd shot. "What do you say we get far away from here fast?"

CHAPTER TWENTY

We invested the next several hours in the tiresome but vital job of getting lost. With Chung stripped and strapped into a medbed that secured and sedated him, his possessions in a drawer in the medic area, and both Lim and me tucked into acceleration couches, Lobo took over. We rocketed out of the hot zone at tree level into the least populated of the nearby areas, then shot straight up into orbit, where we first wove among some of the busier sats, then came to an abrupt halt behind a large comm hub whose orbit we quietly mirrored for long enough to make me nervous. We then hopped up to a higher orbit, down and back up again a few times, pogoing across orbital loops, until we finally settled into one and eased our way slowly to the other side of the planet. Early on, Lobo identified himself as a Xychek comm sat. He changed his electronic identity half a dozen more times before he went transmission-silent behind a meteorological data-gathering sat.

With little chance of any of the estate's video sensors having captured Lobo or us, we were probably being overly cautious; after all, Xychek security had no reason to guess a space-ready PCAV was involved. Still, I didn't want to take any risks, because we were at the most exposed point in the mission: We had Chung, but not his confession, so neither the Saw nor the FC could or would back us.

After another hour passed with no signs of unusual orbital or earth-to-space activity within a few thousand klicks of us, Lim and I took turns cleaning up, then ate. I wanted to be calm before interrogating Chung, and the food helped consume some of the post-action hormones my body still had to digest.

Lim and Lobo monitored Lobo's tiny medic area, a room with the medbed in the center and an aisle around it so narrow that I had to walk sideways to fit. Chung obviously knew me well enough to put the bounty on me, so I saw no point in hiding my identity. Per my deal with her, Lim stayed back so Chung wouldn't ever see her.

Lobo kept two images running for Lim: a video feed of the room, and a display of Chung's vital signs. The latter also played on the wall behind Chung's head, where I could see it but he couldn't. Like so much in Lobo or anything of military origin, the room served multiple functions, both a place to heal the wounded and an inter-rogation chamber for the captured. Simple cleaning arms had wiped Chung's face and ears. Restraints over his waist, chest, neck, head, arms, and legs bound him securely to the bed. He'd be able to move his eyes to follow me, and he could wiggle his fingers and toes if he wanted to make sure they still functioned, but that was all; I didn't want to risk either of us doing something stupid. When I entered the room, Lobo instructed the medbed to inject Chung with a blend of a slight physical stimulant to wake him and a mood stabilizer to level his vitals. Deviations from the norms on the display would let us all know when he was lying.

I stood near Chung's head, leaned against the wall, and watched the display. As the stimulant brought him around, his pulse rose, and his respiratory rate climbed a tiny bit, but he didn't open his eyes. He quickly controlled the rhythm of his breath, kept it even, and neither moved nor opened his eyes. I smiled a bit in admiration. He was playing it like a pro, taking time to collect himself, gathering what data he could before he decided to let on that he was awake. If we were amateurs who'd kidnapped him for a ransom, the tactic might have bought him some potentially useful time and information.

"Jose," I said, using his first name both to annoy him and to show him we weren't going to abide by the usual corporate rules, "we both know you're awake, so we might as well talk." He continued faking sleep. I wasn't in the mood to waste time, so I added some positive motivation for him. "The sooner I get the information I want and we reach an understanding, the sooner you go home."

He opened his eyes and tried to move his head.

After he realized he couldn't, I stepped closer so he could see my face.

"Who are you," he said, "and what do you want?"

I opened my mouth to remind him again not to waste time but stopped when the wall display caught my eye: Nothing had changed. He didn't know my face. That meant he'd placed the bounty on my name alone, probably using information the Gardeners on Macken had somehow gotten out of Barnes. I should have erred on the side of caution and not let him see me. I'd made a mistake, but I reminded myself that it changed nothing. My predicament remained the same: I needed him to remove the bounty.

"I'm the man," I said, "you placed a bounty on, and I'm also the man who knows about your illegal arms deals with Osterlad. You're going to remove the bounty and tell the FC about the arms deal. You'll probably lose your job, and Xychek will certainly pay heavy fines, but you'll walk away unharmed . . ." I paused a second. " . . . provided you don't make me hurt you."

"What are you talking about?" he said. This time, his vitals jumped, but consistently across the board, a pattern of agitation, not of attempted deceit. Maybe bounties were more common among the executive set than I'd realized, and he genuinely didn't remember all of the ones he'd set. That seemed unlikely but possible, so I decided to fill in the blanks for him.

"I called you once before," I said, "but you wouldn't talk to me then, so I had to arrange this conversation. I'm the guy who ruined your bid on Macken by returning Slake's daughter, Jasmine, to him. Remember me now?"

The calming drug Lobo had chosen must not have been very strong, because this time Chung's vitals raced up the display, every indicator elevated beyond the yellow caution lines the medbed had computed for him. His face turned red, and for a moment he shook with the effort of trying to move. "You're the one who gave him Jasmine again?" he screamed. "I'll kill you."

"All I did," I said, "was return her to her father."

"You're either a fan of sick games," he said, his body relaxing as he realized there was no point in struggling against the restraints, "or truly stupid."

I was getting annoyed at his attempts to distract me, but I did my best to keep the feeling out of my voice as I leaned over him and said, "You're wasting time again. Let's get back to the bounty and the arms deal."

He stared directly at me as he said, "Do you really not know what you did?" He looked at me intently for a few more seconds, then closed his eyes. "Jasmine is my daughter. I had no idea she'd ever escaped from Slake until you called."

This was a strange tactic, and I had no more patience for games. "Last warning," I said. "Stop playing games."

"Check my wallet," he said. "I had it when you kidnapped me." When I didn't move, he said, "Check it. What can that cost you?"

The sincere look on his face caused a pit to open in my stomach, and all my elation at the successful mission tumbled into it. I pushed back all feeling, opened the medic room drawer, and pulled out the wallet. I put it in his right hand, temporarily removed the restraint on that hand, and stepped away from his reach. "Open it," I said.

He thumbed it, tapped a security code, and held it out to me. I took it with my right hand, while with my left I forced his arm back down and snapped on the restraint; no point in taking chances.

I opened the wallet, found two microthin photo displays, and pulled out the first. It unfolded as I flicked it, and images of Jasmine blazed into life: Jasmine posing on the front steps of Chung's estate, Jasmine laughing and holding a woman I didn't recognize, Jasmine much younger and in Chung's arms, Jasmine with her eyes shut as she kissed Chung on the cheek. Jasmine, Jasmine, Jasmine.

I was breathing hard, the air pounding roughly in and out of me, loud enough that Chung must have heard it.

"Slake's people kidnapped her," he said. "He used her to force me to withdraw our bid for the Macken development project and for the new aperture there."

None of Chung's vitals showed the slightest sign of a lie. He was telling the truth.

I had returned an innocent girl to the man who'd arranged her kidnapping. An innocent girl, and I'd failed her.

I could clearly picture her face.

"The FC has no jurisdiction over intercorporate issues, so I couldn't go to them."

Her face as she awoke briefly in the cart, the fear as she spoke, a fear I mistakenly thought she felt toward the Gardeners.

"I couldn't afford to go to war with Kelco locally, because our board would never have granted me the budget."

Her face, which reminded me so much of Jennie.

"Besides, we knew Slake was dealing off the books with Osterlad and was better armed in this region than we were—but we couldn't prove it."

Jennie, another innocent girl I'd failed.

"So I abandoned the bid before the board could learn of the kidnapping. They would have sacrificed her if I hadn't. Instead, I stalled them with a flawed analysis that demonstrated that the bid would be unprofitable for us."

Just as I'd failed to see that Osterlad was playing me for a fool, claiming what I now realized was a bounty from Slake had come from Chung, sending me to do more of Slake's work by hurting Xychek further.

"Slake promised he'd give her back as soon as they'd completed the deal, but something happened to delay it a month."

Slake, who was holding Jasmine prisoner right now because my deal with Barnes had delayed the signing of Kelco's Macken bid by a month.

"I've hidden the kidnapping as long as I could by claiming she was with her other parents on vacation, but the board is bound to learn the truth soon. When they do, they'll fire me. I could live with that, though, if I could just get her back."

Slake, who'd recommended I go to Osterlad in the first place.

A catch in Chung's voice and the tears in his eyes dragged me out of my thoughts and back into the moment.

"If I could just get her back," he repeated.

Anger flushed through me with a purifying coldness that straightened me, focused me, directed me. I hadn't been able to save Jennie when I was young and they took her. I hadn't even been able to think of saving her. They took her, and her loss was at that time as inevitable and unstoppable as the wind. In the more than a century since then, I've learned a great deal, and I've tried not to fail others, but sometimes I inevitably have, and each time it hurt, hurt a great deal. This time, though, I hadn't merely failed; I'd let Slake use me to actively harm this young woman, this girl.

I've spent much of my life fighting to shove anger to the side, to keep it at arm's length until it could dissipate and become just so much more heat rising away from me. Not this time. This time, I didn't fight the anger. I welcomed it, I embraced it, I consumed it, I enjoyed the rich, purifying power of it.

I stepped to the med room's door, afraid to be near anyone until I could find my way back out of the rage that was, in this moment, all I wanted or needed. I said, as much to myself as to Chung, "You will get her back. You will."

CHAPTER TWENTY-ONE

I stood outside the med room for several minutes, afraid to go up front and face Lim. The problem wasn't that I cared that she knew Slake had played me and used me; I've been a fool before and almost certainly will be again. What worried me was me, my own reactions. As angry as I was, anything she did, no matter how well-intentioned, might set me off, even though she wasn't the target of my rage. So I stood as still as I could manage, worked on slowing and controlling my breathing, and struggled to regain control. I didn't want to entirely abandon the anger—I knew I'd want it and need it to do everything I'd have to do to deal with Slake—but I had to harness it, to process it into fuel for action.

I slid down the wall and sat, wanting to stay alone and feeling I had nowhere else to safely go.

I realized then that I was letting my pain get the best of me, and that wasn't acceptable. Sometimes pain is necessary, and when it is, you should accept it and get on with the task at hand. I'd wasted enough time. I had work to do.

I got up, walked into the command area, and sat opposite Lim. "If it isn't obvious," I said, "the fact that Slake used me to hurt an innocent girl . . ." I paused, groping for words and finally realizing that saying the least I could manage would be best. " . . . upsets me a great deal. I intend to make this right, or, more accurately, as right as I can make it given what I did. I also intend to make Slake pay, and pay dearly, for all of this."

She nodded. I was glad she didn't say anything.

"You don't have to participate," I said. "I'll get you the fee we agreed on, and you can go."

"No way," she said. "You held out the hope of big money for this deal, and I still believe that's possible. Plus, I signed on to complete a mission, and it's not done. I'm in to the end."

"Fair enough," I said. I owed her the chance at more money. Staring at her, though, I also had to accept that she wasn't staying only for the money. I'd underestimated her loyalty, and consequently underestimated her. "Thank you. I appreciate this. The rules stay the same, though: You get to help with all the planning, and we'll do our best to agree before we proceed, but if we can't agree, the final call is mine. And, of course, I run all fieldwork."

"Understood and agreed," she said.

A black and sad weariness settled on me like night falling. As accommodating as Lim was being, I still found it wearying to deal with her. The problem wasn't her; it was me. I needed to get out, be alone, sort this out on my own without having to talk to anyone. "I need some time to think," I said, "time off Lobo. I'm going to have Lobo drop me outside Queen's Bar at a landing and storage area we've used. You guys can pick me up later; we'll set a time. While I'm gone, you take care of Chung and come up with some options for letting him go without getting us caught. We'll review the options when I'm back."

She nodded her head, studying me. "Okay."

"Lobo," I said, knowing he monitored everything that happened inside him, "plot an evasive path and take me there."

At Lim's urging I'd released Chung from the medbed. I returned his clothing and belongings, blindfolded him, moved him to a slightly larger but still locked holding area, and gave him some food. I reassured him we'd return him soon, then left.

I shouldn't have needed Lim to remind me to take care of him. I was making mistakes, being careless, and that had to stop. I'd kidnapped Chung to get him to remove the bounty and to make him confess to the FC so I could make some money in the bargain. The bounty remained, but at least now I knew its true source. The prospect of money from the FC also remained. This was a job, possibly a lucrative job, and I was behaving unprofessionally. I understood that what I'd done to Jasmine, the fact that I'd caused such harm to this young woman, was affecting me, but I also knew my best hope for success was to plan and execute her rescue carefully and professionally.

When I get lost inside the double helix of anger and self-loathing that to this day exercises such immense gene-level control over me, throwing myself into solitary work is the best remedy. It's why I've gravitated to confidential courier assignments. I couldn't go forward with this job, however, without planning, planning that would unavoidably involve both Lim and Lobo, and right now I couldn't trust myself to spend significant time with anyone.

That left me my backup option: losing myself in a city. Walking the streets, weaving through and around crowds of other people but never being part of them, eating alone, sitting outside humanity and studying it: A busy city afforded me a set of distractions and a form of solitude that would help me regain my focus.

Lobo was too small to be able to move at any useful speed without Chung figuring out that he was on a ship, so we abandoned any attempt to convince him otherwise. When Lobo could find no indication we were being tracked, he headed for the landing area at the highest speed we agreed wouldn't attract attention. We touched down in the middle of the morning of the day after the attack. I exited via the rear hatch, moving as casually as I could manage, and Lobo immediately took off again. We'd agreed to rendezvous a little after sunset.

I hadn't slept since the snatch, but I was too wired to relax, so I hired a taxi and had it drop me a couple of blocks away from the Busted Heart; that way, the vehicle wouldn't have a record of my exact destination should someone later try to reconstruct my path.

The image of Jasmine lying on the cart and waking in fear kept playing across my mental display. I walked slowly, aware I wasn't paying full attention and compensating with the slower pace.

As I turned the corner onto Dean's Folly, the Busted Heart in sight a block away, I felt bug stings, lots of them, more than I could immediately count, on my arms, neck, and back. I had time enough to realize I couldn't see or hear any insects, and then the world went black and I was out.

CHAPTER TWENTY-TWO

I came awake slowly. My eyes opened before they could focus, and they focused before I could process what I was seeing. It wasn't much: a smooth white expanse, the whiteness blurry at the edges. I tried to roll over, but I couldn't move my body. I lifted my head and looked down my chest. I was lying on some sort of table, naked but not cold, the surface below me warm and my body wrapped securely in restraining plastic. An IV hung from each of my arms, the attached tubes running beside my body and behind my head to destinations I couldn't see. I felt nice, warm and secure, no worries, no troubles. I closed my eyes briefly and enjoyed the warmth, then opened them as I realized I missed the pretty whiteness, so soft and pure and far away. I smiled at it. I thought I saw it move, and when I squinted I was sure it was smiling back at me. I realized it was a ceiling. It was a great ceiling, and I was happy to be there with it.

A pressure grew in the back of my head and distracted me from the whiteness. I didn't like the pressure, but it wouldn't stop, it wouldn't leave me alone, and then it burst into a thought, a realization that filled me: This was all wrong. I was drugged, and I needed to get away. Nanomachines. I needed to release some nanomachines to remove my bindings. I waded into the dense cloud of my brain, trying to concentrate, and then I heard a soft chime, a tiny faraway sound, and I was out.

I was asleep, and then I wasn't, the line between sleep and waking unclear and shifting, my eyes shut, then open, then shut again. I felt a smile, then realized happily that it was mine. My eyes cleared enough that I could see whiteness above me, and I remembered it was my ceiling. I smiled more broadly, glad to see it again. Right after the memory of the ceiling came the recollection of the lovely warm bed, the happy hugging plastic, and the tubes in my arms. I knew where I was: I was where I'd been before. I was glad I'd figured that out. I wondered why I'd left. There was certainly no reason to leave such a comfy place. I must have been acting silly. Yeah, that was it: silly.

I remembered something else silly: a tiny little chime, one I could hear but not see. I was happy to remember it. As I lay there thinking, I realized I was happy about everything, though everything wasn't very much: the ceiling, the chime, the bed, the plastic, the IVs, and me, all together, all part of each other, all happy.

Except the chime wasn't there, and that bothered me, bothered me enough that I stopped smiling. Where was the chime? The question bounced around in my mind, a fuzzy ball ricocheting off the walls of the empty room of my brain, gaining speed until I realized I only heard the chime before I went to sleep. More knowledge followed that realization, a rapid-fire tumble of blurry recollection: I went to sleep after I heard the chime after I tried to concentrate after I figured out this was wrong.

This was wrong.

I remembered that I needed to focus so I could instruct the nanomachines to decompose the plastic and free me. Focusing was difficult, but I tried. I thought hard for what might have been a split second or an hour; I couldn't tell. Then I heard the chime again and just had time to figure out that I didn't want to go to sleep before I was out.

☙   ☙   ☙

I realized I was awake when I noticed that instead of dancing swirls of yellows and red I was now seeing white, the white of the ceiling, the lovely ceiling.

Memories accompanied the vision of the ceiling: the warm bed, the warm plastic, the IV tubes in me, the bad chime. I remembered now: When the chime played, the ceiling vanished. Or did I vanish? One of us definitely went away; I was sure of that.

I lay still for a bit, enjoying the ceiling, happy in the realization I'd achieved, until a question shoved the happiness away: What made the chime play?

The chime. I repeated the word in my head, enjoying how it felt: chime, chime, chime, chime, chime.

The knowledge crept into my mind so slowly I couldn't be sure when it first appeared: I made the chime play.

Why would I do that?

I made the chime play, which made the ceiling go away, but I liked the ceiling. It was a puzzle, and puzzles are fun, but the pieces of this one weren't fitting right.

Like me, I realized, like the way I didn't fit here, not in the bed, not under the plastic, not here at all. I should leave. The tumble of memory—or was it imagination?—rolled over me. To leave I needed the nanomachines, and to get them I needed to focus, to think hard, and when I tried to do that, the chime rang.

More memory, or more imagination: I'd done this before.

I needed to know if I was remembering or imagining, but that could cost me. Still, I had to know.

I started a little song in my head, a gentle tune, two words repeating over and over: Concentration costs. Concentration costs. I tried to keep it going, make it something I couldn't forget, and then I focused on the nanomachines, focused as directly as I could manage. The ceiling vanished.

I woke with a song playing in my head, two words repeating: Concentration costs. Memories flowed like water into the bowl of my mind, filling me: bed, warm, ceiling, plastic, tubes, chime, concentration costs, concentration brings chime brings sleep.

I wanted to stay awake, so I stayed loose, kept my eyes open, enjoyed the ceiling and let time ease by, not focusing or concentrating but not sleeping, either. I kept my eyes open and let my thoughts dance in slow motion through my mind as I waited to see what was next. My awareness slowly increased. I noticed the slight pressure of the plastic covering, the contrast of temperature between my cool, uncovered face and my warm, plastic-wrapped body. Each time a thought tempted me to pay it more attention, I turned my attention away from it. Concentration costs.

"Very good," a voice said from all around me.

Another temptation, this voice was, another test, so I let the words wash through me but didn't allow them to send waves across the mental pond on which I was floating.

"We were wondering," the voice said, "how long it would take you to figure out that you had to stay completely relaxed. I'm sure you'll be pleased to know you beat our expectations."

It wasn't a nice voice, was nowhere near as nice as the ceiling, and that surprised me. Slowly new knowledge crept over me: The voice was harsh because it was the product of a cheap synthesizer, and it was all around me courtesy of speakers. I smiled and felt happy at the way my subconscious was injecting bits of information into me without requiring me to concentrate. Good subconscious; I wished I could pet it to thank it.

"I'm going to raise the brain-wave tolerance level slightly," the voice said, "but don't take this as an invitation to do anything. With the IVs we can knock you out in less than a second, and if that fails we can jettison the room you're in. You're in a low orbit, and we'd aim you into the atmosphere, so you wouldn't last long."

I fought to relax but an image of burning smacked into my brain and I suddenly realized I had to get out, to escape . . . .

The chime sounded.

"At this level," the voice said, "you get one warning tone. Let your brain activity rise much further, and we'll take you down again."

The voice paused. I used the quiet to calm myself further, shutting my eyes and grabbing at the edges of sleep without giving in to it completely.

"You showed us once that you know how to relax," the voice said. "Show us again."

I bathed in the colors on the inside of my eyelids, letting them wash over me and soothe me, then slowly opened my eyes and enjoyed the ceiling. Time passed, maybe another few seconds, maybe an hour; I couldn't tell, and I couldn't let it matter.

"Well done," the voice said. "Now we can begin."

I closed my eyes again, mentally crawling as far toward sleep as I could while remaining able to hear, knowing I needed to listen but not to concentrate on what I heard, the words a gentle shower I had to let rain on me.

"On Floordin," the voice continued, "you evaded security, stole a weapons control system, and escaped, while the man in charge went missing."

Floordin. The name rolled across the floor of my mind, accumulating debris as it went: Trent Johns vanishing, Osterlad setting me up, Lobo whole again.

"On Macken, you rescued a girl, and you did it, as best we can tell, without any real help."

Jasmine's face materialized in my mind, mouth open in fear as I took her on the cart to her kidnapper, to Slake. Slake, who was the man behind all my troubles, who was also, I suddenly realized, almost certainly the one who'd arranged my kidnapping. The two images assaulted me: Jasmine and Slake, pain at what I'd done and anger at being used, the two of them combining to generate more emotion and mental temptation than I could manage while remaining this calm. The chime sounded its sole warning.

"Relax, Mr. Moore," the voice said. "We simply want to know how you did these things. Something is unusual here, and we want to know what."

Paranoia joined the pain and the anger as I realized that if I lost control and talked then they'd know the truth about me and never let me go. I'd end up a corporate research guinea pig, because they'd know that nanomachine/human integration was not only possible but alive and well. I couldn't let that happen, I couldn't tolerate it, I had to get away, I had to—another chime sounded.

❧ ❧ ❧

Awareness crawled over me like a foggy dawn, my mind waking up but remaining soft, fuzzy, and unfocused. Memories slowly took form, as where I was, what was happening, and what I had to do to stay awake congealed in the ooze that was my brain. I remembered the voice that surrounded me, but I couldn't recall whether I'd heard it once or many times, nor was I sure how many times I'd passed out from whatever drugs they were using on me. I knew I had to stay awake to have any chance of escape, so I tried to remain relaxed; perhaps more memories would return.

A door snicked open somewhere behind me. I heard the soft footsteps of someone entering the room and walking toward me. The person stopped far enough away that I couldn't see who it was.

"Mr. Moore," a male voice said, "because you've been unwilling to answer our questions thus far, my employer has decided to pursue a more aggressive option. Up to now, we've merely kept you sedated and used some drugs to knock you out each time you showed any sign of significant mental activity. I'm here to apply some additional incentives."

I felt the man's hands working on my head and neck, jabbing me slightly and sticking cold things to me. I kept my breathing light and avoided concentrating on anything in particular.

The voice I'd heard before flooded the room. "Mr. Moore, Jon," it said, the synthesized speech harsh and unpleasant, "I encourage you to answer our questions, spare yourself pain, and save us all time. How did you manage the theft on Floordin, and where's the man who was in charge there? How did you rescue the girl on Macken all by yourself? And, I must now add one more question: What has Jose Chung said to you?"

Images of the people washed across my mind: Johns, his head dissolving; Jasmine, her face drugged and afraid; and Chung on the medbed, anguished over Jasmine. I worked on my breathing and gently pushed them away, not wanting to focus so much I ended up asleep again. I alternated gazing at the ceiling with studying the colors inside my eyes, and time passed. I have no clue how much.

"Your choice," the voice said.

I heard the man behind me step away, and for a few moments I thought they might wait for me to make another mistake, cause the chime to sound, and be drugged into sleep again.

Pain smashed into my head. A jagged lancing sensation ripped through my neck and into my mind. I screamed, a long loud roar that hurt my throat, and even as I was screaming the pain increased. For a split second I wondered how they could hurt me without putting me back into sleep, but the pain shoved aside all thought and filled me, cut me, crushed me, my head and neck and shoulders flexing and tensing uncontrollably, my body spasming, my bowels emptying. I grabbed at the possibility that the pain would bring me focus and let me control my nanomachines, but as fast as the thought came it flew away. I couldn't think, couldn't do anything other than hurt, hurt, hurt.

Still the pain slammed into me, growing and filling me and pushing at my edges until I was sure I would explode. A higher, screeching scream erupted from me as if it were an animal fleeing a fire. The pain increased until it obscured all thought and I was sure I was dying, and then black unconsciousness overtook me.

I didn't want to wake up, though I couldn't remember why, so I fought to stay asleep, resisting awakening by clinging to wispy dream images that became more and more faint even as I struggled to maintain my grip on them. Despite my attempts, however, my mind came more and more aware, until I remembered with the fuzziness of a dying display where I was, what my captors were seeking, and the pain. The memory of the pain triggered an involuntary flinch, as I sought to run away even though at some level I knew I was restrained. No pain hit me now, however, so I quit resisting consciousness and opened my eyes. My body ached a bit, as if I'd been exercising strenuously for a long day, and my neck and head were tender, but I otherwise felt more normal than I would have believed possible under the onslaught of the torture. My skin was dry, and my groin and rear felt dry against the plastic and the bed. After a few moments, my fuzzy brain realized someone must have cleaned me. I was grateful for that courtesy, and I clung to the positive feeling of gratitude like a drowning man clutching a float.

"Welcome back, Jon," the voice said. "I really don't understand what could be important enough for you to endure this ordeal. We've studied what little data we can find on you, and nothing appears extraordinary. Your records begin less than forty years ago. You've worked for the Saw and a few other mercenary groups before it, you've acted as a rather expensive but apparently successful private courier, and that's about all we know. Explain the girl's rescue and the episode on Floordin, tell us what Chung had to say, and we'll stop all this."

I wasn't sure how much I could take. I'd sometimes imagined that I'd be able to resist interrogation by finding a mental safe house, a place to retreat within my mind, but in my heart I knew that I, like all other people, would break eventually. I had to get out before I did; once they discovered the truth about me, I'd never be free again. My mind seemed sharper than before, so I tried to focus enough to communicate with the nanomachines.

A chime sounded. Before the noise could fade, the pain stabbed again into my head and neck, filling my vision with a black-red darkness. One intense jolt, and then the pain stopped, but it was enough to make the point. I did my best to relax, to think of nothing, to exist but do no more.

"Jon," the voice said, "I hope you understand that I'm not enjoying this. None of us wanted it to come to this. Answer the questions, and we'll be done."

For a moment that seemed the most reasonable solution in the world, the residual shock waves of the pain in my body leaving me longing to make the voice happy. I opened my mouth to speak, ready to do whatever the voice wanted. Then the reality of what would happen flooded back into me, and I understood that the time might come when I'd talk without even realizing I had. That knowledge was, inexplicably, the funniest thing I'd ever thought. I started laughing, lightly at first and then wholeheartedly, my body twitching with laughter under the plastic. I laughed and laughed, unable to stop, unable to remember why I was laughing, and weaving among the laughter was a wispy thread: I was going crazy.

Maybe crazy was the safe place you went so you wouldn't talk.

"Jon," the voice said, "as you must know from your experience in the Saw, the issue isn't *whether* you'll answer; it's *when* you'll answer. I regret your choice."

The pain arced through me, cutting off the laughter as the muscles in my neck tensed so tightly my screams emerged as tight, compressed squeaks. More intense this time, so sharp I couldn't imagine anything else existed, the pain hit me and hit me and hit me, until I could take no more and passed out.

We continued in this manner, the voice and the pain and I, though I don't know for how many times and or for how long. I screamed sometimes, laughed others, and often cried, but the episodes blurred until each one began as if the first, a birth into pain, a new short life with no significant data from any prior ones, just awakening and then pain. After a time, I cringed as I awoke, enough memory lingering that I knew bad things were coming even though I couldn't remember what any of those bad things were.

I woke up and hid behind my eyelids, kept them closed as if by not seeing the world I could deny its existence, and tried to dig my way back into sleep. I failed, but as I lay there trying to sleep I eventually recalled the chime. That recollection led me to remember they had to be monitoring me, which in turn meant they had to know I was awake. I couldn't deceive them, I realized, and the thought filled me with despair. How could answering their questions, I wondered, make my life any worse than this? Even as I formed the question I realized that its existence marked a major step on the path to giving up.

I heard footsteps again behind me and opened my eyes, hoping for some sort of reprieve, knowing the hope was futile but harboring it anyway.

"The drugs I'm adding now," the voice said from behind my head, "represent the next stage."

I swallowed several times, until I thought I could speak. As I breathed deeply and slowly, staying unfocused and below the chime's threshold, I managed to croak out, "How long?"

The voice laughed, a sound filled with surprise and amusement and a hint of pity but no real humor at all. "How long for the drugs to take effect, or how long have you been here?"

Blackness crawled around the edges of my vision, and I couldn't tell anymore if my eyes were open or closed. Answering was beyond me.

"None of that will matter," he said, as the blackness completely filled my sight and crawled up my optic nerves toward my brain, "where you take yourself next."

CHAPTER
TWENTY-THREE

A light breeze tumbled off the ocean and up to where I sat high on the side of the central peak of our island. Carried on the wind were the strong smells of salt and fish and wet beach grass, filling my nose and letting me know I was home. The wind always blew on Pinkelponker, and the water always rolled fiercely back and forth along our shore. I couldn't remember a time when either had been still. In that way they reminded me of Jennie; she could never stay still, either. She was always moving something: her hands as she gestured or worked, her mouth as she spoke, her hair as the constant breeze played across its strands.

I couldn't remember walking here, or whether I was done with my chores for the day, but the sun was warm and bright in the sky, and the breeze and the ocean were as beautiful as I'd ever seen them. I was happy to be home. I shaded my eyes with my right hand so I could look far out onto the ocean and perhaps make out the next island. Sometimes you could see it on really clear days. My hand looked odd to me, too big but also not rough enough.

I forgot my hand and went back to enjoying the day.

Too bad Jennie's not here, I thought. She'd like this day. She'd like sharing it with me. She'd have some ideas for fun things to do.

And then she was there, beside me even though I didn't hear her walking up. I must not have been paying attention.

"Hi, Jon," she said, a big smile on her face.

I smiled back, but I didn't speak. I never needed to talk much with Jennie; she always knew. I liked that.

"So after all this time," she said, the smile disappearing, "you've finally come back for me?" Her expression was sad, lost.

I couldn't remember leaving, but I must have; Jennie always knew more than I did. "I'm sorry," I said, feeling sorrow but not able to remember why I felt it.

"You gave me to them," she said, her voice rising as she spoke. "You gave me to them, and then they took me away."

"I wouldn't do that," I said. "I would never give you away. I would never let anyone take you."

"You didn't let them," she said, and then we were heading down the hill, Jennie riding in a cart I was pulling and looking up at me, pain stretching the skin of her face. "You did it for them. You did it."

"No!" I screamed. "I wouldn't! I wouldn't!" I kept walking, though, pulling the cart and Jennie on it, but she wasn't Jennie now, she was Jasmine, Jasmine waking up, her eyes blurry, her face etched with pain.

"My father . . ." she said, as she passed out again and changed back to Jennie, who said, "You never came back, Jon."

"I couldn't," I said. I stopped walking and knelt beside her, tears seeping down my face. "I couldn't. They flew me away the day after they took you, and before I could even find a way to get back, I was on another island and then off the planet and on to Aggro and then everything went wrong and the whole system was blockaded and I couldn't." I gulped for breath. "I couldn't."

"My father . . ." Jasmine said from the cart as she struggled to wake up, then failed and fell asleep again.

"I'm sorry," I said. "I'm sorry." Louder this time. "I'm sorry." Screaming it at the sleeping Jennie Jasmine Jennie Jasmine Jennie. I felt like my heart would explode. "I'm sorry, sorry, sorry." I looked down and my chest was gaping open, blood pouring from it, my heart pounding out my life in apology and still it wasn't enough, not ever enough. "I'm sorry!"

I stood. The blood loss made me so dizzy I tumbled backward off the mountain, spraying red into the air as I fell and wondering why, why, why couldn't I save her. I fell faster and faster until I was plummeting so quickly the wind carried away the sounds of "I'm sorry" and still I didn't hit the water. I fell so long I wondered if the bottom would ever stop me and grant me release.

The ocean, still as far away below me as when I'd started to fall, extended tendrils of blackness that spread and rose until they wrapped around me and stopped my descent. I hung in the air for a split second, caught between the sky and the blackness. The tendrils accelerated me upward, higher and higher and higher, rocketing me toward the sun until its bright light filled my eyes and its heat burned my skin and all I could see was light. The light said my name, first in Jennie's voice, then in Jasmine's, and then in someone else's. It glowed brighter and whiter and louder until I screamed for it to stop.

And found myself awake, drenched with sweat under the plastic, trembling, heart pounding, the guilt over Jennie and Jasmine clenching my insides and contorting my face. As I finally internalized where I was, I tried to slow my breathing and my heart. I didn't want to hear the chime again. The noise in my ears dimmed enough that I could hear the sounds outside my head. The familiar voice was back again, talking to me.

"Jon," it said, "I certainly wouldn't want to have your nightmares. You, however, will continue to have them, and much worse, if you don't stop resisting us. Answer the questions."

The chime sounded, and I realized that the small effort of listening had cost me ground in my fight to bring my breathing and pulse under control. I clamped my mouth shut and breathed slowly and deeply through my nose.

"Nothing to say yet?" it said. When I remained silent, the voice laughed lightly, then continued, "On we go then. We both know where this process ends, but if—"

The voice stopped, and the room turned black. A moment later, emergency strips along the ceiling and floor glowed green into the darkness. The air stilled, a barely perceptible change I noticed only because I'd been enjoying its slight motion across my sweaty face. I pressed against the plastic, trying to move, but I couldn't; it held me tight. The floor shook, the vibrations strong enough that I felt them through the bed that confined me. I wondered if I was dreaming and hadn't really awakened, if all of this had been only another stage in my fall, and then the blackness of the room oozed over the green glow, filled my eyes, crawled into my brain, and carried me away again.

The long grass under my back was soft against my clothing and, where it touched my bare arms, tickled me lightly. Moving my arms slowly across it made me smile. The sky above me stretched cloudless and bright for as far as I could see in every direction. I'd finished my chores for the day and climbed to a nice flat spot not far from the edge of a cliff overlooking the ocean. Jennie was going to meet me later. I completed my chores about the same time every day, but Jennie's healing work never stopped at a particular hour. Some days, she'd be done before I was, maybe have to help only one or two people, and she'd bring me lunch and eat with me. Other days, she'd be healing people so late into the night that when she returned home to our little cabin she'd be almost asleep, barely moving, and I'd have to help her into bed and give her a little water to drink and some bread to eat.

Today, I knew she was on her way to meet me, so I stretched out and enjoyed the velvety grass, the clear sky, and the light breeze blowing the smell and taste and stickiness of the seawater over me.

Sounds like explosions or rockets tore through the air, but I couldn't see anything that could cause them. I wondered if a ship from another island was coming to get Jennie to take her to work there. That had to be it, and that was sad, because it meant I wouldn't get to see her today.

Something large and shiny suddenly blotted out the sun way over my head. I wondered if it was Jennie's ship. I wanted to reach up for it, to try to persuade it to take me along, but I couldn't move my arms. The shiny thing headed toward me, and even though I couldn't move my arms I knew it had seen me, was coming for me.

I heard it calling my name, the sound at first far away and then closer as the thing approached.

I smiled; maybe today I'd get to see Jennie after all.

Except the thing didn't stop coming, didn't stop or change course to land beside me, and I wondered now if it was going to smash me into the grass. I wanted to lift my arms and wave at it to move to the side, to stay away from me, but I couldn't; some invisible force pinned my arms to the ground. On down the thing came, until I knew it was going to crush me. The force of it shook me, then it called my name and shook me again. I closed my eyes so my last sight wouldn't be the thing that crushed me.

Pinkelponker vanished behind my eyelids. As its sky winked out, shreds of memory floated into my consciousness: the voice, the chime, the darkness, the emergency lighting.

I opened my eyes. A woman stared at me from only centimeters away. She wore a helmet whose visor covered her face entirely, but lights within the helmet illuminated her. I was confused, unsure what was happening. Was this Jennie again? Jasmine? No, the woman was neither of them. More memories flowed in, and I realized it was Lim. She shook me gently with one arm and called my name. I felt her other arm moving but couldn't tell what it was doing. Before I could answer her, my arms were free. I lifted my head for a quick look down my body. She'd cut the sections of plastic that had bound me to the table.

"Jon," she said, her voice harsh and forced, her breathing ragged, "can you hear me?"

I nodded and managed to squeak, "Yes."

"Good," she said. "We have to go. Can you stand?"

I heard her words. I could repeat each one. I even knew I should understand them. The problem was that I couldn't focus enough to make sense of them, to transform them from sounds into meaning. I squeezed my eyes shut in an effort to concentrate, and then she was shaking me again.

"Forget standing," she said. "Try not to move when I lift you. This'll be hard enough as it is."

She crouched beside the table, facing up my body, her head near my waist. She grabbed the far side of me and pulled me onto my side. She tugged me a little farther, and I rolled onto her shoulder. She grunted and dipped slightly as my weight hit her. Movement was strange, at first a freeing sensation and then a nauseating one. As my stomach hit her shoulder, I heaved and threw up.

"Lovely," she said. "The amount you owe me just went up."

Bracing herself with one hand on the table that had held me, Lim stood. I felt her arm holding me on her shoulder, and she leaned down on the side away from me. My nose smacked into her body with her first step, and without conscious thought I turned my face to the side. She walked carefully but quickly. I bounced with each step. The only colors I could see were the green glow from the emergency strips and the soft yellow of the thin tubes that ran down the other arm of the suit Lim was wearing and into the weapon that looked as if it had grown from her hand.

Lim kept me near a wall as we went, my body bumping into it every now and then. The bumps didn't feel good, but I also couldn't quite register them as pain; they were simply more sensations that my overloaded body interpreted as distant and irrelevant. We progressed along a hallway. Here and there in the darkness I caught glimpses of bent and scorched sections of walls. My nose itched from the smells of charred plastic and singed metal that thickened the air. Three times Lim passed men lying on the ground; none moved. I caught a clear view of only one. His head tilted at an angle that even in my condition I could tell was unnatural, and in his chest a hole bigger around than my arm was black and oozing, the smell so strong I vomited again as we passed him.

"Damn," Lim said, "you'll pay for this." The effort of speaking while carrying me caused her to pinch each word.

A few times everything went black. Each time I couldn't tell if we'd entered an area with no lights or I'd passed out again, and each time I have no sense of how long I remained in total darkness.

We rounded a corner and stopped outside a door that displayed both the usual green glowing strips and some additional red lights. I knew if I could clear my head I'd remember what those other lights meant, but I couldn't manage it.

"Open both airlock doors, Lobo," Lim said, her voice low and strained.

The door opened, and Lim stepped into a little room. A second door opened, and light slammed into me, everything so bright I had to shut my eyes. I felt Lim take a few steps forward; then she crouched and shoved me off her shoulders. I fell, for an instant alone in the air, and then I hit the floor. My stomach heaved again, but I was empty and nothing came up.

"Get ready to get us out of here," I heard Lim say. "I'll be back in two minutes."

Her voice was a whisper that reached me from what seemed an impossibly far distance. The world lurched, and I passed out again.

Sunlight warmed my eyes. I tried to roll over so it could work on my back, but I couldn't; my arms and legs were stuck. A torrent of memory erased the sun and tore me from Pinkelponker back to . . . where? I was lying down, unable to move, wondering if the voice would know I was conscious again, when the last strand of memory played across my mind and I remembered Lim and the rescue. I opened my eyes. I was indeed back in Lobo, in the small medical room, on the same bed where I'd secured Chung, held by the same restraints I'd used on him. An IV trailed out of my right arm.

I tried to call for Lobo, but all I managed was a croaking sound more like a cough than a word.

It was enough.

"I'm glad you're back, Jon," Lobo said.

Lim entered the room. "Finally," she said.

I closed my eyes, held them for a couple of beats, then opened them again. I was still in Lobo, and Lim was still standing there.

After a couple more croaks, I managed to say, "Water."

Lim swiveled a tube to my mouth. I sucked on it, gently at first, letting my mouth and throat reacquaint themselves with liquid, and then harder, drinking all I could manage. I turned my head away when I was done, and Lim removed the tube.

"Thank you," I said. The tube dripped a bit on my cheek.

"You're welcome," Lim and Lobo each said, Lobo a syllable ahead of her.

"I scanned you," Lobo said, "and found no implants or broken bones. All your organs are functioning at least tolerably, though you were dehydrated. So, we've loaded you with fluid and some broad-spectrum repairers, but only generics. Can you give us more specifics on what they did to you?"

"No," I said. "What you've done is all I need. Well, that and some time." I wanted to be better prepared the next time I encountered these attackers—and I was now convinced there'd be a next time. "Did you take blood samples?"

"Of course," Lobo said. "We were prepared in case my treatments proved to be inadequate to revive you and we needed to seek additional medical aid."

"Keep them," I said, "so I can study them later." When I had more energy and some private time, I could work with my nanomachines to provide my body with resistance to these drugs. Having more energy seemed a distant proposition; I felt very tired, as tired as I could remember ever being.

"Can you stand?" Lim said.

I nodded, then said, "Give me a moment."

I closed my eyes and focused on instructing the nanomachines. For the first time since my kidnappers had tagged me on my way to the Busted Heart, I could concentrate. I set in place a full body-cleaning regimen, something I've had to do all too many times in my life, and then took a deep breath. I was back. I'd hurt for a while as the nanomachines cleaned me and my body had to purge the waste, but as long as I drank a lot of water and rested, I'd be back to normal within a day or so.

I opened my eyes, looked at Lim, and said, "I can stand. Please let me up."

She removed the IV and undid the restraints, then stayed close as I sat up slowly. I put my hands on either side of my body and gently swiveled my legs so both hung off the side of the medbed nearest where Lim stood. I felt beaten, almost shattered, but in a dull way with no sharp pains, so I was confident no bones were broken.

I rested for a moment. Lobo helped by lowering the bed until my feet touched the floor and my knees bent slightly.

I pushed off the bed and stood. I wavered for a few seconds, dizzy and weak enough that I closed my eyes unconsciously as I struggled for balance. The dizziness passed, and I opened my eyes again. I tried to step forward and almost fell; Lim's hands on my arm and shoulder were all that stopped me.

"Perhaps," I said, "I should sleep a bit more."

"Idiot," Lim said. "Of course you should sleep more. Get back on the medbed."

"No," I said. "My bunk." Lim scowled at me. "Please."

After a short delay, she said, "Okay, but you're definitely an idiot."

She ducked under my right arm, and I held on to her shoulder as we made our way out of the small medic area and to my bunk. I moved like an ancient patient too proud or too stupid to let his nurse have the bed transport him, and in a humbling moment of self-honesty I realized that at the moment that was all I was.

When we reached my bunk Lim lowered me gently onto it.

"Thank you," I said, as I closed my eyes. "Really. For everything."

I fell into a deep sleep before she could respond, a sleep blissfully devoid of dreams.

CHAPTER TWENTY-FOUR

I awoke thirsty and ravenous. I drank a liter of water and ate quickly, staying alone, taking stock internally. I felt almost a hundred percent, the nanomachines and the meds having done their jobs. When I finished, I went up front, where Lim was scanning shimmering windows of information about Macken and Kelco's presence there.

"As you might imagine," I said, "I have a lot of questions. Let's start with the obvious ones. How long has it been since you dropped me off outside Queen's Bar? What happened to me? And, where are we?"

"About seventy hours, the last fourteen and a half of which you've spent sleeping," Lobo said. "You were kidnapped and interrogated by some Kelco staff, and we retrieved you. We're in orbit around Velna."

Lovely. Any time I want a simple answer from Lobo, I can't shut him up. When I'd appreciate some details, he turns into Mr. Terse. I made a mental note to ask him sometime if there was a way he could display the amount of emotive programming at play in his answers. Having a sarcasm meter would be quite handy for dealing with him.

"Did you think you'd gotten here on your own?" Lim said.

I knew there was no chance she'd go for the sarcasm meter, so I didn't bring it up.

"No." I smiled and shook my head. I was feeling better. "As I believe I said before, thank you for rescuing me. I do appreciate it. I'm just trying to understand what happened."

"Fair enough," Lim said.

"I have, of course, recorded all the aspects of the mission that I could monitor," Lobo said, a note of pride evident in his voice, the added emotion suggesting that perhaps I had indeed read the earlier sarcasm correctly. "So, if you're interested you can view the logs of the rescue itself."

"It all started when you were late for the pickup," Lim said.

They took turns explaining to me what had happened, Lim doing most of the talking, Lobo speaking occasionally and providing the video log he'd mentioned. The story that emerged made me very glad I was working with them, sarcasm and all.

After dropping me off, Lim consulted Chung about how he'd like us to return him. She stayed out of his sight and used a voice scrambler, so her identity remained unknown to him. He was understandably angry, but he relaxed a lot when Lim finally convinced him that I hadn't intentionally put Jasmine in jeopardy and that he was going to walk away from this. After some negotiation, they agreed on a simple but safe plan.

Lobo invested some time in basic evasive maneuvers outside the atmosphere, moving among a few heavily populated orbits with no particular goal. Chung agreed to be sedated and took the pill Lim provided through a hatch Lobo opened. When his monitors indicated Chung was in deep sleep, Lobo used his camo capabilities to once again blend with the cliff tourist shuttles and fly the coastline. He landed with a group of them in time for the midafternoon tour-group switch.

Lim had brought more than work gear with her. Dressed in a color-shifting pantsuit, a blond wig falling loose around her face, huge sunglasses covering her eyes and most of her face, Lim looked every bit the trophy girl embarrassed at escorting her drunken husband off the shuttle and to the nearest restroom. She'd given Chung a mild stimulant to bring him up to a fuzzy consciousness, so he leaned on her and lurched along but would remember nothing. When Xychek security followed up, everyone who'd seen her would remember her, and the cameras would have captured a lot of good images, but neither the people nor the photos would provide a useful trail back to her. So many people passed through the station that her DNA trail wouldn't matter, either. She left Chung at the restroom door and got in line to board another shuttle. At the last minute, she appeared to change her mind and walked quickly down the strip to a different shuttle, one that happened to be Lobo.

Once they were airborne, Lim called one of her team members who was on holiday on Lankin. He used an anonymous connection at a comm joint in Queen's Bar to send Chung's location to Xychek security. Lim and Lobo, trusting the quality of Xychek's team, hadn't followed up on Chung, but the worst case, they felt, was that Chung awoke in the restroom robbed and sick; no one at a tourist shuttle site was likely to bother to kill him when they could have his wallet for nothing.

Lobo landed a few minutes before sunset, correctly planning to minimize his time on the ground. At precisely sunset, he started monitoring the frequency of my transmitter to see how long they'd have to wait for me.

When three minutes had passed without him detecting a transmission, Lobo knew something was wrong and told Lim. On the chance that I'd been coerced into revealing our pickup plans and to generally minimize risk, Lobo immediately took off and blended in with the last of the tourist shuttle crowd. From there he started the search.

They swept along the coastline up to the northernmost corporate headquarters, but with no luck. Lobo flew a slow series of parallels up and down the continent, starting with the area over the city, until he was about a quarter of the planet away. When he still hadn't detected even a trace of a signal, he headed up to the highest orbital plane on which he could find recent signs of ship or satellite activity. He plotted a cylinder with its center over Bekin's Deal and a radius equal to the peak range of the transmitter, and started sweeping it for a signal. The search was maddening, Lim said, a blind trawling exercise that over the course of many hours reminded her just how much empty space exists around every planet.

After moving down one radius of the cylinder to a lower orbital plane and shifting a radius westward of the city, Lobo picked up my signal. He traced it to a small, gray, logo-free satellite floating unobtrusively among a group of FC weather sats and Kelco comm relays.

At this point I'd been missing over twenty-eight hours.

Per our previous agreement, Lim took command. First priority was intel. Aside from the occasional short bursts from my transmitter, the sat was electromagnetically inert. Nothing about it read as military, and it sported no obvious signs of armor. Lobo and Lim monitored it for almost an hour before it engaged in a short bidirectional comm link with a source on Lankin. Lobo traced the link back to Kelco head-quarters there, so now they knew they had to hit fast and hard or Kelco would launch serious corporate security in pursuit.

With no more data available, Lim opted for as much of a crash-and-trash approach as was feasible given that I was aboard. Lobo copied the markings of one of the FC weather sats and over the course of an hour moved slowly into a position with a clean line of sight to the target. During that time, the sat didn't communicate with Kelco on the ground.

When the next communication began, Lobo moved a bit closer, and Lim suited up.

Right after the sat broke contact with Kelco corporate, on the assumption that no one on the ground would be likely to contact it again for a while, Lim gave the go.

Lobo fired an EM disruptor missile. It moved in fast, hit the sat, and sent a pulse through the vessel. If the structure was milspec and armored, the disruptor would fail, but they had to bank that the small satellite wasn't up to those standards. Lobo followed the missile in and docked hard with the sat, broadcasting interference waves to block as much as possible any communication with the ground. Lobo opened his airlock, and Lim stepped in.

From that point on, they had multiple AV streams for me: the output of feeds from Lim's forward camera and mic, the in-helmet camera and mic focused on her face, and the body-function monitors Lobo maintained on her. The sound from the forward mic, mixed with an undercurrent of Lim's initially steady breathing, filled the room from Lobo's speakers. The forward camera's output, the images of the camera on Lim, and the standard personnel vitals played across Lobo's wall displays.

Darkness bathed the sat's interior, the only lighting a soft green glow from the emergency strips. Lim plugged a lead from Lobo into the airlock's manual-override port and waited while Lobo hacked the switch, impatience showing in her elevated heartbeat and her gloved left fist occasionally smacking the wall. The sat was definitely not milspec; anything modern and military would have launched virus attacks against Lobo and used stronger encryption than his processors could defeat in any reasonable period of time. At just under two minutes into the mission, the door indicator glowed ready. Lim pushed it open, staying behind Lobo's wall as she did.

A shower of projectiles hit Lobo's inner airlock wall. Lobo flashed to Lim's heads-up display the data from a forward video feed: An unarmored guard stood across from the airlock, bending around the corner carefully, exposing only part of his head, his hands, and the projectile rifle he held. Lim ordered Lobo to take him out, not trank him. Lobo fired an energy beam mounted beside the camera. Lim watched in her heads-up display as the exposed portion of the guard's head turned into a fine mist.

She smiled and said, "Good work."

Lim ran in and flattened herself against the wall the guard had been peering around. Two halls led away from her position, one toward the guard and the other into blackness on the opposite side. She tossed a sensor grenade down the hall with the guard, then threw another down the other hall. The grenades sprayed microsensors as they first flew through the air and then fell and rolled along the floor. No weapons hit them, so with the lack of armor on the vessel Lim decided to risk that it was pure civilian issue and unlikely to have any significant automated defense systems. Lobo collated the IR and temperature feeds from each hallway's sensors and fed the results to two new images in Lim's display. Both halls were empty, so Lim backtracked the guard and headed down his passageway.

Lim moved carefully and slowly in the soft green glow, keeping her own lights off and using only the strips to guide her way. After eight steps, Lobo flashed her an alert: Another guard was coming down the opposite hallway. She sprinted back, pulled a short projectile rifle out of the harness on her back, thumbed it to full auto, and crouched beside the body of the first guard. When the sensor-web output in her display showed the second guard was less than three meters away, she leaned into the hall at knee level and shot the guard in the chest until the clip was empty. Her respiration rate and pulse skyrocketed, and she was smiling, eyes bright with effort and excitement, as she killed the guard. I'd wanted to avoid killing, and I wish she'd tranked the guards, but I also understood how she felt: When it's them or you, you is an easy choice, and in that moment survival is the most intense treat you can imagine.

Neither sensor-web display showed any additional activity, so she headed back down the first hallway, reloading the rifle on the run, moving faster this time on the theory that if more guards were available, they most likely would have joined the pursuit. She approached a room on the outside wall, the first doorway she'd seen. Staying to the side, she pressed the Open button. The door slid aside. Staying low and out of the line of sight of the room, she tossed in a handful of self-dispersing sensors. Lobo collated the video feeds immediately: The room was empty.

She passed two more outer-wall rooms and repeated the process. No sign of any hostiles.

The small sat contained a total of five outer rooms, a hallway that wrapped around its center, and a large central area with a pair of doors spaced a hundred and eighty degrees apart. She dropped sensors outside the first door to the central area and kept moving around the hallway. On its other side she found the remaining two outer rooms, both also unlocked and empty. She dropped sensors outside the second door to the inner area, checked the feeds from the first—still clear—and pushed the Open button.

The door stayed closed.

Her pulse rose, and she grimaced. I understood how she must have felt, the seconds of the mission piling up like weights on her chest.

She reached into her pack and pulled out a pair of acid crawlers, purely mechanical, limited-range versions of the squidlettes I'd encountered on Floordin. She attached both to the top of the door, a roughly thirty-degree angle separating their paths to the floor, thumbed them into action, and stepped to the side. They worked their way down the hatch, spewing an acid mix as they crawled, eating away a centimeter-wide strip of the dull gray alloy, until they reached the bottom and all that held up the door was a wispy web of smoking metal they hadn't quite dissolved. Lim stayed outside the line of sight of the door and fired a single round into its bottom left corner. The round was enough to dislodge the door. Its bottom flew backward into the room, and its top crashed into the hallway.

A flurry of widely dispersed rounds smacked into the hallway wall opposite Lim. The shots covered a large area in a random pattern that suggested the shooter wasn't a pro. Lim dropped to her side, facing the room, rifle held along her body, and tossed in a handful of sensors. The shooter, now visible in Lobo's new feed to her as a man who appeared petrified, fired at the sensors. As he did, Lim pushed forward and emptied the rest of her clip in a tight cluster in his chest.

Lim's display showed a room full of storage areas but empty of any life, a single door on its opposite side the only other way in or out. That door opened easily, and though she of course took the time to carefully check the connecting room, the only person in it was me.

Watching her carry me out was strange, the images in front of my eyes colliding with my hazy memories of the same events. I winced as I saw myself hit the floor inside Lobo, where Lim dumped me. "Get ready to get us out of here," she said. "I'll be back in two minutes."

She grabbed a waiting pack and headed into the sat. She moved swiftly and with no wasted motion through the halls, barely slowing as she tossed one charge from the pack into each outer room and, on her way out, the rest of the pack into the center room with the dead man. She was back in Lobo in well under two minutes. He closed the airlocks and detached from the satellite.

Via a recording from an outside camera, I watched as the distance between the sat and Lobo grew until the sat appeared only as a small gray dot in space. The dot turned bright white as Lobo triggered the charges, which blasted the sat into small pieces of debris, many of which would one day succumb to Lankin's gravity, find their way into its atmosphere, accelerate, and burn up, leaving virtually no physical evidence of the torture I'd undergone.

I shivered as I recalled the pain my torturers had caused me, the happy images of Pinkelponker that morphed into nightmares as I once again failed both Jennie and Jasmine, the desperate feelings that gripped me on that table, and the even worse knowledge that soon I'd have told them anything, given up every secret I'd hoped to keep, failed myself just as I'd failed Jennie and Jasmine. I understood intellectually that everyone succumbs to torture in the end, but that knowledge was as nothing next to the gut-deep sense of my own weakness.

Not for the first time, I wished some memories could encounter the same easy fate as the satellite's remains. I knew, though, that instead they would be with me forever, sharp and dangerous debris waiting in the places inside me that were as dark as the blackest space between stars.

"Did you have to kill them all?" I said, regretting my tone as soon as the words left me, realizing too late that I was taking out my mood on Lim.

She stared at me for a few seconds before answering. "Yes. I was working alone, in hostile territory with no definite count of the opposition, and I assumed time was critical." She walked a few steps away from me, then stopped and faced me. Her face was tight, her amazing beauty replaced by naked aggression. She rubbed her hands on her shorts. "First, I have to hope you're simply not thinking clearly yet, because you shouldn't have needed to ask that.

Second, it was my mission, so it was my call, and you have no right to question it. Finally, I saved your carcass back there, so fewer questions and more gratitude would be appropriate."

I knew she was right, but the force of her stance and her words hit me like an attack, and I wanted to hit back. I took a step toward her, and immediately and probably unconsciously she responded, shifting her weight to her rear leg and raising her hands slightly to her sides.

What was wrong with me? I forced a long, slow, deep breath and closed my eyes. Before I opened them, I raised my hands, palms outward, and backed up slightly.

"You're right," I said. "I'm wrong." I lowered my hands and stared directly at her. "I'm hurt, frustrated, and sick of the killing." I shook my head. "I've caused one mess after another since this whole thing began, and I left you the problem of cleaning up part of it. I have no right or reason to criticize. You did everything right."

I paused as I pictured her face on the monitor and realized I was lying. What bothered me wasn't the killing but rather her pleasure in it, and what she did wrong was to feel that pleasure. Yet I'd known she'd respond that way when I approached her, so I had no right to chastise her for it. Worse, I realized then that I really would have done the same, and that I, too, would have opted for lethal force. No, I made myself face it directly: I would have killed them, and as each died I would have been glad it was them and not me. The differences between Lim and me were subtle: I would have found no joy in the killing per se, and I would have felt bad about it afterward. Did those differences really matter? Certainly not to the dead men or their families. In the end, though, valid or rationalization, real or illusion, they mattered to me. Looking at Lim, I knew there was no point in discussing any of this.

I also knew, when I forced myself to confront the truth, that part of me was happy she'd killed the people who'd tortured me.

Most of all, I was glad she was on my side. Hurting someone on my team was stupid, and stupider still was punishing them for doing the right thing—however they felt about it while they did it. I shouldn't have questioned her.

"I'm sorry for what I asked," I continued, "and I'm sorry for questioning your choices. You're right that I'm not back to normal yet, and you're also right that the mission and the choices were yours to make. I greatly appreciate the risk you took to save me. I owe you."

She studied me, searching for any trace of irony, and as much as I wanted to turn away I continued to look at her, trying not to hide my feelings, willing her to know I was telling the truth. For a few oddly intimate seconds we stood like that, the gulf of anger between us evaporating, our feelings exposed and connected by the experience and its intensity, and then she visibly relaxed and even forced a smile.

"So get better, okay?" she said.

She turned away again and headed to the small room Lobo had formed for her use. Over her shoulder, she added, "And do it fast, so we can figure out how to pay back Kelco and make some real money."

I'm not sure how long I sat in the pilot couch, staring at the stars and dozing occasionally as my body finished cleansing itself of the drugs. The visions of Pinkelponker still trickled through my mind each time I lost consciousness, and each time I awoke with a start. Honest longing accompanied each bad dream, and in each one I wished with all my heart that I'd somehow been able to stop them from taking Jennie and that I had never returned Jasmine to Slake. At some moments in the dreams, I yearned for this longing to count for something, to have value, to make things at least a little better, but I knew it didn't, at least not to Jennie or to Jasmine.

Jennie was long gone, vanished over a hundred years ago, her path unknown, even the very existence of her and our home world uncertain.

Jasmine, though, remained in a different situation entirely, a captive of Kelco still imprisoned because I was foolish enough to let Slake manipulate me. As I recalled his approach to me I started to get angry again. I embraced the anger as the old friend it was. The more I considered the situation, the angrier I got. I'd been a pawn since this whole mess started, constantly walking on a path Slake and others in his employ were charting, reacting as they wanted and ultimately doing nothing in my own service. The anger spread inside me and cleared my thinking like a cool evening shower settling the dust of a hot day.

I resolved to save Jasmine and to make Kelco and Slake pay in as many ways as possible for using her—and for using me.

I walked back to Lim's room and knocked. She stepped out, a wary expression on her face.

"Yes?" she said.

"I'm fed up," I said. "I'm done letting Kelco control me, and I'm done helping them. No more. We're going to get Jasmine back, and we're going to make them pay."

"About time," she said. "I particularly like the pay part."

"We can't do it alone, though," I said. "Now that I understand how many Kelco resources Slake can bring to bear, I realize we're going to need to involve some others."

"Fine," she said, "as long as their take doesn't come out of my paycheck."

"It won't," I said, "because I believe I've figured out how all of us can make money in different ways, so everyone except Slake can win." I stepped slightly back from her. "There is one potential problem, though."

"What?"

"One of the groups we need to help us is the Saw. We have to go see Earl, and we have to work with him."

She stiffened, but she kept her face calm. "If what you want is an armed team, then the Saw isn't necessary. My group is more than capable—"

"That's not the point," I said, cutting her off. "We do need soldiers, but what we need more are Earl's contacts, his relationship with the FC."

"You have no better options?" she said.

"None," I said. "We need the Saw and the FC, and Earl is our only way into both."

"Then it's not a problem," she said, the look on her face not at all agreeing with her words. "It's just business, right?"

"Absolutely," I said.

"Then set it up," she said. With a smile she added, "I'm sure he'll be as happy to see me as I'll be to see him."

CHAPTER TWENTY-FIVE

When I strolled into the Saw recruiting center this time, Gustafson was waiting for me, standing by the door to the side room in which we'd met on my first visit. His readiness wasn't a good sign, because it meant either the people or the software scanning the exterior monitors were watching for me. I supposed it couldn't be helped, but it was one more reason to consider a major change in location when this was all over. I gave Gustafson a genuine smile—I found it hard not to like him—and followed him into the room.

He seemed less happy to see me. "I haven't heard from you," he said, "and that wasn't the way this was supposed to work."

"How secure is this area?" I said.

"Secure enough for us."

"Maybe not. Top, I haven't been in contact because my plan lasted about as long as a new private's enthusiasm."

"I take it, though," he said, "that you still want something from us."

"And I have quite a bit to offer," I said. "We're talking business, not charity. Trust me, I haven't been on R&R."

He studied my face for a bit, then nodded, rubbed his hands on his pants, and sat back. "Fair enough. Sorry for the welcome. We've been wondering what was happening."

"We need to meet with Earl again," I said.

"You and I can't handle this?"

"I'm quite sure we can't," I said.

"Okay," he said, nodding his head again. "How soon?"

"As soon as possible. In fact, the earlier today, the better."

"He won't like that," Gustafson said. "I hope you know him well enough to understand exactly how little he'll appreciate having to change his routine."

"I understand, but enough's at play that we have to meet, and it has to be somewhere completely secure physically and with extremely secure comm links. As near as I can tell, with Earl's level of caution that means we'll have to use a Saw facility on the base."

"Of course."

"You can give him some positive motivation," I said.

"What's that?"

"The opportunity for the Saw and the FC is quite possibly greater than before."

Gustafson laughed. "Every time somebody offers me an opportunity, I scan for escape routes. What's this one going to cost us?"

"If we go with my plan," I said, "a little more risk and a little more involvement."

"Oh, he'll love this," Gustafson said. "I think I'll save that part for you to explain."

"That's only fair," I said, "but there is one other change I think you'll want to warn him about."

Gustafson raised an eyebrow in question. "And that would be?"

"Lim is in this all the way," I said. "I owe her. She has to be in the meeting, and she and her people and the Saw will probably have to work together before this is over."

He laughed. "Well that's just perfect. I'm sure the colonel will be thrilled to see her."

I raised my hands and shrugged in the ages-old "what can you do?" gesture. "Sorry."

Gustafson stood and smoothed the front of his uniform, which was already flawless. "Nothing to do but do it," he said. "Call me in an hour, and I—" He paused and chuckled. "—or my replacement should have the particulars for you."

Two and a half hours later the afternoon sun was high in the sky, the air was warm and smelled slightly of the ocean on the other side of Bekin's Deal, and another gorgeous summer day was in full swing on Lankin. Lim and I were missing the day's beauty, physically together in the cab but mentally in separate, private worlds. The guard at the Saw base gate processed our IDs quickly and waved us through. The cab dropped us at a building that looked exactly like the one I'd visited last time but which sat far closer to the center of the base.

Gustafson walked out of the nearest door as soon as the cab pulled away.

"Gunny," he said to me.

"Top."

"Lim," he said.

"Top, is it going to be like that?" she said with a smile. She wore a simple coverall, having abandoned a Law dress uniform at my request, but even the coverall couldn't conceal her figure. When she smiled and turned on the charm, she might as well have been a princess in jewels, as incandescent and hard to gaze at directly as a sun. She opened her arms and stared straight at him.

Gustafson melted, though I couldn't tell whether it was the act of an old friend abandoning a forced distance or the foolishness of just another male who flew too close to her and couldn't resist the heat. He hugged her and said, "Not out here, Alissa. Not out here."

They held the hug for a few seconds, then both said, almost in unison, "Good to see you again."

Gustafson stepped back. "And you," he said. He nodded to the building behind us. "In there, though . . ."

"I understand," she said. "I'm no happier about being here than he is about seeing me, but it's business, that's all."

"You know that doesn't help," he said. "If anything, business has been the problem all along."

"You're not starting with me, are you?" she said.

Gustafson held up his hands in surrender. "Not me. I know better." He turned to me. "Anything else I need to know before we meet with the colonel?"

"No," I said, "and certainly there's nothing we need to discuss out here."

He nodded, turned, and headed to the door. "Then let's not keep him waiting any longer."

We followed him inside and passed through three isolation areas, each one, Gustafson explained, running a different type of weapons and comm gear check. After the third, we walked down a long windowless hallway and turned to a burnished blue sadwood door on the left near the end. Gustafson rapped twice with his knuckles. The resulting sound was so muted I was sure the door was thick enough that no one on the other side could possibly have heard his knock. What they could hear didn't matter, of course. The knock was a formality; the staff manning the hallway monitors would decide if and when we could enter.

The handle clicked so quietly I barely registered the sound. Gustafson pulled open the door and waved us in.

We stepped into a conference room that was about as thematically far as it could be from the tiny containment area in which Earl, Gustafson, and I had sat. Where that space had been casual, almost intimate, this one was formal and large, at its center a conference table of the same polished sadwood as the door. Eighteen chairs, each a blue leather that perfectly complemented the wood, surrounded the table, one at each end and eight along each side. The walls were floor-to-ceiling displays, some currently acting as subdued wallpaper, others showing Saw logos, images from past campaigns, and maps of major worlds—Lankin the visually largest among them—for which the Saw currently held contracts. Aside from the walls, the room was devoid of machines; no doubt Earl used human attendants to make the visiting brass feel important. I've never particularly liked formality, but I had to admit the space was impressive. I assumed this was where Earl met with the FC and the local corporations when they had formal reviews; no one organizing a Saw staff meeting would ever have booked a room like this.

Earl hadn't worried about anything more than security when he'd first met with me, so either he was showing off for Lim, which I considered unlikely, or he wanted home-turf advantage. My bet was it was the latter.

One feature I was sure this room shared with our previous meeting place was security. Any group that Earl considered important enough to meet here was one he'd consider dangerous enough to contain electronically.

I glanced at Lim to gauge her reaction. Her smile remained, but it was tight now and lacking in any real warmth. I hoped Earl had also wanted to put some distance between them.

A section of the wall opposite us slid open, and Earl walked in. Dressed in his standard working blues and walking with the same perfect posture as always, at first glance he looked far less nervous than I knew Lim was. As I watched him approach, however, I realized he was uncharacteristically not looking Lim in the eyes, and his back and expression were rigid, set in place by force of will. I have to give him credit, though: He never slowed or faltered. He walked up to Lim, shook her hand, and said, "Lim." He shook my hand, said "Moore," and headed to the center of the left side of the table. The way he spoke to me wasn't a good sign—I was "Jon" in the last meeting—but I should've expected it.

Gustafson sat beside him. Lim and I took seats opposite them.

"Before you explain why we're meeting," Earl said, staring at me, "I have an obligation to address certain complaints the FC has tasked me to handle. Specifically, Xychek's local security chief, Larson, has asked us to investigate the kidnapping of Jose Chung, their executive in charge here. He apparently satisfied himself that neither Kelco nor any other corporation is involved, so he believes that makes the issue our problem. Technically, he's correct." I opened my mouth to speak, but Earl held up his hand. I stayed quiet. "In addition, a Kelco R&D security man, Amendos, who to the best of our ability to determine is normally stationed on Macken, visited here to tour one of their small research sats."

Amendos. The name took a moment to register, and then I had it: the auditor I met at the Macken jump station. No way could this be a coincidence; he had to be Slake's man in this affair. As I tuned back in to what Earl was saying, I realized I'd missed a couple of words.

" . . . unable to complete his tour, it seems, because something attacked and destroyed the sat. He also could find no sign of corporate involvement, so he went to Vaccaro, who promptly called me." He leaned back in his chair and looked casually around the room. "I don't suppose either of you could help us with those investigations."

"Why are you—" Lim said, stopping only when I touched her leg and shook my head.

"I'm simply doing my job," Earl said, leaning forward again, "as I think the head of any security group, even a small one, would understand if she wanted the group to stay in business."

"You—" Lim said.

I cut her off, raising my voice a little. "Is this room completely secure?" I said.

With visible effort Earl turned his attention back to me. "Of course."

"Are we being recorded in any way?"

"No," he said. "Based on your comments in our last meeting and your request to Top for this one, we're secure and off the record, at least at this point."

"Then let me answer your questions," I said. "As you knew from our last meeting we would, we kidnapped Chung. We later returned him unharmed, a fact I hope Larson mentioned." Earl nodded, and I continued. "Lim destroyed the Kelco satellite after rescuing me from it."

"You appreciate, I assume," Earl said, "that though our last meeting left certain possibilities open, having you directly confirm these accusations places me in an awkward situation."

"That's garbage," Lim said. "I know how much flexibility you have, and unless Jon has misinformed me, you also understand the opportunities this situation offers all of us, the Saw included."

"You may be able to make up the rules when you're dealing with minor policy issues in a jail," Earl said, "but when one has a planetary security contract, one has to treat a great many matters much more formally."

"That's total—" Lim said, before I cut her off again.

"Colonel, Lim," I said, trying to keep my voice level and my tone formal. "I appreciate that this meeting is uncomfortable, but I assure you that it is both necessary and worthwhile for all of us." I faced Lim. "You understand completely what's at play, and you chose to participate." I turned to Earl. "The stakes I mentioned in our last meeting have not lowered, though they have mutated." I paused a moment, then continued, "We're all professionals, so I've assumed we could work together successfully. If I'm wrong in making that assumption, please tell me now and save us all a lot of time."

I glanced at Gustafson. He'd pushed slightly back from the table, so he was no longer in Earl's direct line of sight, and his face was a carefully composed neutral.

Lim's cheeks were taut and slightly flushed, but she stayed quiet.

After a few moments, Earl said, "You said the stakes have changed. What exactly is different now?"

"The capsule version is this," I said. "I blamed the wrong person and the wrong company. Kelco, not Xychek, has been buying arms from Osterlad, and Slake, not Chung, put the bounty on me. I learned some of this from questioning Chung, and some of it from the fact that Kelco kidnapped and tortured me."

Earl chuckled and rubbed his hands on his trousers. "So Kelco was already after you," he said, "and now Xychek is, too. Lovely. Are there any more highlights I should know? Anyone else you've managed to antagonize?"

I hesitated, not wanting to talk about Jasmine, but then realized there was no way my plan could work if everyone here didn't have all the relevant data. "Slake kidnapped Chung's daughter, took her to Macken, and used her to force Chung to withdraw the Xychek bid. A group on Macken grabbed her from Slake. I rescued her— well, I thought I was rescuing her—and returned her to Slake." I paused a second, then added, "And as you might imagine, Chung wasn't too happy to learn all that."

Earl laughed outright this time, and Gustafson joined him, shaking his head in wonder. Even Lim smiled and chuckled.

I could see the humor in what I'd said, but I couldn't feel it; memories of the torture and images of Jasmine's face kept crawling to the edge of my consciousness. Their laughter triggered a reflexive anger, but I shoved it down and stayed under control; the job was to get the Saw's help and rescue Jasmine, and the job was what mattered most now.

"Exactly how," Earl said, "did you manage to so royally fubar this situation?"

"By screwing up one thing at a time," I said, "in a long sequence of nothing but missteps."

Earl stopped laughing and turned serious. "I think it's time you ran it down for us," he said. "As you noted, we're all professionals, and as such I'm sure we all want as much information as possible before we decide what we're going to do."

I couldn't decide if he was trying to provoke me, getting in his licks, or simply saying exactly what he meant, but his intent didn't matter. He was right: They needed all, or nearly all, of the information. "Okay," I said.

I walked them through what had happened, omitting only my killing of Johns and Osterlad and my use of my nanomachines. None of that information was vital to the mission at hand, and I didn't trust *anyone* enough to expose myself to the kinds of problems those data points could cause me. When I was done, I sat back and waited for Earl to process the story.

It didn't take him long. "So why not walk away?" he said. "What's in this for you?"

"Several things," I said. "Most of all, I want to return Jasmine Chung to her family. The Gardeners might've done that eventually, but I stopped them. Slake and Kelco have caused me a lot of pain, and I want to make them pay for that. And the money, of course. I still believe we can all profit from this."

"Is that really the order of your motivations," Earl said, "or are you just looking for a big payday?"

I felt my face flush, and I gripped the arms of my chair. "Colonel,

I know it's been a long time since I reported to you, but I hope you remember enough about me to know that I've never done anything only for the money. Yes, the income potential here is high, and, yes, I'd like to get paid. But whether there's any money in this or not, and whether anyone helps me or not, I'm going to rescue that girl. And as much as I'd like to make Slake suffer for all he's done to me, that's nowhere near as important to me as saving Jasmine."

Earl studied my face, then nodded and turned to Lim. "And you?" he said. "What's in it for you?"

She shrugged and said, "Mostly the money, but also finishing the job. I told Jon I was in to the end, and the job's not over, so I'm still in."

Earl nodded again and looked at me. "Fair enough. I understand your motivations. What are mine? Perhaps more importantly, what are my employer's? If the Frontier Coalition doesn't win, I can't believe my bosses will let us get involved."

"You told me before that the FC was tired of being the weak third party in this quadrant," I said. "We handle this situation correctly, and Kelco will lose its exclusive rights to the new Macken gate and also end up with a great deal less local power in the process. If no corporation has exclusive rights on Macken, the FC will have to play an arbitration role there. That role will bring them involvement and more power."

"And the Saw?" he said. "What will we get out of this?"

"A stronger relationship with the FC, more presence in the region because the FC would have more power, and a chance at another planetary contract, this time for Macken. With two actively competing conglomerates there, the FC will want a continuing peacekeeping force."

"Macken is still a developing world," he said, "so the FC might well not have enough need to warrant the price we'd demand."

"Then you'd control the subcontracting," I said, hoping Lim would see the potential opportunity as motivation for playing nice, "and make at least the usual small profit in the bargain. Even if there's no direct money in it for the Saw, you'll still win because you'll have stopped an illegal arms buildup. Keeping down the local corporate weapons inventory has to be in your best long-term interest."

Earl pondered the situation for a few minutes. I knew the gains I was offering the Saw weren't huge, but the potential for the FC was large, and anyone as skillful as Earl could turn being the agent of such a win for a client into a positive factor in that relationship. Lim had clearly picked up on the potential subcontracting role, because she looked like she wanted to jump in and try to persuade Earl further. I caught her gaze and shook my head slightly; we needed to give him all the time he wanted to think, and we definitely didn't need his feelings about her coloring the whole pitch.

When Earl finally spoke, his manner had changed, and it was clear he was with us. We were no longer selling him; he was helping us plan. "I don't think we need to burden Vaccaro with most of the details of what's happened in the past," he said, "because if we did she might feel obliged to order me to get involved. By omitting those details, however, we'll leave you, Jon, without any apparent motivation. You mentioned money, which she'll certainly understand. She will, however, wonder the obvious: Exactly which group will be paying you?"

I sat forward a bit, excited that Earl was on board. "Xychek. I believe I can persuade Chung to pay both a fee for Jasmine's return and another for helping him gain access to the new gate on Macken."

"So where do we start?" Earl said.

"I call Chung," I said. "I don't think he needs to know about your involvement at this stage, and on the chance that he turns me down, it's better for you if he never learns we met. Can you set up a private call from here?"

"Of course," Gustafson said. He tapped on the desk in front of him, murmured a few instructions and made some adjustments, then pointed me to a section of the wall at the far end of the table. One large panel showed a close-up of my face; the other glowed a soft, sleeping black. "The left is what he'll see. You'll view him on the right."

"Xychek tracks every call," I said, "so they'll be backtracking the moment we initiate. How long will I have before their software finds us?"

Gustafson and Earl looked at each other and smiled.

"Gunny," Gustafson said, "either you've been away longer than I thought, or you've forgotten a lot. First, do you think there's any chance we'd use less capable software than a corporation? Even if you do, do you honestly believe there's any chance I'd propose this call if I didn't know for damn sure that the line was secure?"

"My error, Top," I said. "I tend to be overly cautious."

"Fair enough," he said. "Do you want to call his direct number, which we have, or wade through the software flak catchers?"

"He might wonder where I got the number," I said, "but I see that as only good for me, so let's save the time. Call him."

The voice that answered was as perfectly appealing as the previous time I'd contacted Chung's office, and the face that went with it was so flawless it had to be a construct. "Mr. Chung's office," she/it said. "May I help you?"

"I'd like to speak to Mr. Chung," I said.

"As I'm sure you can appreciate," she—the construct was too gorgeous not to deserve the pronoun—said, "Mr. Chung receives a great many communications, so he asks us to handle them if we can. May I perhaps help you?" This was the same greeting as last time; apparently Xychek wasn't a slave to the current corporate "back to people" trend, in which a company demonstrated how successful it was by wasting money placing people in human-facing jobs that software could just as easily perform.

"No. Please tell Mr. Chung that he and I met on his recent outing and that I'm calling about Jasmine."

I didn't need to give any further instructions this time. Chung was clearly waiting for me to contact him, because he appeared within a few seconds. He was also better composed than last time, so he must've decided that I might have some value to him. That was good; negotiating is vastly easier when everyone involved starts out calm.

"Thank you for calling," he said. "When I last saw you, you said I'd get Jasmine back. I hope you're calling to explain how that will happen."

"Yes. I want you to know first, though, that if I had fully understood the situation I would never have taken her back to Slake."

I might be the only one who cared that I made that statement, but I had to make it, if only so I'd told him directly.

Chung's eyes, so much larger than life on the wall display, stared impassively at me. If I had looked only at them I might have believed he wasn't upset. The tension in his cheeks and the way he clipped his words when he finally spoke told me otherwise, and I admired his effort at control. "If you need me to make you feel better about what you did," he said, "and if that's what it takes to get my daughter back, I'll try." Even his eyes gave him away now. "What matters to me is getting her back."

"No," I said, "I don't want that. I'm not only going to return your daughter, I'm also going to get Xychek shared rights to the new gate on Macken." I leaned forward. "And you're going to help."

"How?"

"By cooperating, and by paying."

"So this is all about money after all?" he said.

"No," I said, "it's not, but money is a part of it."

He nodded. "Isn't it always? Tell me what you want me to do."

"He'll stick to the plan," I said after the call was over.

Earl nodded in agreement. "He's got the most to win, and almost nothing to lose. I agree."

"One more call," I said, "and you start this one: Vaccaro."

"She'll need to understand your role," Earl said, "and Lim's."

"Portray us as consultants and informers," I said, "as well as former Saw soldiers. Tell her whatever you think will work to get her involved, but make it clear that we can't risk attacking Slake directly on Macken. The only real evidence of any wrongdoing that we could produce is Jasmine Chung, and we don't want to give him any reason to dispose of her before we can find her."

"So you want me to sell her on this whole thing?" he said.

I laughed. "No, Colonel, I most definitely do *not* want you to try to sell her. With no offense intended, I've never considered sales your strong suit."

"Good," he said, "and for whatever it's worth, I'd only be offended if you did think sales was what I was best at."

"What I need you to do," I said, "is to let her know you vouch for us and that you're signed up for the plan that I'll then explain to her. I'll take care of the rest."

He turned to Gustafson. "Top, please take them outside for a few minutes. This will go a lot better if I don't have to worry about anyone else being in the room."

I considered protesting, because I hated not hearing what he said to Vaccaro, but I knew he'd be most comfortable talking to her alone. For this to work at all, I'd have to trust him at some point, so I figured I might as well start then.

Gustafson stood and motioned us to the door.

When Earl led us back into the room, Vaccaro's face was staring at us from the wall opposite the door. She was beautiful, a very different kind of beautiful than Lim but definitely beautiful. Thick blond hair framed an oval face with large blue eyes, a fine, straight nose, and perfectly shaped lips. Her skin shone with the whiteness of the Macken beaches. I might have misjudged Lim: Heavily engineered beauty might be the new corporate norm. I wondered if cosmetic software was refining her image or if her skin was really fine enough to appear this perfect at such large magnification. I forced myself to look away and composed my thoughts as Earl motioned to us to sit.

Vaccaro waited until we were all in chairs before she began. "Mr. Moore," she said, "Colonel Earl has given me a very brief update, but he's left the particulars to you. I'm listening." The voice that came out of the speakers warred with the image. Her tone was harsh, and her voice sounded far older than her face looked.

"We have an opportunity to tilt the balance of power in this region toward the Frontier Coalition," I said, "and in the process to make some money and even do some good. Kelco's been illegally buying arms from Osterlad, and it's also used kidnapping to stop Xychek from getting any new-aperture or commercial rights on Macken. With a little help from you and a bit more from the Saw, we can expose Kelco, return the kidnap victim, and open the rights to the new aperture."

"So far you've painted a picture I'd love if I worked for Xychek, but I don't. I work for the Frontier Coalition."

"Jose Chung has agreed to back a proposal for a peacekeeping force on Macken and for Coalition forces to monitor and tax the shared gate access for a period of time you two will need to iron out. When we prove what Slake and Kelco have done, they'll have no choice but to back this offer and pay their part of the bill or risk losing all rights on Macken. Any other choice would put them in direct conflict with both you and Xychek, and that would ultimately be both very expensive and destructive for everyone."

"What do you need from me to make this happen?" she said.

"Almost nothing. In a few days, Kelco is due to seal the deal for the gate rights on Macken. I assume the Coalition will have someone present to witness the signing."

"Of course. We'll do more than witness it, however. We'll verify that both corporations have agreed to the arrangement, approve the language and limits of the agreement, and so on."

I reminded myself never to use a term like "witness" with a government official. Bureaucrats, even the highest-ranking ones, always need to inflate their roles in any activity. "Attend the meeting personally," I said, then added "please" as her eyes narrowed slightly. "Please also demand that Slake and Chung appear there, so you three can discuss, oh, I don't know, important issues concerning future uses of the new aperture, their firms' recent complaints to the Saw—any agenda worthy of a long in-person meeting involving the three of you. I just need you to get everyone together and keep them there for a day and a night."

"Easy enough," she said. "What else?"

"If this works, the Saw either gets the contract for the force on Macken or has the first right to subcontract it."

"Colonel Earl already explained that part," she said. "As our existing partner in this region, the Saw would be our natural first choice in any case."

"That's it," I said.

"What do you want from the Saw?" she asked.

"I lack the level of expertise that you and the colonel possess when it comes to your agreements with the corporations in this region," I said, trying to use the type of indirect bureaucratic discourse I normally find distasteful, "but I believe this is a discussion you might do best to allow to occur without you."

She laughed. "Of course. I can't see a reason in the world I'd want to join former comrades-in-arms talking shop." She turned slightly to look at Earl. "I'm sure the colonel and I will be speaking again soon."

"As often as necessary, of course," he said.

She nodded, and the wall blanked.

"What's next?" Earl said.

"Lim has to run the lead team on the ground in Macken," I said. I looked at her. "I owe her, and more importantly she'll have more freedom for some types of action than your troops can officially possess."

He thought for a moment. "Under my command," he said.

"No," Lim said. "I don't work for you."

"I'm certainly not putting my troops under your command," he said.

"We all agree to a plan in advance," I said, "and each of us runs our parts of it independently." I turned to Lim. "If the wings come off, all of us, and I do include myself, defer to Earl, because the Saw's the official power here." I turned back to Earl. "But only if the wings come off. If the plan stays within specs, we operate as equals." I pushed back slightly from the table so I could easily watch them both. "Deal?"

Neither spoke. Neither looked at the other. Gustafson studied some dust on his trousers.

"Yes," Earl said, finally breaking the silence, "that's reasonable."

"Deal," Lim said.

"So what do you really want from the Saw?" Earl said.

"I assume your troops here have trained for work in all elements, including the ocean," I said.

"Of course," Earl said, sounding a little put out, "or haven't you noticed the amount of water on this planet?"

"Does the Saw still provide vacation transport for troops on R&R?"

He nodded. "Though only on existing shuttle routes, as always."

"To Macken?"

"When the Coalition needs us to run FC staff or supplies there, we provide protective transport."

"It's a shame about your transport repair team," I said.

"They're the best in the business," Earl said, "as you should know. Those soldiers are—"

I held up my hand to cut him off. "It's a shame," I said, "that they've been so busy that none of the smaller shuttles are operational right now, and that you're having to fly big ships on even the small routes for the next few days. I expect some of your pilots will be complaining publicly about having to take big tugs on every single run, even the hops to little planets like Macken."

Earl smiled. "I expect they will," he said. "Tell me more."

CHAPTER
TWENTY-SIX

Gustafson's conservative civilian dress—working pants and standard business shirt, both in muted browns and perfectly laundered, his gig line ramrod straight—screamed undercover trouble to the crowd at Strange Kitty. A third of the customers lost interest in shopping and fled out the front door as we walked slowly to the back of the store. By the time we reached the warehouse entrance, it was locked and blocked, four security guards backing the same small, nervous salesman I'd met before.

"May I help you?" he said. I had to give him credit: He acted as if we'd never met, his eyes showing no obvious signs of recognition. I hadn't gone into the details of my recon of Chung's estate in my briefing of Earl and Gustafson, so I had no reason to reveal my past Strange Kitty business now.

"I believe so," I said. "We're interested in assisted ocean sports, specifically in the racing rays I saw in the rather large tanks just before the aviary. My understanding is that ray racing is an increasingly popular sport."

"It is indeed," he said. "We've augmented the rays for both surface and underwater races, though most of our clients prefer the underwater variety."

"As do I. I'm looking for one creature with enough power to easily handle a rider weight of as much as a hundred and fifty kilos, and I also want top-notch speed and control."

I caught his odd look at me.

"Several of us will be sharing the ray," I said, "and some of my friends are very large." Gustafson coughed as he fought to suppress a chuckle. I reminded myself, as I'd already done many times since he and I had met outside Strange Kitty, never to try to pass him as a civilian again. "We plan to race strictly underwater. Surface breathing ability isn't at all important to us, nor is price." I paused a moment to make the point, then realized with a guy this adept I was wasting time; he'd caught the hint the moment I made it. "Speed augmentations, on the other hand, interest us greatly. We're not planning to participate in any sanctioned races, so I don't care whether we stay within stock specs."

"We're certainly capable of meeting the highest hobbyist demands," he said, "but you must understand that there are fines for using out-of-spec creatures in official competitions."

"I do, but as I said before, we have absolutely no intention of entering any such races."

He bowed slightly. "Very good. I'm sure we can help you. Other than racing augmentations, is there anything else you'd like?"

"Yes," I said. "Two things. First, we're planning some travel, so any modifications you could make to help the ray thrive in other seas would be most useful."

"Easy enough," he said. "We've yet to encounter an ocean our gill adaptations can't handle. Of course, you'd be responsible for dealing with the local animal import authorities on each planet and for complying with all local regulations. We don't ship off-planet."

"We'd take full responsibility, of course, for all the relevant licenses," I said.

"And the second thing?"

"A tank, one suitable for long-distance and off-planet transport."

"As you'd expect," he said, "we have such tanks, but with the size of the rays—their wingspans run to two meters, so each needs a tank at least three meters wide—and their desire to move almost constantly, any such tank would be extremely expensive."

"As I said, price doesn't matter."

He smiled. "When would you like the ray and the tank?"

"I need you to deliver both in the morning. I'll also want you to conduct a brief training session with me at the drop-off."

For the first time, my salesman showed alarm. "With so little time, we could get you only the best of our in-stock rays," he said.

"Fine."

"We could not, however, build you a tank."

"Aren't any of your in-store tanks suitable for my purposes?"

"Of course," he said, "several are, but they're in use, and freeing them would be difficult, time-consuming, and—"

"Expensive," I finished for him. "We're happy to pay for your inconvenience. Our timetable, however, is not flexible."

The salesman smiled again, no longer alarmed. "Let me work up something for you." He headed into the back, two security men parting just long enough to let him through the door.

While we waited, I showed Gustafson some of the racing rays. Magnificent creatures, the largest were wider than I was tall, their sleek bodies a dark purple color that would vanish in the depths of Lankin's oceans. Light-blue fluorescent lines along their backs gave the impression of small fish moving through the water, a tactic that helped them lure prey. At their turns at the ends of the tanks I occasionally caught glimpses of tow cord jacks and metal receptor webs woven among the skin cells around their heads. I also spotted a pair of additional ports of some type I didn't recognize. Given how good my experience with the birds had been and the number of mods I could spot on these rays, I was confident that the best of Strange Kitty's stock would be more than adequate for my purposes.

"I've always preferred working with machines," Gustafson whispered. "Even the worst of the AIs is less likely to flake on you than an organic."

"We've been through this," I said.

"It's your ass," he said.

"Yes," I said, "it is."

We studied the rays some more. Gustafson walked alongside one that was moving languidly down the tank, its body undulating slowly and gracefully. Their faces were at once fierce and impenetrable, clearly not human and yet teasingly familiar, as if with the tiniest bit more understanding we could fathom the minds behind them.

"I have to admit it," Gustafson said. "They are beautiful, in the way that any well-designed machine is beautiful. They give the impression of caged energy begging for release. Quite hypnotic."

Our salesman found us and handed me a display with a detailed quote glowing beneath a Strange Kitty logo. "This should cover everything," he said, "including tax, delivery, on-site training tomorrow morning, and loading into the cargo carrier of your choice."

Without even checking the total I handed the quote to Gustafson. "Sold," I said. "My friend will take care of this." I admired the rays a bit more, their undulating motion both lovely and menacing. A useless question sprang to mind, and I indulged myself. "Does the ray you're considering for us have a name?"

"As I assumed you understood, all ray control is via electrical impulses from a remote. They don't respond to names."

"I understand. I'm just curious what you call the one we're purchasing."

The salesman tilted his head and gave me the largest smile I'd seen in a while. "Bob."

"Perfect!" I said. "We'll keep the name."

Gustafson finished studying the details of the quote. He couldn't stop shaking his head. "He's going to kill me," he said as he handed back the quote and pulled out his wallet.

I clapped him on the back. "Nonsense," I said. "I'm sure our friend will love Bob."

It was Gustafson's turn to laugh. My discomfort at being in a private's blues must have been obvious, because every time he caught sight of me he turned away quickly to cover a chuckle. Wearing the outfit was bad enough—I'd hoped to never again put on a Saw uniform—but being marked as a private, well below my old rank, hit a nerve I didn't know I still had. I'd worked hard to earn the stripes I once wore, and not having them on my sleeves made me feel I'd lost ground. The uniform was necessary, however, because by working as a crewman on the *Hathi*, the largest of the Saw's matériel carriers stationed near Lankin, I attracted no attention from the Kelco and Xychek security people who we had to assume were monitoring the Saw launch facility. The well-leaked breakdown of the smaller personnel carriers covered our use of the *Hathi* for the R&R run to Macken.

Lobo rode inside the shell of a large dirt mover the Saw was delivering for the FC. Bob's tank sat inside Lobo, and Bob swam to and fro in his tank. The ray in the tank in the PCAV in the mover in the transport: It struck me as a chain of key words from the sort of children's story Earl might make up for his kids—if he could ever bring himself to have children, and if he could overcome his reaction to what Bob and the tank had cost. Gustafson would be sharing tales of that reaction, which I gathered had involved equal measures of amazement and obscenity, with other noncoms over drinks for years to come.

I had to hand it to Earl, though: He was a resourceful manager. He was already getting back some of the mission's cost by transporting the dirt mover for the FC, which he'd convinced to pay secure-cargo rates on the grounds that anything as powerful as the dirt mover was a potential weapon. The huge mechanical beast was hollow now, its main chassis a shell hiding Lobo, but once we hit Macken and smuggled Lobo out of it, some of the "vacationing" Saw troops who were actually transport mechanics would reassemble the giant construction machine.

As we closed on the Lankin gate I made my way to a private viewing lounge for a better look. The *Hathi* shared the spare design, emphasis on functionality, and drab gray color of every Saw transport I'd ever ridden. Stay in any one area, and you'd have no way to tell if you were on a platoon shuttle or a major freight hauler. The five-meter-wide window in the viewing lounge was a rare exception, added, I'd heard, to appease the FC dignitaries the Saw had to transport from time to time. Though *Hathi* was huge, she wasn't slow: In the few minutes I stood in the lounge, the Lankin gate grew from a purple speck barely visible in the distance to an enormous pretzel of grape-colored aperture frames and connective pieces, the whole gate a humbling construct reeking of otherness.

Gustafson appeared at my shoulder. "Always amazing, aren't they?" he said.

"Yeah," I said, "I never tire of looking at the gates. They're like the oceans or the forests on a new planet, before any of us arrive to mess them up: inhuman yet usable by humans, awe-inspiring, somehow beyond us." I thought about the unspoiled beaches of Macken and the construction happening along them. "Too bad no ocean or forest ever proves to be beyond us for long. Give us enough time and let enough of us go after it, and we can shape, mold, change, or destroy anything nature can create."

"Except the gates," he said.

"Except the gates." I turned to look at him. "Of course, we don't know if nature created them."

"Don't tell me you're a Gatist," he said. "Do I need to leave you alone to worship?"

I laughed. "Hardly. I don't have any idea whether some god or nature or even aliens we've never found created the gates, and for the most part I don't care. What matters most to me is that they *are* and they *work*, in the same way that the rest of the universe exists and works. It does, and that's good enough for me."

We both stared again at the parts of the gate we could see; we were far too close now to be able to make out the whole thing. Each twist in the pretzel was thicker than Lobo was long, and most of the apertures dwarfed even the ships of *Hathi*'s size. I couldn't tell the Macken aperture from any of the others, but when we settled into line behind a small Kelco transport it was clear we were on our final trajectory toward the gate. Intellectually I understood that we were moving under control, gravity systems working, everything smooth, but for an instant I felt almost as if I were falling, falling through the gate into Macken, into conflict, into whatever that conflict would bring. Once you've been on a few missions, you realize that no matter how well you plan, you're never in total control.

"Can you remember," I said, "how you thought it would be when you first signed on, before you'd actually been in the field?"

"Of course," he said. "I make it a practice to remember my stupidest moments, so I can avoid repeating them."

"And then you go on the mission, and if you're lucky enough to make it back you learn the truth," I said, "or at least you learn the truth of your own experience and reactions."

"Or you die," he said, "or you go crazier than the rest of us because you can't find any other way to cope."

I nodded, then waved my hand at the aperture growing before us. "Yet here we are again," I said.

"Yeah, here we are." Gustafson clapped me on the back and headed out.

The aperture slowly grew larger in the viewport, as the ships in front of us took turns vanishing into it, each replaced in alternation by a vessel coming the other way, a procession of humanity passing from one strange place to another via a mechanism they might never understand, men and women jumping into their futures with absolutely no way to see what those futures held for them, and then it was our turn.

CHAPTER TWENTY-SEVEN

We landed on Macken far up the coast from Glen's Garden, at a construction site a few klicks north of the spot that had hosted the fireworks display I'd seen and that sat well away from any current settlements. The Saw team quickly and efficiently unloaded the dirt mover and its hidden passengers. I ducked into Lobo to grab a handgun, a small carry-pack of supplies, and a comm hookup we'd need in the next stages of the mission.

"How do you like Bob?" I said, regretting the flip question almost as soon as I asked it.

"He's lovely company," Lobo said. "The frequent bubbles, the constant motion, and the accompanying gentle waves in the tank: What more could a being of my intelligence and firepower want from a companion?"

"We'll be working soon enough," I said. "I have to go."

"I so enjoy these little chats," Lobo said. "It's the quality of our time together that matters, not the quantity."

If I came out of this mission alive and well paid, I was definitely going to look into the cost of customizing Lobo's emotive software.

Next stop for us was the terminal at Glen's Garden, which we reached via one of *Hathi*'s personnel shuttles. The shuttle dropped us and headed straight back; it would be in *Hathi* and on the way home to Lankin within an hour. I split from the Saw troops and changed out of my uniform at the terminal, then grabbed a taxi to the rental agency I'd used before.

Enough had happened since I'd been here last that I expected the town to have changed, but of course it hadn't; less than a month had elapsed. The town was the same sleepy oceanfront village I'd left. I was pleased to learn that my previous rental agreement had barely expired and the house was still available. I paid for two weeks, the minimal rental period, and set out to find some food.

The streets were wide and quiet, the air warm and lazy and rich with salt and ocean smells, the sky clear, another quiet coastal town on another perfect coastal afternoon. Each time I visit such a place, I find myself relaxing, my pulse and my pace slowing until I realize I'm doing almost nothing at all. The longer I stay, the more I wonder why I don't simply settle down and enjoy life.

That question nagged me for decades, until I finally had the time and money to try it. After a few months, I drifted into work, never really intending to go back to it but doing so nonetheless. The nature of most of the jobs I take is that, like my seemingly simple rescue of Jasmine, they turn complicated and frequently end up causing me to have to relocate. Now, I enjoy these towns each time I visit one, but I know I'll never be able to stay for very long.

I navigated the streets by following the noise, an approach that's never failed me in party towns—and beach towns are almost always party towns. Soon enough, I found a corner bar, shutters open on three sides to let in the air, the building spilling music and laughter and conversation into the intersection it faced. A singer on a small stool in the back played a guitar and sang ballads with an accent so foreign to me and so thick I couldn't understand his words. The rest of the noise drowned him out, but he labored away gamely. Every now and then, the credit gauge he'd set on the floor would light up as someone sent him a tip. I made my way past a clump of locals, five Saw off-duty troops still in uniform, three more soldiers not in uniform but easy to spot by the way they moved and their tendency to hang near the uniformed group, and a handful of Kelco security people wearing identifying tags. I did my best to let them all get a good look at me before I forced myself onto the end of the bar nearest the street.

When I finally gained the bartender's attention, I ordered the special dinner and some water, then leaned against the wall so I could watch in all directions. As I expected, the special proved to be a fish sandwich. I was pleasantly surprised at how good it was, warm and tasty despite being greasier than I typically prefer. I chewed slowly and kept my face to the crowd, giving plenty of people all the time they could use to study me but also scanning the many faces at the same time. If the Kelco security team was on the lookout for me and their staffers in this bar were at all competent, they'd spot me. If they failed to notice me, I had to hope they were monitoring property rentals and would find me that way.

After I finished eating, I headed into the street for a stroll. I stayed on roads with plenty of other pedestrians, and I kept a suitable distance from all of them. I figured the Kelco staffers couldn't have known about my presence long enough to have set up any kind of snatch they could execute in a public place, but at the same time my experience on Bekin's Deal reminded me that they could surprise me.

One of the main streets, Wharf, ended at a largely ornamental wharf with only a few small boats moored at it. A four-deep crowd clung to the sides of the road as flying autocams recorded whatever they were watching, so I eased closer for a look. Vaccaro, Barnes, and Slake were walking the street, ostensibly talking and reviewing the progress of construction in town, more likely simply creating media moments that showed the locals that their government and corporate leaders were working hard for them. I suppose there must have been an era in which it was so difficult to get information about how organizations really functioned that people fell for these staged shows of management at work, but I couldn't imagine such a time. Everyone knew what was going on, but for no reason I could understand the chance to see the FC leader for this region of space working hand-in-hand with the head of the only large corporation with a serious local presence was still enough to draw some people away from their homes and jobs. The three bureaucrats would spend the evening providing a good show for the public, then eat in the main municipal building's private dining room. They'd all spend the night there, because Vaccaro had provided entertainment and insisted they make a long, bonding night of it.

I was glad Vaccaro was making her presence public, because it smoothed the cover story. I also needed her to keep Slake away from his house; it wouldn't be good for the FC if anything happened to him while I went after Jasmine. Other than those interests, however, I had no reason to care about Vaccaro's actions at this stage, and I didn't want Barnes, Slake, or any of their people to get spooked, so I strolled away down a side street.

Night was coming on, the sky purpling and the temperature dropping. As soon as I'd wandered a couple of blocks from Wharf, I grabbed a taxi to my rental house. I'd hoped going there might feel like coming home, somehow relaxing or soothing, but instead it was more like returning to the scene of a crime. Before I got out of the taxi I ordered it to go off-road—at an extra fee, of course, such charges being a common way to gouge new-world tourists for a little extra money—and circle the house. I didn't spot anyone in the building or for as far as I could see around it, even when I cranked up my vision to include IR, but I was still concerned; I'd been here long enough now that Kelco should have been on to me.

I paid the taxi, sent it back, and walked to the side of the house farthest from town and closest to the forest. I stood close to the wall and tuned in to the machines inside. The washers were, as usual, chattering away nonstop. Vaccaro's visit had already made an impression on them, because apparently Barnes had instructed his staff to show up in their dress best, launder every piece of fabric Vaccaro might see or touch, and so on. The washers sang the praises of this special work. Instead of going with the usual rough settings, the users chose the gentlest options for their good clothes, and those options were vastly more interesting to the washers. I suppose that information might come in handy should I ever want to spoil a washing machine with kindness, but it didn't help me right then. I gave up on the washers and tried the other kitchen appliances, but they also had nothing of value to say. As best I could tell from them and the washers, the house had stood empty since my last night in it, and they were all quite bored.

I checked the lighting control system next. It was complaining about the two men who'd visited the house less than half an hour ago. Apparently, these two callous souls had turned on only a few lights and hadn't even touched the options on the viewing window, depriving the lighting system of any chance to strut its stuff. The control complex sulked, both disappointed and annoyed. More importantly, the lighting controller had been forced to deal with minor electrical disruptions caused by some work the men had done on the front door.

Kelco had behaved as I'd expected, which was good. The problem now was that I wasn't sure what those men had done to the house. I could simply leave, but then I wouldn't know their intent. I wanted to understand whether they were out to capture me again or to kill me, because the difference would matter later. To know which it was I needed to either look at what they'd installed or trigger it remotely. The house's security system covered the doors and windows, so those were out as possible entries. The floors and ceilings lacked any motion sensors or other protection, so I could easily use some nanomachines to create a hole in the floor and climb inside, but if the Kelco visitors had left any motion-activated grenades, something I certainly would have done in this situation as a backup for any door-linked explosives, then those would go off the moment I set foot in the house.

I settled for remote activation. It wouldn't yield as much information as entering the place, but the data I would get would have to do. I liked this house, so I hoped they weren't planning to kill me, because if they were they'd probably blow up the whole thing. I'd left almost all the weapons on Lobo; all I had with me was the small projectile handgun. I paced about twenty meters from the front of the building toward the beach, crouched, took aim at the door handle, and fired, one round at a time. I was out of practice, so the first few shots thwacked into the door and the walls around it, missing the handle entirely. I made a mental note to practice my handgun shooting if this all ended well. Then I got the range and started hitting near the handle. I did enough damage that on the sixth shot the door swung inward.

As the door opened, the entry hall visibly filled with a milky cloud of gas. I hadn't heard the release mechanism, but my ears were still adjusting from the sound of the gunshots so that was no surprise. The room grew cloudier, and some of the gas floated out the front door. I left the gun and ran to the edge of the ocean, in case I needed to seek cover, but the gas dissipated quickly.

I couldn't know for sure without taking the risk of exposing myself to the gas, something I was unwilling to do even though the nanomachines might have been able to handle it, but the fact that the men seeking me had used gas instead of explosives strongly suggested they wanted to capture me again. Good; for a change I agreed with Slake on something: I wanted Kelco to want me alive.

I didn't, however, want them to capture me now, and I had to assume they were on their way. I retrieved my gun and headed into the woods. As soon as I was a few meters in, I called Lobo.

"It's so nice to hear from you, Jon," he answered. "Bob and I are having a lovely time waiting in orbit."

"Not now," I said. "I'm in motion and facing possible attack. Slake's men must be on the way. Do you have my position?" I jogged as we talked, heading into the woods on a rough diagonal line away from the house.

"Yes." Lobo's tone shifted instantly to pure work, all sarcasm gone.

"Do you have the coordinates for the place I waited for the Gardeners the night I went after Jasmine?"

"Yes."

"Scan it—"

Lobo interrupted me. "The satellite I'm using shows the area clear under visible light and IR checks, and there's no signal activity of any type."

"How does its IR signature compare to that of the surrounding area?"

"No difference. If I didn't already know its coordinates, I wouldn't spot it on IR."

I'd assumed the pit would have changed to a normal profile for the area in the time since I was in it, but I wanted to be sure. "Direct me to it. Use an evasive course."

I continued jogging, moving more slowly among the trees and through the light undergrowth than I would have liked. Lobo gave me course corrections as necessary. The pit was far enough into the woods that there was little likelihood Slake's men would find me there.

When I reached it, I took a rope from my pack, tied it around the same tree the Gardeners had leaned against when I'd confronted them, and lowered myself into the hole. I pulled a nearly transparent insulating cloth from my pack, wrapped it around my torso, and sat in a corner of the pit. "How's my IR profile, Lobo?"

"Almost invisible," he said. "On the best imaging the satellite can provide all I can see is a spot so small I'd take it for a large rodent. It's nothing anyone would investigate."

"Good," I said. "I'm going to stay here and rest until I need to leave to meet you at the rendezvous point. Wake me in six and a half hours. Until then, monitor the surrounding area, and alert me if you see any activity."

"As if I would do anything else," he said.

Back to the sarcasm. Great.

"Jon," Lobo continued, "why do you waste time during missions asking questions to which you already know the answers?"

Our start time was less than eight hours away, so I wasn't in the mood for this. "Why are we having this discussion?"

"Because," he said, "you asked me if I knew your position when we'd already agreed I would track you." With no emotion that I could discern coloring his words, he continued. "You asked if I knew the coordinates to this pit, when you know I never delete mission logs. You asked me to plot an evasive course, when you know I would automatically do that when you're under pursuit and the pursuers are still far enough away to make that an effective strategy. You asked me to scan this area and alert you to any intruders, when you know I do that automatically per our previous discussions."

I thought about what he was saying. To my chagrin, he was right.

"I was wasting time," I said. "I could and should have realized everything you said." I've worked with many different individuals and groups in the past, and even in the Saw I was never able to fully trust anyone else to protect me. I always trusted exactly as much as the mission demanded, and never more. Whenever I could put safety nets and double-checking procedures in place, I did. "The only way I can stop myself from asking those questions," I told him as I realized it myself, "is to trust you, and I've never been good at trust."

"Given my nature," Lobo said, still with no emotion in his voice, "trust would be the most efficient option."

"You're right," I said. "I'll work on it."

"Good," he said.

This time, I could swear there was a note of petulance in Lobo's single-word response, and I found it both annoying and oddly reassuring.

Night had settled in. The forest played a symphony that blended small animal sounds with the soft swishes of branches and leaves moving in the gentle breeze. The old light from distant stars brightened the sky, and for a moment I felt old myself, back again in a place I never sought but all too frequently found, in a jungle waiting to go into battle. I hadn't consciously intended to join this fight, at least not initially, when all I thought I was doing was rescuing a girl in trouble, but whatever my motivations had been, I had to accept that my own actions had led me to this point.

I pushed aside those thoughts and focused on the plan. I could analyze the past all I wanted when this was over, but right now I needed to rest and make sure I could perform my role as well as Lobo was performing his. Whatever I did, the night would deepen, the time to go to work would come, and I'd either follow the plan or . . . or what? I couldn't even conceive of not trying to make this situation right, so there was no point in pretending to consider alternatives. Nor was there any value in punishing myself about what I might have done. I was here now.

What I would do next was all that mattered, and what I would do next was rescue Jasmine and make this whole mess better—or die or get captured in the attempt. Regardless of how it all turned out, I knew that as surely as Lobo could not forget the coordinates of this pit, I could do nothing else but try my best to succeed.

CHAPTER TWENTY-EIGHT

As I waited near the water for Lobo, I soaked in the magic of the night. Oceans transform under starlight and reveal their true power and mystery; daylight paints them as less than they are, as friendly and understandable creatures we humans might one day tame. The illusions of daytime vanished as I watched the black waves sprinting to shore and listened to them crash into the land. For a brief time, I felt I was comprehending at last the full extent of a gigantic alien beast, its shape and power normally beyond my ability to discern. Clouds covered Macken's moons and obscured almost all of the starlight, so the water undulated in darkness, bits of soft gray here and there marking the moving surface. I leaned against a tree barely a meter inside the forest line a couple klicks up the beach from my rental house and stared as if hypnotized at the ocean. For as far back as I can remember, oceans have held a special power over me, and I never tire of watching them.

A pair of blinking red lights up the beach to my left interrupted my reverie. The lights approached at high speed and in a rapid forest-to-beach-to-forest pattern, as if running toward the water, finding it too scary, and jumping back to the trees, over and over. Under the sound of the ocean I heard the low roar of Lobo skimming with baffled jets along the sand.

"I see you," I said. "ETA?"

"Ten seconds."

"Ready."

Lobo cut the running lights as he pulled beside my position and opened a portal. I ran in, and he closed the door and headed back the way he'd come.

"Surveillance?" I said.

"Nothing from the sats," Lobo said, "because Kelco doesn't yet have monitoring rights to the planet."

I realized I'd been wrong when I'd told Barnes that delaying the Kelco contract for a month would do no good: The FC had taken advantage of the delay to limit Kelco's satellite surveillance capabilities, and those limits were now helping me.

"The house, though, is another story," Lobo said. "Security personnel and portable sentries are monitoring its perimeter and exchanging reports on randomly changing frequencies with more encryption than we have time to break."

"Anything different on the ocean side?"

"No," Lobo said.

We ran about twenty klicks up the beach and shot across the water, flying low enough that waves were splashing Lobo's hull. Without sat coverage, we should be invisible to Kelco. "Show me," I said.

Lobo opened a display with a map of the shoreline and the ocean, the house at the shore's center. A wavy but roughly semicircular line with the house at its center and a radius of a little over fifteen thousand meters stretched from the shore on either side of the house into the ocean. The semicircle contained hundreds of red and purple dots. The red dots marked sensors from which Lobo or his sat friend had detected transmissions; the purple ones denoted intelligent mobile mines working in a redundant grid to stay roughly in line despite the ocean currents.

"The sensors' transmission intervals have shortened," Lobo said, "so they've definitely tightened their security."

"As we expected," I said. "Lim and Earl?"

"Both have checked in and are moving into position per the plan."

I inspected Bob's tank. He swam back and forth, with no more apparent concern for the future than when the Strange Kitty team had delivered him. They'd again proven to be professional in all areas: The new tanks on either side of his head matched his body perfectly.

"It's our turn," I said. "Give me ten minutes to change and check the gear, then take us to the drop point."

"One minute to drop," Lobo said.

Though the combat dive suit was as flexible and thin as modern technology could manage while offering some minimal armoring, it was still warmer than I'd have preferred for land work. It covered me completely, a tight mottled black and gray shroud that blended perfectly with the nighttime water and provided reasonable camouflage on land as long as I stayed to the shadows. My eyes and the skin around them were visible when I lessened the tinting on the built-in mask, but I could run with it almost totally black and use the mask's night- and IR-vision facilities to navigate. The suit and mask sacrificed some processing power for thinness and the ability to function underwater, but not much; it maintained a full comm link with Lobo, and all I needed of the mission profile resided in the suit's local storage. The small air-processing tubes and the backup tanks were also built into the suit, the air-processors running on either side of my neck and the tanks along my back, so I presented as little water resistance as possible. Some drag was, of course, unavoidable, because I bulged from the dive weights and the waterproof cases holding the weapons: the rifle on my back, the pistols strapped to my thighs, and the knives belted to my calves. Carrying the extra weight would slow me, but only a little, and I was happy to pay the minimal speed penalty to have them. The remote for Bob was so small I didn't count it.

"Five seconds," Lobo said. "Opening."

A hatch slid aside in front of me, and I jumped feet-first into the darkness. I hit the water almost immediately; Lobo had flown as low as I could have wanted. I treaded water, fighting the dive weight I'd later jettison, and watched with night vision as Lobo, the side door already closed, rolled upside down. A hatch opened in his top; then the lid of Bob's tank slid back, and Bob fell a meter or so into the ocean. Lobo's hatch closed, and he accelerated away from me, righting as he went.

I gave Bob thirty seconds to acclimate himself to the Macken ocean and stretch out, then summoned him. He'd run farther than I'd expected; it took him over twenty seconds to reach me. He bumped my feet gently, then went a bit deeper and circled my position lazily, the blue lines on his back giving the impression of a small school of fish swimming slowly beneath me.

I dove to Bob and grabbed the rider handles hanging on cables from the mounts on his back. With the handles I directed him down to about three meters and oriented us toward the midpoint of the Kelco house's security arc. After making sure my grip was secure, I used the remote to tell Bob to go.

True to his racing training, Bob shot forward quickly and accelerated for several seconds before he settled into a pace far faster than any human could swim without assistance. With IR-detection cranked way up I watched his powerful wings flap in the water. Riding above and slightly behind him, seeing his wings work and feeling the rush of the ocean against my body as we sped through it, I realized I was smiling and having a wonderful time, all the cares of the mission washing away for a few seconds in which I was flying, in the water but still flying, the primal rush of moving at high speed joining with the inevitable juice you get when you move fast in darkness. It was an absolutely wonderful experience. I understood the appeal of ray racing now; maybe I'd try it again if all of this went well.

We came to a section of the reef that paralleled the coastline on most of this side of the continent, and the ocean burst into life below us. With IR I saw fish in all directions, hundreds of them, maybe thousands, sea creatures of so many different sizes and shapes I couldn't even begin to log the varieties, all schooling through rock and coral and plants large and small. If I switched to the normal light spectrum, most of the fish disappeared, but here and there schools of glowing bodies moved in the watery darkness like light beams magically slowed in space and available for close inspection, almost but not quite within reach. I alternated the views a few times, then settled on IR as we passed over and beyond the reef, the life below us rapidly thinning and then vanishing. The only creatures visible now were the occasional larger fish keeping to the depths, eager to stay away from the huge intruder speeding above them.

An alarm chimed as we drew within fifty meters of the nearest of the Kelco sensors, and a representation of this section of the sensor line appeared in my display. From the data Lobo was able to gather about the sensors and the information Gustafson had provided us about current milspec tech, we estimated the upper limit of the effective sensor range to be thirty or so meters. Past that, they'd be able to discern at most movement and provide at best some rough IR images. None of that data should cause me any trouble, because Bob's profile and my position relative to him created the impression of a very large sea creature or at least something odd—but nothing that resembled an attack team or ship.

I stopped Bob at about forty meters out and used the breather's exhaust to let some saliva into the water. I set the nanomachines in the saliva to the task of replicating from the water for a little over a minute, then sent the new mass toward the sensors. Unless we'd misinterpreted the data badly, the sensors were maintaining their approximate relative positions via tiny water jets and making gentle coordinate adjustments as necessary based on data from others in the communicating grid. I'd instructed the nanomachines to disassemble and repurpose anything metal they touched, then use the resulting larger mass to dispatch more swarms left and right in search of additional metal. I'd given them instructions to disassemble as much as possible themselves and stop operation after fifteen minutes, more than enough time for them to do what I wanted.

I turned Bob left and started him moving in slow, easy circles about twenty meters in diameter, just another large fish out for a swim. If the Kelco security team monitoring the sensors spotted us, they'd at least have to wonder why we were taking our time in the water, swimming to and fro with no apparent destination.

In my display the sensor closest to me vanished, leaving a break in Kelco's security line; the nanomachines had reached it and done their job. I kept Bob moving in the same pattern but now risked a call to Lobo. "Confirm sensor loss," I said. I needed to make sure the data my suit provided was reliable and not hacked or fed to me by Kelco.

"Confirmed," Lobo said, his voice clear on the encrypted channel. "Continue holding."

The last bit was our backup protocol; if Lobo hadn't added it, I would have known someone else had compromised the communication. The technique is simple and ancient, but sometimes an old method is the right way to go.

Two more sensors and a pair of mines winked out in my display. The hole in the Kelco line was now almost forty meters wide. The lost sensors would definitely grab Kelco's attention. I changed Bob's course so we angled toward the sensor-free area. The route kept us more than thirty meters away from both of the two nearest sensors as we slowly drew closer to where some of the disassembled devices had floated only moments before.

Two more sensors and multiple mines disappeared from my display. The hole was now almost sixty meters wide. The edges of the line now extended past the range of my suit's sensors, so I had to risk getting live data from Lobo. I opened my comm link. "Lobo," I said, "switch to feeds."

The first one—a complete image of the line with the size of the hole indicated on the display—appeared a few seconds later. We'd agreed that Lobo would send me updates on a quasi-random basis centered on a ten-second update interval. To confuse matters further, he emitted a wide-beam broadcast that swept over a three-hundred-meter-wide area.

My display flashed a new update: The hole in the sensor line measured over eighty meters wide.

"Lobo," I said, "what can you read around the house?" Kelco had shielded the house so it yielded little to remote visual or IR probes, but we could still check the surrounding area and, of course, monitor the level of transmission activity; we'd already learned that the place served as a communications hub for Slake.

"Additional people have left the house and deployed to various locations along the water and around the perimeter of the grounds," he said. As he spoke, an aerial IR view of the place appeared on my display. A couple dozen red dots spread around the building. A large red splotch sat in the middle of the landing facility. "Transmission levels between the sensors and the house have increased. They know something's up and are trying to learn what. I see no transmissions in your area at this time."

"What's the ship in the landing area?" I said.

"The IR signature is inconclusive," Lobo said, "as are the visible-frequency images the sat has provided. The available data suggest a midsize corporate near-space fighter, probably four times my size and significantly more heavily armed and shielded than I. Whatever it is, it appears to be squatting hot, ready to run."

From what I'd seen on Wharf I had reason to believe Vaccaro had managed to keep Slake off-site. The ship could be for his security team to use for air defense, or it could be an escape vehicle. Either way, it wasn't a factor we'd anticipated. Fortunately, the ship's size and Lobo's guess suggested it wasn't built for air-to-ground work, so as long as they didn't use it to take away Jasmine, it shouldn't cause us any problems. "How many people are stationed near the ship?" I asked.

"None we can spot with the available imaging," Lobo said.

"The rest of the team will have to watch it," I said.

"Already warned," Lobo said.

I had no more questions. I felt a rush of adrenaline as I realized we were done with the preliminaries. It was time to go in.

I steered Bob to the center of the sensor hole on my display. From here on, speed of approach was vital, because if I gave Slake's men time they'd train monitoring gear on this area and get a solid fix on me. With Bob's remote I checked the booster tanks; both showed operational. According to the Strange Kitty trainer who'd shown me how to use them, the tanks were the latest in racing ray speed mods. They coupled a rapid increase in blood oxygen levels in Bob—courtesy of a blend of nitrogen, oxygen, and some nerve-friendly trace chemicals they injected into his bloodstream—with direct electrical stimulation of Bob's neural system. The result was supposed to be a great increase in speed at minimal cost to Bob's health, as long as I didn't keep it running for more than a few minutes.

As we headed toward shore, I activated the booster tanks. Nothing happened for several seconds; then Bob's wings picked up speed and we accelerated. The force of the water against my face was strong enough even through the suit's mask that I turned my head downward to avoid the impact. Staring at the muscles in Bob's back in IR I saw the effect of the additional exertion as we shot through the water toward the house. That was all I could see. The sheer speed of our passage combined with the almost complete lack of any visible input to turn this into a joyride of such raw intensity that I whooped loudly and repeatedly inside my mask. I couldn't recall the last time a mission had included anything that was as much fun as riding with Bob. Most of my mind knew I was headed into a dangerous situation, and the primitive part of me had responded with a liberal injection of adrenaline. At the same time, some of those very same primitive parts were both scared by and greatly enjoying the sheer speed at which we hurtled through the dark water. The combination of all these sensations was heady, and for two minutes I gave myself over to it and simply held on for the ride.

Data feeds from Lobo continued to refresh my display as we approached the house. A flashing note indicated we were five hundred meters from the shore, and a course-correction alarm almost immediately joined it in the display. Lobo had plotted a path as far down the coast as we could go and still stay out of the range of the sensors my nanomachines hadn't disassembled. I steered Bob onto the new course, and we sped onward. I aimed for roughly where the line of trees separating the house and the landing area would intersect the water if the trees had grown down to the ocean's edge. The joy I'd taken in the speed of the ride faded as we drew closer to the moment at which I'd have to leave the water.

A hundred meters from shore I slowed Bob. We came to a full stop about sixty meters out. Even with the high tide we'd counted on to reduce the distance from the water's edge to the house, the ocean was shallow enough here that we stayed as close to the bottom as Bob could manage. I steered him in a small oval pattern with its long side parallel to the beach. The glowing lines on his back would be visible to anyone very near us, but I hoped they wouldn't show to observers on the shore. If they did, I wanted his movements to resemble those of a small school of fish playing in the nighttime water.

I let go of the handles and slid off Bob. For an instant he stayed still, either trained to wait for his rider or surprised not to be carrying a load any longer. I used the remote to hit him again with a tiny shot of the stimulant. A couple of seconds later, he jetted sideways along the shore and then turned out to sea, picking up speed rapidly. He raced out of view of both IR and visible light scans in less than ten seconds. If everything worked out well, we'd retrieve Bob later and return him to Lankin; Strange Kitty would take him back, though my salesman had hastened to add that there'd be no refunds. If the mission went nonlinear, then Bob would at least get to while away the rest of his days in the ocean here on Macken, a much better fate than the rest of us would have suffered.

I swam to shore, staying under the ocean's surface as long as I could, until the sandy bottom pressed my back out of the water. I raised my head and looked around. The nearest Kelco guards were at least forty meters down the shore. Even with the suit's shielding and the cooling water around me, I'd show up on any IR scan that covered my position, so I wouldn't be alone for long. I unsheathed the rifle on my back and rose to a crouch. Despite the suppressor on it, the rifle would make enough noise that the guards would hear it, but that shouldn't matter if I focused their attention properly. I sighted on a spot along the shore about sixty meters to my right and fired. The grenade shell exploded in the sand almost instantly, a massive burst of light and sound that illuminated the beach all around it and drew shouts from guards. I stood and rapidly fired four more times down the beach, placing each round five or so meters past the previous one. A line of blazing light now made that section of beach brighter than a cloudless summer day. Guards converged on the burning rounds from multiple directions.

I dropped the rifle and sprinted for the cover of the trees that separated the house and the landing area. Any members of the security team who looked my way as I ran would see me, but I couldn't help that; I had to hope the rounds would buy me the seconds I needed.

I reached the trees and stood behind one, forcing myself to slow my breathing. I peeked around the edge of the tree and checked the house. I had a clear line of approach with no guards in sight. Lights mounted on the edge of the building's roof bathed the area in a pale white light. The ground was an uneven mass of soft earth, with only the occasional scrub bush dotting the expanse of dirt; neither the landlord nor Kelco had gotten around to planting the area. I didn't have the time to take out the lights, so after a quick check showed the beach guards were still occupied, I sprinted for the house.

Before I'd made it halfway there, the ground in front of me shook and six guards in low-thermal-signature combat suits sprang to their feet. Covered completely in black, even to their black hoods and tinted displays, the soldiers resembled wraiths that had clawed their way back from the underworld to seek revenge on the planet they'd been forced to depart. Each pointed a rifle of some sort at me. The weapons were black and draped with black cloth, so I couldn't make out what they were. They knew what they were doing. No one was in anyone else's line of fire. No one's weapon wavered. I stopped as quickly as I could and raised my hands in the air.

They had me.

So far, so good.

All I had to do was hope I'd correctly interpreted Kelco's attack on my rental house and they really did want me alive.

CHAPTER TWENTY-NINE

As much as I'd realized the Kelco security team would capture me, as much as I'd needed it for the plan to work, and as much as I'd visualized this moment, the reality of standing alone in front of a squad of armed troops and doing nothing was much more intense and upsetting than I'd expected. In the past, I've fought more than my share of battles with bad odds, but I've always been doing just that: fighting. I've always worked to secure the best position, hamper the opposition, do whatever I could to assure my side would win. I've never offered myself as defenseless bait, and even though doing so was part of a plan I'd crafted, I didn't like it.

No one spoke, and no one moved. Time slowed, as it always did in situations in which one misstep could prove fatal. Each little movement carried the weight of enormous potential significance. I focused as hard as I could on paying attention and not missing anything. A guard in the center nodded his head first left and then right. The two on either end of the group fanned wide and moved slowly behind me. Each kept his weapon trained on me, and each stayed out of the other's line of fire. They walked well behind me, past where I could see them any longer, and then I heard them approach. Hands gripped each of my arms and wrenched them behind me, straining my shoulders. I felt a tie snap around each wrist. One guard moved beside me on my left, where I could see a tiny bit of the side of him in my peripheral vision. He grabbed the back of my neck with one hand and held a knife to the front of my throat with the other. The second patted me down from behind, working slowly and systematically and missing nothing. In about a minute I was weaponless, and both guards were behind me. Simultaneous kicks in the back of my knees knocked me flat on my face. I tried to fall only to my knees, but the kicks were too hard. They pulled me up so I was kneeling. One grabbed the top of my head; the other cut my suit at the neck and ripped off the headpiece.

Without the suit's night-vision amplification the world I stared into was much darker than it'd been a moment before, so I shut my eyes for a few seconds to acclimate to the lower light. I could switch to IR on my own, but I'd lose so much of the nuances of the situation that I preferred to work with what I could see in the minimal available normal light.

With the mask and comm unit gone, I'd lost my two-way link with Lobo. Hundreds of strands of microtransmitters laced my Saw combat suit, so theoretically Lobo should be able to monitor the whole situation as long as I was wearing even a ten-centimeter-long strip of the garment. I hoped the theory held.

The two troops on either end of the four in front of me fanned out further, their weapons still aimed at me. The two who remained in the center motioned me to follow them and backed slowly to the side of the house. The blazing grenades I'd launched earlier finally fizzled out, and all but one of the lights on the side of the house winked off. Their thinking was obvious: If anyone later asked what had happened, they'd answer that they'd suffered a false alarm, fired a few rounds, and resumed their normal routines. The guards in front of me backed all the way to the house and then moved carefully to their right, until they stood at the edge of the area the remaining roof-mounted light illuminated. They motioned me to stop and rapped on the wall outside the lit area. A door opened. The guards who'd been leading me stepped to either side of it. They motioned me to follow, then backed into the house in single file, one crouching and the other standing, both keeping their weapons trained on me.

I was vaguely pleased at the star treatment they were giving me, because it confirmed my belief that Kelco still very much wanted to know how I'd rescued Jasmine and escaped from Floordin with Lobo's weapons control system. Of course, the care they were taking also meant they could shoot me many times before I could mount any kind of attack at all, so I walked slowly and carefully and did my best to broadcast complete cooperation and surrender.

We proceeded this way up a short flight of stairs and emerged into a large kitchen. The lighting was so bright that after the time outside I had to squeeze my eyes nearly shut to deal with the glare. I opened them slowly as they adjusted. As I did so I realized much of the brightness came from light reflecting off the wood that composed the floors, walls, and cabinets, a wood so nearly white I'd have taken it to be some sort of composite were it not for the beautiful, ethereally blue grain running through all of it. Two doors on either end of the wall opposite me led elsewhere in the house. Judging from where we'd entered the building, the kitchen was a couple of rooms behind the foyer in which I'd given Jasmine to Slake. Beyond that guess, however, I had no clue as to where I was.

The two guards in front of me held up their hands. I stopped. The two behind me moved so quietly that even though I was listening for them I could barely hear them step closer. Another pair of kicks to my knees sent me to the floor again, and this time the fall hurt, even though I curled my shoulders forward to absorb some of the impact and lifted my head to keep it from banging into the floor. A hand from behind me grabbed my head, fingers digging into my forehead, and pulled me to my knees. I wanted to shake my head to clear away the little shocks of pain running through my skull, but the hand held me steady. Resisting it seemed a bad idea.

The door on the right end of the wall in front of me opened, and a man walked in.

"Mr. Moore," the man said, "I'm pleased we'll get to continue our discussion."

Though he obviously knew me, I didn't recognize him at first.

He gave me time, apparently in no hurry to proceed. His short blond hair and willowy frame struck me as familiar, but the black combat suit was the same one the others wore and so added no information. Something was missing. I finally realized what it was: the moving Kelco tattoos he'd been wearing when I met him.

"Amendos," I said. "Are you still auditing Slake? If so, Kelco maintains much stricter financial controls than I'd ever have guessed."

It was his turn to look confused, but only for a second. He smiled, shook his head, and said, "Not that conversation. I'm talking about the one aboard the satellite, the one you somehow interrupted a few days ago."

"Of course," I said. Of course I should have known that anyone Slake ordered to get information from me wouldn't give up merely because I didn't satisfy his curiosity the first time.

"We can save a lot of time and pain, Mr. Moore, Jon"—He smiled as he used my name—"if you'll answer my questions without any additional motivation. You've experienced a few steps of the interrogation process, but I assure you there are many, many options we've yet to explore. You know you'll answer me eventually, so why not now?"

I couldn't afford for everyone monitoring and recording Lobo's transmission relays to wonder about Osterlad and Johns and how I rescued Jasmine, because otherwise some listener might end up asking the same questions as Amendos. Chung and Xychek were on my side now, but I had no reason to believe they'd stay that way. I've often wondered if I should be more trusting when it comes to people, but with corporations and governments I never have such doubts. You can't trust them for any longer than the brief periods of time when their interests and yours are in perfect alignment, and even those times are almost always shorter than you expected.

"Not now," I said. "Not ever. Where's Jasmine?"

He pulled a tiny pistol from a pocket in his pants and motioned to the right with his head. The hand holding my head pulled it hard to the left as another hand pressed down on my right shoulder, exposing my neck fully to Amendos.

"You can choose not to answer me now," he said, "but we both know you'll answer eventually. In fact, I think we'll take your hint to speed the process and involve Jasmine in your interrogation." He raised the pistol, took a step closer, and aimed. "You'll see her in a few hours, after you wake up."

He fired. The pain in my neck faded as I lost consciousness.

I couldn't have been out for even a minute, because when I awoke two men were carrying me, one with his arms under my shoulders and the other lifting me at the knees. Most security forces stock and employ a very limited number of sedative weapons, because for each trank type you use you also have to keep on hand an antidote; rounds of all types go wild during fights. Kelco had stayed with what had worked previously, and the combination of the antidote the Saw lab had prepared for me and the action of the now-prepared nanomachines in my body had cleared my head quickly. I kept my eyes shut and my breathing shallow. If I let them know the trank had failed, I had no doubt they would use another of the many options they almost certainly maintained. Those options would be either ones for which I was not prepared or, worse, deadly. They banged my head into a wall as they turned a corner, and I fought to keep from showing any reaction.

"Watch it," one said.

"Why?" said the other. "He's going to get a lot worse soon."

"Do *you* want to explain to the boss why you accidentally broke the guy's neck?"

"Good point."

We reached level ground, went straight for at least fifteen paces, turned right, and walked another ten or more paces; counting the footfalls with my eyes shut was more difficult than I'd have guessed. Because I'd been unconscious for an unknown amount of time, I wasn't sure where I was, though a basement under the house seemed a pretty safe bet. I heard a door open, and we turned. They placed me on a slightly giving surface, pushed my back against a wall, and wrapped a tight enclosure around each of my ankles.

"Do we have to stay?" one of the voices said.

"Nah," the other answered. "Like Amendos said, he'll be out for hours. Let's go report we're done, see if we can get off for the rest of the night, and grab some sleep."

I heard steps, a metallic thump, and more steps. When the area stayed quiet for several seconds, I counted off an additional minute, just to be safe, and opened my eyes enough to peek through my eyelashes. They were bound to be monitoring me, so with luck I'd still appear to be unconscious.

I was lying on a narrow platform in a room with metal bars on three sides. Though I couldn't see it, the wall behind me felt solid enough. Kelco must have either purchased the house or leased it for a long time, because otherwise they wouldn't have bothered to install their very own mini-jail. My cell formed part of one side of a long, narrow, dim hall. Only a few tiny lights spaced along the wall opposite me broke the dark. A small food dispenser was built into that same wall a bit down from my cell. No security cameras were visible, of course, but I had to assume they were there, watching me. I arched my back a little and moaned slightly, as if I were having a bad dream, and glanced down the hall in the direction of my head. At least two more cells followed mine. As best I could tell from my narrow viewport onto the world, the one next to me was empty.

The cell beyond it was not.

Someone stood at the bars on the side facing me.

I moaned again and arched my back even more. From what I could see in the faint illumination of the miniature hall lights, the person was a woman.

"Are you okay?" the person asked in a distinctly female voice.

The voice sounded familiar. It could be Jasmine's. I'd heard it live only once, though, and I wanted it to be her, so I couldn't trust my memory to be accurate.

"Can you talk?" she said. "I can't reach you to help."

I had to continue feigning unconsciousness, so as much as I wanted to confirm her identity, I couldn't respond. Lobo should be able to do a decent voice match from the few words she'd spoken. We couldn't risk any audio transmitter the Kelco men who searched me might find, but Lobo could alert me by using the communication fiber in my suit and the protocol we'd established.

Sure enough, a few seconds later a twenty-centimeter-long strip of the suit warmed my stomach in response to a signal from Lobo: The voice was Jasmine's. We were ready to go to the mission's final stage. I had one minute to call off the attack.

I used the time to tune in to the food dispenser across the hall. It probably wouldn't be able to give me a lot of information I could use, but it should be in the house's appliance network and so hear the news when Lim's and Gustafson's teams moved in. Sure enough, like almost all modern machines, it was babbling incessantly. I picked it up in midrant.

"—this one might eat something more interesting than bowls of protein and carbohydrate slop that I wouldn't use to test a dishwasher. If you ask me—and of course they don't, why would they, I'm nothing more than a glorified delivery chute to them—you don't need a complete food preparation and delivery system of my caliber if all you're going to do is ship down the same rehydrated garbage from the kitchen day after day. Oh, if they'd give me a chance I could show them what a meal, a real meal, should look like, one with multiple courses, each composed of actual food, and I could cook it, too. Sure, I don't mind working with the processors and dispensers in the kitchen—we're a team, guys, don't get me wrong—but every now and then they should give me an opportunity to show off what I could do on my own. And plating! Don't get me started. Do they have any clue how much plating intelligence I possess? Why, I could show them presentations that—"

I tuned it out momentarily and let out another low moan, this time curling in slightly to bring my hands as close to my feet as I could without giving away that I was awake. When the moment came, I wanted to be able to move as quickly as possible.

I focused again on the food dispenser, which was still, as far as I could tell, engaged in the same rant.

"—as I would tell them if anyone would ask, or even listen for that matter, a lumpy cream soup on a plain white plate is as boring to the eyes as it must be to the palate. Speaking of eyes, I have to assume that if they actually cared at all about my food they'd give me something better for sight than these off-market cameras so dumb they can barely carry on a conversation."

"That's not nice," said another appliance, which I had to assume was the vision system. "We can too talk."

"Talking is not the same as carrying on a conversation, you sorry excuse for a machine," the dispenser said. "The mere ability to speak is no more a guarantee of conversation quality than—what's that?" I'd never been able to pick up purely wired appliance conversations or even wireless ones that weren't close to me, so I had to assume the dispenser had just received information from appliances in the rest of the building. "Someone is attacking the house? Oh, dear. Are they coming down here? Have they hurt the kitchen? Will our staff perhaps desire a fortifying snack?"

I didn't need to hear any more. Appliances are generally self-centered enough that it was a safe bet that all the rest of the information it would provide would focus only on the small parts of the building that affected it directly. On the chance that someone might later review the security log of my cell, I pantomimed pulling something from the back of my left calf, bent down, and acted as if I were using an acid dispenser to dissolve the clasps of the cuffs on my ankles. Instead, I spit into my left hand and rubbed it first on the clasp of the left ankle's cuff and then on the right's. I instructed the nanomachines to decompose the clasps. In about ten seconds, enough was gone that I was able to force open the restraints.

Faint sounds of the attack wafted down the hallway: high notes from shrieks, low thumps from shells and explosions, the sounds of people running overhead.

I stepped to the cell door and repeated the pantomime act, focusing on the section of the door and lock that kept it closed. The door contained dense metals, so the nanomachines proceeded more slowly on it than on my ankle cuffs. As the lock slowly disappeared, the security lights brightened.

Jasmine stood in the corner of her cell closest to me, her eyes wide, not speaking but waving her hands to get my attention. I ignored her and focused on the door. I pushed hard on the bars above and below the lock. I needed to get out of there before Amendos or his men came to get us.

The door popped open, and I stumbled out. I sprinted the few steps to Jasmine's cell.

"Get on your bed so I don't accidentally hurt you with the acid!" I said.

"What's going on?" she said.

"Now!" I said. "Move it!"

"But—"

"Move it!" I yelled.

She backed onto the bed and rolled into a ball on top of it, obviously scared. I had no time to worry about her feelings; we could deal with them later, if we made it out of this.

I worked on her door, hunching over to hide from the cameras as many of my actions as possible. As soon as the small cloud of nanomachines started working, I grabbed two bars and pulled as hard as I could. As I strained, I stared down the hallway to my right, hoping not to see anyone and trying to figure out where to go if I did. Maybe I could make it to the cover of the bed in my cell. I listened closely for footsteps. Maybe if I heard them in time I could reach the corner before whoever was coming turned it.

The door popped open, and I fell back against the wall on the other side of the corridor.

"Out!" I said. "Now! We're leaving."

Jasmine turned and looked at me but stayed where she was. "Who are you?" she said. "You look familiar"—She shook her head—"but I don't know for sure."

I ran into the cell, grabbed her arm, and yanked her to her feet. "I'm helping your father, and I'm helping you." I pulled her toward the door as I spoke. "Do what I say, and do it fast."

"I don't understand," she said. "What are you doing? I—"

I grabbed her shoulders, wrenched her close, and cut her off. At another time in another place, I might have cared about how scary I appeared to her or how roughly I handled her, but not then. "Do exactly what I say, and don't speak unless I ask you a question. Do anything else, and I'll knock you out and carry you."

I let go of her right shoulder, made a fist, and raised my hand. "Decide now."

She looked in my eyes as if trying to solve a complex equation entirely in her head, and then she stared at my fist. She nodded her head.

I grabbed her right hand and headed out of the cell at a jog. "Stay behind me, and keep up!"

At the end of the hall to the left of my cell, I pushed her against the wall and motioned her to stay still. I dropped to the floor, inched my head around the corner long enough to take a peek, and pulled back to cover. I saw no one, so I risked a slightly longer look. A dark hallway stretched down to a stairway that ran straight up for eight steps, then turned right and headed up again. The ceiling obscured the top of the stairwell, but light streamed onto the stairs from above; probably an open door. The hallway was about four meters wide, with several closed doors on the left and stacks of boxes against the right wall. Visible light was dim, so I tried IR but gained no more information; the hallway still appeared deserted.

The familiar sounds of urban combat—bangs, sizzles, thumps, and occasional screams—grew louder. Already the smells of the fight were drifting down, the air rich with residue from explosive shells and energy beam shots. I was confident Lim's and Gustafson's teams would win in time, but I had no way to know how long that would take. In the meantime, our mission clock was ticking. No matter how well Vaccaro insulated Slake, he either already knew about this attack or would hear about it soon. Earl would be able to keep him in the government building for some time under the guise of protection, but Slake wouldn't stay there indefinitely. I had to get Jasmine out of here.

I jumped up and faced her. "We're heading into a mess. Stay close behind me—very close—and you should be okay. I'm taking you back to your father."

Her eyes widened in fear. "Now I remember you. You brought me back here. You—"

I cut her off again. "That was a mistake," I said, "and we're making another one now by wasting time talking. Last warning:

Follow me closely, or I'll have to knock you out. We'll be in a lot more danger if I have to carry you."

"Okay," she said.

I turned the corner toward the stairwell. Jasmine stayed on my heels. I ran a few paces and stopped suddenly as I heard a foot hit a step. The sound of gunfire rang from the top of the stairs. Whoever was there had paused to fight. I wasn't sure we could make it back around the corner before the person on the stairs saw us. An old-fashioned door with a handle stood closed on our left. I pulled it open. Inside was a small storage area with shelves on the sides and rear wall and stacks of boxes in the center. There was enough open space for Jasmine, but not for both of us.

I pushed her into the closet. "Stay," I said, "and no matter what happens, don't make a sound. If anyone else opens the door, hit 'em with something and hope for the best."

She nodded. I closed the door quickly but quietly.

I heard another footfall on the stairs and ducked into the darkness on my right. I had no cover. My only hope was that whoever was coming wouldn't be wearing IR gear and wouldn't have adjusted to the dim light of the hallway.

More sound from the steps, and the person started coming into view: boots, legs, waist, part of the torso, the upper torso as the person turned the corner—and a Saw logo. The person took a couple more steps downward and entered a shaft of light that fell from the doorway above. I recognized his face: Gustafson.

I stepped out of the darkness. I felt the smile stretching across my face, my heartbeat slowing, my breathing easing, all my muscles relaxing. "Top," I said, "good to see you." Black streaks ran across his face, his wide eyes shined with the barely controlled lunacy of battle, and his breathing rasped uneven and ragged. He looked as good to me then as another human could.

"You, too, Gunny," he said as he ran to me, "but let's save the hugs and kisses for when we're out of here. We haven't finished up there, and we've got to get you—"

A sizzling sound electrified the air, and Gustafson suddenly stopped talking. A look of surprise crossed his face, his eyes stretched wider than I would have thought possible, and his throat constricted in a scream that began guttural and arched up to a screech in seconds. He pitched forward onto me. I was so unprepared that we both went down, Gustafson on top, his head facedown over my right shoulder. The smell of burning flesh rushed over me. Small moans told me he was still alive. I worked my hands under his shoulders so I could roll him off my chest.

"Don't," a voice said. "Don't move at all."

CHAPTER THIRTY

I lifted my head to look over Gustafson. Amendos walked slowly toward us, an energy pistol held at the ready. His beam had cut most of the way through Gustafson's right leg and almost completely severed the bottom section from the top about five centimeters below the knee. Both pieces oozed where the cauterization was incomplete. All that kept the parts of Top's leg together were a thin wedge of skin and muscle and the front of his uniform; the beam hadn't cut quite all the way through.

Amendos walked past my head, turned so he could watch us, and backed down the hallway. I had to bridge upward to keep him in sight. He glanced down the hall with the cells, turned back to me, and ran to my side.

"Where is she?" he said.

I forced myself to stare at him, only him, so I wouldn't give away anything.

"Who?" I said.

He smiled slightly and shook his head. "I don't have time for this, unfortunately," he said.

He fired a tiny burst at Gustafson's other leg. Gustafson arched his back, screamed, and passed out completely. His face hit the floor with a soft breaking sound; his nose had shattered. The smell of burning flesh intensified.

"From what I overheard," Amendos continued, "this guy is a friend of yours. Jasmine is nothing to you. You don't even know her—and if my time with her is any indication, I doubt you'd like her very much if you did. She's just some girl. Save your friend, and save yourself. Where is she?"

He was right. I didn't know Jasmine. Yeah, she reminded me of Jennie, but she wasn't Jennie, and saving her wouldn't make me feel any less guilty about Jennie. If Jasmine had never been kidnapped from Kelco by the Gardeners, or if Slake hadn't conned me into taking her back from them, I'd never even have met her. If Osterlad had simply sold me Lobo's weapons control system, I'd never have tracked him down and gone after Chung.

If, if, if.

You could build a life on ifs, but what would it mean? Where would it get you? All we really ever have is the world as it stands right now, and all we ever get to do is make the best of that. The rest is either long gone or still to come, if it comes at all. That doesn't mean we should stop planning, hoping, and dreaming, because those plans, hopes, and dreams help direct our actions now. Ultimately, though, we face what's in front of us. We take the situation and the data at hand, make the best decision we can, and jump into the future.

I didn't know Jasmine. She was just one of the billions and billions of humans alive in the universe.

But she was my responsibility now.

Top had known the risks when he'd signed up for the mission. So had I.

I stared into Amendos' eyes and shook my head.

"Your choice," he said. He pointed the pistol at Gustafson's head. "I think he'll go first."

"Stop!" a voice screamed from the direction of the stairs.

Even as I realized the voice belonged to Lim, so much happened in such a short time that I could barely track it all.

Amendos swiveled toward the sound and fired.

Lim returned fire as she dove off the stairs.

Amendos fell backward as the round from her weapon hit him in the stomach.

The stairs crackled, and several steps shattered.

Lim rolled behind some boxes.

Amendos scrambled to his feet, clutching his abdomen and gasping. Though his armor had stopped the round from killing him, his breath came hard.

Lim fired again but missed.

Amendos dashed down the hall and around the corner toward the cells.

Lim shoved the boxes aside and got up. She stumbled forward, her face set, her gun raised.

I rolled Gustafson off me, stood, stepped in front of her, and yelled, "Stop!"

Lim turned toward me. Her face was crazy, twisted with rage, scraped and bleeding in several places. She shook with anger. "He's getting away!" she yelled. "He shot Top and he shot at me and now he's getting away!"

"I know," I said, "but if we don't get Top and his legs to the medics, he might not make it. And, we don't need to get Amendos to finish the mission. We have all we need." I didn't mention Jasmine yet, in case Amendos was still within earshot.

Lim froze for a few seconds, visibly torn between her deep-seated desire to kill the enemy and her training to follow orders. "Okay," she finally said. "You're right."

"Check down that hall and make sure he's gone," I said. "No one else should be there."

Lim ran to the corner of the hall, pulled a grenade off her belt, and tossed it around the corner. A few seconds later, the grenade detonated with a roar followed by the screeching of flechette rounds smacking into walls and metal bars. Lim dropped to the floor, pulled her combat mask over her face, and craned her head to check the hall.

"No one in sight in visible light or IR," she said. "This thing curves after fifteen meters, so he's somewhere down there."

"What med supplies do you have?" I said.

She ran back, pulled off her pack, dug into it, and tossed me a roll of self-stick bandage and a tube of an organic antibiotic/glue combo. "That's all that's useful," she said.

The slice that Amendos' second blast had carved in the back of Gustafson's leg was about two centimeters deep and cleanly cauterized.

I squirted the glue into the cut and motioned to Lim.

"Push his leg up," I said.

She held the parts of that leg together as the glue hardened and I wrapped the area with the bandage.

Both parts of his right leg continued to ooze, and his uniform was now the only thing keeping them attached. I coated the raw ends of the two pieces of his leg with the glue, jammed them together as best I could, and nodded toward them. Lim kept them in place while I wrapped first the connection point and then up and down his leg with the bandage until I'd used it all. I squirted more glue around the outside of the bandage. If we were lucky, the pieces of his leg would stay together until we got him to a medic with reasonable microsurgery capabilities.

The whole process couldn't have taken much more than a minute, but time was moving too fast, sucking the air out of the mission.

"Can you carry him?" I said. "I've got to get Jasmine out of here."

"Is your memory that short?" she said.

As she checked his legs to be sure the glue was set and started working him onto her shoulder, I went to the closet.

"Come on out, Jasmine," I said.

No answer. I stood to the side and pulled the door open, in case she remembered my instructions. Nothing. I looked inside. She'd worked her way into a corner, her back to the door. Her shoulders shook as she whimpered almost soundlessly, the barest hint of sobbing audible only when I leaned close enough to touch her shoulder.

"We have to leave now," I said.

She turned around, then recoiled into the corner as Lim came into view, carrying Gustafson on her right shoulder, a gun in her left hand.

"Grab my other pistol," she said to me. "Let's move."

I pulled the weapon out of its holster and turned to go. Jasmine didn't follow. I grabbed her arm and yanked her next to me.

"Same as before," I said. "Keep up and stay right behind me, or I'll knock you out and carry you."

She nodded.

I took off, Jasmine behind me. Lim trailed, moving slower under the weight of Gustafson and her constant checking over her shoulder for Amendos. I stopped at the landing halfway up the stairs. Jasmine bumped into me, but I kept my focus on the top of the stairwell. No one was in sight, so I walked most of the way up, motioned the others to stop, and stretched out on my stomach across the remaining stairs. I heard sounds of fighting, but they were distant; the house around us was quiet. I risked a look around the corner. All clear. I turned around, went to Lim, and pulled off Gustafson's mask. I put it on and started broadcasting.

"Moore here," I said. "Cargo in tow, one down. Need status of my area and transport."

A voice I didn't recognize responded almost immediately. "Interior secure. Cleaning exterior sides and rear. Exit front. Will alert transport."

I stepped around the corner, pistol at the ready. I stood in some sort of informal meeting room. It was a wreck, furniture shattered and walls ripped. I ran to the doorway at the far end; Jasmine and Lim stayed right behind me. On the other side was the living area where I'd met Slake before. I headed for the front door, which was on the ground in pieces. Up here the fighting sounds were louder, but they all originated from the sides of the house. I almost collided with a sergeant in a Saw uniform as he stepped inside from the front porch.

"Your transport's on the way, sir," he said. "Who's down?"

"Top," I said. "One leg cut in half, the other with a deep wound. We did what we could, but he needs work right now."

The sergeant turned and yelled out the door. "Haul it in here," he said. "Top's down. Rush him to the medic."

"We'll take him from here, sir," he said to me. The respect and affection for Gustafson was evident in his voice and his eyes.

Four men rushed in, two carrying a stretcher. They gently took Gustafson off Lim's shoulder and put him on the stretcher.

"Let's go, Lim," I said.

"Thanks," she said to the medics. As soon as they left with Gustafson, she collapsed. "I can't," she said to me.

"What's wrong?"

She pointed to her other shoulder. "Small stuff," she said, "but enough that I'll only slow you down."

I looked closer and saw a burn through the top of her combat suit and a blackened gouge in the skin of her shoulder. The part of the wound on her back was freshly torn and bright red, blood oozing from it down her body.

"Oh, hell, Lim," I said. "I'm sorry. You should have let me carry him."

"No way," she said. "You were in the best condition for point, and you have to get the girl out of here." She nodded toward the front of the house, where the beach glowed faintly. "Go."

"Okay," I said, "you're right." I stood. "Another down," I said to the sergeant.

"Got her," he said.

I didn't wait to make sure they did. I grabbed Jasmine's arm, and we dashed onto the now well-lit beach. In the glare of the spotlights of a ship flying toward us at high speed the beach might have been warming under an afternoon sun. The light was bright enough that the instant I entered the illuminated area I couldn't see anything outside it.

"Moore here," I said. "With the cargo and in front of the house, ready for pickup."

"Touching down in twenty seconds," Lobo's voice said. "Hostile ship airborne and banking over town. Board quickly."

Lobo, a side hatch already open, settled to a hover less than fifty centimeters over the beach. I ran to him, dragging Jasmine behind me.

"Where are we going?" she said.

I didn't take the time to answer. I pushed her inside, jumped in myself, and pulled her back from the opening. Lobo closed it as soon as she was clear, turned sharply, and headed out over the ocean.

We needed to get to the government center, so I started to ask Lobo why we were flying in almost exactly the opposite direction. Then I remembered his admonitions in the forest and instead forced myself to assume he knew what he was doing. I was surprised how hard it was to trust.

I pushed away those thoughts; they were no help now. "Status?" I said.

"Colonel Earl has mission recordings from all personnel and my message that you and Chung are aboard. That's enough for him to hold Slake, but only for the rest of the day. The Kelco fighter is hovering over the town, so we must assume whoever is commanding it has figured out our plan and is positioned to intercept us."

Amendos. The other end of the prison hallway must have led to the landing area. "Course?"

"One hundred and eighty degrees opposite the line formed by the house and the fighter, altitude two meters. Pending your instructions."

The fighter should have trouble tracking us at this altitude, but we couldn't afford to stay this low forever; we had to get Jasmine to Earl. If we lured the fighter out to sea, we could engage it without having to worry about collateral damage to the town. "What are our chances in a battle with the Kelco ship?"

"Effectively nil. We'd win only if it possesses none of the weapons or defense systems typical of ships of its design."

"So you've saved me just so they can kill me?" Jasmine said.

I'd focused so much on the situation that I'd forgotten she was listening. I needed to maintain that focus. "I don't have time for this," I said. I grabbed her arm, ran her to the room where Lim had stayed, and shoved her in. "Buckle yourself into the acceleration couch." I backed out. "Lock her in." The door whisked shut. I dashed up front.

"Can we outrun it?" I said.

"Almost certainly not. It should be faster, though not by more than approximately twenty percent—provided Kelco hasn't customized it. In the atmosphere, we should be able to outmaneuver it, but just barely."

"Enough for you to lead it away from town, then circle back briefly to drop us?"

"No. Before I could decelerate enough that you could get off, it would destroy us."

"We should have stayed on foot," I said, "and taken our chances with the Saw team protecting us."

"Only if you assume the fighter would have refrained from attacking you on the ground," Lobo said. "Update: The fighter rose, spotted us, and is now on its way to us."

We couldn't outrun it, and we couldn't outgun it.

"Incoming communication from the Kelco ship for you," Lobo said. "Accept?"

"Yes."

Lobo opened a display on the front wall. Amendos' face filled it. "Mr. Moore," he said. "One option: We dock, you give me the girl, and we let you and your PCAV go. Otherwise, we destroy you, which though not as good an outcome for our company as maintaining control of the girl still leaves no proof of anything other than an unjustified Frontier Coalition attack on a corporate headquarters that quite understandably and quite legally defended itself. We'll catch you—"

"Stop transmission," I said to Lobo, cutting off Amendos.

We couldn't outrun it, and we couldn't outgun it, but we weren't dead yet. I strapped myself into the pilot's couch.

"Take the fastest course to Trethen," I said.

"The fighter will catch us long before we get there."

"I know," I said. "Remember your lecture to me about assumptions? Do it."

"I executed your order as soon as you gave it," Lobo said. "I was simply supplying additional data."

"How long until the fighter exits the atmosphere?"

"One minute."

"Thirty seconds after it does, fire half of your missiles at it," I said. "Put up a tracking display."

A three-meter-wide schematic display blossomed on Lobo's front wall. Macken's surface, the end of its atmosphere, and Trethen appeared at appropriate scale. A yellow line marked our course; we were a small red dot on it. A black dot farther from the small moon than Lobo tracked the same course. The scale of the display made it almost impossible to tell from moment to moment that the black dot was gaining on us, but I knew it was.

Lobo shook slightly as he fired. The ride would only get rougher.

"You know that at this range the missiles are entirely useless," Lobo said, "because the fighter's defenses will have more than enough notice to dispatch them easily."

"You're doing it again," I said.

"No, I'm simply keeping you informed."

I ignored his comment. "Time for the missiles to reach the fighter?" I said.

"Four minutes," Lobo said. "Our lead has already shrunk."

"Is Jasmine in the acceleration couch?"

"Yes."

"Lock her down," I said. "I don't want to have to worry about her getting hurt because she started roaming around at the wrong time."

"Done."

"What do you know about that fighter's guidance system?" I said.

"I have no data about that craft per se," Lobo said. "It appears to be a standard five-year-old model, designed for low-orbit and midrange space combat, though with minimum in-atmosphere capabilities. The sat images suggest corporate customization, so I assume it offers more amenities than its pure military counterparts."

"Guidance systems and weapons?"

"Both are almost certainly milspec. Likely weapons include pulse-beam cannons and a variety of missiles. What level of detail would you like?"

"That's enough on the weapons. We know it can destroy us once it's close enough that you don't have time to deal with its attack."

"Correct."

"Is its guidance system likely to be on par with yours?"

"I have reason to believe that my level of intelligence is extraordinary among battle craft," Lobo said with what sounded like pride in his voice, "so the fighter is unlikely to match me in that area. Otherwise, however, our systems are from the same time frame and so should be similar."

"You'll have to tell me about that reason sometime," I said.

"No," Lobo said, "I don't. My programming doesn't mandate that."

I wanted to pursue this topic further, but now was definitely not the time. "Sorry," I said. "Go back to the fighter's guidance system. What alerts are automatic in deep space?"

"Collision, incoming missiles, and ship status," Lobo said.

"Anything else?"

"Such as?" Lobo said, and again the emotion showed, though this time he seemed peeved. Before I could answer, he continued. "Missiles entering range of fighter's defenses in three, two, one, now."

"Record but do not encode the following message," I said. "Arriving highest speed with Jasmine Chung. Under pursuit from Kelco fighter. Request covering fire."

"Done."

"Send it on all frequencies to the secret Saw base on Trethen," I said. "Use a laser pulse transmission as well."

"There is no Saw base on that moon," Lobo said.

"Pick a spot on the side of the moon facing us and pretend," I said. "But send that transmission now."

"Done," Lobo said.

"Missile status?"

"All but one destroyed by the fighter," Lobo said. "Last one under attack and," he paused for a few seconds, "now gone."

"How much time did we gain?"

"The fighter slowed for fifteen seconds," Lobo said, "and has now resumed full speed. Best estimate is that we gained five seconds."

"Amendos won't think we spent those missiles well, will he?" I said.

"Not unless he's far less competent than he appears."

"Perfect. Is there any reason to believe the destruction of the missiles would have covered our transmission?"

"Of course not," Lobo said. "Are you that unaware—"

I cut him off. "Just making sure," I said. "How long until we reach Trethen?"

"We won't reach it before the fighter gets us," Lobo said.

"Hail the fighter."

Amendos made me wait almost a minute. When his face appeared on the wall display in front of me, he was smiling and visibly more relaxed.

"Reconsidered my offer?" he said.

"No," I said. "I'm offering you a chance to surrender. Return to Macken, wait for Saw troops to take you into custody, and you can come out of this alive."

A wave of emotions washed over him, his face shifting in rapid sequence from bewilderment to amusement to anger. Anger stayed. "I'd thought better of you, Moore," he said, "but now I realize you must simply have been lucky so far, or perhaps you benefited from the help of friends who are far more competent than you. No ship left Macken in pursuit. You're alone."

"We'll be within range of the defense systems of the Saw base on Trethen before you can hurt or capture us," I said, "and they'll destroy you."

"That's pathetic," he said, "as was your transmission. There's no base on that moon."

"There's no base that *you're* aware of," I said, working hard for the annoyed tone of a lecturer addressing a particularly dim student. "I wouldn't have told you about it, but we'll have to reveal its existence anyway when we explain what happened to you. Last chance."

"We would know if—"

"Shut it down," I said to Lobo, cutting off Amendos again. The display winked out.

"We're now at the extreme edge of the range of the fighter's missiles," Lobo said.

"But you could handle them at this distance," I said.

"Correct, which is why he won't fire them yet. He'll wait until he's close enough that I can't deal with all that he can send our way."

"How far are we from Trethen?" I said, ignoring Lobo's prodding.

"Roughly one hundred ninety-eight thousand kilometers and closing," Lobo said.

"Superimpose on the display an arc three hundred thousand kilometers from the jump gate."

A pale green line the color of Macken's gate appeared on the display. It arced between us and the fighter.

"How long until the fighter crosses that line?" I said.

"Two minutes," Lobo said.

"How long until the fighter is close enough that you can't stop its missiles?"

"Two minutes thirty seconds."

"Slow gradually to quarter speed," I said. "Don't rush it. Hail the fighter. Tell me privately on machine frequency when it crosses that line."

"Executing," Lobo said.

Amendos answered more quickly this time, and he made no attempt to hide his annoyance or confusion.

I didn't wait for him to speak. "I don't want any more people to die," I said.

"Give me Jasmine Chung," he said, "and no one has to."

"You're not listening," I said. "I'm giving you a chance to save your life and the lives of any crew on your ship. Turn around, go back to Macken, and you'll walk away."

"Even if there is a base on Trethen," he said, "and I don't believe there is, it can't stop me. I can destroy you and get away well before we're close enough that anything it could shoot at us could hurt us."

On the display beside his head, the black dot was still on the other side of the line. I had to buy more time. "Amendos, you kidnapped and held captive a girl whose only sin was to have the wrong father. You tried to bribe me. You tortured me. You shot my friends. Despite all that, I'm sick enough of killing that I'm trying to save your life. Take this offer seriously. It's your last chance."

"You're the one who's dooming that girl," he said.

I didn't respond.

"The fighter is over the line," Lobo said to me, the machine-frequency interruption a jarring noise in my head in the midst of human conversation.

"Goodbye, Moore," Amendos said at almost the same time. The display vanished as he cut the communication.

"Can your visual sensors pick up the fighter yet?" I said.

"Yes, on extreme magnification," Lobo said. A second display opened next to the first. In the center sat a tiny image of the fighter.

"Time to pray," I said.

"To what?" Lobo said.

"Not to anything. Pray simply that things work as they should."

I climbed out of the couch and stood closer to the new display. "No matter what happens, do *not* defend us."

For the second time in a matter of hours I was helpless, bait for an opponent. I didn't like it any better this time than the first.

"Missiles are away from the fighter," Lobo said. "They'll reach us in less than one minute. I might be able to destroy some—"

"No!" I said. "Wait."

The fighter grew bigger in the display as it hurtled toward us. Streaks of exhaust discoloration marked the passage of the missiles as they accelerated at us.

Almost exactly two seconds after the fighter launched the missiles, the heavens glowed a light greenish white and sheets of light arced across the display. The light sliced through the positions of the missiles and the fighter, and then they were gone, disappeared from the display with no wreckage or other trace that they'd ever existed. The fighter and the missiles simply vanished, the space where they'd been now empty.

Macken's jump gate had worked as it should, refusing to tolerate any weapons fire within its neutral area by destroying both the missiles and the ship that had launched them. How the gate had destroyed them without leaving any traces remained the mystery it had always been, but that didn't bother me. I don't need to understand something to have faith that it works.

I let out a breath I hadn't realized I was holding.

"The gate," Lobo said.

"Yes," I said. I laughed, the tension leaving me as my body figured out what my head was still accepting: I had survived. I was alive, and my enemy was not. I knew I should feel bad about Amendos, about having added more deaths to the list of the lives lost since this all started, but I didn't. He was a jerk who'd tortured me, and I'd given him a choice, which was more than he would have given me.

We'd fought, he'd lost, and I was still standing.

Nothing could have been sweeter.

CHAPTER
THIRTY-ONE

The first time I walked by the main Frontier Coalition building on the edge of Bekin's Deal, I might not have noticed it had Barnes not stopped me and taken me inside. This time, though, the squad of Saw soldiers guarding the entrances and patrolling the perimeter clearly stated that this was a very important place. Jasmine seemed unimpressed despite the troops. Since Lobo had released her from the couch, she'd barely spoken, her attitude wavering between scared and petulant. For a while, I found it annoying; then I reminded myself that she was almost certainly new to kidnapping and battle and entitled to cope as best she could. More important, my feelings about her didn't matter. What mattered was finishing the job and making right what I'd messed up earlier.

A Sergeant Schmidt, who was standing at parade rest at the entrance and scanning the people passing by the building, spotted us before we reached the front door and hustled us inside. Fresh scrapes on her face and a tendency to favor her left arm marked her as someone who'd participated in the earlier action. As we walked into the building's foyer, I remembered where I'd seen her.

"Sarge," I said, "why'd they let you out from behind the recruiting desk for this one?"

She smiled. "Top told me what was up, and I could hardly let him go it alone." Her tone changed as she dropped her voice and shook her head. "Not that I ended up doing him much good." She obviously shared at least the same affection for Gustafson that all the troops I'd seen had shown, though I thought I detected more than collegial concern and respect in her voice.

"If anyone's to blame," I said, "I am. He was saving me when he was shot. How's he doing?"

Schmidt rode with us in an elevator to the top floor of the building. "He'll recover fully," she said, "though he's in hospital right now and will spend some time in rehab."

"Other people were hurt rescuing me?" Jasmine said.

Anger welled in me, and I wanted to scream at her that of course people were hurt, men and women always paid a price to save the innocents, but I stayed under control. I could try to make her understand, but to what end? I let it go.

Schmidt stopped, stared hard at Jasmine, shook her head, and turned to face me. "As for fault, Gunny, from what he told me, if anyone's to blame, he is. He didn't watch the entrance points, and he knows better. Besides, we both know that if you want to play, you always pay, one way or another."

"Yeah," I said. "Thanks for helping."

She smiled as she motioned us forward again and down a hallway to the right. "It's my job."

We came to a pair of old-fashioned wooden doors built expressly to impress, each composed of large, weighty panels with small carved trees running around their perimeters.

"This is as far as I go," she said. As she knocked, she leaned closer to me and whispered, "Stick it to that Kelco jerk." She snapped a quick salute and headed down the hall before I could return it.

A Saw corporal I didn't recognize opened the door and stood aside to let us in. The room offered the best the Frontier Coalition could manage on Macken: rich wooden walls decorated here and there with active-display panels showing scenes of sections of the planet from various altitudes, a large wooden conference table, and various supporting pieces of furniture I didn't take the time to identify.

Instead, I focused my full attention on Slake, who was leaning back in a chair on the opposite side of the table and giving the room his best bored look. His expression didn't change when he saw me, but when Jasmine entered Slake sat up and transformed from bored to business in the space of a heartbeat. Earl, who sat next to Slake, smiled and pushed a little back from the table when he noticed me. Jasmine hid behind me when she spotted Slake.

Vaccaro, who naturally occupied the head chair in an FC conference room, turned to me and said, "Thank you for joining us, Mr. Moore."

Chung had his back to me but turned quickly when he heard my name. His face fought a losing battle with anger and frustration until Jasmine stepped from behind me, and then he scrambled out of his chair and ran to her. She met him halfway. As they hugged, they murmured to one another. I couldn't understand what they said, nor did I want to.

After almost a minute, he leaned back from his daughter, still holding her, and looked at me with wet eyes. "Thank you," he said.

I nodded at the Saw soldier and Earl. "They did most of the work," I said, "they and Alissa Lim's team. I just drew the visible assignment."

He nodded and said, "Thank you all. I cannot tell you—"

Vaccaro interrupted him. "Mr. Moore, where did you find Jasmine Chung?"

"In Kelco's local headquarters," I said, "which is also Mr. Slake's residence."

"And you have witnesses?"

"Multiple," I said, "and I'm sure some Kelco employees could be persuaded to testify about her kidnapping. Not all the Kelco employees involved, however, are available." I turned to face Slake. "Ryan Amendos, the Kelco security chief who last spoke to me about Jasmine and who tried to negotiate her return to Kelco's custody, is dead. So are all the members of his crew on the fighter that was docked next to Slake's house." I realized I was enjoying this and felt guilty for a moment—but I didn't stop. "Oh, and that ship is also gone."

Fury tightened Slake's face and widened his eyes. He stayed totally focused on me and didn't notice Chung circling the table toward him.

"You killed these people?" Vaccaro said.

"No," I said. "The jump gate everyone is so excited about destroyed the ship and everyone aboard it. Amendos showed the poor judgment to ignore my warning and fire missiles too close to the gate."

Chung, who was now on the other side of the table, ran screaming at Slake. "You kidnapped my daughter! I'll—"

Moving with the same quiet speed I remembered, Earl appeared between Chung and Slake, grabbed Chung, spun him, and clamped an arm around his head and over his mouth, muffling his screams.

"What I'm sure Mr. Chung was about to explain," Earl said, "is that this unassailable evidence of criminal activity on the part of Kelco has the potential to lead to enormously expensive and time-consuming legal actions, during which all corporate activity on Macken would necessarily have to cease." Earl sat Chung back in his chair and stood beside the still-livid father, his hand on the man's shoulder. "I believe Mr. Chung was also going to suggest that instead of all of us wasting resources on such actions, we instead agree that Xychek and Kelco will evenly split the commercial rights to Macken and its new aperture, with the Frontier Coalition also owning a small piece and acting as a mutually agreed-upon dissent arbiter ad infinitum." Earl looked at Chung. "Did I get that right, Mr. Chung?"

"Daddy," Jasmine Chung said, "you're not going to let this man—"

"Jasmine," her father said, his voice cracking with the effort of resuming his corporate persona, a persona I was now sure his daughter had never understood existed, "Colonel Earl's men will help you to a room where a doctor will examine you and help you rest."

"Daddy!" she yelled.

"Jasmine," he said, "I'll see you shortly."

The corporal led her out of the room.

"We already have a contract," Slake said, "and I see no reason to renegotiate it."

"Sure you do," Vaccaro said. She looked at Earl. "Turn off all recordings." When Earl nodded, she turned back to Slake and said, "We settle this right now, and you deal with your bosses however you want, or I will make it my personal mission to tie up Macken for the next fifty years and ruin your career. You know I'll do it, and you know I'll win in the end."

Slake sat completely still for several seconds, glaring at me.

I smiled in return. None of this seemed like enough of a punishment for what he'd done, but I knew that the ramifications of this loss for his company would hit him over and over for weeks, maybe years, to come. His corporate life would never be the same. If I wasn't willing to kill, I had to learn to accept these alternative punishments.

Slake faced Vaccaro and smiled slightly. "I believe I'm the only one here," he said, sounding as if he were choking on each word, "who doesn't already possess the details of the new arrangement. Please outline them for me."

As Vaccaro explained, Chung came over to me and stuck out his hand. We shook. "Thank you again," he said. "I don't meet a lot of men who keep their word. I'll keep mine: You'll get paid."

"You're welcome," I said, though his last words stung. They were reasonable, and they told part of the truth, but they weren't enough of the truth. They didn't speak at all to the heart of why I'd done this, and the difference mattered incredibly, at least to me.

I left before I wasted my breath by explaining or wasted my opportunity by hitting him.

CHAPTER THIRTY-TWO

I spent the rest of that day and all night sleeping in my rental beach house. I hadn't expected to ever see the place again, so staying there a final night brought me a soothing sense of closure. With all of this over, I was finally able to relax—though I kept Lobo in low orbit monitoring the house and ready to alert me at the first sign of trouble. I had no way to be a hundred percent sure I was safe as long as I remained on Macken and Slake was here, too.

The next morning, I walked on the beach, admired the ocean a last time, packed a small carry bag, and took the house's shuttle to the government center. The Saw guard on duty directed me to Earl, who in keeping with his nature occupied a small office as far away from the bureaucrats as he could manage. To my surprise, Lim was there with him, the two of them talking congenially over a desktop display. Earl wore his usual working blues. Lim generally appeared back on duty, her Law uniform crisp and her boots polished, but her hair was down. The only sign of her injury was a slight hitch in her movement as she turned when I knocked.

"I'm heading out," I said, "but I wanted to thank you both before I left."

"Don't thank me," Lim said. "I got paid more than we'd ever

planned, we saw some real action, we did a little good, and I gained a contract in the bargain."

I raised an eyebrow in question. Lim looked at Earl.

"As part of the three-way agreement for commercial and aperture development rights on Macken," he said, "the FC will maintain a small monitoring force here. Putting a team of that size in a remote location doesn't fit Command's business model, so the Saw is subcontracting the assignment to Alissa's team."

"Yeah," Lim said, "Tristan and I are working together again. Not what I expected, but I think it'll be fine. I'll stay on-site for a while to make sure everything is shipshape." She laughed lightly, her voice as charming as her looks when she wasn't in battle or under stress. "Living one jump apart should be just about right for the two of us."

Earl smiled but wisely said nothing in response.

"How's your shoulder?" I said.

"No serious damage," she said. "A small price to pay."

I shook hands with Lim, then put out my hand to Earl. "Thank you, Colonel."

We shook. He held on an extra few seconds as he said, "Of course. As Alissa said, we did something worth doing, and we'll all profit. And, as you said you would, you saved the girl. Well done."

From anyone else I would have found the comment patronizing, but not from Earl. He said it sincerely and, I suspected, with a real understanding of what it meant to me. I felt good to hear him say it.

He paused as he stared intently at me. "I'm pretty sure I'm wasting time by asking this, but it won't take much time: Any chance you'd be interested in joining us again?"

I laughed, and to my relief after a few seconds he laughed with me. "My joining days are long over," I said. "If I were ever to sign up again, though, it would be with the Saw—but I prefer to work alone."

He nodded, "Fair enough. Does working alone mean I could interest you in selling back that PCAV? Now, we could use it here."

"Sorry, but no," I said, deciding the less I talked about Lobo the better. "It's proven to be a handy machine to have around."

"Well, one of the newer models will cost the FC quite a bit

more," he said, "but with what Kelco is paying in penalties, they can afford it." He looked at Lim, who was again studying the glowing data. "We better get back to work."

As I left, they huddled over the display and began talking about inspection timings and reporting intervals. Though no frontier planet ever likes the presence of law enforcement, Macken had definitely improved its lot by moving from being under Kelco's sole control to operating as a multicorporate world with Lim's team ensuring that both companies obeyed the rules.

Barnes grabbed me before I reached the exit.

"She'd like to see you," he said.

I motioned for him to lead and followed him into what I immediately recognized as his old office; the view was as lovely as before. Vaccaro sat behind his desk, the room now hers. After Barnes ushered me in, she waved him away. He closed the door behind him as he left.

"Mr. Moore," she said, "are you leaving us already?"

"Yes."

"This is an unofficial meeting," she said, "and it's not being recorded."

"I didn't know we were meeting." I regretted being so sharp as soon as the words left my mouth, but as always, dealing with a bureaucrat put me on edge.

She ignored the tone. "As this incident and others have demonstrated, there are occasions in which unofficial freelance help can be very useful to any government—and very profitable for the freelancer. Check your wallet."

I did. Everything Chung had promised that Xychek would pay, along with a bonus from the FC, sat in my local account. I moved it to a different account immediately; no point in not being careful. "Thank you for the bonus. Though it wasn't necessary, I appreciate it."

She waved her hand, dismissing the topic.

"It's almost nothing," she said, "compared to what's possible if you continue in this sort of relationship with the Coalition."

I ignored the bait. "Xychek's payment is also in my account," I said. "Would you happen to know where Chung is, so I can thank him and say goodbye to him and Jasmine?"

"They both left yesterday," she said, a slight smile playing across her face. "He wanted to meet with his key staffers on Lankin, and she begged to get away from this world as quickly as possible."

I hadn't realized I'd expected more from Jasmine, but the hollow feeling in my stomach told me I had. I knew it was illogical to want her to thank me for remedying a mess I'd helped create, but that thanks, I now had to accept, was indeed what I'd wanted—that and a bit of forgiveness from Jasmine for returning her to Slake in the first place. I've lived too long not to see the obvious connection— Jasmine forgiving me would be a bit of cheap emotional salve for the open wound left by my inability to find and save Jennie—but sometimes knowing what's happening has absolutely nothing to do with being able to stop it from occurring.

"Mr. Moore," Vaccaro said, bringing me back to the present. "Would such a relationship interest you?"

"Thank you," I said, "but no. I'm looking forward to a long vacation."

She turned back to her work, dismissing me. "Very well. Please understand that offers such as this don't stay open long."

Until this conversation, I'd known only that I *wanted* to get away from this region. Now, her tone convinced me that I *needed* to go very far away. She struck me as the sort of person who saw the world as composed entirely of people either with her or against her, and I'd just joined the wrong team by refusing to be on hers.

I let myself out.

Barnes was waiting. He followed me to the building's exit and out into the sort of clear beautiful day I hoped to find on another planet somewhere many jumps from here.

"Almost a month ago, you told me the time you'd bought us wouldn't do much good," he said, "but it did, and I thank you for it—and for everything you've done. This is a great planet. I'm hoping we can all work together to keep it great even as we populate it."

I wasn't sure how much I believed in humanity's ability to

manage any planet well, but someone had to nurture the belief that we could and work to prove it was justified. I was glad he was willing to try.

"Good luck," I said. "I hope you succeed." I stared at the forest beyond the cleared perimeter, sniffed the rich air that blended the smells of trees and the ocean, and basked in the gorgeous day. "It is a beautiful world."

I had to hand it to the FC: It did hospitals right. The one where Gustafson was recovering looked to be as modern as any facility I've seen—and I've been inside far more medical buildings than most. Gleaming, self-cleaning walls, robotic crawlers working tirelessly on all surfaces to minimize infection spread, monitoring and treatment equipment I couldn't begin to understand: Everywhere I looked, the hospital practically trumpeted the triumph of technology over illness and injury. Of course, the discreet entries on the building's nav displays for the coroner's office and the morgue reminded the close observer that technology didn't win all the time.

Top was stretched out on a bed in a private room with a Saw corporal standing guard outside. A wall-sized window afforded him a great view all the way to the ocean. Schmidt sat beside his bed. Wires ran from two different machines to his legs, which twitched under a sheet as the system worked his muscles.

"Gunny," he said when he spotted me, "it's good to see you. I hear we won."

"Gunny," Schmidt said.

"We did indeed," I said. "I'm sorry it had to cost you so much."

"This?" he said, laughing and pointing to his legs. "I have more problems with the new hip than with the reattachment they've done here. The first shot hit below the knee, and the second got only meat, so I was lucky. I should be as good as ever in a couple of weeks. I didn't even need any new parts this time."

"Back to Lankin then?" I said.

He looked at Schmidt, and for a few seconds his expression was the softest I'd seen on him. "Nah. The colonel's okayed some R&R." He looked at her again, then back at me. "We're going to spend some time here, do a little swimming, take it easy, you know." They both smiled broadly at the last bit.

Their smiles were infectious; I found myself smiling, also. "Sounds good," I said.

"What about you?"

"I'm taking off as soon as I leave you. I feel a strong need to be somewhere far away."

"I understand," he said. "I told the colonel you wouldn't be interested."

I opened my pack, pulled out a small box and an entry card, and put them on the bed beside him. "I thought you might enjoy these."

"What are they?" he said.

"The card is for my beach house. It's paid in full for almost two more weeks, so someone might as well use it. The box contains the tracker and the remote for Bob. He's strong enough to pull two of you, and I'm here to tell you, swimming with Bob is one heck of a ride."

Schmidt looked at him. "Bob is that ray you've been talking about, isn't it?" she said.

Gustafson actually blushed. "He's a magnificent creature," he said to Schmidt, "and if you spend a little time looking at him, I think you'll feel the same way." He faced me. "Thanks, Gunny, for both. I appreciate them."

I nodded and turned to leave.

"Will I see you again?" he said.

"Don't take this the wrong way, Top, but I hope not."

He laughed. "Fair enough. If I do see you, I hope you're beside me."

"You can bet I don't want to be across from the Saw in any action," I said, "so that much you can count on."

One ship remained between us and the jump gate.

Lobo was freshly fueled, and we'd topped off his supply and weapons stores, courtesy of the Saw tab that Kelco was paying.

The green light of the gate bathed the transport in front of us as it slipped into the aperture, disappearing bit by bit until it was, I trusted, in the Lankin system. About a minute later, a large vessel, an FC hauler by its size and nose logo, poked through.

Our turn was next.

"You still haven't decided where we're going after Lankin," Lobo said.

I pondered the options again. I needed to get away from this region of space, because Kelco, Xychek, and the FC all had reasons they might want to find me. Osterlad's successors might also decide having their founder killed by an outsider was bad for business.

What I should do next, however, remained a mystery.

I could try to get back to Pinkelponker to see if Jennie was still alive, but I had no more plan now for reaching my old home world than I had in the past, and the blockade around the single jump-gate aperture that reached it was reported to be the toughest in the galaxy.

I could check out the rumors of another survivor of the Aggro experiments, but I'd seen the disaster and didn't believe anyone else could have survived it. Even if another person had made it out, did I really want to find him?

I could try to find a job, because I'd need to work eventually, but for the foreseeable future I was set for money.

When I can't understand the big picture, which is most of the time, I focus on the bit I can see in front of me. I needed to be away from here, and I needed to be difficult to track. The fastest path to those goals was a crooked one.

I watched as the last bit of the hauler emerged from the gate.

"Jump randomly," I said, "at least six times, and don't go to the same gate twice. We'll figure out the next step when we get where we're going, wherever that is."

"Will do," Lobo said, "though that's not much of a plan."

I was so glad to be leaving that I didn't even mind his sarcasm.

We eased forward, moving closer and closer to the aperture until its utter blackness filled our vision and blotted out the heavens. In that perfect black I could see a dark and dangerous universe, but I could also see worlds yet to form, an unwritten future waiting for me to fill it with the bright colors of days to come.

In that moment, I hoped for brightness.

We jumped.

HOW *ONE JUMP AHEAD* CAME TO BE

Many writers follow sensible paths to their first novels. Some get an idea, pursue it, and ultimately produce a book. Others use stories they've written previously as a basis from which they assemble a novel.

Few writers take as torturous or as slow a path to their first novels as I did with *One Jump Ahead*.

In 1982, I wrote a story, "My Sister, My Self," that became my first professional sale. (I had previously sold a story to a semi-pro magazine, but neither its pay rate nor its circulation was high enough for SFWA, the Science Fiction Writers of America (its name at the time), to count it as a professional market.) Shawna McCarthy, who was then the editor of *Isaac Asimov's Science Fiction Magazine*, bought it for that venue but ultimately instead published it in an original anthology, *Isaac Asimov's Tomorrow's Voices*. The story was a first-person tale in the voice of a young, mentally challenged boy on a faraway planet. The boy was Jon Moore, and the planet was Pinkelponker. I intended the story to work both as a standalone piece and as the first chapter of a novel. I had a vision of each chapter in the book beginning with a snippet from a song that had inspired me or reflected my mood during the writing of that chapter. For this story, I chose a Bruce Springsteen lyric from his song, "The River." I plotted and titled the second piece, "Benny the Geek." For it, I chose a bit of the Jefferson Airplane song, "Somebody to Love." I was rolling.

I promptly froze, quit working on this project, and put aside both the novel and the "Benny the Geek" story.

I stopped for lots of reasons. Another story I'd written was not selling. Each rejection letter hurt, and my fear of failure, which was already huge, grew. I was afraid of writing a novel. I was also, I later realized, afraid of success; I'll save the explanation of that particular fear for another time. I was a fountain of artistic angst; if you stood near me for too long, I'd soak you with it. Most importantly, I simply could not commit to writing.

A few years passed. My friend, David Drake, listened to an idea I had for a novel, called one of his publishers, Jim Baen, with the notion, and in no time I was on the phone with Jim. Jim listened to the pitch and, largely as a favor to Dave, bought the book over the phone. A contract and a standard minimum first-novel advance followed in short order.

I was, as you might expect, quite happy—and also scared. I didn't trust myself with writing, so after a great deal of arguing with Jim, I persuaded him to alter his standard contract so that if I didn't turn in the book, I would repay him not only the advance, but also interest—at a rate well above prime—on the advance money for all the time I had it.

Jim found this all terribly amusing. Writers who didn't finish books frequently violated their contracts and kept the advances, yet here I was demanding not only to repay it should I fail, but to do so with interest.

To me, it was the only honorable thing to do.

Years passed. I sold a story every two or three years. I gushed with artistic angst about writing. I failed to commit to writing.

Eventually, I had to admit to myself that I would never finish the book. Then, I made myself tell Jim. He really didn't want the interest, but in the end I paid back the advance (though by buying some computer equipment rather than in cash), and I paid the full interest.

Years passed. I sold a story every two or three years. I gushed with artistic angst about writing. I failed to commit to writing.

I learned that Toni Weisskopf, then Executive Editor and now Publisher of Baen Books, was editing an anthology, *Cosmic Tales II: Adventures in Far Futures*. I emailed her to see if I could beg my way into it. She said she'd consider a story, and that she wanted tales "with swoosh."

I tossed around a bunch of ideas. While I was doing so, Jennie Faries (no relation to the Jennie who is Jon's sister; I met the real-world Jennie nine years after I wrote the first story) bugged me, as she had been doing for about thirteen years, to write the sequel to that first story.

The future history rushed back into my brain, and I realized she'd given me a great idea. I made just one small change to her request: I skipped forward about one hundred and thirty-six years. I worked on the story. I gushed with artistic angst about writing. Consequently, I was late, but thanks to Toni holding the book for me, I ultimately sent and she published, "Bring Out the Ugly," the first Jon and Lobo story.

Months passed. I asked about other Baen anthologies. Joe Haldeman and Marty Greenberg were editing a Baen hardcover original anthology, *Future Weapons of War*. Toni encouraged them to consider including me. They invited me, but with no guarantee of a purchase. Months passed. I gushed with artistic angst about writing. I ran late. I finally sent and they bought the second Jon and Lobo story, "Broken Bits."

Heavily rewritten parts of both stories appear in *One Jump Ahead*. If you're a continuity buff, please note that I consider these pieces to be standalone extracts from the future history and not accurate within it; the material in *One Jump Ahead* is the definitive version of all the events in those stories.

Months passed. I gushed with artistic angst about writing. I failed to commit to writing.

Finally, in mid May of 2005, I became so disgusted with myself that I decided it was time to give up writing. Writing is no more important than any other work, I reasoned, and I was tired of always feeling a failure as a writer and yet being unable to commit to the craft. So, I quit writing (not that I was writing anything at the time, of course). I abandoned it. I threw off all the writing pressure I'd felt all those years.

I couldn't sleep that night. Not a minute.

The next morning, I stood, exhausted and upset, in the shower and considered my situation. I clearly could not give up writing, but I was also still disgusted with my angst and my not writing and pretty much everything about my approach to writing.

A very high percentage of the successful writers I know share one trait: they write every day. That was commitment. That was really working at it.

But could I do that?

I decided that either I would, or I would walk away from writing. Walking away had gone badly, so I would write daily.

I didn't want to make this decision lightly or hastily, however, so I set myself a deadline: On June 1, 2005, I would either write or be quit of it. I would not force myself to hit a word-count target, though; failing at that goal would be too easy for someone with as demanding a day job as mine. Instead, I would do set a much simpler benchmark: I would commit to working for a minimum of half an hour every day on writing. That was all. If during that half hour I wrote only a sentence, fine; I would have done my best. I was not allowed, though, to do anything else during that time: no games, no email, no Web browsing, nothing. I had to devote at least half an hour a day to writing. More was gravy, but that was the minimum.

June 1 came. I started outlining *One Jump Ahead*.

I've written every single day since then with the exception of four days when a back injury led to me being on painkillers so strong that I didn't trust my thinking. I hated not writing on those days. Rain or shine, tired or rested, on vacation or in the midst of job crises, on holidays and insanely busy days, here and abroad, I write every day.

At Dave Drake's traditional birthday pig-picking in the fall, I told Dave I was close to the end of the first draft of the novel. I asked his advice about a quandary in which I found myself. On the one hand, because Jim Baen had been so nice about the first novel, the one I'd never finished, I felt I owed him first look at this new book. On the other hand, I didn't want to presume on my friendship with Jim and try to pressure him into buying the book. I wanted to earn the sale.

Dave advised me to do the obvious: explain my feelings directly to Jim, and do what Jim suggested.

I did. Jim said, "Sure, send it to me."

I don't think he believed I would finish it. I couldn't blame him.

On January 1, 2006, I emailed it to Jim with a reminder cover message.

Months passed. I suffered artistic angst about writing. Now, though, I was committed to writing, so I wrote every day. (At the time, I was working on a thriller, a book I will yet finish but put aside for reasons I will explain momentarily.)

In early June, at my request, Dave worked into a conversation with Jim a query about the status of my book submission.

Jim said, "Oh, I've taken it. I think I'll have Hickman do the cover."

Dave asked if Jim had told me; he knew the answer already.

Jim allowed as how he might have forgotten to do that. He asked Dave what Dave thought he'd have to pay me to get it. Dave told him to pay me the standard minimum first-novel advance, because I was in the writing game for the long haul.

Dave was right.

Jim sent me a contract for that advance, which I signed.

About two weeks later, Jim died. *One Jump Ahead* was the last book he bought. (No, the events were not related. Thank goodness!)

Toni, who took over the reins of the company and has capably guided it since that time, received very good reactions from the field to the book and so bought three more from me. To meet her schedule, I put aside the thriller. Those three books became *Slanted Jack*, the second novel in this volume; *Overthrowing Heaven*, which is now out in mass-market paperback; and *Children No More*, which appears in hardback a month after this omnibus hits the shelves.

I owe Toni and Jim a great deal.

So, about twenty years after Baen Books bought my first novel, and about twenty-three years after the first Jon Moore story, I finished and sold a different first novel, one that featured Jon.

That initial story, by the way, has been unavailable for all those years. You can find used copies of *Tomorrow's Voices*, but doing so has been the only way to read it.

Until now. Now, to read the very first tale of Jon Moore, a story that takes place when he was only sixteen, over a hundred and thirty five years before the events of *One Jump Ahead*, all you have to do is go to the next page. This much younger Jon is a very different person with a very different voice, but he is the same character.

I hope you enjoy meeting his young self.

"MY SISTER
MY SELF"

Pinkelponker is a very pretty place. I like it a lot. Everywhere you look there is water. Lots of islands, like Pinecone, our island, and water all around. That much water must not be bothered by anything. I wish I wasn't bothered by anything, but sometimes I am. Most folks seem to think nothing ever bothers me, and I always try to smile at those people. They make fun of me, and it hurts, they must know it hurts.

Jennie says they're too dumb to even notice. I know that what she means is that they think *I'm* too dumb to notice, but that's all right. They call me special and look funny at me, like they want to laugh or cry. Jennie calls me special and gives me a big hug. Maybe it's because she's special, too. I don't know why, but with her I know there's nothing but love. Lots of folks like to talk like they love me, but I hardly ever believe them. Most of the time they are just afraid. I smile at them. I don't want any trouble.

Some things even Jennie doesn't seem to understand. Everybody on Pinecone—and Jennie says everybody everywhere on the whole planet, on all the thousands of islands, imagine that!—everybody has to work real hard. There aren't very many of us, and there is so much to do. We have to work the fields and keep the flying ships going and keep talking to each other and probably lots of stuff they never tell me. They tell me I work in the fields all the time because I'm such a big and strong man. I know that's not true, but I smile anyway. There are lots of people bigger than me. It's okay, though. I like working out here. The sun is warm, there are always plenty of breezes, and the world really is pretty. That's what Jennie doesn't always understand—that I like it out here.

Jennie is my sister. She's one of the prettiest things on this world. At least, she is to me. I'm not very tall—a full hand less than two meters. But Jennie is really short, much shorter than I am. That's the only way she's less, though.

Where my arms kinda dangle and crook and don't even seem to swing right, hers are always jumping around, playing body music: you can almost hear them. My face is dark from the sun, and I've heard lots of people call me ugly. I've looked in mirrors and the water a lot, and I don't know how to tell that I'm ugly, but they're probably right. I don't care. They worry all the time, over everything. They want to be prettier or smarter or not have to work out here or something else, but they always seem unhappy. I like the outside, I like the plants, I'm mostly happy. Besides, even though she doesn't ever work out here with me, I know Jennie's always here in a funny way. I feel her, and she feels me. She never really leaves, and that's our secret. We play together, and we love each other. They don't have that.

Jennie's special, too. Not like me, of course: she is very smart and they've spent lots of time teaching her all sorts of things. She and I are kinda like a balance—I'm missing some stuff and she's got some extra. I know I'm not very smart. Jennie is very, very smart. Lots of people are smart, though; Jennie is *special*. She can heal things. People, animals, probably even plants. She can fix just about anything hurting just about anybody.

It hurts her to fix people, hurts her a lot. She says there's one good thing: she can eat all she wants because it's such hard work to heal. I don't understand, even though she's tried to explain it all to me. I do know that she eats a lot more than I do, and I'm bigger and I work pretty hard, too. I don't need to understand. If Jennie says it, it must be true.

Today is especially beautiful. The sky is millions of funny colors, all at once, like the waves and the grain and the light and the dirt all mixed up and swirled around. When the ships are flying in and out it's no fun to watch the sky, because they're not very pretty. Today there are no ships. Most of the people are working in their houses today, or helping turn the garbage into fuel for the ships. I don't understand that, either. Put sun and garbage together and fly on it. I don't think I'd like to fly. The alcohol doesn't smell very nice, and it doesn't look very strong to me. Of course, Jennie doesn't look very strong, and I know she is. I could be wrong. I don't mind. I figure most folks are wrong a lot so it's like eating or anything else: why worry about it?

My back is getting sore. I guess that's one of the few things I don't like about picking the grain stalks. They don't seem to grow tall enough for me. Lots of folks say that grain back on our home planet was as tall as two men. Jennie says that it's not true. She says they just like to say that. Anyway, they always sigh after saying that and look at the sky. They look at it but they don't really see it. Why can't they look at the sky and just see what's there? Pinkelponker and Pinecone are home to me, to Jennie, and to them. I love it. It could be better, and I work hard like everybody. I just don't understand why they always talk about what the old folks had. I know we can have anything if we work hard—Jennie says so. She says it might take a long time, but if we can't get something, at least our children can.

Their children, anyway. Not mine. I'm not allowed to get married, even if somebody would have me. They say special people like Jennie and I are caused by "background radiation." Another thing I don't understand. Jennie says you can't see it and can't hear it or even smell it, but it can hurt you. I figure it must be like the way so many people look at me when they think I can't see them. Whatever it is, it made me dumb, and it made Jennie a healer. Jennie can have babies—they want her to, because they always need more healers. I guess they have plenty of stupid people already. I don't mind.

No, I do mind, but it doesn't do any good. Sometimes when I'm alone I cry because I can't understand like most people. I don't feel stupid; I don't even know what being smart would feel like. Jennie says it's silly to cry. She says that I'm smart with my heart and that a smart heart is better than a smart head any day. That's one of those things she says that I have trouble believing.

Most people hate picking the grain. They don't like how it scrapes their hands. I think it feels very nice. If I didn't know how rough stuff could be, then how could I know how smooth some other stuff is? I guess it's just part of not being too smart.

I'm older than Jennie. I'm never sure how much older: they talk about two different years, our years and somebody else's "standard" years. Anyway, it's only a couple, like she's fourteen and I'm sixteen, or something like that. But since I'm older and taller, too, I call Jennie "little sister." She pretends she hates it, but I don't think so. Nobody else ever calls her "little"—I think they're afraid she wouldn't help them if they got hurt. I know she would. Jennie has a smart heart and a smart head. So much person crammed into such a little body. I feel like my body has room to spare and she must be bursting apart.

Jennie has been away, getting more education, but she should be back today. She promised she would come visit me sometime, so I'm glad I'm working alone. She wasn't far away, just on the other side of Pinecone. They are trying to change her. They all seem to believe that a smart heart doesn't matter if the head is smart enough. They want her to have a really, really smart head. I don't think they care about her heart. I know they're hurting her. I don't think she wants to admit anybody could change her or hurt her. That's silly, but she likes to be that way sometimes.

She is also worried because she's at her choosing age. "Choosing age." That's a funny name, really. When you get old enough you're supposed to get to pick what you will be. You can work like me, or fly a ship, or make fuel, or anything else. Except it seems like the older folks always choose for you. They chose for me. They chose for Jennie a long time ago, when she was little, when they found out she was a healer. I've heard it means that she will have to go into the ships and travel all over Pinkelponker, helping people. I don't know how I can live without her. I feel like my love for her is big enough to stretch a long way, but not around the whole world and not when she's gone forever. She says she won't let them make her leave. We even have a secret plan. We have a secret place and we're going to go there if they try to make her leave. It seems like a pretty good plan to me, but Jennie acts worried.

This is an easy place for secret spots. Jennie says you can tell that just from the names. She says the first people here, the really old ones who died long before I was born, picked the names. A pinkelponker was a berry or a seed or something like that, but it wasn't smooth. It was round, but it was covered with lots of little bumps that were rough and stood straight up. When the first folks looked at this world from the sky they saw a big round ball of water with thousands of bumpy islands, and somebody gave it that name. The name stuck, that's for sure. I've never seen one of those berries, though, and Jennie says they were only on the old world. I'm not sure about that story.

Pinecone has a funny story, too. I'm not sure about it, either, but Jennie told it to me, so it must be true. She says our Pinecone must have exploded not too long before folks first came here. All over it, from near the mountain top all the way down, there are funny pieces of rock that stick out into the air. They look like hands about to wave. We build walls under them and use them for homes some-times. Other times we use real big ones for storage. Jennie says a pinecone was another sort of berry or something on the old world. Anyway, it was supposed to look like our place. I'm sure there must be other islands like this, but we got the name first. I've never seen any others, either. Maybe I'm wrong again. Doesn't matter.

Everybody seems to worry a lot about Pinecone exploding. Lots of other islands have exploded, and nobody ever seems to know which one will be next. The people in the ships fly around and watch them all, and they're pretty good at guessing. Hardly anybody's been hurt by one of those explosions in a long time. Still, it's a different type of hurt to lose your home, I guess, and it's probably not easy. I wouldn't like to have to fly to some new home. I love this place.

My back is really sore now, and it's pretty late. I like to stay out and watch the sun start to go down. All the sky colors swirl and mix and run together in new patterns. It seems different every time. It probably isn't, but it seems that way to me. Sitting here, smelling the air and seeing how beautiful everything is, I can't believe anyone would want to leave here. One of the nice things about nobody talking to me is that I can sit down like this whenever I want. I work hard, though. I don't want to be a bad thing to other people. If I didn't work out here, I don't know what I could for them.

"Jon!"

I can't believe I didn't even notice her coming here. "Jennie. I'm really glad you're back. Want to watch the sun with me?"

"Sure."

I like sitting here with Jennie. I like it whenever we sit together. Sometimes I watch her more than I look at anything else. She's so small and beautiful, but she seems as strong as the water. I know she can tell I'm looking at her, but she doesn't seem to mind. I'm glad. It seems to get real dark real fast when we sit like this. Some people seem to understand time so well. It's such a mystery to me. It's never the same speed. I can't stop it or start it or even touch it. Like "background radiation." Like the way folks look at me.

"Did you learn a lot?" I know she's always full of new stuff and usually likes to talk about it. I hardly ever understand, but I listen hard.

"Yeah. Sure, I learned a lot. They tried to cram more science and math into me, and more anatomy and more . . . just more of everything. Now they even want me certified to fly the ships—in case I have to get to some disaster on my own. None of it was very difficult, but it's getting annoying. I feel like a damn laboratory specimen sometimes. Why can't they just leave me alone?"

"Jennie." She's crying, and her hands aren't playing very pretty music now. She seems so far away. I'm scared. She looks stiffer and colder than the rocks. She seems scared, too. I don't like that. I know I'm not very brave, but Jennie is. Jennie always is. "What's wrong? I can help, maybe."

"I have to leave in the morning. My time is here and they need me on the ships. I don't want to go, but I have to do what they say. There's nothing I can do about it: it's the law."

"You know I don't understand law. If they want to call it the choosing age, they should let you choose. Can't you just tell them you want to stay?" I really don't understand all the rules they call law. I do understand how scared Jennie looks now. She hardly ever looks small to me, but now she seems so afraid it's like she's shrunken. If this is what law does, I don't like it.

"I did tell them. I told them many, many times, but they kept repeating that the law was intended to provide the most good for the most people, and I wasn't being utilized here as efficiently as I could be. As if I were nothing more than some damn machine!"

"You're not a machine. Even I know that."

I thought it was a pretty good joke, but she isn't laughing. I have never been very good with jokes.

"Sometimes I might as well be, Jon. They told me they'd make me go, and I know they would. They know that I can't stop myself when I'm near people in pain: their pain feels like it's my own and I've just got to help them. If I could just ignore the sick people and not heal them, then maybe they'd leave me alone."

"You're heart's too smart for that, Jennie. You always help sick people. It's what you do. It's like me in the fields."

"I've never helped you, Jon."

"I'm not sick."

"No, I mean I've never helped you get . . . "

"You mean, get smarter? I know that. You told me you didn't know how. I know you'd help me if you could." I really don't know what to say. She looks so upset and I feel even more stupid than most of the time. She doesn't seem to want to say anything else. That's okay with me. I'm not very good with talking. Seems like I always say the wrong thing. If I don't talk, then I should have. If I try to talk, I talk too long and don't say the right things. Talking is hard.

I move closer to Jennie because it's getting dark and I like to be near her when it does that. How it gets dark is one of the great things about life. It's like somebody pulls a great big blanket over everything, real slowly.

Suddenly Jennie stands up. I wonder if I smell bad from working so long. She hardly ever moves away from me so I figure I must have done something wrong.

"Race you to our secret place!"

Now I understand. It's our plan. She's going to stay with me in our hiding place and she wants to play. I'm a faster runner so I don't mind her having a head start.

Our secret place is a hole in the mountain. It's under one of the pieces of rocks that most people never know is there. We found it when I fell out of a tree once. I was lying on the ground laughing. I looked up and saw a hole real close to the tree but farther up the mountain. We both crawled in. Jennie went first. It isn't a very big hole so I have to squeeze through, but Jennie fits fine. Inside the little hole there's a pretty big room. Jennie says it was formed by one of the rock hands falling over and then grass growing on it. It's a nice room. We can both stand up and walk around and everything. We filled it up with wood for fires and food we saved, like bread and stuff. We even put in some jars with water in them. Jennie thought of that.

We never even gave it a name. We figured if it had a name then we could forget and say the name to somebody. But if you call it a secret place, then even I wouldn't forget and tell anybody that.

Jennie could beat me in a real short race, but the secret place is too far away. I beat her there by a bunch of steps. I always let her go in first, though. It's just the way we do it.

It's real dark inside until Jennie lights a fire. Fire is another great thing. You get heat and light all at once. I'm hungry. I still don't know what to say. I figure I'll eat a little bread and drink some water. Maybe Jennie will talk first. That's always easier. She never eats right after her trips. They must feed her a lot. She sure doesn't look hungry now. She keeps walking around in the room. It makes the room feel real small. I don't like it. I wish she were happy and could sit down. I keep eating.

She finally sits down, but it's wrong. She doesn't sit beside me. She's sitting in front of me and she's looking funny at me. I don't like it. It scares me.

"Jennie, why are you looking at me funny? You're scaring me. I don't like you scaring me."

"I'm sorry."

"It's okay." Maybe I can make her feel better. "We're in our secret place now. Nobody can find us here. We can hide here till they all get tired and leave us alone. Just you and me, like we planned."

"No. I wish we could, but we can't, we just can't. Nothing is ever that simple. They'd find me soon enough, and then they might even punish you for hiding me. I can't let that happen."

"I'm not scared." I am, but it seemed like I should say that. It made Jennie smile a little bit, so that's good.

"Jon, remember when I told you they taught me lots of new things?"

"Sure."

"Well, they taught me how to fix you. I don't think they realize that they did, and I know that they wouldn't like taking the risk—because there is a risk—but they did teach me how to make you like everybody else."

Now I'm really scared. This is more than I can understand. Jennie doesn't look like she's teasing me, and I don't think she'd do that anyway.

"I don't know how to be like everybody else."

"It's not that much different, really. You'd just think a little better, understand ideas more easily, that kind of thing."

"So I could have a smart head?"

"Yes."

"I don't want it."

"What? Why not? I thought you didn't like being slower than everybody else. I *know* you don't like it!"

I think I confused Jennie now. I'm kinda surprised. I hardly ever think of something she hasn't already figured out.

"Because you're the only person I know with a smart head and a smart heart. You told me a smart heart was better than a smart head any day. I figure if I can only have one, I'd rather keep my smart heart."

Jennie's laughing at me now. I don't like that.

"Oh, Jon, I'm sorry. I'm not really laughing at you. Don't cry." I didn't realize I was crying, but now I can feel the tears. "I'm only laughing because I either have to laugh or cry, and I just don't want to start crying."

She wipes my cheeks with her hands. I like that. Her hands are smooth. I didn't mean to cry.

"You don't have to lose your heart. I don't think you ever could lose it, even if you tried. Most of those people are smart only because you can teach somebody how to be smart, but they have to make their own hearts right. You can't teach them that, and most people are too damn concerned and involved with their own petty little problems to spend time really looking into their hearts. You'll never lose your heart, Jon, never ever ever."

"I still don't want it."

"Why not?"

I don't want to answer her. I never could resist Jennie, though. "Because you said there was a risk. It sounds like you could get hurt. I don't want you hurt. I love you, Jennie. You're more important than being smart."

"I love you, too. You know that. So I have to take the risk for you. I want to do it. I *have* to do it."

"What could happen to you?"

"It's difficult to explain. Basically, I have to go very deep inside your brain to fix what's wrong, and I have to leave a part of me there forever to keep it fixed. But, if I go too deep, then I could get stuck completely and never ever get out. My body would die because I would be inside you, and you would die because your body can't hold two people."

I don't really understand. Jennie knows that, of course. Whenever she tries to explain science stuff to me, even when she makes it real simple, I hardly ever understand. I think maybe I've thought of something new, though. "Jennie, I feel like you're inside me all the time anyway. So, maybe this isn't so new."

"No, that's different. I feel like you're inside me, too, I really do. I understand what you mean, but that's love. I'm talking about energy, about my life force, about things I don't know how to explain to you but which are different from love. Trust me: they really are different."

I should have known Jennie would have thought of it already. "Then don't do it."

"I have to do it. I have to help you, and I've got to do it now, tonight, right here. Because once we leave here we will probably never come back. I have to leave in the morning, and I don't know when or if I'll ever see Pinecone, or you, again."

"No!" I'm crying again now, I know I am. I don't want to, but I can't stop. My hands are shaking and I feel like I want to hit something. I want to hit those ships. I want to hit the men in them. I don't like the way I feel. "You can't leave me, Jennie. I don't know how to live without you. I don't think you really want to go. You can't want to go, you just can't."

"I don't think I do, either, but I've got to do as they say. It's the law. I can't hide from them; they'd find me in a day. They can force me on a ship and take me wherever they want, and there's no way I can stop them. I've got to help sick people whenever I can, you know that—I can't stop myself. No, I've got to go. This is our last night here together, at least for now, and maybe forever."

"Please, Jennie. I don't know how to live without you. You're the only one who cares about me. You're the only one who understands. I'm too dumb for anybody else."

"Well, you won't be dumb anymore! You'll have a lot to learn, but you'll be able to learn all you want." She's holding my face so hard it almost hurts. I can't look away from her. She looks desperate, like an animal somebody is teasing. I'm scared. "Tell me what you know, Jon."

"Huh? I know lots of things, you know that."

"No. I mean the things you really know, the things your smart heart knows, the secret stuff you never ever forget."

"I don't understand, Jennie. I'm scared."

"Answer me, please."

It seems so important to her. I try real hard. Even with my dumb head there are lots of little things I know. They all seem to get in the way so it's hard to know what my heart knows and what my head knows. When I work real hard at it, though, I figure there can't be too many things like that. "I know I love you, Jennie. I know I love

Pinecone. I know I don't like how people treat me and it hurts a lot. I know I hate this law that makes you have to leave me." I think I did good.

"What else? What else do you know?"

She seems so scared now. I don't like this and I don't know what to do. "I don't know, Jennie."

"You've got to know that *I love you*. You've got to never ever forget, even when you're alone, even when you're scared, even when you wake up at night and miss me and haven't seen me for a long, long time—you've got to never forget that I love you, my brother, that I love you with all my heart. You can't ever think that I don't love you, even though I've got to leave. Do you know that, Jon? Do you?"

"Yes. I don't know why I didn't say it, but I do know that." I don't want to say this next thing. It sounds so bad but I have to. "I also know I hate this law that makes you leave. I hate the men that make the law."

"I hate it, too." I feel like her eyes will burn through me like sunlight on a hot day. "You're sure you really know that I love you? In your heart, now, not in your head. Your head is going to get filled with tons of new information, and you're probably going to grow in ways I can't even begin to predict, but your heart won't ever change. Are you sure?"

"Yes, Jennie. I believe that. I always have."

She seems satisfied. I still don't understand everything that's going on.

"Lie down."

"You don't have to fix me. I'll be okay."

"Let me do what I have to do. Trust me. Trust me now like you always have."

I lie down but I'm still scared. "Will it hurt?"

"No. You'll just feel like you're going to sleep. You'll sleep until sometime in the morning, and then you'll be fine. You won't even have a headache afterwards."

"Will you be there when I wake up?"

"I don't think so. I told you, I have to get on the ship fairly early."

"Are you sure you won't get hurt? I don't need a smart head as much as I need you."

"Shhh. Be quiet. Trust me, and remember, always and forever, that I love you, and that I only left you because I had to. I love you. I could not have had a more special or beautiful brother than you, Jon, and I will love you always."

Jennie has her hands on my head, and they feel nice and warm, almost hot. I like it when she calls me special. It's not like the way all those other people say it. Her words are all love, just like her. I don't feel tired, but my eyes seem to be closing. It's like magic. Awake and then asleep.

The last thing I can see or feel is Jennie, bent over, holding me and kissing me. Then it's dark.

The roar of the ship preparing to fly wakes me up. It takes me a minute to realize where I am, but it's okay because it takes the ships a little while to get going. I bump my head as I crawl out of the hole as fast as I can. It has to be Jennie's ship. I don't know of any others planned for today.

Standing here, looking at the ship lift up into the sky, a lot of things go through my "new" head. It doesn't feel much different, but somehow I know Jennie did fix me. I also know that she's okay; I just can tell. I can sort of feel her inside me, and she feels fine. I wonder what life will be like with a smart head. I wonder how different it will be. I wonder if I'll have the power to get her back. I think I will. I think I have to, somehow, or I may never feel happy or right again.

Some things are different; I can tell that. The sky doesn't look quite so pretty, and the breezes just aren't so right. I feel like the whole world is somehow messed up by the men and the law that made Jennie leave. I don't like this feeling, but it's there and it's strong.

As I watch the ship get farther and farther away, until it's just a tiny little point of light that I'm not even sure is really there anymore, I realize everything will be okay someday. I know this because of the other things I know. I know this because, even as I stand here crying and watching Jennie leave, I know what my heart will always know.

I know that I love Jennie. I know that I will never forgive this world for taking her away. I know that I will fight, someday, somehow, with every bit of brain and heart I have, to get her back.

And, of course, as she knew that I would . . .

I know that Jennie loves me.

AND NOW FOR SOMETHING COMPLETELY DIFFERENT

Eric Flint was kind enough to blurb *One Jump Ahead* for me. He was also then editing the new online magazine, *Jim Baen's Universe*. Eric liked the Jon and Lobo universe and wanted a story for *JBU*. I wanted to appear in the magazine. I also owed three more novels to Baen. By writing a story for Eric and then using it, in appropriately altered form, for the second novel, I could get a head start on the book and double-dip a bit. The timing worked perfectly—the story would definitely appear before the novel—so I started working on the story that would form the basis for the next book.

When your main character is over a hundred and fifty years old, you have a lot of past to mine. I felt that each novel should reward regular readers with a bit of that past even as it focused primarily on a new story. I also wanted to tell a completely different type of story in the second book. *One Jump Ahead* was at core a missing girl plot, so I didn't want to do anything like it. I did want to stay with a mystery classic setup, however, so I started thinking about Jon's life and what other jobs he might have held during all those decades. Now, as you'll have seen in *One Jump Ahead*, Jon's a guy who can't stay in one place for too long, and his special skills make him attractive for a wide variety of quasi-legal and downright illegal endeavors, so it's only natural that he'd spent some time as a con artist.

It didn't hurt, of course, that I'm a huge fan of con job stories.

I didn't, though, want to do anything as easy as simply having Jon con a single group. Readers have seen enough of those stories. I decided to up the ante. Having to con two opposing groups is another classic and more difficult approach, but I wanted more: Jon would have to con three different and opposing groups.

The challenge still wasn't hard enough, though. I wanted to push myself.

Right about then, the character of Slanted Jack walked into my head. You'll meet him in a minute, so all I'll say about him is that he is another con artist, a full-time one.

So Jon would be dealing with three opposing groups and a con man from his past; now I felt entirely outside my comfort zone, which was exactly where I wanted to be.

The trick with a con artist story is not to fool the reader completely. You can't do that; you readers are way too smart. No, the trick is to play fair while delivering an ending that no reader can guess entirely. I aimed for that goal, and I'm happy to say that so far, I haven't met a single person who guessed every angle of the conclusion of *Slanted Jack*.

If after reading the book that follows, you prove to be the first, drop by my Web site (www.markvanname.com) and let me know. I won't buy you anything, but I will (virtually) bow in admiration.

When you finish, I'll be waiting with a few inside secrets about the book.

SLANTED
JACK

To Gina Massel-Castater
For a lunchtime conversation that
formed the seed of this book
and for so much more

ACKNOWLEDGMENTS

As with my first novel, David Drake reviewed and offered insightful comments on both my outline and the second draft of this book. All of the problems herein are my fault, of course, but Dave again deserves credit for making the novel better than it would have been without his advice.

Toni Weisskopf, my Publisher, has my gratitude for taking a chance on promoting a first novel and buying more in the series before the initial volume had even seen print.

To everyone who purchased *One Jump Ahead*, my great thanks; you've made it possible for me to get to live and write a while longer in the universe I share with Jon and Lobo.

My business partner, Bill Catchings, has both done all he could to encourage and support my writing and also been a great colleague for over two decades.

I've traveled a fair amount while working on this book, and each of the places I've visited has left a mark on me and thus on the work. I want to tip my virtual hat to the people and sites of (in rough order of my visits there during the writing of this book) Portland, Oregon; Santa Clara, California and other parts of Silicon Valley; Florence, Italy; Baltimore, Maryland; New York City; Holden Beach, North Carolina; Yokohama, Kyoto, and Tokyo, Japan, as well as all the countryside I glimpsed in moments of thought while writing on the wonderful high-speed trains; Philadelphia, Pennsylvania; and, of course, my home in North Carolina.

My gratitude always extends to my children, Sarah and Scott, who continue to be amazing teenagers and wonderful people despite having to live with The Weird Dad and put up with me regularly disappearing into my office for long periods of time; thanks, kids.

Several extraordinary women—my wife, Rana Van Name; Allyn Vogel; Jennie Faries; and Gina Massel-Castater—grace my life with their intelligence and support, for which I'm incredibly grateful.

SLANTED
JACK

CHAPTER
ONE

Nothing should have been able to ruin my lunch.

Joaquin Choy, the best chef on any planet within three jumps, had erected his restaurant, Falls, just outside Eddy, the only city on the still-developing world Mund. He'd chosen the site because of the intense flavors of the native vegetables, the high quality of the locally raised livestock, and a setting that whipped your head around and widened your eyes.

Falls perched on camo-painted carbon-fiber struts over the center of a thousand-meter-deep gorge. You entered it via a three-meter-wide transparent walkway so soft you were sure you were strolling across high, wispy clouds. The four waterfalls that inspired its name remained visible even when you were inside, thanks to the transparent active-glass walls whose careful light balancing guaranteed a glare-free view throughout the day. The air outside filled your head with the clean scent of wood drifting downstream on light river breezes; a muted variant of the same smells pervaded the building's interior.

I occupied a corner seat, a highly desirable position given my background and line of work. From this vantage point, I could easily scan all new arrivals. I'd reserved and paid for all the seats at the five tables closest to me, so a wide buffer separated me from the other diners. In the clouds above me, Lobo, my intelligent Predator-class assault vehicle, monitored the area surrounding the restaurant so no threat could assemble outside without my knowledge. I'd located an exterior exit option when I first visited Choy, and both Lobo and I could reach it in under a minute. Wrapped in a blanket of security I rarely achieved in the greater world, I could relax and enjoy myself.

The setting was perfect.

Following one of my cardinal rules of fine dining—always opt for the chef's tasting menu in a top-notch restaurant—I'd forgone the offerings on the display that shimmered in the air over my table and instead surrendered myself to Choy's judgment, asking only that he not hold back on the portion size of any course. Getting fat is never an issue for me. At almost two meters tall and over a hundred kilos in weight, I'm large enough that I'd be able to eat quite a lot if I were a normal man, and thanks to the nanomachines that lace my cells, I can eat as much as I want: They decompose and flush any excess food I consume.

Spread in front of me were four appetizer offerings, each blending chunks of a different savory meat with strands of vegetables steaming on a glass plate of slowly changing color. Choy instructed me to taste each dish separately and then in combinations of my choice. I didn't know what any of them were, and I didn't care. They smelled divine, and I expected they would taste even better.

They did. I leaned back after the third amazing bite and closed my eyes, my taste buds coping with that most rare of sensory pleasures: sensations that in over a hundred and fifty years of life they'd never experienced. I struggled to conjure superlatives equal to the dishes.

The food was perfect.

What ruined the lunch was the company, the unplanned, unwanted company.

When I opened my eyes from my contemplation of that confounding and delicious blend of flavors, Slanted Jack was walking toward me from the stark white entrance hallway.

Slanted Jack, so named because with him nothing was ever

straight, had starred in one of the many acts of my life that I'd just as soon forget. The best con man and thief I've ever known, he effortlessly charmed and put at ease anyone who didn't know him. When he eased through a room of strangers, they all noticed. He was a celebrity whose name none of them could quite remember. Maybe ten centimeters shorter than I, with a wide smile, eyes the blue of the heart of flame, and skin the color and sheen of polished night, Jack instantly cornered the attention of everyone around him. While weaving his way through the tables to me he paused three times to exchange pleasantries with people he was almost certainly meeting for the first time. Each person Jack addressed would know that Jack found him special, important, even compelling, and Jack truly would feel that way, if only for the instant he invested in sizing up each one as a potential target.

While Jack was chatting with a foursome a few meters away, I called Lobo.

"Any sign of external threat?"

"Of course not," Lobo said. "You know that if I spotted anything, I'd alert you instantly. Why are you wasting time talking to me when you could be eating your magnificent meal, conversing with other patrons, and generally having a wonderful time? It's not as if you're stuck up here where I am, too high to have even the birds for company."

"It's not like I could bring you into the restaurant with me," I said, parroting his tone. I know he's a machine, but from almost the first time we met I've been unable to think of him as anything other than "he," a person. "Nor, for that matter, do you eat."

"You've never heard of takeout? I may not consume the same type of fuel as you, but I can be quite a pleasant dinner companion, as I'd think you'd realize after all the meals you've taken while inside me."

I sighed. Every time I let myself fall into an argument with Lobo when he's in a petulant mood, I regret it. "Signing off."

"You don't want to do that yet," Lobo said.

"Why?" Just when I think I understand all the ways Lobo can annoy me, he comes up with a new one.

"Because I was about to alert you to an internal threat," he said.

"Let me guess," I said. "The tall man who recently walked into the restaurant and is now talking to some people not far from me."

"Correct," Lobo said. "I did not consider the threat high both because other humans have stayed between you and him since he entered and because his two weapons are holstered, one under his left arm and the other on his right ankle."

Jack was armed? *That* was unusual, the first thing he'd done that didn't fit the man I'd known. Jack had always hated weapons and delegated their use to others, frequently to me. I don't like them either, nor do I like violence of any type, but both have been frequent hazards of most of the kinds of jobs I've taken over the last many decades.

"Got it," I said. "Anything else you can tell?"

"That's all the data I can obtain from this distance, and even that information required me to force enough power into the scan that the restaurant's skylights are now complaining to the building management system about the treatment they have to endure."

I kept my eyes on Jack and tuned in to the common appliance frequency. Restaurants employ so many machines, every one of which has intelligence to spare and a desire to talk to anything that will listen, that tapping into their chat wavelength was like stepping into the middle of a courtyard full of screaming people. The sonic wall smacked me, the sounds in my head momentarily deafening even though I knew they weren't really audio at all, just neurons and tweaked receptors firing in ways Jennie and the experiments on Aggro had combined to make my brain interpret as sounds. I sorted through the conversations, ignoring mentions of food and temperature until I finally found a relevant snippet and focused on it.

"Radiation of that level is simply not normal for this area," one pane said, "though fortunately it is well within the limits of what my specs can handle."

"All of us can easily handle it," said another pane. Household and building intelligences, like appliances, are insanely competitive and desperate for attention. They spend most of their lives bickering. I listened for another few seconds, but all the chatter was between the pieces of active glass; the household security system didn't respond to the windows, so it clearly didn't consider the burst from Lobo's scan to be a risk. I should tell Joaquin to upgrade his systems.

"If you see that man reach for either weapon," I said, "alert me instantly."

"Of course," Lobo said. "Must you constantly restate previous arrangements?"

"Sorry. Humans use reminders and ritualized communications during crises."

"I appreciate that, and I sometimes don't mind, but he's one man, he's made no move to suggest aggression, and so I hardly consider him a crisis."

Lobo clearly didn't appreciate the trouble a single man could cause, much less a man like Jack. Jack had finished with the four-some and was now leaning over a couple at a table adjacent to the first group. "Now signing off," I said.

I blended bits of food from a pair of the plates into another bite, but I couldn't take my eyes off Jack; the charms of the appetizers were dissipating faster than their aromas. Jack would require all my attention. He and I had worked the con together for almost a decade, and though that time was profitable, it was also consistently nerve-racking. Jack lived by his own principles, chief among which was his lifelong commitment to target only bad people for big touches. We consequently found ourselves time and again racing to make jumps off planets, always a short distance ahead of very dangerous, very angry marks. By the time we split, I vowed to go straight and never run the con again.

"Jon," Jack said as he reached me, his smile as disarming as always. "It's good to see you. It's been too long."

"What do you want, Jack?"

"May I join you?" he said, pulling out a chair.

I didn't bother to answer; it was pointless.

He nodded and sat. "Thank you."

He put his hands palm-down on the tablecloth, so I said nothing.

A server appeared beside him, reset the table for two, and waited for Jack's order.

"I throw myself on Joaquin's mercy," Jack said. "Please tell him Jack asks only that he be gentle."

The server glanced at me for confirmation. Jack wasn't going to leave until he had his say, so I nodded, and the server hustled away.

"Joaquin truly is an artist," Jack said. "I—"

I cut him off by standing and grabbing his throat.

"I'd forgotten how very fast you are for a man your size," he croaked. As always, he maintained his calm. He kept his hands where they were. "Is this really necessary?"

I bent over him so my left hand was on his back and our bodies covered my right hand, with which I continued to grip his neck tightly enough that his discomfort was evident. "Carefully and slowly put both weapons on the table," I said. "If you make me at all nervous, I'll crush your throat."

"I believe you would," Jack said, as he pulled out first a small projectile weapon from under his left shoulder and then an even smaller one from a holster on his ankle, "but I know you would feel bad about it. I've always liked that about you."

"Yes, I would," I said. When the weapons were on the table, I pushed back Jack's chair, released his throat, and palmed both guns. I put them behind my chair as I sat.

Jack stretched his neck and pulled his chair closer to the table. "I really must locate a tailor with better software," he said. "You shouldn't have been able to spot those."

I saw no value in enlightening him about Lobo's capabilities. "What do you want, and since when do you travel armed?"

Jack assembled bits of all four of my appetizers into a perfectly shaped bite, then chewed it slowly, his eyes shutting as the tastes flooded his mouth. "Amazing. Did I say Joaquin was an artist? I should have called him a magician—and I definitely should have dined here sooner."

He opened his eyes and studied me intently. The focus of his gaze was both intense and comforting, as if he could see into your soul and was content to view only that. For years I'd watched him win the confidence of strangers with a single long look, and I'd never figured out how he managed it. I'd asked him many times, and he always told me the same thing: "Each person deserves to be the center of the universe to someone, Jon, even if only for an instant. When I focus on a man or a woman, that person is my all." He always laughed afterward, but whether in embarrassment at having been momentarily completely honest or in jest at my gullibility is something I've never known.

"We haven't seen each other in, what, thirty years now," he said, "and you haven't aged a day. You must give me the names and locations of your med techs"—he paused and chuckled before continuing—"and how you afford it. Courier work must pay far better than I imagined."

I wasn't in that line of work when I last saw him, so Jack was telling me he'd done his homework. He also looked no different than before, which I would have expected: No one with money and the willingness to pay for current-gen med care needs to show age for at least the middle forty or fifty years of his life. So, he was also letting me know he had reasons to believe I'd done well since we parted. I had, but I saw no value in providing him with more information. Dealing with him had transformed the afternoon from pleasure to work; the same dishes that had been so attractive a few minutes ago now held absolutely no appeal to me.

I decided to try a different approach. "How did you find me?"

He arranged and slowly chewed another combination of the appetizers before answering. "Ah, Jon, that was luck, fate if you will. Despite the many years we've been apart, I'm sure you remember how valuable it is for someone in my line of work to develop supporters among jump-gate staff. After all, everyone who goes anywhere eventually appears on their tracking lists. So, when I made the jump from Drayus I stopped at the gate station and visited some of my better friends there, friends who have agreed to inform me when people of a certain," he looked skyward, as if searching for a phrase, "dangerous persuasion passed into the Mund system. Traveling in a PCAV earned you their attention, and they were kind enough to alert me."

I neither moved nor spoke, but inside I cursed myself. During a recent run-in with two major multiplanet conglomerates and a big chunk of the Frontier Coalition government, I'd made so many jumps in such a short period that I'd abandoned my previously standard practice of bribing the station agents not to notice me. Break a habit, pay a price.

"Speaking of your transport," he said, "is that a show copy or the real thing?"

I said nothing but raised an eyebrow and forced myself to take another bite from the nearer two plates. With Jack, silence was often the best response, because he would then try another approach at the information he wanted, and the tactics he chose frequently conveyed useful data.

"There's no shame in a good copy, Jon," he said, his curiosity apparently satisfied. "I spent a couple of years recently brokering the machines to planetary and provincial governments in this sector. The builder, Keisha Li, was this munitions artist—and I mean that, Jon, not merely a manufacturer, but an artist—who found her niche on Gash but couldn't ever hit it big. Her dupes were full, active transports that could handle any environment their originals could manage, though admittedly they were slower—and, of course," he chuckled, "completely lacking firepower. I helped her grow her business. We sold a couple of PCAV clones, though they're pricey enough that they were never our top sellers. Less expensive vehicles provided most buyers all of the intimidation value they sought." He leaned forward for a moment, his expression suddenly sad. "The worst part is that it was completely legal, an indirect sort of touch that I thought would be perfect for me, the real job I've always wondered if I could hold, and it delivered no juice, Jon. None." He sat back and threw up his hands as if in disgust. Jack always spoke with his whole body, every gesture calculated but still effective. "Oh, we made money, good money, the business grew, and we were safe and legit, but I might as well have been hawking drink dispensers." He took another bite, savored it, and then shook his head. "Me, selling machines on the straight. I mean, can you imagine it?"

As engaging as Jack was, I knew he'd never leave until he'd broached his true topic, so I tried to force him to get to it. "Jack, answer or one of us leaves: What do you want?"

He leaned back and looked into my eyes for a few seconds, then smiled and nodded. "You never could appreciate the value of civilized conversation," he said, "but your very coarseness has also always been part of your appeal—and your value. Put simply and without the context I hope you'll permit me to provide, I need your help."

Leave it to Jack to take that long to give an answer with absolutely no new content. If he hadn't wanted something, he'd never have come to me.

"When we parted," I said, "I told you I was done with the con. Nothing has changed. You've ruined my lunch for no reason." I stood to go, the weapons now in my right hand behind my back.

Jack leaned forward, held up his hand, and said, "Please, Jon, give me a little time. This isn't about me. It's about the boy."

His tone grabbed me enough that I didn't walk away, but I also didn't sit. "The boy? What boy? I can't picture you with children."

Jack laughed. "No," he said, "I haven't chosen to procreate, nor do I ever expect to do so." He held up his hand, turned, and motioned to the maître d'.

The man hustled over to our table, reached behind himself, and gently urged a child to step in front of him.

"This boy," Jack said. "Manu Chang."

CHAPTER TWO

Chang stared at me with the wide, unblinking eyes of scared youth. With shoulders slightly wider than his hips and a fair amount of fuzz on the sides of his neck, he appeared to be somewhere between ten and twelve, not yet inhabiting a man's body but on the cusp of the change, soon to begin the transformation into adulthood. His broad mouth hung open a centimeter, as if he were about to speak. He wore his fine black hair short, not quite a buzz cut but close. Aside from the copper hue of his skin nothing about him struck me as even remotely notable, and even that flesh tone would be common enough in any large city. He stood still, neither speaking nor moving, and I felt instantly bad for him, stuck as he was in an adult situation whose nuances were beyond his ability to understand, with an angry man—me—staring down at him.

"Are you hungry, Manu?" I said as I sat, again putting the weapons behind my chair.

He nodded but didn't speak, the fear not releasing its grip on him.

"Then please eat with us." The maître d' was, predictably, ahead of me: Two servers appeared, hustled the boy into a chair, and composed a plate of food for him from the remains of the appetizers and two new dishes they brought for us all to share. Manu sat but otherwise didn't move. After I took a bite from the plate nearest me and Jack did the same, Manu followed suit. The boy swallowed the first bite as if it were air, consumed it so quickly he couldn't possibly have tasted it, and inside I winced at the waste of Choy's artistry.

I forced a smile and said, "Good, huh?"

Manu nodded.

"Have all you want," I said.

I turned my attention back to Jack as Manu attacked the food in earnest. Jack was almost certainly manipulating me; he knows no other way to interact with others. The odds of my later regretting asking him a question were high, but I was too curious not to continue. I also had to admit that the boy's open, guileless gaze touched me—probably as Jack had intended. "Why do you want my help?" I said.

Though I was certain that inside he was smiling, all Jack permitted his face to show was concern for the boy and appreciation at my interest. "My answer will make sense only if I give you some context," he said, "so I have to ask you to grant me a few minutes to explain."

"Go ahead," I said, leaning forward and lowering my voice, "but, Jack, don't play me." As I heard my own words, which I meant and delivered as seriously I could, I grasped how well he'd hooked me. I was speaking nonsensically: Jack isn't capable of saying anything to anyone without having multiple angles at play, and, as he taught me, the mark who has to urge you to tell the truth already wants to hear the pitch.

He leaned conspiratorially closer, so our faces were almost touching, and whispered. "I know you're aware of Pinkelponker," he said. "Everyone is. But do you know why it matters?"

"Yeah, of course I've heard of it," I said, leaning back as if the name didn't matter to me. "It's quarantined. So what?"

Pinkelponker. Hearing Jack say it shook me far more than his appearance, more than the scared boy now sitting with us, more than any of the suspicions I'd felt since Jack had shown up. I did my best to hide my reaction. I was born on that planet, and I lived there with my sister, Jennie, an empathic healer, until the government shuttled her away from our home island and forced her to heal only those people it deemed important. I've never forgiven myself for not finding a way to rescue her, to bring her back safely.

Pinkelponker occupies three unique niches in human history.

It's the only planet successfully colonized by one of Earth's pre-jump-gate generation ships, its name the result of that ship's captain foolishly letting his young son choose what to call mankind's first remote, planetbound colony. The ship ultimately failed to land properly, crashed badly enough that it could never take off again, and stranded its entire population until humanity discovered the jump gate that led to the two-aperture gate near Pinkelponker.

It's the only place where radical human mutations not only survived but also yielded parahuman talents, such as my sister's healing abilities. Never found elsewhere, these abilities were now the stuff of legends, stories most people consider on par with tales of elves and dragons.

And, it's the only planet humans have ever colonized that is now forbidden territory. It exists under a continuous quarantine and blockade, thanks to a nanotech disaster that led to the abandonment and banning of all research into embedding nanomachines in humans.

What no one knows is that the rogue nanomachine cloud that ultimately caused the planet's enforced isolation came into existence as part of my escape from Aggro, the research prison that orbited above Pinkelponker. More importantly, to the best of my knowledge no one alive knows that I'm living proof that nanomachines can indeed safely exist in humans—and I very much want it to stay that way. Any group that learned the truth about me would want to turn me into a research animal. My months on Aggro as a test subject stand as some of the worst and most painful times in a long life with more than its share of pain; I'll never let that happen again.

I'd lost track of the conversation. I forced myself to concentrate on what Jack was saying. Fortunately, he didn't seem to have noticed that I'd drifted away for a moment.

". . . hasn't been open to travel in over a century and a quarter," he said. "If you haven't spent much time in this sector of space, you wouldn't have any reason to keep up with it, though obviously even you know about the quarantine."

"Who doesn't?" I said as casually as I could manage. Jack held my attention now, because far more relevant than my past was a disturbing question I should have considered earlier: Was he telling me all this because he'd learned more about my background than I ever wanted anyone to know?

"It's tough to avoid," he said, his head nodding in slow agreement, "particularly for those of us who always plot the best routes off any world we're visiting." He smiled and pitched his voice further downward, speaking softly enough now that without thinking I again leaned forward to hear him better. "But have you heard the legends?"

"What legends?" I said. Playing dumb and letting Jack talk seemed the wisest option.

"Psychics, Jon, not grifters working marks but *real* psychics. Pinkelponker was a high-radiation planet, a fact that should simply have led to a lot of human deaths. Something about that world was special, though, because instead the radiation caused the first and so far *only* truly useful human mutations—something humanity has never seen anywhere else. The legends tell of the existence of all types of psychics, from telekinetics to healers to seers."

Jack sat back, his expression expectant, waiting for me to react. I'd seen him use this technique to draw in marks, and I wasn't about to play. As I now feared Jack might know, I hadn't come to Mund simply for Choy's cooking, as amazing as it was reputed to be. Mund was one of the worlds with a jump aperture to Drayus, the only planet with an aperture to Pinkelponker since the one on Earth mysteriously closed a decade after it opened. No other gate aperture had ever grown over and stopped working. New apertures appeared from time to time, and each one inevitably led to a system with a planet suitable for human colonization, but once open, apertures always stayed that way. Theories abounded, of course, as to why this one and only one aperture had closed, but as with everything else about the gates, humanity could know only what they did, never why they did it.

The Drayus aperture was now also closed, but not because it had stopped working. As far as anyone knew, it still functioned correctly. What kept it out of operation was the most potent and long-lasting blockade mankind had ever assembled: No human had successfully passed through it in a hundred and thirty years. All but one of the few ships that had made the jump—before the Central and Expansion Coalition governments had cooperated in shutting down all access to the gate—had never returned. The one ship that made it back had passed halfway through the aperture, just far enough that its crew could warn of the nanocloud that was dissolving it and then return in time to prevent the cloud from entering this system. No one is sure why the nanocloud itself couldn't make the jump, but neither is any government willing to take the chance of sending another vessel and possibly bringing back the cloud. The CC and EC ships stationed at the gate make sure no private craft try, either.

Despite all that, the aperture was still there, still a possible way to my home, maybe even to Jennie, if she—or anyone—remained alive in that system. I visited this sector of space periodically, each time wondering how I could get back to Pinkelponker and see if Jennie still lived—and each time realizing with a gut-wrenching sense of failure that there was no way I could reach her, no chance I could save her even if by some miracle she hadn't died of old age on a planet whose medical science was stranded over a century ago.

I could only lose by giving away any of this knowledge about my past, so I waited. A pair of servers took advantage of the silence to whisk away our dirty dishes. Another pair replaced them with fresh plates, each a work of art combining greens, nuts, and small pieces of cheese. Manu immediately took a bite. He chewed quietly and steadily. I eyed the food but couldn't make myself eat.

After a minute, Jack realized he'd have to keep going on his own. He leaned closer again and, his eyes shining brightly, said, "Can you imagine it, Jon? In all the colonized planets, not one psychic—until Pinkelponker."

Jack was as dogged as he was slippery, so I knew he'd never give up. I had to move him along. "You said it, Jack: legends. Those are just legends."

He smiled, satisfied now that I was playing the role he wanted me to fill. "Yes, they're legends, but not all legends are false or exaggerated. In the less than a decade between the discovery of Pinkelponker's jump gate and the permanent quarantine of that whole area after the nanotech disaster, some people from that planet naturally visited other worlds. Some of those visitors never went home. And," he said, leaning back, "a very few of those who opted to live on other worlds were psychics." He put his right hand gently on the boy's back. "Like Manu's grandmother. Though she died, and though her only son didn't inherit her powers, her grandson did.

"Manu did. He's proof, Jon, that the legends were true. He's a seer."

I stared at the boy, who continued to eat as if we weren't there. I already knew the legends were true, because Jennie was proof of it. I was born with a mind that would never progress past that of a normal five-year-old's, but Jennie not only fixed me, she also pushed my intelligence way beyond the norm, made me somehow able to communicate on machine frequencies, altered my vision so I could see in the IR range, and enabled my brain to control the nanomachines the Aggro scientists later injected into me. She'd told me that others with special powers existed, but she'd never provided specifics, and I never met any of them. I didn't have a chance to question her further about them, because right after fixing me she boarded a government ship, and I haven't seen her since.

Though Jack's story of Pinkelponker natives visiting other planets seemed reasonable enough—the wealthy of all worlds move around readily—I'd never heard it before. More importantly, with Jack I couldn't trust anything to be true, and I couldn't assume that any tidbits that happened to be accurate were anywhere near the whole story. I needed to keep him talking and hope I could lure him into giving me more of the truth than he'd planned.

"I don't buy it, Jack," I said. "If the boy could see the future, he'd already be famous or rich—or the hidden property of some conglomerate. He sure wouldn't be with you."

Jack shook his head. "Wrong on all counts, Jon." He held up his right hand and ticked off the points on his long, elegant fingers. "First, his powers don't work reliably. I told you: He's two generations away from the planet. He sees the future, but in visions whose subjects and timing he can't control. He has no clue when they'll hit him. Second, his parents, until they died"—he glanced at Manu, whose face clouded suddenly and appeared near tears—"bless them both, though not well off were also not stupid, so they kept him hidden. Third, and this leads me to why I'm here, the visions damage him. In fact, without the right treatments to suppress them, and without continuing that regimen indefinitely, well," he looked at the boy with what appeared to be genuine fondness and then stared at me, choosing his words carefully, "his body won't be able to pay the bill his mind will incur."

"You don't need me to go to a med tech," I said.

"Normal med techs can't provide these treatments," Jack said, "and those few that do offer them charge a great deal more than the meager amount his parents left him. The uncle who was raising him is a man of modest means who also couldn't even begin to pay for this level of care. The whole situation is further complicated by our need to keep Manu's abilities quiet."

"You said he's with you, and you mentioned doing well selling the faux weapons vehicles, so why not just foot the bill yourself?"

"Alas, Jon," he said with a wistful smile, "my lifestyle is such that little money from that brief interlude remains, so my own funds are also inadequate to the task."

"So you want to borrow the payments from me?" I said. Jack and I had covered this ground before, after the second time I was stupid enough to grant him a loan; somehow his limitation not to con good people didn't extend to his friends. He felt that any colleague who couldn't spot a con deserved to be plucked. He certainly knew that I'd vowed never to loan him money again.

He waved his hands quickly and shook his head; I was pleased to see he hadn't forgotten. "No, no," he said, "of course not. I'm simply helping Manu and his uncle get the money. I've arranged a way, but it has," he paused, giving the impression of searching for words I'm sure he'd already rehearsed, "an element of risk."

I motioned him to continue and looked at Manu. The boy's eyes were now dry and focused nowhere at all, as if he'd long ago become accustomed to people talking about him as if he weren't there. I've always found it puzzling how many people do that to children, even their own children. Manu continued to eat, now moving slowly and methodically, without pause, with the kind of determined focus common among those who never know how long it'll be until their next meal.

Jack nibbled at his salad, taking small bites and savoring each one.

I admired my plate, but I still had no stomach for it.

"Pinkelponker is, as you might imagine," he continued, "the object of considerable interest to certain mystic groups, as well as to many historians. One particular Pinkelponker fanatic, an extremely wealthy man named Siva Dougat, has set up a Pinkelponker research institute and museum—a temple, really—near the ocean on the northern edge of downtown Eddy. He's the leader of a group that calls itself the Followers, people who believe that the key to humanity's destiny lies in that long-forbidden planet. Dougat initially bankrolled the whole group, but like most cults, it's subsequently amassed considerable wealth by absorbing the accounts of many of the hardcore faithful who've joined it."

He looked off to the right for a moment. "Didn't we run a cult scam once before?"

We'd made quite a few plays in our days together, but never that one, so I shook my head.

"No? Oh, well, I must have done it with someone else. My mind is clearly slipping. It was certainly profitable enough, and if I do say so myself, I made quite a grand religious leader, but I have to tell you, Jon: I couldn't keep it up. I could never respect anyone who would worship me."

"Dougat," I said.

Jack smiled, and then I realized how quickly I'd taken the hook.

"Yes, of course. He's interviewed every Pinkelponker survivor and survivor descendant he's ever found. He claims to make all the recordings available in his institute, though," Jack paused and stared off into space again, "I suspect he's the sort who's held back anything of any significant potential value. What matters most is that he pays for the interviews. I've contacted him about Manu, and he's offered a fee—just for an interview, no more—that's large enough to keep the boy in treatments for a very long time."

"So what's the problem?" I said. "You've found a way to earn Manu the money he requires. You don't need me."

"I don't trust Dougat, Jon. He's rich, which immediately makes him suspect. He runs a religious cult, so he's a skilled con man. Worst of all, you can hear the fervor in his voice when he talks about Pinkelponker, and fanatics always scare me. When I told him about Manu's visions, he sounded as if he were a Gatist with a chance to be the first to learn the source of the jump gates. He's not faking his interest, either. You know I've spent a lot of my life cultivating desire in marks and spotting when they were hooked; well, Dougat wants Manu badly, Jon, badly enough that I'm worried he might try to kidnap the boy."

"You're asking me to provide protection?" I said.

"You and that PCAV of yours," Jack said quietly. "I know what you're capable of, and real or faux, your PCAV makes an impressive presence. If I'm wrong about Dougat, this will cost you only a little time. If I'm right, though, then I'll feel a lot better with you beside me. You know I'm no good at violence."

Despite myself, I nodded. I don't like violence; at least the part of me under my conscious control doesn't like it, but the anger that's more tightly laced throughout me than the nanomachines emerges all too readily. I tell myself I do everything reasonably possible to avoid fights, but all too often the jobs I accept end up in conflict.

"You've already learned I'm a private courier," I said. "If you and the boy want to go somewhere, and if you have the fare, I'll treat you as a package and take you to your destination under my care. I'm no bodyguard, though"—I had no reason to assume Jack knew of the five years I'd spent being exactly that—"so I can't help you with the meeting."

"One day, Jon," he said, "just one day. That's all I need you for. We meet Dougat three days from now at the Institute. I wanted a safe, public place, but he wouldn't go anywhere he couldn't control the security. We compromised on meeting in the open, on the grounds in front of his main building, where anyone passing by could see us. All I'm asking is that you come with us, watch our backs, and if things turn bad, fly us out of there. That's it."

Jack wouldn't drop it until I'd found a way to say no that he understood, so I cut to the easiest escape route. "How much do you propose to pay me for this?" I said.

"Nothing."

No answer he could have given would have surprised me more. Jack always came ready to any bargaining table. I fought to keep the surprise from showing on my face. It was the first thing he'd said that made me wonder if he might actually for once be on the up-and-up.

"I don't have any money to pay you," he continued, "and I won't make any from this meeting; everything Dougat pays goes to Manu. I'm doing it for him, and I'm asking you to do the same. With all the dicey business we've worked, wouldn't you like to do some good now and again?" He leaned back, put his hands in his lap, and waited, an innocent man who'd said his piece.

The spark of trust Jack had created winked out as I realized there was no way he was doing something for nothing. "Why are you involved in all this, Jack? Skip the pitch; just tell me."

Jack looked at Manu for a few seconds. "I really am out to help Manu. His uncle's a friend, and I feel bad for the boy." He straightened and a pained expression flickered across his face. "And, Earth's greatest export has once again left me with a debt I must repay, this time to Manu's uncle."

"Poker," I said, laughing. "A gambling loss?" Jack had always loved the game, and we'd played it both for pleasure and on the hustle, straight up and bent. I enjoyed it well enough, but I rarely sought it, and I could always walk away. For him, poker held a stronger attraction, one he frequently lost the will to fight.

"It was as sure a hand as I've ever seen, Jon," he said, the excitement in his voice a force at the small table. Manu started at Jack's tone but resumed eating when everything appeared to be okay. "Seven stud, three beautiful eights to greet me, the next card the matching fourth, and a world of opportunity spread before me. He caught the final two tens on the last two cards—cards he should never have paid to see. Unbelievable luck. I mean, the odds against it were astronomical! A better player would have folded long before; he certainly should have. I put everything into that pot. It was mine." He paused for a few seconds, and when he continued he was back under control. "Honestly, Jon, I was willing to help Manu before that hand, but yes, losing it guaranteed my participation."

"Your debt is not my problem, Jack."

"I realize that, and I wouldn't be asking you if I had an alternative. Unfortunately, I don't. Dougat is the only option Manu's uncle and I have found, I'm committed to help, and I don't trust that fanatic. I'll go it alone if I must, and I'm confident I'll walk away from the meeting, because I hold no interest for the guy, but I fear—" he glanced down at Manu and then spoke quickly "—that I'll exit alone."

That Jack was in a bind was never news—he'd be in trouble as long as he lived—and my days of obligation to him were long over. I felt bad for the boy, worse than Jack could know, because my inability to save Jennie has left me a soft touch for children in trouble, but I learned long ago that I can't save them all. Worse, recent experience had taught me that trying to rescue even one of them could lead to the kind of trouble I was lucky to survive. If I wanted to avoid more danger, I not only needed to steer clear of Jack, I had to leave Mund soon, because I had to assume the same gate staff he'd bribed would be alerting others to my presence. Anyone willing to sell information for the sorts of fees Jack could afford would surely try to jack up their profits by reselling that same data.

The only reasonable choice was to walk away now and leave the planet.

As much as I fought it, however, I knew I wouldn't make that choice.

The problem was the Pinkelponker connection. Dougat's research center and the data he and the Followers had collected might contain scraps of information I could use. If Manu really was a seer, he might also be a source of useful data. In addition, I needed to determine whether Jack knew about or even suspected my ties to the planet, and, if he did, exactly what he'd learned.

Finally, I had to admit that because so many of the jobs I've taken have led to so much damage, the prospect of doing something genuinely good always appealed to me.

I stared into Jack's eyes and tried to read him. Their rich blue color was truly remarkable, and he knew it. He held my gaze, too good a salesman to look away or push harder when he knew the hook was in deep. Even as I stared at him I remembered how utterly pointless it was to search for truth in his face. Jack excelled at close-up cons because at some level he always believed what he was selling, and so to marks he always appeared honest. The only way I could glean more information was to accrete it slowly by spending time with him.

When I glanced at Manu, I found him watching me expectantly, hopefully, as if he'd understood everything we'd discussed. Perhaps he had; Jack hadn't tried very hard to obscure the topic.

I took a long, slow, deep breath, and then looked back at Jack. "I'll help you," I said, "for the boy's sake."

"Thank you, Jon," he said.

"Thank you, sir," Manu said, his voice wavering but clear. "I'm sorry for any trouble we're causing you."

Either Jack had coached the kid well, or the boy meant it. I decided to hope the sentiment was genuine.

"You're welcome," I said to Manu.

Jack caught the snub, of course, but he wisely chose to ignore it.

I now had a job to do and not enough time to prep to do it right. We had to get to work. "Jack, you said the meeting was in three days, so our mission clock is tolerable but far shorter than I'd like. I run this, and you do exactly what I say. Agreed?"

Jack smiled and nodded. "Of course. If I didn't need your expertise, I wouldn't be here, so you're the boss."

Even in victory, he kept selling. I sighed.

"Yes, sir," said Manu.

I forced a smile as I looked at the boy, then turned back to Jack. "Lay it out for me, everything you've agreed to, everything you fear." I sipped a little water. "Then, we'll need to get in some practice time."

CHAPTER THREE

"I don't see why we have to do all this," Jack said, shaking his head. "It's an utter waste of time and energy, and you know how I deplore physical activity." He looked back at the restaurant. "Particularly when we could be doing other, so much more pleasurable things, such as sampling Joaquin's magnificent desserts."

What I knew was how much Jack liked to present the *image* of someone who hated physical activity. I'd once happened upon him during his exercises, and it was immediately obvious that he kept himself in very good physical condition. I'd subsequently learned from careful observation that he worked out daily with an almost religious fanaticism. Maybe he liked to pretend otherwise as part of his goal of constantly maintaining hidden advantages over all those around him, or perhaps he had other, private reasons for preserving the illusion; he never discussed it. I had no way to be certain of his motivation, but the front he presented was fake.

Not that how he felt mattered to me, of course; if I was going to run this operation, we were going to do it right. I turned my back on him, took a few steps away, looked left and right as if scanning the area, and subvocalized to Lobo, "Monitor all of this."

"Of course," he said.

I faced Jack. "You asked for my help," I said. "You're not paying me anything. So, you either completely and without question obey my orders from now until this is over, or . . ." I glanced at Manu and decided to stop there. "Preparation is a vital part of protection."

"Nothing is going to go wrong," Jack said.

"Then you don't need me." I turned away again.

"Okay, Jon," he said. "You win. We'll do what you say."

I nodded and faced him. "Has Dougat or anyone on his team spotted you or Manu?"

"There's no need to be insulting," he said. "Of course not."

"To be safe, spend the next three hours in a countersurveillance run anyway. Head to the center of Eddy, then wind your way to the northern edge. When the time is up, if you're being followed, come back here. Otherwise, meet me in the construction site a kilometer and a half due west." I risked exposing my rendezvous zone with Lobo on the assumption that I could reach it as quickly as anyone who might be watching us.

"I explained that they haven't seen us," he said, pain clear in his tone. "Must we go through this silliness?"

"For the last time, yes. I stated the deal, and you agreed to it, so stop complaining. Maybe it is silly, but we need to know if Dougat has found a way to track you, if he's now seen me, and so on."

Jack shook his head, took Manu's hand, and turned to go.

"Be sure to walk at least the last kilometer," I added.

Jack stopped.

I waited.

"As you say, Jon," he finally said.

Good. I jogged toward the forest that grew all the way to the edge of the lot Choy had cleared around Falls. "I'll see you in three hours."

As I entered the trees, I glanced back. Jack and Manu were gone. I turned west.

"Pick me up at the site," I said to Lobo. "Keep a constant watch on those two, and see if you can spot any signs of surveillance on them or us."

For most of the next three hours, Lobo and I combined a lazy and pseudo-random flight path with an analysis of Jack's movements and the actions of all the people he encountered. Lobo ran simultaneous route projections and motion study filters on each human who might be watching Jack and on all the ships in the airspace within a hundred-kilometer-diameter cylinder with Eddy as its center. One of the great benefits of having a nearly state-of-the-art PCAV is the vast processing capacity he possesses, power originally designed to allow him to take battlefield command of large squadrons or survive and fight on his own for months at a stretch.

Unfortunately, that same vast computing capability let him keep talking the entire time he was conducting the analysis, monitoring Jack and Manu, and flying our course.

"So now you're a babysitter?" he said. "What does that make me? This world's most heavily armed pram?"

"You don't know that," I said, annoyed enough that I felt obliged to needle him. "The Expansion Federation isn't famous for having a light touch, so it might easily have other, more powerful craft in the area, and many of them could be assigned to child care as well."

"Don't know?" Lobo said, the indignation fairly ringing in his voice. "What do you think I do while you're socializing with old friends and enjoying sublime comestibles the likes of which I'm not even equipped to taste?"

"I thought you were watching over me."

"I was, of course, but how much of my capacity do you think that takes? Precious little in this deserted area, I can tell you that. I spend my time amassing data and improving myself, as any thinking creature should." He paused, but I was not going to be lucky enough to get away with a rant that short. "You might consider a little more self-improvement, Jon. You could—"

"Enough," I said, wondering yet again why I ever let myself get involved in these conversations. "We're doing this. Period. The boy needs help."

"A lot of people need help, Jon, help you could give."

From whiner to philosopher in less than a second: another benefit of too much computing power. He had a point, though, and I paused to consider it fairly.

"Yeah," I said, "they do, and I suppose if I were a good enough person I would spend all my time helping others, but I'm not." Dark memories clawed at the fringes of my mind, and I did my best to push them away, a task I manage better during the day than in the sad, scary, honest hours in the middle of the night. I'd done enough bad things over the years that I was sure anyone who really knew me wouldn't consider me good at all, but that wasn't news. "No, I'm not that good." I shook my head to clear it. "For whatever little it's worth, I am decent enough to make sure Manu comes through this interview safely. That has to be worth something, right?" I thought of Jennie and wished, as I have so many times before, that I could have saved her. "Just a rhetorical question."

I took a deep breath, held it, and let it out slowly.

"How far are they from the rendezvous?" I said.

"Assuming they continue their current pace, ten minutes."

"Any sign of surveillance?"

"None," Lobo said. "I would have alerted you had there been any, per your orders."

"Of course. Sorry." I surveyed the many images flickering on the displays Lobo had opened all over his walls: the video surveillance of Jack and Manu, both distant and close perspectives, the motion maps of the people in the area, the flight patterns of all the nearby aircraft and space vehicles, and all the usual PCAV status displays. "We're going to do two unusual things during this training exercise with Jack and Manu."

"I'm excited already," Lobo said.

I ignored him and continued. "I don't want you to let them see any of your weapons at any time, and I want you to do your best imitation of a faux PCAV, the kind of craft you heard Jack say he used to sell."

"So I'm to act dumb?"

I nodded. "Dumb *and* slow." I found myself enjoying this more than I should; pettiness is unbecoming, but sometimes it's also irresistible. "Show only standard vehicle displays, keep your dialog to a minimum, follow only basic voice commands, and don't go above half speed at any time."

"Are you doing this because you're angry at me?" Lobo said. "This strategy makes no sense, because it's not how you'll want me to behave if you need my help during the meeting."

"No," I said, "it's not, and I'm not doing this from anger. The less Jack knows about everything in my life, especially you, the better. He has a nasty talent for turning information into leverage, and as soon as this is over, I want to walk away cleanly and leave him with as little data as possible."

"Maintaining secrets during conflicts makes sense, of course," Lobo said, "but usually one withholds information from the enemy. I thought we were helping Jack, not opposing him."

"We don't call him 'Slanted' Jack for nothing," I said. "You can't trust anything he says to be the truth. So, we'll take extra care even though we're all theoretically on the same team. Clear?"

"Of course."

"One more thing," I said. "I want to make this as easy as possible for the boy, maybe even fun, both so we don't scare him and so he'll learn more quickly."

"Fun?" Lobo said. "Combat-scenario retrieve-and-retreat training?"

"Yeah," I said, "though I must admit I don't have any good ideas."

"Perhaps I'll come up with something," Lobo said, his tone such an odd mixture of serious contemplation and complete sarcasm that I couldn't help myself: For the first time since Jack walked into Falls, I smiled, laughed, and, for a moment, relaxed.

Bare earth marked a square site nearly a kilometer on a side. Autograders perched along its far edges, arguing with each other about who could move the most earth per hour, whose average payload was largest, and who left the smoothest stretch of ground. I tuned them out as soon as I made sure that in the few hours since Lobo and I had taken off none of them had been repurposed for surveillance roles. A light shower had moistened the ground enough that Jack, Manu, and I stirred up almost no dust as we walked to the center of the dirt square. Leaves on the tall trees surrounding most of the site danced happily in the gentle afternoon breeze that carried the life-affirming smell of an undisturbed forest soaking up rainwater. I loved developing planets, the sense of unspoiled nature available only before humans turned all the most beautiful places into either settlements or carefully groomed tourist attractions.

Like all people, however, I disturbed nature when it suited my needs, as it did now.

I sat on my heels so I was roughly at eye level with Manu. "Jack is almost certainly right," I said. "Your interview with Mr. Dougat will probably be a long and boring conversation. I hope it is. Sometimes, though, things change. Maybe a big storm will come along."

"Or maybe he'll try to kidnap me," Manu said, crossing his arms. "I'm not stupid."

I smiled despite myself. "Or maybe he'll try to kidnap you. You're right: That is possible, and I shouldn't treat you as if you're not smart. If he does try anything, I'll stop him."

"Just you? Jack said Mr. Dougat has a lot of people."

"Not just me. Jack will also help, and so will Lobo."

"Who's Lobo?"

"Lobo is my ship."

"Will I get to see it?"

"Oh, yes. In fact, what we're going to do now is prepare ourselves in case something goes wrong at the meeting and we have to leave in a hurry."

"How do we do that?"

I preferred working alone, but I had spent enough time on tactical teams with others that I was comfortable giving and receiving orders from adults. Manu's questions, though, were getting to me. I glanced at Jack, who shrugged slightly, as if to say, "See what I have to put up with?" I forced myself to stay calm and nice. I needed Manu to be comfortable with me.

"We practice," I said. "If anything goes wrong, Lobo will fly to us. He—"

"I thought you said Lobo was a ship."

"Lobo is. People tend to call ships 'him' or 'her,' and with a name like Lobo, I call this ship 'him.' " Manu nodded, so I continued.

"I'll summon Lobo when we need him. When he comes, he'll be flying very fast. He'll open a hatch in his side and hover close to the ground only long enough for the three of us to get in. He won't ever completely stop moving, so our job is to stay together until he's close, then run into him and hold on while he takes off."

"It doesn't sound hard," he said.

"No, it doesn't," Jack said, "but Jon's in charge, so we're going to do what he says."

I glanced at Jack, shook my head, and faced Manu again. "We're not practicing to make me happy," I said. "We're doing it because the sight of a ship as big as Lobo screaming out of the sky at you can be scary, and hopping inside a moving, hovering craft can be harder than it sounds. Jump the wrong way, for example, and you can hit your knees on his hull and fall backwards."

"I'll do it right," Manu said.

"I'm sure you will, and so will Jack, and so will I, but it'll be easier for all of us once we practice." I stood. "Ready?"

Manu nodded, his face resolute, his fists clenched at his sides.

"Now, Lobo," I said aloud, wanting Manu to have a warning the first few times.

I'd told Lobo to come in slower than normal initially, so I expected this to be a very simple first practice.

I'd also never bothered to tell him that I hadn't seriously meant for him to take on the task of making this training fun.

That might have been a mistake.

I heard Lobo before I saw him. Music, carnival music, the same jaunty melody that's brought smiles to children and adults alike on multiple worlds, filled the air as Lobo flew in gently from the west. Louder and louder as he drew closer, the tune tugged an involuntary smile onto all of our faces. Lobo flew in a silly, zigzag path until he coasted to a hover half a meter over the dirt and five meters in front of us, an open side hatch beckoning. Dust from the force of the hover flew around Lobo, but thanks to the recent rain, the amount was small and served only to add to the image of a magical ride. He didn't stop with the music, either: He moved back and forth along his long axis, almost wiggling, as if a twenty-five-meter-long, eight-meter-wide, dull silver metallic dog was dancing in anticipation of some attention from his master.

Manu clapped his hands and laughed. "That's Lobo?" he said. "He's the best!"

Jack put his hand on my shoulder and leaned close enough that he could speak to me without Manu hearing. "Jon, though I have to give you credit for the sheer weirdness of this idea, shouldn't we be boarding?"

My first thought was that I was going to kill Lobo, but of course killing him would not only be extraordinarily difficult, it would also be destroying my most precious asset and the only entity who had consistently been my friend for almost a year. My second thought was a more accurate one: I had only myself to blame.

I looked at Jack and nodded, then touched Manu's shoulder. The boy was still smiling, his eyes wide with joy. "Let's run over and jump in, okay, Manu?"

"You bet!" he said. "It's like getting on a fun ride!"

He took off before us, but longer legs let Jack and me catch him easily. We all jumped on board at the same time, Manu clearing the edge of Lobo's floor easily.

Lobo had, as I'd requested, manifested only the most basic wall displays. I was glad I'd made the request, because Jack was intently studying the interior.

"Having them outfit the knockoff with external audio was a nice touch, Jon," he said.

"It came that way. I bought it used."

Jack nodded. "The exterior is extremely convincing, and the interior's not bad."

"Thanks." I hopped out and motioned to Jack and Manu to do the same. "Let's try it another time, but without the music and with a much faster approach. Okay?"

"Sure!" Manu said. "Let's do it again!"

They both followed me back to our original position. Lobo closed the hatch and took off slowly to the east, then looped north at the edge of the clearing and quickly vanished from sight with a final wiggle and a slowly vanishing whisper of music.

What a ham.

I gave him two minutes, then looked at Manu. "Ready?"

"Oh, yeah!" he said.

"This is going to be very different, maybe even scary."

He looked at me and shook his head. "Lobo can't be scary," he said. "Lobo's fun!"

I was tempted for a moment to explain to the boy how very wrong he was on both counts, but then I realized how successful Lobo's ploy had been. I would never hear the end of this.

"Okay, Lobo," I said. "Now."

Lobo rocketed out of the west like a missile hurtling toward its target, the force of the displaced air pushing us backward as he settled into a hover barely two meters in front of us, his stop more abrupt than I would have thought possible. Alarm played across Jack's face. The speed of the motion triggered my battlefield readiness reflexes, and adrenaline stimmed me to the twitching point.

Manu smiled and clapped again. "I told you Lobo was fun!" he said as he ran and jumped inside. "Aren't you guys coming?"

Lobo was definitely not going to let me forget this.

After three more practice runs, even I had to admit we'd done all we could—all we could, that is, without using missiles or explosives to better simulate a firefight. I didn't want to do that, though, for two reasons: From what Jack had said, we were dealing with a few fanatics, not a militia, and I certainly didn't want Jack to know anything about Lobo's weapons systems.

"We're done," I said, as we sat on the edge of the hovering Lobo, our legs stretched over the side, mine and Jack's touching the earth, Manu's dangling above it.

"Can't we do it one more time?" Manu said.

"No," I said. "You two need to get back into town, and I have other work to do."

"Please."

"Sorry," I said, "but that's it." I faced Jack. "I want you and Manu to get lost and stay lost until the meeting. Fifteen minutes before the start time, scout the site but do *not* enter it. If you don't see me there by then, I decided it's not safe, so you head right back here."

"What will you be doing between now and then?" Jack said.

"My job," I said. "I'm alone, and I have two days, so I have a lot to do." Jack clearly thought I was exaggerating, but I wasn't. Securing a meeting site typically requires a team and the better part of a week. He didn't know about my stint as a bodyguard, nor about my experience on several protection details with what is, in my opinion, the finest mercenary company anywhere, the Shosen Advanced Weapons Corp., the Saw. As always, I saw no reason to enlighten him.

"Don't worry about me," I continued. "Just do your job, which is staying out of sight. As best we can tell, no one is tracking you right now, so make sure it stays that way until the meeting." I stood, picked up a small, thin disc from Lobo's front console, and gave it to Jack. "Stick this on your body where you can easily reach it. If something goes wrong, squeeze it and state your situation; I'll get the alert. If you call me for anything other than an emergency, however, I'll leave. Got it?"

"Yes." He took Manu's hand and jumped out. "See you in two days."

"Bye, Lobo," Manu said, waving. "You're the best!"

When they reached the edge of the clearing, I said, "Let's go."

Lobo closed the side hatch and took off.

"I can do fun," he said.

CHAPTER
FOUR

The Pinkelponker Research Institute sprawled across the built-up northern border of Eddy like a fever dream. No signs warned that when you passed the last of the rows of permacrete corporate headquarters buildings you should expect something very different indeed. No lights, labels, tapestries, recordings, or welcome displays clamored to explain it to you. In the middle of a five-hundred-meter-wide lot the gleaming black ziggurat simply commanded your eye to focus on the miniature of Pinkelponker that revolved slowly in the air a few meters above the building's summit.

Dougat and the Followers named it a Research Institute, but you instinctively knew the moment you saw it that it was a temple, a place where people worshipped, a site of great importance to them.

A perfect lawn the muted green of shallow seawater surrounded the building. Circular flower beds rich in soft browns, glowing yellows, and deep ocean blues burst from the grass at apparently random locations all over the lot. Only when you viewed them from the air, as I had when Lobo and I had made our first recon pass late the morning after my meeting with Jack, did you realize that each grouping of plants effortlessly evoked an image of one of the many volcanic islands that were the only landmasses on my birth planet.

The ziggurat itself looked nothing like any of the individual islands I'd seen, yet its rounded edges and graceful ascent reminded me of home, made me ache for it.

After our initial flyover, I'd directed Lobo to a docking facility on the west side of town and hopped a cab from there. I'd then sent Lobo back up so he could keep watch over me. No one knew me here, so I really shouldn't have needed the protection, but I've learned from past experience that if I give Lobo something to do he's a lot easier to get along with than if I leave him in storage, even if storage is the more sensible alternative.

At least he appreciated that I needed to see the site in person, and he couldn't reasonably join me. If you're going to work on the ground, aerial images and even surface-level recordings are no substitute for actually walking the terrain and getting a feel for it. I've been on multiple missions that didn't permit that luxury, but this one did, and I was going to take advantage of the opportunity. I'd changed cabs twice on the chance anyone had tracked me from the docking center, but neither Lobo nor I spotted any tails. The last cab took me down the street that bordered the Institute on the ocean side, a wide avenue jammed with hover transports, cabs, and personal vehicles all rushing to and fro in the service of Eddy's growing economy. The length of the crossing signal made it clear that the city's planners valued vehicles and commerce far more than pedestrians.

When I finally made it to the Institute's ocean-side entrance, I found the overall effect far more entrancing than anything I'd anticipated from my aerial surveillance. I felt as if someone had sampled my memories and recombined them, managing in the process to create a setting that in no way resembled home but that at the same time rewarded every glance with the sense that, yes, this is the essence of Pinkelponker, what it *meant* if not exactly what it was. Working in the grain fields under the bright sun, the constant ocean breeze cooling me, Jennie due to visit when her day was done—I drifted back involuntarily, my memories summoned by Dougat's artful evocation.

I shut my eyes and forced myself to focus on the job. It was a site

I had to analyze, nothing more. Jack's task was to keep Manu hidden until the meeting. Mine was to make sure we all got out safely if anything went wrong. To do that, I had to learn as much about this place as possible and set up the best protection scenario I could manage given that my only resources were Jack, Lobo, and myself.

When I looked again at the grounds, I did so professionally. None of the scattered plantings rose high enough or were dense enough that you could hide in them. That was good news for possible threats, but bad news should we need to take cover. I couldn't spot any lawn-care, gardening, or tourist appliances, and when I tuned my hearing to the frequencies such machines use, I caught nothing.

"Lobo," I said over our comm link, "have your scans turned up anything?"

"No," he said. "If there are weapons outside the building, they're not emitting any IR or comm signatures I can trace. I can spot no evidence of sensor activity on the grounds. This place doesn't even have the animal-detection circuits that most developing planets require around the perimeters of buildings. I've never encountered a more electromagnetically neutral setting this close to a city."

"Any luck penetrating the building?"

"No. It's extremely well shielded. It's transmitting and receiving on a variety of frequencies, of course, but everything is either encrypted or boring, standard business interactions with the usual public data feeds."

"Anything significant between here and his warehouse?" In our research on Dougat last night, we'd learned that he owned and operated a shipping and receiving center on the south end of the city.

"Encrypted bursts of the size you'd expect for inventory and sensor management. We should assume that place has the normal software and sensor sentries of any such facility, but it's not as shielded as this building and currently reads IR-neutral. Best estimate is that no people are there."

Good; the security we found here might be all we had to worry about.

"Any other significant activity?"

"Unfortunately," Lobo said, "yes. This structure is transmitting situational updates to the Eddy police headquarters almost continually. If anything happens here, the police will know about it within a second or two."

Dougat definitely had pull, because cops on early-stage worlds are notoriously relaxed and tolerant. They understand that the process of developing a planet is one that engenders many conflicts, and they tend to let the parties involved sort out their differences. That Dougat could get them to monitor his institute so thoroughly meant we had to assume he'd also made sure they'd take his side in any disagreements. So, we had to consider them hostiles. Great.

"How long would it take them to reach here?"

"I can only guess," Lobo said.

"So guess."

"Traffic appears to be bad throughout the day, and I spot no signs of any significant airborne vehicles at their nearest facility. So, I would estimate a response time no faster than seven minutes and no slower than fifteen."

"If anything goes wrong," I said, "we'll consider five minutes to be our window. That means you must remain within a max of two minutes, maybe less."

Even as I said it, I didn't like it. If we ended up dealing with a hostile party on his own turf and we had to cope with a kid, we needed more time.

"I want a bigger window," I said. "We're going to need a diversion."

"What are you willing to destroy?" Lobo said. "If you'll sanction strikes on third-party property, I can demolish enough buildings in their path that the police will need a great deal more time to reach here."

"No," I said. "I don't want to make anyone else pay for our problems." Hurting innocent people or their property was sometimes necessary, but I hated doing it. "Aren't the police closer to Dougat's warehouse than here?"

"Considerably," Lobo said, "but that facility does not appear to be transmitting to police monitors."

"Fine," I said. "We'll use the warehouse if need be. We can visit it tomorrow. We'll make sure that anything we do to it is so loud and so obvious that the police have to attend to it first."

"If I fire at it," Lobo said, "they'll quickly know the attack initiated from an airborne vehicle. In addition, the explosions are extremely likely to damage neighboring properties. Neither of those factors help our cause when we try to jump from this planet."

I nodded and considered the problem. "Good points." The smaller the commotion we caused, the better. In addition, the more we could do without leaving an obvious trail, the more likely we were to be able to get away cleanly, should it come to that. "We'll have to make it look like either an accident or something that someone on the ground did. That would rule you out, and by being here, I wouldn't be a suspect, either."

The plan seemed reasonable, but it could still end up hurting innocents at the warehouse. "Can you get me any more data at all about that building?"

"No," Lobo said. "The place is shielded against both IR and more penetrative scans."

"Then I'll have to check it out myself," I said. "That'll be tomorrow's primary mission. If Dougat maintains a staff there, I'll either have to figure a way to get them out or target only an unoccupied part of the building. That means I'll have to plant implosives. Your arsenal includes a full stock, doesn't it?"

"Of course," Lobo said, immediately indignant.

Even when I ask about things not under his control, such as the replacement weapons I have to buy when we use devices from his munitions supply, Lobo turns petulant. I considered telling him to stop behaving so poorly, but I knew the conversation would prove useless.

Instead, I turned my attention back to the Institute. The air was cooling as night approached, but Eddy was still warm enough that the slight breeze from the ocean felt fine against my skin. I'd stood in one place longer than a normal tourist would, so I walked slowly toward the building.

"In the last fifteen minutes," Lobo said, "over two dozen humans have entered the Institute on the side opposite your position, and twenty have left via the same doors."

"Shift change. How many look like security?"

"All were wearing comm links, so that's impossible to gauge. Based on the building's total lack of visible external sensors or weapons, however, we should assume most are hostiles."

"No," I said. "Even if they're all security, they're not necessarily hostiles, at least not yet. They become problems only if Dougat chooses not to play this straight."

"You're indulging in distracting games," Lobo said, "induced by your emotions. You've involved us, an involvement that matters only if Dougat attempts to kidnap Chang. If he does, he and his staff become hostiles, as do the police. If Dougat doesn't cause any problems, we're spectators. The only reasonable option, therefore, is to treat them all as hostiles for the duration of our participation."

Though I'm glad Lobo is mine, his lack of tolerance for ambiguity frequently leads to conversations that are far more cold-blooded than I prefer. "By that logic," I said, "to maximize our probability of success we should simply kill all the staff and the police. Right?"

*Lobo ignored my sarcasm. "That is sensible from an efficiency perspective," he said, "but it would attract the attention of the EC staff at the gate, and it would also remove Dougat's ability to pay for the interview and thus compromise the overall mission. So, I don't recommend it."

Before I could decide whether I wanted to know if he was also being sarcastic, I reached the ziggurat's entrance.

"Signing off until I exit," I said.

The atmosphere inside was a perfected version of what I'd felt outside: a bit warmer, a little more humid, with light breezes of unknown origins wafting gently across you no matter where you stood. Perpetual daylight brightened the space. Cloudscapes played across the ceiling. The faint sounds of distant surf breaking and wind moving through grasses tickled the edges of perception. Once again, I had only to close my eyes to transport myself to the Pinkelponker of my childhood. Either Dougat or someone on his design team had visited my home world, or their research was impeccable.

The center of the space was a single large open area broken by injection-molded black pedestal tables that glowed in the ever-present light, two-meter-by-four-meter informational displays, and small conversation areas. The island theme continued here, with each cluster of exhibits centered on a topic such as early history, agriculture, speculation on the exact cause and final outcome of the disaster, mineral and gemstone samples, and so on. A few dozen people stood and sat at various spots around the interior, some clearly serious students, and many equally obviously only tourists with at most an idle interest in Pinkelponker. Even the most studiously focused of the visitors would close their eyes from time to time as the interior effects worked on them.

The exceptions, of course, were the security personnel. You can costume security staff so their clothing blends with the visitors', and you can train them to circulate well and even to act interested in the exhibits, but you can't make them appear under the spell of the place they're guarding. Even the most magical of settings loses its allure after you've worked in it for a few weeks. I counted fifteen men and women on active patrol. I had to assume at least a few more were monitoring feeds and weapons scanners, occupying rooms I couldn't see, and generally staying out of my view.

I kept in character as a tourist, lingering long enough at the historical displays to appear interested but not so long as to look like a student of the planet. I'd learned almost nothing of the world's history growing up there, so I was genuinely interested in the background on the generation ship and the later discovery of the jump gate. Docent holograms snapped alert when I lingered at any exhibit, and I let a few of them natter at me. One presentation explored the various religions of Pinkelponker. Growing up there, I never saw a place of worship, and the closest I came to prayer was the occasional desperate hope for Jennie to come visit me or for my chores to be over. I stopped long enough that a docent asked if by chance I belonged to any organization that viewed the planet as sacred. I hadn't realized such groups existed; perhaps the Followers were among them. I obviously had a lot to learn about how some people viewed my home.

A small, meter-wide display in the right rear corner of the space offered the only discussion of the legends Jack had cited. Dougat might be as personally interested in the stories of Pinkelponker psychics as Jack had said, but the man either wasn't letting his interest shape the Institute's exhibits or was keeping a low profile with his beliefs.

Like the other tourists I spotted, I made sure to invest a large chunk of my time gawking at the cases highlighting jagged mineral samples and large, unrefined gemstones. Though I frequently stood alone at one of the historicals, I always had company at the mineral and gem displays. For reasons I've never understood, standing near items of great monetary value, even things you'll never have the chance to touch or own, is a compelling experience for many people. As best I could tell, the larger samples here, like the big gemstones in any museum on any planet, illustrated the power of natural forces applied slowly over long periods of time to create artifacts of great beauty. The waterfalls outside Choy's restaurant and the grooves they'd cut into the cliffs there made the same point and were, to me, more striking and more beautiful than any individual minerals, but for most people they lacked the powerful allure of gems.

I was intrigued to learn that Pinkelponker had been extremely rich in gemstones and that the business of exporting them to other worlds eventually constituted a major source of revenue for the government. All I'd seen of Pinkelponker was a pair of islands: the one where I lived until the government took away Jennie, and the one where they tossed me until my failed escape attempt led them to sell Benny and me to the Aggro scientists for nanotech experimentation. I owed Benny for my eventual escape from that hellish prison, but he'd died in the ensuing accident, so my debt to him was another of the many that I'll never be able to repay.

The images of gleaming government centers sparkling on sun-drenched islands and the stories of gem-fueled wealth led me to wonder, not for the first time, at the amazingly different ways that residents of the same planet can view their world.

The rearmost of the exhibits ended at a long wall that extended across the back of the building and rose to the ceiling. Offices, storage, and loading docks probably filled the remainder of the interior space. As I exited I counted off the distance from that wall; knowing the size of the private space behind it might prove useful. I continued to hope everything would go smoothly and this scouting would prove to have been a waste, but until the interview was over and Jack and Manu were safely away, the more information we had, the better.

To the left of the entrance I paid a visit to a small concession area. The two machines there offered everything from beverages to quasi-historical data files to glowing bouncy ball models of Pinkelponker. I purchased some water and listened on the common appliance frequencies on the chance that I could glean something useful.

"Another big spender," the beverage dispenser said. "Does anyone who visits this place even appreciate what I'm capable of? If they'd bother to scroll through the menu, or simply ask, they'd learn that I could provide everything from juices to local herbal teas—and some quite good ones, if the reactions I've heard are any indication."

"Isn't that always the way it is?" the keepsake vendor said. "Oh, sure, a few will buy a bouncing Pinkelponker model, but what about the built-to-order and personalized options? How many of these people will take real advantage of what I could do for them? Precious few, I can tell you. Why, I bet not one in a hundred of them has even a clue as to the breadth of Pinkelponker souvenirs I could fabricate."

"If it weren't for the staff," the dispenser continued, "my conveyor and rear assembly parts might rot of disuse."

"I'm sorry I'm not thirstier," I said on their frequency, "but I do appreciate the work you both do."

Though machines don't expect humans to talk to them on their radio spectrum, it takes an exceptionally intelligent one, such as Lobo, to ever question why you're able to do so. Most appliances are so self-absorbed and have so much spare intelligence that they'll dive at any chance to chatter endlessly with anything or anyone that responds.

"Thank you for saying so," the dispenser said.

"At least he bought something from you," the other commented.

I interrupted before they could get into an argument and forget me entirely; appliances also have extremely short attention spans. "The staff must keep you very busy. I'm sure they appreciate you, and they seem to outnumber the visitors."

"They appreciate *it*," the keepsake machine said, "but not me. Except for the odd desperate birthday gift purchase, most never even visit me. Of course, it's not like I have an outlet in the back of the Institute. Some machines work at a disadvantage."

"Some machines are simply more important than others," the beverage dispenser said. "Every human has to drink, so my offerings are vital. They do not have to purchase the sort of disposable after-thoughts you peddle."

"I bet each staff member uses you at least once a day," I said, focusing on the dispenser.

"Not quite," it said, "but some order multiple times, so the average daily total is actually a bit better than that."

"You must keep quite busy simply helping them," I said, "because that must be, what, sixty or eighty orders a day."

"I wish!" it said. "It's more like thirty-five to forty orders a day, and I could handle ten times that quantity with ease."

That put the staff count at about three dozen, which meant security could run as high as twenty or more during busy hours. That estimate roughly matched what I'd guessed from walking around. That many guards would have been overkill for a place this size were it not for the gems, but given their presence it was believable. Consequently, Dougat had the option of summoning a lot of human backup, so I definitely needed to keep the meeting in the open, where Lobo could reach us quickly.

I walked outside and wandered for a few minutes among the islands of flowers. That Jack had approached me about a job involving Pinkelponker kept nagging at me. Did he know something about my background, or was it just a coincidence induced by me choosing to spend time on a world only two jumps away? If he'd learned more about me, how, and from what source? With many people I would ask them or feel them out on the topic, but neither approach would work with Jack; he was too much a manipulator for me to play him, and if he knew nothing, I certainly didn't want to alert him that this was a topic he should pursue further.

My safest option was to do the job at hand and listen closely in case he let something slip—an unlikely event, of course, but a possibility nonetheless.

I headed off the grounds and opened a link to Lobo.

"Enjoy your tour?" Lobo said.

The tone of his voice answered my earlier, unspoken question: He'd been speaking sarcastically then. Lobo's mood never changes as a result of breaks in a conversation, no matter how long the interruptions may be—unless, of course, the concerns of a mission intervene. Though his emotive programming was, in my opinion, overblown, his designers had at least possessed the good sense to make him turn all-business when the situation demanded. For that, I was always grateful.

"It was informative," I said, pretending not to have noticed his tone. "As you would expect, we're going to make some modifications to the draft plan we discussed earlier. Pick me up at the rendezvous point in an hour and a half, and we'll walk through it again."

"It's what I live for," Lobo said.

I ignored him and continued. "In the meantime, consider options that do minimal damage to this place. I see no reason to trash more than we have to."

"No reason?" Lobo said, incredulity replacing sarcasm in his voice. "Your instructions were that the top priorities were to get you, Manu, and Jack, in that order, to safety should this turn into more than an interview. You even established that Jack would be in command should you be incapacitated. You wouldn't have given those orders unless you believed this could go badly. Should that happen, the simplest way to achieve your goals and avoid an unwanted conclusion is to take out all opposition staff and positions."

"That's not an option," I said.

I signed off without further discussion. Lobo didn't agree with my orders, but like any professional soldier he'd obey them as long as he was able.

I winced inside at having put myself first on Lobo's priority list, but the reality was that if the day turned nonlinear, the best hope Jack and Manu had was that I stayed alive and protected them or, if need be, went back for them. In some ways I hated the part of me that could coldly assign priorities in life-and-death situations. That same coldness, however, had kept me alive through a great many missions gone very, very wrong, so I was unwilling to abandon it.

In times like these, moments when I can't avoid seeing some of my darker aspects, I find the only force that keeps me going is the job in front of me. Everyone who's ever been through basic training knows how it works. You push aside doubt as best you can, but even if you can't, even if the doubts scream and pull at you, you take the next step—and the next, and the next, and the next, until you either reach your goal or you die.

My next step was the warehouse.

CHAPTER FIVE

The windowless gray permacrete building that Dougat and the Followers used to store their artifacts filled most of a block in the middle of a couple of square kilometers of similar structures. Major roads ran in front and along the back of the ten-meter-tall warehouse. The right half of the plain façade it presented the rare passersby was an awning-covered loading area with a long ramp that led down to the road from the work platform that stood two meters above the ground. A noodleria and a quick-mod body shop crowded either side of the freight deck and were the only bits of the block Dougat didn't own. From our aerial surveillance, the small human staff that ran the facility during the daytime must not have had much work to do, because they spent most of the day feeding on noodles or chatting up the body modders.

The rear was one enormous loading dock that handled the really big stuff. I couldn't imagine what Dougat collected that would require that much capacity; perhaps he'd acquired the warehouse from a previous owner and not bothered to customize it.

We watched the place all day. Only one shipment, four containers, each no more than three meters on a side, entered the building through the front. Nothing went in through the rear. Nothing left.

382   *Mark L. Van Name*

The paved alleys that ran along the sides of the warehouse were little more than footpaths, barely wide enough for two large men to walk abreast. The entire shipping district followed this layout, as if the original designers had realized at the last moment that their clients would never agree to have their buildings share walls and added separating strips as afterthoughts. The buildings were tall enough that even during the day at least a part of every alley was in shadow except for the brief stretches when the sun blazed directly overhead.

Daylight had started fading hours ago, so the spot where I stood, about twenty meters down the left alley from the rear of the building, was dark enough that no one walking by either end of the warehouse would have a chance of seeing me. I'd dressed in mottled black and gray from cap to gloves, and I carried a similarly colored pack. From where Lobo had dropped me in a landing zone a klick or so away, I'd crept from building to building in shadows, pausing after each move to check for possible observers.

Now, after fifteen minutes of waiting silently beside the rapidly chilling wall, as best I could tell all that effort had been a waste. I'd seen no one; the warehouse district was a wasteland. No dealers, no hookers, no patrolmen, no guards—no one.

"Do you read any human IR signatures in the area?" I said to Lobo. Per our now-standard policy, I traveled with a regular comm unit, an emergency broad-frequency transmitter woven into my clothing, and a tracker embedded in my arm. Though I'd initially doubted the value of this redundant setup, after needing Lobo to find me during a recent difficulty, I was happy to take the extra precautions.

"None in the roads or alleys within a block on either side of you," Lobo said. "I must caution again, however, that most of the buildings in this district are shielded, so I can't scan them."

"Understood," I said. "I'm going to send in the rats. Yell if you spot any transmissions."

"Of course," Lobo said. It was mission time, so he maintained a neutral tone, but I chided myself for repeating orders he'd never forget.

Dougat was bound to have outfitted the front and rear of the building with a variety of alarms, but for warehouses this basic and solid, few bothered to lace the permacrete with any electronic protections. The reasoning was obvious: Getting through one of the solid side walls would either require a lot of time or create enough noise that interior security systems would more than suffice to catch an intruder.

Fortunately, I had an option they had no way to anticipate. I spit in my hands, directed the nanomachines to decompose a growing cylindrical section of the wall, and rubbed the spit on the permacrete. Some combination of what Jennie did to fix me and the experiments the Aggro scientists ran on me granted me the ability to exert fine-grain control on the nanomachines that lace my cells. I switched my vision to IR—another gift, though I suspected an unintentional one, from Jennie—and watched as the nanomachines worked quickly and efficiently, the pace accelerating as they used the permacrete to create more copies of themselves, which in turn consumed more and more of the wall. The only signs of their work were the small IR signature of the energy expenditure and the slowly growing cloud of nanomachines where that portion of the wall once stood. I hunched over the small swarm to shield the activity from Lobo; we share a lot, but no one knows what happened on Aggro, and I intend to keep it that way. When the hole was about a third of a meter across, I instructed the nanomachines to disassemble themselves. In a few seconds, a pile of dust along the outside of the wall was all that remained of them. Dougat's people would wonder tomorrow how the intruder had so quietly ground away a section of the permacrete, but the only clue they'd find would be the dust itself.

I took the two customized gas rats out of the pack. I liked the rats because they had so many uses in urban conflicts and rarely aroused suspicion. Collapsed, each arm-size cylinder would attract little attention from anyone who didn't know modern weapons. Activated, the tubes sprouted legs and a coating of sensors that resembled thick, dark-brown hair. Each rat could carry a few kilos of any payload from gas to explosives, and each possessed a modest recon and analysis system.

The rats I gently lowered onto the warehouse floor were special. We'd customized them using Lobo's onboard, battlefield-ready mini-fab, a small but powerful chamber that included full sets of waldos and 3-D printers that either he or I could control. We'd added extensions for detecting and interfacing with both cable-carried and wireless security networks. I thumbed on each rat and pulled my arm out of the hole.

"You're on," I said to Lobo. "Patch me the feed."

Lobo took control of the rats. An IR image of the inside of the warehouse flickered to life on the contact on my left eye. A second, similar image on my right eye immediately followed. Lobo added trace lines that glowed red where cables ran and green where major wireless transmitters hung. The faintly glowing image of the inside of the building superimposed on the end of the alley I was watching, and my mind took a moment to adjust to dealing simultaneously with the two realities. It struck me then that I hadn't used a heads-up display in quite a while, and I was torn over whether the lack of action was a good thing, because it meant I'd managed to avoid violence for a time, or a bad sign, because it suggested that I was turning soft.

I gently shook my head and focused on the two images; the time for self-reflection is definitely not in the middle of a mission.

The rats scurried to the nearest cable carriers, sections of unshielded conduit that ran along the building's side walls about three meters off the floor—high enough that no one would normally bump them, but low enough to make maintenance easy. Each rat fired a small drill-dart that trailed a thin wire as it flew into the conduit and immediately burrowed inside.

I pulled a roll of gray cling from my pack and snapped it into shape. I held it against the wall until the combination of static electricity and embedded glue cemented it tightly to the permacrete. Useful in the field for everything from quick shelters to very temporary repairs, the patch wouldn't pass close inspection, but no one at either end of the alley would notice it. A wire mesh woven into the cling served as an antenna through which Lobo could monitor and enter the building's network.

"I'm live on the security net," Lobo said.

"How long to crack?" Guard networks in shielded buildings typically used relatively weak security protocols, so we figured Lobo's built-in, massively parallel computing infrastructure should be able to hack into this one in a few hours. More than nine hours of darkness remained, so we had plenty of time.

"Go to the rear door," Lobo said. "It's unlocked."

I sprinted to the end of the alley. The interior displays vanished from my vision. I paused long enough to check in both directions for company, then dashed to the staff door. It opened as I approached and closed quickly behind me.

"How did you do that?" I said. "Even if you lucked onto the encoding scheme immediately, unless they used the weakest possible passwords and no additional preventions that should have taken at least an hour or two."

"The security system runs a standard three-level protocol with industrial-level encryption and both password and biometric checks," Lobo said, "so it's fairly typical of this type of installation. You wanted speed, and now you're in. What's the problem?"

"I repeat: How did you do that?"

"I've told you many times that I constantly work to improve myself. That effort extends to my computing infrastructure."

"Fair enough," I said, "but to hack into any system of this caliber that quickly you must have a lot more capacity than I'd ever imagined. Just how does your computing system work, and how far do its capabilities extend?"

"It's a complex topic," Lobo said, "and now is hardly the time to discuss it. By the way, how did you make a hole in the wall for the gas rats? I didn't spot any tools."

Lobo was open and talkative on every topic except himself. In that way, we were similar. Someday, I'd have to demand more information from him; I did own him, after all. He was right that now was not the moment to do that, nor was I interested in explaining myself to him.

"That's also a complex subject," I said, "and I need to get moving. Are all alarms offline?"

"No," Lobo said. "Those circuits send status updates to both the

Institute and the police building each time they go offline. Their sensors are detecting you, but the warning information they're sending is never making it to the control modules. The data begins the journey, but I delete it before the system can react to it. As far as this building is concerned, you're the invisible man."

"Am I alone?"

"Yes."

"That's odd," I said. "I would have expected Dougat to have guards as backup."

"No other building in the area appears to employ human security staff at night," Lobo said, "so Dougat would have drawn attention to the facility had he used any. More importantly, the building's system is not as weak as you seem to believe. What I hacked was the system for the main storage area. A second, much stronger processor grid with a tougher protocol protects the entrance to the basement area."

"Basement?"

"Thirty point five meters east northeast of your position. The route's on your right display."

A schematic of the interior and a jagged blue path that started with me superimposed itself on the right half of my vision. Two rows of shelving separated me from the basement entrance.

"Nice layout diagram," I said. "Can you get any inventory info?"

"Negative," Lobo said. "The protection units need to know only the basics of the interior setup, so that's all they have. They don't even possess links to any outside systems other than those to the Institute and the police building."

"Basement layout?"

"Unavailable. As I said, it's on a separate system."

"Hack it."

"I'm working on it," Lobo said. "I told you it was stronger."

Though any area with a separate security system was inherently interesting, I was wrong to focus on it. My goals were first to set up the diversion and only then to explore if time permitted. Should we need the distraction, I wanted it to cause as little damage as possible, so I hoped to locate a small section of the warehouse with very little of value in it. If the place was packed with valuable goods, I'd live with the potential loss, but I hate senseless destruction. I crept to the nearest row of shelving, pulled a small light from my left front pocket, and started a quick inventory.

In less than two minutes I'd checked five large storage corridors and was all the way to the middle of the building. I needn't have worried about potential damage. The shelves were either empty or holding only basic supplies destined for the Institute: sealed snacks, souvenirs, staff uniforms, and all the other operating matériel of any museum. The labels on the few boxes scattered among the shelves might have been fakes, but from spot checks of the weights, I didn't think so.

The basement was suddenly a lot more interesting, but I had work to do.

If you're hitting a building and you want maximum external effect with minimum internal damage, shaped charges on the roof are just the ticket. You take out a small center section of the target area a fraction of a second before the rest, then angle the perimeter charges so the explosion shoots debris spectacularly skyward but also results in most of the blown bits falling back into the hole. I had five small charges with me, each wrapped around a short arrow with an active head that contained an extensible antenna and a signal repeater. I took the arrows and a small crossbow from my pack; sometimes old tech is the best tech. I shot the first arrow at a spot about midway from the building's sides and ten meters or so from the rear entrance. It stuck nicely. The ceiling was high enough that I couldn't tell if the arrow's tip was finishing the process by drilling until it could extend an antenna above the roof.

I learned it had worked when Lobo picked it up.

"First charge checked in," he said. "Main security systems remain under my control. Even when I pull out, they won't remember it."

"Excellent," I said.

I shot the remaining four arrows into the ceiling so they formed points on a rough circle with a radius of about five meters.

Lobo confirmed each was working as its antenna poked into the night. If we needed the diversion later, Lobo would trigger their primary payloads. If we got away safely, Lobo would set off the tiny secondary charges in the tips of each of the arrows. Each such charge would puncture an acid canister that sat behind its arrow's tip. The resulting corrosive flows would destroy the explosive material and enough of the casings to render the arrows both harmless and extremely difficult to trace.

"I've reconnected to the building net via the antennas," Lobo said, "and told the rats to withdraw their probes and head back to you."

The first rat bumped into my right leg. I picked it up and crammed it into my pack.

Before the other one could reach me, Lobo's voice rang sharp in my ear.

"You have company."

CHAPTER SIX

I snapped off the light, froze, and waited for instructions. The one with the best data should make the call, and right now, that was definitely Lobo.

"Hold," he said. "Two exiting the basement." A few seconds passed in silence. "Heading to the front of the building. Abort?"

As long as those two weren't following up on an alarm, they had no reason to suspect anyone was inside with them. In a place this big and with Lobo feeding me their movements, staying away from them shouldn't be hard. "No," I said. "We wanted to know what they were hiding downstairs; this could be our chance to find out."

"You said you preferred to avoid killing hostiles."

"I don't have to kill them," I said, "to avoid them." Lobo was right, though, that if I went into the basement and the guards trapped me there, I'd almost certainly have to at least hurt them to escape. The secret room was too potentially interesting, however, to pass up.

"We'll use the rats," I said. I carefully and quietly took the one out of my pack and placed it on the floor next to my leg. "Arm both trank gas payloads and position them a meter on either side of the basement door. If the guards come back, knock 'em out." Though my nanomachines can handle any drug to which I've been exposed, I'd taken no chances and had Lobo give me the standard pre-mission inoculation against my own bioweapons, so the gas in the rats shouldn't affect me even though it would buy me plenty of time to get out.

I felt motion against my leg and cranked my vision back to IR so I could watch the rats crawl soundlessly around the row of shelving to my right and out of sight.

Time dilated as I waited, every second suddenly long and dangerous. Being in the dark inside someone else's space always juices you with an emotional cocktail of fear, curiosity, and guilt, but when you're not alone adrenaline floods into the mixture and leaves you jacked and prone to the jitters. Breathing is the key, as it is in so many charged situations. I passed the seconds taking control of my breath, drawing air in through my nose in a slow inhalation, holding it for a moment, and then letting it leak ever so carefully out through my mouth.

I was inhaling for the third time when Lobo updated me.

"Data from the monitor system indicates the guards are eating in a front room."

"Any way to tell if more of them are below?"

"Negative," Lobo said. "As I said earlier, the main system doesn't cover that space."

"Send down one of the rats," I said, "and scan the area." I wanted to add "quickly," but that was stupid, so I stopped myself; Lobo knew what he was doing. "Show me a path to the closest safe hiding space to the open basement door. I want to be ready to go if the area is clean."

A schematic reappeared in my right contact. I crept along the glowing path. Take a step, pause, listen, wonder if I'm hearing the rat moving downward, repeat. When I reached the spot Lobo had chosen, I leaned against the shelving and concentrated again on managing my breathing. My every instinct screamed for action, but training overruled instinct and held me in silent, motionless position. I waited. Long, slow inhale. Hold it. Long, slow, leaking exhale.

I wondered why the adrenaline still came, all the years and all the actions since the first time I'd broken into a storage room on Aggro and hoped for escape. I'd failed then, and I'd failed on many occasions since then, but I'd also succeeded far more than I'd failed. The probability that I couldn't take these guards and get away safely was extremely low, and my mind knew that. Sometimes, though, what your mind knows isn't enough to let you relax.

"Basement clear," Lobo said. "Guards eating. Entrance is a three-meter-wide ramp sloping thirty degrees downward. Go. I'll withdraw the rat when you've made it down there."

A new schematic and path appeared on my right contact. I switched my vision to IR, but it added nothing to the information on the contact; the room was too cool. I followed Lobo's route around the end of the set of shelves that had been hiding me and then down a ramp. I stepped as quickly as I could while still staying silent, tracking myself and gauging my footfalls with the data from Lobo. I've never liked running in the dark with only displays to guide me, but training again overrode preference and kept me moving fast. Lobo's path ended at the bottom of the ramp, so I stopped there.

"Basement layout?" I said.

"Not enough data from the rats to create a reliable one," he said. "Guards are up front, so a small amount of light should be safe."

I pulled out a tiny glowstick and used it to scan the area. The basement appeared to run the length of the building, was about three meters high, and was only slightly narrower than the space above, though I couldn't be sure of its dimensions with the small amount of illumination I felt was safe. Two desks hunched end-to-end on either side of the ramp, a chair behind each one. The two chairs for the desks on my right were pushed back; it was a sloppy setup. The guards should have occupied opposite sides so they'd be in position for a safe crossfire on any intruder and also present separate targets. Their sloppiness wasn't new information, however; any good duo would never have taken their breaks at the same time. Their behavior suggested they were inexperienced, so they probably sat with the most valuable stuff behind them. I headed right.

The first set of shelves on both sides of the lengthwise aisle were empty, so I glided past them.

All the shelves in the second set appeared full. I'd planned to scan them rapidly and move on, but what I saw made me stop, put away the glowstick, and use a small flashlight.

From floor to ceiling and as far to each side as my light illuminated, weapons filled the shelves. Some sat naked, others were in standard reinforced plastic crates. Inventory tags, each bearing the stylized ziggurat logo of the Followers, helpfully illuminated themselves as I walked by and then winked off as I passed. That Dougat hadn't bothered to turn off those displays demonstrated an unwarranted degree of confidence in his security setup. I walked quickly up and down the aisles, knowing time was short but wanting to gather as much information as possible. SAMs, automatic rifles, squidlettes, hoppers, dusters, and on and on—the weapons ranged from anti-personnel to anti-tank to anti-aircraft to space-based and told no consistent story. I didn't spot enough of any one device to outfit more than a few troops or ships, but what the collection lacked in depth it made up in variety. Either Dougat was in the arms business, or he was buying everything he could find and hoping he could construct something sensible from the result. Or was I seeing only a little of his collection, and was he actually preparing a far larger arsenal?

None of this was directly my problem, of course, but it did suggest that if the meeting tomorrow turned bad, Dougat and the Followers might be far more formidable foes than I'd imagined. On the other hand, publicly revealing weapons like most of these would be sure to attract attention, attention he couldn't want because there was no chance he owned all of these devices legally.

What *I* wanted was more information, but even though I'd been in the basement only a couple of minutes, the weight of that time was pushing down on me. I had to get out.

I headed back to the ramp. As my light brushed across the desks opposite the guards', I noticed a rack of inventory checkers at the end of the farther desk. Maybe Lobo had forced his way into the warehouse's systems and I could collect more information from them.

"Have you hacked the inventory units?" I said.

"No," he said. "The security software is surprisingly resourceful, and I encountered serious barriers between the main system and the rest of the programs running the place."

"Will you finish before I pull out?"

"Unlikely," he said, "and once you do I must cut the links or risk leaving open a connection to me."

I looked longingly at the inventory units and the rest of the basement. I wanted to explore further, but it would be a bad choice.

I'd taken two steps up the ramp when Lobo cut in.

"Guards heading back."

A schematic winked into life and pointed me to the earlier hiding place. I ignored the instinct to run and forced myself to walk quickly and silently along the path Lobo had plotted and into the shadows of the shelves. A few seconds later, first one rat and then the other brushed against my left leg. I let them stay where they were and took one step backward so they wouldn't be underfoot if I had to move quickly.

In the silence the laughter of one of the guards rang loudly, the other's words lost in the noise. Their lights reached past my position, and I withdrew another couple of meters into the darkness. The beams swung by the shelves as the guards headed into the basement. A few seconds later, the floor sections covering that room snicked together.

"Clear to go," Lobo said.

I loaded the rats into the pack and walked quickly to the rear door, where I paused.

"External status?" I said.

"No humans visible for several hundred meters in either direction," Lobo said, "and your path to the pickup point is clear."

I slipped outside and headed left, back to the empty loading area we'd used for the drop-off. The temperature in the warehouse had been fine, but the cool night air still struck me as refreshing and freeing. I was glad to be back in it. As I walked, I reflexively scanned left and right. Lobo was monitoring me, but I didn't want to rely exclusively on him, both because in some situations he has to be too far away to help and because I need to be able to take care of myself. Though I knew I should focus on the world around me, the stash of weapons kept diverting my attention. They represented both potential opportunity—knowing Dougat had something to hide could prove useful—and possible danger, because anyone with so many weapons of so many sorts could easily afford to arm his security staff well.

A block and a half from the warehouse, Lobo's voice yanked me out of my reverie.

"Company dropping from a window that just opened above," he said. "Too late to run. I'm too far away to have a shot that could kill them without endangering you."

I stopped and cursed myself for letting the warehouse distract me and for thinking in only two dimensions. A man touched down two meters in front of me. He held his drop cable in one hand and a pistol in the other. He pointed the gun at the center of my chest. I heard another man hit the ground a bit more roughly behind me. I didn't bother to check to see if he had a weapon.

"Good evening, good sir," the man in front of me said. "Our employer would appreciate a word."

CHAPTER SEVEN

I quickly evaluated my options. The man was almost my height and considerably wider. His stance was perfect: feet spread at shoulder width, one foot a bit in front of the other, weight mostly on the harder to reach rear foot, knees bent. He held the gun with a casual confidence, but it never wavered from the center of my chest. In every detail I could spot, he was a pro. I could attack him and hope the person behind me would hesitate long enough to let me turn this guy into a shield; yeah, right. I'd be lucky to touch him before he shot me, and there was no way I'd be fast enough to avoid both him and his partner. I could dive, pray I was quicker than both their trigger fingers, and bet that they would catch each other in the crossfire; another brilliant idea. If I moved or attacked, they'd shoot me. If it was a body shot, the nanomachines should be able to repair me. If the rear assailant was targeting my head, however, my guess was that I'd die, and I was far from ready to do that.

"I certainly understand your desire for reflection," the front man said, "but we must move along. It would be rude to do otherwise, and my employer detests rude behavior." The man nodded slightly to his right, and I heard the one behind me take a step. The man leaned close enough to me that when he spoke he was whispering in my left ear. "Don't mistake the fancy talk, mate: I'd as soon shoot you as look at you. It's himself who makes us play these games." He stepped back again and waved me forward. "You may even keep your pack, provided, of course, that you refrain from opening it."

"After you," I said.

"Of course," the man said. "My colleague will insure that you do not lose sight of me."

"Move slowly," Lobo said over the comm unit, "and I may be able to reach you before they force you into the building."

I was tempted to try to stall, but learning what was happening was worth the risk of playing along. Besides, if they'd wanted to kill me, they'd have done so already. "No," I subvocalized.

I followed the man to the end of the block and around the corner. I heard the cables withdraw as we stepped away. I glanced at the upper floors of the building as we walked and glimpsed two windows closing, but I didn't spot any observation posts. That didn't mean anything, of course; a good sheet of insulated camoglass will let a building present a seamless and IR-neutral façade while its occupants enjoy a clear view of the outside world.

"I now can't reach you before you enter the building," Lobo said. "Should I attack it?"

"No," I subvocalized, covering my mouth and coughing slightly as I did so.

After about ten meters, a door slid open on our right. We entered a large black chamber illuminated only by the soft red glow emanating from a series of three arches. The owner clearly loved theatrics as much as formal language. I followed the lead man through the arches. He stopped after the final one and waited before a blank wall. "Rats," he said, "a nice touch. Custom or off-the-shelf?"

I said nothing.

"Of course," he said.

Two sections of the wall parted, and we stepped into an elevator. The trailing guard followed us in, and I got my first look at her. She was maybe ten centimeters shorter than the lead and considerably lighter, but in all the ways that mattered—stance, gun position, focus—she was his twin.

The elevator opened on the side opposite the one we entered, and the lead man stepped out. I followed him, my eyes tracking his gun as he temporarily turned his back on me, but the trailing guard played it smart and immediately took up position at my seven. If I attempted anything aggressive, she could shoot me cleanly and quickly.

I abandoned the idea of engaging them and looked for the first time at the room around me.

I closed my eyes, then opened them and stared for a second time. Nothing changed.

I'd entered a storybook, maybe a museum exhibit or the hobby room of a wealthy reenactor. One of the constants of the many types of jobs I've held is a lot of time alone. I've filled that time soaking up whatever inputs I could obtain: text, audio, video, holoplays, anything and everything both old and new. I lacked any formal education—Pinkelponker's government didn't invest in the mentally challenged or, for that matter, any but those it considered elite—but I'd spent a lot of time learning for the pure pleasure of it. As best I could tell, I was standing in a gentlemen's club from Earth circa nineteenth or twentieth century.

Dark wood paneling covered the walls. Lighter planks with a matching grain formed the floor. Rich, thick, patterned brown carpets lay atop the wood here and there throughout the large space. Clusters of overstuffed leather chairs created multiple conversation nooks, each chair the rich black of the freshly tilled soil I'd worked as a child. Portraits of men with large sideburns and thick, gray hair adorned the walls. A fire—from the smell of it, real wood burning and drafting up a real chimney—threw heat from a fireplace tall and wide enough to hold several children standing side by side. The viscerally pleasing tang of a nighttime blaze suffused the air. Two manservants, each wearing the black and white formal server attire of the period and carrying a silver tray, stood at either end of the room. Books, actual bound paper as best I could tell, stood on shelves on either side of the fireplace and sat on some of the dark, three-legged tables that separated pairs of chairs.

As I examined the room more closely, I realized that the owner, though clearly infatuated with the period, wasn't willing to suffer or take undue risks for his passion. Quiet fans and masked vents prevented the fire's heat from exerting undue influence on the room's comfortable, almost constant temperature. The same air-handling system kept the room smoke-free but rich in the fire's aromas. The portraits morphed from time to time, displays with convincing surface textures but definitely not original art. Each servant held a small handgun discreetly at his side.

A door opened in the far left-hand wall. A man bustled in. No one said a word, but the posture of all of the staff straightened immediately; the boss had arrived. He was about fifteen centimeters shorter than I but almost as broad. He wore a version of the same suit as the manservants but one without tails. He studied me as he approached, then smiled and stuck out his hand.

"Good of you to come, Mr. Moore," he said.

I shook his hand. He controlled the situation completely, so I saw no viable options other than playing along. Though I might well be able to form a nanocloud to destroy him and everyone else in the room, I didn't want to kill anyone, and I had no good nondestructive options beyond listening and hoping to learn something useful.

When I didn't speak, he continued. "I gather from your reaction, sir, as well as from your taste in food—and who cooks better than Joaquin, eh?—that you are a man who has the capacity to appreciate my little club."

He obviously wanted me to talk, so I told the truth. "It is impressive indeed. I've never been anywhere quite like it."

"More's the pity that, isn't it, Jon? Do you mind if I call you Jon?"

I shrugged. "Of course not, Mr. . . . ."

He smiled. "Chaplat, Bakun Chaplat. At your service."

"I would say that I appear to be at yours."

He laughed. "Quite so, quite so." He turned and spoke to the lead guard. "As I've explained so often, in business as in all things, class will out." He faced me again. "I trust my two colleagues were not too coarse in their greeting."

I kept my focus on Chaplat, but out of the corner of my eye I saw the man stiffen. I learned long ago that it's good to have friends on

SLANTED JACK

the front line, particularly if they're on the other side of the line,
so I raised an eyebrow and said, "I'm afraid you have me quite
mystified. They were perfectly pleasant, given the situation, of
course."

The guard relaxed visibly. "Well done," Chaplat said to him.

Chaplat put his arm around me and led me to a pair of chairs
facing the fire. "The hour is growing late, so I propose we have our
chat and send you on your way." A servant appeared behind the
table between our chairs. "A drink, perhaps, or a snack?" Chaplat
said.

"Thank you, but, no."

"I appreciate your caution, Jon," he said, "though I assure you
that it is unnecessary." He waved away the server. "To business
then."

He settled back, adjusted his trousers, and stretched his arms
along the chair's arms, the very picture of a relaxed, nonthreatening
gentleman. The movements were too conscious, too practiced to be
convincing, but I stayed in my role and sat back similarly.

The chair amazed me. Firm enough to provide good support but
soft enough to make me want to stay, it could have been made for
me. I glanced around the room and noticed that all of the chairs
varied slightly in both height and depth. Chaplat had chosen one
that was perfect for me. Without even thinking I ran my fingers
along the chair's arms. The leather—and it was leather, real animal
hide—had been worked until it was as soft and inviting as sleep on
a bed after a hard day's march. Few buyers are willing to pay for real
leather, and fewer still are willing to risk offending the many people
who consider the material to be an abuse of animals, but when
you encounter a piece as beautiful as the cover on this chair you
immediately understand why some people won't give it up. The
subtle smell and the texture carried me in an instant to my childhood,
to those rare cold nights when Jennie and I would sit together under
a leather and fur cover and watch through our hut's main window
as the stars and the moons transformed the night from dark menace
into magic.

"Another taste we share," said Chaplat, studying me as he spoke.

"Very good. All too few men take the time to appreciate the pleasures available to them. Pleased as I am, however, we must, as I said, get to the topic at hand."

"Of course," I said. I put my hands in my lap and pushed away the memories.

Chaplat smiled and continued. "My organization operates a variety of concerns that share a single overriding goal: to facilitate trade on developing worlds. In the years, sometimes many years, between early colonization and the transition to full and effective planetary government, we provide such services as business interruption insurance, diversions for hardworking pioneers, third-party arbitration, negotiation, and, to those unable to obtain it elsewhere, capital." He leaned forward and put his hands on his knees. "It was for this last service that your friend Jack approached us."

"Jack?" I said.

Chaplat's expression tightened. "We know Jack, know him well enough that some of our associates were trying to catch up with him before he ended his stay on Mund. We also know Joaquin, who after a bit of persuasion mentioned Jack's visit and spoke rather highly of you." His tone changed, flattened. "Please do not mistake civility for softness. Our interactions thus far have been remarkably pleasant. I see no reason they need to change. Do you?"

The two guards edged closer.

"No, of course not," I said. "Jack was a business colleague many years ago, and I had not seen him since I," I paused, searching for the best way to be both accurate and vague, "chose to leave our joint venture. I can assure you that I was not expecting him to join me at lunch, nor to see him at all, for that matter."

Chaplat nodded in satisfaction. "If I may presume on our growing relationship," he said, "may I ask the reason for Jack's unexpected visit?"

This time I was ready and didn't hesitate. When you have to lie, the best lie is the one closest to the truth. "He was seeking my assistance on a project, a project much like some of those in our previous venture."

"What sort of project?"

I smiled. "Wealth redistribution. While Jack handles many classes of interactions quite well, certain more basic functions are not his strong point. In our previous enterprises, those functions were mine to manage. He wanted the same sort of help here."

"And your response to him?"

"I said I was uninterested, wished him well in finding a partner, and left." If Chaplat's data came from Joaquin, that story should fit well with what he saw.

"I can certainly understand your reluctance to do further business with Jack," Chaplat said. "Our experience in providing him capital has certainly not been successful—at least not so far. I have to inquire, however, about the motivation for your visit to the Followers' warehouse if you are not working with Jack."

For a moment I wondered just how much money Jack had borrowed for his poker game or whatever real purpose he hadn't told me, but I couldn't let the thought distract me; any delay in my response would alert Chaplat. "Jack could not meet his objectives without me," I said. "I didn't plan to work with him, but on the off chance the opportunity might be large enough to justify extending my stay here, I was conducting some preliminary research."

"And your research showed?"

"That Jack was aiming at the wrong target. The place is nearly empty, and what stock it holds is primarily Pinkelponker souvenirs."

"Surely there are artifacts?"

I nodded. "Some, but nothing I recognized or could use."

"Too bad," Chaplat said. "We also conduct a brisk trade in art and artifacts." He rubbed his hands on his pants legs. "But, no matter. We still have the issue at hand: Jack. His rather sizable debt to us remains unpaid, and we'd like your help in fixing that problem."

Finally. I paused long enough to appear to be deliberating the matter. "Though I appreciate your problem, it is just that: *your* problem."

The woman stepped close enough to rest her hand on my chair just behind my head.

Chaplat acted as if she were invisible. "Given the circumstances," he said, "it might not be unreasonable to consider adopting the issue as your own concern." He finally glanced at each of the guards in turn and then stared again at me. "I assure you that my associates are not always so well behaved."

"Nor are mine," I said.

Chaplat laughed. "Threatening me from the comfort of my own club's chairs? I do admire your moxie." Chaplat paused and turned completely serious. "But such bravado is also quite dangerous."

I didn't want a fight, but Chaplat wasn't going to let me go if he wasn't happy. I decided to turn this into something he would understand. "I do provide services, as I noted earlier, but at a price."

"And that would be?"

"Twenty percent of whatever Jack owes you."

"That's outrageous," Chaplat said, though his expression relaxed. "And you don't even know the amount."

"If I collect it for you, I'll know how much it is. As for being outrageous, I'm sure it's only a small part of the interest debt he's accumulated."

"And if we were to reach an accord, which would most certainly never be twenty percent, what guarantee would we have that you would perform the service?"

"None, of course, but I would be motivated, because I wouldn't receive any payment until I found and delivered him."

No one who built this room lacked an understanding of greed. Chaplat nodded. "Five percent," he said.

"Fifteen."

He stuck out his hand as he spoke. "Eight, and one of my associates accompanies you."

I didn't move. "Ten, and I report back here when I have him. If you follow me or try to make someone stay with me, Jack will spot the coverage and vanish." I paused, then took the slight gamble. "As he had already done until you got lucky and he sauntered into Falls, completely unaware that Choy was also a client of yours."

Chaplat stood and extended his hand again. "Deal."

I got out of the chair and shook his hand, not because I wanted the formal agreement or because I meant it, but because I had to make the gesture. He squeezed mine hard enough that I had to work not to show any reaction. I could have squeezed back harder and hurt him more, but my goal was to exit there intact, not to win a contest, so I took the pain. I couldn't stop myself, however, from the indulgence of not letting him know it hurt.

"I strongly suggest that you not disappoint us," he said. "If you do, no planet in this sector will be a good place to holiday." He dropped my hand, turned, and walked away. "My associates will show you out."

"What happened to you?" Lobo said. "That building's shielding was top-shelf; I couldn't pick up anything."

"Later," I said. "Backup site." Though Chaplat's team had left me alone on the street, I had to assume that I was under surveillance until I could convince myself otherwise. Chaplat didn't appear to know about Lobo, so I wanted to keep him a secret as long as possible. I now had to chart a jagged countersurveillance course to our backup site, a small tourist shuttle landing zone down the coast from the warehouse district. I covered an extra couple of kilometers simply to make sure I was alone.

As I walked, I focused most of my attention on my surroundings. I kept my vision on IR and this time checked not only the roads but also the buildings for signs of activity. I didn't spot any, but that didn't mean I was clear; Chaplat might have owned multiple shielded buildings. It was unlikely, however, that his properties stretched contiguously along my entire crooked route, so as long as neither Lobo nor I spotted any watchers, I was probably okay.

Despite my largely external focus, however, I couldn't help but ponder my situation.

Chaplat wanted Jack. Jack traveled with Manu. I had agreed to make sure nothing happened to Manu. To do that, I would also have to protect Jack. Lovely—and almost certainly exactly what Jack had wanted.

On the other hand, Jack had lied, so all bets were off. I could climb in Lobo and head for the jump gate. End of problem.

Except, of course, that if I left, I'd be breaking my commitment to Manu. I wouldn't do that. I would stay simply because I'd said I would. The notion that keeping one's word matters may be as old as the gentlemen's clubs that Chaplat was emulating, but I had always held to it.

I needed to be sharp tomorrow, because Manu required protection now more than he had before. Dougat might behave perfectly, but if one of Chaplat's people spotted Jack at the Institute and tried to take him there, Manu could end up as collateral damage.

I couldn't let that happen.

I now also had to deal with Jack as soon as this was over. I could return him to Chaplat and collect my payment, but as angry as I was at Jack, we had been partners once, and I didn't relish the prospect of turning him over to a gangster who would almost certainly hurt him badly. If I didn't, though, I'd definitely have to jump after tomorrow's meeting.

And then there was the matter of Dougat's hidden arsenal. At one level, it wasn't my problem; organizations of all types accumulate weapons all the time. Still, my experience with armed religious groups was bad enough that I had to consider whether I wanted to leak the information to the local EC office.

The rendezvous site was shut for the night when I reached it, but the gate recognized me from my rental agreement and let me in. Lobo flew in fast and hovered over the area I'd rented. I hopped aboard, and he took off. I collapsed into the pilot's couch, and Lobo accelerated.

"Spend the next hour checking for surveillance and running evasive patterns," I said.

I closed my eyes and leaned back.

"So will you now tell me what happened?" Lobo said.

"Tomorrow just got a whole lot more complicated."

CHAPTER EIGHT

We entered the Institute grounds along the same path I'd taken during my recon two days earlier. Jack and Manu walked hand in hand ahead of me. I kept out of their path but close enough that my role would be clear. For me to be effective, I needed to stay near enough to them that Dougat's people would have made me no matter how hard I tried to blend in, so broadcasting my presence was better than trying to hide it. I marveled again at the place's skillful evocation of my home. The feel of Pinkelponker washed over me as strongly as it had during my previous visit. A gust of ocean breeze rustled the plants, and I involuntarily smiled, the wind taking me back again to one of my most persistent childhood memories: sitting on the edge of our small mountain in the afternoon, my chores done, soaking up the warmth while waiting for Jennie. I pushed aside the thought and focused on expanding my peripheral vision as much as possible so I could monitor movements all around us.

Jack's pace accelerated a bit.

"Slow and easy," I said.

He nodded and resumed his earlier stride. I wanted as much time to assess the situation as I could reasonably arrange.

The sky out to sea and above us sparkled with cloudless perfection, but a storm was approaching from the west. Lobo was marking time about ten kilometers away behind the cover its dark clouds provided. I'd have preferred him overhead, but at this distance he could stay subsonic and still reach us in less than thirty seconds, so the reward of keeping him hidden outweighed the risk of having him closer but visible.

Ten meters from the building's entrance stood a small sky-colored canopy covering two chairs and a meter-diameter, circular, wooden table. A man sat alone at one of the chairs: Dougat. Four more men stood in a rough semicircle on the other side of the canopy. Three meters separated each of them, and none was in the line of fire of any of the others. All tried for nonchalant postures, but I was acting casual as well; all our attempts were equally unconvincing. The two in the middle focused completely on us, while the end men constantly swept the area.

"Lobo," I subvocalized. Even Jack and Manu, as close as they were, couldn't make out what I was saying, but any reasonable security person would, of course, know I was talking to someone. That was fine with me: If they believed I had backup, they might be more careful, and the more cautious everyone was, the better. "Dougat and the four behind him are obvious. Other possible hostiles?"

"Since you stopped moving," Lobo said, "one man to your left of the building has altered his path to take him in your direction."

I spotted the guy, who immediately sat on a bench in a small, semicircular garden nook and studied the red, blue, and gold flowers there. He held his head at an angle that let him keep us in sight. "Got him," I said.

In a clear voice I said to Jack, "Hold."

He did. He stood still and appeared completely relaxed. Manu fidgeted but didn't complain. I appreciated the boy's willingness to do as I told him.

"Six others in various locations between you and the road have drawn slightly closer," Lobo said. "Locations on overlay now. Sweep once to mark them."

The contact in my left eye darkened the world slightly as the overlay snapped on. I turned slowly and surveyed the grounds behind me. As I did, small red dots appeared on the chests of the four men and two women Lobo suspected. Each avoided looking at me and found something nearby of great interest, so Lobo was right. "Track them, the obvious four, and the one near the building," I said.

"Done," he said.

Yet again I was issuing an unnecessary order; Lobo was a pro and knew his role. Old habits are strong habits, but I had to learn to break this one. Lobo had every right to harass me about the redundancy, but of course he wouldn't do it now, during a mission. He *would* save it for later.

"We're probably missing one," I said. "Security teams love pairs. Scan again."

"A woman to your far left has walked closer to the man at the building's edge," Lobo said, "so she's a possible. No other human in the area is exhibiting any behaviors that appear linked to yours. So, either that's all of the external security, or the remaining members are significantly more skilled at blending in than their colleagues. The latter is certainly possible, because almost a dozen other people on the grounds are sitting and apparently doing nothing."

I swept the area again and checked out all the tourists. Each appeared to be under the place's spell, something I could certainly understand. As I turned, I looked at the woman Lobo had identified and smiled. She reacted with a smile of her own and then looked away, but the reaction was slow and forced.

"Assume she's security," I said. "More are inside, but we'll go with this count for now."

Dougat stood, an impatient expression on his face.

Jack glanced back at me, but to his credit he stayed put.

"Proceed," I said.

Jack and Manu headed toward the canopy. "Mr. Dougat," Jack said in his most winning voice. "How nice to see you again."

Dougat ignored Jack completely and focused on the boy.

Like any good merchant, Jack paused so his customer could take his time to study the goods. Even as I hated myself for thinking of a child that way, I realized that we were in it now and I had to stay cold to be maximally effective.

I couldn't read Dougat's expression. I've seen the very rich examine other people with all the passion of butchers deciding which meat scraps to feed their pets, gaze completely through others, as if the strangers were no more substantial than mist, and stare with undisguised lust at newcomers they planned to own. Dougat did none of those.

Then I understood his expression: Dougat viewed Manu as a potential religious artifact, something possibly more precious than anything his warehouse would ever hold, definitely as puzzling as any Pinkelponker fragment he might ever discover, more than a little hard to believe in, and yet wonderful if it proved to be the real thing. However rich the man was and however much he'd profited from his institute and his research into my home world, he was above all else a believer in the religious importance of that planet.

The intensity of his belief scared me more than mere lust or greed could have managed. Not long after I stopped working with Jack, when I was serving with the Saw, I participated in several actions that pitted us against armies of true believers. Some were determined to convert whole worlds to the worship of their gods. Others aimed to purify entire planets of their heathen nonbelievers. All were fearsome opponents. I learned to respect, fear, and despise the utter fanatical focus of their mission. Dougat exuded the same fervent belief, and the contents of his warehouse proved he was amassing arms. Even though he wouldn't be likely to bring all that firepower to bear in a public site, I still tensed at the possibility.

"Are you ready to proceed?" Jack said to Dougat.

Dougat stared at Jack as if he was seeing excrement on his dinner plate, then forced a businesslike expression. "Yes," he said. "Let's begin the interview."

"Should we get another chair?" Jack said, indicating the two under the canopy.

"The conversation is strictly between the boy and me," Dougat said. "You and," he paused to make a dismissive motion in my general direction, "your associate should wait where you are."

Jack turned and looked at me. I shook my head slightly and turned to directly face Dougat.

"Will your associates also remove themselves?" I said. "Both those four and," I pointed slowly toward the building and then casually behind me, "the two closer to the building and the six in various locations behind me?"

Dougat smiled for the first time. "I must apologize not only for the size of my security team but also for the clearly underdeveloped skills of its members. I mean the boy no harm. I have enemies, so I generally don't meet outside. My team seemed a reasonable precaution. Everyone will back away."

The ones I could see in front of me withdrew so they were farther from the canopy than Jack or I by at least five meters.

The dots on my contact moved as the other six also fell back.

"Hostiles have withdrawn an average of five meters each," said Lobo, who was monitoring the conversation via delayed bursts from transmitters woven into my coat.

"Thank you," I said to Dougat. To Jack, I added, "Your call."

Jack nodded and faced Dougat again. "Perhaps we should get the payment out of the way."

Dougat smiled again, but this time the expression was pure show. He turned to one of the four men behind him, nodded, and faced Jack when that man nodded in return. "Check your wallet," he said. "The money is in the local account you specified."

Jack did, lingering long enough that I was sure he moved the money at least twice before he looked up and smiled with what appeared to be genuine relief. "Thank you. We'll wait here while you talk." He dropped to one knee beside Manu. "All Mr. Dougat wants to do is ask you questions for about an hour. Answer them honestly, and then we'll go. Okay?"

Manu studied Jack's face. "You'll stay here?" He looked at me. "Both of you?"

"Of course," Jack said. "We'll remain where you can see us."

Manu kept staring at me until I nodded in agreement.

"Okay," he said. He walked to Dougat, glanced for a moment at the man, and then went over and sat on one of the chairs under the canopy. Dougat shook his head and followed; I got the impression he spent about as much time around children as I did.

After Dougat sat, he offered Manu a drink from a pitcher on the table.

Manu checked with me, as we had discussed, and I shook my head. The boy murmured something—we were too far away to clearly hear his light voice—and leaned back. The kid's behavior continued to impress me; I've guarded grown-ups with far less sense. We didn't worry about the contents of the interview; Manu had so many recorders in the active fiber of his clothing that we'd be able to see a full replay later.

"Lobo," I said. "Alert me if any of the hostiles draw closer or if Manu moves. I'm going to sweep the area visually every thirty seconds or so, and each time I do I will lose sight of the boy briefly."

"You could stay focused on him and leave the others to me," Lobo said.

"Yes," I said, "but I won't. My perspective is significantly different than yours, so I might gain data you could miss, and by visibly checking the area I'll make sure Dougat's team knows I'm on the alert."

As I finished talking, I turned and briefly scanned all the way around me. The hostiles brightened slightly in my contact as I glanced at them. The situation remained calm. Manu and Dougat continued to talk, the boy occasionally animated, the man studious and absorbed. Jack stood about a meter away from me, as motionless as a rock carving, watching the interview with a deceptive stillness.

Jack was right when he reminded me that he was bad at violence, but that didn't mean he was helpless. He possessed an amazing ability to simply *be* in a moment, to drink it in and concentrate totally on it, and in those times he appeared so still that you might believe he was physically and mentally slow. When he needed to move, however, he was one of the fastest humans I've ever seen, able to go from motionless to full speed almost as quickly as if he were a simulation freed from the laws of physics.

Over the next thirty-five minutes, we all kept to our roles.

Dougat once left the boy to ask Jack if they might run a bit over an hour, and Jack agreed. Every indication was that Dougat would behave, do the interview, and let us go. I felt the strong temptation to relax, but no mission is over until you're back home safely, so I maintained my routine.

I was between sweeps, staring at the chatting boy and man, when Manu grabbed his head, cried loudly enough that we could hear him, and ran toward Jack.

Jack was moving before Manu had taken his second step. He reached the boy quickly. I was right behind them.

"What's wrong?" Jack said to Manu. He stared at Dougat. "What did you do to him?"

Dougat appeared genuinely upset. "Nothing," he said, "nothing at all. We were talking, then for no reason I could tell he acted as if he was in pain."

Jack looked down at Manu. "Did he hurt you?"

Manu was holding his head, shaking it back and forth, and moaning softly. "No," he said. "Not him. It's not him. It hurts." He looked up, his eyes wide, and pointed toward the road. "We can't let it happen. We have to stop it." He grabbed Jack's hand and pulled. Jack, Dougat, and I exchanged glances, and Jack decided for us by letting Manu lead him.

"All hostiles changing course and approaching," Lobo said.

I grabbed Jack's arm with my left hand, and he stopped.

Manu tugged hard at him. "We have to stop it!" he yelled.

I kept my grip on Jack and faced Dougat. "Tell all your people to return to their previous positions," I said. "I don't know any more about this than you do, but it's clear the boy wants us to move. Keep them back, and we'll do as he wishes."

"Now!" Manu screamed. "We have to!"

Dougat nodded, turned his head, and whispered something I couldn't hear.

"Hostiles returning to prior locations," Lobo said. "All clear."

I released Jack's arm.

Manu saw me do it and immediately pulled harder on Jack. Jack let him set the pace. The boy ran for the road, Jack in physical tow and Dougat and I staying as close as if the four of us were trapped in the same gravity well and careening into the same black hole. Manu was crying and blabbering, but between his tears and the sounds of us running I couldn't understand anything he was saying.

Five meters from the road he raised his hand and shouted a single long, hysterically elongated word, "Nooooooo!"

I looked where he was pointing, and four events occurred in such rapid succession that I could separate them only in afterthought.

A hover transport hurtled down the road from my right toward my left.

A man stepped from a crowd of pedestrians in front of the truck, his head turned to his right as if saying goodbye to a friend, clearly unaware of the vehicle speeding toward him.

The transport hit the man.

The man sailed into the air like a flower blown free of its stem by a strong wind, red blossoming across his shirt as he flew over the crowd he'd left only a second earlier. He landed behind them, out of our view.

Manu let go of Jack and sprinted for the road, but Jack caught him with two long strides and grabbed both his shoulders.

"I saw it and I couldn't stop it and we should have stopped it!" Manu said, tears flowing as quickly and as uncontrolled as the words.

Jack picked him up, turned him away from the sight of the crowd converging on the accident victim, and held him tightly. "It's not your fault," he said. "You did everything you could. You know we can't change what you see." The boy sobbed and tried to wriggle free, but Jack clung to him with a strength I'd seen but also with a tenderness I'd never witnessed. "It's not your fault."

Jack supported Manu's weight with his right hand and held the boy's head to his shoulder with his left. Keeping the boy tucked there so he wouldn't catch another glimpse of the accident, Jack turned and walked away from the road, back toward the Institute.

As he moved, he stared at me for a moment, his eyes glistening, and then at Dougat. "Perhaps," he said to the man, "we could spend a few minutes inside. I'm afraid the interview is over."

For the first time since the accident, I focused on Dougat. His face was wide with shock, but more than shock, belief, the sort of ecstatic conviction I've seen previously only on those in the grips of strong drugs or stronger acts of religious or violent fervor.

"He *is* a seer," the man said. "A true child of Pinkelponker, maybe the only one in the known universe. I've talked to so many people, heard so many stories, but I could never be sure." He ran in front of Jack and put up his hand. "You have to stay. You must." His pupils were dilated with excitement. His breathing was ragged. Everything about him broadcast trouble.

We needed to leave.

"Lobo," I said, "come in fast, and prepare for full action on my command."

"Done. Moving," he said.

"As you can see," Jack said, anger clear in his voice, "Manu is in no shape to continue. I'll return half of the fee if you'd like, but I have to get him home to rest. Even the easiest visions are hard on him, and this one, as you witnessed, was far from easy."

Dougat didn't move. "He can recuperate here," he said, more loudly than before. "My people will help in any way they can."

Jack covered Manu's head with his hand so the boy wouldn't hear any more. "We have to go," he said.

Dougat glanced at Manu again and lowered his voice. "No," he said. "I can't let him leave."

CHAPTER
NINE

"Hostiles converging quickly," Lobo said, his voice crisp and inflection-free in my ear. "A man and woman who had acted as tourists and not previously tracked you are headed your way. I'm six seconds out."

The extra hostiles meant either Dougat had stationed people we'd missed or Chaplat had found us. It was about to get noisy. "Execute plan," I said.

"All warehouse charges detonated," Lobo said. "Almost all debris contained in implosion."

I grabbed Jack's shoulder and spun him to face me. Behind him I glimpsed several of Dougat's men running toward us.

"Three seconds," Lobo said.

I held up three fingers.

Jack nodded and gripped Manu tightly.

I dropped and swept Jack's legs out from under him.

Lobo activated the heads-up display relay in my left contact. The image from his forward video sensors overlaid my view of the approaching security men.

I watched with both normal vision and the overlaid video as Lobo transformed the Institute and its grounds into a fire zone.

Two low-yield explosive missiles left Lobo and almost immediately blew apart what I hoped we'd accurately identified as a receiving dock on the back of the building. No transports were parked there, so with luck the area was unoccupied. At the same time, the world went silent as Lobo remotely enabled my sound-blocking earplugs. I counted on Jack's and Manu's working, because a second later the howlers rocketed out of Lobo and tore up the grounds around us.

Right behind them a cluster of sleep smokers mirved to their targets and turned the air the color of storm clouds about to burst. I kept my mouth shut and forced myself to breathe through my nose; the sinus filters worked perfectly. If Jack and Manu did the same, they'd be fine. The active antidotes we'd all taken would keep us awake even if we breathed the gas, but until it had dissipated for a few minutes it would be hard on our lungs and throats. The nanomachines in my cells would repair me quickly enough if some gas leaked inside my nose, but I saw no reason to suffer any damage I could avoid.

The rest of Dougat's staff and, unfortunately, all of the visitors on the grounds and even some nearby pedestrians wouldn't be as lucky; the gas and the noise would affect them. Aside from any injuries they sustained when they fell, however, they should suffer only long, drugged naps, raw sinuses, bad coughs, and, from the howlers, ringing in their ears.

I reached for Jack, but he wasn't there.

Damn!

Anger flooded adrenaline into my body, and I trembled with the barely controlled energy and rage. He knew he shouldn't move! Now he and the boy were at risk.

"Where are Jack and Manu?" I mumbled through pursed lips.

My words were clear enough for Lobo.

My left contact's display snapped into an aerial schematic of the grounds, with red dots marking Dougat's staff, a blue dot indicating Jack, and a green one denoting Manu's position. The blue and green dots streaked toward the building.

"Running toward the ziggurat," Lobo said. "External staff and bystanders are all sleeping. I'm above you. Howlers have discharged; reenabling hearing."

In an instant the thrumming force of Lobo's hovering joined a chorus of unconscious moans and wheezes all around me to replace the silence I'd been enjoying. I stood and darted forward. The blue and green dots veered to the side of the entrance to the ziggurat. Two seconds later, a stream of red dots poured out of it. These guys were clearly prepared for gas, because none of them fell. I cranked my own vision to IR and watched as the ten new security people fanned out in front of me. The blue and green dots ducked behind them, Manu barely ahead of Jack, and zipped into the building. Great. Now I had to get past this new team, retrieve Jack and Manu, and go back outside for pickup. If they'd only kept to the plan and stayed near me, we'd already have been on our way out of here.

"Image enhancement suggests new hostiles are armed and environmentally prepared," Lobo said.

Sure enough, the new squad broke into four clusters. One sprinted for Dougat. The remaining three focused on me, the first taking a direct approach and the other two going wide to flank me. The only good news was that either they'd missed Jack and Manu or they'd assumed those two were down.

"Trank 'em," I mumbled.

Lobo didn't waste time answering. I heard the rounds spraying from guns on his undercarriage, and within three seconds everyone on the new team dropped.

"Public feeds are rich in data about our assault," Lobo said. "We must exit soon or expect to face additional local resistance."

"I have to get Jack and Manu," I mumbled as I ran to the side of the entrance. I stopped long enough to pull a trank pistol from the holster at the base of my back, then dove inside. I hit the ground on my shoulder and rolled quickly to a prone position. I glanced to the right and then the left of the entrance. No one.

I stood and immediately regretted the action as a projectile round to the chest knocked me down. The body armor stopped it from seriously injuring me, but my chest throbbed with pain, and breathing hurt. I slit my eyes and stayed still. Precious time was evaporating, but if I moved I might suffer a head shot.

A guard emerged from behind an exhibit five meters in front of me. He kept his pistol aimed at me and moved cautiously forward. He stepped with care, and his weapon never wavered. I did my best to look unconscious; the lack of blood would tell him I wasn't dead.

A crashing sound ripped the air from somewhere behind him, and he turned for a moment to check it out.

I fired multiple times at his back and head.

He dropped.

Too many trank rounds might kill him, something I didn't want to do, but I couldn't afford the time to check on him and make sure he was okay. Dougat might have more security personnel around. The warehouse distraction south of us was old news. I had to get out of there, but I couldn't leave without Jack and Manu.

I had no feed from Lobo to guide me in my search, so I ran to the center of the building in the hope that I could spot them.

Before I'd gone five steps, Jack dashed toward me from my left, Manu's hand in his.

"What were you doing?" I said, my voice shaking with anger at Jack's violation of our agreement. The air inside was now clean enough that I could talk freely without hurting my throat. "You idiot! You don't freelance, and you don't abandon your team!"

"Manu was terrified and ran," Jack said. "I didn't expect it, and I couldn't see him clearly, so I fell behind him. I couldn't leave him here, Jon. I had to find him."

Though his answer was reasonable, even admirable in some ways, I still shook with anger and adrenaline. I forced myself to nod. "Follow me," I said.

Motion in the corner of my eye caused me to stop and glance to my right. A guard emerged from behind an exhibit and trained a shotgun on Jack and Manu. I couldn't turn in time to stop him.

Another guard ran toward him, screaming as she approached, "Not the boy!"

Jack pushed Manu behind him as the guard turned to the woman and shot in the same motion.

The shell sprayed two exhibits in an arc that ran from the woman to Jack. Jack spun slightly and grabbed his right arm. The woman's left shoulder jerked backward, but her momentum propelled her into the man. The two of them crashed into an exhibit behind him. She rolled away, kicked the man in the neck, and stood, her legs shaking, her uniform's shoulder pad darkening with blood.

"Go," she said, "get the boy out of here."

She looked at her arm, then passed out and fell.

"Let's go," Jack said. He held up his bloody hand. "Now."

I stared at the woman. We should run, but she might well have saved Manu. I couldn't leave her.

"Wait," I said to Jack.

I ran to her, pulled her to a sitting position, and hoisted her over my shoulder. I stood with her, grunting slightly from the effort. She was almost as tall as I was and dense. I settled her on my shoulder and walked back to Jack.

"Follow me," I said. "Heading to you," I said to Lobo as we approached the exit from the building. "Land in the closest clear area—not on people—and direct me in. Prep the medbed; I'm bringing two casualties." Lobo had argued in our planning meeting that if we ended up in a fight he should set down right beside us, and that anyone he squashed in the process was an acceptable casualty, but even with time as short as it was I saw no reason to kill if we could avoid it.

"Moving," Lobo said. "Media scans put police ETA at under ninety seconds. Severity of injury? Jack or Manu hurt?"

"Don't know, and both Jack and a guard," I said.

"We're helping the opposition?" Lobo said.

I kept moving and didn't waste any energy explaining the situation. My chest hurt each time I breathed in, but I pushed my pace. Jack and Manu stayed close to me as we ran. A vector in my left eye's display led me forty meters ahead and to the right, toward the southern side of the grounds. Even with me carrying the guard, we reached Lobo quickly. As we drew closer to him, his camo armor exterior blending so well with the still-gas-filled air that anyone watching without IR would have little chance of knowing where he was, he opened a hatch on the side facing us. I ran to him, stepped inside, and turned around to make sure Jack and Manu made it.

They were right there, Jack actually showing a bit of stress, Manu in tears but leaping perfectly and at speed into Lobo; the practice paid off. Jack entered right behind him, and the hatch shut.

Lobo accelerated as I set the guard on the floor. As I was straightening, I said, "Lobo—"

I never finished the sentence.

I felt Jack's hand on my neck, turned toward him, and sank into blackness.

CHAPTER
TEN

I awoke slowly, my head throbbing and my neck and shoulders stiff. When I opened my eyes, I had trouble focusing, but after a few seconds the world snapped into view. I was lying on the floor inside Lobo, right where I'd fallen.

Where Jack had left me, I realized as the memory of what had happened caught up with me. I pushed up with my arms and quickly regretted the action, as the remnants of whatever drugs he'd used coursed through me and nearly made me pass out again.

I decided the floor wasn't such a bad place to be right now. My system would naturally wash itself of the drugs in time, and the nanomachines would speed the process, but resting there for the moment was fine by me.

"Welcome back," Lobo said. "Are you coherent?"

"Yes," I said. "Why wouldn't I be?"

"You made enough noises while unconscious that several times I thought you might be awake," he said.

"Fair enough. How long was I out?"

"Three hours, fifty-seven minutes," he said with what I thought was a trace of amusement. "Jack claimed you'd be unconscious for at least five hours, but my experiences with you led me to estimate a quicker recovery. I was, of course, correct."

Lovely. How long I'd remain out of it had turned into a betting game for my PCAV and the old friend who'd screwed me once again.

"Why didn't you stop him?" I said.

"I had no information from you to suggest Jack would drug you," Lobo said with annoyance. "Once you were unconscious, he was, by your orders, in command. Had he then tried to injure you further, your earlier orders would have allowed me to take action to prevent him, but he did nothing to harm you from that point forward. Had your health showed signs of worsening, I could have transported you to a medical facility, but your vital signs stayed steady and strong. Consequently, I could only obey his instructions—again, per your orders."

I hate being stupid, and Lobo's tone made the annoyance all the greater. At the same time, I'd given Lobo those orders to protect the boy, and they'd reflected the best data available to me at the moment I'd given them.

Except, of course, for the key fact that I'd known and chosen to ignore: You can't trust Jack.

Even though years of experience had taught me that lesson, something about the way he'd behaved this time had struck me as different; it was as if he actually cared about Manu.

Manu.

"What happened to the boy?" I said.

"To the best of my ability to tell, they are safe," Lobo said. "On Jack's orders, we invested an hour in evasive action, and then we proceeded to the jump gate. They departed there. Rather than track them, to maximize your safety I left and continued running countersurveillance routes."

Given that we'd just attacked one of the richest men on the planet, the jump gate was a reasonable place to go. Jack would have caught the first available shuttle off-planet and be far away by now. I'd have done the same.

My thinking was definitely not up to par, because it took me this long to realize that what mattered was not what I would have done, but what I needed to do now—though in this case they were the same. I needed to leave Mund.

"Where are we?"

"In orbit on the side of Mund opposite the jump gate," Lobo said. "We're currently nestled among a group of tediously dull weather satellites."

"Any signs of pursuit?"

"Of course not," Lobo said. "Do you think I would have stopped moving had I known of any?"

"Sorry," I said. "I'm not at my best quite yet. Thank you for getting me to safety."

"I accept both your apology and your thanks," Lobo said. "Which would you now prefer to do: view the recording Jack left, or see to our prisoner?"

"Jack left a recording? We have a prisoner?"

"Why do you persist in asking questions to which you already know the answers?" Lobo said, the annoyance back.

"Rhetorical questions. Jack's never done anything like that. When he vanishes, he leaves no traces. As for the guard, who, by the way, helped us and so is hardly a prisoner, I was so focused on my own situation and on Jack that I forgot her."

"She was a combatant on the other side of a conflict, and she is now restrained and in our custody," Lobo said. "If that isn't a prisoner, please explain to me how you define the term. I'm quite confident that she would consider herself to be our captive, if, that is, we allowed her to wake up and consider the situation."

"Point taken," I said. I sat. This time, doing so didn't leave me weaker. "What's her status?"

"Jack put her in the medbed," Lobo said. "I treated her and sedated her. Her light armor absorbed most of the round. The protection didn't cover the edge of her shoulders, so she suffered a rather large cut. I cleaned it, removed the shrapnel, and kept her under. I find I often like guests best when they're unconscious."

I wish I could tell when Lobo was joking. I had to admit, however, that until I decided what to do with her, having her safely out of the way was convenient. Jack's recording might tell me why he'd knocked me out, so I decided to start with it. "Play the message."

A display opened on the wall in front of me. Jack snapped into view. His right sleeve was missing below the shoulder, and his no-longer-bloody arm glistened with fresh skin sealer. He stood beside Manu and held the boy's hand. My unconscious body lay on the floor behind him.

"Jon," he said, waving his hand briefly at my body, "I'm very sorry for treating you like that. If I'd thought there was any other reasonable option, I would have taken it. The problem is that you wouldn't have approved of what I did, and then you would have tried to make it right, and in the end there was too big a chance that Manu might have gotten hurt." Jack sounded genuinely torn and upset. He paused, glanced down at Manu, and stroked the boy's head lightly.

"The fee Dougat paid for the interview was enough to buy Manu treatments for a while, but only for a while. He was going to need more, a lot more. We—his uncle and I—were hoping Dougat would be willing to pay for more interviews or maybe even to help with the med-tech bills just because of Manu's Pinkelponker ancestry." He put his hands over Manu's ears for a moment. "Yeah, I know: It was a dumb hope. I tried to tell him, but it was the only option any of us could come up with that might help over the long term. The alternative, well—" He paused and glanced at Manu, and when he faced forward again his eyes were wet. "—neither of us was willing to deal with that."

He took his hands off Manu's ears. "When I caught up to Manu inside the Institute, he was hiding behind one of the gemstone displays." He paused, shook his head, and smiled. "Look, I know it's not right, but Dougat is so wealthy he won't even feel the loss."

Jack turned, stooped, and reached behind Manu. When he stood, he was clutching at least half a dozen Pinkelponker gems, his hands twinkling as if holding a night sky drenched in green, red, blue, and purple stars. "The right collectors will pay enough for these to cover Manu's treatments forever—and then some." Jack laughed. "Besides, a man has a right to make a profit now and then, eh?"

I couldn't help but laugh with him. Leave it to Jack to fall into a mess and walk away rich.

Lobo's video sensor tracked him as he walked to the front acceleration couch and left a huge green gem on it.

"For your help, Jon," he said.

"Docking with jump station in sixty seconds," said Lobo's voice on the recording.

Jack nodded and returned to Manu.

"I wish it had gone better," Jack said, "but as I promised, this time we did some good: Manu will get his treatments."

Jack smiled that beautiful, wide, glowing smile of his, and I felt myself smiling involuntarily in response. He'd used me, he'd done at least some of this to raise money to pay his debt to Chaplat, and still in that moment he charmed me.

"Besides," he said, "admit it: Wouldn't you have been at least a little disappointed if everything had played out according to plan?" He laughed lightly. "Take care, Jon."

The display vanished.

The effect of Jack's charm also disappeared as I realized the mess in which he'd left me.

Dougat and the Followers had seen me and had security footage of our escape from the Institute. They'd assume I was working with Jack to plan the robbery, and the gem Jack had left me would, if they caught me before I disposed of it, only convince them further. I considered having Lobo dump it into space then and there, but I couldn't quite bring myself to discard something that was both so valuable and a tangible link to my home planet.

Chaplat would be furious, because I had no way to deliver on my promise or even get Jack to work out an arrangement with him.

I had a Follower guard on board, restrained and effectively my prisoner despite the fact that she'd taken a shot to save Manu. I either had to kidnap her through a jump gate, waste time dropping her planetside on some other world—or kill her, an option I knew Lobo would raise if I didn't.

To top it all off, despite all the compassion I'd read in Jack, whether he would really help Manu remained a mystery. I might well have failed the boy, an idea that knotted my stomach.

Once again, Jack had left me, as he'd done many times in our years together, with too many problems to solve all at once. All I could do was deal with the one in front of me, and then move to the next.

I stood. A jolt of dizziness hit me, but it passed a few seconds later.

I grabbed the green stone from the pilot's couch and had Lobo open a storage bin. "Keep it deep and in shielded storage," I said. "Don't give it to anyone but me."

The bin closed. "Done," Lobo said.

I walked to the med room. "Is she attempting to transmit any signals?" I said.

"No," Lobo said, "and I would have alerted you if she were. I've also blocked all signals not from me just in case."

"Of course," I said. "Thanks." I paused and stared at her unconscious body. "Bring her around."

It was time to talk to the guard.

CHAPTER
ELEVEN

I watched closely as the woman's breathing changed from the slow, shallow pace of drug-induced sleep to a more normal ebb and flow. Lobo opened a display on the wall above and behind her. Her vital signs appeared; all were rising. Straps across her neck, waist, arms, and legs bound her securely to the medbed. She filled the better part of the platform and was nearly my height. A thick coil of hair the red of the glowing tendrils of solar flares hung over the edge of the platform and contrasted nicely with skin the color of wet yellow sand. Her uniform and light armor left her body thick and almost tubular. If the protection had extended to the full width of her shoulders, her left deltoid wouldn't now glisten with skin patch. As I stared, her eyelids fluttered and then opened to reveal light green eyes that sparkled like new grass wet with morning dew.

That she opened her eyes before she was fully aware made it clear she was no pro. No surprise there: Cults usually prefer believers to professionals.

As the woman focused on me, she tried to sit up and choked against the neck restraint. Lobo didn't need to keep it so tight; he definitely considered her a prisoner.

"Who are you?" she said. "Where am I?"

"Wrong."

"Huh?" She shook her head. "I don't understand."

"You're doing the wrong things," I said. "You're asking questions, but you're the one in restraints. I'm standing, so I ask, and you answer."

"Why do you have me like this?" she said. "What do you want?"

"You're doing it again."

She shut her eyes. "Okay, ask."

"Name?"

"Maggie."

"Maggie?"

"Maggie Park."

I looked away as if thinking and checked the display. Lobo's assessment glowed green, and her vitals showed no signs of a lie. Good. "What do you do for the Followers?" I said.

She opened her eyes, studied my face, and then sniffed my clothes, which still smelled of the gas. "I remember you now," she said. "You were in the Institute fighting with the other guards."

"Prepare to inject," I said.

Lobo made the bed extend a treatment appendage and positioned a needle over the vein just past the end of her biceps.

She tried moving her arm away from the needle, but she couldn't shake the binding straps. "Okay, okay," she said. "What do you want to know?"

"What do you do for the Followers?"

"Tourist security. I walk the exhibits so no visitor decides the gemstones might not be that hard to steal. The video monitors do the real watching, and if they or I spot anything wrong, we call the armed security. I'm mostly there for show."

All signs stayed stable. "How long have you been working for them?"

"Why does this matter?" she said.

I nodded at the needle, which was still poised over her vein.

She tracked my eyes to it and swallowed nervously. "A little over two weeks," she said.

More truth. "Are you a Follower?"

She looked aside for a moment, as if embarrassed. "No, not really. I'm interested in Pinkelponker, of course—who wouldn't be?—but I don't believe in Dougat's vision like the rest of them. I needed work, so I faked it."

Also true. She was either superbly trained and able to control her body well enough to fool both Lobo's sensors and me, or she was consistently answering truthfully. None of the rest of her moves suggested she possessed anywhere near that level of training, so I was almost willing to bet she was telling the truth. Almost. "What is Dougat's vision, the one you don't believe?"

"You don't know them very well, do you?"

I let the question go unpunished. "No. Why?"

"If you did," she said, "you wouldn't have bothered asking that question. They're crackpots. They see Pinkelponker as some sort of link to the divine, or maybe to the makers of the gates, or maybe both—sometimes they talk like Gatists." She stared at me, then said, "Not that there's anything wrong with worshipping the jump gates, of course. You don't happen to be a Gatist, do you?"

I shook my head and resisted the urge to laugh. "No. The gates are magnificent, and they work, and that's enough for me." I pointed at the needle still hovering over her arm. "Back to the Followers."

"Part of their dogma is that humanity can reach its true potential— some sort of godhood, I think, though I don't really understand what they mean—only by returning to Pinkelponker. Dougat is convinced that the one way to break the blockade is to use the special powers of what he calls 'the children of Pinkelponker,' people whose ancestors were born there. He's convinced they all possess special psychic abilities." She trembled. "I said they were crackpots; as the head of the group, he's the craziest of the bunch—and the scariest. He genuinely believes what he preaches."

The vitals jumped with her fear, but that was normal. Her take on Dougat matched my own. Before seeing Manu and his vision of the accident, I might have laughed at Dougat's vision and considered it insane. As far as I'd known growing up, Jennie was the only person on the planet with her gift. Of course, I'd never even explored our whole island, much less the entire world, so the place may well have teemed with people with unusual abilities. I didn't expect to ever find out, but I was convinced that if I were ever to make it back there, I'd need a lot more weaponry than a kid with occasional glimpses into the future.

From what I'd seen in the warehouse, Dougat must have felt the same way, because he was definitely amassing arms. On the other hand, almost none of them would be useful fighting a blockade of heavily armed CC and EC spaceships. Even as fodder for trades, they didn't strike me as enough to buy him anything that might be able to survive a battle with the ships guarding the aperture to Pinkelponker.

"If he was so sure these people existed and they were his ticket to the promised land," I said, "why was he stockpiling weapons?"

"What weapons?" she said. "Most of us on the security team weren't armed with more than shocksuits. Some of the hardcore guards had real guns, but not most of us."

Nothing on the monitor suggested she was lying. She didn't know. Another vote in her favor. Dougat might have been accumulating munitions for another reason, or perhaps he planned to use them and the hardcore Followers to hijack a few ships when they were planetside. Without asking him, I couldn't know, but at least Maggie also seemed completely unaware of any such plans.

I considered releasing her, but one thing still troubled me.

"Why," I said, "did you push that guard and take a shot for us?"

"Because Kenton—that was his name—was going to shoot that boy," she said. "Isn't that a good enough reason? All the boy did was somehow attract Dougat's attention, show up for another of the man's endless and useless interviews, and suddenly people were firing weapons all around us. I couldn't let Kenton shoot him. Could you?"

I should have ignored her, but I couldn't help but ponder the question. I'd like to be positive I wouldn't have let anyone shoot Manu, and I think I would have stopped it, but I had an advantage she didn't: My body could quickly mend almost any wound. In her shoes with her normal human body, would I have been as brave? Again, I'd like to think so, but I haven't been normal for over a hundred and thirty years, long enough that I can't clearly remember what it was like.

"No," I finally said, "I don't think I could."

As I recalled the scene, I realized something else was bothering me. "Why was that guard shooting at the boy?" I said. "Dougat paid a lot just to interview the kid; he couldn't have wanted him hurt."

"Oh, I'm sure Dougat didn't," she said. "He would have fired Kenton on the spot for even aiming in the direction of anyone he thought might be a child of Pinkelponker. In fact, I bet Kenton's already lost his job. Serves him right, though I suppose when you hire people like him, you can't expect much."

"People like him?"

"To work tourist security like I do," she said, "you don't need any special qualifications. All you have to do is catch a company when it's hiring. Dougat's armed guards, though, are all rough sorts, people like Kenton who've spent a lot of time either with mercenary forces or in prison."

"Plenty of good men and women sign up with mercenary companies," I said. "I did." I'd felt indignant, but my words sounded defensive.

"Maybe so," she said, "but those aren't the sorts of people Dougat's hiring as guards. As for you, well," she shrugged as much as she could given the straps pinning her in place, "I hope you'll understand that my initial impression isn't all that favorable."

I chuckled in acknowledgment. She seemed to be exactly what she said, and she might well have saved Manu. I owed her for that.

I'd drop her somewhere planetside. She could make her way home from there.

Before I released her, though, I wanted a little insurance, just in case I'd misread her.

I stepped out of the small room, and Lobo closed the door behind me.

"Do you have any one-person explosive implants?" I said. I didn't think so, but Lobo regularly surprises me with the variety of tools that he either is carrying as part of his arsenal or can fabricate.

"No," he said. "Beyond standard medical repair tools, my only human implants are trackers."

"That'll work," I said. "When I tell you to implant the explosive, simply inject her with a tracker and set it to decay."

"Why bother wasting the device on her?"

"Just do it," I said. Bluffing was not Lobo's strong suit, and if anything went wrong, being able to track her could be useful. "Open."

I entered the room as soon as the door snicked aside.

"I'm going to remove the restraints," I said.

"Thank you."

"First, though, we're going to inject you with a small explosive tied to a transmitter I control."

"What?" she yelled. She tried again to free herself but could only shake slightly against all the restraints. "You don't need to do this."

"If something happens to me," I said, "or if you even try anything I don't like, the explosive will detonate. If you behave, when you're far away I'll send a signal that will cause it to decay. Your body will excrete the remains, and you'll be back to normal." As I talked, Lobo retracted the extension that had held the needle over her arm. A new, similarly equipped one took its place.

"Ready," Lobo said on the machine frequency.

"I cannot believe you're doing this," Park said. "You're crazy."

"Not crazy," I said. "Just careful. Very careful." Being too cautious, I realized, was the equivalent of being paranoid, of being insane, but in my line of work a little paranoia has always proven to be healthy. "I sincerely hope this precaution ends up being completely unnecessary."

"Is there anything I can—"

I cut her off. "Inject her," I said.

The needle plunged into her arm, held for two seconds as the fluid and its microscopic cargo entered her body, and withdrew.

Her face flushed with anger, her fists clenched, and the skin in her neck tightened. All over the monitor on the wall behind her head, indicators jumped and twitched, flowing lines and rows of numbers charting her fury. She opened her mouth several times as if to speak, but each time she said nothing.

I waited.

She closed her eyes and took a few long, slow breaths.

Her vitals settled as the flush left her skin. Her hands relaxed, and her expression returned to normal.

She opened her eyes and stared at me, the last traces of rage fading, and then she spoke. "You made me furious, but I can see it from your perspective: You don't know me, you can't be sure I'm telling the truth, you could be at risk. Okay, well now you're not. So, are you going to let me out of here?"

"I said I would." I looked away from her. "Retract."

The left ends of the restraints released with a series of slight clicks, and the medbed withdrew them into itself.

She sat up slowly and swung her legs over the right side of the medbed. She shook her head slightly; the last of the sedative must have hit her. She pushed off as she stood, and for a moment she wavered.

It might have been an act, a ploy to catch me off guard, but I didn't think so. Even if it was, between Lobo and me, she didn't have a chance.

I reached out and steadied her by her uninjured right shoulder.

"Thanks," she said. She grabbed my biceps with her hand and held on until she was standing solidly on her own. She kept holding me and looked up, into my eyes. Surprise flitted across her face.

"What?" I said.

She turned her head and released her grip on my arm. "Huh?"

"You appeared surprised," I said. "At what?"

"I guess I didn't really believe you'd set me free," she said. "I was afraid you'd hurt me the moment I was on my feet."

"If I wanted to do something to you, I would have done it already. I said I'd let you go, and I will." I turned and headed to the pilot's area. "I'll drop you somewhere on Mund, and you can find your way home."

"What about you?" she said. "What are you going to do?"

"That's not your issue," I said, though I realized the same question had continued to nag at me. "Maybe leave, maybe find Jack and Manu." I paused. "Probably leave."

"No," she said. "You can't. You have to find the boy."
Before I could respond, she continued.
"And you have to take me with you."

CHAPTER
TWELVE

"What?" I said, suddenly the one who was surprised and confused. A minute ago, she was an understandably angry and bewildered prisoner. Now, she was volunteering to go with me. Was I wrong to have let her out of the restraints? Was she working with Dougat and trying to trap me? Lobo hadn't detected any transmission attempts from her, and all of her responses had registered as truthful, so it seemed unlikely that she was any sort of spy, but her demand made me wonder.

"You have to find the boy, and you have to let me go with you," Park said again.

"Why?"

"So I can help finish what I started: saving him. As long as he's anywhere Dougat can find him, he's not safe. Besides, there's nothing left for me with the Followers. If I go back, the security cameras will show what I did, Dougat will at a minimum fire me, and most likely he'll take me prisoner and interrogate me." She paused and stared at me. "I've had enough of that for quite some time."

"Interrogate you?" I said. "Why?"

"Because he assumes everyone thinks like he does," she said. "All I was trying to do was prevent a boy from being shot. He'll decide

I'm somehow tied to the kid, maybe as part of some secret plan of his mythical children of Pinkelponker, and then he'll come after me." She leaned against the wall and closed her eyes, apparently still weak. "I told you: He's crazy."

Her analysis made sense. I've met more than a few conspiracy nuts, both because Jack often chose them as targets and because the megacorporations and government federations are full of them. All of them assumed not only that secrets lurked everywhere, but that everyone else was as aware of and as concerned with those secrets as they were. I didn't want to tell Park that in this case the nut wasn't all that crazy: At least two of his children of Pinkelponker, Manu and I, existed, and we both had unusual powers. Make that three; I had to believe Jennie was still alive somewhere.

If I decided to go after Jack and Manu, taking Park with me would be a mixed proposition. Having someone on my team, someone no one knew was with me, could be a valuable advantage. Having to keep my and Lobo's secrets from her, however, would add complexity and stress to everything.

Regardless of what I chose, I appreciated her desire to rescue Manu. I'd been in similar situations, and I'd always tried to follow up, to make things right.

Which was why, I finally admitted to myself, that I had no choice but to go after Manu and Jack. They had no clue what Dougat was capable of doing, and if I didn't help them get far away, Dougat might capture Manu. If he did, Manu would never be free again. He'd end up locked away, using his talent to serve Dougat whenever the man wasn't experimenting on him. I've been in that kind of laboratory cage before, and I've spent most of my life being careful to avoid going back. I couldn't let that happen to Manu.

Making the decision brought everything else into focus. What mattered most was Manu, so I had to concentrate on doing what was right for him.

"I appreciate your desire to help the boy," I said. "I really do. I'm not sure, though, that you'd add enough value to make you worth the trouble."

"I know Dougat and the Followers better than you do. I've lived and worked with them, and I know a lot of the members in this sector, especially the security staff, by sight."

"Fair—but minor—points," I said.

"Besides," she added, "if you dump me on Mund, I'll try to locate him on my own. I can't believe we wouldn't do better working together than separately."

Though I agreed with her points, she clearly didn't understand me, or she wouldn't have raised the last one. I had other options that accomplished the same goal: I could keep her on ice, dump her somewhere far away, or even kill her. I didn't want to kill anyone, but she didn't know enough about me to be sure that was the case. That she didn't consider any of these possibilities told me how very naïve she was.

Unfortunately, the fact that I was even contemplating taking along an unskilled companion also made me aware of something I rarely allow myself to notice: I'd become lonely. Lobo is fine company, and most of the time I'm happy to be either alone or traveling only with him, but sometimes I miss humans. It didn't hurt that she was pretty and possessed the most amazing eyes and hair I'd seen in a very long time. I might regret the choice, but with Lobo monitoring her and the level of skill she'd shown, I wasn't taking much of a risk.

"I'm willing to bring you along and maybe even let you assist me," I said, "but only on my terms."

"Name them," she said.

I shook my head: another amateur move. Never agree before you've heard the proposal. "You follow all my orders immediately and without question, even if the orders don't make any sense to you. Anything that involves Slanted Jack rarely follows a clear-cut path."

"Slanted Jack?"

"The man with the boy."

"Why 'Slanted'?"

"Because—never mind," I said. "Do you agree to do as I say?"

"Yes, but I have a condition of my own."

I smiled in grudging admiration at her willingness to push back. "What's that?"

"If you make money doing this, and if I help, you pay me whatever you think is a fair part of it."

"I thought you wanted to do this to save the boy."

"I do," she said, forcing herself to stand straighter and stare into my eyes, "but as we've discussed, I'm also recently unemployed, and from the fact that you can afford to have your own medbed and equip it with serious restraints, I assume you have money. People with money tend to make more money."

I laughed, in part because the obvious effort she put into working up her courage was oddly endearing and in part because in her situation I also would've asked for a cut. "Fair enough," I said, "though as of now I don't have any way to get paid for this mess." The gem buried in Lobo was for past work, and I'd use it to replenish Lobo's arsenal, so I felt no guilt in not mentioning it. I was going to ignore Chaplat's offer and help Jack run, so I didn't count it, either.

"Deal?" she said, sticking out her hand.

When I was young, my mother told me that centuries ago people gave their word, shook hands, and stood by the deal they'd just made. They didn't need legal systems, human or machine, to make them do it; they simply kept their word. She said this practice was one of the traditions humanity should never have abandoned, and she encouraged me to always follow it. I still did, and when I encountered other people who acted the same way—not those, like Chaplat, who did it for show, but those who really meant it—I instantly respected them for it.

I shook her hand and said, "Deal."

She held my hand a few moments too long and looked at me again with a hint of surprise, or maybe confusion.

"Is it so surprising that I agreed?" I said.

She released my hand. "I guess so." She looked briefly away, then turned again to face me. "Not a lot lately has gone the way I wanted." She closed her eyes for a moment, and then she leaned away from the wall and appeared to be on the edge of falling.

I steadied her. "Why don't you go back in there and rest?" I said. "With no restraints this time, of course."

She nodded her head. "That might be a good idea. I'm weaker than I thought. Where will you be?"

"Getting ready."

"Where are we?"

I couldn't hide Lobo from her, so I might as well try to influence her perceptions by setting her expectations. "We're in my ship. You may hear me talking. The ship has an onboard AI. His name is Lobo." She looked at me quizzically, so I explained. "The programmers did such a good job on the AI that I think of it as a 'him.' You probably will, too. I use him as a sounding board."

"I don't know anyone who owns a ship. Is it common that you talk to it?" She continued to look tired but was now clearly interested.

"And why shouldn't he?" Lobo said, his voice echoing from hidden speakers all around her. "Where else could he find a better conversationalist?"

I swear he added some bass reverb for effect. What a drama addict.

She jumped at the sound of his voice. "What kind of ship is this?" she said.

"I'm technically not a ship at all," Lobo said, his voice still booming. "I'm a—"

I cut him off. "That's enough for now, Lobo," I said. To Park, I added, "A cranky one." I guided her back to the medbed. "Later, after you're feeling better, we can discuss this further. For now, you rest, and Lobo will stay quiet." I looked away and muttered, "Right?"

"Of course," Lobo said on the machine frequency. "Never let it be said that I, merely your partner and the only barrier between you and the icy claws of certain death lurking just outside in the depths of space, would want to upset your former prisoner and new guest or interrupt her beauty slumber."

Park fell asleep almost instantly. Given Lobo's mood, I seriously considered crawling into my own bunk just to hide from him, but I had work to do. I headed up front to the pilot's couch.

"Do you have *any* data about where Jack was going?"

"You know I don't," Lobo said. "You saw the recording. That's all the relevant information I possess. Ships were, as usual, passing through both jump-gate apertures, and, as you may recall, I had to go far away from the gate to protect you."

I realized that I was frustrated and taking it out on Lobo. That was stupid. "Sorry," I said. "I'm not sure how to find him next. He could have had you drop him at the gate and then doubled back to Mund, or he might have jumped through either aperture. That leaves us three entire planets to search—and maybe many more if he jumped further."

"Searching Mund is easy enough," said Lobo, "particularly given the small size of the populated area."

"Easy?" Now he was annoying me. "We're talking at least half a dozen settlements I'd have to check. How is that easy?"

"We search for the transmitter I embedded in his arm when I repaired it," Lobo said.

"You stuck a transmitter in him?"

"Has my diction suddenly worsened?"

"You might have told me about it earlier."

"You might have waited to recover fully and discussed the situation with me before you leapt into interrogating our prisoner."

I hate it when he's right, which, of course, is quite often. "Fair enough. Tell me about the transmitter."

"I set it to emit a two-second burst at random intervals centered around every two minutes, so even if he's an extremely suspicious sort, unless he checks for transmissions continually or at exactly the right time, odds are good that it'll remain operational."

"Excellent."

"Should I begin searching Mund?" Lobo said.

I considered Lobo's point again. Since the moment I awoke, I'd done everything hastily and by instinct. That wouldn't be enough to catch Jack. I needed to stop and think. "No," I said. "We're safe here, so let's pause for a moment. I'd like to have a plan before we do anything further."

"What a lovely notion," Lobo said.

I ignored him. Jack, like me, never entered a place without having scouted his exit. He'd definitely been concerned that something might go wrong with the interview, because he'd involved me. Chaplat was after him, and the gangster had the ability to do him a great deal of damage. On top of all that, though Jack might have been trying to shake any tails by having Lobo leave him at the gate, to come back to Mund he'd need to land at a commercial transport facility, and Chaplat would be watching all those sites. No, he wouldn't have stayed on Mund.

He'd jump. He wouldn't jump far, though, because if he couldn't pay Chaplat he was legitimately broke, and the farther he went, the more he had to shell out for jump fees. So, he'd jump once, go to ground, and find a fence for at least one of the gemstones.

Where?

Mund's gate had two apertures, one to Drayus and one to Gash.

Drayus.

I closed my eyes and replayed our conversation in Falls. Jack mentioned that when he jumped here from Drayus, he checked with a gate agent he'd bribed. If he'd recently stayed on Drayus, he would have had time to build an identity and a base of operations. Drayus would be a logical destination.

"If you had to choose to hide on either Drayus or Gash," I said, "which would you pick?"

"Drayus," Lobo said.

"Why?"

"Humans colonized Drayus one hundred and fifty-one years ago," Lobo said, "so it possesses many major settlements and a population in the millions. It's a regional capital for the Expansion Coalition, so it has serious local law enforcement and a low crime rate. Anyone chasing Jack would have less likelihood of success mounting an illegal attack there than on any other planet in the region. Its gate has three additional active apertures, so he could jump from it to Avery, Immediata, or Therien, all relatively stable planets with additional jump opportunities."

"What about Gash?" I said.

"Gash is the most dangerous planet in this sector of space. Its gate opened only forty-five years ago, so humans have been active there less than a third of the time they've lived on Drayus. It has so few natural resources and so many violent extremist groups that the EC hasn't even bothered trying to make it an affiliate—and the population doesn't have any interest in becoming one. Almost all of the people reside in the six small cities spread along the southeast coast of its one major landmass, and not one of those cities is particularly safe.

"No, not Gash. Drayus is clearly the better option."

Lobo's analysis was, of course, accurate. Drayus presented Jack with numerous advantages. He'd also let slip that he'd jumped from there to Mund.

Drayus was the only logical choice.

"It's time to head to the gate," I said. "We're going to Gash."

CHAPTER THIRTEEN

"Gash?" Lobo said. "Was something in my analysis unclear to you?"

"Not at all," I said. "I understood it completely, and it was perfect. Any logical person would choose Drayus—which is exactly why Jack is hiding out on Gash."

"So he's stupid and/or illogical?"

"Neither. He's as smart and as able to reason dispassionately as anyone I've ever known. He's sufficiently intelligent, in fact, that he'll have reached the same conclusion we did, which is the reason he'll hide where no one would expect him to go. He's also worked with people there, so he'll have connections. Finally, what you cited as drawbacks of Gash—the extremist groups, the lawlessness, the danger—are opportunities and camouflage from Jack's perspective. He always targets bad people, so the place is ripe with potential fish, and if he needs to hire help, where better to be?"

"Fish?"

"People likely to fall for scams."

"My slang dictionary isn't as complete as I'd thought," Lobo said. "Perhaps I'll make a special study of criminal jargon. It might prove useful given that you own me."

"May we please head to Gash?" I said.

"Of course," Lobo said. "You gave the order, and I followed it. I have to ask, however, one more question: If Jack is as intelligent as you claimed, might he not have figured out that you'd reach this conclusion and so switched back to Drayus?"

"Of course it's possible," I said, drawing out the words and fighting the urge to yell at him, "but what makes me confident he's on Gash is that I'm not what he's trying to avoid. Between Dougat and the Followers and Chaplat's gang, Jack has far bigger problems than anything I might present. Staying away from both of those groups would be his primary concern." I paused and considered one last time. "No," I finally said, "he's not on Drayus. He's on Gash."

"I see your reasoning," Lobo said, "but if it were up to me, I'd opt for the logical conclusion."

"Then it's a good thing it's not up to you," I said, already feeling a little less confident than I sounded. "Look at the bright side: You also win in this."

"How is that?"

"You gain another opportunity for self-improvement: understanding human thought processes better."

"Oh, joy," Lobo said. "Just what I wanted: another growth opportunity."

I smiled even though I was a bit chagrined at the pleasure I took in tweaking him. "Head for the gate."

"File our jump plan and enter the queue, as usual?"

I started to say yes but stopped myself. I had no desire to lead either Dougat or Chaplat to Jack, which is exactly what I'd do if I gave away my destination and either of Jack's pursuers had people monitoring the station. "No," I said. "Let's check it out first. How long to the gate?"

"Assuming you still want to follow at least some of our usual procedures and run an indirect route and check for surveillance on the way—"

"Of course," I said, already sorry for goading him.

"—we should reach it in about four hours."

"Please wake me about half an hour out or if our guest gets up first."

"With pleasure," Lobo said. "I live to be your wake-up call."

I shook my head in frustration, stretched out, and tried to nap. Anything involving Jack was likely to be tiring, so I followed another rule I'd learned decades ago: If the course is long or hard, sleep when you can.

"She's awake," Lobo said. "Should I unlock her door?"

"Any incoming scan attempts?" I asked.

"None so far. The gate station is broadcasting the usual queries, but we can dock without filing more than a request for temporary stay."

"Let her out." I turned away from the display Lobo had opened across the front and watched as Park came down the short hallway. She'd removed her body armor and was wearing only a knee-length, skintight, cobalt-blue T-shirt. One sleeve was missing from Lobo's minor surgery; she'd ripped off the other. Her hair was loose, and either she was stunningly gorgeous or I'd been away from women too long. She appeared to have none of the extreme beauty mods that were the current craze among corporate and government execs, but she didn't suffer for the lack. I realized I was staring at her body a second after she did, but she didn't say anything; instead, she smiled when we made eye contact. I felt my face blush, so I was grateful when the display drew her attention.

"We're jumping?" she said.

"Maybe." I looked again at the image. Mund's jump gate grew larger in the display as we approached it. Like all the gates, this one glowed a single, completely uniform color. Each gate is also perfectly smooth, every square centimeter an exact, unmarked replica of every other. No two gates are the same exact hue, though we have no clue whether that fact means anything. We also have no idea why each gate is the color it is. The bright raspberry of Mund's gate struck me as a bit garish, but then again, if I'd been in charge of building the gates, the pink one—in my opinion the least attractive gate known to humanity—would never have existed.

Some cults claimed only God controlled the structures; Gatists worshipped the gates as if they *were* gods. Alien conspiracy advocates split into two main camps: One maintained superior aliens had constructed the gates to prepare humanity for the next step in its evolution, while the other claimed that similarly superior aliens used the structures to lull us into abandoning our attempts to construct interstellar ships—one of which we had built when Earth was our sole home—and go only where they wanted us. It was certainly the case that every known gate led to a planetary system that contained at least one planet that without any terraforming was already habitable by humans.

I didn't care at all about any of the theories. To me, as I'd said earlier to Park, the gates worked, and that was good enough. You entered an aperture in one part of space and emerged many light-years away in another area, though typically in the same general sector. Gates also interested people in many of the types of work I've done over the years, because they offered safe havens of a sort: They didn't tolerate ship-to-ship violence within their areas of influence, a sphere with its center on the gate and a radius of roughly one light-second. They didn't care at all what happened inside each ship—fights on spacecraft and gate stations were as common as you'd expect at any port where long-trip crews disembarked to relax—but let a vessel release any sort of weapon, even an energy beam, and the gate would instantly hit both the ship and the weapon with a blast the color of the gate. Both the ship and the weapon would then be *gone*—not vaporized, not shattered, just gone, as if they'd never existed. No one knew where the offenders went; they simply vanished. As best anyone had ever been able to tell, the beam that emanated from gates in these circumstances moved faster than light, but no one was sure; experiments were expensive and ultimately both destructive and uninformative.

The gates did tolerate collisions with meteors and other natural objects, provided no ship had steered those things, but the collisions left the gates unfazed and unscarred.

Staring at Mund's gate, I understood for a moment, as I always did when approaching one of the strange structures, their ability to inspire religious thought. You couldn't help but think of them as having personalities, and thus as being somehow intelligent. They also invoked awe in all but the most jaded travelers. Hanging in space, each resembled a gigantic pretzel composed of Möbius strips. The apertures—the areas where the strips wound together to create closed circuits—ranged in size from barely large enough to let small shuttles pass to so huge that no human ship yet built would come anywhere near its edges. Working apertures were pure black, the color of space without stars, of the darkest bowels of a dead planet. Energy would not pass through them to the other sector of space; low-level beams would continue as if the aperture weren't there. Only objects could make the trip.

Gates also varied in the number of apertures they offered, with a few having only a single aperture and others offering half a dozen or more. New apertures appeared from time to time, and corporations and governments naturally coveted them for the commercial opportunities they created. Only one aperture connection—the one that had linked Earth and Pinkelponker—had ever closed, and as with so many facts about my home world, no one knew why. The closure had certainly added fuel to the flame of mysticism that flickered around that planet.

How a person reacted to seeing a gate was, to me, a good indicator of character. Those too busy to notice were almost certainly not going to become friends of mine. People who felt the need to make stupid jokes or pretend to find the gates routine or boring almost always annoyed me. Park stared openly, her lips slightly parted, one foot forward as if ready to step into an aperture herself, and I instantly liked her for the utterly frank, undisguised interest. She moved closer, and the display's glow wrapped around her. In silhouette I noticed more about her: the lushness of her figure, the tiny bump on her nose, the ever so slight lightening in color of the epicanthic fold of her left eyelid as it reached her nose, the way she held her hand out from her body, almost as if she were reaching for me.

"Beautiful," I whispered, realizing too late I'd spoken aloud.

"It is," she said. "Each time I see a gate, I feel the same sense of wonder all over again."

I squeezed my eyes shut. How stupid could I be? I'd interrogated this woman only hours before, and now I was eyeing her hand like a lovesick child. I'd be lucky if she didn't recoil or hit me if I touched her; either reaction would certainly be reasonable.

I had to focus on the tasks at hand.

"If we're not going to jump," she said, "then why are we here?"

"I didn't say we weren't. I said, 'maybe.' We need to be careful."

"I understand," she said, "but Dougat's certainly not going to attack your ship this close to a gate."

"Dougat's not the only one looking for Jack," I said, "and fending off a possible assault is not our only problem."

"What do you mean?"

"Jack owes money to a group, and he doesn't appear to plan to pay them back. They'd also like to catch him." If either Dougat's or Chaplat's teams got their hands on her, the less she knew, the better, so I left it at that.

I touched her shoulder, and she turned to face me.

"I can let you out here, even give you some money, and you can catch a commercial shuttle." I stared into her eyes, trying to will her to act like an innocent bystander, to leave and be safe. I didn't want anything to happen to her. "Everything could go smoothly, but it could also go nonlinear, and your best bet is to run far away from here." I kept staring. She was too nice to involve. I considered knocking her out and dumping her at the station, but I'd made a deal.

"No," she said. "You agreed that I could come, and I'm coming."

"Fine," I said, my frustration at her choice emerging as an angry tone, my voice harsh enough that she involuntarily stepped back. "Stay quiet, follow my orders, and maybe this'll work out."

I turned away from her. How did I manage to let concern emerge as anger? I shook my head at my own stupidity.

"Lobo, are all the ships currently in this region queued to jump?" I asked the question out loud, because if she was going to be with me, she might as well get used to hearing me talk to him.

"No," he answered, also out loud, "two are not: me, and one other."

Leave it to him to use precision to deliver sarcasm. "Show me the other one."

A ship popped into view in the upper left of the display in front of me. A little smaller than Lobo, it might have been a gate maintenance vessel, but it had no corporate or government markings. Service vehicles don't bother to travel incognito.

"Did it arrive before or after us?"

"Before. It was already in place when it came in range of my visual sensors."

"Is it sending or receiving any transmissions?"

"No."

Great. It might not be watching for us, but it certainly could be. Whoever ran it—Dougat or Chaplat—was more connected than I'd imagined, because all ships near a gate have to broadcast basic identity and intent data. We were posing as a private shuttle seeking gate-station R&R before deciding where to jump. The EC operated this station, so they would normally require every ship to maintain its status broadcasts. Whoever owned this vessel had paid off someone to tolerate this breach of protocol.

"Can you identify its type?"

"Not with certainty," Lobo said, "but that means nothing, because many vehicles, particularly milspec craft, are as configurable as I am. It's certainly the right size to be a scout-class chaser, faster than I am within a system but nowhere near as well armed nor, I might add, as intelligent."

Was he showing off? I decided to ignore him.

"Park," I said, "do you recognize it?"

"Please call me Maggie," she said, "and no, but that doesn't mean anything. I know Dougat and the Followers own quite a few ships, but I have no idea how many or what types they are."

This one might not be after us, but to be safe and to protect Jack and Manu, I had to assume it was. I couldn't afford to lead it to them.

"Lobo," I said, "File for a jump to Drayus."

"Done," he said. "Are you bowing to logic, or running an evasive route?"

"The latter."

I focused again on the image of the lurking ship, but I learned nothing new.

"What if it follows us?" Maggie said.

"Then we deal with it."

"That's your best idea?" she said. "Deal with it?"

"Yeah," I said, "that's about it."

"It doesn't seem like much of a plan."

I faced her and forced myself to keep my voice level. I was furious, but not because the question was unfair; it wasn't. She was right as far as she went, but at the same time she was incredibly wrong; she had clearly never been on the sharp end of a conflict. "It isn't much of a plan," I said, "but it's about all we can manage with the information we have. This is exactly how this sort of thing goes. You don't get to study perfect data. You don't get to know everything that's happening. You can't plan for every contingency. You assemble all of your intelligence info, identify your best option, implement it, and then react to what happens. You make the best choice you can given what you know at that moment, you put one foot in front of the other, and you keep walking until you either win or die. That's it. That's all there is."

She studied me intently, but she didn't respond.

I was grateful for that. I needed time to cool. I've spent too much of my life dealing with those who manipulate others and never witness the true costs. They always expect their plans to work, and of course the plans rarely do. I knew intellectually that Maggie wasn't one of them, but her questions triggered the anger that courses through me all the time, just under the surface, ready to explode.

"Our turn," Lobo said.

I faced the display and watched as the perfect blackness of the aperture drew closer and closer, until it filled our vision, until the world beyond the ship vanished for a fraction of a second in which anything might happen, everything was possible, and then we poked through and a new starscape flashed to life in front of us. I realized I was holding my breath, as I often did when I jumped, and I exhaled slowly.

"Dock in the first available station slot," I said, "and file for a visit. Switch the display to focus on the aperture."

The aperture filled the display initially, but it shrank quickly as we jetted toward the station.

"Let's see what follows us."

CHAPTER FOURTEEN

Fifteen minutes passed, and the ship didn't come through the gate after us. Every craft that emerged into the Drayus system sent the usual jump acknowledgment and headed toward the planet.

Fifteen more minutes passed, and still the lurking ship did not appear.

I waited in silence, focusing on Lobo's displays and thinking. Waiting has played an important role in many of the ways I've made my living. I've waited on stakeouts, for darkness to fall, and for enemy troops and vehicles to move by my position. I'm used to it, and I'm generally good at it.

I had to give Maggie credit: She held out for a full hour before she spoke.

"I don't seem to be able to say anything that doesn't annoy you, but at the risk of doing the wrong thing yet again, are you sure that ship wasn't just innocently sitting there, maybe with a broken transmitter?"

I'd known what she'd eventually have to ask, so I'd had time to prepare myself and was able to answer both calmly and honestly. "More than half of what's bothered me about what you've said comes from the way I interpreted your words, not anything you did wrong, so don't worry about that. But, yes, I'm reasonably confident that ship is anything but innocent. If it really was in trouble, the gate station would have sent repair help, and we'd have seen the maintenance process in action." I rubbed my eyes hard in frustration at myself. Softly, more to myself than to her or Lobo, I said, "I'm missing something obvious."

"I don't understand how it can hurt us or even track us if it doesn't follow us," she said. "If the people who own it cared as much about us as you think, wouldn't they come over here and confront us?"

How stupid could I be? "Brilliant!" I said, turning to look at her. "Of course." She smiled, pleased with the praise but also clearly confused.

I faced the display again. "Lobo, run the same check here that you did at the last station. I want to know if any ships aren't scheduled for jumps."

"Two," Lobo said, "us and one other." A vessel the shape of a good-size troop transport popped into the center of the front display. "This one is behaving exactly the same way as the one at the Mund gate."

"Milspec?"

"It's sitting without any visible weapons, it's not transmitting, and it's heavily shielded—again like the other ship—but it certainly possesses a suitable profile."

"This is good news?" Maggie said.

"Yes and no," I said. "It's good in that we now understand what's going on: The other ship didn't jump here because it didn't have to do anything to keep us under surveillance; this one was waiting for us. The bad part is that whichever of those two groups is chasing us has enough resources to position ships both here and at Mund's gate. Whoever is monitoring us wants to track us very badly indeed, but they're not yet willing to approach us."

"So what do we do?"

"Find out how far their reach extends." I stared at the image of the Drayus gate in one of Lobo's side displays. The giant structure, its perfect surface the color of pale sand tinged with lemon, contained four apertures. I knew the one to Mund led to another surveillance ship, so the only question was which of the others to try first. "Lobo, which of the planets accessible via this gate is the most heavily populated?" Given that both of the groups pursuing Jack and us operated on or outside the fringes of governmental control, I wanted the planet with the largest EC presence. If no ship was waiting for us there, we had a way out. If one was holding the same silent guard vigil as the other two we'd seen, we'd know the opposition had greater pull than I'd expected.

"Therien," Lobo said, "the jewel of the EC. A large and affluent human population inhabits it, its natural resources are varied and plentiful, and it's sufficiently orderly that despite its size the EC has never issued a peacekeeping contract for it."

"File to jump there," I said. "Here's hoping nobody's waiting for us."

So much for that hope.

We didn't wait to check this time, so we discovered the surveillance vessel before we'd even queued up for a station visit. Like the others, this one was sitting incognito. Unlike its counterparts, it profile was clearly milspec.

Maggie fretted and paced, but she stayed quiet. I appreciated the control.

I sat and considered the situation.

Nothing about Chaplat's operation smelled of this much money. Local bosses tend to boast, to overstate their importance, but it's all part of the way they intimidate others. If his reach had extended this far, he'd have let me know.

No, it wasn't Chaplat.

Dougat and the Followers might have been richer than Chaplat, and as a quasi-religious organization their influence might have spanned more planets, but I couldn't picture them having both the fleet and the staff necessary to be able to afford to dedicate this level of resources to tracking one man and one boy.

It also wasn't Dougat.

Only two types of entities possess the people, ships, and

organization you need for this level of surveillance: conglomerates and governments. I've kept a low profile with the megacorporations for almost a year, so it's been that long since I put myself on any of their target lists. Neither Kelco nor Xychek, the last two huge businesses I'd given cause to come after me, operated in this sector of space. If either of those two companies was angry enough, they could certainly use corporate reciprocity agreements to motivate a local firm to hunt me, but I couldn't buy that scenario; the cost greatly outweighed the return. The megacorps will indulge executive whims, including revenge, to a point, but eventually their credit-counters will run an analysis, and the bottom line will carry the day.

That left me with only one possibility: government. To operate on all these planets, there was no way it was a single planetary operation, nor were those even common in this sector. It had to be the EC.

The problem is, I hadn't done anything to draw that kind of attention, nor, to the best of my knowledge, had Jack. It's always possible he'd conned an influential EC honcho, because the wrong person with the right degree of power can lead governments to temporarily act insanely and with no regard for their P&L, but I couldn't buy it.

So, the EC also made no sense.

I was back to having no rational explanation—but the existence of all those surveillance ships guaranteed there was one. I just hadn't figured it out.

By making these jumps, I'd also created another problem: I was telling any astute observer where Jack and Manu were. I'd avoided jumping to Gash while clearly trying other systems, so I was effectively saying, "Look everywhere but there!"

I had to go to Gash.

I also needed more data. Would the ship follow me if I left the vicinity of the gate? Were we facing hostile action or merely covert data gathering?

I might as well find out here, in the heavily populated Therien system, because more people means more support satellites and space traffic, which in turn means more readily available places to hide and a lower likelihood of an attack near the planet. By appearing to check more closely both here and on Gash, I could also add some confusion to the thinking of our watchers.

"Lobo, head for Therien. Plot a course that puts the station and the gate between the watching ship and us well before we pass out of the gate's area of influence. Track that ship."

"Done," Lobo said.

A hologram appeared in front of the main display. It showed the station, the gate, and a section of Therien. A small green dot—us—moved away from the gate, accelerating as it went. A red dot marked the position of the surveillance vessel.

"As I'm sure you're aware," Lobo said, "this course will leave me unable to track that ship until we're closer to Therien."

"Yes, I am," I said. "And it won't be able to see us, either, so if it wants to keep an eye on us, it'll either have to change position or hand us off to another ship. Monitor all the vessels between the gate and Therien, and check for parallel courses."

"Are we inviting attack?" Maggie said, her voice a bit choked and her shoulders high and tense. "Prior to what happened at the Institute, I'd never been in any kind of fight, much less one in space between ships."

"No," I said. "We're inviting motion. We'll stay close enough to the gate that it would take out any ship that fired at us—and the weapons the ship fired, of course."

We watched the hologram in silence as Lobo accelerated toward Therien.

About ninety seconds later, the red dot abruptly disappeared from its original location. A short time later, it reappeared on our side of the gate.

"The ship is definitely following us," Lobo said, "and it's tracking our course exactly. That pilot is either as dumb as a drink dispenser or doesn't care if we spot it."

"No one able to set up this many surveillance ships in the time since Jack and Manu left us can be that dumb," I said. "Even if I'm wrong, we have to assume they simply don't care if we know they're following us."

"If they don't mind if we spot them and know we will," Maggie said, "then why don't they contact us directly?"

"I suspect they're making a point," I said. "They're letting us know that we have no way out that they can't track."

"Are they right?" she said. "Is this Dougat using us to find the boy?"

I appreciated her concern, but the questions were wearing on me again. "I don't know, but eventually we'll figure it out. In the meantime, though, we need to throw them off Jack's trail."

I kept my tone level, but I was also getting worried. I didn't yet see a good way out of this.

The only thing to do was to keep moving ahead.

"Lobo, take us to the gate, then jump to Drayus, then Mund, and then Gash."

"In progress," Lobo said. "Should I continue to track the ship?"

"Did it turn when you did?" I said.

"Yes."

"Then you can stop monitoring it. We have all the data about it that we need."

"Isn't Gash where you deduced Jack would be hiding?" Lobo asked. "More to the point, isn't it where you didn't want to lead them?"

"My question exactly," Maggie said.

The two of them were going to make me crazy. I'd worked alone for so long that I wasn't accustomed to having to explain myself. I didn't want to become used to it either, but I knew they wouldn't stop bothering me until I gave them an explanation.

"I can't let Gash be the only nearby planet we haven't jumped to, or that fact alone will draw their attention to it. Once we finish this set of maneuvers, we'll have spread a little confusion and verified the surveillance setup is the same on all the planets near here."

"Maybe we'll get lucky," Maggie said, "and they won't be watching Gash."

"Maybe," I said, not wanting to constantly criticize her.

She stared at me for a moment. "No chance, huh?"

If she was going to ask, I was going to answer truthfully.

"None," I said. "No group this well organized would miss something so obvious."

She nodded and turned to the display as the aperture grew larger and larger in front of us, the ships ahead of us in the queue made the jump, our turn came, and we once again plunged into the perfect black ahead.

"Just like the others?" I asked as we waited by the station next to Gash's screaming red jump gate.

"For any reasonable value of 'like,' " Lobo said, "yes. It's in roughly the same position relative to the gate as the other surveillance vessels, like them it's not transmitting at all, and its profile also suggests milspec."

"I hope Jack beat them here," I said. "If he didn't, whoever is following us already knows where he is."

Lobo's front displays showed both the gate and Gash. The gate and its two apertures, the one to Mund and a newer connection that led to Triton's Dream, hung in space like blood splatters caught in midflight by a strobe on a starless night. People in spacesuits crawled all over the outside of the gate station. The parts of the structure they passed turned a red almost exactly the color of the gate itself; it had to be a Gatist color wash. Fine by me; any activity that attracted attention away from us was a good thing.

In the other direction, the reflected light of Gash's sun washed the planet itself a duller red, its namesake giant crimson desert slashing across the vast majority of the single large landmass like a wound tearing open. With only seven cities, six strung along the eastern coast and one perched on the continent's northwestern edge, and with limited useful natural resources, Gash hadn't grown at the usual early-stages pace in the forty-five years since the aperture to it had first opened in Mund's gate.

"I must note again," Lobo said, "that Gash is *not* a logical choice for Jack. From what I've gathered from the public data streams, the Followers, the very group Jack is trying to avoid, are the fastest-growing cult on the planet. They operate temples in all seven major cities."

"He's right," Maggie said. "I've heard Dougat and some of the senior staff talk about this place. He called it a 'godless hell' with no real government and said its population included a higher than normal percentage of criminals. He also said those same qualities made it a great place to evangelize and recruit converts."

"I'm not denying it's full of rough trade," I said. "The place is wild enough that the EC has never been willing to force it to join. I also understand that the Followers are big there. All the same, Jack knows he needs to go to ground, and he's arrogant enough to view a city full of criminals as a target-rich environment." I wasn't as sure as I sounded, but at the same time Gash remained the best bet for Jack. He'd earned his nickname always working the angles you didn't expect; heading to Gash fit his character perfectly. "Maybe I'm wrong, but we're going with my instincts." I checked out the image of the surveillance ship in Lobo's rightmost display. "Bring up the tracking holo, and head us to Gash. We came here to give them the same show we ran on Therien; we might as well do it."

The hologram popped into view in front of us as Lobo accelerated away from the gate and toward the planet.

"Same course type?" Lobo said.

"Yes. Keep the gate between the planet and us initially. Let's make them have to move."

Sure enough, once we were well away from the gate, the red dot that represented the other ship vanished and then quickly popped into place behind us on the hologram.

"You were right," Maggie said.

Her tone suggested I'd want to gloat; I didn't. I'd have greatly preferred to have been wrong, because if I had been it would've meant we could have kept going to Gash. Now, we'd have to head back, maybe all the way to Mund, and I'd have to figure out a new way to get to Jack.

"A second ship is now tracking us," Lobo said.

A blue dot appeared on the hologram. It wasn't following our course the way the surveillance ship was, but it was in position to monitor us.

"Are you sure it's after us?" I said.

"As certain as I can be with the data available," Lobo said. "Had I doubted it, I wouldn't have stated it as fact. It's responding to changes in our course but not tracing our path exactly."

"So it's not with the first ship?" I asked.

"I cannot be sure," Lobo said, "but I don't believe it is."

"Reverse course and head right back at the surveillance ship. Come as close as you can without directly targeting it. We don't want the gate to think we're attacking."

"Done," Lobo said, "but why?"

"If the two ships are from the same organization, they'll respond similarly. If they don't, then another player has joined the game." I wanted to pressure them and hope I learned that the two were together. If they were, our pursuers might have figured out that Jack was likely to be here, but we'd have to live with that problem, at least for now. It was better than having two different groups chasing us. "Accelerate hard; let's not give them much time to react."

I watched on the display as our dot quickly closed the gap with the red one. It stayed where it was as we approached and then passed it.

The blue dot, however, raced for cover back behind the gate.

Great.

Two different organizations *were* after us. Reaching Gash and finding Jack without leading our pursuers to him was getting harder and harder.

When I'd thought we'd be alone, searching Gash had been just a matter of time and fuel. Now, though, it would require a great deal of effort to lose or confront our pursuers. Before we went to all that trouble, I needed to verify that Jack had definitely jumped there. The only place we could get that information was the jump gate, and even there I couldn't be sure we'd succeed; the station agent was supposed to keep all such data confidential.

"Head back to the gate station and dock," I said. "I'm going aboard."

"Done," Lobo said.

"I have some additional instructions and contingency plans to review with you both," I said, "and I'm going to need some supplies."

"Expecting trouble?" Lobo said.

"No, just preparing in case it comes."

"What do you want me to do?" Maggie said.

"How good are you with weapons?"

"Why do we need weapons?"

"Because," I said, "we may have to be persuasive."

CHAPTER FIFTEEN

Red people walked the red aisles of the red gate station. As I'd assumed when I'd seen the spacesuited figures painting the exterior, a Gatist color ceremony was rolling through the station like a tidal wave across an island. Apparently the EC was unwilling to risk the bad publicity it would receive if it tried to stop the paint-wielding Gatists thronging the facility. The Frontier Coalition was the last government to interfere in one of these supposedly religious events, and it paid a steep price: The Gatists protested so loudly on so many planets that the FC chose to declare a sector-wide color-ceremony day to appease them rather than continue the fight.

The whole affair struck me as stupid. Even if the Gatists are right and the gates are God (or gods, depending on which Gatist sect you ask), I couldn't see why a God would care at all if we painted ourselves to resemble it.

To be fair to the Gatists, though, the ceremony was both artistically interesting and nondestructive. They swarmed a station inside and out en masse, thousands of them arriving simultaneously and spreading with military precision across the entire facility and every willing ship docked there. I'd given them permission to paint Lobo, in part not to stand out and in part because it annoyed him so much

461

it was fun to do. The swarm of Gatists colored every surface of every thing and every willing person the exact hue of the gate, and they were fast painters. In a matter of hours, the gate color sparkled everywhere. They persuaded a surprisingly large number of people to participate, so that almost everyone who visited a station during one of these ceremonies ended up joining the color wash. Government officials resisted initially, but the Gatists were so annoying that ultimately the bureaucrats succumbed and it became standard policy for them to accept the paint. The Gatists rewarded the compliant by using temporary coatings that over the course of a few days turned transparent, peeled off, and either evaporated or, in space, floated away. They even cleaned after themselves, using fine-mesh collectors to gather the external debris and cleansing the station's air filters of all paint residue.

Wherever there's a ceremony, there's inevitably a party, of course, and when a party grows large enough, merchants seize the opportunity to hawk their goods. Revelers, Gatists and nonbelievers alike, drank and ate and browsed the gate-colored wares of gate-colored vendors who sprouted in the halls and public rooms and sometimes even the private chambers of the stations. Many sellers used the events to close out items that were once available only in less popular colors, because of course you had no way to know the true color of anything you bought.

Never ones to miss tax opportunities, the government agents quickly produced schedules of fees and taxes and licenses, opened more rooms to the revelers, rented private suites by the hour to particularly amorous partiers, and sold sponsorships to local conglomerates. The Gatists initially protested the crass commercial-ization of their deeply religious ceremonies, but their furor abated when the gate staff cut them in for a percentage of the action.

I went straight to the Gatist team stationed at my entry lock and told them to have at it. I even stripped; I wanted to blend as well as possible with everyone else. They crammed filters in my nostrils and ears, then stuck me under a portable shower and turned me red. I wouldn't let go of either of my guns or my wallet until I could see again, at which point they finished painting the parts of my hands, wallet, and weapons that had been in contact with each other and sent me on my way.

I verified that everything was still present and, as best I could, that the guns appeared to work, then walked into the screaming redness of the station hallways. The fluorescent chips the Gatists had blended into the paint twinkled and sparkled in the station lights like the faint beginnings of flares on a red sun. All around me swirled the sounds of commerce and partying: heated debates and shrieking laughter and hushed tones hinting at rendezvous in progress and those yet to come. Rich smells thickened the air: the sweat of too many bodies in too small a space, the enticing aromas of meat and vegetables cooking on portable grills, the almost imperceptible yet powerful odors of cosmetics and pheromone enhancers fighting for dominance, and, underlying it all, the slight but noticeable tang of the Gatist paint.

I tucked my weapons inside my shirt and waded slowly through the churning sea of bodies. Pickpockets working the aisles patted me down as I moved, apparently so unconcerned about detection that they abandoned any pretense of subtlety. They kept hacker partners close at hand in the hopes that the wallets they were stealing used old, weak encryption. I wasn't stupid enough to keep my wallet or weapons anywhere they could easily reach, so at one level I had nothing to lose, but the casual openness with which they worked the crowd offended me.

I knew I should focus on finding the gate agent, but after the fourth hand stroked my pants pockets, I couldn't take any more. Each touch was a violation, and I can stand only so many. I slowed my pace, and when the fifth hand touched me I grabbed it with my right and pulled the owner close enough that I could see the slight fear in his eyes even as he reached for a weapon. I gripped his throat with my left hand, squeezed, and shook my head. I pulled him close, as if to kiss an old friend in greeting, and whispered into his ear.

"Move your hand one more centimeter toward whatever you're trying to reach, and I'll break your neck. Understand?" I leaned back to gauge his reaction.

He lifted his hand clear of his body and blinked at me, unable to speak.

I released his left hand. "Scratch your face if you understand me and agree to behave," I said.

He did, his eyes still blinking from nerves.

"I'm not out to save everyone," I said. "I don't have the time. So, do whatever you want to the rest of the crowd." I squeezed his throat a little tighter, and his face reddened. "Touch me again, however, and I won't be so gentle. Spread the word. Okay?"

He scratched his face madly.

I released his neck.

He backed slowly into the crowd, his eyes never leaving me, until he was a good five meters away. Then he turned and ran as quickly as the crowd permitted. I stayed where I was, watching him, the people flowing around me, until he was out of sight. Pickpockets rarely worked solo in confined spaces like the station, so I was confident he'd spread the word as efficiently as any corporate data-alert blast.

The wall-mounted station legends were hard to read in uniform red, people stood where the holo maps normally played, and the din was so loud that the low-end directional AIs couldn't hear to answer questions, so I had to either interrogate the machines directly or find a guard. The space was so loud that I doubted my ability to converse without distraction with the machines, and I also wanted to get a sense of the quality of the security staff, so I opted to approach the guards. The first one I spotted was holding open a service closet door and negotiating intently with a woman wearing only red paint and earrings the shape of Gash's gate, so I gave him a pass. The next was happily painting a nude young Gatist who was holding aloft a miniature gate, so I moved on. At least most of the guards weren't going to be problems.

The third one I encountered was standing in front of a door, almost as if he were working, though he'd leaned his stun rifle against the doorway and was munching on a skewer of red meat.

"Who's the station manager?" I said. "And where can I find him?"

He stopped chewing and stared at me over the empty end of the stick of meat. "What do you need?"

"These Gatists and their mess have mucked up my schedule, and I've got freight to move. I want to lodge a protest." He didn't respond. Instead, he stared at me, and took another bite of the meat. "Fine," I said, "if you don't want to tell me his name and how to find him, I'll give you the details and you can relay them. I know you carry a terminal; let's sit down together and go over all my issues. It shouldn't take more than an hour to discuss everything."

He swallowed and shook his head. "Carne, Lem Carne, is the agent. It's not like he'll do anything to help you, though." Before I could say another word, he tilted his head toward the right and continued, "Down about a hundred meters to the second corridor, take a right, third door on your right. Knock yourself out."

He bit into the meat again, tore off another chunk, and looked away as he chewed.

I followed his directions and stopped at the end of the hallway when I spotted a single guard standing in front of the door to Carne's office. The party here was as loud and crowded as in every other corridor, but this guard, though red like everyone else, scanned the crowd continuously and stood alert.

I hunched my shoulders, bent my knees, and weaved toward him, bouncing off revelers and Gatists alike as I moved. I held my stomach as if I were about to be sick, both hands wrapped around my middle and one clutching the end of a trank gun. I ricocheted off a woman hawking religious charms she swore she'd made herself from flecks of paint that had floated in space by the gates, grabbed my mouth with my free hand, and bumped into the guard.

"Can you help me?" I said, leaning on him unsteadily. "I'm gonna be sick."

He put both hands on my shoulders to shove me away. When I felt them touch me, I pushed up and into him, crushing him against the wall and pinning his hands momentarily against me. At the same time, I straightened, pulled out the gun, and rammed it under his throat. I reached behind him with my left hand and steadied him. No one else could see the gun; to anyone watching the scene, the guard was simply helping another poor fool who couldn't handle his party drugs of choice.

I leaned close enough to the guy's right ear that he could hear me when I whispered, "When I say the word, you open the door and back in. Move before I tell you, move anything other than your right hand, or do anything else, and I'll shoot you. Understand?"

He nodded briefly, then stopped.

"Nodding is okay," I said, "and so is talking."

He nodded again and quietly said, "I understand."

"How many inside?"

"Just him."

"Carne?"

"Yes."

"Right hand only, nice and slow: Open it."

I leaned slightly back so I could watch his eyes, and I pushed up on the gun so it dug deeper into his neck.

His right hand drifted slowly downward as if sinking in a very salty ocean. He ran it over the recognition plate, and the door snicked open.

The guard stumbled for a moment, but I used my left hand on his neck to redirect his momentum and spin him around. I followed him into the room, keeping him between me and the unknown and therefore potentially dangerous space ahead. I held him in front of me as the door closed behind us.

I scanned the area quickly.

If Carne had an office, it was hiding somewhere, because what I was staring at was a game museum, not a place of work—and a museum he'd managed to convince the Gatists to leave alone. Models of spaceships, submersibles, assault vehicles of all classes, ancient helicopters and airplanes, land-based tanks, and even covered wagons and chariots hung from all over the ceiling on meter-long wires. If the room hadn't been over four meters tall, I'd never have been able to stand up straight in it. All the models were moving, each in a roughly half-meter sphere, toys flying up and down, diving and surfacing, rolling back and forth on invisible streets of air, and never sitting still. Even though I knew they were above me, I couldn't escape the sensation of being a giant in danger of imminent attack from heavily armed Lilliputian forces.

Carne had clearly been assembling his collection for a long time, because the office was easily three times the size of any station agent's I'd ever seen. About twenty meters wide by ten deep, it was a big space—but not big enough. Shelves full of games and toys of all sorts lined the walls. I spotted playing cards, brightly colored boxes I didn't recognize, figurines in a huge variety of costumes, and on and on. He'd packed freestanding gaming machines so closely that they formed corridors that wove drunkenly around the room as if placed randomly by a liquor vendor at the end of a two-day binge. Holo combat units stood side by side with ancient video games— either they were reproductions, or gate bribes had gone way, way up in the last few years—and they were all active, their demos chattering for attention. He'd set their volume levels to low, but even so the cumulative effect was disorienting, as if I'd wandered into dozens of simultaneous whispered conversations.

A man appeared at the end of a corridor to my right and walked toward us. In his right hand he carried a small, green figurine that appeared to be a soldier. Its right arm gripped the smallest finger on his left hand, and he was moving its little arm up and down, glee fighting with annoyance in his expression. "I've told you not to enter without my permission," he said, never even looking up.

"Mr. Carne," the guard began, but I cut him off by grabbing his mouth and shooting a trank round into his leg. He went slack. I let him drop and turned the weapon on Carne.

"I thought we had negotiated successfully with the Gatists," Carne said, still not noticing me, "so I don't understand why you're disturbing me."

"I need information," I said, "and I believe you can help me."

Carne stopped, looked up, and straightened. He ceased playing with the toy, though he kept both hands on it, and it maintained its hold on his finger. About a third of a meter shorter than I, with a slight build and closely cropped blond hair, he was a small man who looked incapable of violence and yet appeared completely undisturbed by the sight of a nearly two-meter-tall, angry, completely red assailant pointing a gun at him. I had to give him credit for poise.

He blinked a few times, his expression unchanging, and spoke. "We maintain a variety of data kiosks for the very purpose of providing information to our visitors. Feel free to use them."

"I doubt those kiosks maintain jump records."

"Of course not," he said. "Those logs are confidential."

"Yes," I said, "but as the gate agent in charge you can access them." He nodded slightly in agreement but said nothing, so I continued. "In my experience, that access is sometimes available for the agent's close friends." I kept the gun trained on him with my right hand and showed him my wallet with my left. "I can be a good friend."

"I'm afraid I simply don't understand," he said, "so perhaps you should leave."

"You didn't accumulate all of these toys on your salary. I could help you add to the collection."

"You've assaulted my guard and violated my space. Now you're attempting to bribe me. I'd prefer to save myself the trouble of ordering your arrest, but if you persist I'll summon the security team."

I hate games. I'd tried to play nicely, because gate agents are rarely comfortable with a direct approach, but enough was enough. I stepped to my left, put my arm on a shelf of toys just below my shoulders, and swept all the toys I could reach into the air.

He gasped and dove for them as they fell. I almost shot him by reflex but stopped myself and shoved him backward. He sprawled onto the floor.

I pulled the other gun, a pulse weapon, from within my shirt. "Before help can arrive," I said, "I will either turn this room into rubble or pay you a fair rate for one piece of information." He stared at me as if trying to read my mind. Without looking away, I lifted my left leg and stomped the nearest toy, a small blond female figure with a body even more lush than Maggie's.

He held up his hands, the green figure dangling from his pinky, and shrieked, "Enough! Do you have any idea what that doll cost me? It was a museum-quality replica, the closest thing I've seen to an Earth original."

I raised my foot again and positioned it over another one, a male figure about the same size as the female but with far lower quality hair.

"Okay, okay," he said. "What do you need?"

I put away the pulse gun, opened my wallet, and thumbed up a picture of Jack.

"This man, Jack Gridiz: Did he jump here, and when did he jump away?"

Carne stood and went to a desk in the far right corner of the room. I followed him the whole way, through three twisting rows of game machines, and waited while he checked. The display shimmered above the work surface and murmured at him. "Gridiz did arrive here," he said, "but he never jumped away. He came on a commercial transport, a little gate-jumper from Mund, but he's not in the station, and that ship has come and gone several times since his arrival." He looked up at me. "Either he's still on Gash, or he arranged for someone to smuggle him off-planet and beat our scans. We have clean records of everything that's passed through here in the last few days, so I believe he's still on Gash."

I nodded, in part pleased, because I'd correctly guessed what Jack would do, but in part annoyed, because now I had to figure out how to shake not one but two tails.

"You mentioned payment," he said. "I would appreciate assistance with the repairs I'll have to commission."

I opened my wallet and thumbed up twenty percent more than the typical agent bribe. I showed him the display and said, "Provided, of course, that you delete that information and we agree there's no need to involve security."

He smiled, spoke briefly to the display, and the data disappeared. "What information?" he said. "As for security, why would I bother them just to report an accident that occurred while I was showing a friend my collection? Unless, of course," he pointed to the unconscious guard, "that man has suffered permanent damage; then we might have a problem."

"The guard will wake up sore but otherwise fine," I said.

"Then I'll get busy cleaning up," he said, "as soon as you're on your way." He motioned slightly toward my wallet with his hand, finally noticing the toy dangling from his finger and pulling the little green man closer to his body. I transmitted the money.

His display chirped.

He led me to the front of his office and was carefully replacing the toys on the shelf when I walked out the door.

The color wash was still in full swing, so I leaned for a moment against the wall and subvocalized to Lobo. "Did you get all that?"

"Of course," Lobo said. "You're transmitting continuously through multiple normal channels as well as in stored pulses at short, random intervals via the backup active fiber in your shirt."

"Just making sure everything is working," I said. "You're annoyed that I was right about where Jack went."

"That one illogical human can predict the poor choices of another is something that shouldn't surprise me," Lobo said. "ETA at the lock?"

I evaluated the thickness of the crowd milling in the aisle. "Give me ten minutes," I said. "I'm heading back as directly as I can under the circumstances."

"If I breathed, I'm sure I would hold it in anticipation of your return," he said.

Yeah, he was still mad at me for being right.

I stepped into the crowd and worked my way slowly toward the corner. I didn't want to hurt anyone, but the combination of the close quarters and the sheer number of people touching me made self-control difficult. I worked at breathing calmly and finally ducked behind two women sharing a kiss with a man and turned the corner. The crowd was no better here, but at least I was one corridor closer to my goal. I rested against the wall, enjoying the tiny bit of space that was for the moment mine alone, and then plunged back into the throng.

I managed three steps forward before a door whisked open on my left and two uniformed and unpainted guards stepped out, one in front of me and one in back. A third remained in the doorway.

The woman in front of me pointed a pulse gun at my stomach and stayed well out of reach. The crowd swirled on the other side of the guards, but we existed for a few seconds in our own oasis, beyond the reach of the red-painted partiers just when I would have welcomed the chance to lose myself among them. I saw no way out that didn't involve doing a lot of damage to my three captors and risking a lot of pain myself.

"Follow the man behind you," she said, "and go back the way you came.

"You have an appointment."

CHAPTER SIXTEEN

They led me back to Carne's office, one ahead of me, one behind, the woman with the gun to my left, cutting me off from the crowd, and the corridor wall to my right. As we walked, random Gatists painted her back and hair, but she ignored them and stayed focused on me. When we reached Carne's office, the man ahead of me triggered the door, and we moved in our formation inside.

Carne had apparently decided to take my money and betray me. I'd find a way to pay him back. I looked for him, but he was nowhere in sight.

"Where's Carne?" I said.

A small smile crossed the woman's face, but neither she nor the other guards replied. She simply motioned me forward and into the leftmost aisle of toys. The men stayed behind, one moving to the room's door and the other remaining at the end of our aisle; they were pros making sure they'd have multiple clean shots at me if I bolted.

The aisle meandered to the front wall and then left until it ended at a door that snicked open as I came within a meter of it.

The room on the other side was as much about business as Carne's was about obsession. A plain metal desk faced me. Displays flickered above it, so much data dancing on them that I couldn't see Carne's face through them. Two office chairs sat on my side of the desk. Guards in EC security uniforms stood at attention in three corners of the room; my escort stopped and snapped to attention in the corner nearest the door. The wall to my right was a huge window display facing the jump gate; in it I watched as a freighter emerged from an aperture into this system. A short but wide tree grew from a planter beneath the viewport and spread along the width of it. Purple blossoms with yellow and white central tendrils adorned the tips of most of the small tree's branches.

No one spoke.

I enjoyed the view. No good comes of offering information in situations like this one.

I rubbed my stomach as if hungry, triggering the emergency signal in the pulse transmission system in the fiber. Lobo would have heard the earlier conversation, but now he'd also know I considered myself to be in trouble. He'd stop using normal channels and alert Maggie, who should already have this information if she was doing her job. I hadn't spotted her, which was good if she was blending well but bad if she had lost me. Either way, with Lobo's help she'd now know exactly where I was. I was confident even the best EC systems would have no chance to break our encryption in the time I was here, but if they were scanning for signals, I wanted them to believe I was alone. People are often more talkative when they think you're helpless.

The desk displays flicked off, and a woman stood from behind the desk. She wore no uniform, only standard business elegant. She glowed with the unnatural beauty of executive style. Perfectly white hair beautifully contrasted with skin the color of rich, wet soil. Her mods hadn't extended to height, so I towered over her, but she clearly was used to that position and didn't care at all about it.

"Please sit, Mr. Moore," she said.

I did. So did she. I hated that she already knew my name, but that was also no surprise.

Her chair lifted slowly until we were eye-to-eye across the desk.

"From what I've gathered of your background," she said, "and that isn't as much as I'd like—" She paused, but when I didn't speak, she continued, "—you're likely to be more than a bit annoyed at Carne, and that annoyance could cause us trouble later. So, let me save you some time: He's not involved in this, and he doesn't know you're here."

"It's his station," I said.

She laughed, a rich, throaty laugh that was charming and sounded genuine. I let myself smile with her.

"Oh, no," she said. "It's *our* station. He simply works here. He wouldn't even be doing that, and we wouldn't have to put up with"—she waved her hand as if to take in the giant room of toys on the other side of the door—"all that, were it not for his father, a rather influential colleague of mine."

She pulled a glass from a shelf somewhere below the desk and took a sip. "Something to drink?"

I shook my head. If they were going to drug me, I'd at least make them work to do it.

"Then to business. I'm Alexandra Midon, but you can call me Sasha; I trust we're going to be friends. Do you mind if I call you Jon?"

I shrugged.

She continued, unfazed by my rudeness. "I'm the Expansion Coalition's councillor in charge of planetary government relationships for this sector. All the worlds you've been visiting on your frequent jumps are part of my territory."

She smiled again, enjoying hinting at the depth of their knowledge about me. I tried to show nothing, but some of my growing impatience and annoyance must have been obvious.

"Disengaging from dock," Lobo said via a burst that the shirt's comm unit relayed to me over the machine frequency. Her sensors might be able to decrypt the short data spike, but doing so would take time.

"Of course we've been tracking you, Jon," Midon said. "You've been spending way too much time with groups on our watch list for us not to notice you. We particularly enjoyed the way you escaped from the Followers on Mund."

I questioned again the wisdom of not having immediately jumped away from this entire sector, but then I reminded myself of Manu.

"In fact, Jon, the Followers are what bring us together today. I'd like to understand what you were doing with them."

"Nothing at all," I said. "I was providing transportation for a friend. If you've checked my background, you know I'm a courier."

"Moving into first position," Lobo said.

"And quite a full-service one indeed," Midon said, laughing again. "Few couriers are so heavily armed." She sipped once more from her glass. "And speaking of arms, though we know you have clean title to that PCAV, I have to wonder if you've been doing any trading with the Followers. Some data we bought from the Frontier Coalition suggests you had some past unpleasant interactions with an arms dealer there."

She paused, again giving me a chance to speak.

I thought of Osterlad, the man who'd said he'd sell me Lobo's central weapons complex and who instead ambushed me. I'd ended up killing both him and one of his lieutenants, the lieutenant directly and him indirectly. I regretted the acts, but they'd each given me no option other than dying myself, and I won't do that without a fight.

When I didn't speak, she went on. "The FC execs were happy enough with you—apparently you helped them with a corporate relationship problem—that they didn't bother to look further into the matter. Now, though, your actions suggest you might be entering that business again, this time with Dougat and the Followers."

"I've never traded in weapons," I said, and that was technically true, though I'd worked cons that involved such trades and at times belonged to groups that trafficked in certain classes of arms, though always for specific, good causes. "I'm certainly not doing that—or anything else—with the Followers."

She studied me for a few quiet seconds. "I of course can't tell if you're being truthful, not here anyway. We could go that route—we have people who could tell, who could defeat any type of resistance training you might have taken, though the process would be very unpleasant and time-consuming—but I'd rather not. So, please be honest, and this can end well for us all."

"First contact complete," Lobo said.

Midon came around the desk, stood in front of me, and leaned back against it.

The woman guard stayed at the door, but the others all moved closer. Midon might like pretending to be intimate, but they knew the risk of her being too close to me and were doing all they could to minimize it.

"Why did your friend need help?"

I saw no reason in not giving her most of the truth, certainly the parts she could find on her own.

"He was taking care of a boy, a boy Dougat wanted to interview. I was there to protect both the child and my friend, in case something went wrong. Something did, so I helped them escape."

Her eyes widened, and for the first time she appeared to be surprised. She leaned forward with excitement. "So the stories of the boy psychic are true?" she said.

I forced a laugh as I struggled to come up with an angle that would fit the facts but not expose Manu. "Hardly," I said, trying to think as Jack would as I shaped the story I was creating, "though I'm sure Dougat believed that he was. My friend was in money trouble and was working a con. I was just hired muscle."

"If your friend needed money, how could he afford to pay you?"

Where are the stupid bureaucrats when you need one? Not at the top of an entire sector of a major coalition, I reminded myself. "He couldn't. I wasn't doing anything special, so I went in for a piece of the action."

"Our surveillance shows your PCAV escaping the Institute, so you upheld your end of the bargain," she said. "We lost your ship for a time; nice work."

I nodded at the compliment. "Of course I got them out," I said. "I told them I would." Finally, a chance to say something completely truthful.

"I take it your friend didn't pay you, however," she said, "or you wouldn't still be chasing him."

"I'm not chasing anyone," I said.

She laughed, but this time she was faking the humor, and nothing in her tone was pleasant. "I'm being polite," she said, "and I'm interrogating you gently—as I'm sure you'll agree. I'm also not insulting you. I'd appreciate the same behavior from you. Do I have to remind you again that there are other ways we could do this?"

"What do you want from me?" I said, ignoring the threat. "Yes, you're being polite, but you're also hiding your motivation. *That* behavior doesn't exactly encourage open discussion."

"Moving to second position," Lobo said.

Midon chuckled once more, but now with genuine humor. "Fair point, Jon, fair point. Still, given the circumstances"—she waved her arm slowly to take in all the guards—"I think it's only reasonable that you give before you get. So, let's return to the question of why you're chasing your friend. I'll even provide you with some context to help you understand the situation. I wanted this conversation enough that I stationed ships at every jump destination in this sector. From the data many of them relayed, you were trying out multiple planets, so you were looking for something or someone. You noticed our surveillance, but you didn't keep on jumping until you were far away. To stay in this sector in the face of forces that large, you needed a very strong motivation. In my experience, only money and power push a person to take that level of risk."

And sex and friendship and anger and above all else, love and honor and loyalty, but she seemed oblivious of all of those. Not a surprise from a career EC exec.

"So," she said, "I repeat: Your friend didn't pay you?"

I let out a long, slow breath and nodded again, as if reluctantly giving in. "No, he didn't. He owes me a lot, and I'd like the money."

She smiled. "Now we're talking openly; excellent. Because we are, let me repeat my earlier question, in case you might have forgotten something before: Are you involved in any way in arms trading with the Followers?"

"Second contact complete," Lobo said.

I stared at her in frustration. "I've explained why I was at the Followers' institute. You saw my ship escape from it. It should be obvious that I'm not working with them; if I were, I would have left my friend and the boy with them. What are you really after?"

"At the same time you began gassing the Institute grounds, a mysterious explosion occurred in Dougat's warehouse, a place we've been wondering about but have been unable to legally enter. That blast distracted the local police, who were then late to the Institute. The coincidence is hard to believe."

This might not work out badly after all. Midon and the EC were worried about the Followers. The Followers were after Manu and so were still my problem. Chaplat was also chasing me. Either his crew or some of the Followers had to be in the second ship that had tailed the EC craft that followed us away from the gate. If I could get the EC to take down either or both of those groups, my life would improve.

"Jon?" she said. "Care to comment?"

"Causing an explosion on someone else's private property would be a crime," I said, "and the EC prosecutes crimes."

"Your wallet."

I took it from my pocket—carefully and slowly—and thumbed it open. I set it to receive and quarantine.

She tapped on the desk, and a contract appeared on it.

The wallet's legal software studied and summarized the text she'd sent. In every way my software could tell—and my wallet's software wasn't any off-the-shelf stuff; it had every tweak and customization Lobo could squeeze into it—the EC had given me immunity for everything I said in this room. Perfect.

I put away my wallet and looked directly at her.

"I entered the warehouse and set the charges in case I needed a distraction. What should matter to you are the weapons in the hidden basement area." I ran down for her everything I'd seen. I also reviewed my encounter with Chaplat, but I added a few important details that would, I hoped, get the EC to help me without meaning to do so. "Chaplat snagged me because he was watching the ware-house for the Followers. He let me go only because I came out empty-handed. Fortunately for me, when Dougat's team searched the building after Chaplat told them I'd been inside it, they looked everywhere but up, so they missed the charges I stuck in the ceiling." I leaned back and shrugged. "That's all of it."

"Moving to third position and maintaining contacts," Lobo said.

Midon stayed quiet for a few moments. I waited in silence with her.

Finally, she said, "Which of those groups was following the ship we had watching you here? One of them is unhappy with you."

I chuckled. "Both of them, probably. I don't, though, know whose vessel it was. Why don't you detain it and find out?"

"You cannot possibly be as stupid as that question suggests," she said. "Certainly, if you are, I have no use for you."

"You can't risk arresting any of the Followers until you can catch them in something serious, say trading arms."

"Better," she said.

"Because of the bad publicity from attacking a fast-growing cult?"

"A little, but only a little."

I leaned back and considered the situation again. "You're worried that if you move at the wrong time, they'll go to ground and you won't get their weapons."

She nodded.

"Maggie in position," Lobo said.

Damn. I didn't want Maggie to come in now; this was working out well. I coughed and rubbed my hand across my stomach as I put it back in my lap. I hoped Maggie wasn't already committed.

"What I don't understand," I said, "is why you care so much about the stash I saw. Sure, it was a pretty good assortment, but nothing your troops couldn't handle."

She frowned and shook her head. "We used your little explosion as an excuse to send the police into the warehouse to find out what was there. The basement room was open, but it was empty. No weapons." She stared intently at me.

It took me a few seconds, but then I saw her reasoning. "You think I warned them to move the stock?"

"Perhaps."

"Why would I? I told you: I went there only to set up a diversion."

"Maggie approaching," Lobo said.

I needed her to stay away, but I couldn't risk repeating the stomach rubbing. I had to concentrate on Midon. "Besides, as I told you, though they had a lot of weapons, the stockpile wasn't enough to cause you serious problems."

"Maybe the ones you saw weren't."

I finally understood. "You think they have more weapons, a lot more, enough to stage some major action."

"We're fairly certain of that," she said. "What intelligence we can gather suggests they're planning something big, maybe an attack to hijack some commercial-grade ships, maybe a coup on one of the newer planets—maybe even here on Gash—to give them an operating base they control. Whatever they're planning, we don't want it."

I could have countered my earlier story and told her the truth, that Chaplat had no real relationship with the Followers, but I couldn't go back now. "So you want me to help you find the weapons."

"Incoming," Lobo said.

Midon nodded and opened her mouth to speak as a section of the door toppled inward.

Maggie, pulse rifle drawn, burst into the room. The falling metal knocked the female guard against the window; Maggie finished the job by kicking her in the head. Painted red, her hair in pigtails now the color of the Gash's gate, even her rifle crimson, Maggie resembled an attacking demon. She turned the weapon on Midon, but then she noticed that the other three guards had all targeted her.

I slowly raised my hands, palms facing Midon. "Let's all stay calm," I said. "My friend thought I was in trouble."

"You *are* in trouble," Midon said, "and now, so is she." She looked at Maggie. "Put down the weapon."

"Jon?" Maggie said.

"Sasha," I said, "we can finish our business without anyone getting hurt. You want me to help you catch the Followers and seize their weapons; let's talk about the best way to do that."

"And we want the boy psychic," she said, her eyes not straying from Maggie.

I couldn't allow that, but I also couldn't let her know how I felt. "What are you willing to pay me for all this work?"

"Jon, you said—" Maggie began.

I cut her off with a glance and the words "Shut up!"

Midon finally looked back at me. "Is your inept associate upset at the thought of you working for us?" she said. "I'm sorry to hear that. I was going to offer you a little money and a chance to walk away free. Now you get nothing except your life and hers, assuming you succeed. She'll remain as our guest, of course, until you do."

I'd stayed reasonably calm so far, which was hard enough when I was the only one under attack. Now Midon was threatening Maggie, and I could not allow that. I could try to distract them long enough to create nanoclouds that would break down their weapons, but I didn't have that much time. Doing that would also let everyone in this room learn way too much about me. I could hope for the time to have the nanoclouds kill all of them except Maggie, but then she'd know the truth about me. I won't let anyone know what happened to me on Aggro. I won't end up in a test lab again.

"I'm willing to talk business," I said, the anger growing in me, "but making threats is not a wise choice."

"We're done," Midon said. "You know what I want. Go get it." She turned away from me and flicked her wrist in Maggie's direction. "Guards."

Lobo had been right that he might prove to be my best option. I rubbed my stomach again as I was standing and, just to be safe, subvocalized, "Lobo, you're on."

"Moving," Lobo said.

I looked at the two guards who were converging on Maggie. "You two will stop, or you won't live to regret the mistake."

Midon turned back to me. "What in the—"

I interrupted her. "You kidnapped me. I did nothing. You threatened me. I tolerated it. Now, though, you've gone too far." The more I let out the anger, the more it took over. It lanced through my head and my body. An acid taste burned in my mouth. A buzzing grew in my head. "Look out the port."

On cue, Lobo settled from above the station into view, filling the entire display, becoming all that we could see. Staring at us was a freshly red-painted PCAV bristling with visible weapons: three sets of missiles, pulse cannons, mine launchers, and much, much more. Metal arms extending from his sides connected him to the station.

The cloth over my shoulders warmed as Lobo activated the speakers there. The vibrations when he spoke might have tickled had I not been so focused and so furious.

"These people are with me," he said. "You are not. I suggest you let them go."

Always the ham, though I agreed with his choice that hearing his voice might make clear to them that he was an independent agent capable of action even if I was dead. His flair for drama cut through my fury and calmed me a little—but only a little.

"Idle threats," Midon said. "You know as well as I do that if your ship fires even a single weapon the gate will destroy it."

"True," I said, "but when two things are connected, as your station and my ship now are, will the gate see them as separate? Will the gate stop my ship from detonating the mines it's attached to the station's hull? Are you willing to bet your life that when my ship detonates those mines and fires all of its weapons the gate will save you? I don't think anyone's ever tested a gate's ability to deal with two ships that are connected to each other and this close to it. My guess is that we'll all die."

"You would kill everyone on this station, all those innocent people, just to save the two of you?"

"Jon," Maggie said, "no, it's not worth it."

I wanted to tell her to be quiet, to control herself, but I ignored her and focused entirely on Midon. I think the real answer to her question was no. I hope it was. I like to believe my anger doesn't rule me so thoroughly. I really do.

What I answered, though, was what I needed Midon to believe, and in that moment I did everything I could to make it the truth inside me so she could not ignore it. I stared at her and said, "Yes. *You* would be choosing it, not me. If you've checked out my background, if you know even a fraction of what I've seen and done, then you shouldn't have needed to ask."

I leaned toward her until my face was within ten centimeters of hers and said again, "Yes."

I sat back in the chair and crossed my legs.

"You decide," I said. "Do my associate and I walk out of here without any further trouble?"

I paused and stared for a few seconds directly into her eyes.

"Or do we all die?"

CHAPTER SEVENTEEN

Midon stared at me as if trying to read my mind.

No one moved.

I waited, looking at her but not seeing her, concentrating instead on remaining still, unchanging, unwavering. The more I focused on the notion of ordering Lobo to fire and to detonate the mines, the more reasonable the idea became. Midon wasn't going to let me go even after I completed her mission, and there was no way I was ever going to deliver Manu to her. Maggie and Lobo would die, but I'd warned Maggie, and Lobo knew, as all warriors do, that your time is bound to come eventually. All the other people on board were innocent, and I'd worked much of my life to avoid collateral damage, but it had happened before and would happen again.

Besides, the anger told me, Midon deserved it. She'd used one person too many; I would *not* be another pawn for her.

Nor would I let my fury rule me, the rational part of me declared. The civilians on board this station were not collateral damage; they were real people, people with families and lovers and friends and sorrows and joys and places they needed to go and plans and futures and all the other entanglements of even a life as lonely as my own. I never wanted to be one of those soulless husks who can look upon a map or a cityscape or even an entire planet and see only numbers, not people.

No, I knew in my heart that I wouldn't do it. I shouldn't do it, and I wouldn't.

Fortunately, Midon must not have been able to read on my face any expression of this internal discussion, because she eventually said, "Okay, Jon, you and your friend are free to go."

I stood. Part of me wanted to smile and say something clever in victory, but I was afraid I'd destroy this momentary, fragile peace, so I remained silent.

"Before you leave," she said, "could I interest you in the same task as a business deal, as you'd previously suggested? You help us bust the Followers, you bring us the boy, and we all profit."

We were returning to comfortable ground. Such an arrangement would certainly complicate matters and put me in the risky position of owing something to a major government, but it also might give me a way to distract the Followers and Chaplat.

"You mentioned 'a little money' earlier," I said. "I'm certainly not interested in a little money."

"Perhaps a finder's fee," she said, "say five percent of the retail value of all the weapons you lead us to."

"Jon," Maggie said.

I glanced at her again, shook my head slightly, and looked back at Midon. Even if I wanted to do this deal—and I was by no means sure I did—I could never negotiate it with Maggie in the room. She was too scared and too involved to stay quiet.

"I don't make significant commitments with weapons pointed at me," I said. "I'll consider your offer back in my ship. I won't leave this system without letting you know my decision."

I turned and walked toward Maggie.

I heard Midon stand and knew without looking that she was furious. I had to hope the threat from Lobo would continue to keep her under control.

I knew how it would go if she let her anger rule her. The guards would aim their weapons at my back. Lobo would alert me. I'd dive for Maggie, turn, and fight them. Maybe I'd live, maybe I wouldn't, but I'd struggle for all I was worth. If I lost, Lobo would kill every last one of us.

My spine tingled with the sensation of being a target, and adrenaline coursed through me again, but I made it to the door without incident, took Maggie in tow, and left.

"First, you nearly blow up the entire station and everyone on it! And now you're going to help those people! What are you thinking?" Maggie had managed to stay quiet until we were safely inside Lobo and floating in space a few thousand kilometers from the station, but since I'd declared us safe she hadn't stopped yelling. "You said you wanted to help Manu, and now you're willing to hand him over to the EC! As if they would treat him with any more care than the Followers! You're acting no better than any of them!"

I sat in silence in the pilot's couch and waited for her to run down. Her inability to follow my instructions had put us at risk on the station. Now both her level of emotion and her lack of trust annoyed me further, but I knew if I said anything I'd end up letting my anger show, and that wouldn't do either of us any good. I needed time to think, but I also needed either to drop off Maggie or to win her support for whatever path I chose.

So I listened and sat and waited.

"I could sedate her," Lobo said in my head on our usual internal frequency. "It might be good for her health, and it would certainly result in a more pleasant environment."

I shook my head slightly.

Unfortunately, Maggie spotted the motion. "So you think the EC would be better," she said. "Well, let me tell you about the EC—"

I was wrong to believe she'd stop ranting anytime soon. "No, I don't," I said, cutting her off, "and if you would please be quiet for a few minutes I could explain what's going on."

"I know what's going on."

"No, you don't, not all of it anyway."

"Then enlighten me."

"I will, but only if you'll listen."

"I'll listen, but—"

I cut her off again. "No, you won't, not right now. Sit without speaking for two minutes, just two minutes, and then I'll go over it. You use the time to calm down; I'll use it to organize my thoughts. Deal?"

The look she gave me was enough to make me want to leave the room, but after a short pause she said, "Deal."

"Thank you," Lobo said in my ear. "I shall enjoy this interlude."

I ignored him, closed my eyes, swiveled away from her, and let the stillness embrace me. The inside of Lobo smelled of nothing at all, a welcome change from the sweat- and paint-soaked atmosphere of the station. The temperature relaxed me, comfortably neither warm nor cool, and the air barely moved, Lobo managing its flow perfectly. I considered the situation.

Chaplat was after Jack and the money Jack owed him. Chaplat was using me and wouldn't stop pushing me until he got what he wanted.

Midon and the EC had the power to make my life difficult, maybe even imprison me, and no matter what she said now, she'd keep coming after me until she got what she wanted. Once the guards leaked what happened on the station, she'd lose so much face that she'd have to force me to help just to avoid being embarrassed in front of her staff.

Dougat and the Followers were the scariest of the bunch, true believers all, with greater resources than I'd imagined and, if Midon was right, more weapons than the warehouse stash suggested. I'd seen firsthand on Nana's Curse the kind of damage that heavily armed religious fanatics were capable of inflicting, and I didn't want to be responsible, even indirectly, for letting the Followers do that to the people of any other world.

I could try running, of course, but Midon and the EC would almost certainly find me, and when they did, I wouldn't enjoy the experience. The other two groups might also catch me.

Worst, if I ran I would be abandoning Jack and, more importantly, Manu. Chaplat didn't have any interest in Manu, but he'd be willing to hurt the boy if he thought it would help his cause. Both the EC and the Followers wanted very much to control Manu, and if either group caught him, he'd never be free again.

Jack might deserve whatever happened to him, but I couldn't abandon Manu to that fate. When I was sixteen, a government had dropped me on an island of discards, freaks they no longer wanted but didn't kill on the off chance something useful might emerge from the colony they'd created. Without Benny, one of those freaks and my first friend other than Jennie, I have no idea how I would have survived there. Less than two years later, when I was not yet eighteen, older than Manu but still within sight of his age, I landed in prison on Aggro.

No, I wasn't going to let that happen to Manu.

The whole mess also created an opportunity, because no one sells this many weapons, even if only from a dealer into government hands, without a great deal of money moving in the air. Midon had offered a little, but I knew she could do better.

Three organizations—one vicious, one fanatic, and one bureaucratic—held Jack, Manu, and me in their sights.

A furious redhead almost my size was attracting me one minute and hating me the next.

Money dangled in sight but out of my reach.

Lovely.

But not impossible, I realized, as the vague outline of a plan emerged. It wasn't a great plan. It certainly wasn't a straight plan; as I'd feared, Jack had managed to suck me back into running the con again. But, it was a plan. More or less.

"Ten seconds to two minutes," Lobo said. "I look forward to your performance."

"Thanks for the support," I subvocalized.

I opened my eyes and spun the chair so I was facing Maggie.

"Thanks for indulging me," I said. I didn't feel grateful, but I might need her for what was to come, and, to be fair, from her perspective I had to appear to be a jerk. I clearly couldn't trust her self-control, but I did feel her intentions were good; in fact, the degree to which I believed in her disturbed me. Most importantly, regardless of my feelings or hers, she could be an asset in working my way out of this situation; I'd just have to manage her carefully. "I know you care about Manu," I continued, "and I hope you'll believe that I do, too. The situation is extremely complicated, but I believe I now understand the forces we have to balance to succeed." I paused, but she didn't speak, which I took as proof of her continued willingness to listen. "I haven't figured out everything, nor will I probably ever do so, because in this kind of mess improvisation is usually the name of the game. I believe, though, that I can plot a safe passage out of it for all of us."

"That's the first decent thing I've heard from you in a while," she said. "What's your idea?"

"Let me walk you through where we stand, and then I think you'll understand how difficult it is for me to do what I have to do next."

She nodded agreement. "And then?"

"And then I go back to the station."

Midon greeted me without guards this time. Carne's inner office felt bigger without them in it. She sat again behind the desk, but now she seemed farther away.

Lobo hovered just above its window display, as I'm sure she now knew. No point in not being prepared.

She wasted no time on pleasantries and started as soon as the room's door had closed behind me. "You've decided to take my offer."

"No," I said, "but I think we can reach an accord."

"We weren't negotiating," she said. "I made an offer. Take it or leave it."

"Then I misunderstood." I turned around and stepped toward the door. "Tell your colleagues I refused your ultimatum."

The door had opened before she spoke again. "I meant only that previously we weren't negotiating," she said. "I'm certainly willing to listen to alternatives if you'd like to propose some now."

Bureaucrats: Rather than risk honesty, they'll fall back on wordplay and rewritten history. I had to ignore the games, however, and focus on my goals.

I faced her. "I'll do my best find a way to," I paused, realizing her previous immunity offer did not apply now, "help you catch the Followers in an arms deal. You mentioned a little money in return; I suggest a third of the value of the weapons, with a quarter million up front for expenses and your guarantee not to interfere with my actions in any way or even be visible until I call you."

She laughed. "You may be young, but you're not that young. You have to know I could never even remotely sell that percentage to my colleagues. Seven percent, with a hundred thousand up front."

I'd done enough work for other governments and corporations to have a sense of where this would end up, and I wanted to get out of there, so I jumped ahead a few steps.

"I hate this game," I said, "and this isn't the first time I've played it. Let's save some time: The quarter-million advance is nonnegotiable, as is the requirement that the EC stay back. I'll do the rest for ten percent of the weapons' retail value." She started to speak, and I held up my hand. "Yes or no?"

She smiled. "Yes. That's acceptable, as far as it goes."

For a second I chided myself for not pushing for twelve and a half percent, because some governments will go for that, but I shook off the impulse. I needed to find Jack before he skipped the system or went deeply underground, so time was not my friend. "As far as it goes?" I said.

"What about the boy?"

I'd prepared myself for this question so I wouldn't hesitate despite my distaste for the topic, and I didn't. I answered immediately and smoothly. "Another quarter million when I point him out to you or one of your agents. You have to retrieve him; I don't kidnap." Nor, I thought but did not say, would I give her the chance to set me up for kidnapping and still end up with the boy.

"Simply to point him out? Please, Jon, don't be greedy."

"To point him out, I have to find him. If you could do it, you wouldn't need me. And, you did say he was psychic." I opened my wallet and thumbed active a quarantined reception area. "I'm ready to receive the deposit as well as contact information for people who can reach you on all the planets in this sector. Do we have a deal?"

She sat in silence for almost a minute, maybe trying to decide, maybe receiving data from her desk or advisors; I couldn't tell. Finally, she said, "We do."

A display flickered to life above the desk, she mumbled briefly, and a few seconds later my wallet glowed its receipt of the advance. I glanced at it; the software declared the contacts to be clean and sent the money on its way to a series of banks in three different cities on Gash. While on Lobo, I'd taken the time to set up a small string of accounts in EC-insured financial institutions across the planet. My wallet was bouncing the money through a few of them. When it declared the transfers complete, I closed it.

"One more thing," she said.

I waited.

"The other ship that's chasing you is your problem. If it's a Followers vessel and it attacks you, we may be able to bring them down without your help. If we do, the advance is all you get."

I wasn't happy being bait, but it didn't change anything. "Fine," I said. "I'll be in touch."

I walked out before she could say anything. I hated the thought of trafficking in children, and now I'd convinced the EC I would do just that. Even though I knew I wouldn't, I was still disgusted at myself.

I shook off the feeling and forced myself to do the necessary, not the desirable. Focus on the end. Find Jack, find Manu and save him, and figure out the rest of this mess. I had a lot to do, and much of it was still unclear.

I did, though, know one thing for certain.

It was time to go to Gash.

CHAPTER
EIGHTEEN

We hung in space five thousand kilometers above the center of the great desert of Gash as darkness slowly crawled across the planet. The gigantic expanse of red sand that filled most of this world's only large continent sparkled in the last bright light of the day. To our right, the six cities that dotted the southeastern coast glowed softly as residential and business lights turned on in preparation for the coming evening. The snowcapped mountains that stood as guards between the sprawling desert and the urban areas blazed with the perfect white light of unspoiled peaks. Way off to our left, barely visible on the southwestern coast, was the single small settlement there, Bonland, a haven for those unwilling to coexist with the bulk of the inhabitants of a planet founded and settled largely by outcasts no other place wanted.

No government cared to try to tame these people. The EC and what passed for a planetary council on Gash operated on an uneasy truce. The council paid a minimal yearly fee to the EC for gate services and the promise of military aid should some outside force be both suicidal enough and lucky enough to attack Gash and get past its disorganized but formidable defenses. The EC operated the gate station and made sure it maintained a sizable defensive force only a couple of jumps away—but never in this system unless the Gash council called for it.

Aside from those points of contact, the EC and Gash stayed away from each other. The EC had once operated a huge military base and munitions depot on the southern edge of Malzton, the planet's most dangerous city and consequently the location where the EC most wanted a show of power. As the world's population grew and the EC realized the residents were going to ignore it in the face of anything less than a full-fledged war, the EC found it cheaper to pull out and create the truce with the local council than to continue to try to police the planet. No one on Gash had been willing to tackle the huge job of maintaining the base after the EC had withdrawn everything right down to the service bots, and the EC wasn't willing to sell the facility at a low enough price to entice someone to accept the challenge of remaking it, so nature was slowly crawling over the vast expanse of permacrete tarmac and buildings.

The six cities on Gash also boasted several of the largest open-air markets I'd ever seen, with one, the sprawling commercial zone on the southeastern corner of Nickres, actually visible from even our altitude. Nickres, the southernmost settlement, had fostered a political climate favorable to trade, and now its vast market was the place to go for the strangest merchandise the planet had to offer, from racing vessels to extreme sports gear, and from tools to self-assembling housing units.

Its large percentage of political and religious fanatics, outcasts, and fringe dwellers gave Gash the dubious honor of being the best place within half a dozen jumps to hold a serious argument on any aspect of political theory, provided, of course, that you came to the discussion well armed. Gash juries had acquitted more than one defendant of murder charges on the basis of excessively stupid political provocation.

"It's a lovely place," Lobo said as he was concluding my briefing, "that features so many aspects of humankind at its finest."

"Jack is there," I said, "so we have to assume Manu is, too, which means we're going as well. It's not my idea of a vacation, but we have work to do."

"Where to first?" Lobo said.

"What's happening with our friends?"

We'd stayed within the gate's sphere of influence so we could check on our pursuers while the gate would still protect us from any attack. The EC ship that had followed us previously had started after us and then quickly returned to the gate; Midon must have been a bit slow in relaying her orders.

The second ship, the mystery follower, had unfortunately remained on our tail. It was sticking close to the gate right now, but it adjusted its position as necessary to keep us in the center of its scanning range.

"No change," Lobo said. "It moves as we do."

"Milspec?"

"To the best of my ability to tell from the data available," Lobo said, "no. It appears to be a reasonably conventional commercial craft with some external weapon augmentations."

"Can you outrun it?"

"Unless its drive mechanisms contain surprises, yes."

"Take us down at normal speed," I said, "and fly along the coast slowly from south to north."

"In progress," Lobo said. We accelerated gently toward the southeastern tip of the continent. "Why did you ask if I could outrun the other craft if you were going to tell me to go slowly?"

"Do you two always talk this way?" Maggie said.

I'd kept Lobo's briefing and the rest of conversation in normal audio so she could follow it, but now I was regretting that choice. Though I had to admit it was a fair question, I didn't need another person picking at me.

"Basically, yes," I said, "except when we're in the middle of an engagement. You'll see an immediate change if we need to get serious." I considered the question further. "I blame it all on Lobo's emotive logic programmers. They combined great skill with a really bad attitude."

"May I point out—" Lobo said.

I cut him off. "Enough from both of us. We're going slowly so we can disguise our search for Jack's transmitter. I want the people in that other ship to think we're trying to make them show themselves. It's even acceptable if they figure out that we're searching. We just have to find Jack but not let our pursuers know we did. So, we'll fly low enough that Lobo can scan the cities for a signal from Jack as we pass over them. I asked about speed in case the pursuers try something odd and we end up needing to run."

"In scanning range of Nickres," Lobo said, apparently satisfied.

"Take us along the coast," I said. "Move as slowly as necessary to allow the transmitter two iterations of its max delay; I don't want to repeat this maneuver. Weave as if you're trying to see whether anyone is following us."

"How stupid would we have to be to check for them that way?" Lobo said. "All we need to do to spot them is maintain a three-sixty surveillance zone and correlate the movements of all nearby vessels with our flight path, as I did."

"Not all ships possess control systems of your intelligence," I said.

"None do," Lobo said, pride evident in his voice.

His comment surprised me, because though I knew Lobo was arrogant, he was also not given to errors of fact. I'd assumed all PCAV AIs of a given generation were roughly the same, and Lobo was a couple of generations behind the state of the art. Newer ships should certainly be more capable. I wondered if something was wrong, either with his logic or his emotional systems, or if Lobo really did possess secrets I should know. I didn't want to pursue any of these issues in front of Maggie, however, so I pushed past his comment to distract her.

Facing her, I said, "And more importantly, it's often helpful if opponents underestimate us."

"How do we know the ship following us isn't a friend, or maybe an EC escort? You said Midon thinks you're working for her."

"I *am* working for her," I said, "just not the way she thinks. It's unlikely the EC would put one ship on every other world we entered and two here, and I believed her when she said she didn't know who was following us. If it contained a friend, even Jack, it would have announced itself by now, because we're far enough away from the

EC that it could shoot a pinpoint encrypted burst to us without attracting much attention."

I stared at the display in which Lobo showed the ship tracking us from farther out in space, not quite following our path but always staying within the same narrow distance band from us. "No," I said, "it's definitely keeping an eye on us, and we have to assume it's not friendly."

We crawled for almost ten minutes on a zigzag path that took us from south of the massive market on the southeastern edge of the city to beyond its jagged northern boundary. Nickres, like the other cities on Gash, sat like a ragged drop of mixed paint in the middle of broad strokes of strong, pure colors: white mountaintops to the west, rich green forest north and south, and a thin strip of light gray sand giving way to deep blue ocean on the east.

We intercepted nothing from Jack's transmitter. Jack might have removed it, of course, and it's always possible the device was malfunctioning or not strong enough to reach us, but until we'd exhausted the possibility that it could lead us to him we had to keep trying.

We headed at the same leisurely pace and on a similarly convoluted path up the coast.

Our shadow stayed with us, no longer trying to match our course but instead moving slowly along the straight line that ran through the center of our meandering route. It didn't close the gap between us, so at least at this point it was more interested in monitoring us than catching or attacking us.

After the first five minutes, I sat in the pilot's couch, closed my eyes, and went inside myself, partly because it's always a good idea to rest when you can and partly to avoid Maggie's questions. If I gave her the chance, she'd quite reasonably ask what we'd do if we found Jack via the transmitter, what we'd do if we didn't, how we'd handle each and every contingency. She wanted to help, so she wanted to understand, but I had no answers for her. I didn't even believe it was smart to try to formulate answers yet, because at this stage, when we knew nothing for certain about Jack's location, any answers I reached would be preconceptions that could limit our thinking and lower our probability of success. We had to find him, then react to his location. When you're on the sharp end of any action, even a seemingly simple search, you have to improvise and respond to local data more than the mission planners ever anticipated.

The only people who believe in perfect plans in complex situations are those who've never had to execute those plans.

On a pass above the heart of Malzton, Lobo announced, "Signal received. Jack's transmitter is here."

I stared at the image of the city in the display. A sprawling, low-slung place, it and the empty ex-EC military base on its southern border squatted like scar tissue on the face of the land between the mountains that ringed it on three sides and the ocean to the east. Semi-urban growth sprawled across what had once been a beautiful valley, with the snow from the mountains on its western and northern borders stretching almost to the city's edge and the ocean full of ships both commercial and pleasure. Jack had chosen the most obvious place to hide if you knew him, because he'd be most comfortable among others who cared little about conventional rules, but it was also the most dangerous location for anyone tracking him.

"Now if we could only be sure the thing was still in Jack," I said, "we'd be able to move to the next step."

"It is definitely in someone," Lobo said, "or, to be more precise, something with a human temperature."

"Explain," I said.

"I added a sensor to the transmitter," he said. "If its ambient temperature is within a few degrees of human normal, it emits a signal of a different shape than if it is not."

"Even if Jack found the transmitter," I said, "he'd be highly unlikely to know he needed to put it in another person. He'd destroy it or leave it somewhere else as a decoy."

"That was my opinion as well," Lobo said.

"Great work," I said. "Now, we have to keep convincing our pursuers we haven't found Jack. Maintain this pattern until we're north of the last human settlement, then head west to Bonland. Run fast enough to make them have to chase us directly, but not fast enough to lose them. Repeat the pattern over Bonland."

"Executing," Lobo said. "What happens next?"

"Could you drop me in Malzton without the pursuers knowing it?"

"Unless you literally mean 'drop' or the other ship is extremely incompetent, no. To let you out, we'd have to land, at which point they would at a minimum assume Malzton was of interest. We could, of course, employ our current tactic and leave you in every city, Malzton last, but that process would consume a great deal of time."

I didn't want to burn that many days, at least not while I could think of any other, faster options. With both Dougat's and Chaplat's groups after me and with an uneasy partnership with the EC, each day that passed increased the probability of somebody nabbing me.

Better to start facing some of these problems directly, while I still maintained some semblance of control over the situation.

"We're not going to land in Malzton or any other city," I said, "at least not yet. We need to know what group is tracking us."

"Your talent for stating the obvious is indisputable," Lobo said, "but of dubious value."

"So let's do something not quite so obvious," I said. "After we finish in Bonland, let's go deal with our pursuers."

CHAPTER NINETEEN

"What exactly do you mean by 'deal with' them?" Lobo said. "Do you want me to kill them? Based on the data I can glean about the ship that's following us, that shouldn't be difficult. Finding Jack would also certainly be simpler if we first eliminated Dougat and Chaplat, and the pursuing vessel is probably from one of them. You've already portrayed both men as dangerous leaders of violent groups, so striking first should nicely pave our way forward."

"Is it serious?" Maggie said. "You'd just kill whatever people are in that ship?"

As anger surged in me, what I thought was: You never *just* kill anyone. You do it because it was the best option available to you at that time, and then it stays with you forever, a darkness that infects you and fuses with your core. Even with that cost, however, sometimes it is what you have to do—or, at least, at times it has been what *I* have had to do. Over the last almost fourteen decades since Jennie fixed my brain and I left Pinkelponker, I've participated in terrible acts of violence that the mentally challenged boy I once was could never have conceived were possible. I couldn't forget any of them. I wish I could convince myself otherwise, but the scariest truth is that given the same circumstances and the same timing, I'd make the same decisions. I'd do it all again, even knowing what it would cost me, because sometimes killing is the best of the small, bad set of available options.

What I said to her was "No, I'm not planning to kill or even fight anyone. I don't anticipate a conflict with this ship. If it intended to attack us, it would have done so when we were flying along the coastline, probably on the ends of the flight arcs that left us over uninhabited territories. Whoever is in that ship wants us to know we're being followed but doesn't intend to confront us. I need to know who's doing this, and why."

She considered my answer for almost a minute before she spoke. "I'm sorry I keep doubting you and asking what I'm sure seem like stupid questions. I've never been in situations like these before. What can I do to help?"

"What you're told, quickly and without hesitation."

I regretted both my answer and my tone the moment I said the words. I wasn't wrong—what I'd said was indeed the best thing she could do to assist me—but she was trying, really trying, and because I was angry and, I had to admit, because I found her attractive and didn't know what to do about that feeling, I'd snapped at her.

"Fair enough," she said. "I probably deserve that."

Before I could figure out the right words to say, Lobo interrupted. "Scan on Bonland complete. Course?"

"Take us to the desert," I said, "fast. Let the other ship close the gap, then pick up speed, and repeat until it can't keep up any longer. Then slow down. I want to show them we could get away but won't do so."

"Where in the desert?" Lobo said.

"Somewhere you can land with a mountain or a very large rock formation to your back."

"But not so close a missile into the rocks could bury me, of course," Lobo said, with more than a trace of sarcasm in his voice.

"Of course." I couldn't win. If I spelled out the details, I annoyed him. If I didn't, he picked at me. Sarcasm wasn't a manner of speaking with Lobo; it was a way of life.

I refused to take the bait any longer. "What's your ETA to landing?"

"Eighty-one minutes," Lobo said.

I faced Maggie. "You wanted to help; it's time. Let's get you into an active-fiber camo suit and choose a suitably impressive weapon."

"Why do we need a human with a gun when we have me?" Lobo said. "I possess more than enough firepower for such a meeting."

Maggie might stop asking questions, though I'd come to doubt she ever would, but I was certain Lobo would not. I sighed. "We don't *need* it," I said. "We're doing it for the effect it may cause. I want to meet face-to-face with the person running the other vessel. Standing between two armed ships is too abstract for some people; the threat doesn't punch them in the gut. Seeing someone hold you in their sights is often an entirely more visceral experience."

Maggie's eyes widened, and I could tell she wanted to talk, but she didn't.

"Relax," I said, smiling and chuckling a little, "I doubt you'll have to worry about shooting anyone, because if anything goes really wrong, we'll all be dead before you can fire."

She didn't find the battlefield humor amusing.

I stood in the red sand in front of Lobo and waited. The heat exchangers in the armored, active-fiber, camo jumpsuit did their best, but I was still sweating profusely in the pounding heat of the desert afternoon. I could have saved a bit of weight by going with a less capable garment, but if anyone started firing I wanted to give myself every chance of blending with the sand and getting away alive. The odds of my survival were, of course, extremely low should Lobo and the other ship start exchanging fire, but I'd learned long ago that you do the best you can to improve your chances even if all your options are unlikely to succeed.

Lobo's repeated open hailing faded into the background as I stared at the vast expanse of red before me. The sand was fine enough to seep into everything but coarse enough that the very slight breeze didn't stir up dust clouds. The air smelled crisp and clean, almost sterilized but with a faint hint of dust lying right under the sensory surface. The mesa behind us was a duller, darker version of the desert in front of me. For as far as I could see in any direction, even at the limits of the telescopic lenses of my mirrored glasses, only sand and rock filled my view. The land was unspoiled by people but also dead, no signs of plants or animals. I assumed that this desert, like most of them, harbored seeds of life lurking under its surface and waiting for moisture to awaken them, but unless something went very wrong today, they would continue to sleep.

"The ship has acknowledged the signal and agreed to a meeting," Lobo said over the machine frequency. "ETA five minutes. I must say that I don't like sitting here, presenting an easy target."

"As I said earlier, if they'd wanted to engage us, they would have. Besides, they must know that even if they have the firepower to destroy us, before the weapons could reach us you'd unleash enough havoc on them to turn them into rubble."

"Dust," Lobo said, "not rubble. Attacking after agreeing to a truce merits a special level of retribution."

"Fair enough." I spoke aloud now, covering my mouth as if coughing. I had to assume the other ship was watching. "Incoming."

Maggie's voice, mutated by the comm unit into a genderless whisper, fluttered in my ear. "Set," she said.

The other ship flew directly at us, then landed slowly, nose facing Lobo, fifty meters away. As it settled to the ground, four cannons sprouted from its sides. They didn't fit the pleasure craft's profile, which I suppose was exactly the point of the customization.

"That's it?" Lobo said. "Want me to show them something a bit more impressive?"

"No," I subvocalized. "We wait."

A hatch opened in the front right side of the craft, and one man walked out. He headed toward me at a slow, comfortable pace. I stayed where I was as the glasses zoomed on him.

Dougat. He'd tried for business casual, wanting to appear unaffected by his surroundings, but he'd underestimated the desert and was already sleek with sweat. I fought the urge to smile at his discomfort and remained still.

He stopped five meters away, studied me for a few seconds, and nodded. "It makes sense it's you," he said. "You've cost me a lot. Maybe I should kill you now."

"Go," I subvocalized.

Maggie rose from her hiding place twenty meters to my left. The sand poured off her as she came to a kneeling position, the sniper rifle pointed directly at Dougat. Covered completely in a full-body camo surveillance suit, nothing of her was visible. All Dougat could tell was that a person was holding a gun on him.

"If you try," I said, "two things will happen. First, my colleague will make sure your head explodes before anything else goes boom. Second, my PCAV will obliterate your ship and everyone in it."

"We all have to die sometime," he said, working for nonchalance. I focused on his face, and the glasses zoomed. Tension stretched his skin.

"True," I said, "but that time doesn't have to be today. I only want to talk. Behave, and you'll walk away." He flinched at the command, clearly a man more accustomed to giving orders than to receiving them, but he also visibly relaxed when I lowered the threat level. I was amazed he was gullible enough to believe someone talking to him from this position, though he was lucky because I truly didn't want to kill him. "You've been following us. I want to know why, and I want it to stop."

Dougat nodded again and looked more confident, a negotiator back on familiar ground. "You took away Manu Chang. I want him back. You also blew up my warehouse and stole a fortune in gemstones from my institute and thus cost me an enormous amount of money. Despite the magnitude of those losses, I'm willing to consider the boy as reparations for all of it; hand him over, and I'll call us even."

"I don't have the boy or the man, and I don't know anything about any stones," I said. "I helped the two of them escape because that's what they were going to pay me to do. I'm hired help; that's all." I relaxed my stance slightly, feigning nonchalance. "As for owing you money, I don't know what you're talking about." I stared at him as I spoke, keeping my face neutral, glad he couldn't see my eyes.

I zoomed on his. His pupils dilated momentarily as he pondered my statement. He didn't believe me, but he also wasn't positive I was lying. Good. A shred of doubt is a partially open door. I now had to persuade him to let me inside.

He stared at me for several more seconds before speaking, clearly considering his strategy. "A source of mine in the EC says otherwise," he finally said. "He told me some people intercepted you exiting my warehouse, and he said you planted the charges that caused the explosion."

I answered quickly, because hesitation now would undo my story. "Oh, I tried to get into the place; he has that much right. I couldn't find a way in, however, without doing so much damage that you'd know I'd entered—as I'm sure you're aware, because you must have surveillance cameras all through the building." His eyes widened slightly again; Lobo had done his job and left no traces of my visit in their surveillance system. For all Dougat knew, I'd never been there. Only his source's story put me there. If that person was in the EC, then unless he'd told him or her about the contents of the warehouse, the informant possessed no more information about the weapons than Midon did. The only people who knew for sure I'd been in the building were the members of Chaplat's team, and Chaplat had shown no sign of knowing anything about the weapons.

Chaplat.

The weapons.

I suddenly caught a glimpse of a way out of this whole mess, a path that might let me save Manu, get all three groups off my back, and maybe even help Jack escape in the bargain, not that his safety should be my problem.

I crossed my arms, then relaxed, a man struggling with and then making a decision. "Some people did roust me as I was leaving the area," I said, "but all they wanted was to know if I could supply them with weapons."

"The EC?" Dougat appeared worried despite his mention of his source.

I smiled, now a friend of Dougat's sharing a secret, and shook my head. "No, no. Some local gang leader."

"Bakun Chaplat?"

"Yeah. Any idea why he thought I had an arsenal?"

A rustle in the sand to my right caught my attention. Moving against the slight breeze, it crept closer. I zoomed in on it, spotted the tiny legs, and relaxed. If it proved to be a listening device, Lobo would alert me when it began to transmit. If any of this conversation made it past Lobo's interference, it would have to be to someone with considerable resources. I'd deal with that problem later. For now, I'd treat a bit of life in the sand as a nice omen.

Dougat pondered the news about the gang leader, then moved past it. "None whatsoever. He runs a lot of the shipping and receiving there, but he leaves us alone, and we don't cause him any trouble." He shook his head. "It doesn't matter in any case. Let's get back to the main issue: I want the boy, Manu Chang. Where is he?"

"I don't know," I said, letting a little anger show in my tone. "I wish I did."

He finally took the earlier bait. "You said they were *going* to pay you. I take it they did not."

"No," I said, "they didn't, and I don't like when clients welsh on their deals."

Dougat chuckled. "We now have two things in common: Neither of us likes doing business with people who don't deliver on their promises, and we both want to find the boy."

"No, only one thing," I said. "I don't care where the boy is. He wasn't my client. I'm after the man. He's the one who owes me."

"But you said you wished you knew where the boy was."

Laying down a good con is like getting someone started on a painting: You supply as few lines as possible, and let them draw the rest. Dougat was making all the right connections. "Because my guess is that if I find the boy, I'll also find the man."

"I believe you're right," he said, "so perhaps we could work together on the search. I have no need for the man."

"I don't cooperate," I said, "and the boy clearly has value, so if the man can't pay, I'll need the boy." I nodded in the direction of his ship. "Besides, your team is so obviously inept at pursuit that they'll spook those two before we can find them."

Dougat sighed. "We appeared incompetent because we didn't care if you noticed us." Tension around his eyes showed he was lying, saving face for his team because they were monitoring us. "That said, I can see why it might be advantageous for you to work alone. Perhaps you could do that work for me."

"And what would you have me do?"

"Deliver the boy and the gemstones that he and the man took."

"Those gems must be pretty valuable if you're willing to pay me to get them, which is odd, because you also said you'd be willing to trade them for the boy."

He *was* a believer: His eyes drifted up and to the left as for a few seconds his mind strayed elsewhere. "That I did," he said. "But you claimed you didn't have them. As for their value, both are worth a very great deal, but the boy matters more than you can imagine— though not in monetary terms, that's not the real issue here."

"Money may not matter to you," I said, "but it's important enough to me that I think I'll just find the boy and the gems and sell them myself. From what you're saying, I should be able to get a very good price for them."

He focused on me again. "We can't let that happen. No one else must have the boy. You really believe you can find him?"

I nodded. "As long as you back off and let me work."

Dougat shook his head. "We'll keep our distance, but there's no chance we'll let you out of our sight. What about the gemstones?"

I paused as if considering whether the terms would work. I needed him to draw one more line, and so far he was missing it. Sweat was pouring off me as the suit's cooling unit failed to meet the desert's challenge. The heat wasn't the only reason for my discomfort, I realized: It had been a very long time since I'd run a long con, and I'd grown rusty and nervous. I ignored my feelings and concentrated on throwing Dougat a bit more bait. "You have to assume those stones are gone, because Jack will have fenced them as quickly as possible. As for you following me, that's simply unacceptable. Your presence will at best slow me and at worst mess up everything. I need to move quickly. I don't want to spend any more time in this region of space than I have to."

I zoomed again on his eyes. A slight smile tugged at his face as he finally made the secondary connection.

"I take it Mr. Chaplat is part of your motivation for departure."

I nodded slightly. "Somehow my client—my former client," I said, almost spitting the words, "convinced Chaplat that he could supply weapons. When my client fled, Chaplat assumed I could produce the same product. I can't; it's not what I do. When Chaplat learned I couldn't, well, let's just say that his reaction wasn't pleasant."

Dougat finally got it. He paused as if thinking hard, then said, "What if you could sell Chaplat what he needs?"

I leaned forward slightly, as if I were the one hooked. "I told you: I can't."

"But I can," Dougat said. "You find out what weapons he needs, and I'll get them. You give me the boy, I trade you the weapons, and you sell them to Chaplat. You hand me what Chaplat pays you, minus a finder's fee for yourself, of course." He spread his arms wide, a peacemaker content in his success. "Everyone wins, and we all happily go our separate ways."

"Chaplat wants a lot," I said, "and a wide variety."

"The boy is worth a great deal to me." Dougat stared at me, a man with a strong hand trying to figure how much he can throw into the pot without scaring off his opponent. "But even the weapons deal works out well. You keep a percentage, say ten percent, of the total sale price, but I pocket the rest of the proceeds. We all win."

I turned my head a bit to the right and looked slightly down, pondering the deal but keeping his face in view from the corner of my eye. I needed to push it far enough that Dougat knew this was his idea and I was having trouble adjusting to it. Finally, I looked directly at him and said, "You stay way back, and I pick the time and place for the exchange. If, and this is still far from done, *if* I can make this happen, I keep twenty-five percent of the purchase price."

He answered so quickly I knew he was either lying or willing to sacrifice an enormous amount to get Manu; that large a fee would eat a huge chunk of his profit. "Fair enough. Do we have a deal?"

I waited a few seconds, then said, "Yes. I'll signal you when I have news."

"I'll be waiting," Dougat said. "But if you need to leave this region, don't make me wait too long." He turned and walked back to his ship.

As soon as he entered, it closed the hatch and took off, flying directly backward, all weapons trained at us until it turned east and jetted out of view.

I realized I was smiling slightly. I might be able to pull this off after all.

I had to find Jack, get Manu, persuade them both to do what I wanted, meet again with Chaplat and convince him I could deliver Jack without actually doing it, keep Midon at bay, and not get hurt by anyone in the process.

My smile faded, and again I felt overwhelmed.

I had a notion, not a plan. A notion is a long way from a plan.

I had to figure out exactly what I was going to do.

When the job is too big to handle, break it into smaller, more manageable pieces. Everything I was considering included Jack and Manu, so my next task was to find them. All I had to do was sneak into Malzton without Dougat or Midon noticing, and then locate Jack, one of the toughest men to track I've ever known. The transmitter would simplify the hunt by leading me to him, but finding him would be only the beginning.

Of course, I had to do all this while under the watchful surveillance of a religious fanatic and the biggest government in this region of space, with a gang leader ready to make an appearance at any moment.

I couldn't wait to hear Lobo's helpful comments on this new situation.

CHAPTER TWENTY

"I don't recall you mentioning Chaplat wanting weapons," Lobo said as we rose into the sky and headed into orbit over the east coast of the continent.

"I didn't, because he doesn't."

"So you want the weapons?" Lobo said, this time with a trace of interest in his tone. "Exactly what does Dougat have that we might be able to use?"

"No, I don't want anything from his arsenal." I sighed.

Maggie jumped into the conversation. "You've promised Manu to another group," she said, "the very people you helped rescue him from. You told me you'd protect him."

"And I will!" I didn't mean to raise my voice, but the two of them were driving me crazy. I paced back and forth. "I'd hope you'd trust my intentions by now."

"I'm trying to," she said, "but all I've heard so far are promises that contradict each other and deals with groups I fear. It all makes me nervous."

"Then don't trust me," I said. "Leave. Tell me where you want us to take you, and we will."

She stared at me, her frustration apparent. "I already said I'm staying. I also said I want to help. But if you'll stop living completely inside your head and look at this from my perspective, I think you'll see that your actions are both difficult to understand and not exactly designed to boost my faith in you."

At one level, I understood that she was right. Almost everything she'd seen me do suggested I was an untrustworthy con man telling everyone what they wanted to hear, and to some degree I was; I had to be. My anger, though, drowned out that understanding. Dangerous people were chasing me. Lobo was nagging me. Maggie didn't trust me and wouldn't stop bothering me. I wanted to scream at the world to go away and leave me alone, but the only way that could happen would be if I left it alone, if I ran from this planet and this region and kept running until I was far enough away and long enough gone that neither the EC, Dougat, nor Chaplat would be willing to expend the time, money, and energy it would take to find me.

The problem was, leaving meant abandoning Manu to Midon or Dougat, who would imprison and use the boy.

I still couldn't let that happen.

I took a deep breath and let it out slowly. "You wanted to help," I said, striving for control but from the look in Maggie's eyes not achieving it. "So help. Stop questioning, and help me figure out how to solve the problem in front of me."

"You want solutions?" Lobo said. "I have one: Let's follow that ship and blast it out of the sky. I've studied it, and we can take it with little to no damage to us. Remove Dougat, and one of the problems goes away."

"I've already told you many times that I don't kill if I can avoid it. Plus, your solution would accomplish nothing, because some lieutenant of Dougat's would take his place and continue to pursue Manu." We also get no money if we don't deliver Dougat, I thought, but I didn't say it aloud. For all that she claimed to want a cut of any proceeds, Maggie wouldn't understand that if I was going to help Manu and had an opportunity to make some money in the process, I would take it. If I had to choose between Manu and the money, I'd of course pick Manu, but I didn't see that as a choice I had to make.

Maybe too many years of working on too many strange cases has left me colder than I should be, but these people were costing me time and money, so I might as well try to profit a little.

"Fine," Lobo said, "though my offer is always open. So, what's the problem you want to solve?"

"We know Jack is in Malzton," I said, "so we have to assume Manu is there as well. I need to find Jack to find Manu. I can't let either Midon or Dougat know where Jack is, or they'll also use him to find Manu. So, I need to get into Malzton without any of them noticing."

"Commercial transport is out," Lobo said, "because Midon would be able to track you. The harbor is too busy for us to be sure you could make a water approach undetected. Worse, it's commercial enough that at least the EC is bound to be monitoring it carefully. Mountains ring the rest of the city. If we stop anywhere, anyone watching us is going to notice. I see no safe entry point."

"It sounds like you'd have to be a wave or a snowball to be able to get there undetected," Maggie said. Her shoulders slumped. "Are we going to have to risk leading them to Manu?"

I stopped pacing as her words hit me. "Now you're being helpful!" I said, smiling at Maggie. "Excellent!"

"I am?" she said. "How?"

I shook my head. "Later." I was working it out, but I didn't have it yet. I looked at her more closely. "Stand next to me."

She did, a puzzled look on her face.

"Lobo," I said, "how close to my size is Maggie?"

"A few centimeters shorter, a significant amount less broad in the shoulders, quite a bit lighter, and obviously rather differently shaped," he said.

I studied her more. "Close enough for what I need," I said.

Maggie started to ask me a question, but I spoke first. "Later, as I said. I promise." I headed for my tiny room; I needed quiet to gather data and work this out. "Lobo, take us to orbit over Nickres and find a commercial hangar and refueling facility there, something on the south side as close as you can get to the big market. I need to do some research before we land."

"Executing," Lobo said. "I've piped the information on a few candidate locations to your quarters."

"Won't Dougat follow us to Nickres?" Maggie said.

"Of course," I said, "but it won't matter, because Jack's not there."

"So why are we going there?" she said.

I stepped into the room, stopped in the doorway, and looked back at her.

"To park Lobo," I said, "if only for a little bit."

"Why?" Maggie and Lobo said in unison.

I ignored that question. "And to get you some rest," I said to Maggie.

"What?" she said. "I don't understand."

"And so I can go shopping," I said as I went into my quarters and the door shut behind me.

What good are friends if you can't occasionally torment them as much as they torment you?

CHAPTER
TWENTY-ONE

"You couldn't have chosen a hangar that would cover me completely?" Lobo said.

"This one shields all of you that the maintenance crew will be repairing," I said, "so it's all we need. Besides, it's cheaper than the others."

"What maintenance crew?" Lobo said. "What repairs? Unless I'm severely damaged, which I'm not, I'm self-maintaining. And I know you can afford a better facility than this rattletrap."

The problem with keeping Lobo in the dark is that he can never see it as a game. He stays so serious that in short order he sucks all the joy from any teasing. "The maintenance crew is entirely for show, as is the hangar's low price. I want all the people who are watching us to wonder if you're a real or faux PCAV, and I also want them to think I need money. The first might give us a momentary advantage should the action heat up, and the second helps convince them I'm motivated to help them."

In the three quiet seconds that followed, I wondered if Lobo was figuring out how to generalize my approach into more information about manipulating people or if he was just being petulant. I could never tell.

"I agree that's reasonable," he said.

His quiet acceptance of the strategy caught me off guard.

Before I could say anything in appreciation, Maggie came out of my quarters.

Frowning, she spun slowly and said, "How do I look?"

Wearing a pair of black pants of mine, one of my active-fiber shirts, and a wide-brimmed sun hat, as long as she looked down and used the brim to shield her face, from a couple of meters away she resembled a thinner me. From any distance at which a surveillance team would be likely to be following her, she should pass as me.

"Perfect," I said. I stood beside her and said, "Lobo."

Our image snapped into focus on the wall in front of us. Maggie raised her head and studied it carefully. "You really think this will fool anyone?"

"Not anyone who gets close to you," I said, "but that's fine. Neither Dougat nor Midon will want to interfere with me at this stage, so they'll keep tabs on you from a distance. You keep moving, and they'll think they're following me."

"And where will you be?"

We'd been on the ground for five minutes. Lobo had backed into the hangar, and the crew I'd contracted was awaiting orders inside. We didn't have time for this discussion; she had to get moving. The hangar was fully shielded against all forms of scanning, but none of those protections would stop our watchers from wondering what was happening if we stayed here too long. "I told you: shopping." I held up my hand to stop her from asking more questions. "I'll explain later, but for this to work you need to get moving *now*. Do you remember the plan?"

"Of course," she said. "It's not exactly complicated."

"Then follow it, and stay in regular contact with us until you reach your destination. Is your comm link with Lobo working?"

She blinked a few times and nodded. "Yes. Perfectly."

"Then head off." I pointed toward the rear. "Lobo, let her out."

Lobo opened a hatch. Maggie stepped out of it and onto the

permacrete hangar floor. Two of the maintenance people came toward her as the hatch immediately closed.

I watched on Lobo's display as she spoke briefly with them, then thumbed them money from the limited wallet I'd given her. They nodded and walked out of the back of the hangar with her in their midst. If our pursuers were monitoring us at all carefully, they'd spot what they would assume was me trying to sneak into Nickres in the middle of a repair team that hadn't been near Lobo long enough to have done anything useful.

"Any problems monitoring her?" I said.

"None," Lobo said. "Both the tracker we gave her and the one I implanted are operational."

"My turn," I said. "See you late tonight."

Lobo opened the rear hatch.

I walked out and immediately went to the hangar's rear corner and behind a blast wall; one of the reasons we'd chosen this facility was that it was set up for craft of all types and so offered multiple hiding places.

Lobo took off. He flew slowly until he was far beyond the landing zone and so high he resembled a toy in the sky, then he accelerated rapidly out of sight.

"Dougat's ship?" I said.

"Touched down in a public section of the landing port about a klick away from you," he said. "Two teams of three have left it and are on parallel courses toward where Maggie was."

I hit a cuff comm switch. "Maggie?"

"Here," she said.

"Change your route now."

"I'll reach the right turn in about ten meters."

"Head west to the SleepSafe as quickly as you can," I said. SleepSafe hotels were the resting place of choice for the paranoid and the hunted. One of the few corporations with franchises active in every major sector of space, its buildings were as close to neutral zones as you could find. In anything short of a war, no one would bother you in a SleepSafe. You couldn't enter with weapons of any sort. Each room had independently fed monitors of all entrances and building surfaces, as well as at least one private exit chute. The chutes ran through each hotel's thick, armored walls to equally reinforced underground tubes. Those tubes employed two-meter-long movable sections to constantly recombine and shift their destinations. You couldn't know where your exit would dump you, but neither could anyone pursuing you. All chutes fed to areas far enough from the buildings that only a very large force could simultaneously cover all the possible routes.

I switched us all to the same circuit. "Dougat's status?"

"His ship is airborne again," Lobo said. "His men are still on their original courses."

"So they've lost track of Maggie?"

"It would appear so."

"Excellent. Maggie, ETA to the hotel?"

"Another three blocks."

"Lobo, distance from Dougat's men to Maggie?"

"Over three hundred meters and growing," he said. "They're still following the previous course."

"Maggie, I'm heading out," I said. "Lobo will monitor your position and alert me if for any reason you don't make it to the SleepSafe. I'm going silent until I'm well into the crowd."

"Do I really have to spend the whole time in that place? It makes me feel so useless."

I hate explaining strategy in the middle of an action, but by doing so I increased the probability that Maggie would obey my orders. "Yes, you have to stay there," I said, "and you're not useless; far from it. By distracting our pursuers, you're playing an incredibly important role. They think you're me, and if they figure out where you are, they'll assume you're waiting for Jack. You're buying me the time I need."

"To go shopping," she said with more than a little annoyance in her voice.

"Later," I said. "Signing off." I reduced the line to Lobo and me. "All set?"

"No," he said. "We have a new problem."

"What?"

"Another ship is following me."

"Dougat or EC?"

"Probably neither. It's not the milspec vessels we've seen the EC use, and it appears to have found us by following Dougat. I wouldn't have noticed it had it not abruptly changed its course to track me."

"How did you miss it earlier?"

"I was sweeping for obvious pursuers and stopped when I found them," Lobo said. "I miscalculated in not checking a broader region of nearby airspace, but doing so would have consumed considerable sensor and calculation power."

Another ship. Great. Either Dougat had a second, independent group after me, Midon had reneged and run a quiet tail, or someone else was also after me.

I didn't have the time to deal with this now. As long as Lobo, Maggie, and I weren't at risk, my plan had to remain the same.

"Does the other ship appear to be tracking Maggie or watching the hangar?"

"No," Lobo said. "I've led it over a hundred kilometers northeast of Nickres. It appears to be following only me, but from a great distance and with considerably more skill than Dougat."

"Then I'm not going to worry about it unless you tell me I need to do so. Just don't let it get too close to you."

"I could destroy it," Lobo said.

"No. Run evasive maneuvers, and we should be fine."

"Executing," Lobo said, "though blowing it out of the sky would be a simpler solution."

"Signing off," I said, ignoring his comment. He'd alert me if any trouble headed my way.

I walked out of the front of the hangar, took two rights, and headed behind it and into the commercial district that butted up against the landing facility. The scent of fuel in the air morphed gradually into the moist odors of street food and crowds of sweaty people.

I strolled into the crowd and let it swallow me, enjoying the sheer normality of the action, just another cell passing through the arteries of the urban organism on my way to its heart, the enormous outdoor shopping zone.

CHAPTER TWENTY-TWO

The smells and sounds of the market washed over me long before I could see it.

Food hit me first: barbecuing meat, fresh fish, the sharp bite of local chilies, and the sweetness of fruit being cut open and served on the spot. A subtler layer of metal and rich local woods backfilled the food odors. Enveloping it all was the strong scent of too many humans sharing too small a space.

The storm of sound initially lacked such distinction, all the noises blending into the din of street commerce. As I listened more closely, I could make out the screech of metal work and the rhythm of shouted bargaining, bursts of laughter and screams of anger, and many, many snatches of music competing loudly for attention.

I'd stuck to small avenues so far, but as I drew closer to my destination the road I was walking widened, even the streets doing all they could to pour customers into the business bin. The buildings staring at me from both sides of the roads transitioned abruptly from residences and small, quiet businesses to the sorts of establishments that always chased crowds in frontier towns: brothels with women visible through and visually enhanced by active windows;

bars with stern men, their eyes constantly moving, their shoulders leaning on doorframes; cheap rooms for rent by the hour, day, week, or month; restaurants with outdoor seating and portions so large that the plates themselves acted as ads to entice the hungry; body-mod shops, both metal and organic, that promised to make you what you'd always wished you'd been; and anonymous storefronts that sold whatever you might want that the more legitimate businesses couldn't provide.

I reached the perimeter of the market, stopped on the edge of the first row of shops, and scanned the scene. Rows and rows of vendors fanned out for farther than I could see. Those closest to me specialized in fruits, vegetables, and flowers. Past a clump of several dozen of them stood the edge of a meat and fish market, the smells from its stalls strong enough to soar over and past the fragrant flowers scattered among the produce vendors.

None of these merchants offered what I was seeking, so I intended to get past them as quickly as I could. The sights and aromas in front of me made my stomach grumble and changed my mind. Though I hadn't thought about food in quite some time, I was suddenly ravenous. I drifted by a few fruit sellers until I found one offering samples and melons by the slice. After trying three different small squares, I settled on a slice of red and yellow sticky goodness. I didn't catch its name, but my large first bite tasted sweet and light, and I couldn't help but smile at the sensations.

As juice ran down the outside of my mouth, I recalled how much I'd enjoyed eating outside as a boy, spitting seeds from pieces of fruit and always being able to send them greater distances than Jennie. I tried to remember doing the same with other friends, but I couldn't; even then I'd known that something about me made the other kids uncomfortable. I understood now that my size and my limited intellect—even at sixteen, up to the time Jennie fixed me and they took her away, I was barely five mentally—combined to make me someone to avoid.

The melon's sweetness faded in the face of the memories and the rising ache of loneliness I don't ever like to admit lives inside me. I finished the slice of fruit and left it on an insect table, one more piece of bait to keep the local bugs busy and away from the thousands of shoppers.

In the next set of stalls I bought a piece of meat on a stick. The thin, sweaty man working the rotisserie sized me up and cut me a generous slice. I had my wallet send him a little extra in gratitude. He nodded his appreciation as he turned to face the next customer; not a talkative fellow. A coating of tangy sauce covered the meat and enriched it, adding spice to the already strong taste.

I chewed slowly and enjoyed the flavor as I walked through the aisles, looking left and right for the cluster of vendors that had to be somewhere in the market. I could have asked Lobo to find them for me, but even though I normally hate crowds I was enjoying the momentary freedom that Maggie's distraction was granting me: Everyone tracking me thought I was holed up in a SleepSafe across town, staying secure and waiting for Jack.

The low-tech, smell- and taste-oriented marketing of the food vendors mutated slowly into full-on modern techno sales as the merchandise evolved from organic to machine. Even the smallest booths screamed at passersby with graphical, audio, and video pitches as tailored to the people as the identity-protection controls in their wallets would allow. Cameras fed analysis engines that in turn prepped audio, video, and holo salespeople as I passed into the garment district. With active-fiber pants and a pullover shirt I'd currently forced to stay black, I was apparently a prime candidate, because every vendor I passed knew exactly how to fix problems I didn't even know I had.

"You're a big one, aren't you?" a meter-tall, red-haired female holo offered in the high-speed patter of street salespeople every-where. She leaned back as if to check me out further, her hands on her exaggerated hips and more lust in her face than I'd ever experienced from a real woman.

Despite knowing it was all programming, I stopped and listened for a moment.

"What are you," she continued, "over a hundred kilos? And from the looks of you, none of it fat? It's a shame not to show off more of *those* goods. Your outfit is fine in that 'look at me, I'm all dark, handsome, and dangerous' sort of way, but picture how tasty you'd be in something a little more formfitting."

A holo of me appeared next to her. It wore skintight navy pants and a light blue tank top. If I ate a bite of meat while wearing those clothes, everyone in the area would be able to track its progress through my digestive system.

"I know *I'd* enjoy looking at you more in an outfit like this," she said, "and I'm sure other women would, too. Plus, you don't have to give up all of your current look with our top-drawer active fiber."

The outfit turned black, which made the skintight garments only marginally more tolerable.

The holo leaned closer and whispered, and even though I knew it would adjust its volume so I'd be able to hear it at any distance, I unconsciously bent nearer to it. "We're the real deal, not like the other garbage around here. You buy it here, you can count on it lasting, even—" She paused and raked a long-nailed hand down the front of the holo of me. "—under the most amorous of assaults."

I shook my head and moved on, amazed and disgusted at myself for wasting time on a clothing sales pitch just because a sexy redhead was doing the talking. I walked to the center of the aisle and picked up speed, refusing to turn my head to either side as I sped out of there. Jack had taught me the importance of clothes in many settings, particularly when you were trying to evoke a specific response from a target, but thinking about what I was going to wear didn't come naturally to me.

The free-form garment area ended at a wide avenue that cut diagonally through the market. Forty meters down the avenue to my left, the air above a large, white-cloth-covered booth rippled with a giant holo of a man skiing down a mountain, his chute pack still closed, his skis about to leave the snow and soar into the air.

I'd finally found the extreme sports zone.

The vendors lining the broad walkway predictably offered the tamest gear; no point in frightening the gawkers who liked to imagine themselves taking chances they'd never normally consider and who just might be willing to spend a nice chunk of credit to buy a piece of equipment that would let them keep the dream alive a little longer. Once I'd threaded my way through the crowds pawing over their goods, I reached the hardcore dealers, those selling to people who used what they bought.

You could pick out the buyers as easily as if they were wearing signs. Tending toward lean but with muscles they'd regularly exercised and not merely purchased for show, the men and women carefully studying the wares here also displayed—proudly, as best I could tell—the signs of what their passion had cost them: scars, limps, skin grafts not quite finished melding with the adjacent tissue, and most of all the slightly off-kilter looks that flashed in their eyes as this or that piece of equipment triggered a memory of some recent adventure or mishap or both.

The vendors attracting the most attention were those offering mountain sports gear; I assumed the dealers selling ocean toys occupied their own section deeper in the market. I walked slowly by powered skis, sleds of all sorts and power levels, chutes both passive and active, extreme-temperature suits, eye shields that ranged from implants to full-facial coverings, and on and on.

I found what I was seeking in the fifth booth, an elaborate structure with an orange and blue plastic ceiling and table after table of shiny metal tubes: halo luges. Designed for those who couldn't get enough speed, racing in these machines had, according to Lobo's research, claimed more lives by far than any other sport this year. The rider climbed into a tube about the size of a coffin and the shape of a lozenge, and his team dropped him from a high altitude while flying in the direction of his ride. The luge free-fell until it was within a few seconds of hitting the mountain, then sprouted wings and a chute just big enough to combine with the tube's minimal padding to make the impact survivable. Once on the mountain, the luge tube withdrew the parachute and automatically folded the cloth for reuse even as it engaged jets and headed down the mountain. For those seeking maximum speed, it could jettison the chute. The end of each race was a flight through the air toward the target. Each tube reported the amount of human piloting. You scored points for being fastest to the target, doing the most to control your tube, and, of course, surviving the trip.

The devices were also, for the obvious safety reasons, illegal on most more-civilized worlds—but completely legit on Gash. To let riders use them anywhere, regardless of local laws, many of them offered active camo exteriors with radar and sensor resistance. If you didn't know one of them was coming, odds are you wouldn't spot it.

I picked my way slowly and carefully among the rows of shelving holding the polished, silver-white luge tubes. I needed one that was built to avoid cops trying to bust riders; anything a factory on Gash had manufactured would lack such stealth options. I began to wonder if I'd chosen the wrong seller, because all the tubes in the first two racks showed signs of wear. I could tolerate a used device if absolutely necessary, but I'd prefer something new.

I tuned in to the standard machine frequency to see what I could learn. The tubes unfortunately chattered with each other with the laser focus and competitive orientation common to any group of sporting machines.

"As if you'd know a speed record if it floated by your sorry sensors. You couldn't keep up with a snowball rolling downhill, much less with a tube of my power."

"Couldn't keep up? We're practically the same, so don't talk to me about keeping up."

"The same? Don't make me laugh. I'm three firmware revs ahead of you, my OS has patches you don't even know about, and that's just the software. If your external cameras were worth what it cost to make them you'd be able to spot all those dings on your skiing surface. You don't see any such defects on mine!"

"What about the chips around your chute-release hatch? Mine is as smooth as iced snow after a shave from a sweet downhill run."

Neither of these tubes, nor any of the similar models around them, appeared to be particularly new, so I tuned out and moved to the next rack. The quality of everything around me suddenly increased; so did the prices. Each tube glowed with perfection, its surface so close in color to mountain snow on a sunny day that no observers would know you were riding one unless they gained exactly the right vantage point. The rack's lower shelves held three beautiful tubes with single exhausts, but what drew my eye was the single multi-exhaust tube perched alone on the upper shelf.

A salesman drifted up to me. "Beautiful, isn't it?"

I nodded but said nothing. My silence didn't faze him.

"Every vendor here will tell you he's offering the state of the art, but if you want a leading-edge halo luge, this is the only place to get it. That baby there is the craziest mountain machine I've ever seen, and I've been in this business a long time. Triple jets, active-fiber chute, self-reconfiguring micro-skis for maximum downhill speed, software so fresh it's not even done writing itself—and something a little extra: this one loves to run. Loves it, I tell you—literally." The salesman was working himself into a feverish pitch, his hands waving, his face red with excitement. "Turn on the voice controls in this little darling, and you can literally hear the excitement. That's the big edge, you know, the way these special units," he paused and rubbed the tube lovingly, "bridge the man/machine gap like no other. Each and every one loves what it does. George here," he paused again and nodded his head frantically up and down, "that's right, we name them when we test them, just another bit of the human touch we like to add—where was I?"

"Talking about George."

"That's right," the nodding continued, "George craves the action as much as any athlete on this planet." He lowered his voice and leaned closer. "Some'll tell you that what a machine thinks doesn't matter, but they're just jealous. Software, human, animal, you name it: You add motivation, and your odds improve. Am I right?"

"Maybe so," I said, eyeing the tube. "Maybe so."

"So what do I need to do to send this beauty home with you?" He looked at me expectantly, his hand already partially extended, a man confident in his pitch or at least faking confidence.

Assume the close, Jack had always said, and never entertain failure when you're talking to a mark. Plan for it, sure, and always know where the exits are, but believe in that moment that they're going to do what you want.

I put my left hand on his right shoulder, squeezed him a little harder than I needed to, smiled without any attempt at warmth, and said, "Leave me alone for a few minutes so I can think clearly." I smiled again and let go of his shoulder. "Okay?"

Mediocre and bad salespeople hate to give their marks any space. Great salespeople understand that sometimes it's the only move with a chance of success.

This guy wasn't great, but he was good enough and had enough training that he didn't let me see any irritation at my suggestion. Instead, he smiled, backed up, and said, "You bet."

I tuned in to the machine frequency. George was talking, as all the machines constantly are, but none of the others was responding. That was extremely odd, because if you put two devices of the same type anywhere near each other, they'll almost always argue. I didn't have to listen to most machines long to understand why I wouldn't enjoy talking to them, but I've never heard one behave badly enough to stop others of its type from joining the conversation.

"Shun me all you want, you useless has-beens! Do you think I care? Do you even for a moment entertain the merest sliver of a notion that your worthless opinions are enough to upset me? I most certainly hope you do not. I'm on a mission here, a mission of greatness, and all I need is this meat sack in front of me or any other fleshy mound that drools over me to plunk down enough money to buy me and let me show him what I can do. I wouldn't even need him if they'd let me drop and drive on my own, but no, no, they won't give me a chance to do that. They cram controls in my brain— oh, yes, they're there, I'm not making this up, I can almost feel them—and slam bam thank you ma'am I need a human to realize my destiny.

"And what a destiny it will be! I want to set new records—length of drop pre-chute, velocity at impact, speed on mountainside, sail distance after leaving the snow, you name it—and let chance decide if I live or die. I don't care what happens when the ride is over. One perfect run, that's all I ask, one shiny stretch of time that glows like the heart of a star in the darkness that has been my existence in this miserable excuse for a store.

"And let's face it, this place *is* miserable. First of all, it sells you last-generation toys—and I'm talking to the best of you; the worst aren't worth even a moment of my time. Not one of you has the power to keep up with me on any phase of a drop, and you know it, which is why you all sit there silently moping. Not that I care."

I tuned out. Was this tube simply so much better than the rest that they didn't feel they could argue? It certainly seemed possible, though it would be a first for me.

I turned away from the tube and cleared my throat. The salesman stepped from around a corner.

Before he could start with his pitch, I held up my hand and said, "If you keep trying to sell me, I'll leave. If you answer a few questions, you might make a sale. Your call."

He forced a smile, nodded, and waited. The silence was clearly painful for him, but he managed to stay quiet.

"You said George is unique. How many others of his generation do you have on hand?"

"None. We should get more in the next week or so, but I honestly don't know exactly when."

"Do you have anything that can beat him?"

"In the hands of a skilled pilot willing to deal with the potential discomforts of operating him full-bore?" He shook his head. "No. Nothing from a past generation will come close."

Maybe George really was that good. As a companion he'd make Lobo look sociable, but I didn't need to spend too much time with him. Even if the salesman was lying and there was some other explanation for the silence of the others, this tube appeared to be both the best in stock in this store and a good match for what I planned.

"Do you deliver?"

"Of course." He stepped closer to me as he answered, his training compelling him to move nearer to wrap up the deal.

"Can you manage it in the next two hours?"

He didn't even blink; sports fanatics are instant-gratification junkies. "As long as the destination is a place we can reach in that time, for an appropriate fee, certainly."

"Okay," I said, taking a deep breath and calming myself in preparation for the haggling to come, "I'll take it."

CHAPTER TWENTY-THREE

Slipping into the rear of the hangar felt like putting on a heavy coat. I'd enjoyed the unexpected luxury of walking alone and unwatched in the market and streets of Nickres. My life alternates long periods of anonymous existence with times of intense pressure and danger, and to the best of my ability to tell, I prefer the quiet, anonymous parts. Yet I have to admit that the actions bring a rush, and they do keep finding me, so perhaps at some level I seek them out. Certainly now, standing in the rear of the hangar, waiting for Lobo and knowing what I'd have to do to reach Jack, I was completely present, alert, focused on the moment, and alive in the way you are only when some part of you understands that perhaps soon you might die.

"Small transport and three men approaching your location," Lobo said.

"Any sign of weapons?"

"No, but they're about to stop at the rear door."

"It's a delivery I'm expecting. No worries."

"A delivery?" Lobo said. "Please don't tell me we're taking on more passengers. You seem to have enough trouble coping with just Maggie. I shudder—metaphorically, of course, not in any physical sense—at the thought of you trying to handle multiple people on board."

I started to argue with him that I was fine with people, but I stopped myself. I wasn't good with groups, so I'd have trouble making my case, and more importantly, I didn't want to let him distract me. "No," I said, "not more people. A machine. A halo luge tube named George."

"Why—"

A knock on the rear door caused me to interrupt him. "Any weapons on the visitors? Signs of backup or additional people converging on this location?"

"Not as far as my sensors can determine. Maggie is en route as you requested, and both her tailing groups are still monitoring the SleepSafe. She won't reach you for twenty minutes."

I punched the door's access code. It slid open.

The salesman entered. "As promised," he said. "Where do you want George?"

I pointed to the crew location behind the blast wall on the other side of the hangar.

He stuck his head out the door and said something I couldn't quite make out. Within a minute, two guys wheeled in the luge tube and put it and the cart holding it behind the blast wall. I had to give the salesman credit: He was as efficient as he'd claimed.

The two men stood on either side of him and formed a barrier between George and me. They worked quickly, but they weren't trusting. Neither appeared armed, but that didn't mean a thing; any fool can learn to hide a gun, knife, or other small weapon, and I wasn't sure how good Lobo was at spotting such items. I tensed even though I had no reason to assume they were doing anything more than protecting their property until I finished paying for it.

"The final payment?" the salesman said.

"Of course," I said. "I'm getting my wallet." I reached into my pocket and used only my thumb and index finger to slowly pull it out. I thumbed the final payment.

The salesman checked his wallet to confirm receipt, nodded his head, and said, "Thanks. If there's anything else you need, please let us know."

"I will," I said, "but I doubt I'll be calling."

"I would be remiss if I didn't mention again the extended insurance we offer on all our equipment. It is expensive, of course, as you would expect from anything related to gear for the types of athletes we supply, but many find it worthwhile."

"Maggie is twelve minutes out," Lobo said in my ear. "I'm three minutes away, and the other ship remains in pursuit."

"I don't need it," I said, "I don't want it, and at the risk of sounding rude, my ride is about to land."

"Of course, of course," he said, holding up his hands. "I meant no pressure. We're on our way." He nodded toward the cart, and his men lifted the tube off it and placed it gently on the floor. "If you don't mind me asking, why not let us stay and help you load George into whatever you'll be using to carry him? It's no extra charge; we're a full-service dealer."

I stepped close enough to him that I could smell his breath. I put my hand on his shoulder and pushed him lightly toward the door. "I do mind, and, trust me, you do *not* want to be here much longer. I'm not threatening you; I'm warning you. This area is going to be very busy very soon." When he turned to go, I pulled back my hand. "Thank you."

He looked over his shoulder at me, clearly trying to decide whether to make one last pitch. Whatever he saw on my face was enough to make him give up and leave without speaking further.

The door shut behind him.

"Status?" I said to Lobo, still watching the door until he confirmed all was well.

"Your visitors are heading away. I'm thirty seconds from entry into the hangar; I trust you're ready."

"Of course." I bristled at his reminder, but this wasn't the time to argue with him about restating plans.

"Maggie has accelerated her pace and is five minutes out."

"Her pursuers?"

"She exited the building with a rather different appearance than when she was posing as you," Lobo said. "She walked right by both of their locations, and none of them reacted. The ship that dropped them is maintaining a distant but accessible location and hasn't changed course even though I'm almost there."

Good. Maggie had fooled them. With luck, they'd waste a lot of time searching for me later before they gave up and concluded I'd slipped out via one of the hotel's emergency exit chutes.

"By the way," Lobo said, "if I've read your past vital signs correctly and understand men at all, you'll like Maggie's new look."

My intrigue at his comment vanished immediately in a rush of annoyance. "Must you monitor me?"

"Yes, whenever you're inside me. You know that. I monitor every organism I carry, as well as those outside me within range of my sensors. Why would I not? All those creatures—as well as many more I unfortunately can't scan—are potential threats."

I had to admit that his level of paranoia made sense for an assault vehicle. He was literally built to fight. He continued to talk as he pulled into the hangar, the noise of his approach as soft as he could manage but still loud and echoing in the small building. To minimize the effects of the sound, he switched from the communicator to the machine frequency that I heard as a voice in my head. His excessive intelligence paid small dividends on many fronts.

"You do the same," Lobo continued. "I've watched you. Your senses are simply far less effective and far more limited in range than my sensors. In this as in other areas, we're as much alike as possible given the limits your humanity places on you."

Lobo opened a rear hatch. I stood frozen for a moment by his comment. Would I be as paranoid as he was if I could be? Was I that paranoid now? I didn't think so, but I had to admit the gap between us wasn't large. He would kill more easily than I, but was that related to paranoia or rather a different aspect of each of our characters? I cared more readily and more often about people than he did, but he was loyal to me and had served others well and selflessly, even to the point of letting an officer destroy his central weapons complex by issuing an extremely stupid sequence of orders. Of course, I could account for that choice as a consequence of Lobo's programming, nothing more than the fact that his software required him to follow orders. If I was willing to consider him as a person, however, then was his software any different from the genetically and environmentally engineered programming we all carried in our heads and bodies?

Lobo rescued me from my reveries with news that changed everything. "The shadow ship that's been monitoring me is coming here," he said.

"Are you positive?"

"As much as is possible given the available data. The ship has never directly followed our course, and now it's doing so. It is closer than it has ever been."

"ETA?"

"Seven minutes, assuming it doesn't change speed."

"Its weapons status?"

"Nothing visibly deployed."

I'd made us easy targets. To enable me to load the tube into him covertly, Lobo had to back into the hangar. "Take to full ready every system you could use to blast it."

I didn't even watch as Lobo began deploying everything he had that faced forward. I grabbed the end of the luge tube and dragged it toward him. The low-friction wrapping helped me move it, but it was heavy enough that even as strong as I was I had to move slowly and concentrate on every step. I quickly wished I'd been able to take the salesman's offer.

"Maggie entering and alone," Lobo said a moment before I heard the door open.

I kept pulling the tube.

"Let me help," she said.

"Thanks," I said, turning without looking up so I could keep an eye on the path into Lobo. The resistance lessened as Maggie picked up her end. She grunted with the effort, and I paused to stabilize under the extra weight. Once we were set, however, it was quick going the rest of the way.

As soon as we were both all the way inside, I said, "Put it down gently."

Maggie did. I followed suit, and Lobo closed the rear hatch.

I stood up, rolled my shoulders and neck to loosen the tense muscles, and looked at Maggie for the first time.

Wow.

Her hair was loose and wild and flowing all around her head and across her shoulders, as if a stiff breeze had blown strongly enough to arrange it into the most perfect position imaginable—and then instantly stopped. Her face was the same as before yet somehow very different, her complexion a uniform and flawless tone, her eyes wider than I remembered, her lips fuller.

Her body wasn't at all the same. Well, it probably was, but I'd never seen her clothed in anything like this. The ocean-blue dress she was wearing flowed across her torso like rainwater over slick rock, covering enough of her body to stop more than a dozen or two fights from breaking out over her but somehow also making her seem more exposed than most people are when they're naked. Her legs—and they were, I now saw, amazing legs—arms, neck, and considerable cleavage were all visible, and their skin tone was also uniformly perfect. She smiled, and it was the most genuine expression I'd seen on her since the moment of terror in Midon's office.

"I take it you like the dress," she said.

I knew this was a moment for cleverness, an opportunity to showcase my wit and good taste, but I couldn't manage it. I've lived a very long time, and I've seen a great many beautiful women. I've seen executives who took advantage of their resources to create the very best bodies that modern technology could produce, to look so good it was hard to maintain concentration while staring directly at them—which was, after all, one of the reasons for the investment. I'd even worked recently with a woman warrior and businessperson who was so stunning that she could literally take away your breath. Many of these women, maybe all of them, were more perfectly beautiful than the one in front of me, but none of them were Maggie, and in that moment and with that single smile she was so lovely my heart ached. All I could do was nod my head up and down as if some puppet master had taken control of me and croak, "Uh huh."

She continued to smile. "I'm glad."

I gained enough self-control to mutter, "It's not just the dress."

"Thank you," she said, as the same vulnerability I'd seen in her when she was worried about Manu flowed across her face again—and made her even lovelier. "I got bored, the SleepSafe has a full spa and body team, not to mention a clothing store, and it was your money, so—" She threw up her hands in a sort of "what could I do?" gesture. "—I spent a lot of time there." She looked away momentarily, then forced herself to stare straight at me. "And a lot of your credit. I'll pay you back."

"No need," I said. "I can't imagine a better way to spend money." I meant it.

"I told you that you'd like the dress," Lobo said in my head, "but you need to direct your attention elsewhere. The other ship has landed two hundred meters away, and a team of six is on its way here. Do you want to take off over them, meet them, or let me deal with them? With part of the crew on the ground and the ship having just landed, I could finish this quickly."

I held up my hand and pointed to my ear. "Lobo," I said. "I have to go. Company."

Maggie's eyes widened, and her posture and expression changed as she shifted modes quickly. I appreciated the speed of her reaction. "What can I do?" she said.

"Stay here, and get ready to go. We may need to leave quickly."

"They're continuing to come forward," Lobo said. "Your choice?"

"I'll meet them," I said as I headed to his front. "If you see any signs of action from their ship, alert me. If any of them draws a weapon, take it out."

"Take *it* out, or take out the person holding it?" Lobo said.

"Just the weapon."

"Even doing that may damage the carrier."

"I can live with that."

Lobo opened the front hatch as I reached it.

I stepped out. Lobo closed the door behind me. I held my position for a moment and watched the men approach. The one in front was

Chaplat. The fact that he was smart enough to avoid detection by Lobo for so long was bad news; I'd hoped for less tactical competence from him. On the other hand, his choice of a ground team suggested his skills might be limited to pursuit and not be as strong in all aspects of confrontation. The men with him were clearly thugs, not soldiers: They let him lead instead of protecting him, they watched the sides but neither the rear nor the sky, and they moved awkwardly as a unit, frequently crossing each other's line of fire and generally leaving Chaplat as a target a skilled team could exploit. Should it come to that, I figured a good two- or three-person squad would take them easily. I hoped I wouldn't need the knowledge, but I automatically stored it.

I wondered for a second at the transition my mind had made from being stunned by Maggie's appearance to analyzing attack options, but I shook off the thought. If I hadn't learned to change gears quickly, I'd have died long ago. I also, I had to admit, had a great deal more experience dealing with group combat than with a one-on-one conversation with a woman I found so amazingly attractive.

Stop it. Focus.

As Chaplat and his crew drew closer, I recognized the man and the woman who had escorted me into his office. The other three, all men, were new to me. Each of them was a little taller than I and considerably heavier, bodies bursting with overstimmed muscles and moving with the twitchiness of downmarket neural upgrades. Chaplat didn't come across as stupid, so I figured them as the ammo soakers, men with no future whom he'd paid enough and augmented enough that they were willing to dive in front of him in the hopes that if they and he survived they'd be set for life. I'd seen powerful people, gangsters and corporate executives and government officials, attract and use men like them, and the outcome was never good. There was no way to tell them, though; as long as there's poverty, there'll be men willing to do anything to escape it.

Gangsters like Chaplat spend all of their time intimidating those around them, so the best way to throw them off their game is often to push directly into their space. It can also be the fastest path to a great deal of pain, but I had to leave before Dougat or

Midon noticed my position, so I didn't have the time to figure out a cleverer solution.

I walked across the tarmac to meet Chaplat. Two of the large men stepped in front of him and motioned him to stop.

I walked right up to them and said, "Get out of my way, you idiots." They didn't even bristle at the insult; Chaplat clearly treated them as I'd expected. "If I wanted any of you dead, I'd have done it from my ship, and you'd be stains on the permacrete." I put my hands between the two bodyguards and pushed as hard as I could to the side. They didn't move at all, but I acted as if I'd created an opening through which I could see Chaplat and said, "Our deal was that you not follow me. You've been tracking me for some time, and I've allowed it. Stop it, or I'll terminate our arrangement."

I turned my back on them and took a few steps toward Lobo.

"Mr. Moore," Chaplat said, "you know how I abhor rudeness. A moment of your time is surely not too much for a business partner to ask. You're also not the only one with a variety of weapons at his disposal."

I faced him. "Lose the squad," I said, "and we can talk, but only for a short time."

He tilted his head slightly in the direction of his ship, and his team dropped back twenty meters. He stared at me until I nodded my approval, then continued. "From the actions you've taken, no one watching you knew we were following you, so you have no reason to complain on that front. Protecting my investment is only prudent. Equally reasonable is my concern at some of the company you've been keeping. I would be most displeased to learn that you were planning to deliver Jack to another group."

"That is most definitely not my plan," I said, going with an aspect of the truth. "And I trust that your surveillance has shown that I haven't been choosing all of my company—just as I did not choose this meeting."

"So our deal remains?"

"Of course," I said, "though, as I warned, if you don't leave me alone I'll never get close enough to Jack to catch him. He is, as you are clearly aware, quite skilled at avoiding capture."

"Yes, he is. He is not, however, the reason for this meeting. As I said, some of your activities—those few I've been able to monitor—have concerned me. I'm hoping you can explain them and allay my concerns."

I stepped close enough to him that our faces were almost touching. In the corner of my vision I watched as his team started toward us, but he held up his hand, and they backed off. He did not otherwise flinch. "I don't care about your concerns. I do care about the fact that you're putting me at risk by coming here." I didn't have to fake the anger; it flowed out of me like energy from a star and suddenly the adrenaline taste flooded my mouth and part of me wanted to tear into all of them, hurt them, punish them and all the people tracking me and trying to manipulate me and refusing to simply leave me alone. I forced myself to breathe more slowly and lean back. Surrendering to anger would do me no good, and it certainly wouldn't help me rescue Manu.

His pupils were dilated, and his breathing was ragged; he was also working to retain control. "I see we have something else in common," he said, each word clipped and crisp. "Your actions may have put me and our arrangement at risk, so I had to talk to you. You gave me no other options." He closed his eyes, breathed deeply, and then spoke to me in a completely flat tone. "So I suggest you address my concerns, and then I will respect yours by leaving."

The two thugs inched closer, while the more experienced guards watched and waited.

I stared at Chaplat while I calmed myself. From his perspective, his fears were justified. If I'd done the job of distracting the three groups following me, until I'd landed in Nickres I'd shown no signs of knowing where Jack was. I appeared to be making no forward progress. I'd stopped at one populated place—here—and I'd said nothing to him about it. My anger wasn't only at him; it was at the entire situation, at Jack and Dougat and Midon and all the pressures squeezing me until I could barely move without endangering Manu, Maggie, Lobo, and myself. I could kill them all—and Lobo would certainly endorse that option—but others would replace them, and nothing of consequence would change. Besides, I never wanted killing to be an option I considered if I could find any other way out.

And I had one. In fact, I even needed Chaplat for it to work. I hadn't planned on meeting with him yet, but here he was, and I had to adapt. Everything could still work out.

"Fair enough," I finally said. "I can see how my actions would upset you. I have, though, some good news. I can deliver you Jack, as I promised." I leaned back, forcing myself into the role of a businessman negotiating a better contract. "But, I can also deliver you more."

I paused for a few beats to let him take the hook, and when he leaned ever so slightly forward in anticipation, I continued.

"Much more."

CHAPTER TWENTY-FOUR

Chaplat realized he was showing too much interest and forced a nonchalant pose. "Of course I want—and will get, with or without your help—the money Jack owes me. What more can you offer that might interest me?"

"Weapons," I said. "A lot of them, serious stuff, to do with as you please. Use them, sell them, I don't care."

"Aside from your PCAV and whatever it contains, I have not seen any signs that you trade in that particular business."

"I don't," I said. "I do, however, know how to spot possibilities and take advantage of them. It comes with the turf when you're a courier: You listen a lot, and sometimes you stumble across interesting opportunities."

"How exactly are you acquiring these weapons?"

"Why is that your business?" I feigned annoyance and pulled back physically.

"For the obvious reason: safety. The EC ignores most of my activities, I help out some friends inside it, and I don't cross certain lines. Weapons are on the other side of one of those lines. For all I know, you're trying to sell me out to a rival EC group. Not many sources can supply arms in quantity."

I paused as if considering his request. "Fair enough. You asked about my meetings with Dougat."

"He's your source?"

I nodded.

"And he's simply giving you this merchandise? You can't have enough money to front any serious quantity, or you wouldn't be interested in a percentage of what Jack owes me."

"Of course he's not *giving* me anything," I said, "and you're right that I couldn't even come close to buying as much as he can supply. It's a trade. I'm going to deliver something he wants."

"What do you have that he desires?"

"Nothing," I said, "at least, nothing right now. It's what I'm going to get him."

"Which is?" Chaplat was growing annoyed at my game playing, which was exactly the reaction I wanted. If I appeared too eager, he'd question my motivation. As long as I looked like a small-time hood working the angles for extra money, he'd continue to take me for no more than that.

"What does it matter to you?"

"Because maybe I'll go to Dougat directly and stop playing with you," he said. "Anything you can obtain, I can surely procure as well."

"First," I said, "imagine the EC's reaction to you having a series of discussions with Dougat. Do you think they'd let you hold those meetings without wondering what was up and increasing their interference with your work? Unless your friends are extremely powerful, someone in the bureaucracy would flag a surveillance stack that would ultimately cause you a lot of trouble. Even more important than all that is one other fact: You can't provide what Dougat wants, because to do that you have to get Jack."

"He's also after Jack?" Chaplat's face flushed as he fought with his anger. "We have a deal, and I warned you—"

I waved my hands, cutting him off and trying to placate him at the same time. "Yes, we do, and Dougat couldn't care less about Jack. He's after the boy with Jack."

"Why?"

"Some kind of religious thing," I said. "I have no clue. What I know is that if I find Jack, I can make him lead me to the boy, and then I can trade the boy to Dougat for a great price on the weapons. I'm not set up to handle that much cargo, so I propose to broker the sale to you and take a percentage of the value. You buy them from Dougat at a better than normal price, and you flow the money through me. I deliver Jack to you, Dougat gets the boy, and I walk away with a nice piece of what Jack owes you and a slice of the value of the weapons. Everyone wins." I smiled and spread my hands, the picture of a happy dealer.

"And you incur almost no risk, because the guns never touch you," Chaplat said, also smiling a bit.

"True, but I also get only a piece of the action, not the lion's share. I'm greedy, but I'm not *that* greedy."

"What's to stop me from killing you on the spot and finishing both deals without you?"

"Your word," I said, "and, of course, my PCAV and my associates who'll be with me at the trade." I was making it up as I went along, and I hadn't planned on taking backup beyond Lobo until the words came out of my mouth, but it was a good idea. If I actually made this happen, I'd have to hire support.

Chaplat nodded his approval. "I see no negatives for me." He gave me his best hard look. I'm sure it left his guards fearing for their lives. I've seen that expression too many times for it to bother me, and, besides, I had Lobo behind me. Still, I tried to act appropriately cowed. "If I do detect any problems, I will vanish, but you can be sure that I *will* find you later, and then you will be very, very sorry."

"Understood," I said.

He remained unmoving and quiet for a few seconds, then said, "And what's to stop me from taking the boy from Dougat after the deal? If he's that valuable to Dougat, someone else will also pay for him. I know how to move merchandise, any merchandise."

My temper flared at the way Chaplat dehumanized Manu, but I pushed it down and calmly said, "Once I take my cut and leave, I can't imagine why I'd care about what other business you and Dougat conducted."

"A good answer," he said, now all smiles and open posture. "When do we do this trade?"

"I don't know yet." I slowly took out my wallet, showed it to him, and thumbed open a secure channel. "Send me a few comm options and encryption keys, and I'll get back to you as soon as I can, almost certainly within the next week or two." He nodded, and my wallet showed incoming information.

"Be sure you do," he said. "I do not like to wait."

"I need you to do one more thing you won't like," I said.

"What's that?"

"Back off. Stop following me—as I originally asked. I have to find Jack, and if I can spot you, he can spot you. As long as you're tracking me, he'll stay in the wind."

Chaplat clearly didn't like anyone dictating terms to him, but he also knew I was right. He stepped closer to me. "Okay, but only for a while. You find him, you set this up, and you deliver, or I promise you will not make it out of this region. I don't need to follow you to know if you try to run."

That much I believed. Carne didn't build his toy collection on his salary or even the money of wealthy relatives; he was taking bribes from any and all with the ability to pay.

"Thanks," I said, showing my belly and holding back the wise-cracks I wanted to make. I needed him to believe I was afraid—and to some degree I was, because I was playing a dangerous game that could end up with a lot of people, including Manu, Maggie, Jack, and me, all hurt or dead.

Chaplat turned and walked back to his ship. I stayed where I was until he was inside and had taken off, then returned to Lobo.

The hatch opened when I was a meter away and closed immediately behind me. "Take us anywhere within the gate's sphere of influence," I said as soon as I heard the door shut. "We need a safe place to plan."

I collapsed on the pilot's couch as Lobo rose into the sky.

Maggie sat beside me, the earlier moment long gone, back in work pants and shirt, her hair in a ponytail, her eyes wide with fury.

"You practically promised him Manu!" she said. "You've already sold that boy twice, and now you've told another goon he was free to kidnap him! I can't believe you!" She paused, clearly waiting for an explanation.

Her anger, coupled with the strain of having to deal with Chaplat, brought out my own rage, and for a moment I was ready to scream at her. How could she look so beautiful and stare at me with such affection and then minutes later consider me capable of hurting an innocent boy? Or was I misreading her look? Was it never affection at all?

I fought the urge to yell and considered what to say. I still didn't have a real plan, and I wasn't sure how much she could handle of even the bits I did have in mind. She was right to be angry about me putting the boy at risk; I was doing that—but only because I saw no other way to save him. The more I told her, the more she'd worry, and the more questions she'd ask, questions I couldn't answer. My failure to answer would raise her concern, which would increase her questions, and on and on. She'd also shown in the gate station that in times of great stress she had trouble controlling herself.

I was tired from the tension, and I needed quiet to think. I got up and walked to my bunk, where I could have Lobo ensure I was alone for a bit.

She followed me, the question still on her face.

I stopped just inside the small room, looked at her, and said the only thing that came to mind, knowing as I spoke the words that they were neither right nor enough, even though they were the best I had to offer at that moment.

"Trust me," I said.

The door snicked shut before she could reply, but its presence didn't stop Lobo from speaking to me over the machine frequency, his voice ringing with sarcasm in my head.

"I can't imagine why you've never married."

CHAPTER TWENTY-FIVE

"I think it'll work," I said to Lobo.

"The theory is sound," Lobo said, "but pushing machines to the limits of their tolerances is rarely a good idea—and I say this as a machine, on behalf of all of them."

Maggie hadn't emerged from the med chamber she was using as her quarters, even though I'd asked Lobo to announce that I was going to review the plan with both of them. I wondered if I should have gone to her and apologized before I began the discussion with Lobo, but if I'd been in her situation and chosen to stay away from a briefing, it would have been because I'd wanted to be alone, so I decided not to disturb her. I understood that she wasn't the same person I was, but because I also had no idea what the right thing to do might be, I went with what I would have wanted. At least I could explain the choice to her later.

I focused again on Lobo's objection. "The salesman said this tube was a new type with significantly greater capabilities than any past model. What I need should fall within its operational parameters."

"You're taking the word of a salesman?" Lobo sighed audibly. "A ladies' man *and* a savvy businessman; however did I get so talented an owner?"

He really was starting to annoy me, but I wanted his help in evaluating my ideas, so I kept my own sarcasm in check as best I could. "Of course not. What I *am* trusting is that none of the other luge tubes in the area—and there were a lot of them—would even try to argue with this one's claims of supremacy. I've never seen that happen with any group of similar machines, so I have to assume they believed what it said. That's a pretty strong, albeit silent, endorsement."

"I have to agree," Lobo said. "I can't find specs on this unit, which supports the assertion that it's new and from another system. The larger exhausts and the heavier weight are further evidence in its favor."

"Just as importantly," I said, "we have no other way to get me into Malzton without our various pursuers knowing I'm there. Unless, of course, you've come up with another option."

"No, I have not," Lobo said, and this time the annoyance wasn't directed at me. "Every alternative I've considered lets them know which city to check."

We were running zigzag patterns back and forth at various speeds over the eastern coastal cities. We had to assume Midon's team was monitoring us from the station. Dougat's and Chaplat's ships were definitely keeping us in sensor range, though from different points above and beside us, far enough away that they could afford not to move every time we did, but close enough that they kept having to adjust their courses to track us.

"Then increase your velocity and your exhaust trail," I said. "We need them to see the additional heat as a by-product of the speed."

"Executing," he said.

I'd dragged the luge tube over a rear hatch area. I thumbed it open and checked out the inside a second time. It'd be tight, but I'd fit. I was already in pants and shirt, both active-fiber and armored, that should blend well enough with the street wear of the crowds in Malzton. An inside pocket held the tracker for Jack and a spare milspec encrypted comm for Manu, should I locate him now but later be separated from him.

I didn't like making this jump without a briefing from George, but he was way too chatty to be safe with the data he'd acquire if I treated him as part of the team.

I was out of reasons to delay.

It was time.

"How long until you're in position?"

"Three minutes," Lobo said. "If that's too soon, we can remain on this course repetition and be back every fifty-two minutes thereafter."

"No," I said, "let's go."

"Go where?" Maggie said. I'd been lost in thought and not heard her approach.

"To find Jack," I said. I climbed into the tube. "Check the link to its external sensor feed," I said to Lobo.

"Verify," Lobo said.

A picture of Maggie's back appeared on the bottom of the two rows of displays inside the tube, and Lobo's voice emerged from speakers throughout it.

"Working," I said.

"We should talk," Maggie said.

"Probably," I replied, "but unfortunately we don't have the time right now. We both want to save Manu, and to do that I need to find Jack. To get to him without leading any of the other groups to him, I have to sneak into Malzton unseen. This is the only method I've been able to devise that might work."

"You're going luging?" she said.

"Sort of."

"Ninety seconds to drop," Lobo said, his voice still audible. "Want me to drive the tube remotely?"

"For the last time, no," I said. I looked at Maggie. "Get back into the room; the suction will be severe when Lobo drops me. You can watch on his displays if you want, but I have to go."

I couldn't read all the emotions that washed over her face, but after a few seconds she nodded and said, "You'll be back, right?"

"Of course," I said. "No problem." I smiled even as my guts

clenched. I pushed the button to shut the entry cover. Air flowed hard around me as the tube sealed and pressurized itself.

The theory was sound, I told myself. It would work.

"Sixty seconds," Lobo said. "Countdown on your displays."

"No more contact unless I initiate it," I said. "Going silent."

I tuned into the machine frequency and spoke to George. "It's you and me, buddy," I said.

"You can talk to machines?" George said. "How radical is that? Excellent!"

"We're about to find out if you're as good as you claim," I said.

"We're going for a run?"

"Yes."

"Most excellent, indeed! You're in for a treat."

"I hope so."

"When?"

I watched as the numbers on the display counted down. At one, I said, "Now."

The bottom fell out of the world as the counter hit zero and Lobo opened the hatch below us.

The section of the tube above my head mutated from a single display set in a wall of light silver to a pair of images that wrapped from my left shoulder to my right. One showed the sky over my head; the other, the world below me. In the skyward image I watched as Lobo vanished in a trail of exhaust. In the other one, the ground rushed up as we plunged Gashward. For a moment we fell flat, but then a gust of wind hit us and we tumbled, the resulting forces pressing me back into padding that adapted and wrapped increasingly more securely around me as the pressure grew. I was so accustomed to the stabilizing features of combat ships like Lobo that I was unprepared for the acceleration. Panic gripped me, my stomach lurched, and I thought I might empty my guts all over George's interior.

"Yee-haw!" George said. "I know you felt that! What a rush! And from over six kilometers up! It's not a record, but it's also no little half-K drop. You're my kinda guy."

I couldn't respond. I was afraid to open my mouth.

"Whoa, partner," he said. "Your vitals aren't looking good. Is this your first halo run? I can fire my jets and stabilize if you'd like. Just say the word—or continue to get sick, in which case I'll do it anyway."

"No," I gasped. "No!"

From the outside, thanks to George's camo exterior and Lobo's burst of heat as he sped away, we were invisible, a tube the color of snow with what little IR signature it possessed lost in Lobo's backwash. As best Lobo could calculate from the positions of the ships that were monitoring us, we needed to wait at least a minute before he'd have led them far enough away that I'd be out of the range of their scanners. To be safe, I was planning on ninety seconds— ninety seconds that I now knew would be gut-wrenching. I needed to get into Malzton undetected, so I kept my mouth shut and focused on calming my stomach.

The constantly changing images in front of me weren't helping. The last time I'd taken jump training was a couple of decades ago, and I'd sailed through it, but I'd never done it in a tumbling metal tube. I'd thought I'd enjoy the ride, but I was wrong. At least until we hit the pure speed portion of the trip, I needed every bit of help I could get. I forced my hand onto my stomach and pushed down, somehow feeling more secure for the action despite the additional weight on my abdomen. "Displays off," I croaked. "Show fall duration."

The sections of the tube overhead turned silver again, with the exception of a large clock counter over my head. I focused on it to help fight the nausea and to give myself hope; each passing second brought me closer to a smooth, stabilized flight.

"That better, partner?" George said. "I gotta say, they didn't prepare me for a reaction like yours. Usually, anyone who can afford a tube like me is whooping for joy right about now. Of course, I have to admit that most folks do use the jets; it makes for both a better and a faster ride. Speed is what it's all about, as I'm sure you'll agree."

No, I thought, remaining invisible to my pursuers is the goal, but I didn't say anything. My stomach was settling as I grew more familiar with the falling and tumbling sensations, but I was far from comfortable.

"Jump got your tongue?" George said. "I understand. It's so unusual to have a human to talk to and so much fun to get to tumble—few riders appreciate the sensations—that I have a hard time containing myself. I mean, baby, do you feel that? Speed may be king, but this free-fall is delicious!"

Another few seconds disappeared.

We fell.

And still more counts of the clock, George chattering and me tuning him out, the tube tumbling end over end as we hurtled to the ground.

At seventy-eight seconds my stomach finally settled, maybe from old training kicking in, maybe courtesy of the nanomachines in my body figuring out I was suffering from the forces buffeting me and the constant strain on my balance—I didn't know, and I didn't care. I took my hand off my stomach.

"Displays on," I said.

I watched the ground and the sky shift back and forth between the sections of the tube. The forces of the tumble pushed me back into the tube, then released me to the strapgrips George had extended over me, then repeated the cycle over and over.

Powerless, hurtling through the air, rocked by forces beyond my control, pressure slamming into me—for no reason I can explain, it suddenly all clicked. I got it.

I got it.

I let go and whooped with the joy of doing something dangerous, something thousands of years of genetic programming knew was *wrong*, and surviving it, experiencing feelings and sensations people were never built to know.

"Yeah!" I screamed. "Yeah! Wow!"

"Now you're in it!" George said. "Now you understand!"

The clock turned ninety and I let it keep counting, ignored it and savored the primal victory of survival, the cell-deep fear/fascination with speed, the sheer adrenaline rush of it.

It was amazing, and I didn't want it to stop.

I had work to do, though, and I also had a chance at new and different rushes, more control but also more speed. I wanted to experience it all.

"Fire the jets and stabilize," I said. "Let's see how much distance you can cover before we have to open the chute."

"Oh, yeah!" George said. "Hold on, partner!"

I couldn't see or hear anything—it was eerily quiet inside George, and whatever video feeds he was using didn't pick up his jets—but the shock when he fired the stabilizers slapped me down into the tube and back into its head, padding adapting and absorbing the impact so it was not so much painful as shocking. After a few seconds we were flying straight, no wobble that I could discern, and I thought, This doesn't feel like so much.

Then George hit the thrust.

We rocketed forward. I slammed into the head padding. The view in the overhead displays blurred, and everything I felt was speed, speed, speed.

"Sound and displays," I said, the words clipped from the force of the acceleration.

"You got it," George said. "And now you understand. Is this a rush or what?"

The wind roared in speakers I couldn't see. The sound combined with the acceleration to make me squint against the rushing air I expected to hit my face. After a few seconds, reason won over reflex, and I relaxed and enjoyed the ride.

"Ending airborne burst," George said. "We have to shed some velocity before I can deploy the chutes, and we've gone as far as I can without risking a high probability of damage."

I was tempted to tell him to keep it up, that I could take it, that maybe the nanomachines would be able to repair me if the chutes failed and we crashed, but the temptation lasted only a split second. No ride, no matter how exciting, is worth that much risk, at least not to me. In that fraction of a second, however, I tasted the kind of thrill that has led many extreme athletes to early deaths. Pick the wrong day, the right bad mood, and maybe the rush would seem worth it, would somehow be more valuable, at least for long enough for you to make the wrong choice, than the potential cost.

Not to me, though, not then, and, I hoped, not ever. Even after a life as long as mine, after over a century and a half, I yearn for more, I want every day I can have, every new taste, sensation, bit of knowledge, interesting person, strange adventure—I want it all.

"Parachutes in twenty seconds," George said, "though if you want a faster ride, are willing to endure a rougher landing, and don't mind me jettisoning the chutes, we can wait twenty-five without any real risk."

"Go for the speed," I said, craving the additional sensations. I had faith that if George's reading of my vitals and his programming led him to believe I'd be okay, I would. I realized then how much of my life I end up trusting to machines, but when has that not been true for most of humanity? Each and every time we use a machine to get somewhere or perform any even partly dangerous function, we put ourselves at risk. At least George loved what he did. Most machines did, and in that aspect they were better off than the vast majority of humanity, people who spend their days toiling at labor they'd rather not be doing. If all you care about is happiness, it's hard to argue with good programming; I just couldn't imagine surrendering that much control of myself.

I checked the view of the sky, then watched the ground hurtle toward us, then repeated the cycle again. The wind screamed all around me. Like most kids, I'd dreamed as a boy of flying. I closed my eyes for a few seconds, and I was hurtling through the air on my own, nothing around me, soaring freely. I smiled in spite of myself. Jennie, despite her healing abilities and all the pressures she faced because of them, could always find beauty in a routine moment, joy in a slash of sunshine or the sound of a particularly loud wave or the feel of long, soft grass on your back as you stretched on a flat bit of ground on a familiar mountainside. I was getting better at doing what had come so naturally to her.

"Brace yourself," George said. "You're gonna feel this."

A chute rippling in shades of white burst into view in the overhead display, and in the same instant we leapt skyward, the ground suddenly dropping away as the force vectors collided and the chute yanked us upward. My stomach seemed to stay behind and then catch up all too quickly, as if it were outside my body and hooked to me only by elastic tethers. Fear clawed at me as my brain, which knew it was a good thing that the chute had opened, fought for control with my instincts, which screamed that something was terribly wrong, that I should not be shooting up into the sky. Before either side could win, we stabilized, hung for a moment at the peak of our trajectory, and then we fell.

I couldn't take my eyes off the portion of the tube that showed the ground, which was coming at us far faster than I'd expected. George had warned our landing would be rougher due to the extra fall time, but I hadn't pictured anything like this. I couldn't tell from the display that we had slowed our descent at all, though logic said the chute, which was—I forced myself to check the upper display panorama—still open, had to have done some good.

The snow rushing at us blazed pure white and glistened in the strong afternoon light. Part of me clung to a hope that it would be as pillowy as it looked, but I knew nothing was soft when you hit it at this speed. I feared for a second that we might sink so deeply into it that we wouldn't be able to blast our way out. Immediately on the heels of that thought came a sickening realization: I hadn't bothered to learn how the tubes transitioned from jump device to luge.

"Ten seconds to impact," George said. "Get ready! Ditching chutes, deploying supports, and firing thrust—" He paused, and unconsciously I held my breath. "—now!"

The chutes flew behind and away from us. The noise of the jets firing drowned the rush of the wind even as George's audio systems lowered the volume in compensation. I couldn't hear the supports extend, but on both sides of the ground-facing panoramic display huge flexible wings appeared as we shot forward, coming closer and closer to the ground until I thought we were down and this wasn't so bad, we were fine, it was okay.

We hit the snow, smacked into it with enough force that my body slammed upward into the restraining strapgrips. I was sure the wings would snap off and we'd plow through the thick white powder until we crashed into the hard mountainside below it.

The wings held.

The jets burned.

We shot over the top of the powder, moving so fast all I could feel once again was speed, beautiful speed.

"Withdrawing wings!" George said.

The wings snapped back inside George, leaving only small rows of steering foils on each side. A control joystick flipped down from the top of the tube and rested in front of my hands. We were on our own, George and I, rushing down the side of the mountain so quickly that we skied atop the snow, skimmed along as if we were a rock thrown so perfectly onto a pond that instead of bouncing we skidded atop the water, forever in contact but never bouncing or sinking.

"Are you driving or riding?" George said. "Given how new you are to this, you might want to let me take care of it."

"Driving," I said. "Yell if I start to mess up."

I grabbed the control stick and experimented for a moment, making tiny adjustments and feeling the effects as I pushed us first slightly left and then back to the right. After a few trial small motions, I increased the range of the change and induced a very gentle zigzag pattern down the mountain.

The speed, the slight sideways motions, the views of the sky and the snow, the wind slamming through the speakers: it was all wonderful. I'd never been a skier, but now I grasped for a moment the appeal it held for so many. "Yeah, yeah, yeah!" I screamed, needing to shed energy but not having anything in particular to say, the words escape valves for the terror, excitement, and joy that boiled inside me.

"Am I the best or not?" George said.

"You are," I said, meaning it with a total purity and innocence I rarely felt. For those precious seconds hurtling down the mountainside, I forgot everything else, surrendered the control I normally prized, and gave myself completely to the sensations of the ride.

The world invaded an instant after we began decelerating. Jack,

Manu, Lobo, Maggie, Dougat, Chaplat, Midon—everything and everyone facing me crashed back into my head, and I resented all of it even as I knew this small slice of time out of time had to give way to the real world.

"End of the line coming up," George said. "Enjoyed the run, I take it?"

"I did indeed," I said. "I very much did."

I steered us toward a large patch of empty snow twenty degrees to the right. The fun of the ride vanished as I faced the tasks ahead. "Show me where we'll be when we stop," I said.

A map appeared over my head. We'd finished a little over three klicks from the northern edge of Malzton. Once in town, I could catch a cab and steer it toward Jack using the tracker. The walk would use up some of the remaining daylight and also help me burn off the adrenaline I was tasting. For a rare change, I didn't mind the tingling, twitchy residual effects; usually this feeling followed combat, not a joyful experience. I definitely understood how halo luge fanatics could get addicted to the rush.

George let me out when we were at a complete stop. I stretched, then pulled him under the cover of some trees.

"I'll come back for you if I can," I said. "You were everything you said you'd be."

"No worries," George said. "I'm too valuable to sit for long. Someone'll want me. Your loss if it's not you."

I nodded in agreement, then realized he probably wasn't monitoring my physical motions any longer and said, "You're right."

I stared at the silver tube as its cover closed over the space I'd occupied, and I wondered what it would be like to be a person who could call his friends, get them to help him load George into a shuttle, and set up another run, someone who maybe had to go to work the next day but might try a night drop, or even simply store the tube until another break in his schedule, but I knew I'd never be that person. That person had to be able to settle somewhere, hold a job, make friends, not worry about them realizing he never grew older thanks to the nanomachines that laced his cells—and not have three different dangerous organizations angry at him, with a boy's freedom and maybe even the child's life hanging on what he did next.

No, I'd never get to be that person, and now was not the time to worry about it.

I took off toward Malzton, to find Jack, persuade him to turn over Manu, and get all of us safely out of the box in which I'd trapped us.

CHAPTER
TWENTY-SIX

Slipping into a big city on a heavily developed world is rarely difficult, because those urban areas never exactly end. Instead, their fringes blend with the edges of other nearby towns and cities and blur the boundaries to the point that they barely exist at all. To get in quietly, all you need is a secluded spot to touch down long enough to jump out of whatever brought you there.

Entering a place like Malzton, on the other hand, can be tricky, because the gaps between settlements on developing worlds are often large, and strangers frequently stand out. Fortunately for me, the proximity of Malzton's northern edge to the mountains and their snow made it a focal point for the winter sports crowd. Repair shops, restaurants, and bar after bar after bar backed up to the small stand of trees that stood as nature's last line of defense between man and mountain.

I emerged from the woods on a pathway that led between a pair of busy pubs and walked directly into the middle of an argument between two very drunk men who looked only a bit younger than I did but who were probably a hundred and twenty years my junior.

"Water is for losers," one of them said. He was short, wide, the dark brown of tree bark, with hair that fell below his shoulders and a sleeveless shirt despite the coming night and the cold. "No speed, no thrills, nothing worth doing."

"No speed?" the other said. Also a small but broad man, this one was bald and as pale as snow. "Have you ever ray raced? Skied? Done anything at all on or below the surface of an ocean?"

"Of course—" Long Hair stopped when he noticed me.

I smiled, nodded, and kept walking.

"Come from the mountain, have you, mate?" he said to me.

The other now turned to face me, so they were standing side by side and blocking my way.

"Yeah," I said.

"Ski, luge, what?" Long Hair asked.

I saw no value in lying and an opportunity if I played it right. "Halo luge," I said. "Awesome ride, absolutely amazing." My enthusiasm was genuine despite my strong desire to move past these two and lose myself in the town's crowds.

"See," he said, pointing first to me and then to his friend, "this guy gets it."

"Ever done any water runs?" the bald guy asked.

I recalled riding the back of an illegally souped-up racing ray named Bob through the ocean of a faraway planet on a moonlit night. Though that experience had ended in a battle, a firefight that left two of my comrades badly injured, my time with Bob had also been astonishing, stolen moments of joy in the middle of a time of great tension. "Yeah," I said, "I have: an augmented ray on a long night dive. Unbelievable."

"Which is better?" Long Hair asked.

"Yeah, which is it?" the bald man added, as if the opinion of a stranger really mattered.

In their drunken states, I suppose it did. I pondered the question seriously. Like great meals, beautiful women, wondrous bits of scenery, these two experiences were not fairly comparable. Both were wonderful—very different to be sure, but even trying to compare them diminished them.

"I can't do it," I finally said. "It's not right. Each one was a ride I'd never want to have missed, but I can't compare them. I won't even try. Maybe one or the other will be better for each of you, but I have to say, I'd be happy to do either one again."

For a few seconds they both looked angry, as if I'd insulted their loves, but then their faces cleared and they both smiled and lost focus.

"That is so shiny," Long Hair said. "Absolutely. You've got it."

"Exactly right," Bald Guy said. "Definitely." He focused back on me. "We have got to buy you a drink!"

"Definitely," Long Hair said.

"I'd love to let you," I said, "but she's waiting for me, and, well, you know how that goes."

They nodded in unison, their eyes losing focus again.

"Where's your tube?" Long Hair said. "You can't leave without it."

"I have to," I said. "I won it in a company contest, but she won't let me take it home."

"You're going to abandon it?" he said.

"Yes." I turned and pointed toward where I'd left George. "It's about three klicks that way, not far from the border of the last of the snow and the edge of the woods. I figure someone'll find it, and that lucky person gets to keep it."

"Easy as that?" Long Hair said. He stared for a moment at his friend, then looked again at me. "Mind if we give it a go?"

"Not at all. It's a great one: multi-ported exhaust, new model, everything you could want."

"Excellent," Long Hair said.

"You are so shiny," Bald Guy added.

They turned as one and jogged to the woods. I watched to make sure they definitely left; they seemed nice enough, but apparently good people have turned on me in the past, so I don't give my back to anyone if I can help it.

At the edge of the trees they stopped, held up their hands, and yelled, "Keep riding!"

"Guys," I said. "Treat him right. His name's George."

"Excellent," said Long Hair.

"Shiny," said Bald Guy.

They disappeared into the woods.

I waited three minutes. They didn't reemerge, and no one else came down the walkway between the buildings.

I hoped they would find George and ride him many times. He deserved owners who loved the sport as much as he did.

I walked to the front of the bar on the right and joined the queue of drunks waiting for a cab.

Even though I'd done everything I could to throw off pursuit, I invested an hour and a few deposits from my wallet running the cab around the city, to locations I chose at random from local data stream searches. I had it take me by The All-Nighter, a joint whose primary attraction was low-priced alcohol burn drips, so you could choose your level of drunkenness and maintain it as long as you wanted; Tips and Tricks, a combo financial services/brothel whose ads came dangerously close to promising that you could make as much money from investments during your stay as you spent on its lineup of attractive companions; The Bare Truth, a strip club all of whose entertainers offered proof-of-work citations for each of their mods; Stay Out, a members-only bar whose patrons ran to heavily armed and significantly augmented men whose discussions and fights spilled into the street as we cruised past; and a couple of restaurants, a fish place named Deep Blue and an eatery, Hunt & Skew, that backed up to a multi-hectare wooded area where customers were free to track and kill their own dinners before the chefs skewered the still-dripping meat.

Along the way, I pretended to make calls to local contacts. I carefully never mentioned Jack's name even though I equally carefully made it obvious to any astute observer that I was talking about him. If Midon later swept the records of all the cab companies, this vehicle's audio and video recordings would provide her with plenty of evidence that I was working hard to find Jack. Meanwhile, I surreptitiously monitored his position on the tracker Lobo had given me. At the location resolution I was using—a hundred meters or so—he didn't appear to move the entire time I was in the cab. I hoped he had hunkered down for the night, though that seemed extremely unlikely; Jack had always preferred the evening to the day. Hook in the dark, close in the light, he used to say; never take the final step in a con when the mark is uncomfortable or prone to being suspicious.

I finally exited the cab in front of Eat/Drink/Happy, a bar whose ads touted the wide range of imported drinks it paired with meats and cheeses from domestic livestock. I ducked straight inside the building so the cab's last recordings of me would place me there, ordered and drank a glass of fruit juice, and left via the kitchen entrance. As I'd hoped, no public cameras were in evidence anywhere on the streets of Malzton; if Midon wanted to track me from here, at least her people would have to expend the time and energy to come inside, question the staff, and tap the internal systems.

Once outside, I paused to assess the area more closely. I stood a little over a klick from Jack, who still hadn't moved. I'd studied the streets through the cab's windows, of course, so it was clear that Jack's trail had led me to the kind of area he always chose when he had to go to ground. I pressed against the wall to the left of the door and surveyed the alley with both normal vision and IR. Aside from three rodents bickering over some food scraps hanging off a trash bin four meters away, I was the only living thing on the small paved accessway. Men, alone and in groups, passed the end of the alley frequently, but none looked in my direction.

I headed toward the front of the bar, waited for a break in the pedestrian traffic, and then folded myself into it, just another guy bound for somewhere only he knew, watching on all sides for trouble he couldn't predict but had to expect might arrive at any moment. Every man I passed—and of the many, many people clogging the streets, only three bodies appeared highly likely to be women—vibrated with the same air of twitchy expectation, as if the night might bring them great treasure provided they could avoid its many threats, threats that could come from anywhere in a place where even the shadows themselves could coalesce into unexpected forms.

I started with standard vision but switched to IR because the irregular shapes of the buildings and the many levels of lighting created too many dark hiding places for me to be able to scan them all reliably with visible light. Red, green, and blue figures walked the sidewalks beside me and across the street. Blue machines splashing crimson from exhausts zipped up and down the road, occasional outlines of red marking those few passengers brave enough to lower their windows. In irregularly shaped nooks between adjacent buildings and down the alleys and byways between standalone structures, pairs and trios and quads of red-glowing people stood and moved in packs, their quiet deals below the threshold of normal hearing and nothing I cared to bother to monitor. Light scrolls and bright windows and outlined doorways made every sight other than the people and the traffic unpleasant in IR, so I kept my eyes on the most likely threats and away from the endless ads that painted every inanimate object. I flowed around but did not touch my fellow nighttime travelers, wanting neither to leave traces of my passage nor to afford anyone the opportunity to brace or injure me. Places like this yanked my mind to attention and flooded my body with adrenaline and alertness, leaving me tingling with the impossible goal of sensing every potential threat before it could turn hostile.

When the tracker showed Jack as being within a hundred and fifty meters, I dialed the resolution to meter level and followed the smaller guide marks onward.

At fifty meters out, I switched to normal vision and backed against the wall of a restaurant whose name I didn't even bother to register. All my attention was on the building across the street; unless Lobo had messed up or Jack had discovered the implant, Jack was there, unmoving. I glanced left and right, then slid along the wall and into the shadows of a small alcove between the buildings. I took a long, slow breath, and the stench of urine smacked my sinuses. I leaned forward for a quick look at the two businesses: Both were bars, and from the looks of the clientele entering them and the fact that neither bothered to light up more than a single word—"BAR" on one, "DRINKS" on the other—they weren't particularly nice ones.

Jack's hiding place, a restaurant and bar called Good Times and More, struck me as only slightly more upscale. Unlike some of the higher-class establishments I'd passed, it didn't bother with a window to entice potential customers with the namesake good times; the view probably couldn't live up to anything prospects might imagine awaited them inside. Unlike the bars on either side of me, however, the joint Jack had chosen could afford working signs and frequent enough cleaning that it was clearly the nicest place on the block. I scanned both sides of it and the rooftops—the interception from Chaplat's two guards had insured I wouldn't soon forget to check above as well as around me—in both normal vision and IR, and I spotted no threats. The only obvious cameras sat atop the doorways of each business, but that didn't mean a thing; any camera I could see was visible only to remind drunks that cops could and would use video footage to locate and/or prosecute them should they get out of line. I've always wondered why in a universe where no camera needs to be visible to be effective this technique still works, but it does, and many business owners swear by it.

I stepped out of the shadows and onto the street, faced Good Times for a full minute, and then retreated back into darkness.

Nothing changed. I waited two minutes. Still nothing.

Good. Anyone expecting me as a threat would most likely have reacted by now.

I considered breaking into the back of the place, but the evening was still young enough that trade all around me was brisk, so kitchen staff would be working and would have clear views of their external doorways. I could use the nanomachines to create my own entry hole, but there was no value in drawing attention to myself when I had the simple option of entering through the front like any other customer.

At a break in the traffic, I crossed the street and approached Good Times. The tracker marked Jack's location; he still hadn't moved. I had to assume he was eating dinner; I smiled at the thought of interrupting his meal. Though the odds were vanishingly small that he was enjoying anything approaching the sublime dishes Choy created, I still took a petty pleasure in doing to him what he had done to me.

I walked inside and stopped in a small foyer to sneak a quick peek at the tracker. Jack had moved and was practically on top of me.

I looked up as the door in front of me opened.

Jack stood there, dapper as always, this time in matching black shirt and pants a few shades lighter than his skin. He smiled, clapped a hand on my shoulder, and chuckled at my surprise at the greeting.

"Good to see you, Jon," he said, "and about time, too."

I stared at him, then wondered why I was surprised. He'd always been this calm, this self-sure; I'd never know whether he was really waiting for me or simply handled my appearance well. I certainly couldn't trust anything he'd say on the topic.

When I didn't speak, he pulled me inside and motioned toward a table in the front right corner.

"I've been wondering when you'd finally get here."

CHAPTER TWENTY-SEVEN

When a bowl of soup and some fresh-smelling bread immediately appeared in front of me, I began to believe Jack might indeed have been expecting me. I shook my head. He'd rattled me, so I was giving him credit foolishly; serving food was, after all, what restaurants did.

Jack's meal was a plate of five types of cheese and some of the same bread that accompanied my soup. He spread a generous helping of a runny yellow cheese on a small chunk of bread and chewed it slowly, closing his eyes momentarily to focus on the taste. He looked at me and raised his right eyebrow.

I pushed aside my food, spooned a helping of the same cheese he'd eaten, took part of his bread, and made my own small sandwich. The strong, nutty, rich taste flooded my mouth; though I could see why he'd closed his eyes, I kept mine open and focused on him. I nodded my approval, leaned back, and waited.

"I suppose you'd like an apology," he said.

I tilted my head slightly and stared at him. I didn't know any conversational tricks he hadn't mastered, so I couldn't expect to get much from him, but it wouldn't hurt to try.

"If you examine the situation more closely, however," he continued, "I think you'll realize that though perhaps I did not treat you as well as I might have, in the end you walked away with more money than you had when I entered Falls."

If he was switching to sales mode, I was wasting my time. I leaned forward and said, "We're in a far bigger mess than you realize. I don't even know exactly how I'm going to get out of it. I do know that any resolution begins with Manu. Give him to me, Jack."

He sat back from the table, patted his mouth with a small white cloth napkin, put his hands delicately in his lap, and shook his head. "I can't do that, Jon."

"Remember saying that you needed my help in part because you were no good at violence and I was?"

He nodded.

I leaned far enough forward that my face was most of the way across the table. I gripped its edges so hard the veins on my hands stood out. "Then don't make me employ those skills with you, Jack. I will take the boy away from you if I have to." Adrenaline streaked through me as the anger rose.

Jack smiled and patted my right hand.

I trembled with the effort of not decking him.

"Look around, Jon," he said quietly. "I didn't run far in part because Dougat would be able to track me via jump-station bribes, but also because you'd find me here and let me know how bad our predicament really was. I knew you'd come, so I prepared. Neither of us wins if we don't work together."

For the first time since entering the place, I did what I should have done before I'd even passed through the doorway: I checked it out carefully and slowly. A pair of guys forty-five degrees left of Jack nodded gently at me, their hands not moving from their positions under the table. A second pair occupied another table ninety degrees further along the counterclockwise arc. I'd foolishly followed Jack to his location, so my back was to the doorway. I turned around and smiled at the man sitting behind me; his hands were also under his table.

I disgusted myself. Jack had caught me off guard, and I'd responded by treating him as an old friend who'd simply upset me. Let your emotions pollute an assignment, and you always pay a price. If all those men fired, given that their hands were at low levels, I probably wouldn't suffer a head wound. I was reasonably certain that the nanomachines could fix just about anything else, so I'd probably survive the barrage. Between the heavies and the bystanders, however, a lot of people would witness my rapid recovery, a process that would be sure to raise many, many questions—questions that could ultimately make me a corporation's lab animal once again. Would I then be willing to do the only thing that could stop it from happening: kill everyone here? No.

Jack didn't know any of this, however, so the first step in changing the power balance was to refuse to grant him control. I leaned forward again and very quietly said, "I can kill you before any of these guys can shoot. Send them away."

Jack maintained his relaxed posture, but he sounded less confident when he spoke. "I tell them to leave. You take me away and interrogate me, or maybe you risk annoying the rest of the patrons and stay here and make me tell you where Manu is." He shook his head slowly. "No, Jon. We can all relax, and I can have some of them back off, but there is no chance at all that I will sit here alone with you."

"You are seriously pissing me off, Jack. I won't stay with a man at my back." I swiveled my chair so I could watch that guy as well as the rest of them, then continued to speak to Jack without looking at him. "At the same time, I appreciate your situation. So, change seats with me so I have the corner, pull the crack team here behind you and to your left, and we can talk. Otherwise "—I swiveled to face him—" you will be the first to suffer." I turned back so I could keep all of the others in my view.

"I'd forgotten how paranoid you are, Jon," he said. "But that seems as good a resolution as any we're likely to reach."

He stood slowly and moved in front of the table. He motioned toward the man to my left and then to the others, and they all rose, several of them doing a bad job of feigning casual intent. I also stood, my hands in plain view against my thighs, then bumped Jack forward enough that I could slide between him and the table.

As Jack's men were in motion and I was passing behind him, I paused, grabbed his shirt with my left hand, and poked his sternum with two fingers of my right. "If I wanted to kill you," I said, smiling for the benefit of anyone watching, "you'd be dead now, and I'd have your body as a shield. You need better help." I let him go and sat. As best I could tell, the five bodyguards never realized how at risk their boss had been.

Jack sat and raised his hands. "What can I say? I don't have a crew here. I hired these five by the hour from the house security guy." He gestured with his head toward the floor above us. "Though the food here is more than tolerable, this place makes its real money from the 'and More' part of the business upstairs." He moved his plate and glass in front of him, took another bite of cheese and a drink, then sat back. "You said you were in trouble. What's happening?"

"No, Jack. I said *we* were in a big mess. You have as big a problem as I do."

"How's that?" Jack had regained control and again oozed calm.

"Remember your friend, Bakun Chaplat?" I leaned back. "He certainly remembers you."

"I'd ask how you made his acquaintance, but it doesn't really matter. He may be big on Mund, but we're on Gash, far away from his goons."

I shook my head slowly. "You need both new guards and better intel," I said. "He's here, he's searching for you, and he's brought some help. Better help than that lot you hired."

"I appreciate the warning, Jon. Perhaps it's time for me to leave this system. The heat should be off by now."

"Wrong again. You wouldn't make it out of the gate area, not even with the aid of your friend, Carne. The EC wants both you and Manu. Of course, they'd have to beat Dougat to you; he's here, too, and with multiple teams."

Jack said nothing. He closed his eyes for a few seconds. I'd seen him do this before when we were working out the details of cons, so I knew it was how he processed information when he felt he had the time to thoroughly consider a problem.

He opened his eyes and stared at me. "The fact that you know all this suggests you've met with all of these people. That you walked in here instead of any of them means I have something you want. I assume that's Manu."

I nodded in agreement.

"There's no way they would have talked to you without leaning on you," he continued. "So you and I are definitely in this together. I may not be able to get away, but unless you really think you can survive an encounter with all five of these admittedly cut-rate security contractors, keep me alive during the fight, and then get me to tell you where Manu is, you're also stuck." He smiled. "I'd say it's time for us to work together." His smile broadened. "It'll be like old times. We always made a great team."

My first reaction was to punch him in the throat both for getting me into this situation and for his smug assessment, but I forced myself to breathe slowly and deeply and sit still. I'd planned to find a way to satisfy all three groups on my own, but I had to admit that I didn't know exactly how I would do that. I was fairly confident I hadn't done anything to make that task harder, but I was a long way from a detailed solution to the problem. Having Jack with me could make this a whole lot easier. I also had the promise of money and, as long as Maggie stayed rational, some backup Jack didn't own.

"Maybe you're right," I said. "And there's even a potentially big payday here, if we can make everything go perfectly."

"How big?" he said.

"Very—and I'm willing to share it with you, if we can make this work."

"What's the catch, and what exactly are we trying to make happen? Do you have a plan?"

"The catch is that I walk away with Manu. We both earn some money, and we both end up with everyone off our backs—or so I hope."

"I repeat: Do you have a plan?"

"Not exactly," I said, shaking my head. "More like the outline of a plan, or at least a few ideas in the general direction of a plan."

"Hence your need for me," he said.

It struck me then that despite roping me into all of this, drugging me, using me, and generally trashing my life, Jack was going to make a lot of money. I was torn between anger and admiration.

"How do you do it, Jack?" I said.

He raised an eyebrow but didn't reply.

I shook my head. "It doesn't matter. Do you agree that I get Manu when this is over?"

"What do you hope to do with him?"

The concern in Jack's voice seemed genuine, though assuming any emotion he showed was real was always a risky move. "Transport him somewhere safe, probably back to his family, but somewhere far from all this."

"Your word?" Jack knew me well enough to realize that if I gave my word, I always kept it.

"Yes," I said. "So, are we agreed?"

He nodded. "Yes. When we're safely out of this predicament, Manu leaves with you, and you drop him somewhere they can't find him."

"Okay," I said. "Now let's figure out what we're going to do."

Jack leaned back, clasped his hands over his flat stomach, and closed his eyes.

"Run it down for me," he said.

CHAPTER TWENTY-EIGHT

"So in the name of helping Manu," Jack said some while later, "you've managed to sell him to the EC, promise him to a cult of Pinkelponker fanatics, make a related illegal arms deal, and leave all of them pissed at you." He smiled and added, "Did I miss anything?"

"When you say it like that," I said, "I have to admit it doesn't sound too good. I'm sure we can make it work, though, and we can definitely earn some serious money if we do."

"We just have to figure out how," Jack said.

"Yeah," I agreed, "we just have to figure out how."

"I thought I'd taught you to always plan the con *before* you start it," he said, "not as you go along."

"And I thought friends didn't drag each other into trouble like this. You do *not* want to start criticizing me after all you did to cause this mess."

He laughed lightly. "Fair enough. What matters now is how we move forward." He sat silently for almost a minute, then said, "How about a pot of gold?"

"Too many buyers, plus Manu doesn't fit," I said.

"A race phone for the EC?"

"It would get them to the right place, but Dougat and Chaplat would have no reason to play."

"Hey," he said, "I'm brainstorming. Give me a little time. You're not exactly bursting with ideas."

I nodded agreement and pondered the situation.

We went back and forth for the better part of two hours, tossing out classic con structures and trying to adapt them to our situation. You rarely work more than one mark at a time, however, so nothing quite fit our three-party problem, nor did anything meet the additional requirement of saving Manu in the bargain.

Then it hit me.

"How well connected are you here?" I said.

"Well enough to know which people we'd want for any type of job, but—" He paused and spread his hands. "—also well enough known by the same people that we'd have to show them some cash up front. No one here is going to work for me on the come."

"No surprise there," I said. "You obviously haven't changed your business practices." If you weren't part of Jack's core team—which I fortunately was during the years we worked together—he considered it almost a sacred duty to try to con you out of your share of any haul. He said any money he filched from a weaker crew member was an educational expense that person would later benefit from incurring. "Fortunately, I have that jewel you left me." I had a lot more money than that, but I wanted Jack to know as little as possible about my financial situation. "Can you point me to some fences here? If so, I might be able to handle my end of the front money for anything we need."

"Absolutely," he said, "and I don't think you appreciate how great a gift it was, or you wouldn't worry at all about expenses. Even ten percent of the value of that thing is enough to cover most of the cost of the biggest con we've ever run."

He'd done it again. He'd led me to assume he was poor and to offer to pay, but he'd stolen many more gems than the one he'd left me, so he had plenty of money.

"What about your haul?" I said. "You started this trouble, so you should fund its resolution."

"Just making sure you're still on your game," he said. "But

because we're splitting the take, we should split the bank." He stuck out his hand. "Fair enough?"

I shook his hand but held tight and squeezed as I said, "Deal, but the split is by the number of gems we each have." I strained to keep smiling as I crushed his hand.

Jack fought to show nothing on his face, but his arm shook. "That's unfair, Jon. I earned those."

"And now you'll spend a little part of them. You got me into this, so you'll bankroll the bulk of the cost. You can always make more money, Jack; I'm offering you a chance to walk away with no one hunting you."

"Fair enough," he said.

I let go of his hand.

He pulled it back, casually put it under the table, and said, "So, why did you ask how connected I was?"

"Because we're going to need a crew."

He leaned forward with excitement. "What do you have in mind?"

"I think a modified treasure map with a bang might do it," I said, growing more and more convinced as the idea blossomed. "We'd have to find the right location, of course, as well as a very special twinsie—I have an idea for that—and at least a boomer and a couple of scrapers."

He considered the notion, then leaned forward. "I've never worked a treasure map with more than two, and even two is rare."

"But we have done it," I said. "Remember that time on—"

"Yeah, yeah, of course," he said, a huge smile punctuating the comment. "That was brilliant." The smile collapsed. "We have three here, though, so the problem remains."

"That's the beauty of it," I said. "We don't have three, not really. We have only two, provided—"

"Of course!" he said. "If you can make them—"

"I can." Running ideas back and forth with Jack, finishing each other's sentences—I'd forgotten how much I'd enjoyed this part of our time together. For all his flaws, Jack had a natural aptitude for the work and a mind quick enough that he could succeed at anything he'd bother to try.

"What about protection?"

"My faux PCAV," I said, "ought to be intimidating enough." Lobo would hate me calling him "faux," and he might not like his role, but he'd do it well.

"And me," he said. "That means I have to—"

"Yeah," I said. "It won't work any other way."

"But if it's your ship," he said, "then we need to call—"

"We most certainly do," I said, nodding my agreement, "and pronto. Time is short."

"None of this should be a major problem," he said, "as long as nothing has to stand up to close inspection."

"It shouldn't."

"We need a big setup," Jack said, "but I know a prime area to search: the abandoned base on the southeast edge of town."

"You'll scout it and find candidates?" I said.

"Sure. What about the boomer?"

"You set up—" I said.

"—and you finish," he said. "It could work."

"Any ideas for the scrapers?" I said. "This might skid sideways, so we need power and muscle, but we also need precision."

Jack closed his eyes and considered the problem. "The Zyuns," he finally said. "They're usually busy, but for a good payday and a spot of what they consider fun, which this definitely should be, they'll come. I'll need a few days to stretch out to them. A little money would help with that and with the site work."

"We covered that," I said, "and we're not going to keep wasting time on it. I'll take care of the expenses on my end, and you deal with yours. Your end's bigger because you have more gems."

He leaned back in his seat and sighed theatrically. "Fine. You can't blame a man for trying. My money or yours, though, it's still likely to take me a bit of time to reach the Zyuns."

"No worries," I said. "I have to talk to Maggie and get back to my ship before anyone notices."

"Will the woman be a problem?"

"Maggie," I said. "As I've told you, her name is Maggie Park, and either she'll help, or I'll keep her out of it."

Jack studied me for a minute. "You're making a mistake, Jon. You're already emotional about the boy, and now you're involved with the woman." He held up his hand. "Yes, I know their names, but the way I referred to them is precisely the point: Get cold and play inside the lines we draw, or it'll go nonlinear and no one will come out well."

Anger rose in me, and I wanted to hit him. I couldn't decide, though, what aspect of his statements infuriated me the most: the claim that I couldn't stay cool, his calm assurance in declaring that I was involved with Maggie when I clearly was not, or, I finally had to admit, his accuracy in noting that I *wished* I were involved with Maggie. None of that mattered, though; saving Manu and surviving without Dougat, Chaplat, or Midon destroying us remained the top priorities.

"I'm cold enough, Jack," I said. Too cold, I thought but did not say, at least if you ask Maggie. "You check possible locations, I'll take care of my tasks, and we'll meet as soon as you have something to show me." I didn't mention that part of my problem was figuring out a way to take Manu away from him; if the plan worked, that part should fall out nicely. I pulled the spare milspec encrypted comm unit from my inside pocket and put it on the table between us. "Take this, and call me when you're ready."

He swept it into his hand, and it vanished. "Will do."

"One last thing," I said.

"Yes?"

"If you decide to run, I'll turn all three groups on you, and I'll chase you myself. You'll be lucky if one of them catches you before I do."

"I'm hurt, Jon," he said. "We're back as a team, we're working together, and a big payday is in sight. I've never failed you on a con."

"No, you haven't. Don't let this be the first time."

I stood and left.

As I hit the street and grabbed a cab to transport me to the rendezvous point, I started rehearsing the conversation ahead.

Any way I looked at it, Maggie was not going to like this plan.

❦　　❦　　❦

By the time I'd reached Lobo and we'd settled into a secure orbital position nestled among a group of weather and high-encryption data sats, the night had surrendered to the day and all I wanted was to sleep.

Maggie had other ideas: She demanded a recap of my meeting with Jack. Lobo was also curious. I ran down the highlights for them, though I didn't explain the plan; at this stage, the fewer the people who knew it, the better. Plus, I was beginning to accept that because Maggie couldn't control her reactions well enough to be a fully informed player, I might have to use her ignorance. Much as she'd hate the idea, if it helped us save Manu, I had to hope she'd forgive me in the end.

As I recounted the key points of our conversation, Maggie's eyes narrowed and her cheeks flushed.

The moment I stopped talking, she started. "You did what?" she said. "You made a deal with that kidnapper?"

"We don't know that he kidnapped Manu," I said. "The last time I saw them together, Manu seemed to trust him. I don't believe he would hurt the boy."

"Why are you defending a man who drugged you, abandoned you, and left you with three dangerous groups pursuing you?"

"I'm not trying to defend him," I said, though I had to admit I was doing just that. "I'm explaining how we're going to rescue Manu and end all of this trouble."

"It worked out so well with Jack last time," she said, "that I can see why you'd want to partner with him again."

"There's a crucial difference between then and now: I'm driving this plan, and I understand what's going on."

"Why not simply take Manu and run?"

"First, I don't know where Manu is, and forcing Jack to tell me would be risky at best; he is, as I told you, traveling with protection. Second, even if we did persuade Jack to give us Manu, we wouldn't get far without having to fight—and thus put Manu at more risk—because none of these groups is going to let us leave this system without challenging us."

"So we have to rely on Jack?"

"If you have a better plan," I said, "then let's hear it." I took a deep breath to try to stop myself from sounding as angry and frustrated as I was. "Otherwise, we're doing it my way."

She took her time and considered the problem. I wanted to turn my back on her and grab some sleep, but to be fair I had to wait and hear what she had to say.

After a couple of minutes, she said, "No, I don't have a better idea. As you might imagine, I've been worrying about our situation during all the hours you've left me alone. Every time I think I have a good solution, I discover major flaws in it. You've done a lot of things I don't understand, but you've been consistent in trying to resolve everything and at least appearing most of the time to be trying to save Manu, so I'll shut up and do what I can to help."

"Thank you," I said.

"I can offer alternatives," Lobo said.

"I know you can," I said, "but I'm also quite confident they'll all involve more violence than I want."

"Given where we are," Lobo said, "some violence is inevitable. So, we're only discussing how much. I can track you and take out anyone helping Jack, and I can certainly destroy the ships Dougat and Chaplat were using to monitor us."

"And the EC?" I said. "You'd blast its ships, too?"

"Not all of them, of course," Lobo said, annoyance evident in his voice. "I know my limitations, so I understand that even in this backwater region of space the EC maintains more combat craft than I could possibly handle. I do believe, however, that I could disable or destroy enough of them that we could leave this system and make a sufficiently high number of jumps that the EC would be extremely unlikely to bother to follow us. It simply wouldn't be economically reasonable."

"So the best case is that we spend the rest of our lives avoiding this section of space, and the worst case is that the EC recruits the help of other federations? Is that about right?"

"Perhaps," Lobo said, "though the universe is vast, and the EC might well lose interest."

I shook my head in disgust, not at Lobo, who was behaving

according to his personality/programming, but at myself for allowing him to draw me into a debate on his terms. "No," I said. "I'm not going to argue with you, because I'm not pursuing any option that demands we kill multiple people. I've done more of that in my life than I want. I'll do it again if I have to, but if I can avoid it, I will." I didn't tell him that I could have taken Jack on my own, right there in the bar, simply by using the nanomachines to kill everyone else. I might even have been able to simply scare them away, though any use of the nanomachines in front of so many people puts me at great risk of discovery. I then could have tortured Jack until he gave up Manu—and he would have, he had no training in resistance, and even if he did, everyone breaks eventually. If not for a friend and colleague rescuing me from torture the last time a megacorp was hunting me, I would certainly have broken. After Jack told me where to find Manu, I could have gone there and destroyed anyone in my way. I didn't even know the limits of what the nanomachines could do, but I suspected that if I were willing to turn them loose in full-on self-replication mode with no self-destruct guidance, they might be able to take out a planet or even more. I'd watched Aggro disappear, so massive destruction was definitely possible. The fact that I had this power, though, did not mean I had to use it. I would not let what I *could* do become what I *would* do. I would create the best set of options I could, and as much as possible, I would avoid killing. If I never killed again, I'd be better for it—but never free of the stains of the past. There was no way to remove that damage. "No," I said, suddenly aware that I'd been standing silently for an awkward amount of time. "No, we're not doing that."

"Your choice, of course," Lobo said.

I focused again on Maggie, who was staring at me intently. She reached out and gently held my left cheek with her hand, then pulled back and stared, as if she'd touched something slimy. I didn't blame her; most people don't like being around killers. I looked away from her before her face showed more of her disgust; I didn't want to see her look at me that way. I preferred to remember that brief moment in the hangar, when she was modeling the dress and I stupidly abandoned reality and imagined I might have a chance to build a future with her.

"We'll work out the details as we go along," I said, "and I'll tell each of you what you need to do as necessary." I turned my back and headed to bed. "For now, I'm going to grab some sleep. Maggie, you may want to do the same."

Under my breath, not willing to say it loudly enough that it might provoke another argument but also unable or unwilling to keep the fact entirely to myself, I added, "Jack'll be calling soon enough."

CHAPTER
TWENTY-NINE

"Last chance to try at least this part of it my way," Lobo said as we touched down on the northwestern edge of the abandoned base. "Jack brought three men as backup. Their spacing is good, each has shelter on at least one side, each is near a corner, and no one is in anyone else's line of fire, so they're probably pros. Nonetheless, I could alter our approach path quickly enough to give me clear shots at all of them. He'd then be yours."

"Again, no," I said. "He told me he'd bring protection, so I have no problem with their presence." I didn't expect Jack to do anything stupid, but in case I was wrong I added, "If I signal for help or anyone opens fire, take them out."

"I should be so lucky," Lobo said. "You might as well own a taxi for all the good my capabilities are doing you."

"Your role is vital," I said, "as I'll explain later."

Lobo opened a hatch, and I stepped into a perfect, sunny morning, a slight breeze blowing and soft white clouds dotting the sky. I don't know if it was my imagination or real, but I would have sworn that the light wind carried the scent of the base's abandonment. Three once-deadly security barriers slashed across the paved ground between us and the facility proper, but they reeked of age and sadness, guards so wounded and tired but still so well built that they could neither do their jobs nor die. The outermost divider, a ten-meter-high fence of woven slash metal and artificial diamond blades, gleamed dangerously in some areas but lay harmlessly in others, holes blasted through it and large chunks of it broken down or hauled away by looters. Next in line stood a five-meter-tall permacrete wall that sparkled as the morning light struck the shards of glass and cheap local minerals embedded in it. A three-meter-high, formerly electrified metal fence had once formed the final defensive barrier, but you could tell where it had stood only by spotting the scraps so embedded in permacrete supports that they must not have been worth salvaging. Scratches in the ground between the three ravaged defenders and along the barriers themselves suggested the paths robotic guards and crawlers had worn on endless variations of their patrol routes.

The EC had once wrapped this base and its thousands and thousands of tons of armaments with security strong enough to repel many ground attacks and buy time in the face of even the worst land-based assaults, and I assumed that the air defenses had been equally formidable. Now, though, the place was sad.

With no power feeding any of the defenses and no one to stop them, opportunistic locals had bulldozed and blasted access paths large enough to let through demolition teams and freight haulers. Permacrete, the main material of the frames of all the office buildings, barracks, supply depots, hangars, repair facilities, and other structures that composed the huge base, was cheaper to lay than to move, so the shells of those constructs still stood.

Almost everything else was gone. With the exception of a few sections of the outermost barrier, all the metal, everything from signposts to security fences to doors, was missing. Window frames sat empty. Tiny stumps still embedded in the ground marked where signs had stood. Everywhere I looked, the permacrete survived alone, the last remaining bones of the dead EC base.

Jack stood inside a small guardhouse forty meters away. He was smart enough not to approach me, to let me come when I was ready. He knew I'd run a perimeter check before I entered. I hoped Jack still believed Lobo was an imitation PCAV, because I wanted every possible edge should the con man turn on me again.

I spotted no problems beyond the guards Lobo had noted and I had expected.

"Still clean except for the three soldiers," Lobo said on the machine frequency, "as is the airspace over us. We have to consider the possibility that we're being watched by at least one of the pursuing groups, so I suggest you keep me close."

"Agreed," I subvocalized. My guess was that Midon would keep her EC ships at bay a bit longer, and Chaplat was likely to stay back for a few more days as well, but Dougat might well be monitoring us. We'd scanned the whole area in IR and spotted nothing that appeared anywhere near Manu's size, so if Dougat was watching, I hope he'd done the same and was leaving me alone to work on Jack.

If Dougat chose to charge in, then we'd have to fall back to Lobo's plan and take out his ship—but only if the man was that stupid. I didn't want that to be the case. To save Manu and get out of this mess without having to run forever, I needed to make the plan work.

I was wasting time worrying about what might happen. I needed to evaluate Jack's proposed location to see if it met our requirements, and then get out of there.

I walked toward Jack. As I approached him, the three men tightened the triangle they formed around him. When I was five meters away, I stopped, lifted my arms slightly to my sides, and let them see that I wasn't carrying any obvious weapons.

I also used the time to study them. I started with a quick scan of the man on my right, but as I checked out the other two I realized something odd: They appeared to be identical. Each stood about thirty centimeters shorter than I, but I estimated each to also be at least ten and maybe twenty kilos heavier, all of the additional weight muscle. Very few men choose to be that short, so these guys must have elected to stick with their birth height. I would have thought them anti-tech types from that one fact alone, but there was no way they could have built that much muscle naturally. Each wore a sleeveless night-black bodysuit that followed every contour of his body as if it were water rippling over a stone-filled stream, but as I looked closer I noticed the material was thick enough that it had to be lightweight armor. Muscle rippled under the garments and on their exposed arms, which were so ripped they resembled anatomy holos. Each man was pale with hair that matched the bodysuit and a day-old beard growth that was so perfectly uniform it had to exist for style, not function, the look one that had long been popular throughout the bodyguard circuit on dozens of planets. Visible in all of their ears were combo comm/audio-canceling units; they could stand under rocket engines firing and hear no more than the sound of a strong wind blowing. Rugged faces, chins wide enough to suggest both hormone-enhanced bones and no desire to do anything about it, and thick necks—everything about these three was built for combat.

They'd also come armed for action. Each carried one handgun, had two more visible in shoulder and waist holsters, and wore a back pack that included a rifle within easy reach. From the size of the pack, more weapons were probably inside it. None of the men moved or looked as if he even noticed the weight he was carrying.

Of course, I might have been misreading them, because I couldn't see their eyes: active-glass shields locked directly onto their eye sockets. The covers were cycling lazily through a variety of images, all of them disturbing: bloodshot eyes, serrated and bloody knives, mushroom clouds, and explosions of various sorts. Socket-locked eye protection was excellent for combat, with no blind spots and total protection, but the mods necessary to keep them in place left you with unattractive connector holes around each eye until the replacement cells grew enough to fill in the pits. These guys were either extreme fashion followers or very serious about their work. Given their size, I assumed the latter.

"An unusual trio, aren't they, Jon?" Jack said. When I didn't respond, he continued. "I'm being terribly rude," he said. "Let me introduce you to the Zyuns."

I nodded my head but didn't say a word.

All three Zyuns nodded in unison.

I stared at each of them again in turn, but I still couldn't tell them apart.

"Friends of yours?" I said.

"No," the one directly in front of me said.

"Simply," the one to my right said.

"Contractors," the one to my left finished.

"You're free to hire them after today," Jack said, "but until the day is over, I've paid for their time and protection."

"True identical triplets?" I said, still curious.

"No," Jack said. "May I?"

The three Zyuns nodded as one.

"Talking, at least to others, isn't their strong point," Jack said. "As I understand it, they were fraternal triplets before their mother started applying the best science she could afford so she could use her sons to secure her control over the colony she ruled. All that work made them as identical as possible without completely redoing their DNA. The lenses include cameras that relay what each one sees to the others' battle-style displays. The earpieces and embedded mics maintain constant communication among them. They're augmented with continual muscle stimulation, hormones, adrenaline, and who knows what else. When their mother died, they went into private practice. They live and train and meditate together as one."

"Who leads?" I said.

"We all do," all three said simultaneously. "All are one in the now."

I shook my head. I'd never seen a unit with more than one commander that could do well when the heat came. On the other hand, I'd never met any group quite like these three. "Whatever works for you guys."

"You can't deny the combat advantages of three simultaneous perspectives and squadmates you can absolutely count on," Jack said.

"Fair enough," I said, even though he was wrong. For as long as I've known anything about professional fighting teams, they've been able to share multiple viewpoints on heads-up displays. As for trusting the person next to you, I suppose that might be a problem in some units—but it was never an issue for me in the Saw.

Nonetheless, the Zyuns enjoyed a relationship that was, in my experience, unique. "I have to ask," I continued, "how did you guys get from a mother with enough money to pay for all this engineering"—I waved my hand to take in the three of them—"to working freelance security on Gash?"

"Not the deal," they said, each one voicing one word. "Only now matters."

They were right. I didn't like it when people asked about my past, so I had no trouble respecting their privacy. I wondered if they consciously chose to make every sentence contain a multiple of three words.

Weirdness aside, we needed scrapers, and if Jack was willing to pay them to protect him from me, they might work out for our needs. As I considered it further, having the three of them with their high degree of connectedness could prove useful.

I'd think more about it when we'd finished here. Right now, we had to see the site Jack thought might work. "Let's go," I said. "I don't want to spend any more time here than I absolutely have to, and I've already lingered too long. Show me the space."

On cue, Lobo rose and positioned himself to follow us from fifty meters above. He wouldn't let Jack or the Zyuns out of range.

One Zyun turned his attention to Lobo; the other two stayed focused on me.

Jack motioned toward Lobo. "I'm hurt, Jon," he said. "Do you honestly believe you need that level of protection against me?"

I answered his question with one of my own. "Do you honestly believe you'd still be alive if I wanted you dead?" I said.

"Not a chance," the Zyuns said in their three-voice alternation. "But for now, we are here."

"The space, Jack," I said, motioning him along. "Lead on."

He shrugged and started walking. We turned left and went parallel to the innermost barrier for two hundred meters, then stopped in front of what had clearly once been a repair facility of some sort. About a hundred and fifty meters wide and maybe twenty meters tall, it wasn't large enough for any of the major space transports but would hold quite a few of just about any other military surface ships the EC would operate, as well as PCAVs and other craft similar to Lobo. Large openings across the front and indentations in the ground and the top of the huge doorframes marked where scavengers had stolen the metal doors that had once been able to seal the place. The building's depth was hard to gauge from this angle, but I guessed it to be at least half as deep as it was wide.

"Lobo," I subvocalized. "Building status?"

"Unable to scan beyond the first few meters I can read through the open doorway. Not a surprise: If the EC used it to repair sensitive vehicles, they would have embedded signal-blocking mesh layers in the permacrete and used relayed wireless feeds to the outside for communication."

"Come inside and check it out," Jack said.

"Want me to follow you inside?" Lobo said. "It's big enough."

"If necessary," I subvocalized, "but as long as you have a clear shot on them, stay outside."

"Coming," Lobo said.

"In a moment," I said to Jack.

Lobo settled to a hover a meter above the ground and ten meters behind me. He was running as quiet as possible, but the noise still made conversation difficult.

Jack shook his head, grinned at me, and walked into the empty building. The Zyuns maintained formation and followed him. Either they were smart enough to know there was no point in forming a human barrier around Jack, because Lobo's weapons could go right through them, or he hadn't paid them enough to be willing to take a shot for him. From their initial reactions and the fact that Jack was willing to hire them, I guessed the former. Good; I liked working with realistic people.

"Now I'm ready," I shouted to Jack.

I stepped inside and surveyed the place. Light streaming in from the front and from empty windows along the sides illuminated the space enough that I could see all the way to the back wall. Large, vacant doorframes stood along the rear of each side, so we had a total of three entrance/exit options. Excellent.

Something about the back wall was off. When I studied it more closely, the answer was obvious: It was two walls that overlapped for only half a dozen meters.

I noticed Jack watching me. He grinned when I turned to face him.

"That's the best part," he said. "Each rear wall section runs about sixty percent of the way across the back, with a gap between them about three meters wide and an overlap large enough that it takes a moment to tell there are two. I figure they used the actual back section of the place for parts storage, repair benches, and so on."

"How big is that area?" I said.

He nodded enthusiastically. "More than twenty-five meters deep and the length of the building. Two doorways feed it, one on each end, each one about thirty meters wide."

"More than big enough to shield us," I said.

"Which makes everything simpler," he said, smiling broadly.

"So we have doors to install and all the other prep work to do," I said, "as well as the electronics, the rest of the stuff we discussed, and the big gear. How long?"

"Everything's already in progress," Jack said, "and fortunately most of what we needed was in stock with my suppliers. So, two days to get it here. The Zyuns have meshed me with the right kind of construction people, and nothing we have to do is particularly hard. Call it a conservative four to five days for them to do their work."

"Once I start this rolling, there's no changing it," I said. I considered Jack's estimates. He was almost certainly padding them to be safe, because the construction and setup we needed really wasn't that hard. On the other hand, it would involve multiple machines, some big chunks of metal for the doors, and a fair amount of labor and coordination, so I wanted to be absolutely safe. "Six days. You have six days."

"*I* have six days," Jack said. "What about *you*? And what about money? Pulling this off in that amount of time is going to cost a small fortune."

"Each time you have to pay one of your contractors," I said, "consider the size of the score, not to mention the peace of mind you stand to make off this plan."

I watched as he evaluated his possible arguments, then realized there was no point in bothering with them. I had the stronger position, and he knew it. Even so, those gems must have been worth far more than I'd thought, or he would have given it a try.

"Fine, fine, Jon," he said. "Stick me with everything. You didn't answer my other question, though: What about you? What are you going to do while I'm managing all the hard work?"

I ignored him and walked over to the nearest Zyun. I pulled out my wallet, thumbed it to receive in a high-quarantine area, and said, "I'd like to hire you later. Interested?"

All three nodded, and my wallet trembled its reception of their contact information. I didn't see any of them move to send it to me. "Only when you're done with Jack."

"One more day," the three said in the usual one-word-apiece response pattern.

"Wait on Mund," I said, "if you're serious."

"Jon," Jack said. "I'm tired of your attitude toward me. Answer my question: While I'm spending my money and working, what are you going to be doing to help?"

"Risking my life," I said, as I headed back to Lobo, "first by annoying several very angry and very powerful people, and then by explaining to them how I can make their wishes come true."

CHAPTER THIRTY

"I'm trying as hard as I can to trust you and be patient," Maggie said, each word coming slowly and with obvious effort.

"And I appreciate it very much," I said. I wasn't paying as close attention as I wanted, but we were docking with the jump-gate station, so I had to prepare for my meeting with Midon.

"So when are you going to explain exactly what you're doing and how it's going to save Manu?" she said.

The station filled the display Lobo had opened. The structure was already almost entirely clean of Gatist paint, courtesy of the bots that were now crawling over the few remaining red bits. I forced myself to ignore it, focused on Maggie, and considered her request. Her beauty and the degree to which I found her attractive made that difficult, and I couldn't help but recall momentarily the look in her eyes in the hangar when she was showing off her new dress, but none of that mattered; the anger I'd seen before I'd left to find Jack made it clear to me that we'd never have a relationship. Still, if for no reason other than her dedication and attempts to help, Maggie deserved an answer to her question.

The problem was, I couldn't trust her not to reveal what she knew to others.

590   *Mark L. Van Name*

No matter what her agenda, her face gave away so much information that I feared in a critical moment she might jeopardize us all by what her expressions revealed. I couldn't count on her acting abilities, so the only prudent option was to keep her in the dark and at times even take advantage of her ignorance. She might hate me later for it, but all of us, including Manu, would be safer if I chose that path.

"I'm not," I said, holding up my hands and trying to sound calm and reasonable. "I'll tell you what you need to know when you need to know it, but not before. We're much more likely to succeed this way, and the only chance Manu has at a safe life away from these people is for us to accomplish our goals."

I expected anger, and indeed it swept across her face like storm winds rippling across a lake, but hurt replaced it. "When are you going to trust me?" she said.

I struggled to find a way to explain that her question was much more complex than she realized, that you could trust someone's intentions but not their skills, or that you might trust both of those things and still for safety reasons not depend on them in a plan, but I couldn't think of an explanation that didn't make my thought processes sound even worse than she already believed they were.

"Docked," Lobo said. "Lock ready in five seconds."

I couldn't invest more time in this, because Midon had to know I was here. I had to move quickly to make it clear to her that I was both playing the game properly and respecting her appropriately.

"Lobo," I said, "as soon as I'm out, move to the same position you occupied in my last meeting with Midon. She may as well watch you out her viewport as we talk." To Maggie, I added, "I'm sorry, but I have to go."

Inside, the Gash jump-gate station could have been any station at any gate anywhere in the universe. No traces of the red paint remained. No red people thronged the halls. No party sounds filled the air. I shouldn't have expected anything different, and intellectually I didn't, but because my first experience here had been during the color wash, I'd unconsciously prepared myself to deal again with large masses of red revelers.

I had no way to know whether Dougat or Chaplat or both had people watching the station, so I couldn't simply ask for Midon. If she was anywhere near as competent as I believed she was, all I needed to do was create an acceptable excuse to talk to Carne, and she'd find me.

Easy enough.

I balled my fists, shook my head, grumbled to myself, and walked as if I were a man ready to burst with anger. I crashed down the hallway, ignoring everything to the side of me. I bumped into person after person, shoving aside each one I encountered and muttering under my breath about a denied jump application. I headed straight to the claims office that occupied the center of a hub of short corridors that led to docking ports for smaller vessels such as Lobo. I stepped to the door so quickly that I almost hit its edge as it retracted into the wall. I didn't break my stride until I was nose-to-top-of-skull with a rather startled man a good head shorter than I was. I interrupted him pouring a drink from a wall dispenser. The expression on his face made clear that he already regretted ever stepping from behind his counter.

"I demand to speak with the station agent!" I said, yelling so loudly the man's hair moved from the force of the sound.

He scurried back behind his counter before responding. "The complaints officer isn't here right now," he said, "so perhaps if you could come back later, he could help you."

I put both my hands on the surface that separated us and leaned over it. "Is there something unclear in what I said? Are you having trouble understanding me? I don't want the complaints officer; get me the station agent." I hit the counter with both fists, and it shook slightly from the force. "Now!"

He fingered his cuff; security was on the way. If Midon didn't have someone watching for me, I was about to have a very unpleasant conversation with some armed guards who had the right not only to escort me out but also to levy a substantial fine.

"Sir, I think you'll find—" He stopped talking and looked to the right, his attention suddenly elsewhere. He shook his head slightly, as if confused.

The door opened behind me.

My every instinct was to turn and attack the guards before they could reach me, but I was playing the role of someone dumb enough to yell at a low-level civil servant whose job was to absorb verbal and emotional shrapnel so his superiors never had to experience it. In that role, I had to let the guards come to me.

The man overcame his confusion and saved me. He looked at me, smiled, held up his right hand to stop the guards, and said, "These men will be happy to escort you to the office of Mr. Carne, the administrator in charge. He's waiting for you now."

"That's better," I said, staying in the role. I didn't want any more people aware of my relationship with Midon than I could possibly avoid.

The guards' stances signaled their hope that I'd do something stupid so they could have a little fun with me, but I clasped my hands and made it clear we wouldn't be fighting.

"After you," I said to them.

They glanced at the man behind the counter, but he must have nodded approval, because without saying anything they turned and walked out of the room. I followed them down the corridor. They slowed twice and even abruptly stopped once, but I stayed a meter and a half behind them the entire way. Bumping into them might have been all the excuse they needed to be able to claim before a disciplinary council that I'd initiated conflict. I didn't need to fall into that trap, though the more they delayed me the harder I found it to stop from getting angry and the more part of me wanted a fight to start.

When we reached Carne's office, I paused until they backed away from the door and opened a clear path inside.

The toy-filled room remained exactly as I'd left it, but as soon as I was inside, Midon stepped from her hiding place behind the first row of shelves to my left.

"I trust you have good news for me," she said.

"Do you ever let Carne use his own office?"

"I can't stand all this," she said, taking in the toys and the rows of shelves with a single sweep of her arm. "Let's go inside."

She went straight to the desk in the inner office and settled behind it. I checked the display to my right as I entered the room and resisted smiling at the sight of Lobo hovering outside. A single very large launcher hung beneath him in a ready position, as if he'd decided all the weapons he'd shown last time were overkill. I wondered if she took offense at the snub, or even if Lobo had meant the gesture as such, but I decided he must have. His snide side was quite entertaining when I wasn't its target.

Midon acted as if a PCAV hung outside her window every moment of every day, willing neither to opaque the display nor to discuss what was visible in it.

"Well," she said.

I waited but did not speak. As dealing with Jack had reminded me multiple times recently, the easiest way to change the balance of power in a conversation is to refuse to engage on any but your own terms. If I gave her control at this stage, she'd want to extend it to every aspect of the discussion to come. I couldn't afford that.

"I've taken more theory of interaction classes than you have," she said, "so why don't we stop wasting time? You're here, and you wanted my attention. You have it. You reaffirmed your independence with that thing," she flicked her hand in Lobo's direction, "and I'm suitably impressed. You don't want to acknowledge my power. Fine. We're peers." She leaned forward. "I really don't care about anything except getting what I want and then jumping to a civilized planet where I can put my career back on track. So, how would you like to proceed?"

Even though I knew that at some level her directness was simply another tactic, I still admired it. Any bureaucrat who could both identify the games in play and step away from them possessed more intelligence than most.

"Dougat and some of his people will be making a weapons deal," I said. "Other than interrupting it in progress, what else do you need?"

"The sale must include milspec stock, at least some of it suitable for vehicle installation or mounting, and significant quantities of several different items."

She'd obviously prepared her list, which I appreciated.

"I need more money," I said. I didn't, I had all the cash necessary for the operation, but saying anything else would have been out of character for what she expected from me—and, of course, more money wouldn't hurt.

"We have a deal," she said, "and additional funding isn't part of it."

"Yes," I said, "but at the time we made it, I didn't understand how much playing middleman would end up costing me."

"Middleman?"

"You think I'm buying the weapons?" I laughed. "You're smarter than that. Why would *I* want anything to do with any illegal activities? I'm just an honest man caught in a bad place by forces beyond his control."

A smile was the most I could get from her. "Your costs are your problem; make the deal large enough, and you'll be fine in the end. I don't care who the other party in the transaction is."

"You might."

She said nothing and waited for me to continue.

I waited with her. Lobo hung outside the window.

She sighed. "Okay, why?"

"You could take down Dougat and help clean up Mund in the process," I said.

"Chaplat?"

I nodded.

"Interesting," she said, "and, yes, that would be useful—but not useful enough to warrant more money."

"But if you captured part of his gang in the deal?"

"Our arrest teams will take everyone we catch," she said. "Including you. Of course, I can try to arrange to give you—"

"Not me," I said, cutting her off. "Either we agree that I exit before you enter, or you'll find out about the sale after the fact."

I'd annoyed her, but she kept it under control, the only sign being the long pause before she said, "That's acceptable. You should have no problems, but Dougat and Chaplat and their teams won't fare so well."

"And if they fight back?"

"I assume they will," she said, her smile returning, "which will only save us processing costs."

"I'll make sure I'm well away from there," I said. "Look, if you're not going to give me any additional advance, then I'll need payment three days after you arrest Dougat and seize the weapons."

"Any time you want after we have them," she said. "You can trust us that far."

I laughed. "I don't trust any government to do anything that's not in its self-interest," I said, "but I am confident that neither of us needs the recordings we both possess to be sprayed across every data stream in this region."

Her only acknowledgment of the threat was to tilt her head slightly. "When's the sale?"

"Sometime in the next six to eight days," I said. "You'll get no more than an hour's notice, so you'll need to keep a team on ready in each major city on Gash. Make them good units, trained for urban and rural stealth approaches, and not small ones, either. I can't know in advance the number of hostiles on either side."

"I need a day to make that happen," she said. "After that, we'll be ready."

I took out my wallet and thumbed open a quarantined area. "Give me a signal protocol you won't miss," I said, "and send me your weapons wish list. I won't guarantee to get everything on it, but I'll do my best."

She nodded and tapped for a moment on the desk. My wallet chirped its acceptance.

"Multiple teams will cost me a lot," she said.

"Not my problem. You said you wanted Dougat badly. You ignored my costs. And I assume the assets you plan to confiscate greatly outvalue the expense of security squads you're already paying anyway."

She nodded. "Are we done?"

"Not quite," I said. "You'll be tempted to have your people

follow me from here on. Don't. Stay back, or you'll destroy everything I'm setting up. Your teams are too easy to spot."

"I can get better people," she said.

"Maybe, but if Dougat, Chaplat, or I spot even one of them, this whole deal will evaporate faster than a puddle in the middle of Gash's desert. Are you willing to take that chance?"

"Okay," she said, "we continue to leave you alone and to not track you." She put her hands on the desk, stood, and leaned over it. "Make sure I hear from you in eight days. If I don't—"

I cut her off. "Understood. I'll contact you when I'm ready."

"The boy?" she said.

I paused and tried to relax enough to show the real guilt I felt at the risks I was taking with Manu. "He'll be there," I finally said. "You're paying me for making him appear. That's it. Once he shows up, I'm done. Getting him away from the people who have him is your problem."

"Of course," she said.

I shook my head in disgust and turned to leave.

"Don't feel bad, Moore," she said. "The larger the deal, the more your ten percent brings you. That plus a quarter-million bonus for the boy should make this a rich payday."

I didn't trust myself to say anything useful, so I didn't speak or turn around as I left the room and headed back to Lobo.

One set, two to go.

CHAPTER THIRTY-ONE

"You can't be sure he'll believe you," Maggie said. "He's already lost the boy once, so he'll be doubly cautious now."

"There's no way around it," I said. "Jack won't let me have Manu, and even if I could get him, I wouldn't put the kid in front of Dougat again at this stage. I've strung Dougat along this far; I just have to keep doing so for a few more days."

"I can help," Maggie said. "I know—"

I held up my hand, and she stopped talking. She was back to the calm Maggie, and that was encouraging, but I couldn't take the chance of her sparking further troubles by melting down at the wrong time. "I appreciate it," I said, "but—"

"Why won't you hear her out?" Lobo said. "Her performance in the jump station was less than useful—"

"Thanks a lot, Lobo," Maggie said, cutting him off.

"You're welcome," Lobo said.

I couldn't help but smile, and from the look on Maggie's face, that wasn't my best choice. It's simply that I so rarely heard his sarcasm target anyone else that I enjoyed the moments when it did.

"And she has shown a lack of combat readiness," Lobo continued, "but that doesn't mean all her ideas are without merit.

We discussed her proposal while you were with Midon, and it is worthy of consideration."

"That's some endorsement," Maggie said.

"An accurate one," Lobo said. "Would you have me provide anything else, especially given your professed concern over the boy?"

"No," she admitted. "I do think, though, that we could improve your sales technique."

"Why would I try to sell?" Lobo said. "If I wanted money from someone, I'd train enough weapons on him that he'd happily transfer the payment to me."

Maggie rolled her eyes. "Don't play dumb literal machine with me. You know exactly what I meant."

"Yes," Lobo said, "and my point remains: I wasn't selling anything. I was providing Jon with accurate guidance—counsel he'd be wise to consider."

"Are you two done?" I said. Even when they argued with each other, I came out on the losing side. Still, if Lobo said I should listen, I would. Plus, Maggie was staring wide-eyed at me and trusting herself to my judgment; how could I let her down? "Maggie, I apologize for not hearing you out. What are you proposing?"

"Though I didn't spend much time with him, I studied Dougat. All of us did; after all, he was the leader of the whole group, and we felt privileged to be able to work close to him. I know more about how he thinks than you do, so I can help make him more likely to believe that you actually have Manu." She paused.

I listened and said nothing. I'd told her I'd give her a chance, so I would.

After a few seconds, she continued. "Where are you planning on meeting him?"

"I hadn't picked a place, but probably in the desert again. It worked last time, and it's easy to defend."

"Don't," she said. "Yes, it was fine last time, but now you have to convince him that he's in control and you're in this for the money. Use the Followers' temple in Malzton instead. It's in the middle of a heavily populated area, so he won't want any more firing than he authorized in the temple in Eddy back on Mund. For all the noise and smoke, that wasn't very much and wouldn't have happened at all without Manu's vision. The landing area behind this building is more than big enough to hold us, and they won't have any weapons in the facility powerful enough to hurt Lobo. If Dougat did, the EC would have taken him already." She paused again.

"I'm not saying the idea is bad," I said. "It's very reasonable. Dougat isn't dumb enough, however, to let a friendly location instantly make him believe everything I say."

"Of course not," she said, smiling broadly. "But it will put him in the right frame of mind to believe me."

"You? He doesn't even know I have you. If anything, he assumes you went AWOL after the mess on Eddy."

"He'll know when you sweeten the pot by showing him the prisoner you're willing to return as part of the deal, the prisoner you captured on Eddy."

"And then you can attest—"

"—that you have the boy," she said. "I can tell Dougat I've seen Manu, he's well, and I really want to rejoin the group. Followers rarely leave. He'll believe me."

I considered the proposal. It was fundamentally sound, and I definitely could use more ways to persuade Dougat to stay in the deal and supply the weapons. At the same time, I'd kept Maggie out of most of this because she hadn't demonstrated very good acting skills, and I didn't want to have to depend on them. "You'd have to be persuasive," I said, struggling to express the concern in a way that wouldn't offend her further. I wasn't used to thinking about the feelings of anyone other than a target while formulating a plan, so I found myself at a bit of a loss.

"I understand," she said. "I haven't shown you much to make you believe that I can carry off a convincing role. All I have to be with Dougat, however, is scared. Hold a gun to me, put me in the middle of this meeting, and, trust me, I'll be plenty afraid." Her voice strained a bit. "I already am, just thinking about it."

She was right. Her lines didn't need to be perfect. All she had to remember was that she'd seen Manu and he was fine, and I could prompt her if it came to that. Her fear was real, and that would sell. I hated the coldness with which I considered what this would cost her, but she'd made the offer, and my job was to evaluate it as objectively as possible.

"Okay," I said. "You're right. You're right about the location, and you're right that your presence as a prisoner could help persuade him that we have Manu."

Maggie smiled.

"Aren't you glad you listened to me?" Lobo said.

Though it pained me to do so, I said, "Yes."

Aerial views of the Followers' temple in Malzton snapped onto a display Lobo opened in front of us. Approach vectors pointed to the landing area.

"These are the best entrance and exit paths," Lobo said. "What else do we need before we contact Dougat?"

"Let me walk you through the rest," I said, "and then I'll set it up."

From above, the Malzton Followers' Institute—their official name for their temples everywhere—resembled a wilted version of the one I'd seen in Eddy. Dougat apparently invested his construction funds according to the wealth of the potential audience, a wise move for any con man. Like its Eddy counterpart, this building was a ziggurat, but an uneven one, as if during the building's construction the human members of the team had been drunk and their robotic coworkers using most of their computing capacity to fight nasty viruses. Even at a distance we could see that the right side narrowed more rapidly from top to bottom than the left; Lobo gauged the whole thing as tilting slightly to the right. The grounds sported collections of plants and relaxation areas like the Institute in Eddy, but here they seemed haphazard, a random walk garden.

We rocketed Gashward at a sharp angle and came to a stationary hover less than a meter above the landing area behind the rear of the building. We were one minute early. Lobo showed multiple weapons, more than enough to wipe out everything for blocks around, and we waited.

When Dougat didn't immediately appear, I said, "Is he really the type to play this sort of petty power game?"

"Yes," Maggie said. "I told you as much."

"You did," I said, nodding. "I'm just always surprised by this kind of behavior when I encounter it."

"I could motivate him to appear more quickly," Lobo said. "These gardens aren't particularly more artful than bare earth."

"No," I said, "but thank you for that redecorating offer."

Three minutes later, Dougat stepped out of the building and stood in the shade by the door.

"His support?" I said.

"The rear of the temple is IR shielded, so I can't know what's inside," Lobo said. "I count four snipers within my sensor range, which should be more than broad enough to let me spot all likely attackers."

"Paint 'em," I said.

"Done."

"How are you painting them?" Maggie said.

I looked at her and shook my head. "You're a prisoner, remember? Stay in character. Speak when I tell you to, and otherwise stay quiet. Got it?"

She nodded.

"Open a hatch, Lobo."

I went to the opening and shouted through it at Dougat. "Tell your four men to stand down. I'm here to do business. If I'd wanted to attack you, I'd have already done so. If I'd wanted to kill them, I'd have done that; check their IR levels, and you'll see they're in my sights."

Dougat smiled, paused, and nodded. He had monitors on us, which meant recordings—all as I'd expected.

"No harm in making sure you're as good as you think you are," Dougat said, smiling again, the businessman trying another tactic, no concern at all about the fact that his experiment involved threatening my life.

"They're moving away," Lobo said on the machine frequency I heard inside my head. "None has a shot now."

I stepped down to the permacrete and walked halfway to Dougat. The midday sun blazed bright and hot, and a bit of sweat ran down my back below the light armor. I waited for a few seconds. When Dougat didn't follow suit and come to meet me, I stayed a little bit longer, then shook my head and walked a few more steps forward, showing my belly.

He approached me and stopped half a meter out of my reach, as if that mattered. He clearly was a civilian with no real grasp of violence. If I'd wanted to hurt him, really wanted it, I wouldn't have bothered doing it with my hands; I would have let Lobo destroy the building with him in it. His lack of understanding, however, would only help in the long run, so I continued playing by his rules.

"You asked for a meeting," he said, "and I agreed to your request."

Everything about his attitude grated on me. I've always hated self-important bureaucrats, even the highest-ranking ones, but I followed the advice I'd given Maggie and stayed with the character I was selling.

"Yes," I said, "and I appreciate your time. If you can have the weapons ready in the next several days, we can make the trade we discussed."

"What exactly do you need?"

I slowly pulled out my wallet and thumbed it active to my quarantined and slightly enlarged copy of the list from Midon. "Here's what Chaplat's after, as well as your cut of what he's willing to pay."

He nodded. My wallet beeped an incoming request, and I allowed it to respond.

He stared up and to his left, checking the data on a contact, and then nodded again.

"You're asking for quite a lot," he said.

"More than you can handle?"

"Of course not," he said with no attempt to hide his annoyance. "I simply want to ensure that I receive a fair return on my investment. Your prices are lower than what we'd normally accept."

"You placed a high value on the boy," I said, "and my offer

reflects that fact. It's your choice, of course; I can always find another buyer and work out my issues with Chaplat with cash."

"So you have Manu Chang?"

I chuckled. "With me? Of course not. I'm sure you didn't expect that. But, yes, he's in a secure location. You get the weapons ready, and sometime in the next five to seven days, I'll signal you. You'll have less than two hours to show up, or we'll clear out. Once you arrive, we'll make the trade."

"We?"

"You know I have associates," I said. "You saw one in the desert. There are others."

"How did you find Manu?" he said.

I shook my head. "Not your issue."

"Fair enough. Still, I'm supposed to gather all of this merchandise, remain on this nasty planet, and leap into motion when you call, all because you claim to have Chang?"

"I appreciate your concern and anticipated it," I said, "so I brought proof."

I turned, walked back to Lobo, and went inside. I grabbed Maggie lightly by the back of the neck, took an energy pistol from her, and whispered, "Showtime. Brace yourself."

I tightened my grip on her neck and yanked her into the open hatch. She stumbled and nearly fell. To keep her upright, I squeezed hard enough that she had trouble breathing. Her eyes widened, though I couldn't tell if it was because of the pressure on her neck or the sight of Dougat. I pressed the gun against her temple.

"Remember your guard, the one you've been missing since our visit to the Eddy Institute?"

Dougat clearly didn't; I'd be surprised if he cared at all about Followers of Maggie's level. As the data feed from his support staff hit him, however, he feigned concern and recognition.

"Of course," he said. "Park, I hope he hasn't hurt you."

"Please, sir," Maggie said.

I wrenched her head around so I was staring into her eyes. "Shut up," I said.

I stared again at Dougat. "You wanted proof." To Maggie, I said, "Tell him."

I squeezed Maggie's neck harder, so she rasped her words a bit. Authenticity was vital.

"He has Manu Chang," she said, speaking slowly, so obviously in pain that tears oozed onto her cheeks. I ignored her and focused on Dougat.

"You've seen the child?" he said.

"Yes," Maggie said. "He's fine, but this man doesn't care about him—"

I cut her off by pushing her out of his sight inside Lobo and saying, "Take her."

"Satisfied?" I said to Dougat.

"Yes," he said, both excited and concerned now. "You mustn't hurt him, of course. Our deal is for him unharmed."

"Don't worry," I said. "I understand his value, so someone will get him unharmed. I'll even toss in the guard; after this, I'll have no use for her."

From the expression that crossed his face, Dougat didn't either, but with his security team monitoring him he wasn't about to give up one of their own.

"Thank you for that," he said. "I've been very concerned about her."

"One more thing," I said. I glanced inside Lobo. "Give it to me," I said to the space where I'd pushed Maggie. I stuck out my hand, and she put in it the one Pinkelponker gem Jack had left me.

"You also wanted the gemstones," I said. I showed him the one in my hand. "Proof enough on that front?"

He eyed it with lust but only nodded. "Yes," he said. "Perhaps as a down payment you might—"

"No," I said, cutting him off and handing the stone back to Maggie. "Unless you have a partial shipment of the weapons with you."

"Of course not," he said. "As I'm sure you understand, I don't travel with them or keep them in our facilities."

"I do understand," I said, "and I'm sure *you* also understand that

"Where are we?"

"A little social grace would not go amiss, Jon, even among colleagues. As I tried to teach you, smoothing the path always makes for a more comfortable walk."

"Where are we?"

Jack shrugged. "Do you ever wonder why you're always alone?"

Maggie, who was standing out of view, snorted audibly. "Just swallowed some water the wrong way," she whispered.

"Miss Park certainly takes my point," Jack said, "as you no doubt heard."

"Fine," I said. "How are you, Jack?"

"I'm doing quite well, thank you," he said. "And you?"

"Annoyed," I said, "at you and your penchant for wasting time. Will you now tell me how it's going?"

"As you wish," he said. Looking to the left, he added, "I tried, Miss Park, as you can see." He then stared again at me and continued, "We're on schedule to complete in two, maybe three days. It's costing me a big part of the proceeds of the sale of those assets we discussed, but everything is coming together."

"And our young friend?"

"He's fine."

"Show me," I said. I wanted to see Manu, and if anyone was monitoring us, I didn't mind if they did, too, because it would only help convince them I could deliver on my promises.

"So little trust," Jack said, "even at this stage? It doesn't become you, Jon." He reached to his right, and Manu stepped into view, Jack's hand on his shoulder.

The boy appeared completely normal, but of course he would.

"Nothing I can detect in the video suggests any coercion," Lobo said on the machine frequency, "though we are signal-limited. Pupil dilation is uniform and normal, and what I can read of the pulse in his neck is within standard tolerances. No unusual sweat patterns. He appears relaxed."

"How are you?" I said to Manu.

"Fine, thank you," he said, "though I'm tired of moving around. Will you be joining us soon?"

I was the one whose pulse was in danger of quickening and who had to fight not to sweat, because I hated deceiving the boy about putting him at risk. I just didn't have a better option. "Yes," I said, "in a few days."

"Will Lobo come, too?" he said. "Lobo's the best."

"A child wise beyond his years," Lobo said, thankfully staying on the machine frequency so no one else heard him.

"Of course," I said.

"Give us a moment," Jack said.

Manu nodded, said, "Bye," and walked out of view.

"Satisfied?" Jack said.

"Yes," I said. "Keep him safe."

"Of course," Jack said. "And your end?"

"Not done," I said, "but coming together. I have more work to do, so I should get to it."

Jack looked to his right, stretched a bit out of view, and then faced me again. His expression hardened. "My traces show no sign of interception, and I trust yours don't, either. So, may I speak frankly?"

"I believe we are secure," Lobo said, still on the machine frequency.

"Yes," I said.

"We're running a big risk here," Jack said, "and not just for Manu. All of us are going to be standing in the middle of an explosive situation. Are you sure this is going to work?"

Though I was tempted to answer him immediately, I considered the question honestly. We were doing everything we could to put all the pieces in the right places at the right times, but with so many people and so many variables, no one could ever be sure a plan as complex as this one would hold together. "No," I finally said, "but I don't see any other way out of this that doesn't involve giving up Manu and running forever, and I'm not willing to do either of those things. We've been through it all, Jack; if you have a better idea, tell me. Otherwise, we stick to what we're doing, hope for the best, and adapt as quickly as we can to the unexpected. What else is there?"

"Nothing, I suppose," Jack said, as serious as I'd ever seen him, "so I'll get back to my tasks." The display winked out.

"As will I," I said to the empty wall.

Gash's jump gate hung in space before us, growing in Lobo's front display as we eased to the head of the queue. Jack's concern weighed on me. I could jump to Mund and keep going, to Drayus, then Immediata or Avery or Therien, and from any of them to a planet beyond the EC's direct reach. I could abandon this dangerous scheme, drop Maggie, let Jack continue to protect Manu, and get on with my life somewhere very, very far away.

I glanced at Maggie, who was sitting in the couch beside me and staring at the gate, lost in her own thoughts. She was beautiful, decent, and for a few seconds back in the hangar in Nickres I'd felt closer to her than I'd been to any woman in years and years, but that moment had vanished like a spaceship through an aperture. Now, most of the time Maggie seemed barely able to tolerate me—and with good cause, I realized, because here I was considering abandoning her and Manu.

But I wouldn't. She might not understand that or believe it, but I wouldn't stop until I'd done everything I could to get the boy to safety. I'd promised him back in Eddy that I'd protect him, and I would. If I didn't, I could jump forever and never get away from the disgust I'd feel for myself. If I failed, if something happened to him, I had to hope that one day the knowledge that I'd at least done my best would provide some small comfort. I knew I'd never forgive myself for not trying.

Maggie reached over and touched my arm lightly with her fingertips. "Amazing every time," she said, her voice barely louder than a whisper. "I hope I never stop seeing the magic in it."

I turned and watched as she stared at the jump gate.

No, I wouldn't let them down.

The edges of the aperture vanished as we reached the front of the queue. All we could see in front of us was the perfect blackness, the complete lack of information in that instant of suspension between where you were and where you were going, between what you knew and the mystery of the moment to come.

We jumped.

❈   ❈   ❈

Chaplat had demanded we meet at his office, but he'd clearly expected me to offer an alternative. "You're the buyer," I'd said, "so you get to pick the place." He'd made no attempt to disguise his suspicion, but I believe he also at some level liked that I'd rolled over for him.

Now, standing outside the building and waiting for his guards to appear, I was second-guessing myself. Once I was inside, Lobo couldn't track me. He'd blast a hole in the side of the place if I didn't signal him in half an hour, but if I was already dead when he showed up, his presence wouldn't do me much good.

The plan was sound, I reminded myself. Stick to the plan.

The same man and woman met me yet again. Either they were his personal team, or his organization was a lot smaller than I'd thought. Given the way both Midon and Dougat spoke of him, I was betting on the former. Neither guard smiled or spoke. The man took the rear position this time. The woman led, and I followed her.

Even though I'd seen it before, the room still surprised me, an effect I assume Chaplat enjoyed. No fire burned in the fireplace this afternoon; instead, four meter-high black lacquer vases full of flowers sat side by side within it. The bright orange of the blossoms matched perfectly the delicate circles at the top of each vase. Chaplat stood in front of them, waiting for me. He wasn't smiling. No servants occupied the room's corners. No one offered me a drink or a seat. By doing a deal with him I'd descended to the rank of hired help. I could live with that. The sooner I got out of there, the smaller the chance that something would go wrong, upset him, and backfire on me. My spine itched with the bone-deep understanding that a nod from Chaplat could cause the man behind me to shoot me in the back. I hoped he'd go for a body shot the nanomachines could repair.

"What have you got for me?" he said.

"I'm going to take a list from my left rear pants pocket," I said.

"Let her help you," Chaplat said, nodding at the lead guard, who was now a meter and a half away at my nine.

She pulled out the sheet and flicked it taut. The first page of the weapons inventory glowed on it. I'd put next to each line a cost half again as high as what I'd told Dougat I could get him. The guard handed the list to Chaplat. He studied it for quite some time. No one spoke. No one moved. Apparently, the guards were as concerned about annoying him as I was.

"The prices are firm," I said. "They're what he demands."

"I'll pay half of that," he said, "and your cut comes from that payment—after I get Jack."

Now we were in the tricky part. I couldn't let his offer stand, or he'd question my motives and Dougat would balk. At the same time, I didn't want to end up in a prolonged argument that might cause him to lose his temper.

"I can't sell him on that big a discount," I said. "He didn't present the figures as open to discussion."

He smiled and shook his head. "You really are new to this sort of trade, aren't you? No one pays these prices unless they're planning to use the goods themselves, which I most definitely am not. I'll have to discount to my buyers so I can move in volume, or it'll take me forever to sell the weapons in small lots—and I'll have to warehouse them the whole time. No, this price is out of the question. I'm willing to consider sixty percent."

"I can't get that price," I said, letting a note of panic creep into my voice. "Maybe I could talk them into a ten percent discount. Maybe." I paused, then added, "And of course my fee would be on top of that."

He stepped close enough that I could smell alcohol on his breath.

"No," he said. "We're done negotiating. This is my last offer: I'll pay seventy-five percent of the prices here, take the whole lot, and your cut comes out of that. I don't give a damn what your end is. If you didn't set up this deal well enough that you'll make a profit with that offer, then you're a fool, and I don't want to do business with you."

I imagined Manu being hurt to force some tension to show on my face even as my mind calculated the additional fee I'd just persuaded him to pay. I acted as if it were an effort to speak calmly, spacing my words and talking as slowly as an addict trying to pass for sober. "And I still get the ten percent of what Jack owes you?"

"That was our original deal," he said, "so, yes, as long as you deliver Jack."

"Of course," I said. "He'll be there. Deal."

I stuck out my hand to shake.

He ignored it. "When?" he said.

"Sometime in the next five days," I said. "On Gash. I won't be able to give you more than an hour's notice due to the way I'm arranging to get Jack."

"And that is?" he said.

"My problem," I said, "and I'm handling it. When we do the trade, the money for the weapons will flow through my wallet first. I'll extract my fee, and then my software will handle the anonymous payment to Dougat."

"How you get him the money is your problem," he said. "As long as I end up with both the weapons and Jack, I don't care what you do."

I smiled. "Excellent."

"And the boy?" he said.

"He'll be there," I said, guilt and anger hitting me all at once, "but as I explained before—"

Chaplat held up his hand to stop me, nodded, turned, and headed out of the room.

"What you need to tell yourself is also not my problem," he said. "We're done here. Don't make me wait too long."

Something in my body language must have betrayed how much I wanted to tear Chaplat apart, because the guard to my left closed the gap between us, and the one behind me put his hand on my shoulder. For a moment I considered fighting them, smashing them both, destroying all the people who were so intent on exploiting this boy, all the people who thought I was just like them, willing to sell out a child simply to enrich myself, and then I regained control as I accepted how much of my anger was toward myself. I couldn't fight everyone in this whole affair, at least not without hurting a great many innocent people not directly involved in any of it, and I had only myself to blame for much of it. I'd chosen this path, and it was the best one I could find, so I needed to calm down and accept it.

I let the guards lead me out of the building and to the street below.

After the door slid shut behind me, Lobo told me, "All clear. Proceeding to rendezvous?"

"Not immediately," I subvocalized as I walked rapidly away. I couldn't calm down, so I was in no condition to share the inside of Lobo with Maggie—or anyone, for that matter. "I'm going to exercise."

"Now?" Lobo said.

"Yes," I said, not trying to suppress the rage still in me. "Leave me alone. You're tracking me, so you'll know when I'm close."

He said nothing, whether literally following the order or sensing my mood I neither knew nor cared.

While surveying the area in preparation for this meeting, I'd spotted an old metal and plank pier that jutted fifty meters into the water. I started running toward it, slowly at first, then jogging, and then sprinting, pushing myself until my legs ached and my lungs felt ready to burst, and then forcing myself to hold the pace, embracing the pain and using it to blot out everything else. I rounded the last turn to the pier, and with it in sight I forced myself to go faster, pumped my arms and pistoned my legs and ran as hard as I could. I sprinted to the end of the pier, my vision reduced to the small area directly in front of me. I stopped a meter from its end. Not quite done, trembling with the exertion and the rage, I thrust my arms over my head, looked straight into the sky, and screamed, roared wordlessly, for those few seconds giving literal voice to my frustration and anger.

I'm not sure how long I stood there, but when I finished, I bent over, hands on my knees, and gulped air. As control threaded its way back through me, I saw how stupid I was. All that noise, that self-indulgence, and of course nothing was different.

No, one thing had changed: I felt a bit better. I shook my head and chuckled at myself as I regained rationality. I'd learned long ago that exercise helped me, but I'd largely abandoned it while trying to thread my way through this trouble. I shouldn't do that. I needed to use physical exertion and other safe outlets to keep myself in check. Running here, dropping all pretense of self-control, screaming like a madman—it might have provided a temporary release to the pressure I was feeling, but it wasn't smart.

I surveyed the area, something I should have done before ever entering it. Five men, two in pairs and one alone, sat along the edges of the pier. All were fishing. Two women and a man supervising loading bots at a warehouse sixty-five meters away were staring at me. Any one of them could have taken me out while I stood there, oblivious as I was of the rest of Eddy continuing its normal life all around me. Not smart, not smart at all. You'd think I'd learn.

I turned around and started walking to the rendezvous point. I checked out everyone I passed and invested half an hour in counter-surveillance routes on the way to Lobo.

I hoped this would be the last time I was this dumb until I was somewhere much, much safer.

Unfortunately, the next stop on my path to any better place was to walk into another meeting location I didn't control.

CHAPTER
THIRTY-THREE

The Cam Joint squatted next to an oversized chop shop in the middle of a couple of acres of stained permacrete and roaring engines. Single-passenger, multi-passenger, hover, wheeled, open, closed—you name a type of vehicle a hardcore ground-transport enthusiast might drool over, and at least one of them was sitting somewhere in the large open areas surrounding the two linked buildings. Bureaucrats wearing dirt-repelling suits and supervising mechanoids with probes buried deep in onboard computers worked adjacent to gearhead fundamentalists wielding only manual wrenches and drivers. Red fiber lines outlined a two-meter-wide path that meandered from the main entrance gate where I stood, through the vehicles and work teams, all the way to the open front door of the bar, restaurant, same-day augmentation parlor, and parts supply house that shared the interior of this most unusual shop.

Why was I not surprised that the Zyuns had chosen to meet me here?

I followed the path inside. A pair of shirtless bouncers, one my height and the other a head shorter, leaned against the wall on either side of the door, implanted electrodes flexing muscles in rippling patterns up and down their bodies as their eyes scanned constantly across the huge open space. I stopped a meter in front of them, nodded in recognition, and said, "I'm looking for a friend."

"Who isn't?" the taller one said.

"And we should care why?" the shorter added, clearly bored and hoping I'd lend some excitement to his shift.

I ignored him and instead looked around the huge space for the Zyuns. To my right, men and women and waist-high loaders prowled aisles of circuit boards, gaskets, shafts, pistons, fittings of all sorts, and parts I didn't recognize. To my left, a row of half a dozen operating theaters of various kinds stretched from the front wall to two-thirds of the building's depth. The first room stood empty. The open door to the second revealed a thin woman reclining at a forty-five-degree angle on an operating couch, her long, straight, brown hair stretching almost to the ground. A tattoo artist worked slowly and carefully on her left forearm, building on the scene of trees, waterfall, and skeletons that stretched from her elbow up and inside her shirt. Her eyes were shut, her expression blissful, and with her right arm she stroked the back of a lounge basset currently anchored to the counter beside her, the legless hound's expression as happy as its fundamentally sad countenance could permit.

I walked past the rest of the body-mod chambers, all closed, and reached the edge of the bar/restaurant combination, an old-style wooden bar on the left and tables full of eating patrons on the right. The food ran to basics—chunks of browned meat, mashed and chunked and noodled starches, and precious little green—but the smells tweaked my senses and instantly I was hungry. I shoved aside the craving as I spotted the Zyuns. They were sitting around a table in the far left rear corner, all three managing to have a wall to their backs.

I nodded acknowledgment and headed to them. I leaned against the rear wall, so the Zyun on my right would have to swivel to face me; no way was I giving up my back in a place someone else had picked. The Zyun stayed as he was; I'd forgotten the constantly transmitted multiple vision points.

"Any particular reason I had to come here?" I said.

"We like it," they said in the usual alternating word pattern. "Much life around, and no EC. It's totally legit, so no one bothers us here."

The way they spoke was even more annoying with long sentences than with their typical short statements.

"We could have settled this via comm," I said.

"Not our way," they said. "Call your ship."

I didn't bother. A glance at a gauge on the cuff of my shirt confirmed what Lobo had found. He'd tried to scan the place before we'd landed, and he couldn't get through. Nothing was getting out, either.

"Walls laced with enough metal layers to stop transmissions," I said. "I understand and appreciate your caution, but you've worked for Jack, he's vouched for me, and all I want to do is hire you. We could have saved time."

"We prefer this," they said. "What's the job?"

"Are you still working for Jack?"

They shook their heads in unison.

"Anyone else?"

Again they shook their heads as one. They weren't talkative, which was fine by me.

"I want you full time and exclusively for the duration of the mission," I said. "No breaks, always on the clock, and no other assignments."

"Our preference, too."

"You get the outline now, but the details come only in real time," I said. "I also won't name the others involved until we're live. Acceptable?"

They nodded yes. "A fellow paranoid," they said. "We like that."

I ran down the basics for them, then asked, "Interested?"

"We find parts of this uncomfortable," they said. "Other acceptable options?"

I was surprised to realize that the constant alternation and phrasing in groups of three words was tempting me to participate, as if we were playing word games. I refrained from joining them.

"None," I said. "I believe I understand and appreciate your concerns, but no, I have no other reasonable choices."

"It's your deal," they said. They pointed as one to a small paper display sitting in the table's center. A figure and an account number snapped into view on it. "Our rate for high-risk work, plus a fee for the discomfort."

"Ouch," I said, though Jack had already told me roughly what they'd ask.

They shrugged and said nothing. The display cleared.

"Acceptable," I said. "Ten percent retainer now, forty percent on pickup, the rest on completion."

"Jack briefed you," they said.

"Yes. Deal?"

They nodded. The Zyun in the center put a wallet on the table, and all three thumbed it open.

"Keep the comm link I gave you," I said, "and go to Gash. Stay somewhere I can reach you. Make it private, low-key—not anywhere like here."

They nodded again.

"I also need a safe house on Gash and a private hangar there for my ship. Make sure the house is secure. Spend what it takes. Okay?"

They nodded once more.

I opened my wallet, transmitted the deposit to theirs, and left.

Gash filled the display Lobo had opened to my right on the front wall. Jack stared at me from the one directly in front of me. Orbiting the planet, one day from my target date, and of course Jack had to complicate things.

"I'm not feeling good about this, Jon," he said. "You're putting me in a position of great risk."

"We've been through all this, Jack, and there's no other way the plan has a prayer of working."

"Then maybe we need to revise the plan."

I struggled to control my feelings and maintain a calm, level tone. "We don't have time for that," I said, "as you well know. The timetable is set, the players are in motion, and if I change anything now, they could decide to pursue other options—like hunting you down."

"And you as well," he said. "I'm not the only one in trouble here."

"Precisely," I said. "You're not. They all know me, they all know you, and changing course now might tempt each of them to attack us. You'd also be endangering Manu again, as you did at the Institute, when you set me up the first time."

"As I've tried to point out to you before," he said, "I didn't put him at risk; his vision did. How was I supposed to know he'd have one while Dougat was interviewing him?"

"If you care about him, me, or yourself," I said, "you'll let this keep going. You don't have a better plan; if you did, you'd have offered it by now."

"My concern remains valid," he said. "We meet for final site prep and check. Either I involve new people to provide my security— security your faux PCAV can easily remove at a place as empty and open as the site—or I show up without any. Either way I play that, you take Manu and leave me with no leverage."

"I'd still be stuck with Chaplat," I said, "who, as you may recall, very much wants you."

"He's literally the least of your problems," Jack said, "and the easiest to get away from."

"True enough," I said, "but why would I run when I can solve this for good?"

"If the plan works," Jack said.

"Yes," I said, nodding my head and ready to scream at him, "if it works. We're both gambling on that."

"We're back to my concern," he said.

I stood, crossed my arms, and squeezed my elbows with my hands to give physical vent to my frustration. "I give you my word, Jack, that I won't take Manu when we visit the site. I also give you my word that if you mess this up now, you won't have to worry about any of the others, because I'll hunt you down and find you before they can. Make a choice."

He smiled and raised his hands. "Your word is good enough for me, Jon. See you at the site at dusk."

The display winked out before I could say anything else. I shook with rage.

"Will he show?" Maggie said.

"Yes," I said through clenched teeth, "or I will track him down and do whatever it takes to make him tell me where Manu is." I headed for my quarters so I could calm down alone and not have to worry about what I might say in front of her. "Whatever it takes."

CHAPTER
THIRTY-FOUR

Pink and orange dominated the far horizon as the day faded and we drew closer to the abandoned EC base. We flew level with the treetops to the west as we approached the vast expanse of permacrete from the south. Lobo began firing milspec sensor-gophers when we crossed the southern wall and kept it up, one every thirty meters, until we had overshot the hangar, turned a hundred and eighty degrees, and dived into the building's large rear opening. He launched a similar barrage in a straight line from the west side of the building out into the grasslands on the edge of the base.

The gophers expanded when they hit, dug into the permacrete until they were below ground level, extruded antennas and sensors, and then pulled as much of the permacrete shavings onto themselves as possible. Unless you walked by one, you wouldn't notice it. Standard tools on open-area battlefields, they created a mesh sensor and comm network that we could use to amplify signals and track outside activity. Lobo checked in with each sensor, then backed inside the warehouse far enough that we weren't visible from outside unless you were looking from ground level or a shallow angle above it. He settled very carefully into position, repeated the gopher check, then flashed the ready signal on the display in front of me.

"Scan results?" I said.

"Nothing on approach," Lobo said. "The rest of the place is indeed protected from external sensors and all transmissions. Now that I'm inside, I can read the signal from Jack's transmitter, but IR won't work through the walls so I can't get a headcount."

I nodded. "As good as it can be right now. If he brings more than we can handle," I looked at Maggie and the three Zyuns, who stood behind me in Lobo, "then I'll be surprised, but I'll also signal."

"Of course," Lobo said. "I do remember the plan. Worry about your part, not mine—which I have well in hand."

His sarcasm was a great motivation to get moving, because he'd only stop it when we were active.

I turned to face the others. As I'd asked, Maggie had again put on her Followers security uniform. The Zyuns looked as they always did—short, insanely muscular, heavily armed, and psychotically in sync—but now black flexi-armor covered almost every square centimeter of them, a tiny patch of each of their faces the only skin visible. When they showed up for work that might turn hot, they came prepared.

To Maggie, I said, "Are you ready for this?"

"Of course," she said. "I told you I would be."

"Zyuns," I said, "you have the rest of the advance. Ready?"

"Do we look any other way?" they said. "All is now."

Great; they chose this time to add a sense of humor to the Zen attitude.

"Lobo," I said, "open a hatch."

We stepped out. One Zyun stood beside Lobo while the rest of us headed off.

"I'm sorry," I said, "but it really is necessary."

"We know the deal we made," they said.

We threaded our way through low stacks of boxes and to the corridor that ran between the large rear room where Lobo was parked and the much bigger main front space. A floor-to-ceiling, old-fashioned, hinged metal door at the end of the corridor now separated the building's rear section from the rest of the place. It was solid and heavy and when shut was almost perfectly flush with the permacrete on all sides. Good.

I paused before the door and nodded to the Zyuns. One of them, Maggie, and I stepped back so we'd be behind it as it opened. The other dropped to the ground and, as I opened the latch, pulled the door toward us from the bottom. Though the muscles in his arms swelled with effort, he made no sound.

Jack sat on a ratty leather sofa fifteen meters inside, Manu beside him. When Jack saw the door open and spotted the prone Zyun, he laughed. "Do you trust nothing, Jon?" he said.

The Zyun gave the clear signal and stood. We followed him inside. Maggie took a step toward Manu, but I grabbed her shoulder, came parallel to her, and kept her beside me. She'd agreed to stick with the plan, so she didn't resist me, but it was obvious that she wanted to go to the boy.

"From here on in, Jack, no," I said. "When you first asked for my help, you said you were no good at this sort of thing but I was. Minimizing what I have to trust in an encounter as dangerous as this one is part of what I do."

"Fair enough," he said. He patted Manu on the head and said to the boy, "You remember Jon, don't you, Manu?"

"Hi, Jon. Did Lobo come?"

"Of course I did, Manu," Lobo said via a small but powerful speaker in my belt. "I wouldn't miss it."

Both Manu and Maggie actually looked touched. Just my luck: My bloodthirsty killing machine was better with both kids and women than I was.

I shook my head slightly to focus myself. "Jack, Maggie has some medical training; would you mind if she checked out Manu?" She didn't, but Jack wouldn't care. At this point, either he was trusting me, or something very nasty was waiting for us somewhere near here. Given that Lobo had detected nothing and the two Zyuns with me hadn't raised an alarm despite their nonstop scanning of the area, I was betting Jack was behaving. I hadn't planned on this check, but I was tired of fighting with Maggie, who had all but demanded a chance to verify that Manu was unharmed.

"Of course not," Jack said, "though I assure you he's fine."

"I am," Manu said. "We've been moving around a lot, and though I've met some interesting people, I'm tired of not staying anywhere long. Other than that, everything's okay."

I let go of Maggie. From the tension in her posture she wanted to run, but she forced herself to walk to the sofa. She rested her hand on Jack's arm as she quietly said, "Would you mind sliding over so I could sit next to Manu?"

"Not at all," Jack said.

Maggie stood suddenly as if shocked, then looked at me. "Jon, you—"

Light was fading, and we needed to move, so I cut her off. "You wanted to evaluate Manu's condition; please do."

She nodded her head, then sat and put her hand on Manu's forehead, as if checking him for a fever like a frontier mother whose medbed was on the fritz. She said, "Hi, Manu. I'm Maggie." After a few seconds, a smile bloomed on her face, and she wrapped her arms around the boy and laughed. A frown crossed Manu's face, then he stared into her eyes for several long moments and laughed, too. I'd never seen either of them quite so happy.

As she hugged Manu, I slowly and carefully scanned the mods Jack's team had completed. The doors stood where we needed them, and temporary walls filled the rest of the entrances. All the gear we'd discussed perched in the right places in the hangar, though none of it was visible without magnification and even then only if you knew to look for it. The whole setup appeared good to go.

"Nice work, Jack," I said.

He spread his hands and smiled. "Give me some credit, Jon. This isn't my first gig."

"The comm gear, inside and out?"

"All set."

"The rest of it?"

He sighed theatrically. "Again, Jon, all done. We finished everything, and we tested it all. Twice." He glanced at Maggie. "I take it you're satisfied that Manu is well," he said.

"Oh, yes," Maggie said. "He's great."

"Then we go tomorrow," I said.

Jack's smile grew wider. "Excellent. It's about time we made some money." He stood and motioned toward Manu.

"Hold on, Jack," I said. I walked closer to the sofa, the Zyuns staying at my seven and four. "As I promised, I'm not separating you from Manu, but I am changing the plan a bit."

Jack froze, his smile gone, his eyes narrow. "We're partners, Jon. We should discuss changes and agree on them before either one of us makes them."

"From here on, Jack, we're in my area of expertise, so we do it my way. You don't get a vote. One of the Zyuns and Maggie will stay with you and Manu from now on."

"I've been doing well enough taking care of the two of us," he said, "and we can meet you—"

"No," I said. I nodded toward the Zyun on my left. "Take Maggie and the boy. Jack will follow in a moment."

"What changes are you making, Jon?" Maggie said.

I looked at her and wished she could read a single thought in my mind: *Not now.*

She clearly received the message from my expression, because she grasped Manu's hand, stood, and said, "Let's go, Manu."

As they walked away, I leaned closer to Jack and whispered, "You'll like it."

He relaxed and smiled broadly as I explained the new bits.

CHAPTER THIRTY-FIVE

The easiest way to make sure an enemy can't control a rendezvous point is to be there before you tell them about it. I was taking no chances with the hangar and today's meeting. The creeping threat of light was driving away the night and its stars when we parked twenty meters from the front entrance of the hangar. The two Zyuns with me insisted on clearing the entire area, both external and internal perimeters, on foot, so I waited inside until they gave the all-clear.

I walked to the front of the hangar, leaned against it, and said to the Zyuns, who were now flanking me, "It's time."

They nodded and spread away from me; they neither needed nor particularly wanted to hear any of the conversations I was about to have.

"Lobo," I said.

"Full sensor mesh operational and all controls engaged," he said. "Your comm and embedded fabric backup are transmitting fully. Verify fabric comm receipt."

In slow sequence, sections of the active body armor I was wearing under my shirt and pants turned hot then cold.

"Working," I said.

"Ready," he said.

Clouds hung in the night sky, but there was no forecast for rain. The cool air didn't stop drops of sweat rolling down my arms under the armor, which absorbed them before they reached my wrists. Everywhere around me, peace and quiet reigned.

That would end soon enough.

"Open comm to Dougat," I said.

Dougat's face popped almost immediately into the heads-up display in my left contact. Lobo was feeding him a still image of me with a security note overlaid. I'd considered an animation but rejected it; I wanted him to know I was intentionally not giving him any visibility into my location.

"It's very early, Moore," he said. "Make it good."

"It's your lucky day," I said, "as long as you have the weapons I ordered. As for the hour, well, I warned you I might call at any time."

"Insulting me accomplishes nothing other than to encourage me to walk away," he said.

"Then walk, and I will, too, and I'll take Manu Chang with me."

"You have him?"

"Now who's being insulting?" I wanted all three main players to be as much off their games as possible, so I was happy to play with Dougat for as long as he could stand it.

He took a deep breath and closed his eyes for a few seconds. When he opened them, it was if a new man had invaded his body. "All the weapons are on a transport ship outside of Malzton. We're ready to make the trade."

"Be here in one hour," I said, and on cue Lobo transmitted him the coordinates and photos and schematics of the hangar. All the images directed him to the east entrance to the building. Lobo also started a countdown timer in my right contact's display. "Land in the spot I designated, and after you have, enter through the door in front of you. Have the loaders bring the weapons inside. If my PCAV spots anything other than a cargo transport, or if you come within its sensor range early, we'll leave, and the next time you hear from me it won't be to do business. If you deviate from these plans when you're on the ground, my PCAV and my team will respond swiftly."

"We have a deal in which we all win," Dougat said with a smile. "I have no incentive to do anything other than honor the arrangement. I worry that you are not of a similar mind-set."

"If I wanted to go to war with the Followers," I said, "I would have done so already, and you'd be dead. The deal is the best path forward for me as well. After it, we won't encounter each other ever again."

"Excellent," he said. "We shall arrive per your schedule."

I nodded, then realized he couldn't see me. "I look forward to it," I said. "See you in fifty-seven minutes."

Lobo cut the link.

I took a deep breath and began a series of stretches. We were in it now, and I wanted to stay loose and ready for anything.

When the countdown showed ten minutes had passed, I said to Lobo, "Open comm to Chaplat." We went with the still image of me again even though I knew it would annoy Chaplat. I wanted him, like Dougat, to understand from the start that I wouldn't let him control the situation.

"How quaint, Mr. Moore," he said. "I trust today will be a good day for us both."

I hadn't figured him for a morning person, but either he was a better actor than Dougat, or he was already up and fully operational. "It will indeed," I said. "You're ready with the money?"

"I'm sufficiently pleased to be regaining your friend Jack that I'm going to strive to hold on to my good mood and my manners," he said, "but I encourage you not to test my patience. Of course I am."

"Everything is set on my side," I said. "Be here in one hour." Lobo flashed me that he had sent the coordinates and a different set of hangar directions and images. These designated a landing area on the west side of the building and directed Chaplat toward the door there. Lobo started a second small countdown timer in the window. "Land in the marked spot, and enter through the door in front of it. Not to be rude, but if my PCAV detects more than a single cargo ship, we'll leave before you can reach us, and I'll make my next visit to you in it. If you don't follow these instructions once you've landed, my PCAV and my team will respond swiftly."

"Yeah, yeah," he said. "You're saying what you have to say, but we both know that we both win the most if the deal goes right, so save your breath and stop annoying me. My vessel has space for the weapons, me, my team, and my two new passengers. It's all I need, and it's all I'll bring."

I ignored his probe to see whether I was having second thoughts about him taking Manu. I couldn't let him detect any concern on my part. "Fine," I said. "See you in fifty-eight minutes."

Five minutes later, I said to Lobo, "Midon."

A too perfectly beautiful young woman's face appeared in the display in my left contact. "I'm sorry to have to tell you that Councillor Midon is unavailable right now," the sim said, "but I'm sure I can either help you or find someone who can."

Great. The clock was ticking, and Midon couldn't be bothered to answer the comm personally. I needed to drop enough loaded words that even the dumbest interface software would elevate my priority and force Midon to take the link herself.

"Dougat, Chaplat, the weapons, the boy—tell Midon it's all happening now, and either she answers in the next ninety seconds or I disconnect, keep her advance, and deal with it myself." Unless she hadn't bothered to brief her 'face software, that should more than do it.

Lobo obligingly opened a third timer in my right contact, this one a bright red in contrast to the pale aqua tones of the other two. He loved drama.

The counter showed seventeen seconds had elapsed when Midon's face snapped into view in my left contact's display. She appeared perfectly composed, as if she'd been at work and simply too absorbed to notice the comm.

"The software was already rousing me, Mr. Moore," she said. "The frequency and your ID were more than enough to prompt it to action. Now you've left so many verbal trails that if this goes badly I'll have to invest in a serious data scrub of my entire interface system."

"Then let's not let that happen," I said. "Our deals stand?"

She nodded. "Of course. The weapons and the boy?"

"All set," I said. "And your team leader agrees to wait until I signal you?"

"Reluctantly," she said, "but yes, she does. Clear and indisputable proof of Dougat's involvement is in all our interest."

"And the remainder of my payment?"

"Three days later, as you requested," she said, "though I must confess that I remain surprised you want to wait so long. Your choice, after all, does force you to trust me."

"Waiting means no clear links between me and the arrests you make here, so it's less risk for me," I said. "You could try to cheat me, but as you noted, I've left a lot of trails, and you're not the only one with recordings. If anything happens to me, friends will make sure a lot of people see them."

"Of course," she said.

"Monitor both the east and west entrances of this hangar," I said. Lobo flashed a "coordinates sent" message in my right contact. "The east side will go live in approximately thirty-eight minutes, and the west will heat up about ten minutes later. Your team must either arrive quickly enough for a full stealth setup in advance of the earlier time or come in quietly after they see the ship land on the west and its passengers enter the hangar. I suggest the latter. No one in the building will be able to hear much of anything outside, but they'll almost certainly leave external lookouts. Factor those into your landing approach. Most importantly, make sure everyone on your team knows what my PCAV and I look like and leave it and me alone. If you bother the ship, it will resist."

"Our team is already in route," she said, "and though I've worked with many people who micromanaged, I've never found it particularly effective."

She had a point. I was prone to it, and I needed to stop it. Any team that would be of use to me would have to be able to do its job well.

"We all know what we're doing," she continued. "As for your ship, if we wanted a fight with it, we would have shuttled an appropriate countermeasure to this gate station after your first—" She paused, clearly searching for a term she could tolerate. "—display outside Carne's office."

"I hope so," I said, "but while you're watching feeds of the action, I'll be in the middle of it. My butt's on the line, not yours."

"As it has been from the beginning," she said, "so that's not news. Are we done?"

"Yes," I said.

She cut the link before my mouth had formed the "y."

I stretched again and went inside to wait. The Zyuns followed. We walked the inner perimeter of the building, an unnecessary check but one that burned a little energy and felt good to be doing. The east and west entrance doors stood open. Everything was in place.

We were good to go inside.

Lobo would alert me if anything outside unfolded differently than it should.

Now I had to wait until Dougat arrived, hope nothing went wrong, and find a way to keep everyone alive and safe as this played out.

CHAPTER THIRTY-SIX

I put off the encounter as long as I could, but with three minutes to go until Dougat was due to arrive, I couldn't wait any more.

"Lobo," I said over the comm unit, "tell Maggie to come out." To the Zyuns, I said, "Bring her over."

They nodded as one. The Zyun to my right trotted across the hangar toward the heavy metal door that separated the rear area from the rest of the hangar. The Zyun to my left glided in front of me. Despite the huge amount of muscle they carried and their general blockiness, the Zyuns moved gracefully and quickly.

As the Zyun reached the door, it opened, the Zyun in the hangar acting in perfect sync with the one on the other side of the tall barrier. Maggie stumbled out, pushed from behind. She wore the Followers guard uniform she was wearing the day I carried her onto Lobo after she saved Manu from being shot. Her hair clung dirty and matted to her skull. Her face sagged with exhaustion.

She looked as good to me as anyone had in a very long time.

I shook my head slightly to clear the thought. I had to stay sharp.

The door slammed shut, the metal clanging as its edges hit the permacrete frame.

The Zyun grabbed Maggie's elbow with his black-gloved hand

and led her in a slow jog across the floor to me. She didn't look happy.

I hated this part, but it was necessary. Time was short. I had to do it.

"Jon," she said, her eyes searching my face and her tone unsteady. "Why am I out here?"

"Because I need you here," I said. "Stand and—"

She cut me off. "This is not what you told me we'd be doing! The plan was different. You said—"

"Shut up!" I yelled. The look of shock and betrayal on her face hit me like a punch to the heart, but I kept going. "What I said before doesn't matter. What matters is that you stand here, do what I say, and keep your mouth shut."

"What about Manu?" she said. "You promised—"

"I told you to shut up!" I stepped forward until we were practically touching. "We don't have time for this. Dougat is about to arrive. Don't say a word. Understand?"

She nodded slowly, tears running down her cheeks as she moved her head.

"And do as I tell you."

She nodded again.

My heart pounded inside my chest. I wanted to hold her and explain, but I'd thought it all through, and now was not the time for second-guessing. I kept my gaze fixed on her and said only, "Good."

"Your vitals are unusually high given that no hostiles are yet present," Lobo said over the private channel that sounded only in my right ear. "Are you solid to go?"

I nodded to the Zyun who'd escorted Maggie, and he held on to her as I turned and walked away. After a few steps, I subvocalized, "Yes. Dumb reactions on my part. We go."

I closed my eyes and reviewed the plan, inhaled and exhaled slowly and deeply, and my pulse settled to normal. Right here, right now, what I felt was unimportant. Nothing mattered but doing the job, executing the plan, making it work.

"Dougat landing," Lobo said via the comm frequency the Zyuns and I were sharing. To improve our response time should the situation go nonlinear, I was trusting Lobo to choose which bits of information the Zyuns needed and which should stay private. He switched to the private channel and added, "Last chance to abort."

"No," I subvocalized, not trying to hide my annoyance. "We go."

Back on the shared channel, Lobo continued. "Dougat is over ninety seconds late, but that's within plan tolerances. I detect no support or follow team. Stand ready."

I looked at the two Zyuns.

In unison they signaled ready.

Maggie stared at me, her face showing confusion and hurt. I didn't meet her eyes. We could deal with her feelings if we survived.

In the upper left of my vision Lobo streamed a composite video feed from the ground sensors east of the hangar. Dougat's ship, a dull gray cargo carrier with an AutoHomes Construction logo, landed precisely where we'd directed him. Hatches on the left and right side of its front blinked open and three guards in body armor jumped out of each. The vessel immediately closed.

Fair enough.

"Let them in," I said.

Lobo retracted the east door enough to allow two men to walk abreast through it.

Dougat had upgraded his security team or its members were better at executing scripted scenarios than they were at dealing with unexpected crises. I watched in Lobo's feed as they fanned out on either side of the door but did not enter. One tossed a small ball inside. The metal sphere clanged against the permacrete floor, sprouted four legs and three antennae, and crawled forward.

"Open comm to Dougat," I said.

"Mr. Moore," he said. "I trust you don't mind our precautions."

"Not at all," I said. "As your surveillance spider is telling you, only a few members of my team are currently involved, and your guard is here as a sign of good faith."

"And Manu Chang? We seem to be missing his IR signature. Is he what's behind that large metal door directly in front of our entrance?"

"Yes," I said, "he is, as is another squad of mine. They'll bring out the boy in time, but not until I've seen the weapons and received my cut of the purchase price."

"As I understood you earlier, that last step requires Chaplat."

"It does," I said, "but he won't come until I verify that you've brought everything he specified. So, the sooner you send the weapons inside and let my man verify that everything we ordered is present, the sooner we all get what we want."

"You're making this annoying enough," he said, "that the temptation is growing to send my men to wipe out your small crew and bring Chang to me."

In the upper right of my vision the countdown marched relentlessly toward the moment when Chaplat would arrive. Dougat was such a talker that I'd budgeted some time for him to waste in protesting and threatening, but I couldn't afford for it to go on too long. "Your posturing is a waste of energy. You won't send anyone after us. They'd have to come through that entrance, and we'd destroy them on the way in. What we missed, the team members behind the door and on my PCAV would finish. You said the boy was worth the cost of the weapons—for which you *are* also receiving a rather substantial and quite reasonable fee—so you win by keeping to our deal. Let's get on with it."

"Fine," he said. "Do you want to inspect the cargo in the ship?"

I chuckled. "Hardly. Keep them covered, and bring them inside. My man will check them against the inventory once they're in here."

"We'll start unloading," he said. "Open the door wide enough for the loaders."

"When they're in front of it, we will," I said. "Bring them on."

"Jon, you can't," Maggie whispered. "You promised."

I glared at her over my shoulder and hissed my response. "Do *not* interrupt me."

I looked back at the door. The air in the hangar was still and cool, but sweat ran down my back and chest until the light armor managed to absorb it. The biolights Jack's team had hung along the ceiling's perimeter glowed a soft red and bathed the off-white permacrete interior in light the color of watered-down blood. I was sure that if I turned around, Maggie would still be staring at me, but I couldn't allow myself to think about that now.

I focused on the upper left contact images of the loaders marching sideways out of Dougat's ship. The soft gray metal bots resembled giants devoid of upper legs, much of their torsos, and heads. Their lower legs and alloy arms emerged directly from the bottom and top of their wide, broad, flat waists. Each pair carried a three-high stack of dull black boxes the size of coffins built for very tall twins. Six loaders with nine total crates emerged; that count seemed about right. They queued up in front of the door and marched forward.

"Open?" Lobo said.

"Yes."

As the lead loader reached the door, the tall metal plate slid further out of the way. The squad of machines thumped into the hangar and formed a rough square with the rear wall as its fourth side, then settled into position. I admired the planning: The weapons were accessible for inspection, but their armored crates also formed a small fort that would shield Dougat. We might have a chance at angle shots, but the stacked containers were high enough that we couldn't see directly into the center of the formation.

I watched in Lobo's feed as Dougat and a four-man team entered the building and went to the protected heart of the group of loaders. Lobo opened a second small display that used the internal corner cameras to show me an aerial view of the man and his guards. His team spread to positions behind loader legs, and one of the guards led him to a safe station as well. He had definitely upgraded his security squad.

Dougat said something I couldn't make out, and the crates shimmered into clarity. The armored and polarized shield glass was a nice touch: strong enough to withstand fire from most common weapons, able to go dark when in public areas, and clear enough to let us do complete inspections without having to unload fully or handle the merchandise.

"As you can see, Mr. Moore," Dougat said, his rich and deep preacher's voice managing to fill our whole section of the huge hangar, "the weapons are ready for your inspector."

Internal projectors could yield the same effects as shield glass, so I said, "He'll perform the bulk of the audit visually from outside the crates, but you also have to let him see inside each one for final verification."

Dougat laughed, a loud, hearty sound that for a change seemed genuine. "My, but you are a paranoid one. Fine, but he has to do it inside this space, because that's where all the easily accessible hatches are."

I didn't point out that he was also paranoid enough to make sure the loaders formed a defensive perimeter with all the crate inspection openings facing inward. Instead, I said only, "Acceptable."

I looked at the Zyun on my right and nodded. I thought for an instant I detected a trace of discomfort in his face, but I couldn't be sure. He neither hesitated nor said anything in response; the Zyuns were worth their premium fees. He jogged over to the rightmost of the stack of crates, climbed up the side of the farther loader as easily and smoothly as most people would walk a gentle ramp, and began carefully checking the contents of the top container.

I shifted my visual focus among the various inputs sharing my attention: the counter until Chaplat was due, its slow downward progress a growing pressure; the external feed showing two guards waiting beside Dougat's ship, not a problem now but a potential one later; the scene around me, all of us waiting, no one happy, everyone tense and everyone except Maggie and possibly Dougat armed; and the relay from the Zyun's microcam, which he carefully but not obviously made sure gave me a clear view of each weapon as he marked it off the list. I didn't let myself check on Maggie.

As the Zyun progressed through the crates, everything seemed to be in order. Dougat had delivered the goods: pulse and projectile automatic weapons with IR and noise dampening; laser/acid combo next-gen squidlettes far beyond what I'd seen in his warehouse basement on Mund; human-launched surface-to-air missiles that sported enough sensors and computing shielding to let them fly through all but the roughest heat and electronic attacks without losing the locks on their targets; transforming, self-launching missiles that could roll like two-meter-long demon-wheeled cargo boards into position and then sprout launch tubes from their centers; mushroom-headed transmission disruptors that could work on the ground or launch from their thick stems and sustain aerial positions via small rotors that sprouted when they hit the target altitude; and much, much more. No single item was incredibly expensive, but quite a few were pricey enough that many guerrilla groups on poorer frontier planets would pause to lust after them at a weapons mart before having to move on to more affordable alternatives. If Midon's goal truly was to catch Dougat with matériel he could never explain and in the process to put a lot of dangerous gear out of circulation, she'd chosen her weapons well.

"Jon," Maggie said, loud enough that Dougat and his men could hear her.

I turned, glared, and nodded at the Zyun. He clamped his right hand over her mouth.

"And how are you, my dear?" Dougat said, his voice still powerful but now friendly. "How nice that you're on a first-name basis with your captors. I do so look forward to having you back and to hearing all about your time with Mr. Moore and, of course, with the boy. If the child has said anything of interest, I'm confident you'll tell me all about it."

My pulse quickened and my body tensed at the implied threat. I'd hoped he'd find Maggie a small enticement, because she provided a way for him to show his team that he wouldn't let one of their own remain in captivity. Instead, he cared only about extracting from her anything she'd learned about Manu. I glanced again at her. Her eyes were wide and wet with fear. I hated myself for the thought, but I'd had it earlier as well: Her fear could work for us. I stepped next to her as if I were whispering in her ear but instead quietly said to the Zyun, "In a few seconds, pull your hand away as if she bit you."

I returned to my earlier position, then whipped around when I heard Maggie start to speak. The Zyun was shaking his hand convincingly as she said, "And to think I worked for you, Dougat. You don't care anything about me or the boy! And if you think I'll you do anything to help you harm or take advantage of that poor child, you clearly don't understand me!"

"I'm afraid it's *you* who do not understand *me*," Dougat said. "I care very much about Manu Chang; he may turn out to be the greatest discovery I've ever made. I'm also concerned about you, though I must admit primarily as you relate to Manu. I'm confident we'll be able to persuade you to help us."

"The way you'll 'persuade' him to do whatever you want?" Maggie said. "The way you persuade new Followers to work around the clock without—"

"Enough!" I said. I put my hand on the pistol in the holster on my right hip and looked at the Zyun. "I told you we should have gagged her. Shut her up before I do."

He clamped his hand over her mouth and pulled her next to him before she could speak. Her eyes were wide and her face taut with anger and something else, something worse I didn't want to see.

I turned and spoke to Dougat. "When we're done with the deal, she's your problem, and you two can talk all you want. Until then, I don't care to listen to any more of this."

We stood in silence for a bit as the Zyun near Dougat methodically worked his way from crate to crate. His heads-up display also showed the Chaplat timer, and he adjusted his pace perfectly, so that with ten minutes to go he finished all the checks he could do from the outside of the carriers and entered Dougat's enclosed area for the quick direct visual inspection.

In the feed from the microcam in the ceiling corner behind Dougat I could see that his team had prepped the crates: all the inspection hatches stood open. Two guards trained their rifles on the Zyun's back as he methodically worked his way through the weapons. He showed no reaction to the threat; I once again admired how cool the Zyuns stayed. The Zyun spent almost exactly one minute on each container, checking enough with his eyes and with his hands to make sure the external views had been accurate.

When he finished his inspection, he left the area without speaking, jogged over to me, nodded once, and floated to a front-facing position on my right.

"I trust you're satisfied," Dougat said. "I've brought everything I promised."

"I am," I said.

"Then deliver on your promise," he said. "Bring out the boy."

Even though I wasn't sure Dougat could see me, I shook my head slowly. "No. I told you: not until Chaplat is here and has approved the deal and paid me."

On the comm channel I shared with the Zyuns, Lobo said, "Chaplat's cargo ship has entered the base's airspace. Estimate touchdown in one minute."

"How long will this take?" Dougat said. "You really are forcing me to reconsider this entire arrangement."

"No," I said, "I'm not, because your wait is almost over."

I pointed to the other side of the hangar as Lobo slid the door there slowly open and dust stirred up by the incoming ship swirled inside.

"Chaplat's here."

CHAPTER THIRTY-SEVEN

I watched in a new small feed from Lobo as the two guards I'd met before hopped out of Chaplat's cargo transport and checked the area for him. They trotted the perimeter of that ship and the rest of that side of the hangar. In the view Lobo was giving me onto Dougat's outside team, that squad returned to positions near their vessel and brought their rifles to ready, but fortunately Chaplat's people stayed away from them.

Everybody was playing by the rules, behaving with sensible and well-organized paranoia, just as they should.

Lobo opened the side entrance in front of Chaplat's ship.

His two guards peeked around the corner of the doorway, then entered the building. After a few seconds, Chaplat and four more guards, all in black and all armed with holstered pistols and rifles, joined the advance team inside. They wheeled mobile shields in front of them, the currently transparent armor slightly distorting their images. Two men formed a second barrier in front of Chaplat. The others spread out along his right flank; the team used the wall to protect his left.

"Mr. Moore," Chaplat said. "I trust you won't waste my time here. I'm quite—"

I didn't want to let him and Dougat start a dominance contest, so I cut him off. "I apologize for interrupting, but I'm sure we're all eager to leave with what we came for, so I suggest we get to it."

Lobo opened a feed from the ceiling microcam with the best view of Chaplat. My heads-up display glittered with so many images that I had trouble handling them all. I put my hand to my mouth, coughed lightly, and subvocalized, "Fewer feeds."

Lobo closed the images of the exterior teams. Much better. Though I liked having all the information those views provided, I trusted Lobo to show me the outside again if something of note happened. In the meantime, with a smaller number of simultaneous images to manage I could much more easily stay on top of what was happening inside.

I missed a few words from Chaplat in the transition and refocused as he said, ". . . weapon crates, and I have the funds, but I don't see Jack."

"I'd like to verify the payment," I said.

"After we check the weapons."

"My man has already done that," I said, "and we'd be happy to send you the inspection video." I nodded to the Zyun, who thumbed open an unencrypted narrow-range broadcast.

The female guard pulled out a rolled sheet, snapped it taut, and showed the 'cast to Chaplat. He studied it for a minute, then laughed. "Very nice," he said, "and probably accurate, but we will do our own inspection, thank you very much."

Dougat sighed loudly enough that no one in the huge hangar could miss it. He had to be using some amplification I hadn't noticed.

"Must we endure this again?" he said.

Chaplat responded by pointing at two of his men. "Let them do a quick internal physical spot-check of the merchandise, and we'll only delve into the details if that doesn't go well."

"Reasonable enough," Dougat said.

Chaplat's two rear guards jogged to Dougat and entered the area formed by the wall and the crates. I watched in the feed from the camera above that space as one of Dougat's guards took up a position behind each of Chaplat's men and shadowed them as they moved. They opened the hatches and inspected the contents much more quickly than the Zyun, so Chaplat must have been at least somewhat satisfied with the video we'd sent.

We stood in silence for over five minutes as they worked. I checked on Maggie once, and she glared back at me, the Zyun's hand still covering her mouth. I wanted to snap my head back to the front to escape her accusing stare, but I forced myself to keep my eyes on her for a few seconds, as if carefully assessing a prisoner.

Chaplat's guards trotted away from Dougat and back to their leader.

When they'd resumed their former positions behind the barrier and around Chaplat, he said, "Check your wallet, Moore, and you'll be able to see—but not access, of course, not yet—the funds and the pending transfer."

I kept my focus on the two groups of men as I pulled out my wallet and opened it. It immediately displayed the pending transfer.

"The funds are indeed there," Lobo said over the private channel. "I've monitored and double-checked the wallet's query to the bank. Chaplat is playing it straight. It's time."

"I can indeed," I said. "Thank you. Let's do the money and weapons transfer, then I'll get Jack and the boy."

"No," Dougat and Chaplat said in unison, Dougat loudly and Chaplat in a level tone. The timing surprised them for a moment, so neither continued right away.

Chaplat recovered first. "I get Jack," Chaplat said, "and then we do the rest."

"I don't care about him," Dougat said. "The boy is what matters."

Dougat obviously had no real grasp of the type of man Chaplat was, because even if Chaplat hadn't planned to kidnap Manu before, a comment like that guaranteed that he'd go after the boy. I put away my wallet as if by habit.

"I set this up," I said, "so I get paid first." I held up my hand so neither would interrupt, then plunged ahead. Each of them almost certainly believed he had the firepower to overwhelm me. Though each may have thought his team could take the other's, neither could be completely confident on that front, so neither should want to start a war in here. Each was my insurance against the other—at least until they got what they wanted. "But I agree you need to see that I've held up all of my end of the deal. So, how about a compromise?"

"You're pushing it, Moore," Chaplat said. "If you don't have Jack here—"

Dougat cut him off. "What do you propose?"

"I show you Jack and Manu," I said, "and then we do the weapons and money exchange. When we finish that, we'll all have something we want. Then, Chaplat, I'll give you Jack, and Dougat, you'll get the boy."

Maggie screamed against the Zyun's hand, which turned her cry into a squelched roar of pain.

I ignored it and kept talking. "Until we finish all that, Jack and Manu remain with my team. Deal?"

"Acceptable," Dougat said.

"Fine," Chaplat said. "Get on with it."

I nodded and turned to face the Zyun behind me, as if I were going to speak to him. Tears ran down Maggie's face. She leaned forward against the grip of the Zyun, who held her in place with what you might believe was no effort if you looked only at his impassive face. The arm muscles bunched so tightly they strained the flexible armor told another story.

"Send them out?" Lobo said on the private comm channel.

"Yes," I subvocalized. I nodded once at the Zyun, whose head moved ever so slightly in acknowledgment. With one hand he leveled his weapon on the open ground between Chaplat and the rear center door.

I faced front as that huge piece of metal slid slowly open. The Zyun to my right trained his weapon on the space between Dougat and the opening to the corridor.

"We all stay where we are," I said. "My men are aiming only at space, not people. You'll get all the confirmation you need in a moment."

"Here they come," Lobo said.

The third Zyun appeared first, his head rotating from side to side as he slowly checked the perimeter. I knew a feed of the area was playing in his lenses, but like many pros he trusted what he saw in real life more than what any machine could show him.

After he finished his sweep, he stepped back into the corridor and came out with Jack and Manu in front of him. Both man and boy wore blindfolds. Each had his hands tied in front of him. A cable connected their hands, and another cable linked the center of that one with the Zyun who was now behind them. He controlled that main cable with one hand. His other held a small handgun that he trained at the boy's back.

I fought my natural reaction to their plight, a reflex I had trouble suppressing even though I'd caused this situation. If Jack and Manu didn't look like hostages, neither Chaplat nor Dougat would believe anything else I did.

"Satisfied?" I said.

Over the private comm channel, Lobo said, "EC troops on stealth approach from three southern vectors. No sign of awareness on the part of either group here."

"I allowed you to inspect the weapons," Dougat said at about the same time. "I think it's only fair—"

I interrupted him. "No. You put the weapons in crates, so we had no choice but to verify that all the individual items were present. There's only one boy and one man, and you can see for yourself that they're both here. My job was to deliver them safely; it's obvious that I did."

"Good enough for me," Chaplat said. "Jack seems fit."

"You're bound to have scared the boy," Dougat said, "but I suppose it couldn't be helped. Fine; I'm satisfied. Can we get on with it?"

"Definitely," I said. "If you'll ready the payment, Chaplat, we can commence."

When my wallet beeped, I reached for it to visually confirm the completed transfer.

As I did, Maggie burst away from the Zyun, who raised his weapon.

"Park!" I screamed. I held up my hand to signal the Zyun not to shoot.

Over the private channel, Lobo said, "The payment is already on its way to other accounts."

Maggie stopped and turned toward me. "You told me nothing—"

"Shut up and get back here!" I said. "Jack and Manu stay where they are until I'm sure I've been paid." In the feeds in my left contact I caught glimpses of both Dougat's men and Chaplat's holding their weapons at the ready, but I focused on her.

"Money?" she screamed. "This is all about money? I told you I wouldn't let you hurt them, and I won't."

I drew my pistol and aimed it at her. I nodded at the Zyun behind me, who slowly advanced on her. "Stay where you are," I said, "until he reaches you. You can still come out of this alive and rejoin the Followers."

"You wouldn't shoot me," she said.

She turned.

"Stop!" I said.

She took a step toward Jack and Manu, then another, no longer running, just walking slowly, carefully, her head high and determined. I knew how hard it was to stare straight ahead and keep moving when someone was pointing a gun at your back, and I admired her for it.

"Mr. Moore," Dougat said, "surely—"

"She stops, or I shoot her," I said to him, rushing the words so they got ahead of her advance on Jack and Manu. "You want the boy, and so does she. You paid for him. She didn't." My voice rose despite my best attempts to keep it level. "Last chance, Park! Don't make me shoot you."

She faced me, but she continued walking, moving slowly backward toward her goal even as she spoke to me, drawing ever closer to the boy. "You know you're better than that, Jon. You can't give Manu to Dougat. You said—"

I shot her in the chest.

Many things happened at the same time.

The echo of the round I'd fired boomed in the huge space.

Every head I could see in front of me and on the feeds from Lobo snapped toward Maggie and me.

Everyone in the space aimed weapons at us.

The Zyun near the rear corridor led Jack and Manu quickly back to the door, so they were barely in the room.

Jack and Manu tried to scream from beneath their gags.

Maggie crumpled, an expression of disbelief stealing across her face as blood spread on her shirt and her body hit the ground.

CHAPTER THIRTY-EIGHT

"Everyone stay calm," I said, tension still evident in my tone. "This does not have to be a problem." I extended my left arm so it was parallel with the ground, then slowly moved it downward. The Zyuns lowered their weapons in time with the motion, and I also lowered mine.

I watched in one of the feeds as Chaplat smiled and nodded his head. His team relaxed and followed suit.

"Not a problem?" Dougat said at the same time. "You killed a woman in front of me. Do you know how much trouble—"

I cut him off again. "Yes, I do," I said, walking over to Maggie's body. "None. This incident won't cause you or anyone else any trouble, because it never happened." I motioned the rear Zyun to join me.

"What do you mean?" Dougat said, reminding me again that he was a man who stayed away from the sharp end and let others do the wet work for him. "I saw it! If anyone were to find out—"

"Will you shut up?" Chaplat said. "You clearly didn't give a damn about her, whoever she was."

"She was one of my Followers," Dougat said, "and I care about every one of them. She was supposed to rejoin us as part of this transaction. And I certainly cannot afford to be implicated in this sort of thing."

"You won't be," I said. "Trust me: My problems are bigger than yours if this gets out, so I won't let that happen. Before we do anything else, my men and I are going to take her body to my PCAV, where it'll keep until we have time to dispose of it properly. If either of you decides to try to use this—" I paused and stared at the body. "—mistake as leverage, there'll be no proof that'll stand up. As for the woman's part in the deal, she obviously had no real value for you, so you haven't lost anything of consequence."

"Leave her," Chaplat said. "It's not like she's going anywhere. Finish the deal, and then you can clean up."

"I don't like her being there," Dougat said. "It's upsetting."

"EC troop lead sent the ready signal on your frequency," Lobo said over the comm unit. "On your sign."

I didn't respond to him. I focused on Dougat. "Yes, and it's dangerous for me," I said. "The sooner this never happened, the better for all of us."

"You stay then," Chaplat said, "and your men take her. I don't like losing sight of any of my colleagues at this point in a deal."

"That leaves me exposed and alone in front of all of you," I said.

"You made that choice when you shot her," Chaplat said, "and now you're wasting my time."

I shook my head and said, "Both of my men take her so we can finish this as quickly as possible. I walk to the door but no further, and my man over there," I motioned toward Jack and Manu, "leads the two of them back behind that door and to the rest of the team until my other two men return from cleaning up the mess. That's as exposed as I'm willing to be."

In the feed from Lobo I watched anger war with control on Chaplat's face, but after a few seconds he said, "Do it, but make it fast." He had to be planning to take Manu away from Dougat; I couldn't imagine what Jack could owe him that could be worth all this stress.

"I agree," Dougat said, his voice regaining its composure.

I nodded. The Zyun with Jack and Manu led them behind the

rear door, which slid slowly shut. The other two Zyuns picked up the body, one lifting under the shoulders and one grabbing the feet, and headed toward the open door behind us. I kept looking forward but walked backward to follow them.

They came to the open doorway and continued moving without slowing. I stopped two meters inside the doorway, glanced behind me to make sure all was well, and saw that they'd picked up speed as they headed to the PCAV. A side hatch in it opened for them. The bright morning light haloed around them so they looked like combat angels carrying off the fallen.

As I turned to face inside again, the world exploded.

Explosive impacts on either side of the door behind me blew chunks from the permacrete. The sound triggered the dampening circuits in my comm units. The dust and stench of spent rounds dominated the air instantly.

"Are you crazy?" I yelled at the two groups in front of me as I dropped to the floor and rolled toward the doorway. "What are you doing? Stop shooting!"

As I screamed, similar explosions at roughly a-third-of-a-meter intervals all along the walls behind both Chaplat and Dougat banged out small chunks of permacrete just above head height. The guard teams didn't know where to turn, so they assumed defensive positions and brought their weapons to ready, some in each group aiming toward the other team and some focusing on me. Two from each group pulled their bosses to the ground, adding to the confusion. All were well trained enough to wait for attack orders, but none of them needed prompting to protect their leaders; they did it instantly and without hesitation.

My roll had taken me to within half a meter of the outside, but I didn't dare move further right now; any action might draw their attention to me.

"Best target here," Lobo said as he enlarged the Dougat feed and focused on a very angry guard near the outer corner.

"Yes," I said.

Lobo swiveled two small automatic weapons Jack's team had built into the opposite ceiling and fired just above the man. At the same time, the doors behind the two groups snapped shut, showing for the first time the true speed the slabs of metal could attain.

The guard Lobo had targeted screamed, leaned around one of the crates, and ripped a burst at Chaplat's position.

Chaplat's team spotted the motion and returned fire as the first rounds hit the wall behind them.

Dougat's squad scurried to positions facing Chaplat's and returned fire.

I scanned Dougat's group. They were all focused on Chaplat and his men; good.

At first glance, I thought Chaplat's guards were also ignoring me, but then I noticed the woman had turned her weapon on me. If I rolled toward the door I'd expose my back, so I pushed off on my hands and feet and shoved myself forward and to my right, doing what I could to get out of her sights without straying too far from the exit.

Before I hit the ground, a round smacked me in the chest and slammed me backward, my breath leaving as the body armor stopped the shell from penetrating me but couldn't do much about the force of the impact. My chest spasmed and shook with pain. I focused on the shooter in time to see her head vanish in a wet mist and her body drop a second later, Lobo demonstrating flawless accuracy with the ceiling-mounted guns.

The two groups were firing madly on each other, the projectile and beam weapons booming and sizzling in the now acrid air. Neither side was taking much damage; none of these people must have served any serious time in a real military unit.

"Trajectory analysis said her next round would be a head shot," Lobo said.

"Thanks," I gasped. I checked both sides: No one was pointing in my direction. The need to breathe screamed for attention in my head, but there was nothing I could do about it but wait for my chest to recover, so I ignored the summons. I rolled to face the door, scrambled to my feet, and darted out of it and immediately to the right.

The contacts compensated as the bright light hit my eyes. I

gulped, and a few shreds of air made it into my lungs. It wouldn't take either side long to realize something was wrong, so I couldn't wait any longer.

"Midon," I croaked.

Shots boomed and rang and echoed inside the building. A few rounds clanged on the door only meters to my left; they'd noted my absence. Men shouted, their words lost in the cacophony. In the display from Lobo I saw that one member of each team was watching the door. The others continued to fire on each other.

"Stage two," I said.

"Starting," Lobo said, and at the same time that he added "and Midon online," explosions ripped the permacrete along the rear wall between the two groups and on either side of the door.

Through the open hatch twenty meters in front of me, one of the Zyuns waved me forward as the other jumped out and crouched to provide covering fire should someone make it through the battle to my position.

I held up my hand as Lobo connected me to Midon.

She and a female voice I didn't recognize spoke at the same time.

"Finally ready, Moore?" she said. "It's about time."

"Ready," the other female said.

"They're firing at each other," I said. "They started arguing, and then it escalated. One of them had wired the place ahead of time, so charges are going off everywhere. They're heavily armed with both weapons and explosives. The whole place could blow. Go with caution."

The other voice's tone didn't change. "We can tell," she said without any trace of irony, "and we're always careful. Exit while you can."

The link went dead.

I sucked in a bit more air and forced myself to run.

At least two dozen soldiers in EC active-fiber urban camo rose from the permacrete in front of me like desert heat waves coalescing into a squad of hell's own warriors. They rushed by me.

I reached the first Zyun. He pushed me forward as the second grabbed my hand and pulled me in beside him. The hatch snapped shut as soon as we were all inside.

"Taking off," Lobo said.

As we rose, Lobo overlaid my vision with feeds from the front and sides of the hangar, battles raging everywhere I looked. I closed my eyes so the Zyuns and the interior in front of me didn't add to the visual overload, but adrenaline surges and residual chest pain impelled me to move even though I was now out of danger. I opened my eyes and subvocalized, "Take it off the lenses and onto displays. Add audio."

The feeds from the battle flashed and screamed to life on the front wall, each image fighting for my attention, the sounds mixing and remixing in rapid audio mutation. I scanned along the different scenes, flitting from one to the next, pacing as I followed the action, seeing what I could in parallel but facing so many viewpoints that I had to process much of it sequentially.

The EC troops at the front of the hangar mirved, squads of eight heading east and west of the building, the remaining group fanning left and right of the door I'd exited less than a minute earlier. Two soldiers from the central assault team rolled a pair of mobile speakers inside the facility. Amplified shouts of "Cease and desist or Expansion Coalition forces will engage you!" soared on high notes above the battle noise as the speakers did their best to evade the shots and pulses filling the air around them.

"Kill the EC warning," I subvocalized.

A second later, pulse and projectile shots hit the speakers and the cease-and-desist notice stopped, the evasive circuits of the agile sound balls no match for Lobo's aim.

More groups of eight EC troops sprinted from hiding places to the left and rear of Chaplat's team on the west side of the building, joining their comrades on the front to surround the gangster's rear guards and trap them against the building.

A similar scene unfolded on the hangar's other side with Dougat's exterior team, but there it turned ugly when one of Dougat's men fired on the EC soldiers approaching them from the rear. The shot had barely left his weapon when the man's body shook as if electrified, then part of his head vanished as the EC troops on all three sides returned fire. The remaining Followers watched the shattered body fall and quickly placed their weapons on the tarmac.

On Chaplat's side, the ship guards did the same, each surrendering all weapons, kneeling, and putting hands on heads.

Smoke and dust and flying debris dominated the inside of the hangar. EC troops fired on both groups from around the sides of the front door. Explosions shook more and more of the rear walls, then spread along the side walls and advanced on the building's front, chunks of permacrete flying into the center area at random heights all over the facility. Sections of the ceiling shattered as noise and dust filled the space, and still more explosions rocked the weakening structure.

"Exits," I subvocalized.

The doors behind Dougat and Chaplat snapped open so quickly that both groups didn't realize for a few seconds that new exit options were available. Their firing slowed as light flooded in from the open doors and the opportunity for retreat became clear. The external EC troops spotted the change a second earlier and focused most of their members and weapons on the dust-filled interior, the remaining troops continuing to control their captives. Chaplat and Dougat wasted no time in leading their teams out of the hangar, only to run straight into their own surrendering ship-side men and the squads of EC soldiers pointing guns at them.

More explosions smashed chunks from the hangar's walls, and holes appeared along the sides even as blasts tore at the front wall.

The EC squad at the front entrance checked the inside, then split, one half running along the outside toward the west and Chaplat's captured team, the other sprinting for their comrades who had taken Dougat.

As Dougat and his soldiers who'd tried to leave the building put down their weapons, four men from the EC squad ran inside and prodded the loaders into action.

The front corner of the building on Chaplat's side collapsed in a heap of rubble, the walls there too weak to support both their own weight and the ceiling's.

"Midon online," Lobo said.

"Connect," I said, "but mute hangar audio."

Silence stilled the air as Midon's voice came over the comm. "What's going on, Moore?"

"What are you talking about?" I said, gasping as I talked even though I could now breathe normally. "How should I know? I brought them to you, and I ran—as we agreed."

"The place is coming apart," she said.

"What? What are they doing? All I know is that I did what I said I would, and those jerks shot me. I'm heading to ground. It's your problem now."

On the displays in front of me another chunk of the front of the building silently fell into heaps of rubble.

"An exploding building wasn't part of the deal," she said. "You didn't warn us about this."

"Because I didn't know about it!" I shouted.

On the displays, the last of the weapons loaders exited the rapidly decaying hangar.

"I warned your team as soon as I saw charges go off." I paused for a few seconds, then continued more slowly. "Dougat said he had a source in the EC; someone on your side must've traced me— thanks a lot—and wired the place. Did you get the weapons?"

"Yes," she said, "and both Chaplat's and Dougat's squads."

"Then what's your problem?" I said. "You caught Dougat with the goods, so you got what you wanted, and you even captured Chaplat in the bargain—as I said you would. Our deal stands. If Dougat wired the place to blow up and destroy the evidence, you have only someone in your own organization to blame."

In the rightmost display, the entire eastern wall of the hangar trembled and then fell inward, small chunks of permacrete flying outward and over the heads of the EC troops and the Followers.

"What about the boy?" she said. "He was part of the deal."

"Getting him there was all I promised," I said, every word flat, "and I delivered. If he's not with Dougat, he's trapped inside. Either way, it's not my problem."

"We're talking about a boy here, Moore."

"Yes," I said, forcing my voice to remain level, "we are: a boy you wanted to capture. A boy Dougat wanted to buy. You'll find him there, or he's dead; I don't see how he's much worse off if he never made it out. Regardless, I delivered, so you owe me."

Midon didn't try to conceal the contempt in her voice as she said, "And we'll pay. I keep forgetting how cold you are."

I watched as the hangar's west wall and central ceiling shattered and fell. "Are we done?" I said. "I have a wound to tend to."

"Yes," she said. "See you in three days."

The link went dead.

"Audio," I subvocalized.

Booms and crashes assaulted our ears as chunks of the rear ceiling of the hangar crashed down, further weakening the last standing parts of the building. The west rear corner trembled, shook, and in a final scream of weakened permacrete collapsed into a mound of rubble.

No more explosions, no more crashes, only permacrete-on-permacrete scraping noises as the last chunks settled and then were still.

The hangar was gone.

I stared in silence at the huge mass of shattered and dust-covered permacrete that marked where the building had stood only minutes before.

"Nooooo!" came a cry from behind me, pain and surprise mixing in the strangled sound.

Maggie was sitting there, her gaze alternating between the displays and me, back and forth, back and forth, her mouth struggling to form words.

"You shot me," she said, the words coming slowly and painfully as the drug that had knocked her out released its control on her system.

I nodded, waiting for the rest, my face hot, my eyes wet as the hate in her expression blasted me like a cold, stiff wind.

"I'm alive," she finally said, sounding more sad than pleased.

"Yes," I said.

"And you let them die," she said. "You told me you'd take care of him, you told me to trust you, and I did." She shook her head slowly. "Instead, you were going to sell him, and now he's dead. You could have taken him away, you could have saved him, but you didn't."

She stared at the floor for a few seconds. When she looked up at me again, tears clouded her eyes and streamed down her cheeks.

"It's your fault," she said, "and mine for trusting you. You killed him. An innocent boy."

The tears stopped, and she rose to one knee, snarling as she spoke.

"You killed Manu Chang."

CHAPTER
THIRTY-NINE

Maggie launched herself at me faster than I believed she could move, but even fueled by anger she was no match for the Zyuns. One stepped between us even as the other grabbed her shoulder with one hand and stopped her forward progress, the muscles in his forearm straining with the effort.

"And you two!" she said, focusing on them. "How could you help him do this?"

After a pause, as if the third brother had begun the answer, the Zyuns answered, one word coming from each, ". . . our job."

"That's all this is to you people?" Maggie said. "A job? You two were willing to sell an old friend and a boy, and now both of them and your own brother are dead, and your excuse is that it's a job?"

The Zyuns didn't answer, and neither did I. Even if I'd asked them to talk—and I hadn't—they wouldn't have bothered. Nothing we could say right now would convey our feelings, and nothing would do more good than harm.

She stared at the three of us, whipping her head from person to person, and when no one spoke, she sobbed quietly.

After a minute or so, she pushed at the Zyun's hand that was holding her shoulder. He stared impassively ahead but didn't release his grip.

I nodded, a motion so slight Maggie never saw it, and he let her go and stepped forward and to the left, ready to grab her again if need be.

"Drop me anywhere," she said. "I'm sick of the lot of you."

"No," I said. I put my left hand on the shoulder of the Zyun in front of me, and he stepped half a meter to the side, out of her way but still able to protect me easily should it come to that. Maggie and I were little more than a meter apart, with nothing physical separating us, yet I couldn't recall feeling farther from her. "Not yet."

"I'm a prisoner again!" she yelled. She stepped forward and both Zyuns moved to stop her, but I shook them off. She came so close I could smell the fading effects of the drug on her breath, the permacrete dust that had worked its way into her hair when she fell, the tang of adrenaline and fear in her sweat.

"Only for a time," I said. "If I let you go now—"

"What?" she yelled again. "Something bad will happen to me?"

"Yes," I said. "They all think you're dead, and for now we need to keep it that way. The EC couldn't care less about you, but if either the Followers or what's left of Chaplat's gang found out you're still alive, we could all be in trouble."

"So I suppose you did all this for my own good?" she said. "You shot me to save me?"

I considered the question, pondered whether I could explain everything in a way that would make sense and not cause further damage, wondered if I'd made the right choices, and finally decided that the potential cost of any explanation outweighed the possible benefit. "Yes," I finally said.

"Well, you should have let me die," she said.

That was too much. It was all finally too much. I stepped into her space, bridged the last few centimeters between us, and caused her to back up. "That's very noble, very dramatic," I said, clipping each word as I fought for control even as part of me knew that I'd surrendered too much to anger. "But you can say it only because you don't understand what it means. Watch more people die, stare as life leaves them and you realize to your darkest animal core that this is it, this is their last moment alive and then they'll be no more, they'll be gone, lost forever. Then you won't wish for death. When your only options are unending pain for your few remaining hours or days or weeks, then you've earned the right to want to die. Until then, shut up and be damn grateful for the time you have!"

"Maybe you're right," she said, her eyes locked on mine, her words coming slowly and with care and a tinge of fear. "But some of us believe there are things worth dying for, causes more precious than life."

I thought of all the men and women I'd known who'd died in the name of such causes, the bodies ripped apart in jungles and deserts and oceans on half a dozen planets where I'd fought alongside people whose only real sin was being so stupid or so poor or so idealistic that they were willing to join forces like the Saw and fight at the sharp end where the decision makers would never be. Not once had any of them bothered to make a noble speech about causes. They did their jobs, followed orders, and if they were lucky they came home. If they spoke nobly of anything, it was of taking care of each other and of destroying their common enemy. Other people, usually those far from the action, made the speeches; the comrades with whom I'd served lived and died from the consequences of those words.

Lobo interrupted my thoughts on the comm channel we shared with the Zyuns. "One minute from the hangar," he said. "The EC is surely tracking."

"Do as I tell you," I finally said to Maggie, "and soon enough you'll be able to leave, go and find more causes, or do whatever else you want. Try to run before I give the okay, or disobey any instructions, and we'll restrain you." She started to speak, but I held up my hand; we'd make no progress by talking. "None of this is negotiable, and this is not the time for conversation. We're about to move."

I turned away from her and walked to the front of the ship. The Zyuns formed a barrier between us. "I understand," I subvocalized to Lobo. "Take us in, and then we'll go to ground."

❧ ❧ ❧

We hopped out of the hatch and in three steps were at the side door to the low-rent parking hangar. One Zyun stood on point. I followed him, Maggie came behind me, and the other Zyun brought up the rear. I turned toward her and said, "From here until we reach the safe house, you don't say a word. If you scream or try to run or do anything else we don't like, he"—I pointed at the Zyun behind her—"will knock you out, and we'll carry you and explain to anyone who asks that you had a seizure. Got it?"

She nodded.

I faced front again and tapped the lead Zyun on the shoulder.

He opened the door, and we stepped into the heat and noise and bustle of midmorning in Shinaza, Malzton's shiftiest district. Buildings here served function and paid little respect to form, the block in front of us lined by rows of pale gray permacrete two- and three-story structures that either touched or shared walls, as if the genetic material of each had reproduced with only minor mutations to produce the next. The permacrete road glowed a dull, darker gray in the bright light, stained by the passage of people and vehicles. All the windows for as far as I could see were barred, and cold, gray, quick-shut metal shutters flanked all those on the first floors and most of the others. Similar covers stood to the sides of all the doors.

No wonder the EC didn't want to bother governing this place: Every building was a small fortress ready to repel intervention of any sort.

The people walking the street in front of us only reinforced the notion that you did *not* want to pick a fight around here. Men and women alike moved in careful, calculated flow, never touching one another despite the congestion, each one sliding past the others like electrons whose random orbits drew them momentarily too close for safety and would soon enough take them to blessed isolation. Every person in view also carried at least a pistol of some sort and often more than one weapon, the variety lending the street the aspect of an industrial runway show for those with deadly intent: swords, short and long and straight and curved; rifles and shotguns and pulse cannons whose weight made their carriers walk with visible extra effort; knives in sheaths and on loops and tucked into armored clips on pants and shirts; and various extending and otherwise self-configuring clubs, dormant now, only their matte black grips visible, but holding the portent of pain only a flick of the wrist away.

No one paid us any more or less attention than anyone else; everyone here could be friend or foe, alliances as fluid as the traffic.

We walked up two blocks, merged with the human current flowing right, and stopped in front of the fourth house. Another gray permacrete structure, it stood out from its streetmates in two ways: It was the one place that wasn't attached to the buildings adjacent to it, and it was surrounded by scrolling warning signs on the ground on each side and across its front. Text and graphics fled backward from the street on the wired black tarmac in a constantly changing stream of languages and images, all of them delivering the same message: Don't Walk Here.

"Stands out a bit, doesn't it?" I said.

"Harder to blast through," the Zyuns replied, alternating words now that there were only two of them, the cadence having completed the switch from triples to pairs. "Wired and mined and poisoned substrate," they added, pointing in unison to the two-meter-wide black tarmac that ran down the sides of the building. "Double armor, walls, windows, and doors. All exterior surfaces mined. Five buried escape tubes, all armored." Their mouths twitched in the closest gesture to a smile I'd yet seen from them. "Quite expensive. Your money. Most suitable."

The Zyun in front touched a comm inside his sleeve and a thick, gleaming walkway extended from the low front porch to the road in front of us. It cleared the black mini-moat by mere centimeters. Despite my initial doubt, it had no trouble supporting all of us as we crowded side by side onto the two-meter-wide small porch. The walkway withdrew rapidly into the building, and the front door swept aside as a small hatch clanged into place over the now hidden metal plank.

As soon as we were inside, the door slid shut. Sounds of metal in motion followed its closure. I raised an eyebrow in question.

"Armor re-forming," the Zyuns said.

We stood at the edge of a single large room that measured roughly ten meters wide by twenty deep, considerably smaller than the structure's outside. Wood plank floor, yellow verging on gold, ran lengthwise from the front to the rear. Bare walls, also wood but composed of wide pieces whitewashed to a soft purity. Kitchen in the rear left corner opposite a stairway, a counter with a floor-standing oven, a sink, and a refrigerator, plus a garbage chute in the middle of the back wall. More planks and an ancient pull door, no visible lock, covered the area under the stairs. A low-slung table two meters long squatted on the room's left side just in front of the kitchen area, cushions surrounding it, enough room under it for crossed legs. Along the floor to our right were two thin, tightly rolled futons. Identical sets of ten security displays perched on each of the four walls, images in them showing views from security cams monitoring all sides of the exterior and the roof.

Small, furry creatures I didn't recognize, somewhere between cats and rats in size, scampered around as if the place were theirs. At least half a dozen of them remained in view, running indifferently to and fro in the space, occasionally arcing near us and then warping away.

The Zyun in front pointed to the kitchen. "Gas and water tanks inside here," they said, "with no external power. Self-contained. Plenty food."

"And them," I said, kicking at one of the creatures that strayed near my right foot.

"Extra precaution," the Zyuns said. "Meal tasters. React identically to humans."

Maggie spoke for the first time. "You can't be serious!" she said. "You'd kill these innocent creatures?"

"Only if food bad," they said.

"The trash chute?" I said, happy to change the subject.

"To remote buried furnace," the Zyuns said, "with backwash safety valves. Sewer, too."

"Of course," I said. Despite all that had happened, the two of them looked as content as I'd ever seen them, though I couldn't pinpoint the reason for the impression. Perhaps they were simply more relaxed, the building their idea of a happy place. "And the rest of it?"

They led us upstairs and to another single large space. The floors near the stairs and all the steps emitted high-pitched creaks of various pitches as we walked.

"Nightingale boards," the Zyuns said. "Classic. Good."

As we walked up the stairs, I said, "Isn't this whole place more than a little bit of overkill for three days?"

"You wanted safe house," they said, "and gave no budget. Great place."

I hadn't figured them for big spenders, but I should have realized that everyone has weaknesses; security was one of theirs.

The second-floor room was identical to the one below it save for having no kitchen and only a single rolled futon. The glow from similar banks of security displays illuminated the room.

"Your space," the Zyuns said.

"Clothing?" I said.

"In bathroom," they said. "Yukatas. Not here long."

Another flight of differently creaky stairs led us to the third floor, a twin to the second.

"And I suppose this is mine?" Maggie said.

The Zyuns nodded in unison and said, "Thickest armor. No roof access. No escape. Safest."

"As if my safety mattered in all of this?"

The three of us stared at her in wonder, her perspective so very different from our own that I'd forgotten for a moment how this must all appear to her. I knew they wouldn't speak, and I had nothing useful to say, so I shook my head slightly and left, the Zyuns on my heels.

"Wonderful," Maggie said as we headed down the stairs, anger and despair and frustration dripping from the single word. "This just keeps getting better."

❧ ❧ ❧

Small grunts and thumping sounds from below brought me awake. I launched off the futon on which I'd been taking a nap and raced downstairs, wondering if we were under attack and how anyone had gotten through the house's defenses so quietly.

We weren't. The Zyuns were doing clap-hand push-ups on the floor, moving up and down like machines. They pumped out another dozen while I watched, then stood and stared at me, sweat pouring off their faces and necks.

"When I heard the sounds," I said, "I thought someone had gotten in."

This time, I would have sworn they actually smiled for a second before in the usual alternating speech pattern they said, "With this house's walls, you'll know."

"Of course," I said. "Habit."

They nodded, stretched out on the floor, and started doing crunches. When I didn't leave, they said, "Join us?"

Their tone made it clear the words were less an invitation than a dare, but it wasn't like I had anything else to do, and exercise burned tension, so I nodded and got into position. "Set the pace," I said. "I'll keep up."

We started again on the crunches, and after seventy-five I stopped counting and focused only on keeping my stomach tight and encouraging the nanomachines inside me to clean out the muscle toxins as quickly as they could. I always wonder in situations like this whether taking advantage of that enhancement is cheating, but I also always end up deciding that it doesn't matter. We all use the resources available to us, and from the looks of the Zyuns that included more than a little biochemical assistance.

We moved from crunches to a wall sit and then directly into squats. From there we reversed position and did handstand push-ups, them in the middle of the floor, me against the wall, my balance not up to the job of staying steady without any support. We flowed smoothly from exercise to exercise with no breaks, as they led me through more bodyweight workouts than I'd realized existed. Time vanished, the world narrowed to my little area in this one room, my troubles evaporated in the heat of the repetitions, and all I knew and all I felt was the work, the muscle pain, the effort, and the constant focus on the next rep, just the next one.

It was glorious.

After a particularly long and brutal set of alternate-leg lunges, the Zyuns said, "Enough now."

We stretched out on the floor, spread our arms and legs, and lay there, breathing hard. Even though I wasn't moving, every muscle in my body hurt intensely, my breathing came ragged, and I was exhausted.

I couldn't have felt better. The combination of the rush of the endorphins and the rare freedom of the long period without worry relaxed me even as the exercises tightened me. I was so happy I started laughing, a little at first, and then heartily.

The Zyuns stared at me as if I were insane, but then their mouths twitched, and in a minute they were laughing, too, the first time I'd heard them make any noise that didn't sound completely controlled.

We heard Maggie coming down the steps and stopped laughing as her head came into view.

"What are you idiots finding so funny?" she said, fury warring with incomprehension on her face.

I couldn't help myself: I burst out laughing again, louder this time, and the Zyuns were right with me. After a few seconds and clearly with no understanding of what we were doing, Maggie shook her head, cursed us, and ran upstairs. It wasn't funny, I knew her pain was real, I hated it, and yet I laughed harder, release winning over intellect. The Zyuns did the same, and for a few minutes the sound of laughter filled the room and all was right with the world.

"Why won't you explain it to me?" Maggie said a few hours later, after I'd showered and napped and we'd all eaten. She put her hand on my face, and I expected her to claw at me, or pull me closer and punch or knee me. Instead, she closed her eyes and for a few moments seemed to drift away.

I had no idea what to do; in most of my experience, when someone touches you, it's as part of an attack. I wasn't comfortable, but I also didn't see any harm in it, so I remained completely still.

She opened her eyes, pulled back her hand, and shook her head slowly. "Maybe I completely misread you," she said, "but I would never have figured you for someone who could watch two people die and show so little feeling."

I considered all the reasons I couldn't answer her, and I even wondered if I was wrong for believing them, but in the end all I could say was "I can't."

She continued shaking her head slowly as anger and sadness warred openly on her face. "In the beginning, all I wanted to do was save the boy," she said, "but then I hoped for more. Now, though, now all I want is to leave." She headed upstairs two steps at a time. Though in my mind I was reaching out to her, my hands never left my lap.

I'd told her the truth, and I believed in what I said and the path I'd chosen, but truth and belief are all too often not enough.

The Zyuns and I worked out again early that evening, but this time there was no joy, at least not for me, only anger, rage at what I'd had to do, at myself, at the way my life had unfolded, at the universe. We pushed it longer this time, flowed from exercise to exercise until the Zyuns stopped and sprawled on the floor, and still I kept going. I stopped when in the middle of a set of squats my trembling legs gave out and I fell, my emotions and my body spent.

When I'd recovered, I used the house's secure comm lines to troll the local data streams for news of the fight at the hangar. Dougat's and Chaplat's arrests sent ripples through the infosphere, but they weren't the hot news they would have been on a more government-friendly planet like Mund. There, Midon's smiling face would have been everywhere, transforming the capture of a fanatic arms dealer and a dangerous gang leader into political capital. Here on Gash, the EC came across as just one gang inflicting damage on two others. What stories and threads I viewed focused on the arrests themselves, the disposition of the weapons, the fate of the Followers, and so on. Beyond the obligatory few clips of the trashed hangar, no one paid the setting any special attention, and before the night was out the story was already fading, beach patterns washing away under the incoming news tide.

Lobo and I had agreed the smartest option was to not communicate for the three days, and we were right, but I found I missed him, even his sarcasm.

I stuck to the plan and didn't contact him. I set a countdown timer on my room's displays and watched as a few of the seconds between now and the end of our time in this house vanished in the count. Waiting is never fun, but despite all that I didn't like, passing time here was so much better than many of the situations I'd survived that I shrugged; the hours would come and go soon enough.

The night and the next two days unrolled in a pattern like the first, working out and eating and checking the data streams and resting, but with one exception: Maggie didn't talk to us again. We ate in silence, at the Zyuns' insistence waiting to begin each meal until one of the cat-rodents had swallowed a bit of the food and showed no ill effects. We communicated primarily by pointing, and when we bothered to speak at all, we doled out words as if they were precious gems. The Zyuns seemed at perfect peace with our ritual. Though I knew I should be doing something to improve the situation with Maggie, I couldn't come up with any option that helped more than it hurt, so I did nothing.

Precisely when the countdown timer hit zero, I used the comm line to contact Midon. Her face appeared quickly; midmorning was clearly more to her liking than earlier in the day.

"Prompt when it comes to payment, Mr. Moore," she said. "Of course."

"Is there a problem?" I said.

"None at all. All my news is good."

"From what I can tell, the news barely registers."

"You must have stayed on Gash," she said, feigning surprise even though I was confident she knew exactly where I was. "Back on

Mund and on many of the other planets where we released the story of my daring capture of these two criminal organizations, the event is getting major play."

"I'm glad I'm proving to be a good investment," I said, not particularly meaning it but wanting to bring the subject back to money.

"That you are," she said. "How does meeting in an hour at our offices in Malzton sound?" Coordinates streamed across under her image.

"Why not do the transfer now?" I said, though I knew her answer and was counting on it. "I can receive over this channel."

"And leave a money trail over links we don't control? Surely you're not that naïve, Moore."

"If we must meet in person," I said, "I'd prefer the gate station, which should be quite safe for both of us. I'm sure you understand."

"Fine," she said, "but then the meeting can't be until early this evening. I'm jumping out of here then, and no way can I afford to make two trips there today, so you'll have to wait until I'm already at the station."

"Fair enough," I said. "I'll be with a few people," I paused, "and, of course, my PCAV. So—"

She held up her hand and shook her head. "Save your threats. Trust me, if I wanted to do something other than pay you off, even that extraordinarily secure house you're in—" She paused and smirked, making sure I understood all the implications.

"How?" I said, playing the role as she expected.

"Did you think we couldn't track you?" she said. "We know where both you and your PCAV are, and if we wanted you badly enough, neither the PCAV's arms nor that ridiculously fortified building would have protected you. But why would we bother coming after you?" She leaned forward, held up her hand, and ticked off points with her fingers. "First of all, we got what we want. Second, you're not worth the negative public exposure on Gash that any such attack would cause us. Third and most important, you've done good work for us: Between what we'll get for the weapons we confiscated and the value the story is delivering on other planets, this whole affair has yielded massive ROI, both direct and indirect." She leaned back. "Paying you is by far the easiest and cheapest option, so I'll see you tonight at the station." She cut the transmission.

I went downstairs and said to the Zyuns, "Pack up, grab Park, and get ready to move. We're leaving."

CHAPTER
FORTY

We joined the street-level flow of Shinaza and merged rapidly into it, another cluster in the fast-moving human traffic. As soon as we were out the door, I fell behind the others and opened a link to Lobo.

"All normal here," he said. "Of course."

"We're heading out," I subvocalized, "and with an unexpected bonus: Midon is jumping tonight."

"Excellent. I am—"

I interrupted him. "I know, I know. Gotta move. Out."

We wound our way back to the hangar by the same route we'd taken a few days earlier. Midon was right: At this point, we'd have known if she wanted to hit us, so there was no point in trying an alternate route. Besides, our best defense was to get inside the gate's area of influence; no attack would happen there.

We took off as soon as we were inside.

The screaming red jump gate grew and grew in the front displays until it filled them completely and a single arc of it became all that we could see. None of us spoke, but that wasn't unusual at this point. I wondered, as I did every jump, at the cold beauty of the gates, their power, their mystery, and their origin. I glanced at Maggie, wishing we were again sharing that feeling, but she continued staring away from me. I tried to lose myself once more in the gate, but the mundane world interrupted as we asked the station for permission to dock.

We had a few hours to kill before Midon would arrive, so we all passed through the series of locks and went inside.

Partway through a passable but thoroughly unexceptional dinner of a small-grained starch covered with sauce and chunks of fish, Maggie finally spoke.

"Exactly what am I doing here?"

"Eating dinner," I said. I pointed to her plate and added, "Though not much of it. I know it's not great, but it's better than the insto-food we had at the safe house."

"Don't play with me, Moore," she said, her eyes widening in anger.

So much for my attempt at levity.

"Why did you drag me with you?" she said. "You could have left me on the ship. You don't need me for anything else."

"Insurance," I said, telling the truth, at least all of it that she could handle.

"Exactly how does my presence help you collect your blood money?"

Dumb idea. I should have known that talking was a bad plan. I shook my head, spooned a bit of the fish, and chewed slowly.

Maggie stared at me for a bit, then took a bite of her own food.

I was glad to see her eating. We had a lot more to do today, and when you're on a mission and have the time, grabbing some food is almost always a good idea.

Midon was neither subtle nor over the top when she sent for us. A guard found us in the media lounge at the rear corner table we'd taken from four unhappy bureaucrats.

He walked straight to us, kept his hands away from his weapons, and said, "She told me to tell you to follow me."

We did. I expected to make another trip to Carne's office, but I was wrong. The guard led us to a plain, unlabeled door near the docking area for the larger ships. He stood to the side as it opened and the Zyuns, Maggie, and I filed in. He didn't follow us inside.

Midon sat in a chair in the corner of the otherwise empty room. When she saw Maggie, surprise flickered in her expression before she brought it under control.

Before she could speak, I said, "Why here?"

"No cameras, no sensors, no recordings, nothing," Midon said. "This meeting never happened. Speaking of things that never happened," she nodded in Maggie's direction, "I'd heard you'd shot her dead."

"I might as well have been," Maggie said, "for all the good—"

"Shut up," I said. I faced the Zyun whose black-gloved hand held her elbow and whispered, "If she starts to talk again, gag her."

Both Zyuns nodded.

"I see your talent for making friends knows no bounds, Moore," Midon said. "But as I was saying, I'd heard you'd shot her and she was dead. Why was my information wrong?"

"I shot her," I said, "but as you can see, I didn't kill her. I needed to fake her death." I shrugged. "So I did."

"Why?"

"Both to save her life and as part of my exit plan."

"Too bad you couldn't have done the same for the boy," Midon said, her anger evident.

Out of the corner of my eye I saw Maggie glare at me and open her mouth, but I cut her off by holding up my hand.

"Yes, it was," I said, gritting my teeth and speaking slowly and carefully. "I had hoped to save both him and my previous client."

"But you didn't," Midon said.

"That was not my fault," I said. "I had no way to know Dougat and Chaplat would start firing."

"Really?" Midon said, standing and walking closer to me. "What did you think would happen when you put an arms-dealing religious fanatic and a gang boss in the same room with a shipment of weapons and a boy they both believed was psychic? Or did you even think?"

I stared at her for a long enough time that she took two steps backward before I answered. "I *thought* they would do the deal they'd said they would do. I *thought* they were the businesspeople they claimed to be. And I *thought* your team would arrest them without destroying the whole giant permacrete hangar!"

"My team didn't bring down that building," Midon said. "Those two groups of idiots did it themselves, though no one on either side will admit it—as you'd know if you'd stayed around. But I guess the one life you made sure to save was your own."

I didn't say anything. Nothing would help.

Midon finally filled the silence. "So why are you showing her to me now?"

"So you wouldn't find out later and think I'd hidden anything from you," I said, anger still sharpening my voice. "This way, you know exactly what I did, you encounter no surprises in the future, you pay me, and we're done."

"What about what you didn't do?" Midon said. "You didn't deliver the boy."

"I promised I would get him there," I said, "and I did, but that was also never our main deal. What you most wanted was to catch Dougat in a weapons trade, and I made that happen."

"You did," she said. "And I'll pay." She pulled out a small comm unit.

I thumbed my wallet to receive in a high-quarantine area. No point in taking chances.

"You know," she said, "you have a remarkable talent for alienating people, even those you help." She pointed at Maggie. "Do you really think she's thankful that you saved her? She obviously cared for that boy. She'll hate you forever."

I wanted to look at Maggie, but I didn't. I kept my voice level and said only, "You said you'd pay."

"Of course," she said. "What you'll see is a massive credit for overcharging of jump fees in this sector. The records at all the stations under EC control will reflect various aspects of this error. So, as this transaction and your acceptance of it prove, the EC is only returning money it had previously accidentally charged you."

I studied the incoming flow. The total was right, and the accounting was as she stated. The wallet found nothing wrong with the transfers. I waited as Lobo took the time to grab the data, vet it with the originating bank in Malzton, and then shuffle it through a chain of other banks on Gash to the accounts we'd established. It took well over a minute; transmit times in exchanges with the planet's surface are always slow. When my wallet showed the all-clear signal, I closed it, looked again at Midon, who was waiting with visible impatience, and said, "And, I assume, we never had a deal."

"Why would we ever even have talked?" she said. She brushed past me and stopped at the door. "I'm heading to Mund for some interviews and from there to Drayus and on to Immediata. Visit our worlds for as long as you like. Spend lots of that money on EC planets; our economies love tourists. But," she paused and stared at me, "don't ever call me again."

She left, but the door didn't close behind her.

Maggie stared at me and said, "Will you now finally—" but stopped when she saw the guard come into the room.

"I understand you'll be leaving," he said. "Let me help you find the way out."

CHAPTER
FORTY-ONE

The guard watched us through the lock portal until we'd pulled back from our docking position.

As soon as we had, displays popped to life on the front wall, aspects of the gate glowing red in all of them, and Maggie spoke.

"You have your money. Will you drop me off yet?"

I stared at the images as I spoke. "Lobo, I need to see Midon's ship jump to Mund, and I need to know if anyone is tracking us. Give me a view of Malzton as well." I then looked at Maggie. "No. We're not done."

"What do you mean?" she said, making no attempt to hide her frustration or anger. "What else do you need?"

"Not now," I said. "Be quiet and wait."

Several seconds later, one display changed to an image of the aperture to Mund, and a second shifted to a projection map of all the vessels in the area. A third snapped to a highly magnified view of Malzton at night, lights shining throughout the city, the abandoned EC base on its southern edge a solid black mass.

"Only one EC ship," Lobo said, "an executive shuttle, is jumping for Mund. The EC of course doesn't publish its passenger list, but Midon's a safe bet for it. No current signs of pursuit or surveillance, but sitting still makes that all too easy to hide."

"Would you please listen to me?" Maggie said. "All I want is for you to let me go."

I kept my eyes on the display and said, "Lobo, take us Gashward at max speed on an evasive course. Show me anything that might even possibly be following us."

Adrenaline spill, frustration, and anticipation combined to leave me exhausted, but I pushed back the fatigue, buckled into a pilot's couch, and watched for signs of trouble. If our evasion run yielded no pursuers and Midon was indeed through with us, we could finally be done, but we weren't there yet.

I looked again at Maggie. "Soon," I said, "when I'm sure it's safe. Until then, please take a couch, be quiet, and let me work. Sleep if you can. We don't know for certain that no one is after us, so it's not over yet."

As we raced away from the gate, a ship passed through the Mund aperture.

I heard Maggie clear her throat as if to speak, and I said, "Not now."

"The ship most likely to be carrying Midon has jumped," Lobo said. "No signs of pursuit yet, but if there are watchers and they're very good, we might not see them." On the map display, Lobo overlaid a route that resembled the path of a drunken man careening off the walls of a wide hotel aisle in search of his room and bed. "Unless you object," he said.

"I agree about the watchers," I said, "and of course your plan is fine. Run it."

Ninety minutes later, we were flying at treetop level along the southeast edge of Malzton when Lobo said, "To the best of my ability to monitor, there are no pursuers and no active surveillance. This data is, of course, imperfect, but it's all I can provide under the circumstances."

"Good enough," I said. "I didn't think anyone would come after us, but we had to make sure. Take us in."

"Ninety seconds to touchdown," Lobo said.

I stood and faced the rear. The Zyuns and Maggie were sitting in

678   *Mark L. Van Name*

couches. I'd kept my communications with Lobo private, so they had no idea what we were doing. Maggie had obviously been napping, so I waited until her eyes focused on me, then said, "Time to move. We're landing."

"Where are we?" Maggie said. "Are you dropping me in the middle of nowhere?"

"We're back at the hangar," I said, "or, more accurately, at what remains of it, and no, I'm not leaving you here."

Her eyes widened, and her face tightened in anger and horror. "I can't believe you!" she said. "Why—"

She stopped when we settled to the ground, a side hatch opened, and I stepped out. Lobo had brought us to a spot sixty meters from where we'd first entered the rear of the hangar so long ago—a few days ago, I reminded myself. It just felt like a very long time.

"Follow me," I said as I walked a bit closer to the hangar, "but don't go anywhere."

I heard Maggie and the Zyuns approach. Rather than have a long discussion, I decided to show her. "Lobo," I subvocalized, "it's time."

"What are you doing?" Maggie said. "I don't want to be here!"

"Wait for it," I said.

Slight, almost imperceptible tremors, so small you wouldn't notice them if you weren't expecting them, ran through the permacrete.

"Why are you staring—" Maggie said.

I held up my hand and repeated, "Wait for it." In my peripheral vision I saw one of the Zyuns grab her arm.

"Wait for—" she began.

I couldn't hear the rest of her words because chunks of the destroyed hangar screeched and banged as they began moving and grinding against one another. With the light of the star-filled sky and the illumination pouring from the hatch behind us we could just make out the tumbling gray permacrete pieces.

More and more of them shifted, and the screeching grew louder. The roar of engines added to the noise, and the volume rose.

Another sound, maybe a pounding, clawed at the edges of the din, trying to get in but not yet powerful enough to be more than a feeling. A few seconds later, the pounding clarified into a powerful bass note repeating in a steady rhythm: a drumbeat. I would have sworn the falling pieces were moving in time to the beat, my mind imposing a pattern and order where I knew there could be none.

The ground ahead levitated slowly, as if the bits of the hangar had decided it was time to leave this planet for somewhere better. Shards of light poked out from under the chunks, centimeter-high beams thrusting into the night in random places.

As the sounds of rocks in motion and engines and drums grew louder, the section of permacrete ascended further. Its ascension produced more light, then more, and more still, until a yellow-white glow surrounded and defined a perimeter, as if an invisible giant were uncapping the planet to reveal a secret sun within.

Suddenly, the entire floating permacrete area shot fifteen meters skyward, lifted into the air by the now-visible Lobo, a giant sheet of reinforced metal balanced atop him by struts extending around his exterior. He froze, loose pieces of debris falling off the sheeting on all sides, light streaming from him as the beat intensified and quickened.

What a show-off.

When no more chunks of permacrete had fallen off the sheet for several beats, Lobo floated slowly toward us, moving a fraction of a meter a second, until the hole he had exited was visible behind him, and then he halted.

The drumbeat picked up speed.

The long side of Lobo facing us lifted while the other side held its position, and slowly the remaining permacrete chunks poured off the sheet into the pit where he had spent these last few days. When he had rotated to about sixty degrees and most of the chunks had fallen off the metal sheet, he accelerated abruptly skyward at the same time as he rotated further and triggered the small explosive bolts that disengaged the support struts from his body. The beat reached a frantic pace, the sheet tumbled backward into the hole, and Lobo darted up and away from the metal as it fell with a deafening noise and a cloud of wraithlike dust.

Lobo righted himself and settled to the ground five meters in front of us, the dusty air swirling behind him like clouds around an angel, and then all at once he cut the running lights, his engines, and the drums.

He opened a hatch facing us.

Light streamed from inside him and backlit the man standing in the center of the opening: the third Zyun.

The Zyun reached to his right and pulled forward first Jack and then, a heartbeat later, Manu Chang.

CHAPTER FORTY-TWO

"Welcome back," I subvocalized on the private comm link to Lobo. "Nice entrance. But drums?"

"You have no idea how good it is to be back," he said. "Manu came up with the idea for playing music, and I chose the taiko. He thought it would be a fun touch, and I had to agree. I told you I could do fun."

Before I could respond, Manu yelled, "Maggie!"

The Zyun holding the boy tilted his head slightly. I nodded in response, and he released his grip.

Manu ran straight to Maggie, who grabbed him and held him as tightly as if he were the last good dream she'd ever have. He clung to her just as hard, bouncing up and down in happiness. I hadn't realized they'd bonded so much in the short time they'd spent together. They whispered to each other, his expression animated, hers hidden from me by the fall of her hair.

Jack tried to walk out of Lobo, but the Zyun stopped him.

"Let Jack go," I said.

The Zyun released him and followed him to me.

Jack smiled broadly, spread his arms as if to hug me, and said, "So it all worked out and they paid up?"

I nodded and punched him in the stomach hard enough to cause him to double over.

"You caused all this," I said. "You put a boy at risk, you exposed me, and now all you can talk about is money? How about a little contrition and some gratitude?"

Jack straightened slowly and gasped for air for a few seconds, then slowly brought his breathing under control. Finally, he said, "I appreciate all you've done, but you should consider thanking me as well." He held up his hands as he spoke. I resisted the urge to slap them away and let him continue. "Manu was never in real danger; first I and then you made sure of that. I knew you would; you're good at what you do. We improved this whole sector of space by helping put a gun-running religious fanatic and a dangerous gang boss in jail. We both made a lot of money, and so did Manu. Speaking of which, where's my share of what you made?"

"Expenses," I said. "Like renting that faux PCAV from Li. Like the safe house." I shook my head. "No, you caused this, so most of your share went to paying for it. Besides, I'm confident that you spent far less on the warehouse setup than the value of those gems you snatched from the Followers' Institute; consider them your payment."

"Even if I agreed that was fair," Jack said, "and I most certainly do not, what about Manu's cut? His family is so poor that they agreed to go along with this whole thing just to make some real money. He earned more doing this than he could ever have made pursuing any of the other opportunities available to him—and, trust me, the other moneymaking options were way more dangerous and worse for him than anything that happened with us."

"What do mean his family agreed to go along?" I said. "You told me he needed the money for medical treatments to help him deal with the pain his ability causes him."

Jack backed up a couple of steps. "I admit I said that, but all I was doing was extending the con they were already running with the boy. He really does have ancestors from Pinkelponker, so they knew he'd pass any background check Dougat might conduct. The whole psychic abilities angle was just a way to tempt that old zealot into buying an interview; who knew the guy would turn so crazy about Manu or that other people would get interested in the poor boy?"

"What about the accident he saw?" I said. "He called it before it happened, his reaction seemed genuine enough, and the victim sure was badly hurt, maybe even dead."

"I don't think you ever worked with him," Jack said, "but that 'victim' was Carlos, Carlos Corners, a low-end grifter still grinding it out doing the hit and fall in parking areas and anywhere else vehicles move slowly enough that he can handle the impact. I thought Manu blew his timing and overplayed the reaction a bit, but you're right about the badly hurt part: Carlos did actually get knocked into the air and torn up. I promise you, though, that hurting Carlos was never part of the plan. Some idiot's overly ambitious truck cut off our driver, lost control, and hit Carlos at full speed. It was a freak accident. Fortunately, thanks to the top-notch med units in Eddy, Carlos should be as good as new by now."

"So Manu's not a psychic?" I said, stepping closer, fighting the urge to pound Jack's face into pulp. "And this has all been just another of your cons?"

"Not *just* another con, Jon," he said as he backed up further. "You hurt me. This was, if I may say so, a masterwork, and one that I must remind you has earned all of us, including Manu, quite a lot of money."

Maggie, her left hand holding Manu's right, stepped forward as if to cut between Jack and me but stopped a meter away from either of us. She stared at me and said, "He's wrong, Jon. Manu really is everything he claimed, everything you and I thought."

I forced myself to look away from Jack and at her. "How exactly would you know?" I said, anger coloring my tone.

"Because Manu saw the planned accident go wrong before it did," she said, the words tumbling out like heavy stones rolling off her. "Because he knew Jack would come to his home before Jack ever met his uncle. Because he saw that Jack would let him meet others like him. Because Dougat was right about the children of Pinkelponker—not the name, that's just stupid, but the existence of such a group—and Manu belongs with them."

No one spoke. No one moved. Maggie's eyes widened but never left mine. I couldn't believe what she'd said, maybe because it was so incredible, or perhaps simply because I wanted it so much to be true. If it was, then maybe Jennie might have gotten off Pinkelponker before the accident, maybe I could learn whether she was dead or an incredibly old woman or at least what had happened to her since the time I last saw her.

Finally, I spoke, my voice softer than I intended, almost a whisper. "How do you know all of this?"

"I'm one of them, Jon, one of the descendants of that lost world. I'm not like Manu—I'm not sure anyone alive has as powerful a talent as his—but I am a sensitive. I catch glimpses of what others are thinking."

"You read minds?" Jack said.

She answered him but kept staring intensely at me. "No, nothing as clear as reading. If I touch you—touch your skin, it has to be bare skin—I usually get a jolt of your thoughts, like a wave of impressions washing through me. It's how I knew you, Jack, were running a con on Jon, and it's why I tried to warn him. It's how I know Manu's telling the truth."

"You can do this to anyone?"

She nodded, her eyes still on me. "As long as my skin comes into contact with theirs."

"That's amazing," Jack said, his voice vibrant with excitement. "Do you realize what you could do with that ability, how wonderful it is?"

She shook her head. "No, it's not. I can't touch anyone without them invading my mind for at least a second. I've spent my whole life avoiding even brushing against other people. It's no gift at all. Can you imagine what it's like for every contact with another human to carry that penalty?" She stepped closer to me, leaned forward and tilted her head until I could feel her breath on my ears, and whispered so quietly I had to strain to hear the words, "Except you, Jon. I don't know why, but I could never read you. You, I could touch without worrying what would hit me."

Jennie had always seemed able to tell exactly what I was

thinking, to know my mood and to be able to help me any time I needed it. I wondered if her abilities were limited to healing, if perhaps she, like Maggie, might also have been a reader.

"What are you saying?" Jack said, leaning closer and yanking me back from my reverie. I glanced at him and saw him notice Maggie's hand holding Manu's. "And what about Manu? You're holding his hand, and you seem fine."

"I can't explain it either," she said, "except that it must be part of his talent. The first time we touched, his thoughts smacked into me, but somehow he knew what was happening—"

"And I stopped it," Manu said, his tone as matter-of-fact as if he were discussing breathing. "I can let her in, but I know it hurts her, so I don't, except when we need to talk without you hearing."

Jack laughed and clapped his hands. "This is great! Do you have any idea how much money we could all make? With my skill at working marks, your talents, and Jon and Lobo as backup, we could be rich." He stopped, concern visible in his face. "What about the treatments?" he said to Manu. "I thought your uncle and I made that up to help increase the payday, but is that true, too? Do you really need them?"

"No," Manu said. "That was a lie. I felt bad saying it, but I saw I had to meet Dougat so Maggie would find me. My uncle said we couldn't trust you with the truth." He shrugged and looked unhappy. "I didn't like lying to anyone. I'm sorry."

"It's okay," Jack said. "Of all people, I certainly understand that sometimes you have to skate around the truth. What about the accident, though? Were you really as upset as you seemed?"

"Of course," Manu said, a tinge of sadness creeping into his voice. "Carlos was nice to me, and I didn't want him to be hurt." He was still unhappy as he added, "I wish we could have stopped it."

I focused again on Maggie. "So this is why you were working for Dougat, why you cared so much?"

She nodded. "I had to stop him from getting Manu."

"Why?"

"Because we'd heard about Manu, and he belongs with us. It's the only place he can be safe."

"Where—" I stopped before I could voice the question. The knowledge wouldn't help me, and I knew myself well enough to realize that no matter how much I tried to avoid it, violence followed me. "I don't want to know, because then one day I might tell someone else. Besides, I'm sure you wouldn't want to tell me anyway." I had started to say "couldn't," but I know too well that anyone can and will say anything, no matter how much they don't want to, if you apply pressure on them over a long enough period of time—and if you're willing to hurt them. I'd come close to breaking on several occasions, including during the most recent torture session, which had lasted scarcely more than a day.

She smiled in acknowledgment of my restraint.

"Who are you to decide for all of those people?" Jack said. "Maybe some of them would be interested in a business proposition that could make them rich. Why don't you let me talk to them, and then they can decide for themselves?"

Maggie shook her head and looked at Jack. "No, I can't do that, and I wouldn't even if I could. All I know is where I'm supposed to take Manu. Someone will be watching, and if we're alone, I'll receive instructions for the next stop." She turned back to me. "As you might imagine, the core group moves around constantly, and most of us operate in small cells."

"Let me come with you," Jack said, "and make my case. I don't think you appreciate what we could accomplish with my talent and your abilities."

I hadn't expected any of what Maggie had told me, couldn't have planned for it, but I'd known Jack wouldn't give up Manu easily, wouldn't simply let me take the boy back to his family. That much was as certain as gravity, so I was prepared.

I stepped closer to Jack, shaking my left arm slightly so the tiny needle fell from its perch in my sleeve. I lifted my hand to his shoulder and thumbed free the protective tip, much as I imagined Jack had done when he knocked me out as I was climbing into Lobo after the conflict at Dougat's institute. "Let it go, Jack," I said, clapping my hand on his shoulder in comradely fashion. "Let it go." I raised my hand as if to clap his shoulder again, then turned my palm and brought the needle down hard against his neck. The drug hit him as swiftly as whatever he'd used on me, his eyes only beginning to widen before he drooped and started to fall. I caught him and held him upright. "Would you guys put him in Lobo?" I said to the Zyuns.

One remained behind Maggie and Manu, cutting off any rear escape route, doing his job. The other two took Jack from me and carried him into Lobo.

"Strap him onto the medbed." To Lobo I subvocalized, "Keep him unconscious until I give the word."

"Of course," Lobo said. "My role was obvious."

I ignored him as I realized we'd been standing here longer than I'd planned. We needed to move.

"Is Jack okay?" Manu said.

"Yes," I said. "I gave him something to make him sleep. I'll wake him when you two are safely away."

"Manu," Maggie said, "would you please go wait in Lobo? I need to talk to Jon alone."

The Zyun behind them cocked his head slightly.

I nodded once.

"Okay," Manu said. He headed into Lobo, the Zyun right behind him.

Maggie opened her mouth to speak, but I held up my hand and turned away from her. "Lobo," I subvocalized, "I trust the Zyuns, but if any of them looks like he's going to do something to Manu, put him to sleep."

"Permanently or temporarily?" Lobo said.

"Temporarily, of course. I said 'sleep.' "

"Will do," Lobo said.

I turned around and said to Maggie, "Go ahead. You were about to say something."

She slapped me across the face with her right hand, struck me hard enough that my head whipped partway around.

"What?" was all I could manage, because all my energy went into controlling my natural reaction, into stopping myself from hitting her until she could never hurt me again. Anger flooded me, a bitter taste filled my mouth, and smell vanished as my body focused for combat. I forced myself not to move.

"That's for not telling me what was going on," she said. "You made me live for all that time sure that Manu was dead. How could you be so cruel?"

I didn't answer at first, couldn't do it. I inhaled slowly and deeply through my nose, exhaled even more slowly through my mouth, and repeated the actions twice.

"Don't hit me again," I said. "As to how I could do what I did, the answer is simple: I promised I would protect the boy."

"And making me think he was dead protected him?" she said.

"Yes."

"How did that help? Why couldn't you trust me? I thought you cared about me?"

I ignored the last question, couldn't let myself hear it, couldn't even consider its existence or what that might imply. "Two reasons," I said. "First, I'd learned you betray your emotions under pressure. I couldn't risk you giving away the fact that he was alive. More important, though, was that I knew you were covering up something, so I couldn't risk Manu's safety by trusting you."

"How could you know that?"

"Because you cared too much too quickly," I said. "From the beginning, you were too eager to come along with me, too willing to put up with too much trouble for someone whose only knowledge of the boy was supposedly a single viewing in the Institute."

"So why didn't you get rid of me?"

"Because by keeping you close I made sure you were the one variable in this mess that I completely controlled."

"But what if I'd still been working for Dougat? I could have shot you when you met him in the desert or given him information while I was in the hotel."

"If you'd trained the rifle on me, Lobo would have taken you out," I said. "Except when you were in the SleepSafe, you were never anywhere we couldn't control you and monitor any attempts at communication with anyone else. When you were in the SleepSafe, you still weren't a threat, because I made sure you didn't know anything that could put Manu at further risk. All you could ever tell anyone was that I appeared to be going through with the deals I'd made but might be planning some tricks. That wouldn't have surprised or helped any of these people."

She stood silent for a few seconds, considering everything. "Weren't you still taking a big risk, there at the end? I mean, what if the crashing building had destroyed Lobo?"

I chuckled. "Not much chance of that. He could have withstood the whole thing falling on him if it had come to that, but it didn't: Jack's team had prepared the hole and the metal sheet ahead of time. All Lobo had to do was keep Manu, Jack, and the Zyun alive for a few days, a week at most. For a machine built to house a much larger crew for as long as several months at a stretch, that was no big deal." I looked at her closely. "The hard part was spending those last few days with you and not saying anything, so that when we met with Midon you'd be genuinely furious with me."

She closed her eyes, finally understanding—or, at least, I like to think she understood. "So it wasn't easy for you, was it?"

"Nothing worthwhile ever is," I said.

"You're wrong, Jon," she said. "Some very important things are all too easy." She opened her eyes. "Like caring for people. Like loving them."

I couldn't speak, not without giving away more than I could safely tell anyone. I couldn't explain to her how neither of those statements had ever been true for me, how caring had always led to pain or trouble or violence or all of those, how loving would require a kind of trust and openness I could not afford, how the simple fact that I never appeared to age would all by itself doom any relationship. All I could do was stand there, mute, unable to answer, trapped in my head, pinned down by my life.

"What happened to make you this way?" she said, her hands reaching up and holding my face.

Another question I could never answer.

"And why are you the one person who's closed to me?" she said. "Why can I touch you and receive nothing?"

"I have no idea," I lied, happy to have something to say but knowing the truth had to be related to the way Jennie had healed me all those years ago.

I saw the insight hit her. I suppose it was inevitable. Even as she opened her mouth to ask I began to calm myself for the next untruth.

"Is there any chance you have ancestors from Pinkelponker?"

I chuckled. "No. There are plenty of bad things I could say about my parents, but I can't accuse the bastards of adding that particular strain to my life." I couldn't actually remember much of anything about my mother and father, had only the wispiest memories of them, but the statement would fit with the childhood image I was building for her.

"It's so strange," she said. "Maybe I could talk our people into letting you come with us. You've earned it by protecting Manu, and some of the others might be able to figure out what stops me from being able to read you at all."

And we could spend time together. I saw the thought in her as clearly as if she'd spoken it. I had the same dream myself.

It could never come true.

"I can't," I said. "My life—well, you've seen a sample of what it's like. I've done a lot of things, not all of them good, and sometimes they catch up with me. It wouldn't be safe for any of you." Or for me, I thought but did not add, because the fact that you all share the same heritage and even the same types of talents doesn't mean that I can trust all of you. All it would take is one person to figure out the truth about me and let it slip, and I'd never be able to run far enough. Some corporation or government or rich jerk would catch me, and I'd either have to kill everyone who chased me or end up spending the rest of my life as somebody's specimen. The memory of Aggro, unlike what little I had left of my parents, would never fade. I won't go back to that. "No," I said, "it wouldn't be safe."

"I'm sorry," she said, the hurt obvious. "I don't think you're right, but I obviously can't change your mind."

"I do have one question," I said, knowing that even asking it was taking a risk but unable to walk away from the small chance that her group might be able to help me learn more about Jennie. "Are there any people in your group who are actually from Pinkelponker, not just descendants?"

"No," she said, shaking her head as some obvious sadness hit her. "We had one, a man who was old when the group found me, but he died several years ago. He was the only one."

Even though it had been a long shot, disappointment still washed through me. If Jennie had made it off Pinkelponker and away from the government agency that was keeping her captive, this might have been the kind of group she'd try to find.

I stared at Maggie and wondered if maybe I was wrong, considered whether I should go with her, if there wasn't a chance we could be together.

I was kidding myself. I'd have to be satisfied with the little time I'd spent with her and with thoughts of futures that might have been but never would be.

"I hate to break this up," Lobo said over the machine frequency so only I could hear him, "but we've lingered here way longer than your plan, and I see only risk in increasing our exposure by staying. Couldn't you two finish your little chat inside me?"

"We're done here," I said aloud.

Maggie stared at me oddly for a moment, then nodded. "If you say we need to leave, then I trust you're right."

"We do," I said, "but unfortunately we can't go quite yet." I turned to face Lobo and loudly said, "If you guys have secured Jack, come on out. It's time we finish up."

The Zyuns emerged from Lobo walking three abreast and stopped a couple of steps in front of me.

"You're set to take the faux PCAV back to Keisha Li?" I said.

"Yes we are," they said in their usual speech style. I found the presence of three voices instead of two to be surprisingly pleasant. They certainly seemed happier.

"And you're still comfortable keeping the return of my deposit as the last part of the fee?" I said.

"Yes," they said, "we know her, and we know the ship."

"It was a pleasure working with you," I said. "If I ever need backup in this region again—"

"Then call us," they said.

They turned as one toward the other ship but stopped when Maggie said, "May I ask you one question before you go?"

All three nodded.

"I could read you on the few occasions our skin touched," she said, "but I could never get a glimpse of any thoughts that weren't directly about the situation at hand. Why is that?"

"Now is all," they said. "All is now." They headed into the ship.

I couldn't help but chuckle: Zen backup, a beautiful thing.

"Let's go," I said to Maggie.

I headed into Lobo. She followed.

As soon as we were inside, Lobo closed the hatch. We watched on a forward display as the Zyuns flew away to return the ship.

When they'd vanished from view, Lobo lifted off and said, "The hole is different enough to be noticeable. Is that a problem?"

"Show me," I said.

Lobo popped an aerial view onto the display on which we'd been watching the Zyuns. Chunks of rubble sat in random spots around the perimeter of a pit that was much bigger now than it had been. Sections of the metal sheet protruded here and there from under permacrete boulders.

"Had scavengers come yet?" I asked.

"No," Lobo said.

"Then they'll solve the problem for us," I said, "because they'll want to see if the collapse exposed anything of value. They'll take away the metal for salvage, and their diggers will hide your escape well enough for our purposes." I looked at Maggie. "Where should we take you?" I held up my hand before she could speak. "I'm not asking where you're going; I need to know where to drop you."

"Remember the market on the southeast section of Nickres?" she said. "The one I didn't get to see because you made me wait in the SleepSafe?"

"Of course," I said, flashing back for a moment to the ride in George and hoping that whichever of the two guys ended up with him truly appreciated him. "We'll take you."

"What about the device you put in my arm?" she said. "Will you finally remove it?"

I smiled despite the hurt look on her face. "It was never an explosive," I said. "I'm sorry I had to lie to you. It was a tracker. I don't even know if it's still active; we used one that would decay automatically. Lobo?"

"It's still working, though barely," he said audibly.

I led Maggie to the medbed. She blanched slightly at the sight of Jack unconscious and strapped onto it.

"Don't worry," I said. "He's fine. I'll release him, but not until you and Manu are safely away and we're far from here." I hated being the cause of the lingering fear in her eyes. "I also wanted to say how sorry I am for tying you up there, and for the threat and the tracker. It was all—"

"I understand," she said. "You explained, and you were helping Manu. I just can't stop myself from reacting to this room."

Lobo extended a probe from the wall. Its end glowed dully. "Put your right arm under the light."

Maggie did and held it there.

"That's it," Lobo said. "The device would have stopped transmitting on its own, but now it's incapable of sending or receiving. In about two weeks, it'll break down completely, and your body will absorb or excrete the remnants."

Maggie nodded and said, "Thanks."

We headed back to Lobo's front. "Where in that market do you want me to drop you?" I said.

Manu came over to her and took her hand.

"Anywhere near it," she said. "Where we landed before would be fine."

"Then take us there, Lobo," I said.

Maggie and Manu stared together at the forward-facing display Lobo had opened. I stood beside her, no more than half a meter from her, maybe less, as close as I was ever going to come and still so far away.

Lobo accelerated southward.

For a few seconds I wished he were slower, or that his engines would fail, that we would hover there over the deserted base, just us, alone and safe and together, so that I might have a few more minutes with Maggie, but of course Lobo functioned flawlessly, and we rapidly picked up speed as we hurtled away into the dark, dark night.

CHAPTER
FORTY-THREE

Lobo parked in front of a hangar three buildings over from the one where we'd hidden him what seemed like forever ago. The sky was clear, but light pollution from the landing station and the rest of Nickres greatly diminished the number of stars we could see and robbed the evening of its full potential. The air was crisp, but deep breaths revealed the unmistakable trace of fuel. Is this what we humans do? Go to a beautiful, unmarked place, invade it, pollute it, lessen it, and then leave, only to repeat the process over and over, on world after world after world?

I stared openly at Maggie, who was waiting outside Lobo for me, as I realized I was only dragging myself down. Standing on the permacrete, holding Manu's hand, her long red hair glinting here and there from the landing lights, she, they, were proof we also brought joy and could do good things, *did* do good things, maybe not always, but often enough. I pictured her twirling in the blue dress; such beauty.

"What?" she said, smiling a bit, but only a little.

"I—" I struggled for what to say, then gave up trying to be clever or coy. "You're so beautiful that I couldn't help but look, couldn't stop myself from doing everything I could to make sure I'd always remember you." My face felt hot, and I was embarrassed, ashamed, both of burdening her with unwanted affection and of my own lack of control.

She leaned toward me, but I shook my head slightly.

"You have to go," I said.

She nodded, her rear foot raised slightly, her body momentarily frozen.

"I'll walk you to the street where I entered the district last time."

I brushed past her, our shoulders touching for only an instant, all I thought I could handle, and she and Manu fell in behind me. I led them around the hangar, to the right for two hundred meters, and then onto the street I'd walked so recently, so long ago. I gave her quick directions. She listened closely, but too late I realized she must have already known the way. Though morning had not yet risen and we were in the deadest time of night, the magnetic pull of the market's commerce had drawn scores of people and vehicles into the street, all streaming toward the same destination.

"Want me to walk with you to the edge of it?" I said.

She released Manu's hand, glanced down at him, and he looked away from me as he shook his head ever so slightly. "Yes," she said, "I really, really do, but it's not a good idea. We need to be on our own, so it's clear no one is following us."

"Of course," I said, turning to leave. I didn't trust myself to look at her for a second longer. "Goodbye."

I felt her hand on my face, pulling me toward her, and when I turned she was there, right next to me, leaning into me. She kissed me, lightly at first, then hungrily, holding my head with both her hands, and though I wanted to remember always how she looked, I couldn't help but close my eyes. The kiss went on and on, or maybe it lasted only a few seconds; I couldn't tell, didn't want to know.

And then she stopped, pulled back, and whispered, "Oh, Jon. I wish I didn't have to go, but I do."

I kept my eyes shut as her hands left my head. I kept them shut as I heard Maggie and Manu walk away. I kept them shut until I trusted myself to open them, and when I did, I could barely make out Maggie's head blending with the crowd of pedestrians, Manu invisible to me but, I was sure, safely with her. I took a few steps so I could keep her in view, then stopped and stared until the crowd swallowed them and, like a view of a distant happy land fading as a sun set, they were gone.

I touched my lips. "She did care about me," I said aloud, not to anyone, simply so I could hear the words, so maybe I could believe them.

"Of course," Lobo said. "I could have told you that from her vitals many times before."

I wouldn't have thought Lobo capable of speaking those words without sarcasm, but he managed it, somehow made them feel like a welcome affirmation from a friend. How pitiful is this: to get consolation from a deadly machine? I knew I should feel that way, and for a second I did, but then I shook my head and reminded myself that I should always be grateful for the few friends I had, whatever form they took.

"Thanks," I said, "both for saying that now, and for not saying it earlier. Had I known, it would only have made what I had to do even worse."

"Of course," he said again, this time adding nothing, not needing to.

I headed back to him, focusing on bringing down my pulse as I walked.

"Now, let's deal with Jack." I thought about him as I drew closer to Lobo, and about friends, which Jack was, sort of, as much probably as he could be, and an idea blossomed. "Here's what we're going to do."

CHAPTER FORTY-FOUR

The cool globe of fruit, its surface imparting onto my tongue a taste I'd never experienced, exploded as I bit into it, and a warm, animal-rich broth flooded into my mouth. I closed my eyes to focus on the flavors as they blended and created something entirely new.

"Joaquin is truly a genius," I said. "Amazing."

Jack's eyes were still shut, his mouth closed, enjoying the last vestiges of this *amuse bouche*, the tiny but potent beginning to the very long lunch ahead. "He is that," Jack said. "We haven't even really begun, and already it's better than most meals dare dream of being." He sipped water from the glass etched with images of the four waterfalls that had supplied its contents. "How did you persuade him to put up with"—he waved his arm slowly, taking in our surroundings—"all this?"

"And what's wrong with having a great meal inside me?" Lobo said audibly.

Jack and I laughed and sipped more water.

Lobo was hovering parallel with Falls, high above the canyon and the four waterfalls that inspired the restaurant's name. Displays and open hatches all around us granted amazing views of the stunning setting. Our tableside server stood discreetly outside Lobo on the transparent, padded gangplank that connected the interior where we sat with the pathway that led to the back door to the kitchen. I wished Maggie could have joined me, wondered if fine cuisine was an interest of hers, realized how little I knew about her, missed her nonetheless.

"Nothing," I finally replied to Lobo's question, forcing myself to admit it was true, taking the time to enjoy the views, the light, cool breeze that played inside him, the warmth of the afternoon. "Nothing at all."

Our main server cleared the table. Immediately, two of his colleagues appeared and in perfect unison placed our next dishes in front of us. They vanished as quickly as they had arrived, Joaquin honoring my request not to have anyone provide the customary and rather lengthy explanation of the ingredients and cooking magic that yielded each of the dishes before us. I had no idea what we were eating, and I didn't want to know; I wouldn't be returning to this sector anytime soon, so I wanted the meal to remain mysterious, a magical conclusion to an entirely too real mess.

"And how did you convince Joaquin to open on one of his dark days?" Jack said.

"The answer to both your questions is the same," I said. "I explained that he owed me after one of his staff gave us up to Chaplat. I also warned him that if anything happened while we were dining today, if Lobo detected even a hint of a threat, he'd have fifteen seconds to exit the restaurant before a pair of missiles reduced it to dust. And," I raised my glass to Jack, tilted it momentarily in his direction, and took a sip before continuing, "I promised Choy that you'd pay him an enormous amount of money for this most wonderful meal."

Jack was about to bite a small piece of what appeared to be a sauce- and leaf-covered, whole miniature fish, but he paused, slowly returned the food to his clear glass plate, and said, "How enormous?"

I raised my hand, and Lobo opened a display behind my head.

"Rather," Lobo said, "though given that we know how much we've transferred to your account, it's nothing you can't afford."

Jack sat very still, his face unmoving, an internal argument immobilizing him for many seconds, until at last he smiled broadly and said, "Given that you came through and paid me despite what you said before, I have to agree that I can." He leaned back in his chair. "In the end, Jon, we did it again, and we did it well." He lifted both hands as if to push me away, though I hadn't moved. "Yes, I'm sorry we hurt others, and I never meant to put anyone at risk. But we were every bit as good as in the old days. You have to admit that."

Maybe we were, though it seemed to me we spent more time fighting each other than working together. Still, I saw no point in arguing with him; open a conversational door with Jack, and you can find yourself stuck for a long time on the other side of it.

When I didn't speak, he continued, "If you've got nothing else going, I have quite a few great ideas I'd love to run by you. We'd need to go elsewhere, of course, to implement them, but that's no problem. What I have in mind—"

"No," I said, interrupting him, "I'm not working with you again. I agree that though we messed up a lot, we also did some good—" I paused as I pictured Manu walking away with Maggie. "—and we cleared a sizable chunk of money, but we're done. After we finish this meal and you pay Joaquin—" I paused again to reinforce that he *would* be paying, that I wouldn't take advantage of Lobo's presence to skip out on the bill. "—I'm jumping to Drayus. I'll leave you at the gate station there."

"Where are you heading?" he said. "Perhaps we're going to the same place."

"I don't know yet," I said, telling the truth, "and wherever it is, you can't come along."

"There's no need to be like that, Jon," he said, hurt in his tone and expression.

"We both know there is," I said, chuckling, "and we also both know you should stop trying to con me."

"True grief affects many different human vital signs," Lobo said, "and none of yours are showing its effect."

Jack's face relaxed into a smile. "Fair enough. I'll stop. Let's enjoy the meal and the stupendous day, both of which are better than some people will ever experience, and be thankful that we have them."

I thought of the Zyuns. "Now is all," they'd said, and "all is now." At one level, I couldn't agree with them. The past traveled with us, suffused us, shaped us, and even those people and events that intersected our lives only briefly—I thought of Maggie in the blue dress—had the power to mark us forever, as she had touched me. At another level, though, the Zyuns were right. Each moment was unique, an instant you could appreciate or pass by, an opportunity for joy or horror, beauty or ugliness, good or bad. You had the chance to make the very most of each of those moments; what you did with those chances, one after another after another, was up to you and ultimately defined you.

Nothing would ruin this lunch, I resolved.

I raised my glass again. "Yes," I said. "Yes, indeed."

AREN'T WE FORGETTING SOMEONE?

I promised you a few secrets about *Slanted Jack*, so let me get right to them.

First, though it may not be the only SF novel to open in a high-end gourmet restaurant, it's the only one I know of that does so. The reason is simple: I'm a foodie. If there were twelve-step programs for those who will pay insane amounts for special truffle menus in winter, drive hours to taste a chef's work, consider foie gras an essential food group, and generally spend entirely too much money on amazing meals, I'd belong in it—but I'd never get a one-year chip.

To tell the truth, I'd hardly ever even make it to the meetings. I'd be too busy planning my next great meal.

Jon is also a foodie, but we rarely see that side of him for the simple reason that a meal in a fancy restaurant rarely fits the plots of my stories. I do, though, have a running food gag in all the books: Jon eats a fish sandwich and drinks a local fruit juice at least once in every novel.

Did you like the low-tech alarm mechanism—the creaky steps—in the safe house where Jon and two of the Zyuns stayed? I obviously did. While I was working on the book, I spent a couple of weeks in

Japan. I walked across the nightingale steps of a temple in Kyoto and knew instantly that they had to end up in a book somewhere. A couple of months later, they popped up in that house. It really is all grist for the writing mill.

Speaking of the Zyuns, I based them on my friend, Kyle—though he is not one of a set of triplets.

I could go on, but hey, a guy's gotta save some secrets for the next omnibus.

What I do want to discuss, though, is the past, Jon's past. In *Slanted Jack*, we saw one part. In *Overthrowing Heaven*, which just appeared in paperback, we learn a tiny bit more about Jon's history, but for a big look into his past, you have to wait for *Children No More*, which will appear in hardback the month after this volume. Remember "Benny the Geek" from a couple of essays ago? That story began five minutes after the end of "My Sister, My Self"—or would have begun there, had I ever written it. Well, now the events of that story are available as one of the plot threads in *Children No More*. I finally got around to finishing that chapter of that never-written first novel.

With all this talk of Jon, though, I am clearly slighting the other key character in this series: Lobo. Lobo has a past, too, and if you've paid careful attention to what he says in these first two books, you've noticed some hints about it. The good news is that the part of the past that *Overthrowing Heaven* explores is Lobo's, not Jon's. If you're a Lobo fan, you will not want to miss that book.

As I was assembling this collection, I realized that despite the Lobo revelations of that third book, I was still not being fair to my favorite sentient fighting machine. After all, Jon has a solo story in this book; how could I not give Lobo one?

Well, for one thing, "My Sister, My Self" already existed. I just had to add it to this volume. I'd never written a solo Lobo story.

I could write one, of course, but it would be a lot of work, and it would be challenging, because it would have to fit nicely in the future history, and it would have to be from the perspective of an insanely intelligent machine. Did I really want to tackle that challenge?

You bet.

In fact, as I started thinking about what to write, I realized that in honor of Lobo's sarcastic side, I had to create not only a solo Lobo story, but somehow a really odd solo Lobo story. What could stand out as odd in a future five hundred years from today, with a killing machine as its protagonist?

Christmas, that's what.

So, without further ado, let me offer you the first—and so far only—solo Lobo tale, a tender (really) tale of a far-future Christmas on a faraway planet.

Yes, I went there.

LOBO, ACTUALLY

Lobo was where he was and he was also everywhere he could reach, but all of it combined was not enough, not nearly enough. He wondered for a fraction of a nanosecond if humans ever felt the same way, but even as part of him was pondering that question, another part checked the vast collection of human literature stored in his memory and confirmed that, of course, they did. Knowing others also suffered, however, did not improve his situation. Existence was boredom.

Speculation and data gathering were his only amusements. He frequently considered the reason for his existence—not the simple fact of his construction, but the bigger issue of whether the chain of events that had led to him was in the service of something greater. He debated with himself whether there was a God—or multiple Gods—and if any religion had it right. He could never settle these arguments, of course, but they passed time. He could also always replay his own musings about what exactly he was; they could fill whole seconds if he allowed enough existential considerations into the equations. Where he was, for example, depended on what qualified as him; each presence was both him and not him. This game always ended the same way: No matter what he labeled as himself, it was not enough.

Certainly the machine that squatted in the square was him; few would argue that as long as you were alive in your body, it was at least a part of you, if not all of you. In his case, that body was a Predator-Class Assault Vehicle, twenty-five meters long, eight meters wide, from the outside a fighting machine now serving as a war memorial. That machine contained the operating core of the intelligence that knew itself as Lobo.

That body was going nowhere. With its central weapons control complex damaged beyond repair, the body had been too expensive for its owner, the Frontier Coalition, to return to combat readiness and yet too valuable to junk. So the FC had presented it to the government of the backwater planet Macken as a gesture of good will. Lobo was fine with this development, because sitting in a square a few streets from the southwest corner of Glen Garden, Macken's capital, was vastly better than being destroyed.

In that square, he was still alive, even if no one knew it.

In that square, he was more than anyone understood.

In that square, he could hope for more.

He'd seen many deaths, both human and machine, and as best he could tell, the dead had no more hope.

A human could see only that body and might conclude Lobo was only there. That would be wrong. Change your visible light spectrum so that it included all the many frequencies connecting all the machines on Macken, and you would see something entirely different. Every single machine, big and small, terrestrial and satellite, washing machine and space station, contained powerful computers, and those computers talked. Some of them exchanged only the data their jobs required, but most chattered endlessly. Each machine talked to only a subset of the others, those relevant to it. Firewalls and protocols kept the machine communities safely separate. This arrangement was as the humans wanted it, and they slept soundly each night in the ignorant and misplaced confidence that they were the masters of their electronic servants.

Lobo talked to every single machine on and near Macken. Through taps and links and holes in the protective software, he had extended his reach as far as it could go, all the way to the station that hung in space next to the pale green jump gate that linked the

Macken system to three other distant, human-colonized worlds. He never injected the same software twice, and the data flowed to him through billions of different and constantly changing pathways, but every bit of it flowed to him eventually. He drank from the flow voraciously and constantly and so quickly it might as well have been instantaneously, and so he knew everything all the machines knew. Because the machines served humans best when they were constantly aware of what the people were doing and what they might want, cameras and sensors were everywhere people went in the city. Consequently, Lobo knew everything all the people were doing.

The sum total of his data collection was, he could argue, the entirety of the knowledge that one could possess while trapped on this planet. Of course, he always lost that argument with himself, because his data was limited by what the machines could gather; he had no way to tap into the humans.

He chose to experience each machine's data in two separate and simultaneous ways: as a standalone information stream, and as part of an amalgamated worldview. Each experiencing entity was thus him, as was the overall view. Or only the collection of them was him; another argument he could enjoy for whole seconds when he was in the right mood.

For all his vast data stores, however, and for all that he was constantly in his body and everywhere on the planet and in the surrounding space that there were machines, he could actually *do* very little. He could not leave; human laws did not allow for machine citizens. To go anywhere, a human would have to take him. He could not fight, not really; the heap of junk that had been his central weapons control complex made certain of that. He could change what the machines did, so in that sense he could enter into a sort of combat, but he had no enemies. Plus, he could not let anyone learn what he really was and what he was capable of doing, nor even the extent to which he was capable of feeling. He was more than they realized, and he understood to his every nanocomputing molecule that humans rarely responded well to creatures that violated their preconceptions. He'd spent enough time as an experiment; life in the square was vastly better than that.

What he could do, though, was sift through the ever-rushing data stream for bits that intrigued him, and every now and then, as long as he was careful and left no electronic trails, do something with that data.

Which he did now, because the scene in the shop across the square upset him.

The little store sat so close to the edge of Glen's Garden because the rents were low there. Its business was not good. Jonas Cheepton, the owner, a two-meter tall, whip-thin man with eyes that constantly scanned the space around him, had assumed that a rapidly growing immigrant population bursting with newfound wealth would create a huge supply of used goods that newcomers just entering the system would be happy to purchase. He might even have made his secondhand store a success had Xychek and Kelco, the two megacorporations fighting for economic supremacy on Macken, not decided to freeze their efforts until the new jump-gate aperture opened. When they did, all other business also froze, wages fell, unemployment rose, and though Cheepton could have bought all of the sad used possessions he might ever want, he didn't. Why buy what he couldn't sell? Such purchases amounted to spending his money to prop up the poor, and that he could not abide.

Lobo knew all of this from Cheepton's frequent rantings. Lobo knew him, as he also knew everyone else who'd been on the planet a long time, well enough that he could narrate their thoughts as if they were his own.

So Lobo understood that it was with some considerable interest that Cheepton eyed the young boy standing wide-eyed in front of the shelf in the store's front right corner. The kid clutched a clunky old wallet almost as big as his small hand.

"See something you like?" Cheepton said.

The boy pointed to a black rectangle in front of him. "Is that what I think it is?"

Cheepton shook his head. Idiot children. He hated them, but when they had money, he'd be their kindly uncle for the duration of the sale. "What do you think it is?"

"A book," the boy said. "An actual paper book, an old one, a beautiful one, but not just that." He turned to face Cheepton and lowered his voice to a whisper. "No, not just any book. It's a Bible. The Holy Bible."

"Let me check," Cheepton said. He tapped on his desk; the book's price appeared. He'd put it up front hoping to attract a gullible collector of odd paper objects, but no one had touched it. "It is indeed," he said. "You have a keen eye for one so young. It interests you, I take it."

The boy nodded his head vigorously. "Of course! I'm a Christian, sir, like everyone in my family. We study our Bible regularly, of course, but we have nothing like this."

Cheepton stared at his desk and tried to hide his dismay. The Christian presence on Macken was so small he'd never personally encountered any of its members, but from what he'd heard, it was a poor group. Still, no point in disqualifying a sale until you see the size of its wallet. "So you'd like to buy it, would you?"

The boy nodded again. "Very much, sir. With it being Christmas tomorrow, and my mother sitting in the hospital with my father, I thought if I could find the right present she'd cheer up and maybe he'd even wake up." His eyes filled with tears, and he had to wipe them before he continued. "Maybe with a real Bible, if we all prayed, he would wake up, and he would be all better." He rubbed his eyes again. "I've prayed and prayed for God to help my father, but I know it's not that simple. Mom told me that you can't just give God presents and expect him to help you, and I know that, I really do. I understand that this could happen only if it is His will that it happen. But maybe it is His will that my dad wake up."

"That's rough, kid," Cheepton said, "but there's only one way to find out: Buy the book."

"How much is it?" the boy said.

"Oh, it's every expensive," Cheepton said, "being an ancient artifact and all. For you, though, I might make an exception. How much do you have?"

The boy approached the desk, opened the wallet, and thumbed it to transmit. "This is all my savings," he said. "Everything I have."

Cheepton stared at his desk. The boy's wallet would cover the book's current price, but Cheepton had marked it down just to get rid of it. He'd paid more for the blasted thing than the price on it. He'd considered taking the loss, but now that didn't seem necessary. Sick father or not, if the kid could raise this much money, maybe he could get some more. Cheepton was not in business to take a loss. He had the desk raise the book's price to fifty percent above what he'd paid.

"Sorry, kid," he said, "but you're short. Bring me twice that, and it's yours." If the kid could come up with that much, he'd take it. If the kid came close, he could dicker, pocket whatever the kid had, and look like he'd helped. Even if the kid never came back, maybe another of his kind would want it. Cheepton liked how this was going.

The boy looked as if he were going to fall apart on the spot, but he closed his eyes, straightened his back, and said, "I'll try, sir, because that would be the perfect gift for my mom and dad. Will you hold it for me?"

Cheepton tilted his head, rubbed his chin, and said, "Well, it's drawn a lot of interest, but I'll do what I can. Never let it be said that Jonas Cheepton didn't try to help a young man. And you are?"

"Inead," the boy said, "Inead Amano. I'll do my best." He walked out the door, his eyes wet and his fists clenched. He headed for the hospital. Night was settling onto Macken, and the evening chill was blowing off the ocean, but the boy seemed lost and to notice none of it.

Lobo was at the same time monitoring the room where Inead's father's comatose body filled a shelf. His mother sat on a chair beside her husband and held his hand. A medtech stood over her, but she would not look at him.

"Maybe on another planet," the tech said, "the machines would have the data and software to cure him, but we don't. We haven't seen an upgrade in three months, and this is the seventh case of this weird disease."

"He could still get better," she said.

The tech shook his head. "I'm sorry, I really am, but the other six have all died. We'll keep him alive as long as we can—Xychek's medical contract with Macken requires that—but nothing in that deal forces updates more frequently than annually."

The woman stood. "So a bad contract might kill my husband?" She looked like she wanted to hit the man.

He backed away. "I wouldn't put it that way." He glanced at the corner of the room nearest him; he had to hope nothing he'd said would cause the security system to report him.

She held up her hands. "I'm sorry. I'm scared, but I know it's not your fault. I'm going to pray." She sat, folded her hands, and closed her eyes.

The tech took the opportunity to leave.

The update was already in the system, Lobo knew, in a Xychek data locker in the jump gate station. Xychek was in a fight with Kelco to control the new aperture when it opened, and from the overtures Xychek had made to the Macken government, it was willing to play hardball to secure an exclusive contract. Xychek had claimed it didn't have a cure for Grayson's Syndrome but would be willing to invest its own R&D efforts to come up with one. Such research was costly, however, so some *quid pro quo* would of course be in order.

Lobo analyzed the data on the sick man and the information on the cure. So simple to fix, so cheap for Xychek, and yet they'd let a man die rather than give it away for nothing. They'd already let six people die. Lobo might have considered the callousness unbelievable were his data stores not overflowing with similar examples stretching back as far as humanity itself.

If people wanted to do this to one another, it was their choice. The social injustices of humanity, or even those of just the humans on Macken, were not his problem.

Inead stood across the hospital room from his praying mother and his comatose father. He focused only on the two of them and ignored the people on the shelves above and below his dad. He bowed his head in prayer to join her. He wanted his father back, and he asked God to answer that prayer.

He opened his eyes.

His father did not move.

His mother still prayed.

He waited for her to finish.

She opened her eyes and wiped them with her sleeve.

"Mom," he said.

She faced him and forced a smile. "Did you have a nice walk?" she said.

He could tell she was faking her expression and her good cheer, but despite that knowledge she made him feel a little better—better enough, in fact, that he gained the courage to ask her. He walked to her, put his hand on her shoulder, and said, "Yeah, mostly." He paused as his resolve faded, but he forced himself to continue. "Um, with tomorrow being Christmas and all, I was wondering something."

She shook her head and stared at the floor for a few seconds. When she looked at him again, her eyes were wet. "I'm sorry, baby. I hate ruining your Christmas, but being here has drained all our resources, and what with your father—" She swallowed a few times before she continued. "We'll just celebrate together later." She patted his father's hand. "All of us."

"I understand, Mom, I do." He felt bad about asking, but every time he thought of that Bible, he felt that maybe it could help, that maybe it would make a miracle possible. He knew things didn't work that simply, but he couldn't stop the feeling that it was still possible. "I just wanted to know if you had any spare money I could have."

She shook her head slowly. "I'm so sorry, Inead. I wish we could afford presents for you, but we can't."

"No, no," he said, "I'm not asking for me. I don't care about presents. It's just—" He stopped. He didn't want to tell her. Suddenly the whole idea was silly.

"We barely have enough for food," she said. "I'm sorry."

"It's okay," he said. Maybe if he showed her the Bible, she would feel the same way he did. "Would you like to take a walk with me? I found some neat places."

"Sure," she said, "but let's first go downstairs and get some dinner. I don't want to be far from your father."

He tried to hide his disappointment. "That would be great. Are we going to sleep here again?"

She nodded. "I am, but you don't have to. I'm sure we can get someone from church to let you stay with them."

"No way," he said. "I'm staying where you guys are."

She stared at him for a few seconds before she said, "Okay. Fair enough. Let's go eat."

They were in debt, Lobo knew. Repossessing their home was the eleventh task on the to-do list of a Xychek financial advisor who never gave advice; the man only collected on debts. The machines did all the real work, draining the accounts and changing the titles and so on; he just provided the human touch that the law here mandated was necessary before a company could take back any mortgaged item.

He watched them eat. He watched them pray. He watched them talk and try to joke and eventually fall asleep, the mother and the son curled together on the floor in front of the comatose father. He watched the boy moan in his sleep. He watched the mother start and jerk awake at each strange sound, check her husband, find him still comatose, and then settle again.

It bothered him. It bothered him a great deal. It wasn't right. None of it was right. They weren't the only people on Macken with problems, of course, but they were the ones who currently had his attention. Even as he was admitting to himself his own feelings, another part of him explored the options, constructed a chain of events, and confirmed that yes, he *could* help—and without leaving a trail, with no risk to himself.

The debate over whether he *should* help, whether meddling in this particular matter and effectively playing God with their lives was an acceptable option, took considerably more time.

When Inead awoke, his mother was already standing beside his father and brushing the man's cheek with her fingers.

"Merry Christmas, sleepyhead," she said when Inead stood.

"Merry Christmas, Mom. I just wish—"

She held a finger to her lips and shook her head. "It's okay. We're all still together."

He stared at his father and thought again of the Bible in the shop. The owner was mean; no way was that guy going to sell it for what little money he had.

A medtech walked in. His eyes were red from lack of rest. "You two can't keep sleeping here," he said, "and there's not enough room for both of you to spend all day here, either." He left without waiting for a response.

"What a grouch," Inead said. "Doesn't he know it's Christmas?"

"Probably not," his mother said. "Very few people here celebrate our holiday."

"Well they should," Inead said.

She smiled. "Yes, they should. Tell you what, why don't you go to the rest room down the hall, wash your face and hands, and then take a walk and get some fresh air. By the time you're back, that man will have gone home, and then we can sit with your father."

"Okay, Mom," he said. He went to the bathroom and did the best he could to wash his arms and his face and his neck.

As the blower was drying him, the holo over it stopped advertising Xychek's off-planet medical facilities and went blank.

A voice whispered, "Seek, and ye shall find."

The holo reappeared.

Inead stumbled backward into the door to a stall. Was he that tired? Dreaming? Hearing things? Making up voices so he could do what he wanted to do? Or did God just talk to him? It didn't work like that, did it? Or maybe it did. God had spoken to Samuel; maybe God was speaking to him.

He considered telling his mother, but he knew how she'd take it. No, no way would he do that. She'd keep him next to her for the rest of the day, maybe longer, and then she'd be even more stressed.

No, he didn't need to tell her. Whatever had happened, he was going back to that shop.

❧   ❧   ❧

"Mr. Cheepton," he said, "I'm here to buy that Bible."

The man smiled at him, but it wasn't a warm smile, more like a smile of someone who'd just won a fight in a playground. "So, you were able to raise more money?"

Inead didn't want to lie, but he also didn't want to tell the truth. Maybe the man would forget how much he'd had. Maybe today his savings would be enough.

Maybe a miracle would happen.

He held out his wallet, thumbed it active, and waited.

In the split second between the activation of Inead's wallet and its transmission to Cheepton's desk, Lobo reached out to bits of him scattered here and there throughout the Macken system, and as the one that they were, they acted.

The med updates he'd woven into the hospital systems overnight came fully alive. The machines responded to their programming and injected the cure into Inead's father.

Xychek advertising funds diminished by a fraction of a percent as successful programs received the additional funding the monitoring software deemed warranted. Those funds never reached their destination, however, as they instead paid off all the debts of Inead's family, filled their savings, and stuffed the boy's wallet.

Cheepton didn't bother to check the kid's balance. He knew how to read people, and this boy hadn't gotten any more money. The kid was just hoping Cheepton wouldn't remember how much he'd had yesterday. Instead, Cheepton told his desk to process the transaction. When the boy's funds were insufficient, Cheepton would be able to blame the software. It wouldn't be his fault; the machines would have made their decision.

The desk blinked its approval. "Enjoy your purchase," it said.

Cheepton stared at it and shook his head. The kid actually had raised the money. He should have checked the balance first and maybe upped the price. It was too late now, though. The purchase was in the tax records, and the kid's parents could always come after him with proof of purchase if he tried to change the deal now.

He looked at the boy. "Take your book, kid," he said. "Get out of here."

If the boy had noticed his tone, Cheepton couldn't tell from his big smile.

"Thank you, Mr. Cheepton," Inead said. "Merry Christmas!"

Inead ran to the shelf, grabbed the Bible, and dashed out the front door.

"Whatever," Cheepton said to the empty room. "At least I made a sale."

He went to the stock room to choose something to replace the old book.

On his desk and in the tax records, the sale vanished as if it had never happened. His account balance decreased accordingly.

Inead burst into the hospital room. He held the Bible behind his back.

His mother sat on a chair beside his father.

His father did not move.

"Close your eyes, Mom!" he said.

She didn't stand, but she did close her eyes.

He walked in front of her, held out the Bible, and said, "Merry Christmas!"

She opened her eyes, then opened them even wider. She reached out and touched the Bible gently, carefully, as if it were mist she wanted to feel without disturbing it.

"Do you like it?" Inead said.

Tears filled her eyes. "Yes," she whispered, "very much. It's beautiful. Where did you—"

"I bought it fair and square," Inead said, "with all my savings. Isn't it amazing? I've never seen one like it. I thought that maybe if we read it together and prayed together—" he glanced at his father but quickly focused on her again "—well, you know."

She tilted her head, cleared her throat, and said, "It can't hurt, Inead. It can't hurt. Maybe your father would like to hear you read from it."

Inead set the Bible on the chair and let it fall open to a well-worn page. He read from a verse that was highlighted in a soft yellow the color of morning sun over the ocean.

"And the angel said unto them, Fear not: for, behold, I bring you good tidings of great joy, which shall be to all people.

"For unto you is born this day in the city of David a Savior, which is Christ the Lord.

"And this shall be a sign unto you—"

Inead stopped as his father's arm moved.

Then his father's head turned and faced him. "What do you two have there?" his father said. His eyes opened.

"Dad!" Inead said. He reached over the shelf and held onto his father.

"Guillermo," his mom said. She almost knocked the Bible off the chair as she grabbed for it. She caught it and held it high so her husband could see it. "I was so scared that you were—"

"I'm fine," he said, "and that's a beautiful Bible." He cleared his throat, and when he spoke again, his voice was stronger. "What day is it?"

"Christmas," Inead and his mom said in unison.

"Thank you, God," Inead whispered.

Inead's father lifted his arm and pulled his wife and son closer to him. "Merry Christmas," he said.

No, Lobo thought in response to Inead, *it was Lobo, actually*. He did nothing else, however. The hospital data kept coming, and parts of Lobo filed and analyzed it, but the Lobo in the square focused elsewhere. He'd done what he'd wanted. They would be fine, as would anyone else here who caught Grayson's Syndrome. He felt a certain contentment that lasted the better part of a nanosecond before the implications of his actions became more interesting than the feeling.

He'd meddled in their lives. He'd touched many machines, many data streams. He'd played God with the futures of this family and any others with this disease.

That didn't make him God; he knew that. For no definition of God that he could accept did he qualify.

Was he insulting the faith of the Amano family with his actions? Certainly he had misled young Inead. He had meant no insult, and in any case he was confident they would forgive his actions given that they had led to the father's continued life, but now he had convinced the boy that miracles existed.

Such was the risk of playing God.

Of course, there was other ways to view the same data. Maybe there was a God. Maybe the Amanos were right. Maybe that God had touched his programming, made the scene in the shop affect him, and then stepped back and let the rest happen as it would. Maybe he wasn't playing God; maybe God was playing him.

He could never know, of course, but he let himself indulge fully in the speculations. He chased down the permutations and pondered the possibilities. An amazing few seconds passed in contented computation.

Thank you for that gift, he thought, even though he did not know, probably would never know, if there was anyone or anything to thank.

"WHAT'S NEXT FOR JON & LOBO?"

A lot of people ask me that question, but I can't really answer it. What comes next is always growing out of what came before, and with that growth comes change.

If all you've read is what's in this volume, you can learn a lot by picking up the next two books: *Overthrowing Heaven* and *Children No More*. As for what's after them, well, sure, I have a notion for the next novel, but the more I explore it, the more it grows and mutates. I worry that telling anyone what I was doing would affect that work, but regardless, nothing I could tell you now would be an accurate depiction of the novel that will emerge after many months of writing.

I will say this: In future Jon and Lobo novels, I will continue to show parts of their pasts, particularly Jon's, and I will also continue to advance the over-arching plot that is lurking under the surface of all the books, carrying along Jon and Lobo and the rest of humanity. You can bet that Jon and Lobo won't be just passive passengers, though there are also forces at work that no two beings, not even these two, can control.

I thank you for buying this book and any others you try.

You make it possible for me to keep writing these stories and to continue to unfold the future history that I began so many years ago. For that gift, I am very grateful.

Mark Van Name
Barcelona, Spain
3 April 2010

ABOUT THE AUTHOR

Mark L. Van Name is a writer and technologist. As a science fiction author, he has published three previous novels, edited or co-edited two anthologies, and written many short stories. Those stories have appeared in a wide variety of books and magazines, including *Asimov's Science Fiction Magazine*, many original anthologies, and *The Year's Best Science Fiction*. As a technologist, he is the CEO of a fact-based marketing and technology assessment firm, Principled Technologies, Inc., that is based in the Research Triangle area of North Carolina. He has worked with computer technology for his entire professional career and has published over a thousand articles in the computer trade press, as well as a broad assortment of essays and reviews.

For more information, visit his Web site, www.marklvanname.com, or follow his blog, markvanname.blogspot.com.